**Pain exploded in Gyre's head, a line of fire from
cheek to eyebrow.**

He was falling backward, hitting the floor shoulder-first, feeling nothing
but the searing agony in his face. He mashed his hand against it, and
blood *squished*, torn skin shifting nauseatingly under his fingers. He only
realized he was screaming when he had to stop to take a breath.

Va'aht loomed above him, an outline shimmering in a haze of tears.

"You'll live, with care, though I daresay there'll be a scar." The centarch gave a humorless chuckle. "Let it be a lesson to you."

He limped past, still carrying Maya. She screamed Gyre's name
again, but his thoughts were already fading into a fiery blur of pain. By
the time his father reached his side, darkness was closing in around him.

By Django Wexler

BURNINGBLADE & SILVEREYE

Ashes of the Sun

THE SHADOW CAMPAIGNS

The Thousand Names

The Shadow Throne

The Price of Valor

The Guns of Empire

The Infernal Battalion

ASHES
OF THE
SUN

Burningblade & Silvereye:
Book One

DJANGO
WEXLER

www.orbitbooks.net

Copyright © 2020 by Django Wexler
Excerpt from *Legacy of Ash* copyright © 2019 by Matthew Ward
Excerpt from *We Ride the Storm* copyright © 2018 by Devin Madson

Cover design by Lauren Panepinto
Cover illustration by Scott Fischer
Cover copyright © 2020 by Hachette Book Group, Inc.
Map and chapter ornaments by Charis Loke
Author photograph by Rachel Thompson

Orbit
Hachette Book Group
1290 Avenue of the Americas
New York, NY 10104
orbitbooks.net

First Edition: July 2020

Orbit is an imprint of Hachette Book Group.
The Orbit name and logo are trademarks of Little, Brown Book Group Limited.

The publisher is not responsible for websites (or their content) that are not owned by the publisher.

The Hachette Speakers Bureau provides a wide range of authors for speaking events. To find out more, go to www.hachettespeakersbureau.com or call (866) 376-6591.

Library of Congress Cataloging-in-Publication Data
Names: Wexler, Django, author.
Title: Ashes of the sun / Django Wexler.
Description: First edition. | New York : Orbit, 2020. | Series: Burningblade & Silvereye ; book 1
Identifiers: LCCN 2019044375 | ISBN 9780316519540 (trade paperback) | ISBN 9780316519465 (ebook) | ISBN 9780316519472
Subjects: GSAFD: Fantasy fiction. | Epic fiction.
Classification: LCC PS3623.E94 A93 2020 | DDC 813/.6—dc23
LC record available at https://lccn.loc.gov/2019044375

ISBNs: 978-0-316-51954-0 (trade paperback), 978-0-316-51946-5 (ebook)

Printed in the United States of America

LSC-C

Printing 6 ,2023

For Dad

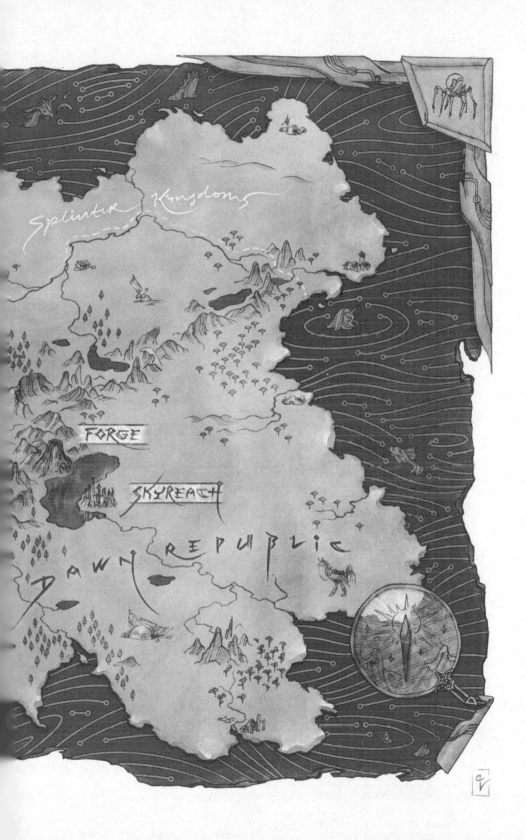

Prologue

Gyre and Maya were playing ghouls and heroes. Gyre had to be the ghoul, of course. Maya would never tolerate being anything less than a hero.

Summer was in full flower, and the sun was alone in a pale blue sky, with only a few wisps of cloud at the horizon. They'd already had the dramatic sword fight, and Gyre had been defeated with appropriate hissing and choking. Now he lay on his back, dead, and Maya had planted one foot on his stomach, hands on her hips in a heroic pose.

"...an' now I'm *queen*," she shouted at the top of her lungs. "An' there'll be peace an' justice an' all, an' everyone's got to do what I say. Stupid Billem Crump an' his stupid brothers have to help Mom dig the new well, an' there's going to be apple pudding every day with dinner. An' my brother Gyre can have some," she added generously, "even if he never beat a ghoul all by himself."

"If we had apple pudding every day, you'd get sick of it," Gyre said.

"Would not."

"Would too. And anyway, queens are for barbarians. We have senators and consuls."

"You shut up. You're dead."

She pressed down on Gyre's stomach, and he let out an *oof.* At five,
Maya was heavier than she looked, plump and broad-shouldered, with
their mother's light brown skin and curly crimson hair. Everyone said
Gyre, darker and black-haired, took after their father.

"I'll be consul, then," Maya said. "Everyone still has to do what I say
forever an' ever."

"You only get to be consul for a year," Gyre said.

"That's practically forever," Maya argued. "An'—"

She stopped, and a moment later vanished from his field of vision.
Gyre sat up, brushing dirt and dried vulpi dung off his back. All
around him, yearling vulpi snuffled over the rocky ground, looking for
tender green shoots. Yearlings were Gyre's favorite age for vulpi, soft-
furred and playful, before they grew into bristly, irritable layers and
then huge, sedentary terminals. They didn't take much watching as
long as the gate to the pasture was closed, which was why he had time
to fool around.

Even so, Gyre had a guilty moment while he made a quick count of
the herd. He relaxed when he came up with the requisite thirty-three.
He was eight and a half years old and had never lost one of his father's
vulpi, not even the time when the fence had washed out in the rain and
six of them had made a break for it.

"Gyre!" Maya shouted. "Gyre, it's a *centarch*! He's riding a warbird!"
She was standing at the fence with her feet on the second rail, leaning
as far over as she could. "*Gyre*, you have to come see!"

"It can't be a centarch."

Gyre hurried to the fence, absentmindedly grabbing the back of
Maya's dress with one hand in case she leaned too far over. Maya was
reckless, and often sick to boot, spending months with fevers and rack-
ing coughs. Keeping his sister out of misadventures was as much a part

of his daily chores as tending vulpi. But her excitement was infectious, and he found himself leaning forward to get a better view of the cloud of dust coming down the main road. It *was* moving awfully quickly.

"It was *too* a centarch!" Maya said breathlessly. "I *saw* him an' all. He had white armor an' a blaster an' a hackem!"

"Haken," Gyre corrected. The legendary bladeless sword, weapon of the centarchs of the Twilight Order. "What would a centarch be doing here?"

"Maybe he's come to arrest Billem Crump for being an ass an' all. Dad said he was going to go to law with him if he kept picking those apples."

Gyre pulled his sister back. "Centarchs don't arrest people for stealing *apples*."

"They arrest people who've got"—she lowered her voice to a stage whisper—"*dhak*." The word, with its connotations of filth, infestation, and immorality, was inappropriate in polite conversation. If Gyre's mother had heard Maya saying it, she'd have gotten a smack on the ear. "Maybe Billem Crump's got ghoul *dhak* in his shed and the centarch is going to drag him away!"

Gyre watched the dust cloud with something less than his sister's wide-eyed wonder. He still didn't believe it was a centarch, and if it *was*, he wasn't sure how to feel about having one of the Order's champions on their farm. He'd caught on to the hard expression his father and the other farmers wore when the subject came up. Everyone knew the Order kept the people safe from plaguespawn. But...

Nothing else, just the significant "but." And Gyre knew, as Maya did not, what was in the locked shed off the south field. Last summer, when a plague of weevils had threatened their potatoes, Gyre's father had taken him out there by night. They'd both equipped themselves with a double handful of bright green seeds, like hard young peas, from a half-full sack, and spent the evening planting them between the rows of potato plants. By the next afternoon, the field was *full* of dead weevils. Gyre had swept them up and buried them in the compost pile, proud and guilty with the shared secret.

Was that dhak*?* Gyre suspected it had been. *Dhak* was anything from the Elder times, before the war that had destroyed both ghouls and Chosen, unless the Order had approved it as safe, sanctioned arcana. But his father had assured him it was fine and that every farmer in the valley had something like it laid away. *A centarch wouldn't come after him, just for that. Would they?*

"We should get back to the house," he told Maya. Or, he discovered, he told the empty space where Maya had been, since his sister had already jumped down from the fence, wriggled out of his grip, and set off up the path as fast as her short legs would carry her.

Gyre looked at the dust cloud. It was rounding the point of the hill now, going past the turn for the Crump farm and definitely heading their way. He wanted to run after Maya, but there were the vulpi to think of—well behaved or not, he couldn't just leave them on their own. So he spent a few frantic minutes rounding the animals up, ignoring their affronted blats and whistles at being turned out of the pasture early. Only once they were safely back in their pen, jostling for position at the water trough, did he hurry toward the house.

The path led directly to the kitchen door, which was undoubtedly where Maya had gone. But a smaller side route led around the low, ramshackle farmhouse to the front, and Gyre went this way. He had a notion that if the visitor *was* anyone important, his father would banish him and his sister to their room before they got a good look. Coming in through the front door, Gyre hoped he would be able to get an idea of what was happening.

There was indeed a warbird standing in the gravel drive, looking incongruous next to their battered farm cart. Gyre had seen one of the creatures before, years ago, when they'd been in town on the day the magistrate's guard had come through. This one seemed bigger than he remembered, its long, curving neck layered with overlapping plates of pale white armor with the iridescent shimmer of unmetal. More armor covered the warbird's plump body. Two long, knobbly legs each had four splayed toes and a single enormous backward claw. The head, ridiculously tiny compared to the rest of the animal, was encased in segmented white plates, with its beak covered by a long, curving blade, shrouded in turn with a black velvet cloth.

It was easily twice Gyre's height. The magistrate's warbird hadn't been nearly as big, he decided, and in retrospect its plumage seemed a bit ragged. It certainly hadn't been armored in unmetal. Whoever the visitor was, he was considerably better equipped than even a county official. *Maybe it* is *a centarch.* Gyre gave the warbird a wide berth, creeping around the edge of the drive toward the front door, which stood partially open.

It led to the parlor, which the family used once a year at Midwinter. The rest of the time, the good furniture was covered by dust sheets, and life at the farm centered around the kitchen and the back door. Gyre and Maya's room was in that part of the house, an addition that leaked when it rained. Looking into the parlor, Gyre had the feeling of being a stranger in his own home, the shrouded shapes of the sofa and end table looming and ominous.

Gyre's father stood in the doorway that led to the kitchen. He was a big man, broad-shouldered, with dark hair tied at the nape of his neck and skin the color of the soil he spent his time tending. Gyre could tell at once there was something wrong, just from the way his father stood. He was slumped, defeated, his eyes on the floor.

In front of him, in the middle of the parlor, stood the visitor. He was tall and thin, with short hair that gleamed purple-black in the light. He wore an unmetal breastplate and shoulder armor and carried a matching helmet under one arm. On his right hip there was an implement a bit like a capital letter *T*, or a sword hilt and cross guard with no blade.

It was, without question, a haken. The highest of arcana, able to manipulate the power of creation in the raw. And that made this man a centarch of the Twilight Order, since only they could use the haken. Gyre had never seen one, of course, but he recognized it from a hundred stories. With haken in hand, a centarch was unstoppable, invincible.

Now that he was confronted with one of the legendary warriors in the flesh, Gyre realized he very much wanted the man to be gone. *Just go away and leave us alone*, he thought. *We're not ghouls, and we haven't got any* dhak *except for seeds that kill weevils. What harm can that do to anyone?*

"You're certain?" Gyre's father said quietly. Neither of the men had noticed Gyre yet, and he pressed himself against the sofa, desperate to hear their conversation.

"Quite certain," the centarch said. He had a highborn accent. "Believe me, in these matters, the Order does not make mistakes."

"But…"

Maya screamed, and Gyre's father started. Gyre's mother came in through the other door, holding Maya under her arm. The girl was kicking furiously, tears running down her cheeks, and shrieking like an angry cat.

"It's all right," Gyre's father said. "Maya, please. Everything's going to be all right."

"Yes," the centarch drawled. "Everything's going to be fine."

"No!" Maya said. "No, no, no! I don't want to go!"

"You have to go," Gyre's mother said. "You know how you get sick. They can help you."

Gyre frowned. Bouts of a strange, feverish illness had been a regular feature of Maya's life for as long as he could remember, especially in the winter. But she'd always recovered, and by summer she was herself again. *Though Mom did say this year was the worst she'd ever been.* Maya hated doctors, who could never find anything wrong and prescribed bitter medicines that didn't work.

Did Dad call the Order to help her? Gyre hadn't heard of the Order doing anything like that, though they had access to arcana medicine far better than any doctor's. *But why would they need to take her away?*

He bit his lip, watching as his mother transferred the squirming five-year-old to the centarch. The thin man donned his helmet, which made him look like a white beetle, and took Maya under his arm, lifting her easily.

"No, no, no!" she screamed. "I don't *want* to go! Mom, Dad, don't let him take me!"

She hates doctors, Gyre told himself. *She screamed her head off when she cut her hand and Dad took her to get it sewn up.*

But something was wrong. The way his father stood, hands clenched into fists. His mother's eyes, brimming with unshed tears, her hands clasped to her chest. *It's* wrong. *Why are they letting him take her?*

Gyre stepped into the doorway, trembling, as the centarch turned to leave. Maya saw him first and screamed again.

"Gyre! Help, help, *please!*"

"Let her go," Gyre said. He wished his voice didn't sound so small, so like a little boy's.

"Gyre!" Gyre's father took a half step forward. His mother turned away, her shoulders shaking with sobs.

"Ah," the centarch said. "You must be the brother. Gyre, is it?"

Gyre nodded. "Put my sister down."

"It is commendable, of course, to defend one's family," the centarch said. "But I am afraid you have made a mistake. My name is Va'aht, called Va'aht Thousandcuts, a centarch of the Twilight Order." His free hand brushed across his haken.

"I know what you are," Gyre said. "Put her *down.*"

"If you know what I am, you know that the Order helps wherever it can. I am going to help your sister."

"She doesn't want to go," Gyre said.

"I don't!" Maya wailed. "I'm not sick, I'm *not.*"

"Children don't get to make those decisions, I'm sad to say," Va'aht said. "Now, if you would stand aside?"

Hand trembling, Gyre reached for his belt. He drew his knife, the knife his father had trusted him with the day he found all the vulpi. It was a wickedly sharp single-edged blade almost four inches long. Gyre held it up in front of Va'aht, heart thumping wildly.

"*Gyre!*" Gyre's father shouted. "Drop that at once and come here!"

"I see," Va'aht said gravely. "Single combat, is it? Unfortunately, boy, I'm afraid I don't have time at the moment. Once you've grown a bit taller, perhaps." The centarch turned. "If there's—"

Gyre moved while he was looking the other way. Va'aht's torso was armored, and Gyre's steel blade wouldn't even scratch the unmetal. But his legs were protected only by leather riding trousers, and Gyre swung the knife down as hard as he could into the man's thigh. It sank to the hilt, blood welling around the wound.

Va'aht shouted in pain, and Maya screamed. Gyre's mother was screaming too. Gyre tried to maintain his grip on the blade, pull it out for another stab, but Va'aht twisted sideways and he lost his hold. The centarch's knee slammed into Gyre's stomach, sending him gasping to the floor.

"Gyre!" Gyre heard his father start forward, but Va'aht held up a warning hand. The centarch still had hold of Maya, who was staring down at her brother, too scared even to keep shrieking.

"That," Va'aht said through clenched teeth, "was unwise."

"He's just a boy," Gyre's father said. "Please, I'll answer for it, I'll—"

"That's Order blood, *boy*," Va'aht said, raising his voice. "The blood of the Chosen. Every drop is worth all the flesh and bone in your body. Consider that, and reflect on my mercy."

"Mercy, sir," Gyre's father said. "Please."

Gyre heaved himself up onto his elbows.

"Let her go," he croaked.

Va'aht put his hand on his haken. He didn't draw the weapon, just touched it, and crooked one finger.

Pain exploded in Gyre's head, a line of fire from cheek to eyebrow. He was falling backward, hitting the floor shoulder-first, feeling nothing but the searing agony in his face. He mashed his hand against it, and blood *squished*, torn skin shifting nauseatingly under his fingers. He only realized he was screaming when he had to stop to take a breath.

Va'aht loomed above him, an outline shimmering in a haze of tears.

"You'll live, with care, though I daresay there'll be a scar." The centarch gave a humorless chuckle. "Let it be a lesson to you."

He limped past, still carrying Maya. She screamed Gyre's name again, but his thoughts were already fading into a fiery blur of pain. By the time his father reached his side, darkness was closing in around him.

Chapter 1

Twelve Years Later

It was hot, and Maya was watching an empty house.

She sat on a rickety chair, staring out a second-story window through the gap between two stained, threadbare curtains. It gave her a perfect view of the alley below, which contained nothing more obviously interesting than a midden aswarm with flies, and a mangy old dog, huddled miserably in the shrinking shadow of the building to try to keep out of the sun.

There was also the front door of a single-story shack that, as best as Maya and her mentor had been able to determine, was the lair of a monster.

Watching this was Maya's assignment, which was all well and good, except that she was convinced the monster wasn't actually home. There had been no movement through the one visible window of the little shack. No movement in the alley, either, aside from the drone of the flies, the panting of the dog, and the heat haze dancing above the baked-mud road.

The city of Bastion seemed designed for misery. It was surrounded by a Chosen relic, a rectangular unmetal wall stretching nearly a kilometer on its long sides and thirty meters high. The human city was jammed inside, like a wasp's nest daubed between joists in an attic, the taller buildings around the edges leaning against the indestructible unmetal for support. All well and good for defending the city against bandits or plaguespawn, but it made for a tangled rat's warren of streets, and the wall kept the air fetid and stagnant. The whole place smelled like a cesspool.

Her vantage point was a second-story room in the sort of flophouse that rented by the hour. At the moment, the room was only slightly more interesting than the alley. There was a bed whose stained sheets Maya had flatly refused to touch under any circumstances, a chamber pot, two rickety chairs that had been smashed and repaired so often they were more nail than wood, and a thirteen-year-old boy lying on his back and tossing baked nuts into the air to try to catch them in his mouth, surrounded by the evidence of his repeated failure at this task.

Maya glared at the boy, whose name was Marn. Against all appearances, he was also an agathios, another student of her mentor, Jaedia, and bearer of the same gift Maya wielded: *deiat*, the power of creation, the Chosen's desperate legacy to humanity.

I refuse to believe the Chosen had Marn in mind, though. They would have taken one look at him and said, "Well, that's it. Might as well close up shop and let the plaguespawn eat everyone."

A nut caromed off Marn's nose. Sensing her stare, he tipped his head back and looked at her upside down.

"What?" he said.

"You're supposed to be studying chapter fifteen of the *Inheritance*," Maya said.

"And you're supposed to be watching the street, not paying attention to me," Marn said, with thirteen-year-old sophistry. "So if you've noticed *I'm* not studying, then by definition—"

"Shut up." Maya glanced guiltily back at the alley, but nothing had changed. The old dog rolled on his back, panting. "Hollis probably isn't even there."

"Jaedia thinks he is. Why else would she go to the Auxies for backup?"

"I don't know why she bothers with the Auxies in the first place," Maya grumbled. The local authorities were usually worse than useless. "Whatever's in there, we can handle it."

"If I had a haken, I could help," Marn said, fumbling for another nut.

"If you had a haken, you'd blow your own head off."

"Would not."

"Would so."

That was about the level of discourse she and Marn achieved, most days. Jaedia told her to forgive Marn for being thirteen, but Maya had been thirteen only four years ago and she was reasonably certain she'd never been *that* stupid. *Or stubborn.* She turned back to the window with a sigh.

If Hollis is there, he's staying out of sight. The *dhakim* known as Hollis Plaguetouch had eluded the Order this long. *Maybe he's already cut and run. In which case . . .*

Maya froze. Shadows moved on the wall of the alley. A moment later, three people came into view, walking single file. Two were large men, in the sleeveless white shirts and canvas trousers of common laborers. One was shaved bald, and the other wore his dark blue hair in a long queue. Between them walked a young woman in a colorful dress, long golden hair unbound. There was something off about the way she moved, but Maya didn't catch it until she'd walked directly under the window. *Oh, plaguefire.*

"Marn!"

"Ow!" Marn rolled over. "Plague it, you made me drop that one in my eye!"

"They're taking someone to the house!"

"Who is?" Marn got up and shuffled over to the window. The two men had reached the end of the street, one of them standing with the girl while the other unlocked the door.

"You think they're with Hollis?" Marn whispered.

"The men are," Maya said. "The girl's a prisoner."

"How do you know?"

"She's gagged and her wrists are tied behind her back."

Marn looked over at her nervously. "So—"

"Shut up and let me think."

The door in the alley opened, and the trio went inside, one of the men pushing the girl along by the arm. *She looks terrified.*

Maya's hand came up, unconsciously, and touched the Thing. It was a bad habit, calling attention to something that was supposed to stay secret, but she'd never been able to break it. The little piece of arcana, like a rounded crystal surrounded by a ring of smaller faceted stones, was embedded in Maya's flesh just above her breastbone. It had saved her life as a girl, banishing the coughs and fevers that had nearly killed her, and ever since, she found herself tapping it when she was anxious, as though to make sure it was still there.

Jaedia won't be back for another hour, at least. Her mentor had assigned her to watch for Hollis trying to leave, not people arriving. And she'd made it very clear that Maya wasn't to do anything more than observe. *But she didn't consider them bringing in a* prisoner, *did she?* Maya didn't want to think about what might happen to a bound and gagged girl dragged into a nest of *dhakim*, but the images came all too readily to mind. *Oh, fucking plaguefire.*

Not much of a choice.

"Don't be stupid," said Marn, who'd been watching her expression.

"I'm not being stupid." Maya checked her panoply belt, threaded under her shirt around her midsection. Her haken was concealed at the small of her back, instead of in its normal place at her hip, but she could still draw it quickly. "Chosen know what they're going to do to her."

"Jaedia said to stay here!"

"*Jaedia* wouldn't stay here and let some poor girl have her skin torn off," Maya retorted. "And neither will I."

"But *you're* not a centarch!"

Not yet. Maya gritted her teeth. "I'm still going in. You go and find Jaedia, tell her to get back here as soon as she can."

"How am I supposed to find her?" Marn said. "All I know is she's somewhere—"

"Fucking figure it out!" Maya snarled as she turned from the window and ran for the door.

The flies scattered into a buzzing cloud as Maya emerged, and the ancient mutt cringed against the wall. Bad as the heat had been in the room, it was worse out here, the air baked dry and stinking of rot. Maya hurried to the end of the alley and paused in front of the door to the shack. Every instinct told her to knock, but under the circumstances it felt ridiculous. *Excuse me, Master Dhakim, but I couldn't help but notice you kidnapped a girl?*

She touched her haken with one hand, and the power of *deiat* opened inside her. Heat flashed across her body, like sparks landing on her flesh. The sensation passed in an instant, replaced by the steady pressure of waiting energy in her haken. Maya threaded a thin strand into her belt and felt the panoply field activate, throwing a very slight blue haze over her vision. Thus protected, she stepped forward and tried the door latch, her other hand brushing against the Thing for reassurance.

The door clicked open, swinging inward on rusty hinges to reveal the filthy interior of the shack. There was no furniture, just a cold hearth against one wall surrounded by a few pots and pokers. Dirt was smeared across the floorboards, as though muddy livestock had been driven through. A small window in the back wall looked out onto a brick-lined carriage yard, but there were no other doors, and no sign of the *dhakim* or their prisoner.

They must have a hiding place somewhere. Maya looked over her shoulder. *No wonder we couldn't spot anyone inside.*

The door swung closed, and only dim light came in through the curtained windows. Maya opened her hand and tugged another tiny strand of *deiat*, conjuring a cool flame that danced blue-white across her fingers. In that harsh glow, she paced in a circle, searching for some sign of the residents. There were bootprints in the dirt, but they ran in every direction.

Where in the Chosen's name did they go? Maya's jaw clenched as she imagined the two thugs dragging the girl through some secret passage, only meters away. *Come on, come on.*

Something made the hairs on her arm stand up. She stopped pacing and paused until she felt it again—a chill draft, lovely in the stifling, dead air. Not from the windows, but from the floorboards. *Underground.* Maya stomped her boot, hard, and the sound was hollow. *Got you.*

With a terrific *crunch* of shattering wood, a ropy *thing* studded with yellowing spikes smashed up through the floorboards, spraying splinters in all directions. It lashed itself around Maya's ankle, and before she could reach for her haken she was yanked downward. The floorboards gave way under inhuman strength, and she felt the panoply field flare as she fell, blunting her impact a moment later. Generating the shield pulled power from her, which she felt as a sudden chill, her heart abruptly hammering loud and fast in her ears.

She'd hit stone, about three meters down, light spilling from a broken circle of floorboards overhead. The tendril-thing was still gripping her ankle, and Maya snatched her haken from the small of her back. She drew on *deiat*, channeling it through the Elder device. The haken, shaped like the hilt of a sword, grew a blade, a meter-long bar of liquid fire that lit up the underground space and threw shifting, hard-edged shadows.

Every centarch manifested *deiat* differently—as lightning, ice, raw force, or subtle energies. For Maya, it had always been fire. *Deiat* was the fire of creation, the raw power of the universe. When Maya swung her haken at the gripping tentacle, water on the damp rocks spat and flashed into steam, and the fleshy appendage parted with no more resistance than a damp sheet of paper. The end wrapped around her ankle spasmed and went limp, and Maya shot to her feet.

By the haken's light, she could see the rest of the tendril, and the creature it was attached to. It was a hulking, heavyset thing, the size of a very large dog or a small pony. There was no confusing it with any natural animal, though. *Plaguespawn.*

It walked on six legs, asymmetrical, one dragging and one extra-jointed. The thing had no *skin*, its grotesque musculature on full display, red-gray flesh twisting and pulsing as it moved. Bones protruded from its body, apparently at random, sharpened to yellow, hardened points. A skein of tangled guts hung loose beneath its belly, dripping vile fluids.

And yet the worst part was not what was alien about the creature, but what was familiar. Here and there, pieces of other animals were visible, incorporated whole in the fabric of the monster's flesh. Half a dog's snout, upside down, made up what passed for its jaw, with a dozen dangling, wriggling protrusions like the tails of rats. One of the legs ended in a five-fingered hand that looked disturbingly human. The tendril that Maya had severed was its tongue, a muscular rope at least four meters long, edged with canine teeth. A dozen eyes of various sizes stared at her from across the thing, all blinking in eerie unison.

Jaedia had once described plaguespawn as the product of a mad taxidermist, given the run of the contents of a butcher shop and a morgue. That was close, but Maya thought that no human mind, however mad, could have matched the awfulness of the real thing. And, despite all its deformities, the thing *functioned*. When it stepped forward, the play of muscles in its flanks was smooth and powerful. Its long tongue coiled under its half jaw, dripping black blood from the severed tip.

In the shadows behind it, Maya saw more of the creatures. They were smaller but no less horrific, each a unique amalgamation of rats and cats and dogs and whatever other flesh they'd been able to catch. Fangs, claws, and shattered, repurposed bones gleamed razor-sharp.

Maya straightened up, forcing a grin. Bravado was wasted on these monsters, of course, but...

"Well?" she said. "Are you coming or not?"

They came, the small ones first in a wave, with the larger creature lumbering in behind them. Maya gave ground, drawing power through her haken, and drew a half circle in the air with her off hand. A wall of flame blasted up from the stones, cutting in front of the plaguespawn with a crackle and a wash of heat.

Maya didn't expect that alone to stop them. The first of the creatures came through only moments later, scorched and smoldering. Its claws scrabbled on the wet stone as it leapt for her, sideways jaws dripping slaver. But it was alone, the others being slower to dare the flames, and Maya was able to sidestep smoothly and pivot to cut the thing in half. Her haken blade went through muscle, bone, and sinew like a wire through cheese, and the separate parts of the thing splashed to the stone behind her, twitching spastically.

The next one appeared in a rush, a crest of hair on its back aflame, and Maya separated its head from its body with a sweeping downward cut. Two more emerged together, coming at her from opposite directions. She intercepted the one that looked more dangerous, smashing it to the ground in a smoking ruin, while the other scored against her hip with a pair of raking strikes. Its claws of splintered bone stopped a few centimeters from her skin, the panoply field flickering blue-white, and she felt the bone-numbing cold of a rapid drain of energy. A gesture with her free hand blasted the thing with a bolt of fire that tossed it backward, burning fiercely.

She had barely a flicker of warning as the long tongue of the largest creature lashed out again, this time for her throat. Maya ducked, swiping upward and missing, the tongue vanishing beyond the curtain of fire. She closed her fist, and the flames died, revealing the creature gathering itself for another strike. Maya didn't give it the chance; she charged through the burning, shattered corpses and dodged when the tongue slashed again. Her haken licked out, a horizontal cut that severed one of the thing's legs and sliced the hanging ropes of guts, spraying the ground with vile fluids. The plaguespawn staggered, eyes rolling wildly, and Maya delivered another blow to its head, slicing the dog's muzzle in two. It retreated, wobbling like a drunk, and she sent a wash of fire boiling over it. Eyeballs exploded in the heat, and after a few moments the increasingly blackened plaguespawn collapsed, settling down to burn with an awful stench.

For a moment, nothing moved, and the only sound was the crackle of dying fires. Maya straightened up from her fighting crouch, haken still held in front of her. Her free hand touched the Thing, just for a moment, and she let out a long breath.

"I did it."

Her heart was hammering in her chest, the adrenaline of the fight rapidly turning to euphoria. Not that she hadn't fought plaguespawn before, of course. *But never without Jaedia looking over my shoulder.* She'd been telling her mentor for months now that she could handle things on her own. Maya felt a wide grin spread across her face.

"I *fucking* did it!"

Someone hit her very hard from behind.

She didn't pass out, in the normal sense. The panoply belt was Chosen arcana like the haken, a tool that used *deiat*, albeit a far more specialized one. It drew power from the user to protect them, heedless of how much energy the user actually had to offer. This drain, rather than the actual impact, was what made her lose consciousness, and so when she awoke it was not to a pain in her skull but rather with the trembling, sore-muscle sensation of *deiat* exhaustion. After suffering that kind of abuse, her connection to her power would take hours before it could be used again.

Okay. Maya shook her head, trying to clear the lingering muzziness, and looked around. *So where am I?*

A single torch burned in a wall bracket, illuminating a circular brick room she guessed had once been a cistern. The open ends of pipes protruded from the walls at irregular intervals, some capped off, others broken and jagged. Maya herself was propped against one wall, her hands tied to a pipe above her head with rough hemp rope. Her ankles were bound as well, and a few brief tugs assured her that whoever had done the binding knew their business.

Her haken was nowhere in sight, though she could sense that it was still nearby. They hadn't stripped her of her panoply belt, but without a connection to *deiat* it was just so much silvery fabric.

All in all, it doesn't look great, does it?

On the other hand, she wasn't dead. *Not being dead always opens up possibilities.*

She took a moment to berate herself for letting her excitement get the better of her, but only a moment. Maya tried standing up a little straighter, putting some slack into the rope at her wrists, and was craning her head back to see if this could give her any advantage when a door in the side of the cistern opened.

She knew the man who came in by sight, though they'd never met. Tall, pale-skinned, with a bald dome of a skull. He wore a leather coat with a high fur lining, too hot by far for this time of year, and there was no mistaking that bulbous nose and those bushy eyebrows.

"Hollis Plaguetouch," she said, settling back down.

"They still call"—he paused for a fraction of a second, then tilted his head and continued in a slightly different intonation—"*call* me that, do they?"

"I am seizing you on the authority of the Twilight Order," Maya said. "You stand accused of practicing *dhaka*. You will have an opportunity to present evidence in your defense."

Hollis laughed, loud and sudden. Maya set her jaw, waiting stoically until he'd finished.

"You are a bold-*bold* little thing, aren't you?" His voice was a rich baritone, but he had a strange nervous tic—not an ordinary stutter, but an odd pause that made him sound like a machine with a broken cog.

Hollis stepped closer, bushy eyebrows rising as he studied her. "Shall I untie you and submit, then?"

"That would be a good start," Maya said. "Though I can't promise leniency."

"What a pity-*pity.*" Hollis raised an eyebrow. "Let me offer a counter-proposal. You tell me how the Order found me and how many of you they have looking."

"And what?" Maya said. "You'll let me live?"

"No, I'm afraid not-*not.* But I can promise you won't be conscious as I tear your body into pieces for spare parts."

"Tempting." A drop of sweat rolled down Maya's forehead.

"You will refuse, of course-*course.* Such a brave girl." He rested two fingers on her cheek, and Maya fought the urge to lean away. "Fortunately, your cooperation is not necessary. I can change-*change* you until you *want* to tell me. Memory and desire are only matters of the flesh-*flesh,* after all."

"That's a bluff." Maya swallowed hard. "You may be *dhakim,* but you're not a ghoul."

"Do not presume to tell me what-*what* I am." Hollis' fingers moved in a line down her chin, forcing her head up and tracing the hollow of her throat down to her collarbone. There was no crude lust in his touch, only a cold evaluation, a butcher turning a cut of meat and deciding how to carve the first steak. "You'll find out soon-*soon* enough."

Maya's heart was slamming against her ribs, so hard she thought it might tear free. *He can't do it. He* can't. She could face the prospect of pain, even death, as inevitable risks of service to the Order. But what Hollis described—being turned into something *else,* something that was her but not—

Would I remember? Would I still be inside somewhere, the real me, screaming?

Peasants invoked the Chosen as though they were gods, begging them for favor and protection. The Twilight Order knew better. The Chosen, powerful as they had been, were gone, and there were no gods to answer. But at that moment Maya understood the impulse. *Help me. Someone. Jaedia, Marn,* anyone, *just don't let him do this.*

Gyre . . .

The *dhakim* stopped, his finger in the center of her chest, resting against the Thing.

"Interesting." A cold smile spread across his face. "Very inter-*interesting.*"

There was a long silence. Maya tried to think of something to say, some last defiance to spit in his face, but her throat seemed to have swollen shut.

"I think . . ." His hand fell to his side, and he stepped back. "I think it is not-*not* worth risking a *disruption.* Not now, when we have come so far." The *dhakim* shrugged. "I will see you again, never-*never* fear. And perhaps we will have a more . . . thorough conversation." He tilted his head, as though listening to something Maya couldn't hear. "It appears that our time here is nearly up in any event. Until next time, *sha'deia.*"

Next time? Maya stared, uncomprehending, as Hollis spread his arms and smiled beatifically.

There was a *crunch,* like breaking bone. Hollis stood stock-still, but something moved behind his head, hidden in his high collar at first, then scaling the top of the *dhakim*'s bald skull. It was black, spiderlike, with four spindly legs, muscles exposed like a plaguespawn but bones that looked like dark iron. A long bundle of thin tendrils, their barbed tips dripping blood, rapidly retracted into its underside.

It gathered itself and leapt, reaching the wall of the chamber and hanging from it like an insect. After a moment's pause, it scuttled upward into an open pipe, feet *tink-tinking* against the metal as it skittered away. At the same time, Hollis collapsed face-first to the wet stones. There was a large, ugly hole in the back of his neck, flesh peeled away as though something had torn its way out.

What the fuck *is going on?* None of it made any sense. *Why would a plaguespawn hurt its master? Why would it* flee? And what Hollis had said—

There was a new sound from outside the room, a whistling howl like a rising gale. *Jaedia!*

The door slammed open, and one of the thugs she'd seen outside stumbled through. It was the bald one, a short sword in one hand, bleeding heavily from a gash across his thigh. He backed up, lashing out with the weapon. It was intercepted by a line of swirling clouds, condensed into the blade of a haken. When they met, wind screamed a rising note, and the steel sword was sheared into two neat pieces. A moment later, a dozen blades of hardened air swept across the thug, and he exploded in a shower of bones and gore, blood splashing the wall of the cistern.

Jaedia Suddenstorm stepped into the chamber. She was tall and thin, lithe and flexible as a snake, with sparkling blue eyes and short, spiked hair the color of young leaves. The howl of the wind gradually died away as she lowered her haken, taking in the sight of Hollis' motionless body.

"Maya," she said, in her lilting southern accent. "Are you all right?"

"I think so," Maya managed. *Though I'm not sure why.*

"Good." Jaedia turned on her heel, eyes blazing. "Because I am going to *skin you alive.*"

After a few moments, Jaedia calmed herself and helped Maya down from the wall, though her expression still promised dire retribution.

"Honestly," she said. "How could you be so stupid? I explicitly told you—"

"There was a girl," Maya said, rubbing her wrists. "Two men brought her in here, bound and gagged. Did you see her?"

"Aye," Jaedia said. "She's scared to death, but she'll be fine." She held out Maya's haken, and Maya took it gratefully. "What happened to you?"

"I got caught up fighting those plaguespawn, and one of those men got to me from behind," Maya said, feeling blood heat her cheeks.

"A centarch of the Order, knocked down by a twopenny thug?" Jaedia glared. "You have to do better, Maya. When you get your cognomen, I'm not going to be here to pull you out of the fire."

"I know." Maya took a deep breath and blew it out. "I'm sorry. I just couldn't—"

"I understand." Unexpectedly, Jaedia stepped forward and wrapped Maya in a hug, something she hadn't done for years, not since Maya was old enough to be a proper agathios instead of merely a child in her care. Her voice was soft, and for a moment Maya thought there were tears in her eyes. "You have the heart of a proper centarch. I just need to knock a little more sense into your head."

Maya said nothing and hugged her back. It felt like a long time before Jaedia finally pulled away, scratching her spiky green hair.

"What happened to Hollis?" she said, looking down at the *dhakim*. "You didn't look like you were in a position to take him on."

"I'm not sure," Maya said. She shuddered at the memory of his exploratory touch, cold and clinical. "He . . . talked like he *recognized* me."

"When he saw your face?"

Maya shook her head and told the story from the beginning. Jaedia's frown deepened as she went on, then turned puzzled as Maya explained about the plaguespawn that had—attacked the *dhakim*? *Escaped* from him?

"I don't know," Jaedia said when Maya asked. "Never heard of anything like it, in all honesty. You're sure it stopped when it found . . ."

She trailed off, gesturing at Maya's chest. Maya nodded.

"That's doubly strange, then." Jaedia's lip twisted. "I need to speak to Baselanthus. The old bastard owes me some answers." She looked again at the corpse, then up at Maya. "And don't think *you've* heard the last of this, either. Now, come on. Marn is waiting."

Chapter 2

Deepfire was a city of many fogs, and after three years Gyre was familiar with the peculiarities of each. There was the black fog that issued from the Pit and meant it was time to take in your washing unless you wanted it stained gray. The rare green fog, which crept out of the crevices like a living thing and could kill a child in minutes. The falling fog, which descended in great gray waterfalls from where the cold mountain winds met the rising hot air from the cracked and broken earth, and the rising fog, billowing in tall columns from the sewers and storm drains.

This last was the most common, and it dominated the streets tonight, as it always did after a rain. It hung in tattered curtains, leaving beaded drops of water on the windows, softening the edges of the streetlights and turning their steady glow into a shifting, uncertain thing. To the east, the fog turned pink and then a sullen crimson, reflecting the glow from the Pit.

For the third time, Gyre's hand came up to scratch at his scar, and for the third time he stopped, frustrated, on encountering the etched metal surface of his mask. *Why did I ever start wearing the plagued thing?* He knew the answer, of course—there were only so many ways for a one-eyed man to hide his identity—but he'd never meant to build a legend. In the taverns of Deepfire, people whispered about Halfmask.

Idiocy. Even if Yora thought it was useful. He tapped his foot impatiently, until the leathery *slap-slap-slap* of reptilian footsteps echoed up from the empty street. *Finally.*

A moment later two shrouded lanterns came around the corner. They hung at the front and rear of a heavily built coach pulled by a pair of ragged-looking thickheads. A driver with a long, spiked prod sat on the box, poking lackadaisically at the lizard-like beasts, while a half dozen men and women in leather vests with knives and cudgels walked alongside, peering through the fog.

Six was more guards than they'd counted on. *At least we know the cargo must be worthwhile. Old Rottentooth clearly isn't taking any chances after last time.* Gyre waited a few more seconds, until the thickheads were just below him, fingering the stunner. The alchemical bomb didn't look like much, just a clay oval the size of his fist. Gyre tossed it over the edge of the roof and jammed his hands over his eye.

The faint sound of breaking pottery was followed immediately by a monstrous *crack*, as though the carriage had been struck by lightning. The stunner's flash briefly lit up the street brighter than midday, and Gyre saw the bones of his hands outlined through glowing orange flesh. A moment later, the light faded, and pained screams rose in its wake.

Gyre blinked a few errant spots from his eye and looked down. At least two of the guards were down, one unconscious on the cobbles and another one writhing and clutching her face. More important, the two thickheads were motionless, bellies pressed against the street and forepaws over their eyes. Ponies or loadbirds might have bolted, but a thickhead's panic response was to hunker down and let predators break their teeth on its pebbly skin. It would be a few minutes before anyone could persuade the beasts to move. *Perfect.*

A rope waited, coiled and ready, on the edge of the roof. Gyre scooped it up, tossed the coil over the edge, then stepped off himself. The cord hissed through his hand as he gripped tighter to slow his fall, and he felt the building warmth of friction even through the iron-studded leather glove. Before it grew uncomfortably hot, his feet touched the cobbles, and he dropped the rope and drew his knives.

Six guards outside, plus the driver. The driver was the one who'd been knocked out, his skin scorched from the small blast. The closest guard, writhing on the ground, wasn't a problem. *That leaves five.* The next nearest, a young man with gray-green hair, had backed against the carriage, waving his cudgel wildly and clutching at one ear. He blinked and tried to say something as Gyre approached, but Gyre's ears were still ringing from the blast. *Not that it matters.* The man only had time to gesture briefly with his cudgel before Gyre extended on his right foot into a textbook-perfect lunge and skewered him through the throat. *Four.*

That left four, as the young man spun away and painted the side of the carriage with spurting blood. The last one on this side was an older woman with stubby red hair and an angry scar across half her face. She tossed her cudgel aside and drew a long knife as Gyre advanced. Gyre dropped into a fighting crouch, feinted at her right leg, and let her parry and riposte. He twisted under the return blow, his forearm slamming into hers and shoving it out of the way, while his off hand came up and punched his short blade once, twice, three times into her stomach under her ribs. Her knife slipped from her fingers, and when he stepped away she stumbled forward and collapsed onto the cobbles.

Three. Gyre heard the scrape and grunt of fighting as he rounded the back of the carriage. On the other side, Yora and Harrow had emerged from their hiding place in the alley to engage the three stunned guards. Yora, long leather coat flapping, held two of them off with her flashing, spinning unmetal spear. Harrow had somehow ended up in a grapple with the third, her leg twisted around his as he pressed a forearm against her neck. They staggered together along the length of the carriage like a pair of drunken lovers.

None of them were looking for Gyre, which made things easy. He stepped in behind the larger of Yora's two opponents and drove his long blade upward at an angle into the man's back. As he staggered forward, his companion turned, cudgel swiping desperately to keep this new enemy at bay. Gyre danced out of range, feinted to keep his attention, then turned away as Yora's spearpoint erupted from the guard's chest, unmetal edge slashing effortlessly through flesh, bone, and leather. *Two and one.*

The guard in Harrow's grip saw her companions go down, and her eyes went very wide. She said something—too low for Gyre to hear, but Harrow paused, relaxing a fraction. In an instant she was twisting, fingers coming up to tear at his face as she fought to draw the knife at her belt. Before she got there, though, Yora's spear licked out, catching the woman in the eye and pinning her to the side of the wagon, unmetal passing easily through wood and bone.

Done. Gyre straightened up from his fighting crouch. Harrow let go of the shuddering body and stepped away, breathing hard. Yora pulled her spear free, letting the dead guard fall to the cobbles, and bent to pick up Harrow's two-handed axe from where it had fallen. It was a heavy steel weapon, but her arm didn't tremble as she handed it back to him.

"There's a time and a place for mercy, Harrow," Yora said. "But this isn't it. Once you've decided to kill somebody, make sure you follow through."

Harrow gave a nod, brushing lank brown hair off his sweaty forehead. He was eighteen, big and broad-shouldered but still with a hint of teenage gawkiness. He was in love with Yora, like half the tunnelborn his age, and Gyre saw the pain in his face at even this mild rebuke. *Idiot boy.*

"Good evening, my friends." Ibb stepped around from the front of the carriage. He looked as flamboyant as usual; he wore a long leather tunnel coat, like Yora's, but decorated with flashing bits of silver embroidery, and he added a broad-brimmed hat with one side rolled up in the Khirkhaz style. A long curved sword rode on one hip, and a blaster pistol in a worn holster sat on the other. "No difficulties so far, I take it?"

"Glad you finally decided to join us." Yora whipped her spearpoint down, spraying the dripping blood across the cobbles. She was shorter and slighter than her legend indicated, but her frame was corded with muscle, and her orange eyes blazed with enough force to make up for any deficiencies in stature. The frown she directed at Ibb could have spoiled milk, but he absorbed it with the aplomb of long practice.

"I was in the agreed-on position," Ibb said mildly. "It's not my fault Halfmask works so quickly."

"We're not finished yet," Gyre said. "Let's make sure we get what we came for before we start congratulating ourselves."

"Fair enough." Ibb hopped up onto the back of the coach and pulled the rear door open, leaning prudently out of the way as he did so. When nothing emerged, he swung back and peered inside. "The chest is here, at least. Thoroughly locked, though."

"We can take care of that later," Yora said. "Harrow, get those thick-heads moving."

The boy was already at work with the big lizards, clicking his tongue softly and offering a handful of squirming earthworms. The treat had the desired effect, and first one and then the other clambered back to their feet, snorting and shaking their heads at the residual effect of the stunner. Harrow let them lick the worms up with their long, spiked tongues, while Ibb pushed the unconscious driver off the box and picked up the reins.

Blood was painted across the cobblestones, vivid crimson in the lamplight. Gyre fought the urge to look away from the corpses. *They deserved what they got.* The woman he'd stabbed in the stomach had managed to crawl several meters before her strength gave out, leaving a slick of gore behind her. *They chose to work for the Order and the Republic. They're a part of the system, just as much as the highest centarch.* Once again, Gyre tried to scratch the scar where his eye was missing, and once again the half mask thwarted him. He swore.

The shrill shriek of whistles cut through the night, echoing weirdly in the fog. Gyre turned, hands dropping to his knives.

"Go!" Yora said to Ibb. "Harrow, stay with him. We'll buy you a few minutes to get clear."

Harrow clearly wanted to object, but Ibb was already snapping the reins, startling the thickheads into lumbering forward. He grabbed the boy by his shirt and hoisted him onto the box as the coach got up to speed. Yora moved to stand beside Gyre, spinning her spear in a slow circle.

"Was there a way out the other end of that alley?" Gyre said as the tramp of booted feet got closer.

"Someone's back door," Yora said, calm and professional.

"Locked?"

"Nothing I couldn't break through."

Lights swirled in the mist. "Give them a look at us," Gyre said, "then head that way?"

Yora gave that a moment's thought, then nodded. Gyre reached into the pockets of his coat and came up with three small clay spheres.

A squad of Auxiliaries emerged from the mist, twelve men and women with long spears and sword belts, in padded leather jerkins and conical steel caps. Their sergeant, a red-faced man with a bushy blue beard, had a whistle between his lips and was blowing for all he was worth. He pulled up at the sight of Gyre and Yora, and the squad clattered to a halt behind him. Gyre heard someone say, "Halfmask!"

"That's right," he muttered. "Here's your stupid ghost story."

He tossed the clay bombs, letting them land at the Auxies' feet. They were crackers, less spectacular than the stunner—too easy to blind himself at this range—and went off with more of a *pop* than a *bang*, but the explosion gushed an enormous cloud of choking, acrid smoke. Shouts of alarm and hacking coughs filled the street. Gyre held out a hand, warning Yora back from the expanding miasma. Only when the first soldier burst free of the cloud and fell to her knees, retching, did Gyre turn and run for the alley.

"They're getting away!" the woman rasped. "To the right!"

Perfect. Any pursuit would focus on them, rather than the stolen wagon and its lumbering team of thickheads. Gyre darted into the alley, Yora close behind him. But another set of footsteps followed, and he turned in time to see someone else turn in after them. His stomach fell.

Legionary.

The Auxiliaries were local militia, indifferently trained and armed with weapons forged by ordinary human smiths. The Legions of the Dawn Republic were another matter entirely. Equipped with Chosen arcana maintained by the centarchs of the Twilight Order, they were the heart of the Republic's military. They were spread thin—Gyre doubted there were a dozen Legionaries in Deepfire—but it was enough.

The soldier was armored in off-white unmetal from head to heel, an insectoid suit of overlapping plates that slid smoothly over one another at the joints. Gyre guessed it was a woman by her height, but there was no other way to tell, with her face obscured behind a pane of darkened Elder glass. On her left arm she carried a large round shield, and a sword rode on her right hip, one of the Legion-pattern unmetal blades. The snub nose of a blaster rifle poked up over her shoulder.

"Halfmask," she said, voice distorted by the mask. "I am detaining you by order of Dux Raskos."

"Get the door open," Gyre muttered. He saw Yora nod out of the corner of his eye.

The Legionary stepped forward, the streetlamps giving her armor an iridescent shimmer. "Put down your weapons and surrender."

Gyre drew his knives and charged, and the soldier drew her sword. Checking his momentum at the last moment, Gyre faded back from her slash, drawing her deeper into the alley. Then, with as little warning as possible, he planted his back foot and lunged.

It was a good move, and it would have worked against any ordinary opponent. His right-hand dagger curved in, wide and obvious, and the Legionary brought her shield up to block. His left thrust upward, fast and tight, even as his knife was skittering over the impenetrable unmetal. There was just a *hint* of cloth visible, where the bottom of her helmet met the articulated breastplate. *Maybe—*

She moved fast, faster than someone wearing armor had any right to. Her blade met his edge on, and where unmetal clashed against steel the Elder creation won easily. Gyre yanked his hand back and found himself holding the hilt of a dagger with perhaps an inch of blade remaining.

Oh, plaguefire. The Legionary advanced again, and Gyre danced backward. Something squishy burst under his feet, and for a moment he lost his balance. She thrust, and he threw himself sideways to avoid being skewered. His remaining dagger scratched uselessly against her shoulder, and she threw herself behind her shield and slammed it into him, driving him hard against the wall. Stars burst behind his eye as his head cracked the bricks.

"I am *detaining* you," she said. "Just hold still, would you?"

Gyre tried to think of a good rejoinder, his mouth coppery with blood, his vision edged with shimmers. He reached into his coat but froze as the Legionary raised her sword to his throat. Then, abruptly, the soldier spun, shield coming up. She wasn't fast enough, and Yora's spear slipped under her guard to slam into her breastplate. The Legionary grunted, retreating a step, and brought her sword down behind the spearhead. An ordinary weapon would have been sliced in half, but Yora's spear was of the same Elder make as the Legionary's gear, and the sword rebounded with a distinctive crystalline ring.

Yora pressed her attack, spear whirling in her hands. Unmetal weapon or not, she was still unarmored, and she fought to keep the Legionary on the defensive. Her blade scraped against the soldier's shield and glanced off her armored side, and the Legionary ducked under a swing that would have sent the butt of the spear into her head. But the soldier's blade licked out, and Yora's parry caught it too late to turn the weapon entirely. The edge bit into Yora's thigh, raising a thin line of blood.

By that point, Gyre had caught his breath. More important, he'd gotten his hand into his coat pocket, grabbing his backup stunner. He ran forward, hurling the little sphere in the Legionary's face. It went off as he collided with Yora, one arm raised so the leather of his cloak covered her eyes.

The bomb exploded with a soft *whuff*, a wave of pressure, and a light much brighter than the noonday sun. The Legionary staggered backward with a strangled cry. Even facing away with his eyes tightly closed, Gyre still saw an orange flash, and afterimages danced across his vision. He could see well enough to get to his feet, though, and pull Yora up after him. Her eyes were watering fiercely, so he grabbed her hand and ran for the door, which now hung slightly open.

It led to a dusty storeroom, which had another door leading into the entrance hall of a small apartment building. Gyre tumbled a stack of boxes behind him, blocking the way, and he and Yora pounded through, boots clattering on the floorboards. The front door was latched but not barred, and in another moment they were through into a dark, empty street.

In theory, Deepfire proper, the aboveground part of the city, was sealed off from the tunnel network that surrounded it at night. Great gates guarded by Auxiliaries blocked off the major entrances, where city streets dove underground and merged seamlessly with the largest passageways. In practice, however, there were too many tunnels and not enough Auxies, and getting underground was just a matter of finding the right forgotten corner or dark oubliette.

Or, in this case, the unused last stall in an otherwise legitimate livery stable. Yora opened the stable door with an iron key and led the way past wooden pens full of the curled-up shapes of sleeping loadbirds. A few interrogative chirrups followed them, but the birds remained calm as she entered the stall at the end of the row, kicked some straw aside, and raised a wooden trapdoor.

"Your leg all right?" Gyre said, indicating the wound Yora had taken from the Legionary's sword. Yora glanced down as though she'd forgotten about it until that moment. "I've got some bandages."

"It'll keep," Yora said. "I want to put some rock between us and Ras-kos' people first."

Gyre nodded. They'd stopped hearing the whistles of Auxie pur-suit several blocks back, but that was no guarantee. *Not if he's sending Legionaries after us.* That meant they had the dux's personal attention.

Yora strapped her spear to her back and climbed down the short ladder under the trapdoor. Gyre pulled off his mask—and scratched his scar, a blessed relief—then followed. The ladder let them into a narrow stone passage, smooth walled except where chunks had fallen away to litter the floor with rubble. Yora took a glowstone from her pocket and shook it to life, its pallid blue light painting the walls with leaping, shivering shadows.

It was possible to forget, on the surface, that Deepfire was not a human place. It had streets and buildings, shops and restaurants, like any other city. If you were wealthy enough to live aboveground, only the deep, smoldering fire of the Pit and the white-capped mountains clustered close in every direction kept you from imagining you were somewhere in the central Republic.

For the majority of residents, though, an open-air dwelling was far out of reach. They lived in the tunnels, dividing up the vast, winding galleries with wood-and-cloth partitions, reclaiming human space from something Elder and intimidating. But no one forgot where they were living, not when every too-smooth curve and vast cavern was a reminder.

Before the Plague War, this had been a ghoul city—possibly *the* ghoul city, their capital, though legends were contradictory—and the endless kilometers of tunnels that honeycombed the mountain had once been their homes and workshops. Not long after the war began, the Chosen had unleashed a terrible weapon, which had smashed the place open like a child taking a shovel to an anthill. No one was quite certain what *kind* of weapon it had been, but everyone agreed it was still down there, sputtering away at the bottom of the Pit. It was the source of both the warmth that kept the city free of the surrounding glaciers and the occasional miasmic gases that strangled children in their sleep.

The surviving tunnels, in the meantime, had been ruthlessly

cleansed by the Chosen and their armies. These battles had left a rich legacy of Elder arcana behind, broken weapons and shattered armor, bits of junk and the occasional marvel. Not long after the end of the war and the final downfall of Chosen and ghouls alike, bold men and women had returned to scavenge for treasure and had raised the beginnings of the modern city in the still-glowing crater.

And then the centarchs decided no one else was allowed to play with their toys.

The small tunnel joined a larger one, which bore a few signs of habitation, bits of trash in the corners and crude messages painted on the walls. This eventually joined another, still larger passage, which became an alley feeding into one of the main thoroughfares. Apart from the smooth stone roof, twenty meters overhead, this could have passed for a street in the poor quarter of any city—a narrow, muddy road down the center, lined by narrow, rickety buildings. Day and night had little meaning down here, and torches and braziers burned nonstop, filling the air with a haze of smoke. There were no carriages in the tunnels, and a sea of bustling humanity pushed and grumbled past one another, mud spattering from their feet.

Poor bastards. It was hard not to pity the tunnelborn, who spent their lives down here, emerging aboveground only long enough to trudge to a job at some manufactory. They were gaunt from bad food and pale from lack of sun, like they were half corpses already.

Yora threaded her way into the crowd, instinctively using hips and elbows to work her way through the press. Gyre stayed in her wake. Even after three years, he couldn't maneuver through crowds of tunnelborn with the ease of a native like Yora. After a cramped, sweaty interval battling the press, they broke through into a less crowded section.

There was nothing marking out the door to the Crystal Cavern as belonging to a pub. Gyre wasn't sure if that was even the official name of the place. An alley led to a side tunnel, which dead-ended in an iron-banded door. It opened to Yora's knock, revealing a tough-looking woman who gave them a once-over, then grunted.

Inside, a long, low-ceilinged cavern was mostly full of a haphazard array of mismatched tables. There was a bar along one wall, made of pieces of old packing crates. The place was mostly empty, apart from a few determined lone drinkers, and Gyre spotted the rest of their crew in their usual spot in the back corner.

"Good to see you in one piece," Ibb said, tipping his hat graciously. He sat in a rickety chair tilted dangerously far back, his boots propped up on an unused table. "Have any trouble losing our helmeted friends?"

"A little more than usual," Yora said, pulling another chair over. "They had a Legionary with them."

Ibb raised his eyebrows. "That's unusual. Maybe we're finally getting to Raskos."

"Are you all right?" Harrow got up from where he was sitting and hurried over. When he noticed Yora's wound, his eyes widened. "That looks—"

"It's a scratch," Yora said, waving a hand. She prodded the wound with her finger and winced. "Sarah will sew it up for me. Right, Sarah?"

"Not really my area of expertise," Sarah said from the corner. "Nevin's the one who's good with needles."

"Nevin's a little busy at the moment," Nevin said.

Harrow pulled up a chair for Yora beside Ibb. A heavy wood-and-iron chest had been hauled onto a table, and Nevin sat in front of it, a pair of lockpicks in his hands, bent in front of a keyhole at one end. Sarah stood behind him, one hand on his shoulder in silent encouragement.

Sarah was their arcanist, a woman in her midtwenties, short and plump with a mass of red-brown curls. She'd been with Yora for years, since before Gyre had arrived in Deepfire, and her cheery optimism sometimes seemed like a deliberate counterpoint to Yora's dourness. Nevin was a newer addition, a tunnelborn thief whom Sarah had taken up with and convinced Yora would be a useful member of the inner circle. He was a tall, lanky young man with dark green hair and long, spidery fingers, well suited to the kind of work he was doing now.

There were more members of their nebulous organization, spread throughout the tunnels and reaching into Deepfire proper. Probably only

Yora knew for sure how many. Certainly among the tunnelborn—the Deepfire natives, born underground and rarely seeing the sun—there was no love lost for the Republic, Dux Raskos Rottentooth, and the Twilight Order that backed them. That resentment kept them alive every time Raskos sent his Auxies into the tunnels, searching for the daughter of Kaidan Hiddenedge and the thief called Halfmask who'd caused so much trouble.

It's kept us alive so far, anyway. If Raskos was calling in the Legionaries, that might not last. *Yora and I need to talk.* He glanced at Yora, who was deep in conversation with Ibb. Harrow, catching Gyre's look, gave him a resentful glare, and Gyre sighed inwardly. The boy's puppy-dog protectiveness of Yora was starting to get genuinely irritating. *He needs to learn that she can take care of herself.*

A loud *clunk* drew his attention back to the chest. Nevin leaned back, brushing his sweaty hair back from his forehead and grinning broadly.

"Told you," he said. "No problem."

"You're brilliant." Sarah bent down and kissed him, then flipped up the lid of the chest. "Let's see what we've got."

The box was full to the brim with small bundles, wrapped in rough cloth and tied up with twine. Yora and Ibb got up, too, and came over as Sarah rooted around, pulling out a few pieces that clunked when she set them on the tabletop. She peeked inside a few of the other bundles and gave a soft whistle.

"These I'll have to take a closer look at," she said, gesturing to her chosen items. "The rest looks like raw alchemicals. Lynnia's going to have a field day."

"A field day for which she'll pay handsomely," Ibb said, grinning broadly. "You know what that means." He glanced at Yora, then raised his voice. "A round for the house, courtesy of our favorite alchemist!"

One round turned into several, as drinks were wont to do. Gyre nursed a clay mug of dark, sour wine and watched Harrow try to keep up with

Ibb. The boy was already weaving unsteadily as he went back to the bar, while Ibb seemed utterly unaffected no matter how much he downed. *The benefits of experience, I suppose.*

Yora was holding court. Word had gotten around about the score and the free drinks, and a steady stream of tunnelborn made their way to the Crystal Cavern to pay their respects and collect their booze. They bowed to Yora, or bent close to whisper words of support they didn't dare say aloud, or raised foaming mugs to toast the memory of Hiddenedge and his companions, who'd first roused the tunnelborn against the Republic and ended up dying in a cell for his pains.

"It's not all that encouraging a story, actually," Sarah said, coming to sit beside Gyre as yet another toast was proclaimed. "From our point of view, I mean."

Gyre glanced at her. She and Nevin had been sitting in a corner for some time, pressed close and lips locked, pausing only long enough to down the drinks Ibb kept bringing them. "What happened to your boy?"

"Having a piss, I think. Or losing his dinner." Sarah gave a cheerful shrug. "You don't look like you're enjoying yourself."

"It's dangerous to be out in public like this, even in the tunnels." Gyre watched Yora shake a gnarled old man's hand, nodding as he told her some story. "I'm just not sure it's worth the risk."

"It lets the tunnelborn know someone's fighting for them," Sarah said. "That's worth something, I think."

"To them?"

"And to us, if it means a friendly hand or a sympathetic ear when we need one." Sarah raised an eyebrow. "Seriously, what's eating you? You're not usually the worried one."

"Just thinking too much," Gyre muttered.

"I know what'll fix *that*," Sarah said, pushing his mug toward him. Gyre took a drink, to appease her, and changed the subject.

"So did you get a chance to look closer at the loot?"

"Only a little." Sarah's eyes lit up. "One piece is a secondary actuator, which looks intact. It might have come off a skyship, but more likely got broken off from—"

She was interrupted by Nevin, returning from the toilet apparently none the worse for wear. Sarah bounced off to meet him, leaving Gyre alone once again with his thoughts.

Enough. Gyre downed the rest of his wine and got to his feet, waving off Ibb's offer to get him another. He stalked out through the now-crowded pub, emerging into the darker, quieter tunnel outside the door with a deep feeling of relief.

Thinking too much. You can say that again. For a moment he hesitated. He badly wanted to be back in his own bed, but fading adrenaline had left him with aching limbs and a throbbing headache. *Maybe I should find a flophouse and head back in the morning.*

The door opened behind him, and Gyre turned to find Yora, hands in the pockets of her tunnel coat. She caught his look and raised an eyebrow.

"Tired of playing host?" he said.

"A bit." Yora had unpinned her hair from the tight bun she kept it in on jobs, and it hung in waves down the back of her coat, gleaming in the faint torchlight like liquid gold. She ran a hand through it and sighed. "Half of them want favors, and the other half just want to tell me how they supported my father all along."

"Easy to say, after the fact," Gyre said.

"I know. If half the people who say they were with him now had been willing to stand up..." Yora shook her head, and there was a hint of pain beneath her usual stoic mask. She'd been ten when her father had died, Gyre remembered. *Barely older than I was when the Order took Maya.*

"Sorry," Gyre muttered. "Didn't mean to stick my finger in old wounds."

She waved it away, then said, "Sarah's worried about you. So's Ibb. Usually taking down a bunch of Auxies is what cheers you up."

Gyre snorted. "Let me guess. They think I should come in and get roaring drunk?"

"They mean well." Yora stepped closer, leaning one shoulder against the rock wall. "What's wrong, Gyre?"

Gyre blew out a deep breath. "That Legionary was waiting for us."

"Raskos can't know exactly what we were going to hit. I bet he scattered a squad across a few likely targets."

"Even so. He wants us badly."

Yora nodded. "We're hurting him. And the best part is, he can't go crying to the Order for help. The last thing he needs is for some centarch to start poking around."

That was true enough. Among the dux's responsibilities was suppressing the trade in *dhak*, which in the modern Republic meant anything Elder, ghoul, or Chosen that didn't come through the Order. Most of Deepfire's duxes had taken advantage of their position to line their pockets with a little light smuggling, from what Gyre had read, but he suspected none had gone quite as far as Raskos Rottentooth— the man had his own *warehouse. So he can't exactly complain to the Order that his illegal shipments are going missing.*

"Right," Gyre said. "So he'll do what he can to stop us—Auxies, Legionaries, mercs, whatever it takes."

"And we'll keep getting past them," Yora said. "We managed tonight, didn't we?"

"Barely." A week of careful planning and smooth execution had nearly been ruined by a single soldier. "But let's say we do. Then what?"

"Eventually, Raskos goes down," Yora said. "He seems strong, but he's on a narrow base, with the tunnelborn on one side, the Republic nobility on the other, and the Order looming over his shoulder. Keep shaking him, and he'll lose his footing."

"And *then what*?" Gyre growled. "We take the city? The Republic will send a hundred Legionaries through the Gate and take it back. Or a centarch wanders through and blasts us back into our holes without breaking a sweat. We had *one* Legionary come after us, and that was almost too much. How are we supposed to fight back?"

"This isn't about taking on the whole Republic," Yora said, her tone stiffening to anger. "This is about bringing down Rottentooth and getting justice for the tunnelborn. When the city rises and the dux falls, the Senate will negotiate."

Negotiate. Gyre closed his eye, breathing deep, and said nothing.

"I know," Yora said, after a moment. "It's not enough for you. You want to burn the whole thing to the ground."

Gyre held his silence, and Yora sighed again.

"You're good, Gyre. There's no one I'd rather have at my back in a fight, and no one who works harder once we have a target. The tunnelborn are starting to talk about Halfmask the way they talk about my father, and that's worth something."

"Not when the centarchs come for us," Gyre whispered.

"Let's focus on tomorrow." Yora's voice had softened again, and she patted Gyre on the shoulder. "And the next day, and the next. When we win, and Raskos has fallen, if you want to take your share of the loot and keep pushing, I certainly won't stand in your way." She smiled—not a false smile, but not genuine either, the practiced expression of a leader who knew how to deploy it to encourage the troops. "Until then, I hope you'll stay by my side."

"Of course," Gyre said. He pushed away from the wall. "Like I told Sarah. Just thinking too much."

"You should—"

Gyre raised his only eyebrow. "Get roaring drunk?"

"I was going to say 'get some rest,'" Yora said.

"Probably a better plan," Gyre muttered. He pulled his coat a little tighter around his shoulders. "Send for me when you've got the next target."

"You know I will," Yora said. "Good luck, Halfmask."

"There you are," said Lynnia Sharptongue from the seat in front of her worktop. She didn't look up from whatever she was mixing. "I was starting to wonder if Raskos' idiots had finally caught up with you."

"Not yet," Gyre said, pulling the basement door closed behind him.

It led directly into a forgotten tunnel, which made coming and going convenient. "But it was a near thing."

"Someday you're going to run out of luck," Lynnia said. "I've been telling Yora that for years. Not that anyone listens to me, mind."

"Good to see you, too," Gyre muttered.

The basement was lit by more glowstones, safer than fire around alchemical compounds, which meant everything was tinged blue. By that pallid light, Gyre could make out a large room, with a long, scarred granite worktop along two opposite walls, both covered in a menagerie of glassware, boxes, and iron devices with cranks and toothed wheels that looked like instruments of torture. Lynnia sat on a swiveling chair, working a tiny grindstone with one hand and peering at the results through a loupe. When she looked up, her eye was grossly magnified by the lens, pupil dark and enormous.

Gyre had no idea how old Lynnia Sharptongue really was, only that she'd been a fixture in Deepfire longer than anyone could remember. She didn't look ancient so much as *weathered*, her skin wrinkled and spotted, her curly black hair hacked off short. She wore an eclectic collection of tattered dresses, sometimes several at a time, with protective leather gear thrown over the top. Given the tendency of the things she worked with to explode or catch fire, it was a sensible choice.

As far as the Republic's tax collectors knew, Lynnia was a respectable spinster, drawing a modest income from family wealth invested in a Deepfire merchant combine. This allowed her to keep a well-appointed brick house in the West Central district, comfortably close to the Pit and far from the chill of the tunnels. It had a ground floor and an upper story, both of which went almost entirely unused. Lynnia spent her days in the basement, mixing, grinding, and very carefully burning the strange substances the ghouls had left behind and turning them into all manner of alchemical cleverness.

This was highly illegal, of course, but that didn't seem to bother Lynnia, any more than the risk of blowing herself up did. At her age, she always said, she welcomed any sort of excitement.

"Everyone's fine, incidentally," Gyre said. "Thank you for asking."

Lynnia waved as though that was of little importance. She flipped her loupe out of the way and peered at Gyre. "And?"

"And what?"

"The new *stunner*," she said, barely able to contain her glee. "How did it work?"

"Well enough," Gyre said. "It got the thickheads hunkered down just like we wanted, and knocked the Auxies sprawling."

"Did you find a use for the other one?"

"Tossed right in a Legionary's face," Gyre said. "It just about slowed her down, but that's about it."

"The glass in those helmets shifts in response to light. Cuts out glare. I bet she'll have a headache, though."

"Good to know we can mildly inconvenience our enemies, at least."

"If you want to take down Legionaries, I'm going to need more to work with than glow dust and black drip," Lynnia said. "A bit of ignition oil, some drive stems—"

Gyre held up a hand. "Take it up with Sarah. She's going through what we got from the carriage. Right now, I'm about five minutes from falling over."

"Get yourself upstairs quick, then." Lynnia spun her chair back to the worktop. "Chosen know I can't carry you."

Gyre edged past her, pushing through the narrow lane down the center of the basement not occupied by alchemical glassware or general detritus. He'd reached the narrow stairway at the far end of the room when Lynnia looked up again.

"There was a delivery for you this afternoon," she said. "One of your mysterious friends. It's on the front table."

Gyre paused for a moment, then continued upstairs. The main floor was furnished much more conventionally than the basement workshop and was distressingly neat and tidy. Gyre shuffled over to the second-floor stairs, exhaustion growing in him with every step, and nearly forgot to pick up the envelope waiting for him on the front table. It was cheap paper, bulging and sealed in wax with the stamp of one of his usual couriers. Gyre put it in his coat pocket and went upstairs.

His bedroom was as ordinary as the rest of the house. Gyre made a point of not keeping anything incriminating here that he couldn't grab in a hurry on his way out, to make sure Lynnia could deny everything if Raskos ever tracked him this far. Even after three years, therefore, the place bore few traces of his personality—just some of his respectable clothes in a dusty wardrobe and a map of the city pinned up over the small desk. Gyre shrugged out of his coat and let it fall, the mask in his pocket hitting the floorboards with a metallic *clunk*. Then he flopped into bed and closed his eye.

Plaguefire. He rolled over and looked down at his coat. The end of the envelope stuck out of his pocket. *It's probably a lot of nothing, just like last week. And the week before.* But there was always a chance...

Sleep first. I can be disappointed in the morning.

He closed his eye again and took a deep breath. A moment later he was sitting up on the edge of the bed, swearing irritably as he broke the wax seal. He pulled out a few folded scraps of paper, along with another, smaller envelope.

Each torn sheet bore a few lines of hurried script, written in several different hands.

Doran Hardskull and his crew returned from the deep tunnels south of southwest. One man lost to plaguespawn. Recovered one antique armored suit, one blaster rifle, assorted trinkets.

Hina of Asclo back from looking for her sister. Found the body, died from a fall, but couldn't recover. No plaguespawn activities.

Carolinus Redeye brought in a wagonload of debris from the dig at Gaston's Fork. Some unidentified arcana that may be of interest.

And more, all in that vein. Gyre flipped through one after another, then tossed them aside.

He'd made the decision when he was eight years old. Lying in bed, skin slick with fever sweat, the gash where his left eye had been swollen and leaking pus. His father had cared for him. His mother, he'd learned later, hadn't been able to look at him without weeping.

Even at eight, he'd understood what had happened and what had to be done. If the Twilight Order could do this—if they could reach into his quiet, peaceful farm, unbidden, and destroy his family's happiness in an afternoon—then the Order could not be allowed to exist. It was that simple.

Only, of course, it wasn't. People fought the Order—or the forces of the Republic, which amounted to the same thing—all the time. Bandits, rebels, smugglers, *dhakim* cultists. None of them amounted to anything, no more than mites on a warbird. How could they? The Auxiliaries were ordinary men, even the Legionaries were only soldiers kitted out in Chosen relics, but the centarchs were something else entirely. They had *deiat* behind them, the fire of creation, and nothing could stand against that. And the power was inborn—if you didn't have it, no amount of wishing or training would ever let you wield a haken.

When he was twelve, he'd left home. He'd done what he had to do— been a thief, a bandit, a whore, a spy. Always working his way north, in the mountains, toward Deepfire. He'd come chasing a pair of rumors. The first was that in Deepfire, even after the failure of Kaidan Hiddenedge's rebellion, there were people who stood up and fought back against the authority of the Republic. The second was that there were wonders still to be found in the tunnels under the Shattered Peaks, ruins so deep that even the Order had never cleaned them out, where the lost power of the ghouls still waited. The only power that had ever been able to stand up to *deiat*, the power to topple the Order itself.

He'd made the difficult journey through the mountains, and it had nearly killed him. The master of the caravan he'd joined had dumped him on Lynnia's doorstep in a delirious fever. Once he'd recovered and gotten his bearings, it hadn't taken long to discover that the first rumor was true enough. Yora's crew was always in need of steady hands who were willing to take risks and do what was needed, and he'd done well.

As for the second rumor, Gyre had plowed his cut from the jobs they pulled into a network of eyes and ears, keeping track of scavenger gossip and notable comings and goings. In three years, it had brought him plenty of wild speculation, but never anything solid. There were ghoul arcana out there, and Chosen weapons, lying broken and forgotten in the dark—enough to make a few scavengers rich, but nothing that could accomplish what Gyre wanted. *Nothing that could challenge the Order.*

So he scouted targets for Yora, stole Raskos' ill-gotten gains, and waited.

With a sigh, he set the pages aside and picked up the second envelope, breaking another thin wax seal. The paper was considerably better quality, and it was written in a clean, educated hand. There were only a few lines.

Halfmask, it began. That made Gyre take a bit more notice. His agents didn't know his real identity, of course, but most of them didn't even know they were working for the mysterious rebel. That someone else had figured it out was worrisome. His brow creased as he read on.

I have been following your activity with interest, and I think we can help each other. I'd like to meet, if you have no objection. Come to the Smoking Wreckage tomorrow night and order the Katre '49. I'll find you.

That was curious enough that it took him a few moments longer to notice the signature. When he read it, Gyre went very still.

Doomseeker.

Chapter 3

A nother problem with a city built inside an indestructible wall, Maya thought. *Traffic jams.*

At Bastion's main gate, four streets merged into one messy thoroughfare, each contributing its load of vehicles and anxious, unhappy animals to the congestion. Whenever the line moved and a space opened up, drivers and teams jostled for position, trading insults and a variety of grunts and squawks. Loadbirds glared at one another and puffed out their feathers, thickheads exchanged clicks and hisses, and a pair of long-horned woodbreakers had to be kept from taking big bites out of the next cart in line. Pedestrians filtered through the mix, and enterprising locals sold food and water from trays.

"I thought," Marn said from his position in the back of the cart, "we were staying another week. You said we could look for those dumplings I like."

"Would you shut up about the dumplings?" Maya hissed.

"Plans change," Jaedia said, with a serenity Maya could only aspire to.

"But *why?*" Marn said, secure in the knowledge that Maya was not allowed to actually set him on fire.

"There'll be dumplings at the Forge," Maya said.

"Not the same kind. At the Forge they make everything with lake shrimp. It's gross." He shifted in the back of the wagon, trying to find a comfortable position on the pile of blankets and rolled-up tents. "If you killed Hollis, why are we in such a hurry?"

"Maybe shout about that a little louder," Maya said. "I'm not sure *every* Auxiliary in the city heard you."

Marn rolled his eyes. In fairness, Maya had to admit that the sound from the various impatient animals did a good job of drowning out casual conversation. But there *were* Auxiliaries everywhere, distinctive in their round metal caps, carrying spears and shouting at carters who got out of line, and the three of them were trying to remain inconspicuous. Up ahead, at the gate itself—thankfully not far now—a half dozen of the soldiers were stamping papers and asking questions.

The truth was, Jaedia's sudden decision to return to the Forge bothered Maya, too, though for different reasons. Her mentor spent as little time in the Order's great mountain fortress as she could manage, and they'd made only a half dozen visits in the last five years. For her to drop everything and go to consult with Baselanthus indicated that their encounter with Hollis had shaken Jaedia more than she let on.

A lumber wagon pulled by a pair of unruly thickheads finally rumbled away, and they were at the front of the queue. Jaedia clicked her tongue, and the loadbirds stepped forward a few paces. Four Auxies started poking around the back of the wagon, while another pair came up to speak to Maya and Jaedia on the bench. The one on Jaedia's side, looking bored, scanned the papers she offered him. The other, a youth about Maya's age with a face badly savaged by acne, gave her a frankly appraising look and a leering grin.

Maya gritted her teeth and, with an effort, kept her hand from going to her haken. It would be nice to teach this lecher-in-training a sharp lesson—by heating his codpiece until it burned, say—but while Jaedia might have managed such a focused application of *deiat*, Maya was still just as likely to incinerate the boy by accident. That would not help them remain inconspicuous.

"You're missing a stamp," the older soldier said, waving the paper. "Ministry of Trade."

"I believe I have that one," Jaedia said.

"It's out of date." He showed her the paper. "Got to get the Trade stamp *after* the Road and Commerce stamp, see? Otherwise you could change what you were carrying and Trade wouldn't know any better. Very important. You'll have to go and get it, then come back."

The thought of waiting through the line again put Maya on the brink of deciding to set the soldiers on fire after all, but Jaedia only took the papers back from the man, frowned at them, and reached into her belt pouch. She handed them back, and Maya saw the green and blue of a wad of Republic thalers go along with them.

"I think you'll find," Jaedia said, "that everything's in order."

"So it is," the soldier said, not even pretending to read the documents. "Go on through, then. You're holding up traffic."

The boy mouthed something at Maya, who made an obscene gesture in return as the cart clattered forward through the gate in the unmetal wall. Outside, another pair of guards waved them onward, down a rutted dirt road flanked by high hedgerows. The loadbirds picked up the pace a bit, and the cart shuddered and bounced over the uneven ground.

"Ungrateful bastards," Maya said, looking over her shoulder at the looming bulk of Bastion. "It's not fair."

"No?" Jaedia held the reins loose in her hands, adjusting the birds' pace with an occasional low whistle.

"We might have saved their whole plagued city. Chosen know what Hollis would have done if we hadn't stopped him." She shook her head. "And they don't even know it happened."

"You'd like a parade, perhaps? Streets strewn with roses?"

"A little courtesy wouldn't be too much to ask for," Maya muttered. "They treat us like—"

"Anyone else?"

Jaedia gave an enigmatic smile. At the moment she didn't look very much like a centarch. They all wore drab travelers' garb, dull and practical, with Jaedia and Maya concealing their haken under shirt and coat. But up close, Maya thought no one would ever confuse Jaedia for a peasant. She had thin, delicate features, deep, knowing eyes, and a smile that quirked *just so* and implied that every conversation was part of a lesson. That smile had been a constant in Maya's world almost since before she could remember. Jaedia's patient, leading questions had taught her to read, to ride, to draw her power, to understand the Order, her place in it, and their place in the world.

Maya loved Jaedia with all her heart. But, she had to admit, there were times when she found her mentor as exasperating as Marn. *Well. Let's not go too far. Nobody is as exasperating as Marn.*

"We're *helping* them," Maya said, trying to clarify her thoughts. "Hollis was a *dhakim*—for the Chosen's sake, he was kidnapping people and taking them to bits! Why should we have to *sneak* out of the city in disguise and bribe some jumped-up night watchman who should be groveling at your feet?"

"He probably would grovel, if he knew who I was," Jaedia said. "But out of fear, not out of gratitude. And once we were out of sight..." She whistled, and the birds picked up speed. "How would you feel, if you were the local dux? A centarch comes to your city and says they've shut down a *dhakim* cult, killed a few people, and now they're moving on."

"I'd feel happy," Maya said obstinately. "And embarrassed I hadn't found out about the *dhakim* myself."

"You don't think you'd be a little frightened?" Jaedia said.

"If the dux hadn't done anything wrong, he'd have nothing to be afraid of."

"Unless the centarch decides otherwise."

"But she wouldn't. I mean you wouldn't."

"And he knows me so well?" Jaedia shrugged. "Besides, what does it gain us to strut around showing off and throw the city into chaos? The chance to skip a queue and save the Order a hundred thalers? Baselan-thus can afford it."

"I know." Maya leaned back against the bench. "It's still not fair."

"Life isn't fair, Maya." Jaedia's expression was suddenly serious. "Is it fair that some peasant boy out there has to fight off plaguespawn with nothing more than a stick, while you could turn his village to ash by waving your hand?"

"That's why it's our duty to defend him!" This was the most basic lesson of the *Inheritance*, the book the Chosen had left behind to guide the Twilight Order. They'd granted the power of the centarchs, to be used to defend humanity in the aftermath of the plague. "It doesn't mean people should be afraid of us."

"Listen, Maya. No one is going to cry for Hollis Plaguetouch." Jaedia frowned. "But there will come a time when you have to hurt someone—even kill someone—to protect the rest, whether or not they deserve it. When that day comes, you'll understand why we have to hide so often. The Order does what must be done, and it does not win us many friends."

Maya swallowed, taken aback. After a moment, she glanced at her mentor, but Jaedia's face was a mask, her eyes on the road.

"You don't hurt people who don't deserve it," she ventured.

"I try not to. And"—she grinned—"I'm pretty good at it. But I'm always *ready*. You should be too."

There was another silence, broken by the chuffing of the birds and the rattle of the cart wheels.

"Ah, plague it." Jaedia scratched her short hair. "I don't mean to worry you. But it won't be long until you get your cognomen, you know. Then you'll have to decide these things for yourself."

Maya looked down at her hands, feeling a quiet thrill. *Not long.* She was seventeen—not the youngest ever promoted to full centarch, but well ahead of most. Her hand went to the Thing for a moment. *Not long...*

"How long until *I* get my cognomen?" Marn said from the back of the cart.

"That depends," Jaedia said. "Have you got chapter seven by heart yet?"

Marn groaned, and Maya laughed. The cart rolled on.

When they reached the turnoff to the forest road, they paused to give the birds a chance to rest. Jaedia cut open a canvas bag of the fat nyfa seeds they liked and scattered them on the ground. The unharnessed animals were soon pecking contentedly after them like enormous chickens.

Marn, to his vocal displeasure, was hard at work on the devious chapter seven. Maya and Jaedia, in the meantime, were sparring.

The power of *deiat* prickled through Maya's skin, and the panoply field shimmered into existence around her. Jaedia stood at the other end of a small clearing, her haken in hand. Her own panoply was invisible at this distance. *Not that she has much need of it.*

Maya raised her haken, and the blade flared to life, a shimmering bar of white fire. At the same time, she let her consciousness expand, feeling the flow of power between them. *Deiat* coiled around Jaedia, tensed like a cat ready to pounce. Maya drew power of her own, pulling it along the flaming blade. A swipe of her sword sent droplets of fire spattering in an arc across the ground, where they hissed and spat like coals dropped in a bucket.

Jaedia stepped forward, bringing her haken up, its blade like a roiling bar of solid cloud. It left a misty trail of vapor behind it as she slipped to the left, her stance open, and Maya matched her with a shift to the right. There was a moment of silence.

Then, as one, they struck.

When centarchs fought, the contest was always on two levels, blade against blade and power against power, and both were crucial. A contest of *deiat* was more likely to be decisive, but the tightest, sharpest control in the world wouldn't help against an opponent who separated your head from your body at the first clash. The combat that resulted felt like trying to turn cartwheels while doing logarithms, or playing chess and dancing a jig simultaneously.

Blade met blade in an explosion of vapor and twisting fire. Jaedia gave ground with elegant parries, and curving razors of solid wind opened around her like a flower. Maya pulled flame from her sword and wove it into a cage of fire, intercepting the intangible blows. She could feel the impacts, *deiat* thrashing against *deiat*, titanic energies grinding into one another. With a thought, she went on the offensive, summoning a snaky, whirling flame that split into four parts and whipped out to strike at Jaedia from unexpected angles. At the same time, Maya pressed the attack with her sword, feinting to drive her mentor against a tree, then hammering her before she could extricate herself.

Jaedia deflected the assault with her customary grace. Air turned solid as her power brushed it, forming curving shields that let the flames wash past instead of meeting them force for force. She parried a few blows, then ducked, letting Maya's blade bite into the tree behind her in a spray of flaming splinters. Maya drew a curtain of fire between them, already anticipating the counterattack, and knives of wind shattered against it. Jaedia rolled clear, popping up like a jackrabbit.

Right where I want her. One of the beads of fire Maya had cast off at the opening of the fight was just at Jaedia's feet. There was power packed in there, more than was obvious at a glance, and now she let it expand into a fireball that sent an earsplitting *bang* rattling through the forest and threw up a dense pall of smoke. For a moment, Maya couldn't see. *Did I get her?*

A rush of air drew her attention upward. Jaedia was above her, level with the treetops, a shimmering shield of solid cloud beneath her. *She rode the blast up!* And now she was descending straight toward Maya, blade coming down in an unstoppable arc with all her momentum behind it.

Maya did her best, sending curving lines of fire upward, but Jaedia blew through them like a descending comet. At the last moment, as Maya swung her sword desperately, Jaedia twisted midflight, letting the flaming blade pass close enough to her side to singe her clothes. As her cloud-sword came around, Maya felt herself grinning.

I should have known I couldn't get to her that *easily.*

Her panoply flared, a sick-making feeling of power emptying out of her like water draining from a broken barrel. Maya didn't even feel her impact with the earth.

When she came to, the late afternoon sun was slanting through the trees, and the world looked as though it had been dipped in gold.

Maya lay with her head pillowed in Jaedia's lap. Her mentor had one hand tangled in her hair, idly letting it run through her fingers like strands of crimson resilk. Maya's body ached from the drain of the panoply, but for an instant she felt utterly at peace, the summer sun pleasantly warm on her skin. She kept her eyes closed, hoping to prolong the moment.

"I can tell you're awake, you know," Jaedia said.

Maya sighed and opened her eyes, finding her mentor staring at her upside down. She grinned.

"I still can't keep up with you," Maya said.

"You're getting better," Jaedia said. "It was a good trick, laying traps for me."

"You always prefer to dodge instead of block," Maya said. "So I thought I wouldn't give you the chance."

"Try to disguise it a little better next time." Jaedia tapped her lightly on the forehead. "And don't forget that just because someone doesn't *like* a particular style doesn't mean they can't use it."

Maya nodded. Jaedia stared at her for a while, eyes distant, then shook her head.

"What's wrong?" Maya said.

"Just…thinking. About what I said earlier." Her lip quirked. "How do you feel about getting your cognomen?"

Maya swallowed. The question had a special meaning among the

Order. Ordinary people might have their final name bestowed by their friends, their families, or even their enemies, but it was different for centarchs. The Council assigned them, based on the nature of an agathios's powers and their standing with their colleagues. When a centarch died, their name would be given to another, a signal of the expectations the Order placed on the new recruit. Jaedia's cognomen, Suddenstorm, was an ancient one of honorable lineage.

When an agathios was granted a cognomen, they were accepted as an equal among the centarchs. Save for the twelve Kyriliarchs of the Council, no centarch stood above or below another, and each was free to carry out the mission of the Order as they saw fit.

I'm ready. Maya fought down her excitement. Aloud, she said, "I'm...not sure."

"I've kept you away from the Forge as much as I can." Jaedia's attention seemed to be far away. "I thought it would help keep you from being dragged into...politics." She pronounced the word like it was something foul. "Sometimes I wonder if I've really done you a favor."

"Of course you have," Maya said. She sat up, rolling over to face Jaedia. "I'd much rather be out here helping people than shut up in the Forge debating doctrine with a bunch of stuffy old scholars."

Jaedia laughed. "Of course you would. But you're going to have to know how to navigate those waters, sooner or later. I'm hardly the one to teach you, unfortunately." She sighed. "And don't think I've forgotten about your stunt with Hollis. Clearly there are some lessons still to be learned."

Maya cast her eyes down. "I'm sorry."

"That's a start." Jaedia clapped her on the shoulder and yawned. "Now, get up, my lazy student, or I'll be the one falling asleep next."

Maya climbed to her feet, wincing at protests from sore muscles. She followed Jaedia back to the cart, where the loadbirds had settled down for a nap, tiny heads tucked under their wings. Marn was napping too, sprawled in the cart atop the lumpy tarp that wrapped their gear. Jaedia left Maya to prod the boy awake while she hitched up the birds.

"Marn."

"Muh?" he said, opening one eye.

"What did Math-Eth-Avra say to the Council of Nine?"

"What?" The boy sat up, blinking. "You made that up."

"Chapter seven. That's what you were reading, weren't you?"

"Course." His face screwed up in thought. "Something about...
being doomed?"

Maya rolled her eyes. "Better hope Jaedia doesn't quiz you."

He scrabbled among the packs and rolled tents for his copy of the
Inheritance, and Maya rather smugly pulled herself back onto the bench
beside Jaedia. The birds clucked softly until Jaedia whistled them into
obedience, and they lurched down the overgrown forest track.

As the sun went down, the shadows grew longer, until only broken
fragments of light were visible between the trees. The track got rougher
and rougher, little better than a game trail. The darkening forest closed
in around them, trees pressing tight on every side. Jaedia lit a sunlamp
with a touch to her haken, and in its brilliant, bouncing light branches
seemed to shift and reach like stretching limbs. Maya ducked under
one that hung low enough to scrape the cart, and giggled as Marn, less
observant, got a face full of leaves.

Up ahead, the light from the sunlamp outlined the edges of a rocky
outcrop, with a few scraggly trees clinging to the top. It looked ordinary enough, but Maya could feel the power flowing under the little
hillock. Jaedia touched her haken again, sending a silent command
Maya could see as darting wisp of golden light. Part of the rock face
slid smoothly aside, shedding a handful of dirt. Within the hill, more
sunlamps woke gradually, as though a new day were dawning underground. The loadbirds balked briefly at the threshold, misliking the
ancient, musty smell, but Jaedia coaxed them forward with a whistle
and a flip of the reins.

There wasn't much to the secret space, just a square room, the walls
and floor of flat white unmetal, covered with dirty footprints and wheel
tracks from previous visitors. Opposite the hidden entrance was a

freestanding arch, tall enough for a warbird to ride through and wider than their wagon. It was made of hundreds of thin strands twisted round and round, like a rope woven from spiderweb. At its base it was as thick as a wagon wheel, but it narrowed as it climbed, until at the apex the arch was completed by a fragile-looking thread no bigger than Maya's little finger.

The fragility was an illusion, of course. It was made of some variety of unmetal, like most Chosen arcana, and thus invulnerable to anything short of a direct assault with *deiat*. This room had been here for at least four hundred years, and unless a mad centarch took it into their head to destroy it, it would exist unchanged for a thousand more. The archway was a Gate, the most important surviving arcana after the haken themselves.

Jaedia twisted in her seat and sent a command to the outer door, which slid closed as noiselessly as it had opened. The loadbirds stamped uneasily.

"Maya?" Jaedia said. "Would you do the honors?"

Maya took a deep breath and nodded. In her mind's eye, she composed the sequence that would wake the Gate, a brief command followed by a code telling it where she wanted to go. There were seventy-nine known Gates, both inside the Dawn Republic and beyond its borders, though the Council had deemed some too dangerous to use. When she was certain she had it right, Maya touched her haken and sent the command sequence into the arcana. It reached back to her, a questing tendril that latched onto her connection to *deiat* and began to draw power, like a thirsty taproot reaching a pond. A brief chill spread through her body, dissipating as her power replenished itself. The space under the arch filled from the top down with shimmering quicksilver, like a mercurial curtain falling. When it reached the ground, the ancient arcana sent back the code that meant it was ready.

Jaedia gave a low whistle, and the loadbirds started moving, squawking curiously as they approached the strange surface. She snapped the reins, goosing them forward, and they were through before the animals had time to panic. Maya always expected to feel *something*, but the transition was seamless, crossing hundreds of kilometers in the space of a breath. The shimmering surface passed over her, and she was somewhere else, a huge, vaulted stone chamber lit by sunlamps. Behind them was the Gate they'd just passed through, and to either side of it loomed another identical archway, dark and inactive. Three Gates, side by side, though two had not been used in centuries.

Ahead of them, a large doorway was sealed by an unmetal door, guarded by a half dozen Legionaries in their faceless white helmets and segmented armor, blaster rifles at their sides. A centarch stood in front of them, his armor more elaborate, trimmed in his personal colors. Green-white-gray, for Querius Doorbreaker. Maya had never met him, but part of her lessons had been the name and cognomen of every centarch in the Order, along with their heraldry and a little bit about their history.

The Gate chamber was the only place where a centarch could be found doing the work of a mere sentry. The Forge was so heavily fortified that no conventional army could hope to storm it, but anyone who had access to the Gates could bypass all the defenses and walk straight into the heart of the Order. The Council did not want anyone entering or leaving their sanctum without their knowledge.

At the sight of them, the Legionaries tensed, and Querius let his hand drop to his side. Jaedia tipped back her broad hat and drew her haken, and everyone relaxed, the Legionaries returning to their watchful boredom and Querius coming over to the cart, his armor clicking as he moved.

"Suddenstorm," he said, bowing his head in acknowledgment of a senior. He had an upper-class Republican accent, his voice distorted by his unmetal helm. "I wasn't told to expect you. I hope there hasn't been a problem?"

"I'm not sure," Jaedia said. She stepped down from the cart, gesturing for her agathia to follow. Maya hopped down beside her, feeling small beside Querius' armored bulk. "But I thought I'd better consult with Basel. Can you send someone to bring my things to my quarters?"

"Certainly." Querius gestured to one of the Legionaries, and the big door swung wide. "Shall I inform Kyriliarch Baselanthus you've arrived?"

"No need. I'm going to see him at once." Jaedia glanced back at Maya and Marn. "Do you remember how to get to your room?"

"Yes, Centarch," Maya said, over Marn's slightly embarrassed shrug. She rolled her eyes and grabbed his arm. "I'll make sure he gets there."

"Good. I'll send for you when I need you, but it may not be until tomorrow morning. Clean up and get some rest."

"Yes, Centarch." She and Jaedia dispensed with Order formality on the road, but under Querius' watchful eye Maya found herself reverting to the official style.

Jaedia nodded again and strode off. Querius gave the two of them a brief look, his expression unreadable under his helm. Maya towed Marn behind her, through the half-open door of the Gate chamber, and out into the corridors of the Forge.

Maya had never seen the Forge from the outside and had only a vague idea what it looked like. She knew it was carved into a single enormous mountain, a long-dead volcano rising by the side of a huge lake. On the other side of the lake, visible from the balconies when the air was clear, was the city of Skyreach, capital of the Dawn Republic. She'd never been there, but she'd seen the impossibly tall Elder buildings from a distance, towers with weird, gravity-defying curves and bridges a thousand feet in the air. Skyreach and the Forge, the twin hearts of what remained of civilization. The Dawn Republic and the Twilight Order, working together to keep humanity safe from the *dhakim* and the plaguespawn.

The founders of the Order had built their bastion on an absolutely colossal scale. The tunnels went on for *kilometers*, boring through the mountain in carefully organized levels, living quarters and storehouses and practice rooms cut directly out of the rock. It had all been done with *deiat*, of course, construction of a size no mere mason would ever have attempted.

Most of it was abandoned now. Jaedia had said that the fortress had never been full; as the Order's numbers had dwindled across the centuries, the Forge had grown ever emptier.

That was why Maya and Marn had their own rooms assigned to them, in spite of the fact that they'd spent barely two weeks at the Forge in the last five years. Maya found her way to the right corridor with only a couple of missed turns. They passed Jaedia's chamber, where gray-robed servants bustled in and out, depositing everything they'd unloaded from the wagon.

Maya's room was exactly as she'd left it, plus a layer of grime. It wasn't large, but it was furnished more comfortably than any inn on the road, with a large, soft bed, clean sheets, and a private toilet. A wardrobe stood with its doors open, empty except for a couple of ancient rags at the bottom. There was nothing that marked the room as hers, apart from her name on the door. Maya sighed and sat down on the bed, raising a faint billow of dust.

There was a knock at the door. Maya cleared her throat and said, "Yes?"

A young man in the dark gray of the Forge servants ghosted in. He was several years older than Maya, but he kept his eyes reverentially downcast. Serving at the Forge was a hereditary position, and some of the servant families had been with the Order from the very beginning, more than four hundred years ago. Jaedia sometimes joked that the old families ran the Order just as much as the Council did. Maya always found their deferential attitude unsettling.

"Greetings, Agathios," the young man said. "I've brought your things." He set down Maya's pack by the door. "Is there anything else you require?"

"Something to eat," Maya said at once. "And my clothes probably need cleaning."

"Of course." He bowed lower. "Set them out, and I will have it attended to."

Maya looked down at herself. *Well. Might as well take advantage of the place while I'm here.* "And can you direct me to the nearest bath?"

It had been a long time since her last visit, but one thing Maya remembered very clearly about the Forge was the baths. Not only was there hot and cold running water—a luxury even in the heart of the Republic, and unheard of in the places Jaedia traveled—but every living section had its own enormous communal bath, with vast pools of steaming-hot water to soak in and frigid ones for a quick dip to firm the muscles.

Baths had always presented a particular challenge for Maya. It was not that she was especially modest about her body—Jaedia was always quick to strip off and dive into any mountain pond or icy stream they encountered, and Maya followed her example, no matter how it seemed to embarrass Marn. The problem was the Thing, glittering in the center of her chest like the hilt of an impaling dagger. Only Kyriliarch Baselanthus, Jaedia, and Marn knew about it, and Jaedia had forced Marn to swear a mighty oath not to say a word to anyone.

Baselanthus, who'd put the Thing there in the first place, had told Maya it had saved her life from a childhood disease, but he'd refused to elaborate beyond that. The less she knew, he'd told her, the better. Maya could understand that, to a point. Implanting arcana in living flesh, even if the arcana in question was clearly of Chosen make, was dangerously close to *dhak*. But it was inconvenient in the matter of baths. Most of the larger towns had bathhouses, where the people would come to clean up at the end of a day's sweaty labor, and after a long stretch on the road Maya often wanted nothing more than to join them. But they offered no privacy whatsoever, and so she had to make do with streams and lakes, hurrying to wash off before her teeth started chattering.

Here in the Forge, while the baths were still communal, the place was so empty she could generally have one to herself. After wolfing down the meal the servant brought her—meaty dumplings swimming in onion soup, thick crusty bread, and slices of summerfruit—she'd changed into her spare shift and left the rest of her clothing in a pile by the door, then set out, padding barefoot down the smooth stone halls. The bath wasn't far, and it was as empty as she'd hoped. There was a space for changing and a stack of big linen towels. Maya took one of these and passed through a doorway blocked with hanging wooden slats that clattered gently as she pushed them aside.

Beyond, the air was saturated with steam. She took a deep, cleansing breath, feeling the tension in her muscles. A waterfall of lukewarm water cascaded down from one wall onto a grating, for bathers to clean off before climbing into the tub, and Maya went and stood under it for a few glorious minutes, letting the torrent thunder onto her back and shoulders.

When she felt clean, she climbed into the big pool, which was deep enough to sit in with her head underwater and wonderfully hot. Like everything else in the Forge, it was carved from rock, but the surface was as smooth as fine porcelain under her feet. Maya found a spot on a shelf about halfway along, with only her head and shoulders above water, and settled in to soak with a long, pleased sigh.

Maybe Jaedia's right, and I should *spend more time at the Forge.* When she had her cognomen, she'd be able to choose her own path. *Maybe that path should involve a lot more places with nice big baths.* She smiled, idly, and closed her eyes. *Did we have a bath at the farm?* She thought they had, a sort of tin-bucket thing. She had a memory of sitting naked on Gyre's lap as their father poured hot water over both of them, thrashing hysterically because her brother wouldn't stop tickling her.

Once I'm a centarch, I could go and visit them. The idea made her oddly uncomfortable. Agathia were not permitted to see their families—it might interfere with their training and moral development—but full centarchs could go wherever they wished. She tried to picture herself striding back into the old farm in full regalia, gleaming white unmetal armor and haken hanging at her side. *Would they be proud of me? Scared of me?*

Gyre hadn't wanted her to join the Order. She didn't remember much about the day she'd left—she'd been all of five years old—but she remembered his screams. *He was only eight.* It was strange to think that all her memories of her big brother, his strong, comforting presence at her side, were of a boy younger than Marn. *Gyre would be twenty now.* Not a boy at all, but a young man. *That* was a strange thought. She made an effort to add him to the picture of her triumphant homecoming, but she couldn't make him fit, couldn't even guess what he might look like now. *Probably turning into a weather-beaten vulpi herder, just like Dad.*

Maya opened her eyes, staring at the ceiling through drifts of hanging steam. Her body felt loose, with limbs like boiled noodles. *I should get out before I turn into a prune.* With an enormous effort of will, she pushed herself across the tub—

And heard the wet slap of footsteps in the anteroom.

Plague it. Maya sank against the side of the pool, heart suddenly beating faster. *It's fine.* She just had to edge over and grab her towel from where it sat. *Not a problem.*

There was a change in the sound of falling water as the new visitor stepped under the shower, and then more footsteps. Maya stood up and hurriedly wrapped herself in the towel just as the stranger entered, pausing in the doorway.

She—it was a young woman, about Maya's age—*definitely* a woman—and—

Oh.

Maya had left home at age five, so it had fallen to Jaedia to explain the facts of life to her. Maya had known some of it—she'd lived on a farm, after all—but she remembered listening with a vaguely horrified feeling as Jaedia went through the mechanics of sex and what she could expect from puberty, and taught her the exercises to use if she ever wanted to become fertile. She'd explained how one could find oneself

attracted to men, women, both, or neither. It had all seemed very theo-
retical at the time, and Maya had doubted any of it really applied to her.

And then, one night a few years later, they'd been at a village dance.
A pretty girl with yellow-gold hair and silver eyes had smiled at her
across a campfire, and Maya had felt her heart lurch and her skin flush
and she'd thought, *Oh.*

Not that she'd had a chance to do anything about it, then or later,
except in the privacy of her own bedroll. That sort of entanglement
was forbidden for agathia, and while Jaedia might have been willing
to bend some rules, Maya had never found occasion to test her on this
one. Now she felt the same lurch, that same *oh*, because the girl standing naked and dripping wet in the doorway was the most beautiful
thing Maya had ever seen.

She was taller than Maya, with long green hair that, wet, curled
down her neck and over one shoulder. Her skin was a few shades lighter,
though not as pale as Jaedia's, and she had a dusting of freckles across
her cheeks that continued down to her shoulders and the upper slopes
of her small breasts. Her eyes were hidden behind thick, gold-rimmed
spectacles. For a moment Maya thought these were opaque, and that
the girl might be blind, but then she pulled them down, blinking, and
Maya realized they'd fogged over with steam. Her eyes were a deep
navy blue, and they narrowed as she squinted at Maya.

"Sorry," the girl said, stepping out of the doorway. "Can't see worth a
thaler without these." She rubbed the lenses against her arm, put them
back on, and blinked. "Ah. Hello."

"Um." Maya swallowed hard, pulling the towel a little tighter around
herself. "Hello."

The girl stared at her a moment longer, then moved to the bath.

Say something, Maya told herself. *Say something say something say
something. You're being weird.* Her throat felt thick. *You're nearly a* centarch, *for the Chosen's sake, you can talk to a pretty girl in the bath.*

At least get her name. Empty as the Forge seemed, there were still hundreds of Order members there at any given time. Finding someone you didn't know wasn't difficult.

The girl tested the water with one toe, shivered deliciously in anticipation, and slid into the tub one leg at a time. The thatch of hair between her legs was a darker green, Maya noted, before she furiously dragged her eyes away.

Ask. Her. Name. She'd paused too long, and it would be awkward. *Plague that. Ask or you'll regret it.*

"Um," Maya said. "I—"

"Beq?" Another girl's voice, coming from the anteroom.

"In here!" the girl in the pool shouted.

In a few moments, two more girls and a younger boy had piled into the bath, sending great waves of warm water sloshing over the side and into the drains. None of them did more than nod at Maya as they passed, chatting and laughing. The beautiful girl, Beq, was laughing with them.

Right, Maya told herself. *I got her name, didn't I?* She tugged her towel a bit tighter and beat a hasty retreat.

Beq featured heavily in some very inappropriate dreams that night, and Maya woke up the following morning feeling irritable and unsatisfied. Her clothes, washed, folded, and patched, were waiting in a neat pile outside her door, along with a breakfast tray and a note instructing her to be at Kyriliarch Baselanthus' office within the hour. She dressed hurriedly, gobbled the bread, jam, and vulpi milk, and set off into the depths of the Forge with only a vague idea where she was going.

Fortunately, before long she ran into a servant who was able to give her directions that got her most of the way. The Council of Kyriliarchs occupied the upper levels of the fortress, where the mountain narrowed, their offices set against the exterior walls to provide windows and balconies. That meant pounding up endless flights of circular stairs until she'd worked up a healthy sweat, and by the time she got to the proper floor the spiraling meant she'd completely lost track of which direction she was supposed to be going.

Up here, at least, there were more people about than in the cavernous, empty lower levels, and the furnishings made the place seem more inhabited. The corridors were still raw stone, but the floors were covered with long rugs, and flowering plants stood at intervals between the sunlamps on the walls, providing a little color. Maya paused to catch her breath, then flagged down a well-dressed middle-aged man making his way toward the stairs.

He was tall, with red-black hair carefully combed and coiffed. When he saw Maya, breathing hard, he raised one elegant eyebrow and gave her an indulgent smile.

"Yes, Agathios?"

Damn. Belatedly, Maya noticed the colors trimming his jacket. Blue-red-purple, that was Nicomidi Thunderclap, a member of the Council. Maya swallowed and bowed, hoping he wouldn't take offense at being buttonholed like a servant.

"My apologies, Kyriarch," she said. "I'm due for a meeting with Kyriliarch Baselanthus, and I seem to be lost."

"Ah." Nicomidi gave a quick, humorless smile. "The Forge can be confusing, if you're not accustomed to it." He paused. "You're Maya, aren't you? Jaedia's agathios."

Maya blinked. While she'd memorized the names of all the centarchs, she hardly expected them to have heard of *her*. She nodded cautiously.

"I am, Kyriliarch. Have we met? I apologize for not remembering."

"No apology needed. I know you by...reputation." He pointed down one of the corridors. "That way, and take the first left. Hurry, now, you wouldn't want to keep old Basel waiting."

"My thanks, Kyriliarch."

Maya bowed again and hurried in the direction he'd indicated. The back of her neck itched, and she was certain he watched her until she turned out of sight. *Reputation? What's that supposed to mean?*

Basel's office door stood open a fraction. Maya slowed as she approached, brushing stray crumbs from her shirt and wishing she'd had time to do something about her hair. She went to knock, then froze at the sound of her mentor's voice.

"It's too soon." Jaedia sounded angrier than Maya had ever heard her. "I won't stand for it, Basel."

"It is the Council's decision to make." Baselanthus' voice, scratchy with age, sounded resigned. "If you fight them, it will only make things worse for everyone."

"You promised me that you'd keep her out of this."

"I promised you that I would keep her away from it as long as I could," Baselanthus said. "I have done all that I can."

"But—"

"Jaedia." There was a hint of steel in his tone. Then, raising his voice, he said, "Maya, is that you, dear?"

I shouldn't have heard that. Maya's heart slammed against her ribs. Her hand came up, automatically, to touch the Thing, but after a few quick breaths she forced it down again.

"Yes, Kyriliarch," she managed, in an almost normal tone.

"Come in, dear."

Maya pushed the door open. Basel's office was small and crowded with bits and pieces of arcana. He collected Elder artifacts, especially those with no obvious purpose, and every square inch had been turned into a shelf for strange little creations with smooth white curves and gemlike protrusions. A few of these were obviously broken, like the gold-veined staff with a broad crack through the center that hung just behind Basel's desk, but most seemed intact.

Basel himself sat behind an unmetal desk, repurposed from some ancient facility. He was surprisingly tall and broad-shouldered for someone with his intellectual reputation, and must have been a powerful man in his youth. Now his skin was spotted and wrinkled, and all the hair from the top of his head seemed to have moved to his chin. His eyes were a bright crimson and showed no signs of softening with age.

There was a chair in front of the desk, and a few more off to one side. Jaedia sat in one of these, looking down at her hands as Maya came in. Maya tried to catch her eyes, but Basel cleared his throat, demanding her immediate attention.

"Maya," he said. His smile was almost lost between beard and mustache. "It's good to see you."

"And you, Kyriliarch." Maya bowed, her hands clenched at her sides.

"Basel, please." He waved a hand. "Shut the door and have a seat."

She did so. Jaedia still wouldn't look at her, and Basel's smile had a forced quality to it, as though he were putting the best face on something unpleasant. Maya's stomach went sour, and she swallowed.

"Jaedia," Basel said, "has given me extremely encouraging reports on your progress."

"I'm gratified to hear that," Maya said, sneaking another sideways look at her mentor.

"And how do you feel?" He touched his chest, about where the Thing would be. "No fevers or weakness?"

Maya shook her head. "A few ordinary colds now and then, but nothing worse."

"Good, good." Basel gave a long sigh. "You don't know how much we agonized over your...treatment. Looking at you now, I'm very glad we made the right decision."

"I..." Maya hesitated. "Thank you, Kyriliarch. Basel."

"Now." Basel leaned forward, clasping his hands in front of him. "You are a very talented young woman, Maya. From what Jaedia tells me, you have the potential to be one of the strongest centarchs the Order has seen in many years. Is that still your desire?"

"Of course." She blinked, a little bewildered.

"Excellent." He sat back. "We believe you're ready for the next step in your education."

"Ready?" Maya shook her head, glancing at Jaedia. "I thought it would still be...some time."

"Yes. Well." Basel looked uncomfortable for a moment. "Circumstances being what they are, the Council thought it best to . . . accelerate things somewhat."

"Circumstances?" Maya said. "I'm afraid I don't understand."

"Jaedia's services are required for a particular task," Basel said. "It would not be ideal for your training to accompany her. But since you are doing so well, she and I agree it will do you no harm to begin your next assignment immediately. Quite the opposite, in fact."

"Begin—you mean *now*?" Maya caught her breath, and all at once she understood. *Whatever she's doing is the important mission, the one I'm not ready for. So she's shuffling me off to a . . . a sideshow.*

"Yes," Basel said mildly, as if he hadn't just turned her world upside down.

"I . . ." *She said I was nearly ready for my cognomen.* Maya's throat felt thick, and she groped for words. *Now she's leaving me behind.* "I . . . understand."

"Very good," Basel said. "I expect great things of you, Maya."

She forced her head up, meeting his gaze. "I won't disappoint you, Kyriliarch."

The red eyes glittered unsettlingly. "I know you won't."

"I should . . . prepare." Maya blinked away tears, determined not to show weakness. She couldn't look at Jaedia. "If you'll excuse me?"

Basel nodded, already looking down at the papers on his desk. Maya turned away and swallowed hard.

"Maya—" Jaedia said.

Maya hurried out before she could finish. She managed to keep her composure until she turned the first corner, wiping furiously at her eyes.

Jaedia found her on a balcony, chin in her hands, looking out across the lake at the distant spires of Skyreach. Mist rising from the water made the city look unreal, shimmering like a mirage. Maya sat on a stone bench between great round planters, listening to the leaves of the potted trees swaying overhead and trying not to think.

"There you are," Jaedia said. Maya didn't look up.

Her mentor came and sat beside her in silence. The midday sun caught the angled glass of Skyreach's towers, making them gleam like liquid gold. Kilometers-long swathes of reflected light shimmered on the waters of the lake.

"I thought you would be happy," Jaedia said after a while.

Maya gritted her teeth and said nothing.

"You'll be on a mission with a group of other trainees, under a senior agathios but with no other supervision. It's an important step forward." Jaedia touched her shoulder tentatively. "You said you wanted to get your cognomen—"

"You don't have to pretend." Maya shifted away. "The Council is sending you to do something important, and you don't think I'm strong enough to help, so you're leaving me behind."

"Oh," Jaedia said, and there was a moment of silence. "You heard."

"I heard," Maya said bitterly. "I wish you could just be honest with me."

"It isn't like that," Jaedia said gently. "Truly. If I was concerned with keeping you out of danger, would I bring Marn with me?"

"You're bringing *Marn*?" Maya looked at her mentor incredulously.

"Marn is going to spend a lot of time stuck in his room reading the *Inheritance*," Jaedia said. "And if I could have you with me, Maya, I would. I swear to you."

Maya blinked away tears and rubbed her eyes with her sleeve. "I don't understand."

"Neither do I. Not completely." Jaedia took a deep breath. "It's the Council. They have...strongly suggested that you get this assignment while I'm away."

"What? Why?"

"Politics," Jaedia said, as though it were something scatological. "I've tried to keep us out of it. But Basel is a Pragmatic, and you and I are associated with him. He says this came from the Dogmatics on the Council."

Though the details of Council politics were a mystery to Maya, she at least understood the basic sides. All members of the Order were sworn to exterminate *dhak* and *dhakim* and protect humanity from unsanctioned arcana, plaguespawn, and other threats; the difference of opinion was on how they should focus their efforts. The Pragmatics believed that by turning a blind eye to small transgressions, the Order could maintain its standing with the people and focus on the really dangerous problems. The Dogmatics insisted that any such indulgence was heresy, and deviations were responsible for the gradual decline in Order power. They wanted strict enforcement and swift punishment.

"What do the Dogmatics want with me?" Maya said.

"I don't know," Jaedia said. "I think Basel suspects, but he's not saying, the secretive old shit. But things must be worse than I thought." She sighed. "It may be that they simply want you to fail."

"Fail?"

"Maybe they think that would embarrass Basel. Or maybe it would make one of their own look good by comparison. I don't *know*." Jaedia's expression was a mask of frustration. "I stayed away for so long because I wanted to keep *out* of this *dhak*."

Maya sat for a long moment.

"All right," she said. "So what do we do about it?"

"Oh, Maya." Jaedia looked down at her and smiled. "It's your greatest gift, do you know that? Nothing slows you down for long." She sighed. "I won't pretend this is exactly what I wanted for you. But you are equal to whatever challenge they set, I swear to you. You understand?"

"I understand," Maya said. The knot in her chest softened a little.

"They may expect you to fail. *I* expect you to disappoint them. And when you come back, they'll have no choice but to give you your cognomen."

"I will." Maya's voice faltered. "But..."

"What?"

Her jaw clenched. "Will I see you again? Afterward?"

Jaedia's eyes widened. "Is *that* what you're worried about?" She grinned and looked suddenly more like her old self. "Once you're a centarch, you'll be able to go where you like, on your own authority. Nothing to say that you and I can't travel together for as long as we fancy. *Somebody* is going to have to keep Marn from getting too big for his boots."

Maya let out a long, shaky breath and gave a weak grin.

"Where are they sending you?" she said. "How long will you be away?"

"I can't say. But it *is* important," Jaedia said. "Basel was right on that count."

"Does it have something to do with Hollis and that black spider?"

"Clever girl." Jaedia gave a half smile. "Once you're a centarch, I'll be able to tell you everything."

Chapter 4

From above, the Pit looked like a knife wound carved into the granite of the mountain, a crevasse a kilometer long and several hundred meters across. Legend said that it had originally been cut as neat as a surgeon's incision with an unmetal scalpel, but four hundred years of caustic fog rising from the depths had eaten away at the rock. The edges crumbled, bit by bit, breaking loose to bounce down the cliff face into the glowing fog that shrouded the depths where the Chosen weapon still gnawed at the earth.

This erosion had been uneven. Outcrops of tougher rock remained as freestanding peninsulas and even islands, balanced precariously on ever-narrowing bases until they finally gave way and toppled into the deeps. As a rule, the wealthiest districts of Deepfire were those closest to the Pit, with the Spike on the east side and the great palaces of the merchant combines lining the west. But only a madman would build on the very edge, where the rock crumbled a little more each day, and only the maddest would try to use the islands themselves.

Deepfire being what it was, there was no shortage of madmen willing to gamble that the inevitable collapse would come just a little later. One such entrepreneur had thrown a spindly wood-and-cable bridge from the east bank to one of the larger islands and constructed a rambling, three-story wooden structure that seemed to less stand on its rocky base than cling to it desperately. It was a bar, a brothel, and a gambling den all rolled together, catering to the soldiers and servants of the Republic nobles who lived in the shadow of the Spike. The owner, foresightedly, had named it the Smoking Wreckage.

The sun was setting behind the jagged peaks of the western horizon. Gyre, loitering in the street opposite the swaying rope bridge, watched the sky go from burning crimson to a faded, bruised purple and straightened his borrowed linen coat. His scar itched something fierce, but he didn't dare scratch.

Well. Here goes nothing.

He'd spent much of the day getting ready, in between arguments with Lynnia.

"You don't think I should go?" Gyre said.

Lynnia scowled. "Of course I don't think you should go!"

They were in the alchemist's workshop. Gyre sat in front of a section of worktop that sported a large mirror, mixing a gooey powder in a metal dish. Lynnia sat in her chair, swiveling irritably back and forth.

"What's the problem?" Gyre said.

"You mean, apart from how this is *obviously a trap*?"

"I would say that it's only *probably* a trap."

"Gyre. Who goes to the Smoking Wreckage?"

He shrugged. "Servants looking for a good time. Merchant combine guards. Caravaneers."

"And *Auxies*," Lynnia said. "The place is practically their second headquarters. You might as well walk into the Spike and offer Raskos your head."

"Hence the disguise," Gyre said, testing the consistency of the goop in the bowl with one finger.

"Which you're going to blow as soon as you use this idiot code word to announce yourself." Lynnia leaned her head back and sighed. "I know how much you want this, Gyre. You've been looking for Doomseeker ever since you first heard his name. But all this means is that the dux knows it, too."

"Maybe." Gyre scooped the goop onto his finger, squinted in the mirror, and started layering it across his face. "We'll find out."

"I have no idea how you've survived this long." Lynnia glared at him. "And if you don't come back, what am I supposed to tell Yora afterward?"

He paused, goop dangling from his finger. "The truth. That I got myself killed doing something stupid."

"All right!" Lynnia got to her feet. "Don't listen. Not that you ever do. And"—she glared at his pack—"not like you ask before borrowing my supplies. I've been keeping you out of trouble since they dumped you half dead on my doorstep, but what do I know?" She clomped up the stairs.

Gyre turned back to the mirror and reached for more goop.

Disguises were hard when you had a twenty-centimeter scar through your left eye. People tended to remember a thing like that. The muscles around the socket were too badly damaged for Gyre to use a glass eye, and in any case the vertical cut Va'aht's power had drawn across his face twelve years ago was clearly visible as a long, raised line.

Fortunately, among Lynnia's many alchemical interests were the pastes and powders used by stage actors, and she'd taught Gyre a few of their tricks. About the only way to cover up a highly visible facial scar was with a bigger, even more visible facial scar, and Gyre had gotten quite creative with these. His current attempt was shaping up to be a masterpiece of the genre, a mottled mess of badly healed burns that covered his eye, his cheek, and part of his jaw. He combined it with a silver wig and a bit of facial hair backed with sticky gum, and he was fairly sure nobody would recognize him.

He went upstairs an hour later, carrying a pack filled with useful supplies. Lynnia was in the sitting room, furiously drinking tea.

"You look hideous," she snapped.

"Good," Gyre said. "That's the idea."

Lynnia scowled and stared into her tea. Gyre walked past her to the door.

"Gyre."

He paused, hand on the latch. "What?"

"What will you do if it *is* Doomseeker?"

Gyre straightened slightly. "He's the only man who's ever found the Tomb and come back."

"So rumor has it, anyway." Her skepticism was apparent. "You're going to ask him to show you the way?"

"Something like that."

"You really think there's a power to match the Order, just lying buried in some four-hundred-year-old vault?"

Gyre shrugged. "If what I need is anywhere, it's there."

"What you need. Gyre…" She shook her head. "Never mind. Go get yourself killed."

It may be a long shot. But it's the only chance I've got. And Doomseeker is the first step. Assuming it wasn't a trap. Assuming Doomseeker was everything he was rumored to be. *Assuming a fucking lot of things.*

Gyre thumbed the latch and let himself out.

The bridge to the Smoking Wreckage was supported on a pair of too-slender resilk cables. Though Gyre knew intellectually that the Elder fiber was related to unmetal and the next thing to indestructible, it didn't help the feeling in the pit of his stomach.

He put that out of his mind and started across. Out over the Pit, there was a constant updraft of warm, dry air, laced with the faint smells of sulfur and acid. Gyre wasn't the only one heading to the Wreckage as the last of the sunlight vanished, and the bridge bounced and twisted with the footsteps of a small crowd. Gyre let out a silent sigh of relief when he could put his foot on solid stone again, even if it was the weathered, precarious stone of the pillar on which the Wreckage sat.

The building was a rambling place, with a three-story hall having sprouted several extra wings and additions. Gyre headed for the main entrance, marked by a painted tavern sign depicting the building as a burnt-out ruin. The charred skeleton leaning on the bar, he thought, was a nice touch. Below it was a pair of double doors jammed open, leading to a long wood-paneled room centered on a heavily built circular bar. Other doors, some of them attended by discreet guards, led off to other parts of the establishment, for those who had more particular vices. At the far end, a grand staircase led up to the second floor.

The general impression was of ostentatious but entirely fake luxury. Gyre looked over the place with a thief's eye, noting the cheap, flaking gilt on the furniture, cut glass in the sparkling lamps, threadbare red carpet, and wallpaper already damp and bubbling in patches. If you squinted, though, you could pretend you were in some nobleman's ballroom, or one of the grand hotels of Skyreach. Gyre guessed that for the clientele—mostly servants and guards of those who really *could* afford such splendor—this was the closest they could get.

Only the bar itself looked like it was built to last, a ring-shaped counter of polished stone with all the barrels and bottles tucked safely inside it. Three uniformed bartenders circled, filling orders, and decithaler coins clattered and slid across the stone. Gyre joined the loose queue, quietly satisfied at the horrified, pitying looks he got out of the corner of his eye. *This scar really is one of my better efforts.*

When he reached the bar, he found himself facing a boy no older than fourteen. The lad said something Gyre didn't catch—he had the rolling, grating accent of the mountains, unsoftened by standard Republican pronunciation. Seeing Gyre's scar, he raised his eyebrows quizzically. Gyre cleared his throat.

Here goes nothing.

"I would like," he said, "a bottle of the Katre '49."

The boy blinked. " 'Scuse me?"

"The Katre '49," Gyre repeated, raising his voice.

"What the fuck is a Katre '49?" the boy said.

One of his companions behind the bar, an older man with a salt-and-pepper beard, leaned in with a growl. "This look like the kind of place that keeps a bottle for fifty fucking years?"

"It's still my order." Gyre drummed his fingers on the bar top and glanced around. "Katre '49."

"Well then, *of course,* m'lord," the older bartender said, putting on an obnoxious Republican accent. "Would that be the north or west side of the vineyard you'd be wanting? And would you care to sample the cherry-crusted sparrow penis?" He barked a laugh, and the boy snickered. "Order a real drink, or piss off."

Maybe it's a test. Gyre's finger tapped a little harder, and he took a deep breath. "I think—" he began.

He got no further, because someone grabbed him by the shoulders, turned him, and kissed him hard. This was so unexpected that it took Gyre a moment to react. He got the impression of a young woman, pressed against him by the crowd, her lips soft against his. His hand went to his back, where a knife was hidden under his coat.

"*This* is my man," she announced, pulling away from him and turning to face the crowd. "And he's a hundred times better than you Auxie scum."

Gyre blinked.

There was a long, dangerous silence.

It gave Gyre the chance to size things up, at least. First there was the girl at his side. She was his age or a little younger, dressed in dark pants and a tailcoat, with a scavenger's leather jacket thrown over the top making a decidedly odd ensemble. Nearly his height, she was long and lean, with only the slightest of curves. Her hair, a brilliant teal, was cut short in wild spikes.

Second was the group she'd been speaking to. There were half a dozen of them, all large men, wearing identical trousers and gray shirts. Now that he was looking at them, Gyre could identify these as the underpadding for Auxiliary armor, dark with sweat at the armpits and collars. *This bunch must have just come off shift.* The closest, with a shock of red hair and a thick beard the color of old blood, was just starting to turn his attention to Gyre.

Out of the corner of his eye, Gyre saw more gray shirts moving in the crowd behind him, heading his way. *So much for a quick exit.* He returned his gaze to the red-bearded man in time for the Auxiliary to grab Gyre's collar with one massive fist.

"What the *fuck* is this, then?" the man said. His breath, of which Gyre was the unfortunate recipient, was thick with alcohol.

"I think there's been a misunderstanding," Gyre ventured. His hand was still on his knife.

"I've been buying this plaguepit drinks for an hour," Red-beard said, glaring at the blue-haired girl. "Now you're gonna come in and take her? Fuck that. She's *mine.*"

The girl raised an eyebrow but didn't respond. Gyre started to make another attempt at politely disentangling himself, then paused.

Plague it. His mission here was totally fucked at this point, whatever happened. *Plague if I'm going to bow and scrape to an* Auxie. The look in the girl's eyes—not afraid in the least, almost expectant—played more of a role than he'd care to admit.

"I don't think she belongs to anyone," Gyre said. "And I don't like your language. And furthermore—"

At this point he kneed the Auxie in the balls. Holding someone's collar, while it might be intimidating, left you open to all sorts of nasti-ness. *Idiot's just lucky I'm not spilling his guts.*

Red-beard doubled over, letting go of Gyre's collar. Gyre gave him a shove to send him to the floor and danced clear. The Auxie's closest companions pushed forward into the rapidly clearing space around the bar, roaring threats. Gyre met the first one with a downward stomp to his extended knee, buckling the leg and turning his shouts into screams of pain. The second one swung a punch at Gyre's face, and he ducked, came up inside the man's guard, and drove an elbow into his jaw from below. There was an audible *clack* as his teeth came together, and he stumbled backward, blood bubbling between his lips where he'd bitten off a chunk of tongue.

There was a brief, hushed silence. The remaining three Auxies had squared off, but for the moment they didn't charge. Behind Gyre, the bartenders had vanished into whatever secret place bartenders go when fights break out, and the rest of the crowd had backed off far enough to be out of danger but close enough that they could still see the show.

To Gyre's mild surprise, the blue-haired girl hadn't taken the opportunity to run for it. She stood beside him, looking down approvingly at the groaning Auxies.

"Not bad," she said. "I'm Kit. Duck."

"What?"

"*Duck.*"

He ducked. A moment later her foot whistled through the space where his head had been, a perfect arc of a kick that connected beautifully with the jaw of another Auxie who'd been creeping up on him from behind. The momentum of it picked the man up and sent him tumbling across the bar top, scattering mugs and glassware.

Gyre looked around frantically. It was worse than he'd thought—there were at least three more groups of Auxies, maybe twenty men and women in gray shirts closing in. At the edges of the room, the establishment's security wasn't rushing to interfere. *This probably counts as tonight's entertainment.*

He looked back at Kit. "What do you say to getting out of here?"

"Probably for the best," she said with a grin. "The beer is frankly swill."

"Great." Gyre stuck his hands in his coat pockets. "Follow my lead."

* * *

Most of the Auxies were between Gyre and the front door, making a quick break in that direction impractical. The stairs, however, had only five gray shirts in front of them. *One decision made.*

His hands came out of his pockets with an alchemical cracker in each. These were smaller versions of the stunner he'd used against the Legionary, not much more than a distraction, but it couldn't be helped. In the dense crowd, a stunner was likely to seriously hurt someone who didn't deserve it; Gyre had no sympathy for Auxies, but most of the patrons of the Smoking Wreckage hadn't done anything wrong. *Well,* he amended after a moment, *they haven't done anything to* me, *anyway.*

Darting away from the bar, he lobbed the first cracker in a low arc behind him. It landed among the groaning Auxies just as their comrades gathered their courage to pursue, detonating with a *crack* and a brilliant flash. He waved the second one in front of Kit, who got the idea and squeezed her eyes shut. Gyre hurled it forward and put a hand over his good eye.

The group in front of him scattered when they saw him hurl the bomb, and the detonation disoriented them. The closest was a dark-haired, well-muscled woman who got her hands up in a fighting stance in spite of eyes streaming with tears. Gyre didn't even slow down, ducking under her clumsy blow and sweeping her legs out from under her. She hit the ground with a meaty thud, and he popped back up, just in time for a younger girl to slam a fist into his face. Gyre wobbled backward, head ringing, but had the presence of mind to grab her wrist and sidestep her next blow, twisting her arm to send her into a painful flip that landed her on her downed comrade.

Another Auxie was down at Kit's feet, and he looked up in time to watch her confront the largest of the group, a barrel-chested man with a much-broken nose. He used his longer reach to his advantage, keeping her at bay for a moment with roundhouse swipes. Kit bulled forward, taking a hard jab to the cheek, and got inside his guard. She bent her knees and popped up, forehead slamming into the taller man's chin, sending him reeling backward. Her kick caught him in the stomach while he was off-balance, doubling him over, and he toppled to the floor wheezing.

The last Auxie, a boy younger than Gyre, scrambled out of their way as they reached the base of the stairs. Gyre, still wobbly from the girl's blow, sprinted up, glancing backward to make sure Kit followed. She was right behind him, blood streaming from her nose and dripping off her chin, a huge grin on her face. A mob of Auxies a dozen strong pounded after them. Gyre hurled his last cracker at the base of the stairs and watched them scatter.

"Sir," a large man in a dark suit was saying, "you can't be up here without an escort—"

Kit did another one of those high kicks, her foot scything through the air at head height, and sent the security goon crashing against the wall with a clatter. Gyre stared at her.

"Well?" she said. "Are we escaping or what?"

"Right." He shook his head, trying to lose the image of her bloody-toothed grin.

The stairs led up to a long hallway lined with doors, with several crossing corridors leading off it. At the other end, a tight spiral stair led upward. Gyre pointed and Kit nodded, blood scattering. They took off down the corridor at a run, as the doors started to open and the footsteps of the Auxies drummed on the stairs behind them.

Men and women leaned out to see what was happening, then ducked back in alarm at the sight of the two disheveled figures sprinting toward them. The Auxies were shouting for help, and a few of the bystanders stepped out to try to block Gyre's path. A pair of shirtless mustachioed men grabbed for him as he went past, but he avoided them with a quick twist and kept moving. From the other side of the hall, an enormous woman erupted from a doorway buck naked, which was startling enough to give Gyre pause. Fortunately Kit was faster, spinning to plant an elbow in the woman's solar plexus that left her sprawled back inside her room. There was more shouting behind them.

The second set of stairs was steeper than the first, with a locked door at the top. Gyre hit it with his shoulder at full speed, and it gave way with a splintering crash, letting them out onto the roof. Gently sloped tiles stretched ahead for a dozen meters, then cut off abruptly as the building ended at the edge of the abyss. In the other direction, one of the third-story additions loomed, cutting off their escape.

Kit skipped fearlessly out across the tiles and turned on one heel. "Now what?"

Gyre drew his knife, and she raised an eyebrow. He understood her concern—the unspoken etiquette of Deepfire bar brawls said that, until there were weapons involved, the losers might expect a beating and broken bones but would probably escape with their lives. Once the blades came out, however, all bets were off.

Gyre wasn't sure where alchemical explosives ranked on that scale. *Not that it matters. I don't plan to lose.* He grinned at Kit and turned back to the door, jamming the knife through the iron handle and driving it as deep as he could into the doorframe. It wouldn't hold for long, but they didn't need long.

At the bottom of his pouch, a pair of long linen gloves was rolled up in a tight bundle. He extracted them, shook them out, and tossed one to Kit.

"Put that on," he said. "I've only got the pair, so put your ungloved hand on top, and for Chosen's sake don't let it touch the line. It'll take your fingers off, never mind your skin."

Kit blinked. Her eyes, Gyre noted inanely, were the same bright blue as her hair. "Line?"

Gyre walked carefully along the tiles to the edge. From here he could see the near face of the cliff, separated from the island supporting the Smoking Wreckage by perhaps twenty meters of empty space. Jagged, splintery rock stretched down into the Pit, disappearing into the sullen red glow of the cloud below.

Aligning himself on the half-broken chimney he'd used as a landmark, Gyre slipped the glove onto his right hand and leaned over the edge. The soles of his feet tingled furiously, as though they expected the tiles to tip him over at any moment. He groped until his grasping fingers found what they were looking for: a cable, about as thick as his thumb, heavy and slick in his grip and so translucent that it was barely visible.

"Just grab hold and step off," he said. "Grip tighter if you're going too fast. If I've set this up right, we should be fine." It had taken him most of the afternoon to arrange, climbing the outside of the Wreckage in a shadowy corner.

"Clever," Kit said, another broad grin spreading across her bloody face. "*Very* clever."

"Well." Gyre felt more pleased at her smile than he probably should have. "I don't like to go anywhere without an emergency exit. Always prepared."

Footsteps sounded behind the door, and he heard angry voices.

"You want me to go first?" Gyre said. "If I plummet to my death, you can take your chances with them."

"I'll go first." She pulled the glove tight. "I trust you."

"Why?"

Kit laughed. "Call it a hunch."

There was a *crunch* from the door. "Better move, then."

She took the line from him with her gloved hand and stood poised on the edge of the roof, staring down into the glowing abyss. "Just step right off, huh?"

Gyre nodded. Kit heaved an exaggerated sigh.

"Story of my life," she said, and stepped off the roof.

For a heart-stopping moment, she plunged straight down and disappeared from sight. Gyre started breathing again when she zipped into view, riding the line's downward slope in a long parabola, sparks trailing from where the specially treated glove gripped the rope. It was only a few seconds before she reached the end and he lost sight of her against the darkened cliff.

The door gave way with a splintery crash. Gyre grabbed the wildly juddering line with his own glove, turned to give a mocking salute to the enraged Auxies, and hopped over the edge.

There was a moment of free fall, until he ran out of slack and the line jerked him upward, brutally hard. He felt it whirring past under his glove and concentrated on keeping his other hand firmly atop the protected one. The lights of the city approached, shockingly quickly, and he belatedly remembered to squeeze to shed some speed. He hit the crumbling edge of the cliff hard enough to knock the wind out of him, and clung to the edge with his ungloved hand.

"That," Kit said from just above him, "was a rush. You could sell tickets."

She extended her own hand, and he grabbed it. Muscles bunched in her shoulders as she hauled him up.

Figures were visible milling around on the roof of the Wreckage. Kit looked at them, eyes gleaming. "You think they'll try to come after us?"

"If they do, they'll probably lose a finger," Gyre said. "But we can make sure."

He dug a firestarter out of his pocket, flicked it open, and applied the tiny light to the end of the cable. It caught immediately, burning with a cool blue flame that zipped up the way they'd come, briefly outlining a curve of light through the red-tinted darkness. Then it fell away in pieces, still burning as it dropped into the Pit.

"*Where* do you get these toys?" Kit said, delighted.

"I know an alchemist," Gyre said, closing the firelighter.

He realized, abruptly, that he didn't have a clue what to do next. They were standing at the end of a dingy alley. A single lamp provided the only light, throwing Kit in profile as she leaned her head back and squeezed her nose.

"Are you all right?" he said.

"I've had worse." She looked down her bloody nose at him. "You?"

Gyre touched his cheek. "I'll be fine."

"I don't know how to break this to you," Kit said, producing a handkerchief from somewhere, "but your scar is coming off."

"My—" Gyre explored his cheek more thoroughly and found that the pasted-on scar was indeed falling apart where the Auxie had punched him. *Damn.* He slapped a hand over it, feeling stupid, and turned away.

"I imagine that's why you usually wear a mask," Kit went on. "More durable."

Gyre froze.

"You *are* Halfmask, aren't you?" She cocked her head, still holding the handkerchief to her nose.

"That depends," Gyre said. He turned back, hand behind his back creeping to the handle of another knife.

"On what?"

"On who's asking."

"Oh." She swept her arm out and performed a wide bow, inadvertently letting a stream of blood patter on the stone. "Kitsraea Doomseeker, at your service."

"Kitsraea—" He stopped. "*You* sent me that note?"

"Mmmhmm."

"And you *kissed* me?" His lips tingled. He'd almost forgotten that part.

"It seemed like a good way to start a fight."

"Why?"

"So that I could see if you could handle yourself," Kit said. "You have no idea how many people don't live up to their reputations."

Gyre's hand clenched into a fist. "This was a *test*."

"And you passed! With flying colors." She looked admiringly back at the Wreckage. "I was not expecting *that*, I must say."

"What did you *think* I was going to do?"

"Start killing people, frankly. Isn't that your line of work?"

"I . . ." He shook his head. "It feels impolite to kill people on their day off. Even Auxies."

Kit barked a laugh. She lowered the handkerchief, waited a moment to see if the blood would resume, then tossed the soiled fabric over the edge. It fluttered down into the Pit, drifting lazily on the updrafts.

"So now what?" Gyre said.

"Now I have a proposition for you," Kit said. "I'll be in touch, the same way as last time. It won't be long."

"But—"

"Thank you, sir, for a very informative evening." She bowed again. "Good luck with the scar!"

Before Gyre could say another word, she was gone, trotting past the lamp and vanishing into the shadows. Gyre prodded the torn edge of his paste scar with one finger, then tore the whole thing off and tossed it over the cliff. He scratched the real scar underneath, which was a blessed relief.

Okay. What in the name of all the Chosen was that?

Chapter 5

This time, Maya arrived at Baselanthus' office early.

She knocked on his door, shifting uncomfortably in her rarely used formal tunic and trousers. It felt like a long time before anyone answered, and she fancied she could hear the low buzz of conversation.

Finally, Basel said, "Maya? Come in, please." Maya opened the door, her posture stiffly correct, and gave him a precise bow.

She and Jaedia had always maintained a friendly, informal relationship. But she had no idea if the same would be true in this new assignment, and after what her mentor had told her, Maya was determined to give the Council no cause to criticize her performance. *If they think they're going to be able to use me against her, they've got another thing coming.*

When she straightened up, Maya saw that Basel was not alone behind his huge, cluttered desk. On one side of the old man sat Kyriliarch Nicomidi, whom she'd met on her last visit. He cut a dashing figure, well-groomed dark hair swept back from a sharp widow's peak, pale skin, and sharp blue eyes. His chair was angled slightly away from

Baselanthus', and something in his tight features and the way he sat spoke volumes about the tension between them.

At the other end of the desk was another centarch, even older than Basel. He sported a long, bushy beard and fiery orange-red hair a few shades lighter than Maya's own crimson. The rest of his face was nearly lost in the tangle, leaving his eyes as bright points of purple. As far as Maya could see, he wasn't wearing any identifying colors, but he leaned back in his chair, completely at ease, and she guessed he had to be another Council member.

"Kyriliarchs," Maya said. "I am reporting as ordered."

"Indeed you are," Basel said. "Kyriliarch Nicomidi tells me you've met?"

"Only briefly." Maya directed a bow in his direction.

"And this," Basel went on, "is Kyriliarch Prodominus."

Prodominus. Now, *there* was a name Maya had heard before. The oldest member of the Council was simultaneously a legend and a joke, famed for his youthful exploits and ridiculed for his devotion to an impossible cause. Alone of the twelve Kyriliarchs, he stood apart from both Pragmatics and Dogmatics, instead declaring himself a *Revivalist.* This group insisted that some of the Chosen were still in hiding somewhere, and the real purpose of the Twilight Order was to cleanse the world of the Plague so they could return to power. In the early days of the Order they had been powerful, but the Revivalists had dwindled as the centuries passed, until they consisted of only Prodominus and a handful of oddballs.

She bowed to him as well, as respectfully as she knew how. "It's an honor, Kyriliarch. I've heard a great deal about you."

"That I'm a senile old fool who wastes Order gold on pointless quests, no doubt." Prodominus grinned hugely under his beard. "No need for flattery, Agathios. My taste for it has worn thin."

Nicomidi muttered something that sounded like, "Not thin enough." If Prodominus heard, he didn't comment. Baselanthus cleared his throat.

"As you know," he said, "with Centarch Jaedia urgently needed elsewhere, the Council has agreed that you will be given an independent assignment. This is somewhat irregular at such short notice, but we have reviewed your records"—his eyes flicked to Nicomidi, and he frowned briefly—"and we believe you are ready."

"Thank you, Kyriliarch. I'm honored by your trust."

"If you insist on being honored by everything, it's going to be a long interview," Prodominus said.

"I..." Maya paused, nonplussed. "I apologize, Kyriliarch."

Nicomidi rolled his eyes and glared at Prodominus. "If you could keep your prodigious wit under control?"

"*In any event,*" Baselanthus said irritably, "you will be serving on a team with Agathios Tanax and two support trainees. Have you met Tanax?"

"No, Kyriliarch," Maya said.

"He is my own agathios," Nicomidi said. "I'm certain he will provide appropriate guidance for you." There was a knock at the door, and Nicomidi raised his voice. "Come in."

The young man who entered was tall, with the very dark skin and hawk nose she associated with the Republic aristocracy. Like her, he wore a formal Order tunic, with a haken on his hip. His lips tightened at the sight of her, as though he were already angry, but he kept his posture rigid as he bowed to the three Kyriliarchs.

"Tanax," Nicomidi said. "Let me introduce you to Maya, agathios to Jaedia Suddenstorm. She will be your second on this assignment."

"Understood," Tanax said, turning to Maya. His dark eyes seemed to evaluate her immediately, and his expression said he was unhappy with the results.

"Honored, Agathios," Maya said with a shallower bow. Tanax responded with a nod.

"Honored," he murmured, then looked back at Nicomidi. "What's the assignment?"

"The support trainees should be along in a moment," Baselanthus said.

Tanax looked impatient, but the sound of running feet from the corridor outside was clearly audible. A girl shot by the door at a dead sprint, grabbing the edge of the doorway to arrest her momentum. She swung herself into the room, breathing hard, and staggered in front of the desk, almost colliding with Tanax. Her bow was so deep she nearly banged her head on the unmetal.

"Sorry..." she gasped. "Running...stairs...sorry..."

"Arcanist-Trainee Bequaria," Baselanthus said, with only the faintest smile. "We try to maintain a bit of decorum here, you know."

"Sorry. I mean. Apologies, Kyriliarch. Kyriliarchs." She straightened up, took a deep breath, and bowed again. "I didn't want to be late."

"Admirable," Prodominus rumbled. "Why don't you introduce yourself to your team?"

"Right!" She turned to face Maya and Tanax. "Apologies, Agathia. I'm Bequaria. You can call me Beq."

Maya felt her cheeks go hot. It was the girl she'd seen in the baths her first day here. She was dressed informally, in a leather vest and trousers, both studded with dozens of little pockets. What Maya had taken for ordinary spectacles were some kind of arcana, with small glowing beads and gold knobs set around the rim and several sets of lenses one in front of the other. Her green hair was bound up in a long, complicated braid.

"It's an honor to be working with you," Beq said with another bow.

"Agathios Tanax will be leading the team, with Agathios Maya acting as his second," Nicomidi said.

"An honor," Tanax drawled.

"An honor," Maya echoed, not daring to look Beq in the eye. She was certain, in that moment, that all her private thoughts were written on her face.

"Now all we need is the scout," Nicomidi said.

"Scout-Trainee Varo, reporting as ordered," said a voice by the door. Another boy was standing there, so quietly that Maya hadn't noticed him. He had light brown skin and thin features, with his head shaved as clean as polished brass. He bowed to the Kyriliarchs, then to Maya and the others. "Scouts is only if you're being polite, though. We're spies, really."

That got a laugh from Prodominus, and Maya ventured a smile.

"Honored," Tanax said. He seemed to be growing as impatient as his master. "Good to have you on the team."

"You'll come to change your mind on that point, I'm sure," Varo said. "But I suspect you're stuck with me, so I'll do my best."

"The assignment, Basel?" Nicomidi said.

"Of course." Baselanthus nodded. "Agathios Tanax, the Council hereby charges you to travel to the village of Litnin, on the northern border. We have received credible reports that a group of smugglers operating out of Grace have been using Litnin as a way station to move products into the Republic, including dangerous *dhak* and unsanctioned arcana."

"Grace," Nicomidi spat. "If we were properly vigilant, that hive would have been purged long since."

"If we were as 'vigilant' as you wanted," Prodominus said, "every city within a hundred kilometers of the borders would be a pile of ashes."

"Perhaps that wouldn't be such a tragedy."

"Gentlemen, please," Baselanthus said. "These young people are not here for a Council debate. Agathios Tanax, your team will go to Litnin and investigate. Take whatever action you deem necessary if you discover that the reports have merit. Any who aided in the smuggling of proscribed items should be brought to justice under Republic law. Do you understand?"

"Yes, Kyriarch," Tanax said, glancing first at Nicomidi, who gave him a quick nod. "When do we depart?"

"Tomorrow morning. The quartermasters' office has been informed, so request what you need. Travel funds and so on have also been allocated." Baselanthus peered at the four of them. "Are there any questions?"

Maya could think of a few, but before she could raise her voice Tanax answered for her.

"No, Kyriarch." He bowed again. "If you'll excuse me, we need to prepare."

"Go on." Baselanthus looked at his fellow Kyriliarchs with a sigh. "I suspect we have other matters to discuss."

Tanax straightened up, nodded again to Nicomidi, and turned to leave. Beq and Varo followed. Maya, feeling a little left behind, hurried after them. She expected to see them gathered in the corridor, but instead the two trainees were already going one way while Tanax stalked in the opposite direction. After a moment of indecision, Maya jogged to catch up with her fellow agathios.

"Agathios Maya." Tanax stopped and turned to face her. "Did you have a question?"

"I just thought...I mean..." Maya gave herself a mental shake. *Remember what's at stake.* Tanax, presumably, would be the one who informed the Council about her performance. *And he and Nicomidi are Dogmatics. If they want me to fail here, to try to get at Jaedia...* "I wanted to offer my assistance. This sort of assignment is very familiar to me." Investigating rumors of smugglers and *dhak* had been half of what she and Jaedia did on their endless circuits of the Republic. "Do you have any thoughts you want to share on our plans?"

"*Our* plans?" Tanax's lips pressed tightly together. "I am the senior agathios on this assignment, I believe."

"Yes, of course," Maya said. "I only meant—"

"When I wish to hear your opinion," Tanax said, "I will ask for it. Until then, all I require is that you follow instructions. Is that understood?"

Maya froze. For a moment, all her effort went into biting back an angry retort.

"Understood," she managed eventually.

"Requisition your gear as you please," Tanax said. "I will expect you tomorrow morning, in the Gate chamber."

Maya had no idea *how* to requisition equipment, actually. The few times she'd been to the Forge, Jaedia had handled it. But she was plagued if she was going to ask *him*. Instead she gave another bow, as shallow as she could manage without giving offense. Tanax waved in dismissal, and Maya turned on her heel.

This is going to be harder than I thought. Her hand kept straying toward the hilt of her haken. *How much trouble would I be in if I lit him on fire just a little?*

The quartermasters' office and storerooms were on one of the lower levels of the Forge, along with the archive and various libraries. A vast central rotunda covered in a checkerboard pattern of tables served as a working space. Like the rest of the Forge, it was much larger than it needed to be, and the few lonely arcanists and servants reading or copying out of tomes were separated by acres of empty seats.

Maya spotted Varo and Beq, sitting together at a table, with a map and sheets of foolscap spread in front of them. She threaded her way to them, doing her best not to show her nerves. She'd never been down here before, and the vast, chilly space had a forbidding air.

"Ah. It's Varo, right?" she said. "And Bequaria?"

"Agathios," Varo said, inclining his head.

Beq frowned at her, touching the dials on her golden spectacles. Lenses shifted, magnifying her eyes. "Agathios," she said after a moment.

There was a long pause.

"Did you require something?" Varo said. His voice was cold.

"I…" Maya looked down at the table and felt a spike of stubborn pride. "No, I'm sure you're busy. Carry on."

Varo immediately turned and started peering at the map. Beq watched Maya for a few moments longer, then turned away as well, shaking her head.

What did I plaguing do to them*? First Tanax, and now these two. This is not going to be a pleasant expedition.* Maya turned, spotted the sign for the quartermasters' office, and stalked across the marble. *I just need a few bits of camping gear. It can't be that difficult.*

Five minutes later, she was back, all thoughts of pride forgotten.

"Scout-Trainee Varo?"

He looked up, eyes narrowed, voice polite. "Yes, Agathios?"

Maya heaved a sigh. "Please help me. I have no idea what I'm doing."

Varo glanced at Beq, and conflicting expressions flitted across his face. Finally he gestured at an empty chair. "Have a seat."

Maya shuffled gratefully around the table. She set down the catalog the bored clerk at the quartermasters' office had handed her, an enormous tome considerably thicker than the *Inheritance*. At the sight of it, Varo laughed out loud.

"Glad to see they're giving you the full treatment," he said. "At least *some* of the old traditions of the Order are being kept up."

Maya glared at the huge book. "This is someone's idea of a joke?"

"More like a ritual," Varo said.

"I've never heard of it," Beq said. "Let me see."

Beq swiveled the book to face her, flipped it open, and twisted a dial on the side of her spectacles, which made something inside the lenses shift. The page was covered from edge to edge in tiny, neat writing, and she leaned forward to read. As she did so, she reached up automatically to brush back a coil of green hair that had escaped from her braid, tucking it behind her ear. Something about the motion, the perfect curve of the neck thus exposed, did strange things to Maya's guts. She felt as though her internal organs were jostling for position.

This is ridiculous, she admonished herself. *You're going to be a centarch, for the Chosen's sake. Have a little self-control.*

"Sorry," Maya said, aware that Beq had been talking but not of what she'd said. "What was that?"

Beq looked up, her eyes huge beneath her spectacles. "I said it's just lists of junk. Listen to this. 'One spherical device, approx. one meter cubed, for the control of flame in piping, nonfunctional. One ovoid device, approx. thirty-five meters cubed, for the purification of water, working order.'" She flipped a page. "'Devices of unknown purpose, cubical, of less than one meter cubed, separated by provenance.'" She frowned and flipped again. "'Three suits of armor, of the Gevaudan pattern, badly damaged.' That's dated two hundred years ago!"

"You know how big this place is," Varo said. "The storehouses go on forever, so the quartermasters never throw anything away. Every piece of scrap that's ever come into the Forge is still in there, somewhere, just in case someone needs it. When someone asks for the full catalog, they take them literally."

"That doesn't seem the most helpful way to behave," Maya said.

"Even quartermasters need laughs, I suppose." Varo shrugged. "If you needed help, why didn't you ask Tanax?"

Maya pulled a face. "Tanax doesn't seem inclined to offer much assistance. Or to talk to me at all, for that matter."

"Oh?" Beq closed the book and dialed her spectacles back. "I thought it was just me."

"He gave me the brush-off, too," Varo said. "But that's centarchs. Not much time for the rest of us."

"Really?" Maya frowned. "I've never worked with any support staff."

"Never?" Varo raised an eyebrow. "Is this your first time doing this kind of work?"

"Not exactly," Maya said. "But it's always just been me and my master and her other agathios. We never spent much time at the Forge."

"That explains why you're so friendly," Beq said with a grin. "I didn't think that centarchs were allowed."

Maya smiled back as her heart double-thumped. Varo cleared his throat.

"This will be Beq's first time in the field," he said, "so I was going over her equipment list with her. Would you like me to draw up something basic for you?"

"Please," Maya said. "I throw myself on your mercy."

Varo smiled a little at that and started pointing at the map and scribbling with a pencil. His efficiency was impressive, as he quickly figured the distance from Litnin to the nearest Gate along the most suitable route and converted that into a list of supplies, including a substantial safety margin. It made Maya uncomfortably aware how much of the basics Jaedia had always handled—their lessons had focused on *deiat*, not how to find water that was safe to drink.

"You've been out quite a bit, then," Maya said.

"More's the pity," Varo said, looking down at his list and frowning. "That's the scout's life, I suppose."

"Better than being stuck in a damp basement fixing old blasters," Beq said. "I've been looking forward to this for ages."

"Travel isn't all it's cracked up to be," Varo said, still working. "It's mostly bad food, no sleep, and getting rained on. And you usually catch something right when it's least convenient." He perked up a little. "Sometimes there's a good laugh, though. A friend of mine once used a Red Spider bush to wipe himself after a shit, and watching him try to walk the next day had all of us giggling. Of course, my other friend laughed a little *too* hard, so the first fellow found another Red Spider and stuffed it into his jock while he was sleeping—"

"Is that why you said Tanax would regret having you on the team?" Maya said. "Because you shove Red Spider bushes in people's underwear?"

"That was my friend's idea." Varo shook his head. "And anyway, he fell through the ice into a lake we were crossing and drowned. Froze so solid that once we fished him out we used him as a sledge." Maya raised her eyebrows doubtfully, but Varo went on. "No, the only problem with me is bad luck."

"I don't believe in bad luck," Maya said.

"That's what they all say, until they travel with me," Varo said. "The other scouts call me Varo Plagueluck." He stood up, lists in hand. "I'll take this over to the clerk, then."

"Do you believe that, about the boy who froze solid?" Beq said when he'd left the table.

"Probably not," Maya said.

"I wouldn't want to be stuck with Plagueluck for a cognomen, I know that." Beq twisted the dials on her spectacles, returning her eyes to a more normal size, and blinked. "It's different for centarchs, I know. The Council assigns your names."

Maya nodded, her throat suddenly dry. For a moment they sat in silence.

"Am I doing something weird?" Beq said. "Sometimes that happens."

"What? Why?"

"You just seem to be alternating between staring at the ceiling and your boots instead of looking at me, so I thought I might have done something weird." Beq shrugged. "They say the more time you spend around arcanists, the stranger you get, so I must be pretty strange by now."

"No, it's . . . nerves, I suppose." Maya took a deep breath and looked straight at Beq, trying to ignore the way her curls framed her round face and the spectacular blue of her eyes. *Self-control, Maya. Come on.* "You've been with the arcanists a long time, then?"

"Since I was four, I think." Beq looked thoughtful. "That's what they tell me, anyway. Since I can remember. I grew up here at the Forge."

"My mentor picked me up at around that age." Automatically, Maya's hand went to the hard lump of the Thing in her chest. "I've been with her ever since."

"That's young, for a centarch."

Maya nodded and found time stretching like taffy into another awkward silence. *Say something.* But what? *"Ever since I saw you naked I haven't been able to stop thinking about you" lacks . . . tact.*

"All set," Varo said, rescuing her. He came back to the table and picked up the big catalog. "I'd better give this back, too. Wouldn't want them to lose their prank piece."

"Thank you." Maya looked between him and Beq. "I'll try not to be . . ."

"A typical centarch?" Varo grinned. "That would be a nice change of pace."

They set out the next morning.

Maya stepped forward, through the rippling mercury curtain, and in the space of a breath crossed most of the width of the Republic. She emerged from the Gate with her panoply raised, one hand on her haken and *deiat* coiled around her like a snake.

Jaedia had taught her to be cautious at these moments of transition, but it was more than that. Every previous time she'd gone through a Gate, she'd been at Jaedia's side. To be without her mentor made her feel *raw*, every sensation heightened, as though something had scraped away her skin and dug cotton out of her ears.

The Gate to which they'd traveled was set into a rocky hillside, obscured from casual view by a screen of tall bushes. Maya pushed her way through the brush and found herself in a sun-dappled forest, the blue sky visible in patches overhead through the leafy canopy. The breeze raised gooseflesh along her bare arms, and the air seemed to be alive with birdsong.

Tanax pushed his way through the bushes behind her, swearing as they tangled in the straps of his pack. Varo slipped out after him, quiet as a ghost, and then Beq. The arcanist was even more heavily burdened than the rest of them, but she still moved lightly. Tanax was already scowling, pulling himself free of the bushes and brushing the leaves from his clothes. He turned in a slow circle, as though expecting to see an obvious direction to proceed. Nothing seemed to present itself, and he frowned.

"Scout-Trainee Varo," he said. "Which way to Litnin?"

Varo checked the crystalline compass hanging from the straps of his pack and oriented himself. He made a chopping gesture.

"That's north," he said, "unless this thing has gone completely haywire." His expression went thoughtful. "That happened to a friend of mine, in fact. He kept following that compass until he wandered into the ocean and the sharks got him."

"You must not have very many friends left," Maya said.

"It's a lonely life, being a scout," Varo deadpanned.

"Litnin is to the northeast, if I recall," Tanax said, turning. "Follow me."

"Ah..." Varo gestured at right angles to Tanax's heading. "Perhaps we should descend to the flat ground near the river first. That would make for easier going."

The look Tanax gave the scout could have frozen him on the spot. "Why don't you lead the way, then?"

"Of course, Agathios." Varo managed to catch Maya's attention and raise an eyebrow, and Maya had to suppress a giggle. "If someone's going to get eaten, it might as well be me."

He hitched his pack up and pushed through the underbrush, moving with an ease that spoke of long practice. Beq, behind him, sounded like a vulpi pup tearing through a pile of autumn leaves. Tanax stalked after them, swatting irritably at branches in his path. Maya permitted herself a sigh before following.

Why, she thought, *do I have a bad feeling about this?*

Chapter 6

The Moorcat Merchant Combine was one of the wealthiest houses in the Republic, rivaling the most powerful nobles in its reach and power. Some said the Moorcats were richer than the Senate itself, while others confidently asserted they had bought the Senate long ago. Conspiracy theories aside, the reality of their influence was obvious enough. While most merchant houses had to make do with buildings in the West Central district, uncomfortably close to the stench of ordinary commerce, the Moorcats were permitted an expansive complex on the East Rim, within a stone's throw of the Spike and surrounded by the sprawling mansions of Republic nobility.

Their land was fenced off, the exterior watched by Auxiliaries and the interior by Moorcat house guards. The chapter house itself was near the back of the estate, surrounded by carefully faked woodlands. It was a magnificent structure, sporting an enormous central dome topped with a gilded statue of Galbio the Moorcat, legendary founder of the organization. Up close, Gyre found the statue unimpressive—the gold was clearly a thin alloy coating, and the details of Galbio's features looked cheap and hastily carved.

I suppose you don't get to be a continent-spanning merchant combine by wasting money on a statue nobody is ever going to get a good look at. He settled against the stone base of the ugly thing. The dome was large enough that it wasn't steeply sloped, but the lead roofing provided awkward footing. It was nearly midnight, and the stars were blotted out by thick clouds.

Fortunately, he didn't have long to wait. It was only a quarter of an hour before he spotted a lithe figure pull itself up onto the edge of the dome and scramble lightly up toward the statue. Gyre had chewed some nighteye before he'd set out for the evening, and in the weird grayish vision the alchemical stuff provided, Kit's features were easy to make out. She wore something close to his own working clothes, well-tailored dark silk with a few reinforcing panels of black-dyed leather, and she bore a pair of long knives on one hip and a blaster pistol in a worn holster on the other.

For his own part, Gyre had brought his full kit, long and short blades in their sheaths, half mask covering his missing eye, the pockets of his dark hooded coat filled with alchemical surprises from Lynnia's supply closet. He crossed his arms, looking down at Kit as she straightened up and sauntered the last few meters. She'd taken nighteye as well, her pupils hugely swollen until her eyes were nearly all black.

"Hello, Halfmask," she said. "I like the look. Very mysterious."

"Doomseeker," Gyre said.

She winced. "Call me Kit, if you don't mind. I try not to spread my cognomen around."

"Kit, then. Can I ask why you wanted to meet *here*? Another test?" He'd had to elude several patrols just to cross the grounds, not to mention a dangerous climb up the side of the chapter house timed to elude the men and dogs on patrol. *I hate plaguing dogs.*

"Something of that nature. Although, fair's fair. I got here too, didn't I?" She half turned and gestured. "Besides, I like the view."

With trees screening the neighboring estates, there was really only one thing to see. The Spike lived up to its name, two hundred meters of unmetal as slender and featureless as a needle. It was a relic of the war, a Chosen fortress that had served as a base for their purges of the tunnels. The Gate was inside, connecting Deepfire directly to the Forge and the heart of the Republic, ensuring that it remained under the Twilight Order's influence in spite of being well outside its nominal borders. In later days, the dux's palace had been constructed around it, a manor even more luxurious than the Moorcat chapter house, surrounded by walls, Auxiliary barracks, and intricate arcana defenses.

"I can't say that I care for it," Gyre muttered.

"Always good to appreciate what you're up against," Kit said. She glanced back at Gyre. "That *is* what you're up against, isn't it, Half-mask? The Order?"

"If we're asking questions, I have a few. Starting with your cognomen."

"Oh?"

"Doomseeker has been a legend since before I came to Deepfire," Gyre said. "I asked around, and people have told stories about him for at least fifty years. You're, what, nineteen? Twenty?"

"That's a rude thing to ask." Kit gave a saucy wriggle. "Maybe I'm just very well preserved." She grinned. "Maybe I found the elixir of youth down in the Tomb, and I'm really a hundred and ten."

"You're not Doomseeker," Gyre said. "Which raises the question of why I'm even talking to you."

"Now, let's not run away with ourselves." Kit spread her arms. "I'll admit that I'm not the *first* Doomseeker. How does that sound?"

"Does that mean you never found the Tomb?"

"That's an awfully personal question," Kit said. "Let me maintain *some* air of mystery."

"I've heard enough," Gyre said.

She put on a pout. "But I haven't even gotten to my proposal."

Gyre turned away.

"Fifty thousand thalers," Kit said. "And the chance to kick the dux in the teeth as hard as he's ever been kicked." She cocked her head. "Not literally, I suppose."

"I wouldn't get anywhere near his mouth," Gyre said. "They don't call him Raskos Rottentooth for nothing."

"Ah," Kit said. "You're listening, then?"

"For the moment." Gyre turned back to her, eye narrowed. "Fifty *thousand* thalers?"

"Fifty thousand," Kit said.

That was an astonishing sum of money, enough to buy a sizable chunk of the building they were standing on. Gyre paused.

"Why do you have that kind of money?"

"My business," she said. "Or, rather, my client's."

"You have a client." Gyre frowned. "Who?"

"Also their business."

"And?"

"Raskos has acquired an item from the deep tunnels," Kit said. "He's currently negotiating to sell it, but he doesn't have the faintest idea what it is he's got. I want you to take it from him."

"That's it?" Gyre's frown deepened.

"Don't make it sound so easy. The item is locked in a stasis web, so we're going to have to acquire a destabilizer to open it. Then we need to get the thing itself." She shrugged. "Most of the mercenaries and scavengers in Deepfire won't go up against the dux, not directly. But I knew there was at least one group willing to take him on. You and your crew are a little bit infamous, Halfmask."

"It's not my crew. And for fifty thousand thalers, I imagine most mercenaries would overcome their reservations," Gyre said.

"Maybe. But they're not the best. You are."

There was a long moment of silence. Gyre looked into her too-wide pupils, and she stared steadily back at him. In the distance, the lights of the city twinkled, and the red glow of the Pit reflected faintly off the low clouds.

"No," Gyre said.

"No what?"

"No, I'm not doing it." He shook his head. "The whole thing stinks. For all I know, you're working for the dux and this is a setup."

"If I was trying to trap you, I could have done it back at the Smoking Wreckage," Kit said.

"Still too risky," Gyre said. "I don't need the money, and there's other ways I can get to Raskos." That wasn't true, of course, but...

"Then why come to meet with me at all?" Kit said. She leaned closer. "Why come a second time, hmm? Just my personal charm at work?"

"Curiosity."

"Birdshit." She smiled delightedly. "I was right. It's the Tomb you want, isn't it?"

"I thought we'd established you'd never been there."

"I didn't say that." Kit straightened up. "So what would it take, Half-mask? You want an artifact from the last city of the ghouls? Something no one has ever seen before?"

She's lying. She's been lying to me all along. But Gyre couldn't keep his pulse from racing.

"I want you to take me there," he said.

"Oh." Kit blinked. "Is *that* all?"

"That's all."

"You have no idea what you're asking for," she said. "Didn't they tell you no one ever comes back from the Tomb?"

"You did. If you're telling the truth."

"The truth is...complicated. But that complexity doesn't apply to you, I can tell you that much."

"Nevertheless. That's what I want."

Kit rocked back and forth on her heels, lost in thought. "You're serious."

"I am."

"And they call *me* Doomseeker." She sighed. "If that's what you want, I'm not going to stop you. Just don't blame me afterward."

It was Gyre's turn to be taken aback. "Just like that?"

"What, do you want to go downstairs and have the Moorcats draw up a contract?" Kit shrugged. "It seems simple enough. You help me get what I want from Raskos, and I'll take you to the Tomb. I assume you'll still need the fifty thousand to get the rest of your merry band on board."

"Definitely." Gyre shook his head. "What proof do I have that you've even been to the Tomb?"

"None that I can offer," Kit said. "On the other hand, once I tell you what we're going to steal, there's nothing to stop you from taking it for yourself and leaving me out in the cold. So we're going to have to trust each other, won't we?"

Very slowly, Gyre nodded.

"Like I said, it's not my crew," he said. "I can't guarantee that the others will be on board."

"Just get me a meeting," Kit said, her grin returning. "I'm sure I can bring them around."

Gyre led Kit on a roundabout route through the city, skirting the north end of the Pit and heading west. They passed the Smokehouse district, with its endless rows of chimneys drooling black streamers that blotted out the stars, and stayed to one side of the road to avoid the continuous rumble of wagons. Beyond were the tunnels, the road running straight into the cracked, crumbling side of the mountain through a massive, irregular archway. The gate was closed, but a quick detour through a side passage brought them to the other side.

Relatively close to the surface, the tunnels resembled ordinary streets, except that the overarching stone meant none of the buildings had roofs. There were shops and cafés, stables and wagonyards. Since the typical ghoul tunnel was much wider than it was tall, these businesses had apartments behind them, with storefronts separated by narrow, anonymous doorways giving access. There were quite a few people about, even at this late hour, and the pair of them attracted no particular attention. Gyre chewed the neutralizer for his nighteye as he walked, letting his vision return to normal to avoid being blinded by the streetlights and smoke. A thick haze filled the air, and soot blackened the tunnel ceiling.

Kit stared around openly, drawing sour looks from the troops of tunnelborn in drab coveralls as they trudged past. Gyre nudged her to one side of the street and kept his voice low.

"You haven't spent much time in Deepfire, I take it?"

"Almost none," Kit said. "I was born in Grace. After that I've been— all over, really, but I haven't spent more than a night here before now." She shook her head. "I knew people lived in the tunnels, but I thought it would be more..." She shrugged. "Improvised."

"There's some of that farther out," Gyre said. "These tunnels are close enough to the Pit that they're always warm enough to live in. Deeper into the mountain, it depends on the time of year, the air currents. People crowd wherever they can manage."

"What are they all doing here?"

"Trying to survive." Gyre started walking again, and Kit fell in beside him, at least trying to look less like a tourist. "In the chaos after the end of the war, people from the mountains gathered around the Legion base here for protection. Once there was money to be made, though, the Republic moved in and pushed everyone else down into the tunnels."

"Why don't they leave?"

"And go where? The Republic border is closed if you're not a citizen, and the Splinter Kings are as likely to sell you into slavery as let you come stay."

"Nobody rules out in the mountains," Kit said.

"Nobody keeps you safe from plaguespawn, either."

"I suppose not," Kit mused. She glanced at Gyre. "And that's what you're fighting for, is it? The rights of these tunnel people?"

"They call themselves tunnelborn. And, yes. The dux and his

Auxies only care about the manufactories and the merchant combines. Nobody else will protect the people down here."

"Hmm," Kit said. She gave him a curious look, as though she didn't quite believe him.

He shrugged and pointed to a narrower alley. "Through here."

Gyre led them past a junction where a pair of fiddlers were entertaining a crowd by the light of a bonfire, and along another street filled with printers' shops. They were all locked up at this hour, though the occasional light in a window showed where someone was hard at work on tomorrow's edition.

The cold stole in gradually, step-by-step, until Gyre found himself rubbing his hands together for warmth. There were fewer people on the street here, and they wore heavier clothes, thick coats and patchwork gloves.

Kit shivered artfully. "I've never visited a city where it goes from spring to winter in a few hundred yards."

"This is nothing," Gyre said. "If you want to come into the deep tunnels with us, I hope you have something warmer to wear."

"I imagine I'll manage." She nodded at a long, low building up ahead, fitted snug against the curving rock. "Is this it?"

"Yeah." Gyre pulled his hood forward a bit. "Keep quiet until we're alone."

The shelter didn't have a proper door, just a heavy curtain to keep the heat in. Gyre pushed through it, eye wrinkling against a burst of warm, humid, foul-smelling air. Several large hearths were glowing, banked to save on precious fuel. The interior was one large room, the walls lined with sleeping mats two deep, crowded with filthy, ragged figures. Most of the residents were asleep, huddled in piles for extra warmth, but here and there small groups sat by the fires in quiet conversation or playing cards.

A young woman, standing out from the crowd in her clean gray robe, put down the bowl she was scrubbing in a basin of dirty water and hurried over to them. Gyre raised his head, enough to let the fire-light gleam on his mask, and she gave him a quick nod of recognition. She gestured toward another curtained doorway, and he and Kit threaded their way through the press of sleeping bodies.

Beyond the second curtain was a small storage area, backing up against the rock wall of the tunnel. There was a large, heavy-looking box, which shifted sideways with surprising ease when Gyre set his shoulder against it. Behind it was a crack in the stone, barely wide enough to squeeze through, with a glimmer of light visible through it.

Kit raised an eyebrow. Gyre smiled and gestured her onward.

"There are maps of the tunnels," Gyre said as he pushed through after her, "but everyone knows they're incomplete. This place was a maze *before* the Chosen blasted it into a crater. The one thing we never lack for is nooks and crannies."

"I can imagine." Kit looked back at the cracked rock wall. They'd emerged into a long, narrow corridor, running at right angles to the street they'd left. "What was that place?"

"The shelter? One of Yora's projects." Gyre took a deep breath—the air smelled better already—and started walking. "For people who can't work in the manufactories anymore, or never could. The bosses just throw them down here to freeze or starve. Yora tries to help them as much as she can. Food and fire is about what we can manage."

"And you don't find her charity admirable?" Kit said, catching up to him.

"Who says I don't?"

Kit shrugged, and for a moment they walked in silence.

"It's just not enough." Gyre shook his head. "Trying to save a few people at the edges. There's always more."

"You want to do something bigger," Kit said.

Gyre gave her a sharp look, and she shot back a knowing grin.

The light from the shelter had faded, so Gyre pulled a glowstone from his pocket and shook it to life, the eerie blue glow lighting up the rock. As they rounded a long curve, another tiny pinprick of blue became visible in the distance. Gyre halted, raised his light, and moved it slowly back and forth. *One, two, three, pause, one, two.*

The other light wagged back. Gyre let out a breath and kept walking.

"Impressively paranoid," Kit said.

"It keeps us alive," Gyre muttered. "I hope you know what you're getting into."

"Your concern is touching."

"I'd just hate to have to slit your throat, after all this effort," Gyre said.

"I must be growing on you." Kit grinned up at him, her features hideous in the blue glow.

The tunnel ended in a circular chamber about twenty meters across. Two other tunnels led off in different directions, but otherwise the junction was a featureless circle of ghoul-cut stone. They'd been meeting here long enough that they'd moved in a few sticks of furniture, a rough-cut table with biscuit crates and barrels for chairs, and a pair of lamps on tall iron stands. Not as comfortable as the Crystal Cavern, but for planning, it was better to have a little privacy.

Harrow was the one standing in the entrance with the glowlight, wearing leather armor with iron studs, his two-handed axe slung across his back with the handle poking up over his shoulder. He gave Gyre a grumpy nod and stared openly at Kit, who returned a sunny smile. Harrow turned and waved his light, and a moment later the lamps were lit, casting a weak radiance across the table that cut the pale green of the alchemical lights.

"About time," said Ibb. "I was getting tired of sitting in the dark." He wore his long leather coat and broad-brimmed hat, with a thin sword on one hip and a blaster pistol on the other. At the sight of Kit, he raised one delicate eyebrow. "Halfmask, you neglected to give us a full description of your guest. Most prospective clients aren't so... appetizing."

"Don't take him too seriously," Gyre said. "Ibb's a family man. A husband in the merchant combines and two children."

"Doesn't mean I can't appreciate beauty when I see it," the mercenary said. He bowed. "Ibb of Gerentia, at your service."

"Kit," said Kit. "Charmed, I'm sure."

"Halfmask," Yora said, careful to use his title in front of a stranger. "Kit, welcome. I'm Yora. This is Harrow." She gestured down at the pair sitting at the end of the table. "These two are Sarah and Nevin."

Sarah gave a smile and a wave, cheerful as always. Nevin sat beside her, hunched over, long-fingered hands moving nervously over the stone table.

"Halfmask tells us you have a business proposition," Yora said.

"It must be a plaguing good one," Ibb said, leaning back in his chair. "I thought we'd agreed to let the heat die down after last time."

Yora shot him a sour look. Gyre cleared his throat uncomfortably.

"I think this might be worth our time," he said. "Kit, say your piece."

"It'll definitely be worth your time," Kit said, grinning. "If you're bold enough."

Gyre watched the rest of the crew while Kit explained what she needed. Ibb's eyes widened at the mention of fifty thousand thalers, and Sarah perked up when she heard about the stasis web. Yora kept glancing between Kit and Gyre, and Nevin just stared at the table.

"That...is quite an offer." Ibb looked down at his hand and pretended to pick grit from under a fingernail. "If it's true, of course."

"You don't trust me," Kit said, her voice pleasant.

"Of course not," Ibb said.

"Halfmask vouches for you," Yora said. "Otherwise you wouldn't be here. But we need more."

"Then you're not interested?" Kit said. "Fifty thousand would buy a lot of food and firewood, wouldn't it?" Yora's face twitched, indicating a hit.

"Assuming the money really exists," Ibb said. "I admit that I'm tempted, but I would need ten percent in advance, and the rest deposited in a Moorcat Bank escrow account."

"Done," Kit said immediately. "That seems only fair."

"It's not that simple," Yora said. "We don't do mercenary work."

"Speak for yourself," Ibb drawled.

Yora sighed and looked at Sarah and Nevin. The arcanist spread her hands.

"It seems…plausible," Sarah said. "Scavengers have dug up active stasis webs before, and they usually fetch a high price, since whatever's inside is likely to be intact. You'd need a destabilizer to open one, at least if you haven't got a centarch handy to cut the web off."

"What's inside this one?" Yora said to Kit.

"The device is called the Core Analytica," Kit said. "It's a cube about a half meter on a side, fragile, nonvolatile. That's all I can tell you. Raskos has the stasis web stashed in his private warehouse."

"And the destabilizer?" Ibb said. "You mentioned we'd need to acquire that first."

"Yes. I have a location for it, but I'll need your help to get there. It's in the deep tunnels."

Sarah frowned. "How did you get its location, then?"

"That I can't tell you," Kit said, still smiling. "Sorry."

"Fifty thousand thalers buys an awful lot of 'no questions,'" Ibb said contemplatively.

"Nevin," Yora said. "You know the defenses around Raskos' warehouse. Can that part be done?"

The green-haired youth looked down at the table, shifting uncomfortably under everyone's scrutiny.

"You'd need a lot of gear," he said in a whisper-thin voice. "It's not just the guards. Rottentooth has everything money can buy around that place—screamerwire, scare charms, you name it. A good alchemist could get us past most of it, but…" He shrugged and lowered his head farther. "It'd cost."

"My client is prepared to pay any reasonable expenses," Kit said. "For quite a broad definition of reasonable."

That had Sarah sitting up and paying attention. The prospect of working with a large budget was always attractive. Gyre grinned to himself, imagining Lynnia's reaction.

"And you?" Yora said, looking back to Kit. "Would you be coming with us on this operation?"

"Of course," Kit said. "Whatever danger's involved, I'm happy to share it. Halfmask can attest that I can take care of myself."

"She can certainly fight," Gyre said. *Even if she gets a little reckless.*

Yora looked around the table. Ibb shrugged.

"You know my opinion," he said. "Provided we get paid as promised."

"Halfmask." Yora got to her feet. "Could I speak to you in private?"

They stepped aside from the others, to the far end of the cavern. Yora toyed with her golden hair, curling it through her fingers. She glanced back at Kit, then turned to Gyre.

"Do you trust her?" she said.

"She's not telling us everything, that's obvious." He hesitated. "She's no friend of Raskos', though. She and I fought our way through a couple dozen Auxies."

"That doesn't mean it's not a trap."

"Raskos doesn't have the imagination for *this* elaborate a trap."

Yora's lip quirked. "Probably not." She paused. "You know she can't be Doomseeker."

"She might have some . . . connection." His scar itched, and his finger tapped idly on his mask. "It's more than I've found in three years."

"I don't like it," Yora said. "We don't know what she's after, who her client is . . ."

"But we need the money." Gyre was careful not to sound too eager, but he knew it was a trump card. "With fifty *thousand* . . ."

"I know, plague it." Yora shook her head. "You think we should do it."

"I think it'll be dangerous," Gyre said. "But the payoff is worth it."

"Be honest with me. Worth it for the crew and the tunnelborn? Or just to get you closer to a myth?"

Gyre was silent for a while. Finally, he shrugged uncomfortably. "Why not both?"

Yora stared at him for a long moment, her expression unreadable. At last she nodded sharply.

"Then we do it," she said.

Chapter 7

I suppose he'd prefer to ride," Varo said. "Everything's easier from the back of a warbird."

"Should I help, do you think?" Maya said.

"I doubt he'd appreciate it."

Tanax's talent for stumbling into every patch of brambles and hanging vine in the forest bordered on the supernatural. At the moment, he'd managed both at once, flailing at the vine that had attached itself to his pack while stumbling deeper into the pricking bushes. His swearing was clearly audible above the rustle of branches.

"If this were a comic opera," Varo said, "about now a beehive would drop on his head."

Maya sniggered.

"Mind you," Varo went on, "a friend of mine died that way. Turned out he was allergic to beestings, and he swelled up like a balloon."

"That's terrible," Maya said.

"Dunno. With his last words, he swore the honey was worth it."

Varo shrugged and started forward. "I'll go and offer my services. Why don't you check in with the rear of the column?"

Maya trudged back through the woods, cresting a low ridge. She looked around for Beq and found her standing stock-still between two trees, frozen in an awkward position.

"Um. Is something wrong?" Maya said.

"Shhhh!" Beq hissed. "Stay there!"

Maya's hand dropped to her haken. "What's going on?"

Sweat dripped past Beq's spectacles, pooling in a drop at the end of her nose. She was breathing in shallow gasps.

"If I move," she said, very quietly, "it's going to bite me."

"What's going to bite you?"

"The snake!"

"What—" Maya looked Beq up and down, spotted the bit of bright green, and let out a long breath. "Beq. That's a well snake."

"I don't care how good of a snake it is—"

"As in the kind you find down wells," Maya said patiently. She crossed the distance between them in a couple of strides and plucked the thing off Beq's shoulder. *She must have knocked it off a branch.* The snake was about half a meter long, and its scales were the bright green of fresh leaves. Maya held it behind the head, and it coiled its length around her arm. "We found these all the time back on the farm. They're harmless."

Beq, who'd flinched at Maya's movement as though she expected imminent death, uncoiled slightly. "Really?"

"Really." Maya put the snake on the nearest tree branch. "I guarantee it was as terrified as you were."

"I doubt that," Beq said. She heaved a sigh of relief, looking distrustfully at the snake as it wound rapidly away. "I thought it was going for my throat."

Maya grinned, and after a moment Beq grinned back at her, a broad, goofy smile that did strange things to Maya's innards. Apparently oblivious to the effect she produced, Beq stretched and adjusted her heavy pack.

"Well," she said. "So much for my reputation as a bold hero."

"Heroes have to start somewhere," Maya said as they started walking toward the others.

"True." Beq looked at her, a little shyly. "Thanks. Can you tell this is my first time out of the Forge?"

"Um. A little." Maya patted her shoulder. "You're doing well, considering."

"You seem like you know your way around the woods."

"My mentor and I spent a lot of time traveling," Maya said. "You get used to it."

"I hope so." Beq shifted her pack again. "This thing is already killing me."

Maya had to admit that she was with Beq on that one. Jaedia had typically traveled with a cart for the heavy gear. Back at the quartermasters', Maya had eyed the list Varo had come up with and thought it was a bit scanty; now every jounce of her pack made her wonder if she really *needed* spare underwear.

They all had good cause to be grateful for the scout's expertise. Maya might have more experience in the woods than Beq, but Jaedia had usually stuck to the roads, so she wasn't much good at finding her way. Tanax was obviously no help, so they relied on Varo to lead, down the shallow-sided valley and over the occasional rocky outcrop. Like many Gates, the one they'd emerged from was in rough country, and the Order preferred not to call attention to their precise locations by constructing roads or trails. *Sensible, but awkward.*

They lunched by a broad pool, aching legs and backs grateful for the rest, even if the hard-traveling food Varo had requisitioned was nothing much to look forward to. The water was delicious and tooth-achingly cold, at least, utterly refreshing after the heat of the morning. Beq ducked her whole head under and came up gasping, coiling her wet braid over one shoulder.

"Had a friend who liked to do that," Varo said. "One time there was a big river crocodile waiting for him. I swear that thing had followed us for kilometers."

Tanax snorted derisively, sitting in the shade of a boulder some distance from the rest of them.

"He didn't talk as much after losing his head," Varo said, "but we all agreed it improved his temper."

"I think we're a little far north for crocodiles," Maya said, trying hard to ignore how the water that soaked Beq's shirt made it cling in exciting ways. "But we should get moving."

They stood, with assorted curses and groans, and got back to walking. By the time the sun started to slide down toward the horizon, the land had flattened out some, the valley widening and the forest thinning out, which made for considerably easier going. Glacial boulders dotted the broadening plain, and Varo laid out their camp in the lee of one of them, constructing a fire pit from flat river stones. Maya stopped him as he started to gather twigs for kindling. She dragged a couple of larger dry branches over, laid a finger on her haken, and twisted out a fine thread of *deiat* until they ignited with a dull roar.

"That's handy," he said, sitting down beside his pack. "I can think of a few times we could have used you. Once—"

"If this story ends with someone freezing to death, I don't need to hear it," Beq said, dropping heavily to the packed earth.

"Nobody freezes," Varo said. Then, after a moment's contemplation he added, "The polar bear got him first."

Beq caught Maya's eye and heaved a sigh. Maya grinned at her.

"We should keep a watch," she said. "We're not that far from the border, and I doubt the Legion sweeps here very often. There could be plaguespawn."

"No need." Tanax dug a small unmetal-and-glass sphere out of his pack, about the size of a marble. Maya felt him thread a bit of *deiat* into it, and it started glowing.

"A watch charm?" Beq said, suddenly interested. "Where did you get one of those?"

"Not from the quartermaster, that's for sure," Varo said.

"It was a gift from my mentor. He said I would have more use for it now than he would." He sounded a little defensive and hardened his tone immediately. "Now, get some rest. We'll move out early tomorrow morning and reach Litnin by midday."

Lying on her bedroll beside the softly glowing watch charm, Maya found herself too keyed up for sleep. She wasn't worried, exactly—the charm would sound if anything came near, and even if there were plaguespawn they weren't likely to be anything two agathia couldn't handle. She just felt too *aware*, cognizant of every rustling branch and snapping twig in the forest. Stars winked at her through the gently shifting canopy.

I wonder where Jaedia is now. It was the first time she'd been away from her mentor for years. She'd told herself she was ready, even eager to move on from the constrained life of an agathios, but now she felt like a part of her that had been tied down was flapping loose. It was made worse by the knowledge that whatever Jaedia was doing, it was certainly important and possibly dangerous. *That black spider-thing...* Maya shuddered at the memory of the *crunch* as it tore itself free from Hollis' neck. *If that's what she's investigating, I should be with her. She needs better backup than just Marn.*

And, of course, there were other distractions. Beq lay next to her, curled up on her side under a thin sheet, her precious spectacles set carefully beside her bedroll. Maya could hear her soft, slow breathing. *She didn't have any trouble getting to sleep.* Maya wondered, idly, what would happen if she rolled over and threw her arm across the girl's shoulders. *Probably she'd think she was being attacked by a bear.*

Varo boiled tea in the morning, which Maya gulped greedily, and they broke camp and set out at a moderate pace. Fortunately, the terrain got easier as they went along, rough ground flattening out, and they made good time. When they reached the point where the little creek they'd been following emptied into a larger river, Varo checked his map and announced they were only an hour south of the village.

"Do we have a cover story?" Maya asked as they refilled their canteens in the shallows. "Or are we going in openly?"

"Openly, of course." Tanax seemed genuinely puzzled. "This is the Republic. Why would we need to conceal ourselves?"

"Jaedia says that people are usually afraid of the Order," Maya said.

"Typical soft Pragmatic." Tanax gave a mirthless grin. "If they're afraid, that's all to the good. We're here to investigate them for heresy and treason. A little fear might encourage the villagers to offer up the guilty more quickly."

Maya frowned. "Assuming there are any guilty."

"There will be," Tanax said, one hand on his haken. "The Council doesn't make mistakes in cases like this. If they've sent us here, there'll be something to find."

He took the lead, now that they were close, the others following behind in single file and in silence. Maya wanted to ask Varo if he'd been on this sort of mission before, and whether Tanax's approach was typical, but there was no way to speak without the other agathios overhearing. *Maybe he's right.* She and Jaedia had often chased rumors to no result, but the Council presumably had higher standards for evidence. Maya touched the Thing and tried to calm her mind. *Remember. I must do well here. That means doing what the Council requires.*

They passed the top of a low ridge, and the village was suddenly in sight. It was set in a fold in the land, with a stream running down the middle to feed into the river, and buildings spreading outward from it up both slopes of the gentle valley. There were perhaps fifty homes, fairly large as backcountry villages went, with a pier for a few small boats jutting out into the river at one end and terraced gardens stretching up the valley at the other. In between were haphazardly placed plaster and timber houses, with clay roofs and windows blocked by rag curtains instead of glass. Quite a few people were visible, and a small gang of chickens ran free in the street, pecking bugs out of the midden. Several loadbirds milled around in a pen by the water, owlishly watching the antics of their smaller cousins.

A small group, headed in their direction, stopped abruptly at the sight of the four of them. There were two men and a woman, all in tough canvas trousers, heavy work shirts with rolled-up sleeves, and thick leather gauntlets. Maya guessed they were loggers; the big felling axes they carried looked more like tools than weapons. The woman's eyes widened at the sight of two haken, and she muttered something to her companions. They tensed up, standing straighter.

"Litnin welcomes the Twilight Order," the logger woman said, stepping forward. "We are honored by your visit."

"Indeed you are," Tanax said. He stopped in front of her and frowned at the realization that she was at least ten centimeters taller than he was.

"Can I ask your business?" the woman said. "Is this a patrol, or —"

"To whom am I speaking?" Tanax said.

"My name is Kaiura Axebreaker, Centarch," she said, bowing. Maya guessed she was in her midthirties, with tanned olive skin, thickly muscled arms, and a curly mop of gray-green hair.

"And are you the magistrate of this village?"

"I suppose." Kaiura scratched the back of her neck. "I'm the one who signs the paperwork, anyway."

"Excellent," Tanax said. "If you could conduct me to your residence, I would like to begin work immediately."

One of the other loggers started to say something, but Kaiura held up a hand to silence him.

"Apologies, Centarch," she said. "Can I ask what work that would be?"

"A thorough investigation of Litnin," Tanax said with a cold smile. "I can't say more at this time. But I value your cooperation."

A little more than an hour later, Tanax was sitting in a chair at Kaiura's kitchen table, examining a bound ledger, where, in crooked handwriting, the lives of Litnin's people were chronicled. Maya, Beq, and Varo stood behind him, unregarded.

"According to this, there are eighty-five adults in the village," he said, looking up at the logger. She stood beside the table, still in her work clothes, though she'd laid aside her axe. "Is that correct?"

"I believe so," Kaiura said. "Though Eskin Badapple's boy is nearly seventeen."

"Very well." He spun the ledger to face her. "I will interview them in order. Can I trust you to arrange it?"

Kaiura blinked, tugging absently at her hair. "All of them, Agathios?"

"Of course. I wouldn't want to be less than thorough."

"Of course," Kaiura echoed. She picked up the book. "Excuse me, then."

Tanax gave a dismissive wave. Kaiura bowed again and went out, leaving Maya and the others alone. Maya glanced at the door and lowered her voice.

"You're going to interview *everyone*?" she said.

"If I have to."

"What's the point?" Maya shook her head. "If these people weren't terrified of us before, they certainly are now. Why would they tell you anything?"

Tanax gave her a sidelong look. "Apparently Jaedia neglected some parts of your education. The Council will be receiving my report."

"Jaedia—" Maya shook her head. Jaedia would have gone straight to the inn, started buying drinks, and gotten the villagers to tell her stories. "She does things differently."

"I imagine." He sighed. "While it's not my responsibility to educate you, if you must know, this is standard procedure. A nervous subject is more likely to slip up under questioning."

"What, they're going to just blurt out that they're smuggling *dhak*?"

"Of course not. But they will make mistakes in their answers, and when we compare one interview to the next, a pattern of lies will emerge, depend on it. Then we will know where to direct our investigation."

"And this is how Dogmatics do things?" Maya said, unable to restrain herself.

"This is how the *Order* does things. I suggest you learn if you ever want to get your cognomen."

Maya shut her mouth, biting back a sarcastic reply. Tanax turned to Beq.

"Arcanist-Trainee, I will require your assistance taking notes. Requisition paper and ink from the villagers."

"Um. Yes." Beq fiddled with her spectacles, lenses clicking back and forth. "You think there's a store around here—"

"Just ask for some," Tanax said flatly. "It's their duty under the law to provide for the Order."

"Right." She gave a worried nod, glancing at Maya. "I'll just...go do that, then."

"Don't dawdle." Tanax looked around. "I suppose you two had better keep watch outside. Make certain no one is eavesdropping, and tell Kaiura to send the interviewees in as soon as they arrive."

"Yes, Agathios," Varo said. He jerked his head at Maya, who'd been biting her tongue only with difficulty.

She glared at Tanax as Varo led her outside, not that the other agathios took any notice. *Arrogant bastard.* He was only a year older than her at most. *Where does he get off—*

"I'm starting to understand what you mean by behaving like a typical centarch," Maya muttered when they were in the hall.

"Well." Varo rubbed a hand across his bald skull. "Tanax may be a bit more snappish than most. I expect you have something to do with that."

"Me?" Maya said, lowering her voice only at the last moment. "What did I do to him?"

"I'm not an expert," Varo said, "but I know it's rare to see two agathia from different factions on the same assignment. Probably 'cause they'd expect them to fight like cats in a sack. Maybe Tanax thinks your being here means the Council doesn't trust him."

"That's ridiculous. The Council—" Maya shook her head. "It has nothing to do with him, I'm certain."

"Try to explain that to him, if you get a chance." Varo yawned. "Well, if the worst we have to deal with is Tanax being an ass, I'll count this as one of my better assignments. Much better than the time—"

"I can guess," Maya said, holding up a hand.

"Tore it right off," Varo said, with a sad shake of his head.

He opened the front door, which produced a couple of high-pitched squeals. Two girls, aged seven or eight, fled from where they'd been pressed against the front of the house, taking cover behind the front hedge. Maya could see several other children of various sizes waiting there, eager for a glimpse of these rare visitors.

She stopped for a moment, affected by a sudden, powerful memory. *I was playing with Gyre, and we saw a warbird coming...* Her chest tightened, and her hand came up to touch the Thing.

"You all right?" Varo said. "No good with kids?"

"I'm...fine." Maya shook her head. "Just memories."

"You come from a place like this?" he said, strolling outside.

Maya followed, looking back at the house, which was a ramshackle two-story affair. It was built on a slope high on the hillside, giving it the look of an animal burrow, partially buried in the rocky ground. A hedge of neatly trimmed blackberry bushes demarcated a small front yard, full of blooming herbs and flowers. Around the side, a dirt paddock was occupied by the massive round shape of a vulpi terminal, its atrophied limbs receding into the rolling bloat of its fatty body, with a pair of more nimble yearlings peering out nervously from behind its bulk. Somewhere, a dog barked.

"Not exactly like this," Maya said. "My parents were vulpi ranchers, near Threecrowns. It was all open country—you could see for kilometers. But...not so different, really." She glanced at Varo. "Where did you come from?"

"Skyreach," he said. "The bad part."

"I didn't think there was a bad part of Skyreach."

"There's a bad part of every city. Some of them are just better at hiding it." He shrugged. "Took a test to get into the Order's scouts when I was eight, with about a hundred other kids. I think I was the only one who passed."

"That's quite an honor."

"I suppose. At the time all I knew was that it meant I wouldn't have to worry where my next meal was coming from." He gave Maya an odd look. "I suppose you didn't get a choice."

"Not really. My parents..." If she pressed her memory, she could recall their worried faces. *And Gyre was screaming.* "They knew it was best for me."

"Of course."

Varo cut off and stood a little straighter as Kaiura returned, a couple of anxious villagers with her. Two of the children had also attached themselves to her, taking a hand each and trailing nervously behind her like reluctant kites.

"These are the first two on the list, Agathios," Kaiura said, pulling her hand away from the older girl and gesturing the villagers forward. They were an old man and a younger woman, close enough in looks that Maya guessed they were family. "Some of the others are out in the woods, or at work in the fields. I don't know if I'll be able to track everyone down before nightfall."

"Just do your best," Maya said. She smiled at the pair, which only made them cower. "You can go inside. He just wants to ask you a few questions."

The two villagers bowed hastily and went in. Kaiura watched for a moment, then looked down at the children, now huddling around her legs.

"Are they yours?" Maya said.

Kaiura nodded. "This is Sayura and Miura. Bow to the agathios, girls."

The two little girls gave half-hearted bows. Maya gave them a smile, too, though it didn't seem to help.

"I don't suppose you can tell me what this is about?" Kaiura said, lowering her voice. "Life has been peaceful here. We haven't seen a Legion sweep in two years, and no one has met a plaguespawn bigger than a rat. And now..." She looked at her kitchen window.

Maya bit her lip. *Tanax is writing my report. It's probably best not to contradict him directly.* "I can't say. But if there's nothing wrong, I assure you that no one has anything to worry about."

"Of course." Kaiura's face was hard, but Maya could see the disappointment there. "Excuse me, Agathios. I should find the next people on your colleague's list."

She turned and stalked out of the garden, the two children hurrying to keep up. On the way out she almost ran into Beq, who was hurrying in the other direction with a stack of paper and pens.

"Sorry!" the arcanist said to Kaiura, and then again to Maya. "Sorry! That took longer than I thought. I had to go to four houses before I found one with some paper, and—"

"You'd better go in," Varo said. "He's started the interviews. Best not to keep him waiting."

"Right!" Beq gave a shaky grin. "I'll go and take notes, then."

When she was gone, Maya looked around. Apart from the gang of kids behind the hedge, there was no one else nearby.

"So now what?" Maya said. "We just stand out here like sentries?"

"I think that's the idea." Varo yawned. "I'm going to go and secure the rear of the house. There was a comfortable little hay shed that looked like it needed…guarding." He winked at Maya. "Give a shout if you need anything, yeah?"

Taking a nap when she was supposed to be keeping a lookout might have been a dereliction of duty, but after several hours it was starting to sound very attractive. They'd been up early that morning, and as the sun rose clear of the tree line, the day was only getting hotter. Maya had retreated to a patch of shade, which was shrinking by the minute as noon approached.

Kaiura had returned several times, escorting families of villagers to their interviews with Tanax. The people she brought were mostly older, plus a few youths in their late teens. She explained that the day's logging parties had already gone out, so most of the young men and women of the village wouldn't be back until evening. That made Tanax scowl, but he had enough to keep him busy in the meantime.

When she came inside for water, Maya got a glimpse of her fellow agathios, delivering crisp questions to a frightened old woman. Beq, sitting beside him, looked miserable as she scratched away at a rough sheet of paper, writing down the answers. Maya had considered offering to take turns keeping notes, but watching Beq even for a moment made it clear that was foolish—the other girl's writing was much faster and neater. *It must be something they teach the arcanists.*

Instead, Maya went back outside, huddling into the little shade that was left and watching the people of the village. After an interval, they'd emerged, cautiously, to go about the day's business, working in their gardens and feeding animals, throwing occasional suspicious glances at Kaiura's house. Even the children at the hedge had drifted off, apparently deciding that nothing interesting was happening after all, or else called back to do chores.

Maya was seriously considering slipping around the back of the house to ask Varo to trade off when another face appeared at the hedge. A girl with a bright purple ponytail and a nervous expression leaned out to look at Maya, then froze when she realized Maya was looking back. Maya cleared her throat.

"Did you need anything?" she said.

The girl took a deep breath to steel herself and approached. She looked about thirteen, with the same golden-tanned skin most of the villagers shared. Maya smiled again, and this time it actually seemed to work. The girl gave a nervous bow.

"H-hello." Her eyes darted to the haken at Maya's hip. "You're one of the centarchs, right?"

"I'm an agathios," Maya said. "A centarch-in-training. My name is Maya."

"I'm Streza," the girl said. "My grandmother told me not to talk to you. But..." Her lip twisted.

"What's wrong?" Maya said.

"My brother's missing," Streza blurted. "Grandmother says he probably just tagged along with one of the logging parties, but I know he wouldn't do that without asking. And she said not to tell anyone in the village, but you're not *from* the village and Father used to say that centarchs would help anyone who needed it even if they didn't have a reason. And—"

"Slow down," Maya said. "Has your brother been gone long?"

"Since yesterday," Streza said miserably. "Some of the logging teams stayed out overnight but I *told* Grandmother I saw him since they left."

"Do you have any idea where he might be?"

"I think he was playing at the old storehouse," the girl said eagerly. "We're not supposed to go up there, but he and I used to play at ghouls and heroes. I saw him on the hill, but I thought he was going to visit Bannie."

"You haven't gone to look?"

"Just...just a little bit." Streza crossed her arms. "There's a lot of holes in the floor down into the old basement. I thought he might have fallen down, but I didn't have a light, and..." She swallowed.

"Okay," Maya said. "Can you wait here for a few minutes? I'm going to go inside and talk to someone."

Fortuitously, Tanax and Beq had just finished their latest interview. An old man with a wild puff of gray hair stomped out, looking irritated, and Maya slipped in before the next villager could arrive. The heat in the closed-off kitchen was stifling. Tanax was leaning back in his chair, apparently perfectly comfortable, but Beq looked miserable hunched over her paper. She perked up as Maya entered.

"Any luck?" Maya said.

Beq started to answer, then looked to Tanax. The other agathios gave a regal smile.

"The pattern is still forming," he said, "but I have enough to know something strange is going on. We'll get to the bottom of it." He leaned forward. "Nicomidi always said that patience and perseverance are the keys to successful work."

"I'm sure," Maya muttered.

"Have you found anything unusual?"

"Not so far," Maya said. "There's a girl asking for help, and I wanted to see what I could do for her."

"Help?"

Maya explained what Streza had told her. As she spoke, Tanax's frown deepened.

"If the boy's grandmother isn't concerned," he said, "I don't see why we should be. Surely she would know best."

"Probably," Maya admitted. "But it's a good excuse to poke around. And it might help build a little goodwill with the villagers."

"It's not their goodwill I need, just their obedience." Tanax sighed and waved a hand. "If you really want to spend your time pulling lost cats out of trees, I suppose you might as well."

Better than standing around here like a stump. "Thank you," Maya said. "I'll let you know if I find anything interesting."

"Very well." He waved dismissively. "Send in the next villager."

Beq caught Maya's eye, shook out her writing hand, and made a pained face while Tanax wasn't looking. Maya winced and mouthed, "Good luck," as she slipped out. In the hall, she told a stout older woman to go inside, then hurried back to the front door. Streza was waiting, kicking nervously at a stone.

"All right," Maya told the girl. "Take me to the old storehouse, and we'll look for your brother."

The old storehouse turned out to be on the other side of the village, atop the rise. Streza relieved her nervousness by providing a running commentary as they walked, pointing out each house.

"This is where Anna Ironbelly and her wife live, and that's Grend Purevoice's place. He once won a county singing contest. *And* his son is in the Legion now." Streza puffed herself up a little at this. When she looked back at Maya, though, her face fell. "Litnin must seem tiny to you."

"You'd be surprised," Maya said. She and Jaedia had spent a lot of time in small villages, although usually not quite *this* small or so far off the beaten path.

"I thought centarchs lived in Skyreach with the Senate and all."

"Some of us live in the Forge, which isn't far from there. But not all of us. I grew up traveling from place to place with my mentor."

"That sounds amazing," Streza said. "When I grow up, I want to go somewhere."

"Where?"

"Dunno. Anywhere more interesting." She sighed. "Nothing ever happens here."

Let's hope not. Maya pointed to a long, low building visible on the top of the ridge. "Is that the storehouse?"

"Yeah." Streza's steps slowed. "Grandmother and the others always tell us never to go up there."

"Why not?"

"The old storehouse caught fire," the girl said, "and part of the floor fell in. They built the new storehouse down in the valley, and we don't use this one anymore. I think they're worried it might collapse."

"People do come up here, though?"

"Sometimes. My brother and I used to come play. And he said he once saw Venli and Firn up here kissing and, you know, messing around." Her cheeks reddened.

Not busy, then, but not abandoned either. If the storehouse was the local make-out spot, it was unlikely that anything really dangerous had taken up residence without being noticed. *Maybe the boy fell and knocked himself out?*

"What's your brother's name?" Maya said as they climbed the ridge.

"Reese." Streza pressed closer to Maya's side. "Do you think he's okay?"

"I'm sure he is," Maya said.

In a few minutes, they were standing in front of the old storehouse. It was a stone-walled building, so the fire had left most of it standing, but the shingled roof had partially collapsed. The big front doors stood open, one hanging from a single hinge, and Maya could see the inside was a maze of burnt debris, carpeted with moss and a few enterprising saplings. One of the roof beams had crashed through the floorboards, creating a large hole into a dark understory.

"I can see why your parents don't want you up here," Maya said.

"I'm sorry," Streza said. "I swear we'll never come up here again. I'll watch my brother every minute."

"It's all right," Maya said. "Stay here at the door. I'm going to take a look."

Streza nodded nervously. Maya touched her haken and conjured a small flame above one hand for light, and the girl gasped in surprise. Maya couldn't help but smile at that. Then, feeling a little foolish, she threaded *deiat* into her panoply belt, the familiar blue haze of protection washing over her. *Better safe than sorry.*

The floorboards groaned underfoot. The inside of the storehouse was mostly open, with the collapsed remains of a loft in one corner. It was silent enough that Maya felt odd raising her voice. She coughed, awkwardly, and called out.

"Reese? Are you there?"

No answer, not that she'd expected one. She went to the edge of the hole in the floorboards and held the flame over it. The light illuminated a packed-earth surface about three meters down, littered with splinters of burnt, blackened wood.

"Streza, I'm going down to look around," Maya called. "Just stay where you are."

"Be careful," Streza said.

Maya grinned to herself and stepped off the edge. She absorbed the fall with a crouch, the panoply field killing some of the energy and sending a chilly wave over her skin. She fed more power to her flame, and the light grew brighter, illuminating a rough-walled underground space. In one corner, stairs led to a trapdoor in the ceiling. Bags and barrels were stacked in rough piles, charred by fire and softened by moss and decay. The air still smelled scorched.

As she turned, a breath of air played across her face. Maya saw a darker half circle in one wall, the entrance to some sort of tunnel. *Odd.*

"Streza?" Maya said.

The girl's head poked over the side of the hole, her expression worried. "Are you all right?"

"I told you to wait at the door," Maya said.

"Sorry."

Maya shook her head. "Do you know where this tunnel goes?"

"What tunnel?"

"There's some kind of entrance down here."

"I've never heard of a tunnel under the storehouse," Streza said. "Maybe it was a secret?"

"Maybe." Maya played her light on the entryway, showing a few feet of well-packed earth. "I'm going to take a look. *Stay there*, would you?"

"Okay."

The cooler air coming out of the tunnel mouth had an odd scent to it. Maya sniffed as she got closer, trying to place it. There was fresh earth, and ashes, and . . .

Old meat. For a moment she was back in another underground cavern, grappling with a tentacled horror. *Plaguespawn!*

Eyes opened in the darkness, five mismatched orbs glowing in the reflected light of her flame. Maya took a step backward, and the monster lunged.

She had enough warning to throw herself to one side. The thing that barreled past was bigger than she was, the size of a pony, with a wolf's snout that had been split down the center and widened with a complex armature of gleaming bone and pulsing red muscle. Six limbs, each of which looked as though it had originally been at least two animal legs, extended up over the creature's back before coming down, giving it the look of a fleshy, skinless cockroach. Several tails twitched at the back end of it, one sporting an additional eye.

It skittered past her, horribly fast, and slid to a halt on the packed

earth. Maya straightened and drew her haken, the blade igniting into a
line of orange-white fire.

"Maya?" Streza's voice came down from above. "What's happening—"

The plaguespawn, hearing her, took a step forward, and it must have
come into the girl's field of view, because her voice rose into a high,
shrill scream. That only captured the thing's attention further, and it
gathered its legs under it, preparing to leap.

Plague that. Maya extended a hand, and a bolt of solid flame flashed
across the room, crashing into the side of the monster. It rocked and
staggered sideways, fire running briefly over its body before guttering
out. It turned again, split jaw working as it glared at Maya with mismatched eyes. She stepped forward deliberately. *That's right. Look at
me, ugly.*

"Streza!" Maya shouted as the plaguespawn started to circle. "I want
you to run back to Kaiura's house *right now.*"

"But—" The girl's voice was a whimper.

"*Now.* Tell my friends what we found. *Go!*"

She couldn't say whether the girl answered, because the monster
charged again, legs blurring as it threw itself into a sprint. Maya waited
until the last moment, holding its attention, then sprang to one side
like a ringfighter. She dragged her haken along its flank, the blazing
sword slashing a long, ugly burn into the slick, wet muscle there.

The plaguespawn made a warbling, gurgling sound, then screeched
as Maya brought more fire boiling up underneath it. It hopped sideways, and this time she charged first, coming at it head-on and bringing
her blade down on its bifurcated head. Flesh and bone parted easily in
the path of *deiat.* Both halves snapped at her, one set of jaws closing on
her arm, the panoply field straining to keep them apart. Maya, fighting
the chill, spun and twisted her blade through the plaguespawn's neck,
sending one half of its head bouncing to the earth.

The stump gouted black blood, but the thing was still moving, the
remaining half head twisting and biting in a frenzy. Maya gave ground,

fading to one side, and waited for it to commit to a lunge. When it did, she sidestepped and slashed at its throat. Another half a skull came free, and the now entirely headless creature wobbled and collapsed.

*That...*Maya was breathing hard, and her heart pounded triple-time. She touched the Thing with her free hand. *That was unexpected.*

"Streza?" she called. There was no answer.

Good. The girl was, hopefully, halfway across the village by now. *I hope she can get through to Tanax.* Maya looked down at the dead plaguespawn, swallowing hard. *At least none of the parts look human.* You couldn't *always* tell, but...

It can't be coincidence. Plaguespawn couldn't restrain themselves. They were constructs of meat and *dhak*, and all they understood was the hunger for more flesh. *If something this size had found its way in here on its own, the villagers would have seen it before now.*

That meant the thing wasn't a wild plaguespawn, following its own instincts. It had been guarding the tunnel.

Only a dhakim *could have set it a task like that. Whatever's going on in this town, I think I've found it.*

The logical thing to do would be to retreat, up the stairs at least, and wait for help. But if Streza's brother was alive, he needed help now, before the *dhakim* knew she'd found them.

She took a deep breath and let the fire fade, plunging the basement into semidarkness. Ahead of her, the tunnel entrance loomed like a black maw. She touched the Thing again.

Tanax, you ass, you'd better listen to Streza. Maya stepped forward, fingers white-knuckled on the hilt of her haken.

The tunnel was long and twisting, so low Maya had to stoop to continue. A light would give her away, so she groped her way along in the dark, one hand on her haken. Dirt crumbled around her outstretched fingers, cascading down into her hair. Long, outstretched roots of plants growing above blocked her path like a stubborn curtain, and she had to push through them.

She was starting to wonder how far it could possibly go when a faint light filtered around a curve up ahead. It wasn't much, but she could make out dim shadows. Maya crouched, moving more slowly, and stopped when she could see out into a larger space.

It was a cave, roughly circular, with a wider tunnel at one end that ended abruptly in a wood-and-canvas barricade. Crates were piled three-deep in the center, with a lantern on top of the pile providing a flickering light. Around the edges of the room, Maya could see long, rectangular boxes with iron-banded sides and metal grates at the front. *Cages?*

Three figures worked near the central pile, prying open a set of crates to examine the contents. One of them, slim and blue-haired in a heavy waterproof coat, stood a few paces back, keeping an eye on the others.

So these are the smugglers. Maya wasn't exactly sure where she was, but they couldn't be too far from Litnin. Listening closely, she could hear the sound of running water. *We must be near the river.*

The important thing was to figure out if Reese was here. If he wasn't—or if he was dead, a possibility she had to force herself to consider—then the thing to do was retreat the way she'd come and return with backup. *But if he is here . . .*

Jaedia's chiding echoed in the back of her mind. Maya pursed her lips. *What am I supposed to do? Let people die?*

"Plague it," one of the figures said. "It's not here. I still say that bastard shorted us."

"I counted the lots myself," the blue-haired figure said. It was a woman's voice. "It's here. You shitheads just put it in the wrong crate."

"We haven't got time for this," another man said. "Just put it in the next load."

"No guarantee we'll have a buyer," the woman said. "Find the fucking thing."

Another voice cut across the cavern, a young girl's, and Maya's blood went cold. "I'm hungry."

There was a chorus of whispers, like someone was trying to quiet the girl, but the woman in the coat had already heard. She stalked away from the crates.

"Did I not already tell you to shut the fuck up?" she said. "Next word I hear out of any of you, I'm going to turn you inside out."

"She's not kidding," one of the men said. "I've seen her do it. Boy was walking around with all his guts hanging off his outside. So, fucking behave."

Oh, dhak.

The child's voice had come from the edge of the cavern. *The cages.* Peering closer, Maya could see that some of them had their doors hanging open, while others were closed and padlocked. Behind the grills, she could see movement. *Have they really got them in* cages?

Whether Reese was there or not, going back was out of the question. She had no idea how long it would be before they discovered the dead plaguespawn, but Maya wasn't going to risk it. *And if I can't go back, then the only way out is forward.* She stepped out of the tunnel entrance and straightened up.

"All of you," she said, her voice shakier than she would have liked. "Stop and drop your weapons."

The three figures froze. After a moment, the closest, a thin man with a ragged fringe of orange-red hair, snatched up a lantern and stalked toward Maya.

"What the fuck?" the woman said from behind him. "How did she get in here?"

"Plagued if I know. It's some girl." The thin man raised his lantern in one hand, a small crossbow pointing at Maya. "You picked the wrong place to wander around—"

Maya could see his eyes go wide as he recognized the haken in her hand. She was already pushing off into a sprint as he squeezed the trigger. His aim was bad, and the bolt flew wide. She'd covered half the distance between them as he scrabbled to draw a sword, letting the lantern and crossbow fall.

"She's a *centarch*!" he screamed, as her haken ignited with a flaming hiss.

Then she was in front of him and he had his blade out, swinging clumsily for her throat. Maya parried, automatically, the brief contact with *deiat* carving a glowing notch out of the ordinary steel. Fast as thought, she went into her riposte, a simple upward slash across his body.

If she'd been fighting Jaedia, this would have rewarded her with the blue flare of a panoply field and perhaps a word of praise when the fight was done. Instead, her haken carved a long, charred path across the smuggler, from his hip to his shoulder, flaming blade shearing through clothes, flesh, and bone and leaving smoldering ash in its wake. The man managed a choking cry as he fell, sprawled motionless in the dirt.

Maya had killed plaguespawn. She'd even killed ordinary animals, deer or rabbits for food, once a loadbird that had broken a leg and needed to be put out of its misery. But, until that moment, she'd never turned her power on a human, never snuffed out a life with *deiat*.

It was horrifyingly easy.

"Plaguing *fuck*!" The other smuggler's swearing refocused her attention. He was a larger man, stripped to a tunic and trousers for hard labor. Another heavy coat lay nearby, and he scrabbled with it, searching for something. Maya leveled her glowing haken.

"I said *stop*," she grated, stepping around the corpse. "You are both prisoners of the Twilight Order."

The big man came up, a blaster pistol in hand.

Maya had been expecting another crossbow, which was hardly dangerous with her panoply up. A blaster was another matter. She threw out her hand, sending a focused wave of flame crashing over the smuggler, but it wasn't fast enough. Bolts of blue-white energy *cracked* across the cavern, slamming into the walls with explosive concussions.

One of the shots caught Maya in the chest, and she felt herself picked up and tossed backward as her panoply flared. The power drain was horrific, as though her entire body had been plunged into a pool full of ice, and her vision darkened. She fought desperately to stay conscious, tucking her body into a ball and turning her skid across the ground into a roll. She came to a halt against the wall of the cavern, white-hot chunks of rock landing all around her. Dimly, she could see a figure in flames rolling wildly on the ground.

The third smuggler, the woman in the coat, stood untouched amid the guttering fire. She was smiling. There was something *off* in her face, as though one side of it were distended, and her right eye was deep purple and bulged like a grape. *Dhakim.*

"Fucking Twilight Order," she said. "Do you know how many people I'm going to have to kill when I'm done with you? *Someone's* been talking." She glanced at the cages. "I thought we had plenty of insurance, but apparently not."

Maya staggered to her feet. *Deiat* was still flowing, and her haken still burned, but it was a near thing. Taking a blaster shot head-on was enough to almost exhaust her reserves.

"I don't suppose you want to lie down and die?" the woman said. "It would make this much easier."

"You. Are a prisoner. Of the Order." Maya gritted her teeth. "Give it up."

The *dhakim* laughed. "Small chance of that." She gave a high, piercing whistle.

Twisted shapes circled the pile of crates. A half dozen dog-sized plaguespawn, bodies rippling with skinless red muscle, exposed bones sharpened to rake and tear. Remade jaws dripped slaver that sizzled when it hit the floor, and long limbs twisted unnaturally. The *dhakim* was grinning wider, and she whistled again, a low, short command. The plaguespawn charged.

Keep moving. It was Jaedia's voice in her head. *Remember, plaguespawn are not truly animals.* For a moment Maya felt detached, distant, watching the scene from afar as her mentor lectured her. Then her heart began to trip-hammer, her pulse a roar in her ears, and she was yanked back into her body. Jaedia's voice faded to a barely audible drone. *They can never hunt as a pack. It is always every creature for itself.*

Maya didn't know whether that applied to plaguespawn under the direct control of a *dhakim*. But *it's the best chance I've got.*

She went straight at them.

There were three on each side of the crates. Maya charged one group, and the leader stood its ground, rearing up on telescoping hind legs until it was nearly as tall as she was. The two creatures behind it, though, couldn't push past, and Maya speared the lead monster through the chest, leaving her haken in place for a moment until its flesh started to bubble and smoke. Then she spun away as the plaguespawn collapsed, the two behind it leaping over the body. The three from the other side had closed the distance, but one was faster than the others, and Maya intercepted it with a downward sweep that severed its misshapen head in a gout of steam and black blood.

Four left. Unfortunately, if the creatures lacked the pack instinct of natural hunters, they also lacked their fear. Even without a *dhakim* to drive them, plaguespawn had no sense of self-preservation. They would attack until they were dead or she was.

And then they'd take me apart. She imagined her own eye staring out from the folds of skinless flesh, her hand twitching at the end of some composite limb. It made her bile rise. The Thing seemed to be red-hot in her chest, pain shooting through her ribs with every ragged breath. Her connection to *deiat* was as unstable as a stumbling drunk, and she dared not draw any excess power.

Not exactly my finest hour.

But there were children in cages, and four plaguespawn still standing.

Two of them came at her together. She dodged left, evading a pair of snapping wolf jaws, but the other creature's face split into a nest of writhing tendrils, and two of them whipped along her side with bladed tips. The flare of the panoply field from even this minor wound was enough that she nearly passed out on the spot, and the flame of her haken flickered. Desperately, Maya wrenched the stream of *deiat* away from the panoply belt, deactivating it. Her skin tingled, unprotected, and the Thing pulsed again.

Behind the monsters, the *dhakim* woman was sitting on a crate, like the audience at a theater. Her swollen eye flicked from side to side, taking in the action, and she smiled at Maya's obvious exhaustion. She had one hand on the hilt of a sword but seemed content to watch.

Fine with me. Giving ground, Maya veered away from the tentacled horror and baited the wolflike one into another lunge. That was easier to avoid, and her desperate chop took off a front leg and most of its face. It was still moving, blood spewing across the earth, but slowly enough that she could afford to ignore it. The tentacled creature came at her again, and Maya stood her ground, aiming a slice right through the nest of whirling blades. Her sleeve shredded, and multiple cuts blossomed along her arm without the panoply field to protect it, but she chopped the thing nearly in half, and it went down with a gout of foul-smelling smoke.

Two. Blood dripped down her arm, sheathing it in red, wet and sticky on her fingers. With a frown, the *dhakim* got down from her crate and drew her sword. It had the iridescent gleam of unmetal, the short, flat style that was standard in the Legion. Maya swallowed hard as the two plaguespawn separated, letting the woman approach, then padded forward at her side.

"Always wanted to kill a centarch," she said. "But they can be hard to come by. They *say* that the ability to touch *deiat* is in the soul and not the flesh, but I've always wondered if you couldn't find it if you diced things fine enough." Her engorged eye stared at Maya, unblinking. "I guess we'll find out."

She attacked, and immaterial haken clashed with unmetal, *deiat* thrashing and sparking against the Elder blade. Maya held her block for a moment, blood dripping from her elbow, but it was clear the *dhakim* was stronger. She danced away instead, evading the next cut, aiming a riposte at the woman's face that was easily countered. The plaguespawn kept pace with the duel as Maya gave ground, slowly circling the pile of crates. The *dhakim*'s mental control of the thing was better than Maya had given her credit for, and the creatures acted as extensions of her will, darting in to nip and slash at Maya when she was distracted and jumping away before she could cut them down.

Fuck. The fact that she wasn't going to win this fight hit Maya like a revelation. *Fuck fuck* fuck. She had to think of something else—not because she needed to do well to impress the Council, to help Jaedia, even to save the children, but because if she didn't, she was going to fucking *die* here, her guts spilled by an unmetal blade.

The *dhakim* came at her with a fast series of brutally strong blows, and when she went to parry, Maya was hammered to her knees. One of the plaguespawn darted in, jaws closing on the meat of her calf, and a scream tore its way out of her throat. Her opponent raised her blade, smiling in triumph—

And a bolt of blue-white energy tore across the room, hitting the plaguespawn and detonating in a burst of pulverized flesh and bone. The whole back half of the creature was blown away. The second monster spun with a gurgling growl, but another bolt caught it and blasted its head and shoulders completely apart.

"Maya!" Beq stood in the tunnel entrance, hair covered in dirt, blaster pistol held in a solid two-handed grip. She fired again, but the *dhakim* ducked, and the blast hit the far wall in a spray of dirt.

"Interfering *plaguepit*—" the *dhakim* growled. She sprinted toward Beq, dodging another blaster bolt. Beq scrambled back, far too slowly.

No. Maya, still on her knees, raised her haken and sighted along it. She called up every bit of power she had left and let it flow through the haken as a lance of white-hot fire.

Somehow, the *dhakim* sensed it coming. She spun and raised her sword, the unmetal catching the beam and splintering it in a dozen directions. Sparks sprayed across the woman, scorching holes in her clothes, but she gritted her teeth and kept her Elder weapon between them. Even unmetal would melt, eventually, but Maya didn't have the strength. She felt herself faltering, the beam flickering out, and darkness clawed at the edges of her vision.

Beq, though, didn't wait that long. She brought her blaster up and fired, and the *dhakim*'s head came apart like rotten fruit.

When Maya opened her eyes, the cavern was full of people.

Beq knelt by her side. Maya's right arm was stretched out on a cloth, and Beq was applying something green and vaguely astringent from a tin. The wound in her calf was already wrapped up, and Maya recognized the numbing sting of quickheal. Beyond her, there were quite a few voices speaking at once, mixed with children crying.

"Maya?" Beq leaned over. "Are you awake?"

Maya gave a cautious nod.

"Thank the Chosen," Beq said. "I'd hoped it was just power exhaustion that had knocked you out, but I couldn't be sure. How do you feel?"

"Not...bad." Maya swallowed. In truth, she felt oddly better than she had in some past scrapes; letting the panoply draw power until the last minute left her connection to *deiat* scraped raw, and she'd avoided that, at least. "Arm hurts, obviously."

"Right. Let me finish up." Beq went back to applying the ointment, twisting a dial on her spectacles. Lenses clicked. "You got cut up pretty good, but not too deep. With some quickheal it'll be all right in a few days."

"Right." Maya lifted her head for a moment to look around, but the effort was too much, and she quickly lay back down. "What happened?"

"After, you mean? Of course you mean after. You remember what happened *before*." Beq looked over, eyes made huge by the lenses' magnification. "You do remember, don't you?"

"I think so. You shot the *dhakim*."

For a moment Beq went still, and then she gave a quick nod and looked away. "Tanax and Varo turned up not long after. That girl—"

"Streza?"

"Right. She came to Kaiura's house, screaming her head off, but Tanax was in the middle of an interview and wanted her to wait. I argued with him and—" Her face flushed slightly. "When he wouldn't listen, I just walked out and followed Streza. Varo convinced him to come along eventually."

"You..." Maya swallowed again. Her chest ached, the flesh around the Thing tender. "You saved my ass."

"I did? I mean, I guess I did. You probably had things under control. I just thought—"

"Nope." Maya turned her head to look at Beq, who was blushing further. "I was definitely going to die."

"Oh." Beq went quiet for a moment. "Then I'm glad I rushed."

"Me too."

There was another silence. Beq pulled a roll of bandage out of her pack and started wrapping up Maya's arm.

"So what's happening now?" Maya said.

"Kaiura and a bunch of the villagers followed Tanax," Beq said. "I'm not sure what they're fighting about now." She lowered her voice. "Tanax is really angry with you."

Maya sighed. "Of course he is."

A few minutes later, she had the strength to sit up, and Beq helped her wobble to her feet. A small crowd of villagers stood by the cages, all open now. Maya recognized Kaiura in their midst and caught a glimpse of Streza clinging to a bent-backed old woman and a filthy, sobbing younger boy in a fierce hug. Some of the rest were also comforting the rescued children, while a small circle around Kaiura spoke to each other in low tones, occasionally glancing up at Maya and the others.

Tanax and Varo, meanwhile, had pried the lids off a few of the crates and were carefully examining the contents. Small jars were packed neatly in straw, beside boxes stacked with waxy tablets wrapped in oiled paper.

"Up and about already, Maya?" Varo said.

"Didn't want to get lazy," Maya said. "Were all the kids okay?"

"Well enough," Varo said. "Just scared and dirty. They were only here for a few days."

"According to Kaiura, they were taken after someone discovered the smugglers moving goods into the cavern." Tanax nodded to the entrance, where the wooden barricade had been. They'd removed it, and Maya could see out to the bank of the river. "Best guess is they use this as a depot before moving the stuff overland. Apparently they grabbed the children as hostages."

"Thank the Chosen we got here, then," Maya said.

"Indeed." Tanax frowned. "It might have been a great success, if you'd exercised better judgment."

Maya stood frozen for a moment, trying to digest that. Beq stepped forward, hands raised.

"We don't have to get into that now," she said. "Maya's still—"

"What do you mean, better judgment?" Maya said. "And how is this not a success?"

"All three smugglers are dead," Tanax snapped. "Two of them at your hands, I might add. We have no opportunity to interrogate them, which might have led us to the rest of their organization."

"I'm sorry I didn't get the chance to take prisoners," Maya said. "I was a little busy trying not to get killed myself. One of them was a *dhakim*, if you haven't noticed."

"I understand your difficulties," Tanax said, and his air of condescension made Maya want to scream. "But you wouldn't have been in such a dangerous situation if you'd gone for backup immediately."

"You were the one who told me I was wasting my time pulling cats out of trees."

"That doesn't excuse charging in on your own," Tanax snapped.

"The children were hostages. If I'd waited, and the smugglers figured out we were onto them, they might have killed them all and run for it."

"Possible. Not likely with all this product at stake."

Maya fixed him with a glare. "It wasn't a risk I was willing to take."

"Which will *certainly* be included in my report." Tanax glared back. "A centarch must be capable of making hard choices for the greater good. Saving a few lives here might condemn more later, if the rest of the smugglers remain undetected. This is what Pragmatics like you and your master never understand."

"I…" Maya forced herself to keep silent. *I can't fight him, not here.* "I think I should get some rest."

"By all means." Tanax nodded to Beq. "Take her back to our headquarters. Varo and I will handle things here."

"What needs to be handled?" Maya said. "The smugglers are dead."

"The complicity of the villagers still needs to be examined."

"Their children were taken hostage!" Maya said.

"So they claim. We'll see." He gave a thin smile. "I still plan to do a thorough investigation."

Maya didn't say much on the journey back to Kaiura's house, which seemed ten times as long in her exhausted state. Beq walked beside her, watching in case she stumbled, but Maya kept her eyes ahead and her back straight.

A thorough investigation. She wanted to scream. *These poor people have been through the plague already, and he wants to keep pushing.* It was no wonder the villagers she saw as they made their way across the valley gave her frightened looks. *If this is how centarchs usually behave, no wonder Jaedia had us in disguise.*

When they reached the house, Beq led her upstairs to a second-floor bedroom. It clearly belonged to a young girl—there were hand-carved toys scattered across the floor, mostly swords and horses, and enthusi-astic if incompetent paintings pinned to the walls—but a bedroll had already been rolled out beside the small bed, with Beq's large pack and Maya's smaller one sitting beside it.

"There's no inn in town, so Kaiura offered to put us up," Beq said in answer to Maya's questioning look. "Her girls are sleeping in her room."

Maya had every confidence that Kaiura had "volunteered" the lodg-ings as easily as she'd given up her home to Tanax's investigation. *Might as well be generous, since we have the legal authority to take what we want, not to mention enough power to reduce the town to ash.* Another coal of anger, added to the already-smoldering fire. *It's not right.* She and Jaedia had stayed with villagers plenty of times, of course, but they'd always paid for their beds, either in money or in chores.

"You can have the bed," Beq went on. "Go ahead, lie down. I'll get you some water."

Maya nodded, suddenly feeling the weight of her exhaustion. She sat down on the bed, yawned, and blinked sleepily.

When she next opened her eyes, the sky outside was dark. The pain in her arm and leg had subsided to a dull ache. She lay in the bed, under a thin summer sheet, stripped of her boots and outer clothes. On the floor, Beq lay sprawled across her bedroll, her own sheet kicked to the side.

The moon was high, and its soft light silvered everything. Maya stared at the childish drawings on the walls without really seeing them.

I won. She glanced down at Beq and found herself smiling. *We won, I suppose. I would have died if she hadn't gotten there when she did.* The memory of that moment of realization brought a twist to her stomach. *But she did get there, and we beat the* dhakim *and rescued the children.*

So why do I feel so bad?

She probed her emotions cautiously, like she was poking a rotten tooth with her tongue. Her mind replayed the fight, the first smug-gler going down with a smoking wound carved across him, the second burning alive in her flames even as he blasted her. *Is that it? Killing those men?*

There was a twinge, but it was less than she expected. *They were trying to kill me. And they were keeping children in cages.* Sometimes centarchs might have to make hard choices, but this hadn't been one of them.

It wasn't getting chewed out by Tanax, either. She could think about that with surprising equanimity. *Let him take his report to the Council. I'll tell them what really happened.* Nicomidi and the Dogmatics might side with his agathios, but she was certain Baselanthus and the Pragmatics would understand. *Centarchs are supposed to be heroes. If the Order isn't for rescuing children from* dhakim, *what in the Chosen's name is* it for?

And that was the real sticking point, the thing that made her heart twist. It was the look Kaiura had given Tanax, the faces of the villagers as she'd made her way back with Beq. The *fear. We're here to help them. To* serve *them. They shouldn't be afraid of us.* It made the victory taste like ashes. *And now Tanax is going to make it worse.* Dhak.

Beq gave a quiet whimper. Maya sat up, too abruptly, and her head swam. She swallowed and looked down in time to see the arcanist shift awkwardly, then moan, as though she were in pain. Her face was twisted, freckled skin sheathed in sweat. Hesitantly, Maya reached down and touched her shoulder.

"Beq," she said. "Hey. Are you okay?"

Beq's eyes snapped open, pupils very wide. Her breath came in quick gasps. Seriously worried now, Maya rolled out of bed and knelt beside her on the floor.

"Hey." She put her hand on Beq's arm and tried to speak soothingly. "It's all right. You're all right. Just breathe."

Maya wasn't sure if her words had any effect, but after a few moments Beq's rapid breathing slowed. She blinked, and her eyes focused. Abruptly, she sat up, forcing Maya to shuffle backward.

"Glasses..." Beq said, groping on the floor beside her. "Glasses, glasses—ah." She flipped her spectacles open and put them on, some of the tension going out of her. One hand went to the dials, twisting new lenses into place. "Maya?"

"Sorry," Maya said. "I wasn't sure if I should wake you. You sounded like you were in pain."

"Oh," Beq said in a small voice. "That."

"Are you…okay?" Maya shifted awkwardly. "If you don't want to talk about it, that's fine."

"No, it's something you should know if we're going to be sleeping together." It was good that it was dark, Maya thought, so that Beq couldn't see her expression. Apparently oblivious, the arcanist went on. "It's been a while, but I guess today…stirred things up."

"Nightmares?"

"I think so. I never remember them when I'm awake, except for little pieces." Beq looked at the floor, light gleaming on her spectacles. "When I was little, after I first came to the Forge, I had them all the time. They had to put me in a separate room. It got better, eventually, but…not entirely, I guess." She took a deep breath and forced a smile. "You can ignore me. Or wake me up, if it bothers you. Either. I just… I'll be fine."

"Okay." Maya didn't want to leave it there, but Beq was so clearly uncomfortable she couldn't press her. She got up and climbed back into the bed. "If you need anything…"

"Thanks." Beq stretched out on the bedroll again, setting her glasses beside her.

There was a long silence.

"Can I ask you something?" Beq said, very quietly.

"Of course," Maya said.

"You've been…out, in the field."

"Most of my life."

"This is my first time. You know that, I told you before. Sorry. I just…" Beq took a deep breath. "Is it always like this?"

"What do you mean?"

"I shot that woman," Beq said. "She was going to kill you, and I shot her. I spent a lot of time shooting blasters in the ranges under the Forge, I know what they can do to rock, but…"

"She was a *dhakim*," Maya said. "You did the right thing."

"I know that," Beq said. "Obviously. It's what I was supposed to do. My duty. But when I close my eyes I keep seeing her head coming apart." Her voice was small. "I did that."

"Beq..."

Maya rolled over. Beq looked up at her, eyes full of tears, and Maya impulsively grabbed her hand. The arcanist's fingers were long and slender, as rough with calluses as Maya's own.

"We saved people today," Maya said. "Try to remember that. It doesn't erase the...other stuff, but it matters, too."

"Do you get used to it?" Beq said.

"I don't know. I hope not."

Beq's eyes had closed, and her voice was fading. "I'm glad...I saved you."

Maya grinned. "Me too."

A moment later, the arcanist's deep breaths told Maya she was asleep, though their fingers were still entwined. Maya shuffled the pillow under her cheek, closed her eyes, and drifted off as well.

When she woke again, in the morning, Beq was already up and about. Maya yawned and rolled out of bed. Her limbs ached fiercely but under the bandages her cuts only itched. *Quickheal is wonderful stuff.* After making sure she was alone, she pulled up her shirt to examine the Thing. The crystalline arcana looked the same as ever, but the ring of flesh around it was puffy and red, painful to the touch. That had never happened before.

I'll tell Baselanthus when I get back to the Forge. Maya found her traveling clothes washed and neatly folded just inside the door. She dressed, with her panoply belt and haken in their accustomed places, and went downstairs. From the kitchen, she could hear an argument in progress, Tanax's familiar arch tones mixing with the voice of a young woman she didn't recognize.

Before she could see what that was about, she ran into Kaiura in the hall. The older woman touched her shoulder and drew her aside.

"I wanted to thank you," she said. "On behalf of the village, and for myself. It could easily have been my girls down there."

"Oh." Maya rubbed the back of her neck, vaguely embarrassed. "I was lucky to find the place. You should thank Streza for taking such good care of her brother."

"I will, believe me," Kaiura said. "But I heard what your leader thought of your decision." She smiled broadly. "I just thought you should know that not everyone thinks you made the wrong choice."

"I'm glad," Maya said. "And I'm sure you have nothing to worry about, whatever he says. The Order won't punish people for having their children held hostage."

"I hope you're right."

"Who's he talking to now? Some of your people?"

"Some of yours, I believe," Kaiura said. "A messenger arrived not long ago."

A messenger? That was unusual. "I'd better go and see."

She nodded to Kaiura and pushed her way into the kitchen. Tanax, Varo, and Beq were already there, along with a young woman in the gray of a Forge servant. Tanax shot Maya a look as she came in, but his attention was on the newcomer.

"Our work here is still incomplete," he said. "The Council has to know that."

"I assume they do, Agathios," the messenger said, returning his glare coolly. "But they did not give me any more details, only your instructions."

"But—"

"What instructions?" Maya said. "What's going on?"

"We've been reassigned," Varo said. Maya thought she detected the tiniest hint of smugness in his tone.

"It doesn't make *sense*," Tanax said. "Why us?"

"As I said, Agathios—" the messenger began.

Tanax waved her away, thinking furiously. Maya caught her eye.

"What are the new instructions?"

"You're to report to Deepfire immediately and deliver a message to Dux Raskos," the messenger said. "Apparently, matters there are getting out of hand."

Chapter 8

S he could be mad," Lynnia said.

"It's possible," Gyre agreed. "But I'm willing to risk it."

"You're risking a plaguing lot," the alchemist said, stalking back and forth behind him with her mismatched gait. "Everyone else's life on top of your own, for starters."

"Everyone heard what she had to say. Everyone agreed."

"They all look to Yora. And Yora looks to you, more fool her. Never trust a man just because he dampens your knickers." The old woman made a noise like she wanted to spit but didn't have the phlegm. "I don't like it."

Gyre let out a long breath and tried to concentrate on his task.

They were in the alchemist's library, and he was copying maps. In addition to shelf after shelf of musings on alchemical studies by long-dead scholars, Lynnia had acquired a surprisingly broad collection of maps of tunnels under Deepfire over the years. More recently Gyre had added his share, purchased from the delvers by his agents.

Kit had given them only a vague idea of where the tunnel they were looking for lay, although she swore that she would be able to find it when they got closer. Gyre had dug out every map from every scavenger who'd explored in that region, which made a substantial pile. Since Lynnia forbade any of her maps to leave the premises, he was using the alchemical paper sometimes called "lazy scribe" to copy them. Pressed against ink and paper, the stuff turned itself into a mirror-image copy; painting another reagent across it and pressing it on a virgin sheet would transfer the text or image back to it right way round.

It was tedious work, and the pot of alchemical goo smelled like rank liquor and piss. But he wasn't going to leave anything to chance if he could help it.

"This Kit won't explain to you how she knows where to look?" Lynnia said.

"She's entitled to her secrets," Gyre said, carefully peeling the sticky paper away from some explorer's hasty sketch.

"Which only wiggles her hooks in deeper, as far as you're concerned," Lynnia said. "You *want* to believe she knows things nobody else does, because that means she's who you hope she is."

"Lynnia…"

She glared at him. "What?"

"Get me another page of this, will you?"

Grumbling, Lynnia retrieved more lazy scribe and handed it over. Gyre shuffled to the next map and started laying it down.

"It's not as dangerous as you're making it out to be, anyway," he said. "Plenty of scavenger crews go into the deep tunnels."

"Should I point out you're not scavengers? You're thieves with a gift for inspiring the tunnelborn."

"We'll have Ibb with us. And Harrow."

"A mercenary fashion plate and a lovesick puppy. Wonderful. Rounds out the group." She shook her head. "Don't come crying to me when you end up lining some plaguespawn's nest."

"I imagine that would be difficult, yes," Gyre said. "Careful, Lynnia. Next you'll have me thinking you actually care about my well-being."

"Don't be a plaguefired fool," she snapped. "I'm just hoping to hang on to a profitable client."

"Imagine the profit when we have fifty thousand thalers to spend."

"Fine." Lynnia sighed and stumped to the door, muttering. "Tell Yora to watch out for herself. Obviously my advice is lost on *you*."

Kit looked in her element, dressed in battered scavengers' leathers, her short, spiky blue hair ragged, a heavy pack slung nonchalantly over one shoulder. She had her blaster pistol holstered on one hip and a curved short sword on the other, both with worn grips that hinted of heavy use.

Gyre himself felt somewhat less comfortable. His black working outfit wasn't meant for tunnel crawling, and his overstuffed pack slowed him more than he liked. There was no way around that, though. As they moved away from the Pit, the temperature would fall quickly, and the fur overcoat he'd crammed in would be a necessity.

"About time we got moving," Kit said. "I don't usually take this long between jobs. Makes me antsy."

"Oh?" Gyre said.

He tugged the edges of his hood, making sure the shadows concealed the dull gleam of his mask. They were standing at an intersection in the tunnels, not far from the shelter where he'd taken Kit to meet the others. Habit made Gyre pause and look around carefully, searching for tails.

"You know the scavenger's routine." Kit stretched, arching her back. "Get paid, get drunk, get fucked, go back out."

"With the money you're spending on this project, I'd have thought you'd have enough to entertain yourself for a while."

"It's my client's money, not mine." She grinned. "Besides, drinking and screwing don't scratch the itch for long, you know?"

"Not really."

Gyre finished his reconnaissance, having seen no indications that Auxie spies were onto them. He beckoned to Kit, who sauntered along in his wake. She was stronger than her skinny frame would indicate, and the heavy pack didn't seem to burden her much.

"Is that why you do this, then?" Gyre said as they walked. "Excitement?"

Carts and riders passed in a steady stream in both directions, along with a small crowd of pedestrians, mostly manufactory hands.

"At first, I suppose. I needed the money, but there's other ways to make money." Kit shrugged. "Later I found other reasons."

"Such as?"

"Sorry." Her smile was predatory. "A girl's entitled to some secrets."

"Fair enough." Gyre pointed at a side street. "Through here."

Close to the surface, the tunnels felt like a normal city under a stone roof. Now, though, as they pressed into increasingly narrow back alleys, the original form of the place became obvious. Long stretches of bare stone, smooth, ghoul-carved surface riven by cracks, were broken by clusters of shacks huddling at intersections. The regular lanterns and glowstones disappeared and a cool wind blew steadily, not yet unpleasantly chill but definitely with a suggestion of more to come.

Eventually, they reached a long, straight tunnel that dead-ended in a kind of gate, a metal grating set into the rock that blocked the way completely. Beyond it, the corridor was in shadow and strewn with more debris and fallen stones. An iron-banded door stood in the center of the grate, secured with a heavy iron padlock.

"The tunnelborn try to block off the deep tunnels," Gyre said. "Past here is scavenger territory."

"Why bother locking the door?" Kit said. "Plaguespawn don't exactly know how to work a latch."

"Because it's not only plaguespawn they're trying to keep out," Ibb said, emerging from the shadows beside the grate. "Hello, Halfmask. Kit." He touched his broad hat, a bit of mocking courtesy.

"There are people who live in the deep tunnels," Gyre said. "Bandits, mostly. *Dhakim*. Some just plain desperate." He shrugged. "Personally, I always figured the locks were to keep idiots from leaving the gate open."

"If that's the case, they should use better locks." Ibb produced an iron key from a pouch with a flourish. "Or take better care of these."

"You've been out this way before?" Kit said.

The mercenary nodded. "A few times. This is an old gate, and everything close by was stripped clean long ago, so it doesn't get a lot of use. Which is perfect, for our purposes. At some of the busier crossings we'd be mobbed by beggars and thieves as soon as we went through." He cocked his head. "You're certain your information about the location of the destabilizer is accurate?"

"It's not *precise*, but it's accurate," Kit said. "If we move in the right direction, I'll be able to tell you when we get close."

Ibb made a face that meant, *We'll see*, but said nothing. Gyre turned at the sound of boots on stone and saw Yora approaching, Harrow's hulking form looming just behind her. The big warrior's face contorted into a scowl on seeing Gyre, as usual. *I'm getting a little sick of his attitude.*

Yora carried her unmetal spear and wore the same light armor, her golden hair bound back in a tight braid. She had no pack, but Harrow carried enough for both of them, along with his big battle-axe.

"Halfmask," she said. "It's good to see you made it."

Gyre raised his lone visible eyebrow. "Why, were you worried?"

Yora shook her head. "There've been some ugly rumors. Auxie activity is up."

"They won't bother us down here," Ibb said. "Are we all ready, then? It's a couple of hours' walk to Beggar's Rest, and then at least another hour to the edge of the map. We'd better move."

"Suits me," Kit said, and clapped her hands together excitedly. Everyone else jumped. "Let's get on with it."

The first leg of the trip, out to Beggar's Rest, was easy enough. After Ibb had let them through the gate, they'd all sparked glowstones and spent the next couple of hours walking amid blue-tinged shadows. The deep tunnels were considerably messier than the more civilized parts of the underground, littered with chunks of fallen stone from the initial collapse four hundred years previously, mixed with detritus and the occasional moldering skeleton of more recent visitors.

As far as live inhabitants went, they saw only distant glimmers, torches or glowstones that vanished as soon as they came into sight. A single scuttling plaguespawn, not much bigger than a rat, skittered down a side corridor as they passed through an intersection. It threw itself at Yora, tiny bone-jaws clicking; disdaining her spear, she simply brought her boot down on the thing, crushing its fragile body to a sticky pulp.

"Sometimes," Ibb said, looking with distaste at the mashed remnants, "I think the only reason Deepfire hasn't been overrun is because even the plaguespawn can't get enough to eat."

"I thought the Legions cleaned these tunnels out," Harrow said, frowning at the mess.

"Nothing stays clean for four hundred years," Kit said. "There's hidden entrances all over the mountains. Plaguespawn can find their way into anything, given long enough."

"The Auxies are supposed to sweep down here periodically," Yora said, scraping her boot against a rock. "Not that Raskos can be bothered."

Beggar's Rest was visible long before they reached it, the flickering yellow-orange light of its fires gradually painting the walls of the tunnel as they approached and drowning out the fainter blue of the glowstones. A slight upslope led to a large, round chamber, with a dozen tunnels projecting in all directions like spokes from a wheel. There was a single large fire at the center of the room, with a crowd of hunched, shadowy shapes clustered around it, and a few other campfires and makeshift tents scattered about. A pair of big men with long staffs gave them a cursory look as they came in, and Ibb gave them a friendly nod.

"Last bit of warmth before the deeps," Ibb said. "Take this chance to get your coats on. Stay close. I want to ask some questions."

Harrow walked behind Yora as they picked their way through the crowd. People turned to stare as they passed, and Harrow glared at anyone who got too near. Most of the people clustered by the bonfire seemed to be beggars in truth, skinny, ragged men and women, dressed in scraps, with a few children drawn in close. Their skin was a uniform gray with dust and grime, and filthy hair hung in sticky clumps. Nearly all were maimed somehow—missing arms and legs, hands and feet, gaping eye sockets that made Gyre's own scar itch, big patches of scabby, diseased flesh.

Besides the crippled and the diseased, though, there were the *changed*. A woman curled in the fetal position on a scrap of blanket, her legs trailing off into a dozen slim black tentacles, dripping a clear fluid. A young boy was missing most of his lower jaw, and his grotesquely elongated tongue twisted and curled underneath it, agile as a third hand. An emaciated man with the compound eyes of a fly, shrouded in translucent gauze.

Gyre hadn't been aware he'd been staring until he felt a nudge in his ribs. Kit, standing close at his side, nodded quietly at a hairless woman whose skin glistened with mucus.

"You know what happened to them, don't you?" she said under her breath.

"*Dhaka*," Gyre said. "Ghoul magic. Either they fell in with a *dhakim* cult, or else they—"

"Went someplace they shouldn't have gone, and messed with something they shouldn't have."

"Like the Tomb," Gyre said flatly. "Is that what you mean?"

She gave a small shrug. "I just don't want you to say I didn't warn you. It's not too late to renegotiate."

Gyre shook his head and kept his eyes on the ground.

"Your business." Kit shrugged. "Your friends are attracting some attention."

"Everyone knows Yora. Even down here."

"Your crew has quite a reputation."

"It's not that. At least not *just* that." Gyre shrugged. "Yora's father was Kaidan Hiddenedge."

"He was a bandit, right?"

"That's what the Republic would like you to think. But it doesn't explain why they went to such lengths to destroy him." Gyre gestured at the beggars. "If you ask these people, they'll tell you he was a hero who fought for the freedom of the tunnelborn against the corruption of the dux. Yora's spent her life living with that legacy."

"That's a hard road to follow." Kit eyed him sidelong. "You respect her, don't you?"

"She pushes back against the Republic and the Order. That's more than I can say for almost anyone else."

"But you still want to find the Tomb," Kit said.

Gyre pressed his lips together and didn't reply.

On the other side of the fire, Ibb had found what he was looking for. Two women, Gyre's age and nearly identical, sat side by side, wearing slightly better garb than was typical. Ibb squatted opposite them, and Gyre saw a couple of coins change hands. Ibb gestured him over, and the pair looked at one another. One of them closed her eyes with a sigh, while the other spoke.

"That's a bad road to be taking right now," she said. "New gang moved in from down-tunnel, and they're hungry. Got a flesh-twister boss, maybe. Couple of scav packs went down and didn't come back."

"How many?"

The woman shrugged. "Enough. If you're looking for a score, you'd be better going to the Roaring Well to try your luck. I heard Rodrig Axebite broke open a new tunnel there, and there's been some scuffles over it. Plenty of old loot and new loot lying about, I should think."

"Thanks for the advice," Ibb said. He glanced at Kit. "But we've got a client. Is there a path that'll get us around this new gang?"

"'S possible." The woman, pale-skinned and so thin her face seemed half a skull, gave a shiver and a nod at Ibb's purse. "If you've got a map and another decithaler."

"Halfmask?" Ibb said.

Gyre pulled the roll of copied maps out of his pack and handed them over, along with another coin. Ibb flipped through until he found the one he wanted, and both women bent over it. The silent twin pointed while the other kept up a running commentary, and Ibb took notes in pencil.

Kit, bored, had wandered away, and Gyre found Yora by his side, with Harrow standing protectively behind her. Yora had her arms crossed tight, gripping her elbows, and her face was uncharacteristically pained. Gyre shifted toward her.

"Something wrong?" he said.

"These people," Yora said. Her voice was tight. "The Republic built gates over the tunnels to keep us underground, and we tunnelborn turned around and did the same thing to the people we'd rather not see. Half of them won't make it through the winter."

Probably not. Gyre looked over the crowd of beggars. *And another lot of luckless wretches will move in to replace them in the spring.* That was an old argument between them, but here and now he found it hard to voice it. Instead, he said, "You're doing the best you can. Like Kit said, fifty thousand thalers buys a lot of food and firewood."

"Not enough," Yora muttered.

"It'll be a start."

"It's getting cold," Harrow said, coming up behind them. He gave Gyre a glare, then offered Yora a fur-lined coat. "Here."

"Thank you, Harrow."

Gyre took the opportunity to dig his own warm coat out of his pack. The air was definitely turning cold, and it would only get colder.

Ibb returned, frowning at his annotated map. "This is going to be harder than we thought," he announced.

"How so?" Kit said, drifting in behind him.

"If we want to stay clear of trouble, we'll need to avoid this set of galleries." Ibb slid his finger across the map. "That means working our way through the side tunnels here. Once we're past this junction, we can shift back over, I think." He looked up at Kit. "If that's all right with you, of course."

"Like I told you," she said, "I'll let you know when I see something familiar."

"If you've never been here before, how can it be familiar?" Yora muttered.

Not a bad question. But Gyre didn't speak up, and Kit just smiled.

Beyond Beggar's Rest, the temperature dropped with every step forward. The choking, red-hot fumes of the Pit were a long way behind them, and without that warmth there was no avoiding the fact that they were climbing through the bowels of a mountain in the tallest, coldest range in the world. Somewhere above his head, Gyre supposed, through thousands of meters of rock, were the glaciers that shrouded the Shattered Peaks in permanent winter. It was a strange thought.

Following the twins' advice, they'd veered away from the main galleries, working their way through an interconnected network of narrow passages and round, nearly featureless rooms. Until this point, evidence of the original inhabitants of these tunnels had been scanty, with even worthless debris scraped up by some hopeful scavenger. Here they started to find scraps.

The ghouls, masters of *dhaka* but without access to *deiat*, hadn't wrought their creations in unmetal and crystal like the Chosen. Much of their arcana had been biological, tools and implements grown to fit their purpose. Some of their tools had even been alive in their own right, a living creature used as a modern arcanist might wield a plier or a scalpel. Four hundred years had reduced most of these wonders to decomposed slime, but there were hints at what had been. Strange skeletons, coiled in nooks and crannies, and multichambered shells like mollusks. Bits of crystal and glass mixed with patches of phosphorescent fungi, marking the place where some ancient bit of arcana had found its resting place. On the ceiling, more glowing patches flickered fitfully to life as they approached.

Lynnia would have a field day. It was remnants like these that alchemists used as raw material.

There were signs, too, the queer spidery ideograms of ghoul script carved into the stone. Kit stared at each marking they passed, but if she understood them, she wasn't saying. She'd put on a heavy coat of her own, so big it dwarfed her thin body, making her look smaller. Every breath puffed into steam around her face, shrouding her in mist.

Finally she halted in front of one set of signs, studying them intently. Gyre stopped beside her. His scar itched under the chilly metal of his mask, and he fought the urge to scratch it.

"Can you read them?" Gyre said.

"Of course," Kit said. "I told you I could find what we were looking for once we got close." She turned to the others and pointed. "We need to go that way."

Ibb glanced at the map and pulled a face. "That will take us across the main gallery. If we keep on from here for another few—"

"No guarantee we can find directions again farther on," Kit said, tapping the Elder sign. "If we go too far, we might miss it entirely."

Ibb glanced at Yora and Harrow. The big warrior gripped the handle of his axe.

"It's too much of a risk," Harrow said darkly. "If we get caught in the open by a large group..." He shook his head.

"Halfmask?" Yora said.

"It's a big gallery," Gyre said. "They can't patrol the whole thing all at once. Maybe we'll get lucky."

"It's a gamble," Ibb said.

"I like gambles," Kit said, grinning.

In the end, in spite of Harrow's grumbles, there wasn't much option. Nobody wanted to come this far and miss their objective.

A few twists led them back to the main gallery. It was a wide tunnel, the size of the streets out in the warm, living part of the city, but littered with stone and wreckage and rimed by frost. Curiously regular piles of metal and crystal lay about. A few had been scattered by scavengers, but most were intact, the inorganic wreckage sunk in black slime and ranks of mushrooms. A few more glowing patches came to fitful life on the high ceiling.

"There," Kit said, pointing to another mark incised into the wall. "That way."

Ibb gave her a dubious look but followed as she scampered down the corridor. The others fell in behind, with Gyre bringing up the rear. The larger space made Gyre's skin crawl and set his scar to itching. Side tunnels branched off every dozen meters, leaving innumerable ways they could be outflanked and surrounded. *Harrow was right. It's too open.* His jaw clenched.

But trouble, when it came, didn't arrive from ambush. There was a chunk of fallen rock in the middle of the corridor, and as Ibb and Kit got within a few meters, a lantern came on, blindingly bright for eyes adapted to glowstone light. Gyre blinked away tears and saw a single figure clad in shabby black sitting on top of the rock. It looked like a man, but something was wrong, and it took another moment to process what: curling horns sprouted from his head, curving back on themselves and winding to a vicious-looking point.

"Hello, friends." There was something strange about his voice, too, deeper and more resonant than it had any right to be. "You're in Beloriel's territory now. I assume you're willing to pay the appropriate toll."

Kit gave a quiet snort of derision, and her hand drifted toward the blaster at her side. Ibb stepped in front of her, signaling her to wait.

"That depends," he said, "on how much the toll is. We're fully prepared to be reasonable."

"Oh, wonderful," the horned man said. "I do love dealing with reasonable folks." He cocked his head. "You're well armed, for scavengers. Surely you don't need two blasters, especially if you have our protection."

"We'd prefer to pay in thalers, truth be told," Ibb said, hands spread. "You know how one gets attached to one's gear—"

The *crack* of a blaster going off ripped through the silence of the cavern, and the bright flash left dazzling afterimages in Gyre's eye. Kit had her weapon out, aimed not at the horned man but at one of the piles of debris behind them. The bolt tore it apart, sending bits of stone and metal flying in all directions, and Gyre had a glimpse of a human figure pinwheeling away among the shrapnel.

For a moment, everyone was frozen. Then the horned man gave a *roar*, an echoing cry like a lion's that filled the cavern. He leapt forward, unnaturally fast. Ibb swore and clawed for his own blaster, even as misshapen figures swarmed toward them from all directions.

Gyre offered a choice oath of his own, drawing a blade in each hand. The bandits had emerged from behind the mounds of rotting wreckage in twos and threes, dressed in thick leather and ragged furs. They were armed with a mix of knives and spears, with a few sporting improvised metal shields. Gyre could see at least a dozen, with probably as many behind him.

Kit fired twice more, one bolt sizzling high to explode against the rocky wall of the corridor, the other catching a charging bandit head-on and blasting him into grisly chunks. She had time to holster her blaster and draw her curved saber before two more were on top of her. Pivoting with a dancer's grace away from a spear thrust, she brought her weapon down on the haft and cracked it, then ducked in time to evade the swipe of another man's blade. Her momentum brought her sword around, striking sparks from his metal shield, and she rebounded off and turned the motion into a spinning kick that sent him stumbling. Before he could recover, she darted inside his guard and opened his throat with an easy motion.

Gyre had three opponents of his own, coming in fast but coordinating poorly. The first, a teenage girl with dark skin and fiery orange hair, screamed a war cry and swung her sword for his head with more passion than sense. Gyre sidestepped her, opening her bowels with a twist of his short knife and leaving her to collapse with guts spilling through her fingers. The man behind her had a shield and spear, jabbing expertly and keeping Gyre from closing. Gyre gave ground, letting the third bandit, a skinny boy with a pair of knives, get closer. Hopping over the shuddering body of the dying girl, Gyre circled, and the boy followed, swiping with his short blades.

Too tentative. With a knife that size, only a committed attack was going to cause any damage. Gyre waited until he wound up for another strike, then stepped forward, blocking one descending blade with a forearm and parrying the other, then punching the bandit in the mouth with his pommel. The boy staggered backward, drawing his knife along Gyre's arm, but without his weight behind it the blade scraped off his leather bracer. More important, he was now between Gyre and the spearman, and Gyre kept pressing forward, driving the boy back and spoiling the more experienced man's stance. Desperately, the boy lunged again, and Gyre ducked and swept his legs out from under him, then popped up inside the spearman's guard. The older bandit dropped his spear and went for a sidearm, but Gyre's knife took him in the throat before he could reach it.

Twisting to finish the boy on the ground, Gyre saw Yora and Harrow fighting back-to-back. Yora's spearhead darted like a leaping fish, unmetal iridescent in the twisting, strobing light of glowstones and blaster fire. One bandit was down in front of her, and she held two more at bay. As Gyre watched, her spear licked out, the unmetal blade slicing clean through the ordinary steel of her opponent's shield and opening a long gash on his arm. Behind her, Harrow fought with wild swings of his axe. A lithe young woman slipped inside his guard with a long knife, slashing his leg, but the boy slammed his forehead into hers, leaving her reeling. Before she could recover, he caught her on the backswing with his big axe, and she folded up around the blade like a limp rag and spun away in a spray of gore.

Ibb seemed to be having the most difficulty. The antler-man was quicker than he had any right to be, and his nails were as long and sharp as a thickhead's claws. Ibb's rapier was faster, but under his rags the *dhak*-twisted bandit was armored like a thickhead, too, and the fine-tipped blade skittered off his scales. The mercenary gave ground, bleeding freely from a cut to the scalp and another to the thigh.

Gyre moved in to assist, slashing wildly at the antler-man to draw his attention. He ducked as a clawed swipe whistled past, and lashed out with his short blade, but the cut that should have opened the man's stomach only slashed his clothes and glanced off his scaly armor. Gyre dropped his long blade just in time to catch the man's wrist before the claws found his face, but the bandit's prodigious strength forced him back, first one step and then another. For a moment they stood locked, sweat standing out on Gyre's brow as he strained to keep the vicious razors back.

"Duck!"

This time, Gyre needed no further warning. He let go of the bandit's arm and threw himself flat. The antler-man stumbled forward against the sudden lack of resistance, and Gyre felt a wave of heat and heard the *crack* of a blaster bolt. He raised his head and found Kit walking past him, blaster leveled. The antler-man was down but getting back to his feet. The huge crater blown in his chest, exposing the ragged, shattered tips of his ribs, barely seemed to slow him.

"Just die, would you?" Kit said. She fired twice more, and the third bolt caught the bandit in the head, blowing his skull to fragments. When she was satisfied he wasn't getting up again, Kit holstered the blaster and reached out to help Gyre up. "You all right?"

"Somehow." Gyre took her hand and stood. The fight seemed to be over, the remaining bandits having melted away into the darkness with the death of their leader. The five of them were left standing in a circle of bluish glowstone light, along with the bodies of the fallen. Somewhere a woman was shrieking in pain, and a man repeated frantic prayers in a gurgling voice.

Ibb, his face painted with blood from the wound on his forehead, limped to face Kit and leveled his rapier.

"What the *fuck* was that?" he said.

"What?" she said, raising her hands. "Saving your life? Or saving Halfmask's, I suppose, after he saved yours?"

"You *started* this fight," the mercenary said. "We could have paid them off."

"With a blaster?" Kit snorted. "I hope you were willing to hand yours over, because I'm plaguing sure they weren't getting mine."

"We were negotiating," Ibb growled.

"He was stalling while his friends got into position," Kit said. "I saw them coming and decided not to wait."

"You put us all at risk."

"Coming down here at all is a risk." Kit cocked her head. "I didn't take you for a coward."

"That's enough," Yora snapped. Harrow was on one knee in front of her as she bandaged the bleeding cut on his leg. "Ibb, come and let me look at you."

For a moment, Kit and Ibb held their locked gazes. Then the mercenary turned away, growling, and sheathed his rapier, limping over to Yora. Kit caught Gyre's eye and shrugged, then started prowling through the bodies.

Gyre caught up to her, picking his way cautiously through the still-cooling debris.

"Thanks," he said.

"Not a bad fight, honestly," Kit said, grinning at him. She did her cat's stretch again, rolling her head from side to side. "A little quick for my taste."

"Doomseeker," Gyre said, shaking his head. "You're crazy, you know that?"

"I never claimed otherwise."

Kit stalked forward. She'd found the source of the shrieking, the young woman who'd taken Harrow's axe to the midsection. It had opened her, messily, and her eyes were wide and glassy as she plucked feebly at her guts with gory hands. Kit grabbed her by the hair, jerked her head back, and slashed her throat.

"That's better," she said, when the bandit's shudders had ceased. The praying man's gurgles had died away, too, leaving the gallery in silence. "Now, let me see that map?"

In spite of his wounds, Ibb insisted they start moving again as soon as possible, lest the bandits return with reinforcements. If there were more members to the gang, though, they didn't show themselves, and Gyre and the others walked down the gallery for a time in silence. Kit held her glowstone high, examining each marking on the wall they passed, sometimes hesitating for a moment, then muttering and moving on.

"You're sure we haven't missed it?" Yora said.

"Pretty sure," Kit said, without looking around. "Mostly sure. Kind of sure." The bloody melee seemed to have improved her mood.

"Wonderful," Ibb grated. He had a circle of bandages around his head and another wrapping his leg.

Finally, Kit came to a halt, bouncing excitedly on her heels.

"Here!" She pointed to the carved character. "This way. It's not far."

"Someone could be waiting—" Ibb said, but Kit was already darting forward. The rest of them followed more slowly, leaving the main gallery for a short side corridor. They caught up with Kit at a dead end, the smooth-walled passage stopping abruptly.

"This is what you've been looking for?" Ibb said.

Yora stepped forward, raising her glowstone. She took another step and ran her finger along the wall, knocking away bits of grime. "Is this a door?"

"It is!" Kit said, sounding delighted. "Still sealed."

"Which does us what good, exactly?" Ibb said. "Unless you brought a centarch or a wagonload of alchemicals to blast it open and forgot to tell us."

"Better than that," Kit said. "I brought the key."

She fished in her pouch and brought out a small device about the size of a drinking cup. It was flat on one end, while the other sprouted an organic-looking spray of metal and crystals. Ibb's eyes widened.

"Is that a *code-key*?" he said. "Where in the plague did you—"

Kit shrugged. She stepped up to the door and placed the code-key's flat side against it, where it stuck like a suction cup. The crystals began to glow, flashing a complex pattern in several colors. Then, with surprisingly little fuss, the rock wall slid open, each half retreating smoothly into the wall along a noiseless track. It made a doorway wide enough for two people abreast.

Beyond the door, a smaller corridor stretched out to a T-junction. It was much neater than the raw, rocky space outside, the walls colored off-white and without cracks or fractures. On the ceiling, circular patches glowed with a flat, deadening radiance, giving the whole place a sterile look.

"What in the name of the Chosen?" Harrow breathed.

"It's still *alive*," Yora said.

"More or less," Kit said. "I imagine there's been some degradation, but it's better off than the rest of this place."

"How did you know this was here?" Ibb said. His usual calm, which had been severely shaken by the fight with the bandits, was now gone entirely. "I've never heard of a live ghoul tunnel anywhere close to Deepfire. Plague, I haven't heard of one being found for a hundred years!"

"I imagine there aren't many left," Kit said. "Unless you know where to look."

"And you knew where to look," Ibb said. His lip twisted. "I don't like it. We have no idea what's in there."

"It's been closed since the war," Gyre said. "It can hardly be infested with plaguespawn."

"Halfmask's right," Yora said. "We need the destabilizer to finish the job."

"But..." Harrow began, then stopped at a look from Yora.

Ibb sighed and made an effort to compose himself. He straightened his hat, knocked askew during the fight, and put one hand on the hilt of his rapier.

"I suppose we do," he said. "Stay close, then. And be ready for anything."

He paced forward, and the other four fell in behind him. Gyre, walking beside Kit, leaned close to her ear.

"I've never heard of *anyone* with a functioning ghoul code-key," he said. "The Order has some Chosen ones, but…"

"It's amazing what you can dig up," Kit said with a smile. "*If* you know where to look."

What did she find, down in the Tomb? Gyre had pictured a ruin, like the tunnels under Deepfire, only grander. Now he imagined something perfectly preserved, kilometers of neat white tunnels like this one. *And what else? Workshops? Arsenals?*

The ancient tunnel here even *smelled* different, the air fresher and without the stench of rot. Down at the edge of hearing there was a faint whirr, and Gyre felt air currents brush over his face.

At the first junction, there was a gray metal sign on the wall, labeled in incomprehensible Elder script. Kit peered at it, then pointed, and Ibb led the way onward. They passed steel doors on either side of the corridor, labeled with more glyphs. Most were closed, but a few stood half-open, revealing chambers full of long, low tables strewn with strange metal-and-crystal arcana. One room was full of long-dead plants in metal pots, long-dead trunks in neat rows surrounded by their fallen, skeletal leaves. In another, the corpse of something had decayed in a dark smear, covered in mushrooms.

"Every scavenger in Deepfire is going to want a chance at this place," Yora said. "Nobody has found anything this intact since before I was born."

"They're welcome to it, once we're finished," Kit said. "Sell a map, if you like. Consider it a bonus." She gave a giddy laugh. "Nearly there, I think."

The corridor ended in another steel door. This one was open just a crack, enough to see that there was a large open space beyond. Ibb put a hand against it and shoved, and it swung inward. Lights in the ceiling began to glow, and the whirring sound grew louder.

In the center of the room was a dais, clearly the focal point of everything here. Tables surrounded it on all sides, as though whatever had sat there had needed to be observed from every angle. Whatever it had been, it seemed to be gone now, and the dais was empty except for a few trailing silver wires.

Kit was unconcerned by the absence. She waved everyone into the room.

"Look for the destabilizer," she said. "It's a black rod about half a meter long. Probably in one of those closets." She pointed at a set of upright metal lockers along the far wall.

Ibb caught Gyre's eye, and Gyre only shrugged. Ibb sighed, and together they crossed the room and started opening doors. Yora followed, while Harrow stood guard by the entrance. Kit was poking around under the tables, though whether she was searching or merely idly curious Gyre couldn't say.

"I can't say our employer is endearing herself," Ibb muttered.

Most of the lockers were empty, revealing only puffs of four-hundred-year-old dust or clusters of decaying mushrooms. Gyre poked through these with his dagger, then moved on. Another door revealed a leather case full of queer metal tools. It was exactly the sort of thing most scavengers would give their eyeteeth for, and he was considering jamming it into his pack when Yora straightened up.

"I think I found it." She lifted something that matched Kit's description, a black rod about as thick as her wrist, inlaid in places with fine silver wire. "Kit?"

"*Yes*." Kit crossed the room at once, grabbing the thing like it was her long-lost child. "Perfect. *Perfect*." Her face was a mix of glee and relief. "Now let's get the fuck out of here."

"Maybe we should rest a bit," Ibb said. "Only one way in here. It'd be safer than out in the gallery."

"Not really," Kit said. "Trust me. Let's move."

Ibb's eyes narrowed. "What aren't you—"

Something else spoke.

The voice was deep and resonant, making the tables rattle and Gyre's teeth buzz. The words were incomprehensible. For a moment, everyone froze, looking for the source.

Except Kit, who was already heading for the door. "Run," she said. "Run *now!*"

In one corner of the room, a shape began to unfold. It started as a stone cube about a meter square, which Gyre had dismissed as part of the architecture. Now the surface split along invisible seams. Inside was a roughly humanoid shape, curled up with its head bowed. It began to straighten up, interlocking fragments of rock clinging to its body like plated armor.

The flesh underneath was dark and striated, with visible, shifting muscles that put Gyre in mind of a plaguespawn. But this was no haphazard monster built from scavenged corpses. It looked *designed*, and it moved with the smooth purpose of a well-made machine.

Standing, it was a head taller than even Harrow, with subtly inhuman proportions. Its articulated stone armor must have weighed half a ton, but it loped forward with strength. Kit was already halfway to the doorway, but Gyre, Ibb, and Yora were on the other side of the room.

Harrow, directly in the creature's path, drew his axe and stood his ground. He shouted and swung a two-handed blow as it charged, aiming for the base of its neck. The thing threw up one arm to block, blade rebounding from stone with a *clang*. Its other arm swept forward, slamming into Harrow's chest, and Gyre heard the *crunch* of breaking bone as Harrow went tumbling.

"*Fuck* me," Ibb swore. His blaster was in hand, and he fired as the creature started to turn. The white-hot bolt of energy crackled across the room, but several inches from the thing's armored skin it *splashed*, rippling outward like a droplet of water hitting a window. Gyre saw a blue translucent field shimmer around the creature for a moment, like a second skin, before it faded to leave the stone-armored thing unharmed.

"Running sounds good," Gyre yelled.

They ran. Gyre vaulted the tables, putting them between himself and the monster, and Yora stayed close behind him. Ibb took a more circuitous route, still firing, but every blaster bolt simply splashed into nonexistence before touching the thing's armor. The creature came at them, a single blow flattening the metal tables like tissue paper. Gyre tried to slip past, but it cut between him and the door, and he barely jumped back from the sweep of a boulder-like fist. Ibb's blaster gave the high-pitched whine of a dead sunsplinter, and he swore again.

"Harrow!" Yora shouted.

The big warrior was back on his feet, his lips flecked with blood but axe still in hand. He charged the creature from behind, sweeping the big crescent-shaped blade down at the back of its leg. It was a well-judged blow, slipping between two armor plates and biting into the dark flesh between. The rock-thing twitched but didn't make a sound. Before it could swing around to deal with Harrow, Yora leveled her spear and jabbed for its shoulder. The unmetal blade left a notch in the stone but failed to penetrate, and she had to dance back out of range.

"Move!" Yora said, pushing Gyre past her. "Harrow, get away!"

With an axe in its leg, the creature was a bit less mobile. Gyre threw himself past it, barely outrunning a hammering blow that sent bits of table flying. At the same time, Ibb circled in the other direction, breaking into a run for the doorway. The rock-thing turned to follow, but as it tried to take a step it found Harrow still holding on to the axe buried in its flesh.

Gyre couldn't tell if Harrow meant to hold the creature in place, or if he was only too stubborn to abandon his weapon, but either way the result was the same. One huge, rocky hand slammed down onto the warrior's head, smashing it open like a melon against the monster's armored flank. The other ripped the axe free and tossed it away.

"Harrow!" Yora leveled her spear, ready to charge the thing. Gyre hastily grabbed her by one arm, and Ibb by the other. Between them they dragged their leader out the door.

"He's dead!" Gyre shouted. "Get *out*!"

"Fucking *plaguefire*!" Yora snarled, but she turned to run.

He'd hoped the stone thing might be restrained by the doorway, but the steel proved to be no more of an obstacle than flesh and blood. It burst through in a shower of rock chips and metal shards, coming to a halt in the flat white corridor. Though no eyes were visible, Gyre was certain it was watching them as they ran. The deep voice boomed again, and then the thing was running, slowly at first but picking up speed with every step, like a boulder rolling downhill.

Yora was just ahead of Gyre, and Ibb farther on. Gyre looked up to try to find Kit, which proved to be a serious mistake. His foot caught on a loose piece of debris, and he went down in a tangle. Yora heard the sound and skidded to a halt, then started back toward him, reaching out a hand. The monster's thumping stride accelerated as it closed.

"Yora, don't!" Ibb shouted from up ahead. "Go!"

Some part of Gyre's mind, calmly judging distances and speeds, told him he was right, that neither of them would make it. Yora grabbed his hand and yanked him to his feet, the rock-thing only paces behind. The ground shook as he got his legs under him and started to run, the creature now moving faster than a galloping warbird, *no chance—*

A blaster *cracked*, the white-hot bolt ripping past Gyre's shoulder. Kit stood square in the corridor, weapon held cool and steady in both hands. Gyre waited for the blue field to intercept the shot, as it had with Ibb's, but the bolt was poorly aimed and slammed into the ceiling. It detonated with a roar, and chunks of rock cascaded downward.

Not poorly aimed at all. The creature staggered under the rain of stone, its momentum checked.

"Fucking *run*!" Kit shouted. She fired again, her aim tracking along the ceiling, bringing the ancient tunnel down on the thing's head. Gyre put his head down and ran, Yora pounding along at his side. As they passed Kit, she holstered the blaster and joined them, skidding around the corner at the T-junction.

"Come on, come on!" Ibb shouted, already outside the hidden door. He had one hand on the code-key.

Gyre gritted his teeth, sweat stinging his eye, and ran with everything he had. The three of them passed through the doorway as the rock-creature, dust-covered but intact, made it to the corner. As soon as they were clear, Ibb ripped the code-key from the door, which obligingly slid quietly shut and sealed with a final-sounding *hiss*. A moment later, the thump of footsteps from the other side came to an abrupt halt, and there was silence, aside from their labored breathing and the occasional crash of falling rock.

Kit let out a whoop of triumph, brandishing her prize. Ibb fixed her with a poisonous glare. He'd lost his hat, and without it he seemed smaller. Yora had tossed her spear aside, fighting for breath, face dark with anger. Kit glanced between them, caught Gyre's eye, and shrugged.

Sitting on the table in their meeting room, the black rod that Kit called the destabilizer didn't seem like it was worth the effort. Sarah examined the thing with a practiced eye, running her hands over the random patterns of silver wire that shimmered beneath its surface. Nevin, the thief, was nervously sketching on a long roll of thin paper. Yora herself sat several paces back from the table, jaw tight.

Ibb, for his part, had replaced his hat and regained some of his aplomb. He sat, most of his face hidden, at the end of the table that was farthest from Kit. The look he threw Gyre when he came in was impossible to read.

Kit swiveled on her own chair, as though the effort of holding still was too much for her. Her eyes were on the thing they'd retrieved with such difficulty.

"Well?" Yora said quietly as Gyre entered. "What do you think?"

"Frankly," Sarah said, "your guess is as good as mine. I've certainly never seen anything like it."

Yora looked up at Kit, her eyes hard. "You say this thing will destroy a stasis web?"

Kit nodded eagerly. "It takes all of a minute. Maybe less."

"That certainly makes things more possible," Nevin muttered, not looking up. "Stasis webs are heavy, and unless you've got a centarch to help you, the only way to open them is with blaster fire. Risks damaging the contents, and it's noisy. You said this thing we need to steal—"

"The Core Analytica," Kit supplied.

"—you said it's not very large?"

"I could carry it easily," she said.

"Then we have a lot more options." Nevin glanced shyly at Yora. "With a good team and the pick of the alchemists' shops, I think we can do it."

"Assuming this thing works," Sarah said, setting the destabilizer down. "Which I can't guarantee."

"It'll work," Kit said.

"If," Ibb said, pushing back his hat, "we do this at all."

The room went quiet.

"You know I'm not going to pay for half a result," Kit said. "If you want your share—"

"I understand." Ibb shook his head. "But my share will be a small comfort to my husband and kids if I come back as a corpse."

"I'm sorry about Harrow—" Kit began.

"No you're not," Ibb said. "Do us both a favor and don't lie about it."

"Fine," she shot back. "He knew the risks. We all knew the risks."

"Did we?" Ibb's eyes narrowed. "You *knew* that thing was waiting for us. No wonder you were so eager to get out of there."

"I hoped it wouldn't still be active," Kit muttered.

"And you didn't think we could have used some kind of warning?"

"What for? All we could have done was run away, and we did that anyway."

"He's right," Yora said coldly. "You should have told us."

"Fine." Kit shifted uncomfortably in her seat, unrepentant. "I'm sorry. I was worried that if I warned you, you'd back out."

"I gathered that." Ibb got to his feet and stared at Yora and Gyre. "And maybe we should."

Nevin was hunched farther over his drawing, looking miserable. Sarah, silent through this conversation but watching closely, now turned to Yora.

"If we back out now, then Harrow died for nothing," Yora said. "And we need the money."

She looked at Gyre. Ibb turned to him, too, and Kit was watching out of the corner of her eye. Gyre swallowed.

The Tomb. Everything that had happened—Kit having a code-key to an intact tunnel, the stone-armored guardian—pointed to her telling the truth about having been there. *How else could she know everything she does?* And if she *had* found it—

He gave a slow nod. "I'm staying."

"Fine." Ibb swept his coat from the back of the chair. "It's been a pleasure working with you. Come and find me when you come to your senses."

"Ibb—" Yora began.

But he was already stalking from the room. Kit watched him go, then turned back to the others and smiled brightly.

"Fair enough," she said. "Let's see about this plan, shall we?"

Chapter 9

The villagers of Litnin assembled to see them off, offering Tanax stiff, formal bows when he told them to expect a further inquiry from Republic authorities. Maya suspected the villagers knew very well that this was an empty threat, as neither Council nor Republic was likely to spare much effort chasing down a few potential conspirators now that the smugglers had been destroyed. She herself got smiles and nods as she walked past, especially from the children. She saw Streza, waving goodbye with one hand and hugging her brother tight with the other.

Varo, morosely apologetic that he hadn't arrived in time for the fight, seemed determined to make up for it by setting a quick pace on the return journey to the Gate. Maya's legs soon ached, and the straps of her pack chafed, but she had the satisfaction of seeing Tanax no better off. He did his best not to show it, however, possibly because their new companion, the messenger girl whose name turned out to be Dhira, loped along behind the scout without the slightest sign of being winded.

And Beq—Maya didn't know what to think about Beq. They'd had a moment of connection, alone in the night, and she'd worried at the time that it would make things awkward between them. Beq's attitude the next morning had been relentlessly normal—normal for Beq, anyway—and only occasionally did Maya catch the girl watching her, when she thought no one was looking. She did her best to force herself not to read too much into it. *For all I know, she's embarrassed she ever talked to me.*

Maya talked to Dhira instead, at least for as long as she could keep up. Messengers were a unique and well-respected group among the Forge servants, because the nature of their assignments could bring them into considerable danger and strand them with no way to return. It took a centarch to open a Gate, so while it was always possible to travel *from* the Forge, for a messenger the return was never certain. A messenger sent to find a centarch who'd been killed—or even left their post unexpectedly—could find themselves stranded weeks or months from home.

Dhira seemed to take this as a matter of course. She was a tall, muscular girl, with short-cropped gray hair and the humble bearing that all Forge servants affected in the presence of centarchs. Like Varo, she glided through the woods with an effortless grace, while behind her Maya fought down spikes of pain in her thighs and Tanax stumbled through the underbrush, face sheathed in sweat.

"You really have no idea why the Council pulled us out?" he said between labored breaths. He'd been harping on that theme since they'd departed. "It doesn't make sense. Surely you could deliver the letter to the dux as well as we can."

"I'm afraid I only have my instructions. The letter is ciphered, and only for the eyes of Dux Raskos himself. After delivering it, you're to assist the dux and await further word from the Council. Beyond that, you know as much as I do."

"We could just return to the Forge and ask," Maya said. "It wouldn't delay us long."

"No," Tanax said, apparently coming to a decision. "If those are our orders, we will obey them. I'm sure the Council has its reasons, as always."

"Reminds me of a friend of mine," Varo said from ahead of them. "He and I were out on the road, and we got a message to head back to base by the following evening or there'd be plague for everybody. We rode all night, nearly killed ourselves doing it, and when we got there it turned out the messenger had got the wrong patrol. So we got chewed out, even though we'd only obeyed orders, and had wall duty for a month."

There was a pause.

"That's it?" Maya said. "What happened to your friend?"

"Eaten by a pack of rabid thickheads," Varo said promptly. "But that wasn't until later."

Maya grinned, and then grinned wider at Dhira's perplexed look. Behind her, a crash indicated that Tanax had had yet another encounter with a thornbush.

They reached the Gate early on the second day, after Varo and Dhira persuaded Tanax that "as soon as possible" didn't mean they should try for an all-night march. Grumbling, Tanax had insisted that they at least keep their rest to a minimum, so they'd set out as soon as the sun peeked hesitantly through the interlocking branches overhead.

Maya was once again glad to have Varo in the lead, because without him she'd never have spotted the entrance to the Gate. There was no secret door here, just camouflage hiding a narrow cleft in a rocky hillside, which had been carved into a niche just wide enough to accommodate the delicate twisted arch.

"Do you have any message for the Council?" Dhira said, standing in front of the Gate.

"Just that we're proceeding according to instructions," Tanax said. "I will deliver the letter to the dux personally."

Maya badly wanted to ask for an update on Jaedia's mission, but she doubted the Council would share anything, even if they knew. She shook her head when Dhira glanced at her. Tanax touched his haken and sent mental commands to the Gate, and the curtain of silver descended. Dhira gave a deep bow and stepped through back to the Forge. After a moment, the silver cleared.

"Dux Raskos is an important ally," Tanax said. "He's to be given due respect. Is that clear?"

Maya nodded. Varo said, "Do we know what sort of work assisting the dux is going to involve?"

"Whatever he requires," Tanax said, which Maya guessed meant he had no idea.

She felt the ripples in *deiat* as he sent the unfamiliar sequence for the Deepfire Gate, and the archway filled with liquid silver once again. Tanax stepped through, unhesitating, and Maya followed close behind. As usual, there was no sense of transition, as though she'd walked through an ordinary doorway into a room that happened to be hundreds of kilometers away.

The other side of the Gate was in a chamber similar to the one that housed the Gates at the Forge—bare stone except for the Gate's delicate arch, and a single heavily reinforced door. Two Legionaries stood beside it, looking like inhuman statues in their off-white unmetal armor and blank faceplates. At the sight of the two agathia with their haken, the soldiers lowered their weapons and thumped fists to chest in salute.

"Agathios Tanax," one of them said, her voice distorted by her enclosed helmet. "Please excuse me. The dux asked to be informed immediately when you arrived."

Tanax nodded, and the Legionary pushed the door open and slipped out. The other soldier remained at attention until Maya gave him a bow of acknowledgment. He relaxed slightly and inclined his head.

"Welcome to Deepfire, Agathia," he said. "We're grateful for your assistance."

"Are we in the Spike?" Beq said eagerly. She fiddled with her spectacles, lenses clicking and whirring.

"Uh...yes, Arcanist," the soldier said, nonplussed. "Formally, it's the Ducal Palace, but the Spike is its common name."

"One of the last Chosen-built structures," Beq said to Maya. "After the Chosen burned the ghoul city here, Filo-math-Beria raised the main spire in a single day before installing the Gate. Founder Volute led some of the cleansing here, before the formal establishment of the Order."

"I had no idea," Maya murmured, grinning at the arcanist's enthusiasm. Whatever awkwardness lay between them was no match for the wonders of the Elder world, clearly.

"I've always wanted to visit Deepfire," Beq said. "Do you think we'll get the chance to explore the tunnels at all?"

"That's up to the dux, I imagine." Maya glanced at Tanax, who was looking at the door with obvious impatience.

"Of course the strike did a lot of damage, but the area is still very well preserved," Beq said. "It's on par with Grace in terms of the discoveries that have come out of it. That's why the Republic maintains a presence."

"How many Legionaries in the garrison?" Tanax said, chiming in.

"Ten, Agathios," the soldier answered. "And approximately one thousand Auxiliaries."

The door swung open. Four more Legionaries waited, two on each side, blaster rifles at the ready. Beyond them was a long line of more conventional soldiers, in steel breastplates and round caps, spears at their sides as they stood at strict attention. Between them, a short, heavily built man in flowing purple-and-gray silk offered a deep bow.

"Agathia," he said. His voice was moist and breathy. "You honor me with your presence. Please convey my utmost thanks to the Council for their assistance. I am Dux Raskos, and I hold this garrison on behalf of the people of the Republic."

He straightened up and smiled. His teeth were a horror, brown and splintery, gleaming here and there with precious metals like coins shining out of a sewer. Maya felt an overpowering urge to keep her distance, but Tanax had already started forward, and she had no choice but to follow. Beq and Varo came after her, the arcanist looking curiously at everything, the scout seeming distinctly ill at ease.

"Thank you for your service, Dux Raskos," Tanax said, with a shallow bow of his own. "I have a message for you from the Council."

"Of course." Raskos took the letter, a slim envelope, from Tanax. The dux wore a fixed smile. "My gratitude."

"Until we receive further instructions, I am to place my team at your disposal. I hope we will be able to resolve your difficulties."

"I have no doubt you will," Raskos said. His smile grew more genuine. "But that can wait. I understand you're coming directly from another assignment, and you must be tired. Let us see to your accommodations."

The Gate room, it turned out, was deep underground, connected by a broad spiral staircase with the rest of the Spike. After several revolutions, it emerged into a large, luxuriantly appointed hall, where a phalanx of liveried servants waited like a second contingent of guards. The dux waved his hands like he was conducting an orchestra, and four dark-coated footmen peeled off to stand expectantly in front of Maya and the others. It took Maya a moment to realize that the servant was waiting for her pack.

"I've taken the liberty of arranging a small gathering this evening," the dux said, as the travelers handed over their gear. "Everyone in Deepfire is eager to make your acquaintance, though of course only the best people will be invited. I trust that will be satisfactory?"

"Is that really necessary?" Maya said. Tanax shot her a look, and she hastily added, "I thought we would be at work as soon as possible, is all."

Tanax cleared his throat. "Agathios Maya is correct, Dux Raskos, that we don't require any courtesies."

"Of course not," Raskos said, bowing again. "But the situation here in Deepfire is delicate. It may be some time before your aid will be required. Until then, I hope you will take advantage of my hospitality."

Tanax nodded, apparently mollified. Raskos, purple robe rustling, gestured to a sweeping wooden stairway, and the pack-bearing footmen trooped up it in formation. Tanax strolled along behind them, with Maya and the others following in his wake.

"You'll be summoned this evening," Raskos said. "Until then, please ask if you require anything at all."

He remained at the bottom of the stairs as the servants led them away. When they reached the second-floor landing, Maya exchanged a look with Varo, then made sure Tanax was several steps ahead.

"Is this...normal?" she muttered, in a low voice. "All the bowing and scraping."

Varo shrugged. "You're the centarch."

"I usually slept in a cart beside the road, or in bed with three other people at some cheap inn." The servants were leading them down a corridor now, and Maya looked around at the polished woodwork, thick scarlet carpets, and sunstones in cut-glass sconces. "This is all new to me."

"Me too," Beq said, fiddling with her spectacles as she peered up at the ceiling. "I think this is a later part of the structure. The construction is all wrong for a Chosen building."

"I know one thing," Varo said. "The dux didn't look happy to see that letter."

"He didn't, did he?" Maya said. "I'd love to know what it said. Maybe then we'd have some idea what we're supposed to be doing here."

"It'll be ciphered," Beq put in. "Until the dux uses his copy of the key to write it out, it'd just look like gibberish."

Tanax looked around, and the three of them quieted. They followed the footmen through several twists and turns until Maya was thoroughly lost, ending up in a corridor with blue carpet instead of red and a line of elaborately inlaid doors on one side.

"Here we are," one of the footmen said. Struggling under the weight of Beq's enormous pack, he opened the first door. The room beyond could have swallowed Kaiura's entire house from Litnin, with high ceilings and a broad expanse of carpet. Bookshelves lined the walls, full of matching leather-bound volumes, and broad-paned windows looked out across the city. Several more doors led off, presumably into the rest of a suite.

"I imagine we'll fit," Maya muttered, a little shocked.

"Oh, this is for Agathios Tanax," the footman said. "Agathios Maya, if you'll follow me? Jonathon, take the others, please."

It turned out he wasn't joking, as Maya had initially assumed. There was another suite next door, just as luxuriantly appointed, which was apparently reserved for her exclusive use. Two more sets of rooms on the other side of the hall, only slightly less princely, were for Varo and Beq. After sorting out whose packs went where and demonstrating the discreet bellpull that would summon someone to attend to their needs, the footmen bowed and departed, leaving the four of them in the corridor.

"Okay," Maya said. "This *can't* be normal. Who treats a pair of agathia like visiting royalty?"

"We're here at the Council's request," Tanax said. "By honoring us, he honors them in turn. He's eager to demonstrate his loyalty."

"Maybe a little too eager," Varo muttered.

"As I said, the dux is a valued ally," Tanax intoned frostily. "You will treat him with courtesy. Is that understood?"

"It would be easier for us to help him if we knew why we were here," Maya said. "He wasn't exactly forthcoming."

"He's hardly going to explain everything in front of the servants," Tanax said. "I'm sure we'll find out when it's necessary. Until then, it's not our concern."

He gave them a firm nod and turned away. Maya exchanged looks with the others, then went into her room. The size of it was still shocking—she'd considered her assigned space in the Forge generous, but compared to this suite it was barely a monk's cell. Opening one of the side doors let her into a bedroom nearly as big as the sitting room, with a bed that could have slept a dozen. It did look invitingly soft, however, and a glance into the attached bathroom showed that the

Spike had not only running water but private baths, which made up for a multitude of sins.

Another door, she found, led out to a small balcony. It overlooked a set of opulent gardens, riotous with colorful flowers in neat beds, well-trimmed trees marking the edge of the grounds. Past that, more grand houses rose, each sitting in its own square of gardened perfection. The horizon was defined by a set of colossal mountain peaks, rising like the broken teeth in Raskos' smile, as though they were at the bottom of an enormous bowl.

Most striking of all, though, was the view to the west. She could see the city of Deepfire, block after block of warehouses, tenements, and office buildings, built mostly of stone and slate and presenting a dour facade of gray and brown. Lying between the Spike and this more urban part of the city was an enormous scar on the landscape, where the ground simply fell away in a dizzying chasm that extended a considerable distance north and south. Islands of rock hung far out into the emptiness, supported by slender columns. Plumes of white smoke drifted skyward, all up and down its length, illuminated by a crimson glow.

The important cities of the Republic had been part of Maya's education, and she'd heard of the Pit, the scar left by the Chosen weapon that had vaporized one of the great cities of the ghouls. But it was one thing to read about and another to see in person. The forces unleashed in the war beggared the imagination. *The Chosen had weapons that could crack mountains in half and are still burning four hundred years later. And they* lost. It was a humbling thought.

She shook her head, went back inside, and started filling the bath.

Maya started awake to the tinkling of a delicate brass bell and for a moment struggled to remember where she was, marooned in an ocean of crimson silk and dark brown furs. The remnants of a dream flitted across her mind, a skittering sense of something vile lurking beneath the surface of the world, and her heart hammered.

More insistent ringing brought her back to herself, and she scrambled out from beneath the suffocating bearskin and struggled to the edge of the monstrous bed, the too-soft mattress sinking beneath her hands and feet like quicksand. Eventually she slipped over the side, her tumble cushioned by the thick carpet, and popped to her feet, breathing hard. She was wearing only her underthings, and gradually she remembered—sliding out of the sinfully hot bath after much too long, overheated and dizzy, and flopping onto the bed for a moment's rest. By the light coming in through the windows, she'd slept for several hours.

The bell rang again. Maya put her hand on the Thing, felt the frantic pounding of her heart, and took a long breath to calm herself.

"Just a moment!" she called, looking around frantically. Her traveling clothes were scattered across the bathroom floor, soiled and sweat stained. But one of the wardrobes stood open, and there was a selection of dressing gowns inside. She grabbed one that looked roughly her size and slid into it, silk whispering across her skin. It was embroidered, she noted absently, with rearing warbirds, the stitching astonishingly intricate.

Thus decent—and, more important, with the Thing concealed— she hurried to the door. Thankfully, it wasn't Tanax who was ringing the bell, but one of the dux's uniformed footmen, who bowed politely.

"Agathios Maya," the man said. "The dux is hoping you will honor him with your presence in half an hour, in the minor court. Is there anything you require?"

"Require?" Maya blinked.

"To assist you. A perfumer, perhaps, or a face painter?"

"Oh." Maya shook her head. "No, I'll be fine."

"Very good."

Her stomach gave a warning grumble. "Will there be food?"

"Of course."

The very slightest smile might have crossed the footman's face, and Maya felt her cheeks warm. She drew herself up in what she hoped was a haughty fashion.

"Thank you. That will be all."

"Very good," the man said again. He closed the door.

Chosen defend me, is this how the nobility lives? She couldn't imagine what it would be like to have people around all the time, *watching* you. *I suppose I had Marn. But I could punch him if he did something I didn't like.*

There was no question of wearing her traveling clothes, of course, not even with her spare sort-of-clean shirt. Her formal uniform was tucked into the bottom of her pack, somewhat wrinkled after several days on the road. She hadn't thought to ask whether it would be suitable. *I suppose the dux isn't likely to throw us out.* Maya shucked off the gown, tossed it in a corner, and dressed rapidly.

Her hair presented another problem. Even after a long soak, it wasn't exactly *clean*, and the nights in the woods hadn't done it any favors. She attacked it with a hairbrush, heedless of the tangles that yanked at her scalp, and when it was tolerably smooth she tied it into a tail with a leather cord.

There. She examined herself in the mirror. *Still no beauty, but it'll do.* At least the formal Order uniform looked a bit dashing, with its black and silver. The boots were the same ones she'd worn in the forest, that couldn't be helped, but she'd at least taken the worst of the dust off them. And her haken hung from her belt, crystal gleaming.

There was a rap at the door. Maya gave the mirror one last look, then hurried to answer it. Once again, she'd expected Tanax, but this time she found Beq, and the sight made her pull up short.

The arcanist wore her own formal uniform, similar to Maya's but with deep blue piping denoting her place in the Order. It was well tailored, flattering her curves, but what really took Maya's breath away was her hair. Beq normally wore it in a thick braid, easily pulled aside for practical work. Now it hung loose in brilliant emerald waves, falling past her shoulders like a curtain and leaving Maya distinctly short of breath.

"Um. Hi," Beq said, fiddling nervously with the dials on her spectacles. "We're supposed to go downstairs soon, I think."

"I'm ready," Maya said. "You look...nice."

Beq shook her head. "I don't...I mean..."

"I don't know about you," Varo said, coming down the corridor, "but I could eat a loadbird." He was in his uniform, too, though he seemed more comfortable than either of them. His bare skull had the gleam of a fresh shave. "Not that I recommend eating a loadbird, to be honest. We had to do that once, and my friend got one of the little bones caught in his throat—"

Maya gave an exaggerated sigh, and Beq giggled, which seemed to break the tension. Varo looked around. "Where's Tanax?"

"I'm ready." Tanax opened the door to his room and came out. To Maya's annoyance, he looked perfectly elegant in his uniform, his hawk-like profile the very picture of the Republic aristocrat. He glanced around for a moment, then said quietly, "I hope I don't have to tell you to be polite and cautious this evening. We are here to help the dux and represent the Twilight Order."

"Of course," Varo said, bowing. "I will be the very soul of courtesy."

Tanax scowled at him, then met Maya's eye and scowled harder. Before he could say anything further, a footman appeared to lead the way, and they fell in behind him in silence.

It was a good thing the dux had sent a guide, because the layout of the palace remained incomprehensible to Maya. They followed several long corridors, descended one flight of stairs and ascended another, and finally wound up at a set of broad glass doors that had been thrown open to admit the early afternoon air. Outside was a tiled square, bigger than most village greens, with an elaborately decorated white gazebo in the center and broad circles of grass around the edges. At least a hundred people were milling around, not counting the liveried servants who moved through the crowd like ghosts, distributing drinks and hors d'oeuvres. Under the decorative roof of the gazebo, a dozen musicians in somber suits played softly, ignored by everyone.

Maya, who had been expecting something along the lines of a dinner table and a dozen guests, swallowed hard. At her side, Beq went very still and made a whimpering sound deep in her throat.

Tanax brushed past them, stepping through the doors and out onto the tile. Maya forced herself to follow, and Beq stumbled after, Varo gliding at her side. Maya could hear a ripple of whispers spread through the crowd, and heads turned to follow them.

Raskos was there, still swathed in resplendent silks but now dripping with jewelry as well—gold and silver, but also the weird, twisted shapes of Elder relics, crystals and bits of unmetal cleverly melded with human artistry. When he bowed, something gave a gentle chime. Maya couldn't help but wince at his smile, which was as horrific as ever.

"My guests of honor," he said. "I hope you're not disappointed by your reception. It was a bit of short notice, I'm afraid."

"It's lovely, sir," Tanax said smoothly. "You honor us."

"No more than you deserve, surely." The dux beckoned. "Come, I'll make the introductions."

Maya found herself whisked away behind Raskos, vaguely aware that Varo and Beq were being hustled off in another direction by obsequious servants. There followed a confusing whirlwind of meetings, with the dux introducing a rotating cast of nobles, bankers, and other notables at breakneck speed, a blur of tasteful suits and intricate gowns. She wondered if the rapid-fire names meant anything to Tanax; judging by the rigid smile on his face, she guessed not. Raskos didn't seem particularly interested in letting them *meet* anyone, and Maya got the distinct impression she was being shown off, like a new pony or a dazzling jewel.

"—and this is Lady Vance, of the Moorcat Combine," Raskos said, gesturing at a stiff-looking older woman in a green coat and trousers. She gave the two agathia a cursory glance, then fixed her gaze on Raskos, not looking pleased. "Lady Vance, this is Agathios Tanax and Agathios Maya, of the Twilight Order."

"Honored," Vance said, with a bow so slight it was barely a nod.

"And—" Raskos paused as the music swelled. "Ah. I see it's time for the first dance. Would the pair of you do us the honor?"

Maya felt like she was suddenly in the center of an expanding circle of inquisitive eyes. She stopped herself from touching the Thing and swallowed hard.

Tanax leaned close to Maya's ear. "I don't suppose you dance?"

"I can dance," Maya said. She turned to glare at him. "Can you?"

"Of course." He looked skeptical. "A proper centarch must be fit to socialize at the highest levels."

Jaedia had not given Maya any lessons in decorum that would have helped her socialize at the highest levels. But she *had* learned to dance, at village fairs and festivals all across the Republic. *How different can it be?* She turned to face him, chin jutting out, and stiffened as his hand found her hip.

Tanax sighed. "Are you sure—"

"It's fine." Maya clamped her hand on his shoulder. "Go ahead."

The music picked up, and they were off.

Annoyingly, it turned out Tanax was quite a good dancer. His style was a little rigid for Maya's taste, but he had a feel for the rhythm of the music, which was a formal piece Maya didn't recognize. After a few almost-graceful turns, she let herself relax a little. Other couples joined in, progressing in a stately ring around the gazebo and the musicians.

"I must admit I'm surprised," he said, quietly enough that only she could hear.

"That I can dance?"

He shrugged. "I didn't think you Pragmatics approved of cultured pursuits."

"You don't know anything about what I approve of," Maya said as they took another turn. "What's your problem with me, anyway?"

"Problem?" He raised an eyebrow. "I don't—"

"Save it," Maya hissed. "Varo said it's always like this when two cent-archs from opposite factions are on the same team. Is that it?"

"Don't pretend you don't know."

"*I'm* not pretending anything."

The music thrilled faster, and Tanax drew her closer for a quicker step. He kept his voice low.

"My *problem*," he said, "is that this was supposed to be the end of my apprenticeship. My chance to get my cognomen. And instead I wind up babysitting an agathios who's never been away from her master before."

"That's not fair. I—"

"And don't think I don't know why. Everyone knows Baselanthus and the Pragmatics would do anything to inconvenience my master, and he and Jaedia are still close, for all she professes to be neutral. If our mission fails, Nicomidi will be embarrassed." He bent closer. "I will not let that happen, whatever you do. Some of us are more interested in defending humanity than scoring political victories."

"If it *fails*?" Maya was momentarily speechless. Her mind raced as they went through the steps by rote.

Jaedia warned me that he *might try to sabotage this mission*. Either Tanax was a very good actor—and she knew he wasn't that—or he hadn't been let in on any such plan. *He's worried about* me? It explained, a bit, why he'd been so cold from the very start. *He might have tried talking to me about it, though.*

The music ended with a flourish, and the couples separated, bowing to one another. Maya followed suit, belatedly, and her gaze met her fellow agathios's. Tanax's eyes were narrowed, in suspicion or curiosity.

"Wonderful!" Raskos glided up, throwing an effusive arm around each of their shoulders. "Now. Who's up for a drink?"

Much later, she was sitting on the grass, trying to guess if the lamps overhead were really spinning. Probably not, Maya decided. It was more likely she was spinning instead.

She wasn't clear on *how* much later it was. Night came early to Deepfire, surrounded as it was by mountains, and the dux's servants had lit the lamps hanging from beams crisscrossing the courtyard not long after the festivities had begun. There had indeed been food, in bewildering variety and quantity, tiny portions of candied meats and honeyed fruit and little bits of who knew what that added up to Maya feeling like she'd swallowed a couple of bricks. Other servants had brought flutes of light, bubbly wine, followed by small cups of dark, thick stuff that smelled like molasses and tasted like fire. Maya had started waving them off a little too late, which was probably a contributor to the spinning.

Everyone seemed to want to talk to her. It was a distinctly odd sensation for Maya, out in the open with her haken on her hip. Jaedia had generally preferred that they remain unnoticed. In Litnin, the villagers had been terrified of them, but here people were fascinated instead of fearful.

In Litnin we were there to investigate them, a deeper, cynical part of her mind answered. *Here we're supposed to be* helping *the dux, and these are his friends.*

A small circle of younger guests had gathered on one of the greens, catching their breath from the endless dancing. Maya had lost most of their names almost immediately, but the slim young man in the dark robe was an under accountant at a merchant combine, and another boy with an arm around his shoulders was a prince of some sort. A blue-haired girl, who refused to stop trying to get everyone to sing, was heir to a manufactory fortune, and her amiable, chattering friend was an officer in the Auxiliaries and related to someone important.

Most of Maya's attention was on Elodel, and not just because she was sitting next to her. Elodel was a head taller than Maya, broad-shouldered and well-muscled, with short brown hair artfully mussed and wide violet eyes. She worked in one of the appraisal houses, assessing the stream of relics and arcana that the scavengers pulled up from the tunnels under the city. It was fascinating work, or at least Elodel made it sound fascinating, with her musical laugh and sly smile.

Elodel smiled a lot. When she'd broken up laughing at a joke

someone across the circle had told, a few minutes ago, she'd slapped
her own thigh in amusement, and her hand had ended up resting on
Maya's knee. Maya felt frozen by that hand, pinned by it, breath held,
as though in fear of disturbing a butterfly that had just alighted.

"Of course, with Yora and Halfmask on the loose, it's a wonder anything interesting ever makes it to the appraisal house," Elodel was saying, to nods from around the circle.

"Why?" Maya said. Her mind was not fully on the conversation.
"Who are Yora and Halfmask?"

"You haven't heard of our little homegrown rebellion?" the prince
drawled. "I suppose the rest of the Republic doesn't have much reason
to pay attention to the news from Deepfire."

"They're thieves, not rebels," the accountant said. "Yora talks about
freedom for the tunnelborn, but it's all for show. She's no better than a
mountain brigand."

"*I* heard she hands out free bread and blankets down in the tunnels,"
the blue-haired girl said.

"Which will only encourage the rats to multiply." The prince sighed.

Maya glanced at Elodel, who took pity on her confusion. "Yora runs
a criminal gang out of the tunnels. They steal from the Republic and
say it's on behalf of the tunnelborn, the people who live on the other
side of the city border."

"Ungrateful is what I call it," the prince said. "As though providing
them with jobs and protection from plaguespawn isn't enough."

"*I* heard that was why the dux brought you here," the accountant
said. "To make yourselves useful and put a stop to it."

"That would be a first," the prince said, and barked a laugh.

Elodel glared at him. "Don't be an ass, Rench."

"Apologies." He raised an imaginary cup in salute. "I'm sure Agathios Maya will do whatever it takes to clean up the city."

Maya smiled uncertainly and nodded. Elodel shifted, still glaring,
and took her hand off Maya's knee, which briefly made Maya hate
the prince more than anyone who'd ever lived. Only briefly, though,

because Elodel grabbed Maya's hand instead as a new round of music filtered out of the gazebo.

"These triples are my favorite," she said. "Do you want to dance?"

"I…" Maya put her free hand to her chest, feeling her heart hammer under the Thing. "I'm not sure I could keep my feet under me at the moment."

"Come to think of it, I'm not sure I'd trust myself not to do something stupid." Elodel laughed again. "At least it's not a long ride home. You're staying here at the Spike, I assume?"

Maya nodded. Elodel was still holding her hand, their fingers entwined.

"I bet the dux has given you one of the nice suites," Elodel said. She leaned forward, as though sharing a secret. "I'd love to see it."

I can't. Maya missed a breath, and in that moment the automatic refusal died on her lips. *Can I?*

On the road with Jaedia and Marn…no one had ever *told* Maya she couldn't share her bed with someone, not in so many words. There just wasn't a great deal of opportunity. They slept under the stars, or all together in a single room, because the kind of poor travelers they pretended to be couldn't have afforded separate beds. And Jaedia was far too smart and sharp-eyed for Maya to have thought of sneaking away.

Here, though…

I could, couldn't I? She had her own room, that soft bed with the slick silk sheets, and no one to object or even notice. Elodel's hand was so warm in hers. *I…*

She'd lost track of her companions some time ago, though she'd caught a glimpse of Varo dancing with surprising competence in the arms of a handsome young man. Tanax had been in his element, comfortable with the people who'd flocked to him just as they'd flocked to Maya.

Beq had just vanished, until now. Scanning the courtyard, automatically looking for Jaedia's stern but understanding glare, Maya caught sight of a wave of bright green hair and a pained expression, headed rapidly through one of the glass doors that led back into the palace proper.

"I...have to go." The words forced themselves out, past a thick throat.

Elodel cocked her head. "Really?"

"Sorry. My friend..."

"Of course." Her smile seemed genuine. "Go and help."

Maya extracted her hand, fingers tingling from the contact, and got unsteadily to her feet. Mumbling goodbyes, she hurried through the now-shadowy courtyard, following Beq. The glass doors led into a long corridor, soft carpet over polished stone, lined with small trees in decorative pots. Beq sat a little ways in, deep in shadow, her arms wrapped around one of the planters like it was a lifeline.

"Beq?" Maya said. "Is that you?"

"Mmm-Maya?" Beq's voice was a drawl. "'S'that you?"

Maya padded over and knelt beside her. "Are you all right?"

"Feeling..." Beq shook her head carefully. "A bit better now. A little bit." She looked down. "Hope nobody liked this pot."

Maya examined the planter and wrinkled her nose at the sharp smell of vomit. "How much did you drink?"

"Dunno." Beq waved a hand vaguely. "They kept bringing them."

"Okay." Maya held out a hand. "Let's get you to bed."

"'S'okay." Beq leaned against the pot, fiddling with the gears on her spectacles. Lenses clicked and whirred. "I'll be fine. Go back to the party."

"I'm about done anyway."

"Liar. Saw you with that girl." Beq blinked, her eyes magnified hugely. "She's pretty."

"I wasn't..." Maya shook her head. "It's fine. Really."

She took Beq's hand and with a little effort managed to hoist the other girl back to her feet. Maya draped Beq's arm around her shoulders and got them staggering more or less straight. A footman, not bothering to hide his superior look, gave Maya directions.

"'M not good at parties," Beq said.

Maya laughed. "Probably not many formal dances back at the Forge."

"The other apprentices used to sneak down to the empty levels," Beq said. "To drink an' play games. And..." She lurched against Maya, voice lowered. "Fuck. You know."

"Beq," Maya said, trying hard not to think about the body pressed against her. "Walk straight, would you?"

"Sorry." Beq swung back into line. "I was never any good at them. Stopped getting invited, after a while. Silly Beq, rather read and mess with crystals than sneak out and kiss boys. Scared, wimpy Beq."

"You're not silly," Maya said, shepherding her charge carefully up a spiral stair. "And you're definitely not scared. You saved my life back in Litnin."

"Was scared. Thought I was gonna pee myself."

"You saved me anyway, though." With some relief, Maya recognized their corridor and headed for Beq's door. "That's what matters."

Beq fell silent. Maya thumbed the latch, and they made it as far as the couch in the sitting room. Beq slipped away from her arm and sat down heavily, pulling her spectacles aside to wipe at her eyes.

"Thanks," she mumbled. "Sorry. I didn't mean to ruin your party."

"It's fine. I'm not here for parties, anyway."

"You should go find that girl." Beq made a shooing motion. "Go. I'll be all right."

"You're sure?"

The arcanist gave a weary nod and put her spectacles back on. "Go."

Back in the corridor, Maya leaned against the wall and let out a long breath. *Parties.* Her own room wasn't far, but she thought she should at least find Tanax and explain what had happened. *Assuming he's not stumbling drunk by now, too.*

Unfortunately, reversing the directions the footman had provided proved to be more difficult than she expected. Most of the Spike was quiet and gloomy, the sunstones set to a gentle twilight glow, and all the corridors looked similar. She was reasonably certain she was headed in the right direction, but the courtyard full of life and light eluded her.

After a third wrong turn, Maya felt her head start to pound. *Should have gone back to bed after all.* She heard voices ahead and hurried toward them, willing to put up with a servant's arched eyebrow. At the last minute, though, she pulled up short, recognizing one of the voices. *Raskos.*

"You're certain?"

"Yes, sir." The other voice was a man's, clipped and professional. "Yora and Halfmask are there."

Rebels? Maya eased forward. The dux was in a small study, the doorway half-open. He sat at a desk with several pieces of folded paper in front of him. On a torn envelope, Maya recognized the seal of the Council's letter. The other man, tall and gaunt in an Auxiliary uniform, stood in another doorway, beside a hearth where a fire popped and crackled.

"Very well," Raskos said, setting down his pen. "What do you need?"

"Ten squads, at least. Halfmask is tricky."

"He's a roach," Raskos snarled. "You don't need a blaster to crush an insect."

"You want to ask your Order friends to assist?"

"Don't be stupid. We can't have them blundering about."

"Then I need ten squads," the man said.

"Take them," Raskos muttered. "Just be certain you get them all."

"Of course, sir."

Booted footsteps walked away. Raskos looked down, mopping his sweaty forehead with a handkerchief. His eyes shifted, reading, and then he swore quietly. He crumpled the page into a ball, tossed it into the hearth, and got up, coming in Maya's direction. Maya quickly scrambled back from the doorway, arranging herself in the hall as though merely lost, but Raskos didn't even glance her way when he emerged, turning in the opposite direction and striding off.

Maya held her breath until he was out of sight, trying to think. *Ten squads is a big part of the garrison.* That implied that Raskos thought Yora and Halfmask were a serious threat. *So why doesn't he want us "blundering about"?*

She glanced around the doorway again. The torn envelope was still on the desk. *I shouldn't. But...*

Before she could talk herself out of it, she slipped into the room. There was a sheet of folded paper still on the desk beside the envelope. Maya reached out, then hesitated. *The dux just left it here. So how secret can it be?* Jaedia probably would not have approved of that logic, but for the moment it quieted Maya's pangs of conscience. She flattened the sheet with her hand.

She was almost immediately disappointed. It was written in neat, block capitals, on good paper, but the letters spelled only nonsense. *Ciphered.* Beq had mentioned that. *No wonder Raskos doesn't worry about anyone reading his mail.* She glanced at the hearth. *He must have burned the legible copy—*

Maya paused. It had been a hot day, and the servants had only laid a small fire after dark. Flames leapt from the front of the hearth, but the back was dark and gray with soot. *He threw it pretty hard. So maybe...*

She touched her haken and closed her hand, and the fire went out. *Yes!* Wedged in the back of the grate was a small wad of paper, slightly singed but otherwise untouched. Maya knelt to dig it out, careful to avoid getting ash on her uniform. Excitement warred with guilt as she pocketed the crumpled page, straightened up, and reignited the fire with another brief touch to her haken.

Slipping back out into the corridor, she rounded a corner and found herself faced with a couple of footmen. Maya flagged one down.

"Yes, Agathios?" the man said with a bow.

"I was looking for the party," Maya explained, "but now I think I'm feeling a bit poorly after all. Do you think you could direct me to my room?"

"Of course," he said. "Follow me."

Maya followed, fingering the stolen letter, heart thumping hard.

Chapter 10

The sketch on the table was growing more elaborate by the moment. It had begun as a simple outline of Raskos' private warehouse, an unassuming square building with a sloped roof and high, small windows. Then Nevin had started adding annotations in colored pencil, with accompanying mutters.

"Screamers here, here, and here. Reverser coils behind the walls here. Thread ward on the doors. Windows..."

The picture that took shape was practically a fortress. Raskos had spent years skimming off the scavengers, keeping the best finds to sell under the table for his own benefit. Gyre had known that, but he hadn't realized that the dux had also been grabbing every nasty trap dug out of the ghoul warrens—often at considerable cost in blood—and installing them around his own private safe house. *What in the name of the Chosen is he keeping in there?*

Well. The Core Analytica, apparently. Whatever that is. He glanced at Kit. She sat at one end of the table, watching the preparations with hooded eyes, apparently bored. Yora, on the other hand, seemed to grow more restless with each passing moment, walking back and forth with her spear in her hand, tapping the butt against the ground. She tried not to show it, but Gyre knew Harrow's death had hit her hard, as had Ibb's defection.

Sarah was the only one who seemed immune to the oppressive atmosphere. She worked away on her own notes, writing as fast as Nevin could sketch. If anything, the prospect of tackling the dux's trap-laden storehouse seemed to excite her.

With Harrow and Ibb gone, Yora had pulled in a few hands from outside her core team to act as security. A couple of broad-shouldered manufactory workers leaned against one wall, carrying cudgels and knives, and she'd posted lookouts in the approach tunnels to their secret meeting room. The newcomers seemed competent enough, but Gyre had to admit that he would have rather had Ibb with his blaster and rapier.

"I think that's it," Nevin said. "That we know of, anyway. None of our people have been past the anteroom, so there could be more inside."

"Which leaves us with a whole set of contingencies," Sarah said, scribbling rapidly. "We wouldn't want to get past all the outer defenses and get stuck—"

"Can you do it?" Kit said. "Or not?"

Sarah blinked and looked at Yora, who gave a quick nod. The arcanist shrugged.

"We can do it," she said. "We'll need time and a fair bit of cash to line up the appropriate countermeasures. Lynnia can make some of what we need, but the rest we're going to have to buy from the black market, and we don't want to attract attention."

"Cash I can manage," Kit said. "Time may be in shorter supply. Raskos is trying to find a buyer for this thing. If he does, he may move it out of our reach."

Sarah spread her hands. Nevin laced his fingers together, looking down at the table, and said, "If we run into a screamer and don't have a way to shut it down, we'll all end up buried under the Spike."

"Every job has risks," Kit said, waving a hand.

"She told you what we need," Yora said. "We've already *risked* enough for this project."

Kit raised her eyebrows but said nothing. After a moment's glare, Yora turned away, tossing her spear from hand to hand.

"How much cash are we talking about?" Gyre said.

"Hard to say," Sarah said. "I can make a scouting trip tomorrow—"

"*Boss!*" A young woman in rough laborer's garb burst into the chamber, panting. "Auxies!"

Gyre was on his feet instantly, and Kit bounced up with her usual grin.

"Where?" she said. "How many?"

"Twenty at least," the scout gasped. "Coming this way. I left Villam to keep an eye on them."

No sooner had she spoken than a rumble echoed through the tunnels, attenuated but clearly recognizable. *Blaster.* Yora slapped her spear into her other hand and turned to the pair of guards.

"Gul, Hil, check if the other exits are clear. Go!"

Nevin was frantically gathering up his maps, and Sarah had pocketed her notebook, pulling down a pair of dark-tinted goggles. For a few heartbeats, they waited in silence.

Gyre knew—because he'd mapped it himself—that of the six tunnels exiting the meeting room, three were dead ends. Only one had originally been open, but a little patient excavation had cleared a narrow path through the others, precisely for this sort of situation. Unfortunately, the tunnel the scout had come down was one of the backups, which strongly suggested that the dux's people had stolen a march on them.

Which leaves us with plan B. He'd never been particularly happy with plan B.

The *snap* of crossbow bolts echoed down one of the other tunnels, and a moment later the responding roar of blasters. One of Yora's people emerged, badly cut up and bleeding from splinters of flying rock.

"Parak's dead," he reported. "Lots of 'em coming, loaded for fucking thickhead. Not getting out that way."

Yora glanced at the third tunnel, where there'd been only an ominous silence.

Plan B it is, then.

"Get away from the table," Gyre said. "Back up. *Now.*"

Nevin scrambled back, clutching his notes, and the others followed suit. Gyre dove underneath, pawing through the dirt until he found the long, coiled shape of the fuse. He sparked it with a firelighter, then shuffled backward as fast as he could. Flame raced across the floor and then down into the stone.

A batch of Lynnia's special mix went off with a muffled *boom*. A cloud of dust and smoke engulfed the room, and stone and bits of furniture pattered down all around them. Where the table had been there was a dark hole in the floor, parts of it still crumbling away from the force of the explosive.

"You never bothered to mention we were meeting on top of a *bomb?*" Sarah said, waving away the smoke.

"Never came up," Gyre muttered. "There's more tunnels down there, but I don't have a full map. We should split up, get as far as we can, hide if we have to."

"Right." Yora waved. "Come on, everyone down!"

The sound of many footsteps was getting closer on three sides. Yora tossed her spear into the hole, then jumped after it. Sarah, Nevin, and the rest of her people followed suit. Gyre looked to Kit.

"After you, Doomseeker."

"Always prepared, right?" Kit's grin widened.

"Right."

She hopped over the edge. Gyre followed, absorbing the fall with a crouch. Only a trickle of light from the lanterns in the meeting room filtered through the smoke, and the ground was a mess of stone fragments. Vague silhouettes moved about. He felt someone take his hand and recognized Kit's slight shape.

"We're headed north," Yora's voice came out of the murk. "If we get clear, I'll get you a message."

"I'll take the other way," Gyre said.

"Good luck, Halfmask."

"Good luck." Gyre pulled Kit into a run and fled into the dark.

"Always prepared," Kit whispered in Gyre's ear.

"Right."

"But not to the extent of . . . you know. Knowing where you're going."

"The thing about unexplored tunnels," Gyre muttered, "is that nobody's made a map."

This is why I didn't want to go to plan B.

His hope had been that the hole he'd blasted in the floor would link up quickly to some inhabited part of Deepfire's tunnels, allowing for a quick escape. Unfortunately, that did not appear to be the case, at least in the direction he and Kit were moving. They prowled through the blackness, feeling their way along the smooth-walled passages and navigating chunks of fallen stone, Gyre mentally kicking himself for not carrying any nighteye with him.

Gyre had a pair of glowstones in his pocket, but using them would announce their presence for a kilometer in the pitch-darkness. And it hadn't been long after they'd started moving that he'd seen the flicker of torches behind them and heard the muttered sounds of conversation. The Auxies were sweeping the cavern—slowly and cautiously, alert for ambush, but they were coming.

And now . . .

"This is a dead end," Kit said, feeling her way along the wall. "I'm back where I started."

Gyre looked over his shoulder and didn't see any light. He took out his firelighter, flicked it briefly, and looked around in the glow of its transient sparks.

"Dead end," he agreed. It wasn't even a collapsed tunnel, just a smooth wall of rock. "We'll have to go back."

"There were a couple of side passages at the last junction, I think," Kit said. "But the Auxies have to be getting close."

Gyre couldn't see her expression, but there was certainly no fear in her voice, no more than there had been in their fights in the deep tunnels. Danger simply didn't seem to matter to her. *What did I expect from the Doomseeker?*

"We could try to jump them," she said. "Cut our way through and get back to the meeting room. It might work if we catch them by surprise."

"They're playing this safe," Gyre said. "And they've got blasters. We'd never make it."

"Then we'd better hurry." He would have bet good money she was grinning again as she took his hand.

They backtracked a few hundred meters, until a change in the echoes told him they'd reached a junction. Farther on, tiny reflected gleams of torchlight showed on the walls, and he could hear the sound of quiet voices.

"Left or right?" Kit said.

Gyre struggled to remember Lynnia's map and where they were in relation to the inhabited tunnels. In the end, he shrugged and pulled Kit to the left. They followed the tunnel around a long, descending curve, like a spiral ramp. The farther down they went, the more Gyre's spirits sank. *This is not going to end in a way out.* He wasn't sure if heading into the deep tunnels in total darkness would be more or less suicidal than simply trying to fight his way through dozens of Auxies.

Ultimately, however, the point was moot. Kit pulled up short, her hands groping sideways along another blank wall. *Dead end.*

"Well," she said. "Ideas?"

Gyre flicked his firelighter again, throwing sparks across the stone, looking desperately for a way out that wasn't there. The murmur of approaching voices echoed off the rock.

"How many shots left in that blaster?"

Cloth rustled as she shrugged. "Maybe half a dozen."

"That might get us back to the junction. After that . . ."

"Hang on," she said. "Let me have the firelighter."

He found her hand, pushed the little device into it. Reflected torch-light was growing behind them as she flicked sparks into the air.

"There's a room," she hissed.

"What?"

"Come *on*." She grabbed his hand and yanked him forward. "In here."

Blind again, he felt rock close on both sides. Kit, ahead of him, turned and pulled him forward, sliding into a niche just across from her. The space didn't qualify as a room, or even a closet—it was just a sideways cut in the rock, about as deep as a man and taller than Gyre, but so narrow that he and Kit were wedged practically in one another's faces.

"Can they see us?" Gyre said, as quietly as he could.

"I fucking hope not," Kit said. "Because if they catch us in here, we're not exactly going to be able to fight our way out."

That was true, Gyre reflected. He couldn't even reach his blades without elbowing her in the stomach, and any attempt to draw them would have badly injured somebody. *The deadly Halfmask, discovered jammed into a ghoul's old closet. Maybe they'll laugh so hard we can get away.*

The voices were getting closer. Gyre closed his eyes and tried to hold still. Kit's breath tickled his cheek, warm and distracting.

"Another dead end, sir," a woman's voice said.

"Chosen fucking defend," a man answered. "All right. Wait here. I'll go back to the filiarch for orders."

Two sets of footsteps receded for a few moments. Then one stopped and the other continued. Gyre opened his eyes and saw the glow of a torch not far away.

"Just one stayed behind." Kit's voice was a quiet breath. "I can probably kill her before she calls for help."

"No," Gyre mouthed. "He said *filiarch*. That means Legionaries."

"The dux only has a couple of squads of Legionaries."

"He only needs *one* to kill us." Gyre swallowed. "Stay quiet."

Time passed, in silent and excruciating slowness. Kit shifted her weight, brushing against him in the process. He gritted his teeth.

"We could fuck," she whispered. "If you're bored."

"Very funny."

"Not the most comfortable position, I admit, but there's something about trying to keep quiet. Knowing that if you gasp too loud you're definitely going to die." Her hand brushed against his cheek, playing over the silver mask. "No?"

"Please be quiet."

Her other palm pressed against the front of his trousers. "Aha. I *knew* you'd be into it."

"*Kit*—" He cut the word off in a strangled gasp at the sound of approaching footsteps.

"Head back up," the man's voice said. "We'll hold the junction until we've secured the area."

"Yes, sir," the woman barked. Then, mercifully, both sets of boots headed back up the corridor.

Kit tweaked him through his trousers. "Missed your shot, Halfmask."

Before he could warn her, she wriggled past him, pushing out of the niche. Gyre took a few quick breaths and followed.

"What the plagued *fuck*—" he began.

"Oh, relax." Kit was still invisible, but he could *hear* the grin. "Just breaking the tension."

"You really are insane, aren't you?"

"I've been told that before. You're the one who wants to go to the Tomb." She flicked the firelighter, outlining herself in a brief shower of sparks. "You think we can get past them?"

Gyre ordered her to stay put and padded back up toward the junction, moving with the smooth silence of long practice. Well before he got there, he could see the light of more torches. Risking a peek around the last corner, he saw at least a half dozen shadowy figures, and one who gleamed in a rainbow of iridescent colors. *Legionary.* There was something insectoid about the faceless unmetal armor. The man—or woman; there was no way to tell—carried a short sword on their hip and a blaster rifle slung over their shoulder. Gyre swore silently and eased back down the corridor.

Kit was where he'd left her, for a wonder. She answered his quiet call with a flick of the firelighter.

"They're still at the junction. Auxies and a Legionary," he said. "We're not going to get past them. We'll have to wait."

"So we wait." Kit sighed. That prospect seemed to disturb her more than the idea of fighting their way out. "Until they get tired and go home."

"Or decide to come double-check."

He heard the rasp as she slid down the rock wall. "And not even anything to read in the meantime."

"We could—"

"Very funny," she snapped.

Gyre sat down beside her, his back to the wall. "You're not good at waiting, are you?"

"Nope." He heard the firelighter clicking, open and closed. "Clock's ticking, you know?"

"What clock?"

"You know. The clock."

"On life, you mean?" Gyre shrugged. "Given your line of work, is getting old really something that worries you?"

"You have to plan for the best case, right?" She flicked the firelighter again.

"How old *are* you, anyway?"

"Nineteen." She cocked her head by the light of the sparks. "Maybe twenty by now? I haven't been keeping track."

There was a long silence. Gyre stared into the darkness, the firelighter's sparks dying away. He went to scratch his scar, was blocked by the mask, and shifted uncomfortably.

"Tell me a story, then," Kit said.

"A story?"

"Something about your life."

"I'll make you a deal," Gyre said. "A story for a story."

"I suppose that's fair." Cloth shuffled as Kit stretched. "You want me to go first?"

"If you don't mind."

"What do you want to hear about?" She paused. "Not the Tomb. Not until we're finished."

Gyre made a face. *I suppose that was inevitable.* "Did you really know the . . . other Doomseeker? Where did you get the name?"

She grunted as though he'd struck her. "Suppose I should have expected that."

"If you don't want to trade—"

"It's fine." She paused. "It's just a little hard to look back, sometimes."

"It can't have been *that* long ago."

"I was fifteen, maybe." She shifted against the rock. "I got . . . some bad news. I was living in Grace at the time, and I marched down to the tavern and signed up with the scariest scavenger expedition I could find. The real madmen, who go out way past where anyone else has gone, hoping for a big score. A virgin tunnel, or a piece of skyship. There were eight of us when we left. Three came back."

She was quiet a moment. "There was a boy I liked. Not even a scavenger; he just kept the thickheads from running loose. I don't think he knew how dangerous the run was. Stupid, pretty boy. I let him crawl into my bedroll, and a week later a plaguespawn the size of a cart peeled his face off."

"I'm sorry," Gyre said quietly.

"Wasn't my fault," Kit said. "But it felt like it. We got out with a decent haul, and I blew the whole thing on drink and whores in about a week. Then I went back out with another team. Down into the tunnels under Crackskull Peak. Came back with four busted ribs and a broken arm, plus a new blaster. Waited until it healed, then went out again. You get the idea.

"After a while I guess I was kind of a legend." She gave a short laugh.

"They were calling me Doomseeker, and I didn't mind. Bought me a lot of drinks. You'd think they wouldn't want me on their crews. Every run I went on went bad, one way or another. I kept waiting for my luck to run out."

"Why?" Gyre said.

"That's another story. You only get one." He could hear her grinning again. "About a year after this started, I was in one of my drinking and fucking phases, and a guy comes to see me. Old guy, which is rare enough, because there aren't that many old scavengers. He sits down and tells me that he's heard I was using his name. Doomseeker."

"Really?" Gyre leaned forward. "The original?"

"No idea. But going by the way old-timers treated him, he could have been. I was a little drunk, so I told him if he wanted to fight, we could fight. He said that wasn't how he preferred to handle things. He just wanted to make sure I was *worthy*. I tell you, I almost shot him just for saying that. But he pulled out a deck of cards and sat down.

"I mostly gambled as another way to lose money as quickly as possible. We played a few rounds, back and forth, up and down. I'm just throwing in whatever I can, and he's starting to look disappointed. I finally get a really good draw, and I throw everything I have in the pot, and he looks at me real quiet and says, 'I bet my life.'

"'What the fuck does that mean?' I ask him.

"'If you win, you can take me out back and shoot me. If I win, I can do the same to you. Real stakes.' And he leans forward, and I get the feeling this is what he wanted from the start."

"You called?" Gyre said.

"Of course I called." Kit snorted. "I'd been betting my life every time I went down into the tunnels. What's one more time? But he starts flipping up the last draw, one card at a time, and none of them help me. When he gets to the last one, he asks me if I want to keep going. I look him in the eye and tell him I do. He grins at me.

"And then he gets up and walks away. Leaves a whole stack of thalers on the table." She flicked the firelighter again, another cloud of sparks shimmering in the darkness. "I looked at his cards. He had me cold. I guess he found out what he wanted to know."

"Did you ever see him again?"

Kit nodded in the dying light. "I tracked him down, obviously. Told him if he'd folded, then he owed me his life. He thought that was funny. But he taught me . . . a few things." She shook her head as the last of the sparks died. "That's another story, too."

"Is he still alive?"

"As far as I know," Kit said. "But now it's my turn."

"What do you want to know?"

"The obvious," she said. When he didn't answer for a moment, she heaved a sigh. "What happened to your eye, idiot."

"My eye?" Gyre's scar itched under the mask. "What about it?"

"I saw you at the Smoking Wreckage, remember? You don't have to play dumb."

"Right." He tapped one finger on the blank silver eye just above his empty socket. "Okay."

"Well?"

He cleared his throat. "I was eight years old. My parents were vulpi farmers—"

"If it turns out you lost it in a farming accident or something, I get another story."

"Relax," Gyre said with a slight smile. It quickly faded as the memory played itself out in his mind. "My sister was five. Maya. She was fearless, smart. You would have liked her. But she was always getting sick, and doctors were no help."

"Did she die?"

"For someone who wanted a story, you're not a very good listener."

"I told you," Kit said. "Clock's ticking. Get on with it."

"One day in the summer, a centarch turned up at our door. His name was Va'aht Thousandcuts, and he told my parents he was here to take Maya away to the Order. She was getting sick because she had the potential to be a centarch herself."

"I've never heard of that."

"Me either. But who were we to talk back to the Twilight Order? My parents were just going to let him take her, but I didn't want to. So when Va'aht wasn't looking, I jammed my knife in his leg. I thought I might be able to grab Maya and run, I guess."

"I take it it didn't work."

"Of course not. My parents were screaming, but Va'aht wouldn't listen. He took my eye as punishment." The scar gave a dull throb. "Then he took my sister, too. I never saw her again."

There was another pause.

"You hate them, don't you?" Kit asked after a while.

"I hate them," Gyre said. His voice was surprisingly calm.

"So that's why you work with Yora? To hurt the Order?"

"It's...more than that." Gyre drew his knees against his chest. "I hurt them, but it's not enough. It's not just about *me*. The Order is..." He shook his head in the darkness. This was the part that he had a hard time expressing. "They're the *past*. The Chosen ruled over humanity for who knows how many centuries, and then when they were dying they built this *thing* to keep us on the path they wanted."

"The Order defends the Republic against plaguespawn and *dhakim*," Kit said mildly.

"Because they're the ones with the power," Gyre said. "They decide what's sanctioned arcana and what's *dhak*. They tell us what power we're allowed to have. And just coincidentally, anything that might be able to challenge them, to do *without* them, isn't allowed." He swallowed. "Maybe we needed them once, after the war and the Plague. But now..."

"So you want to go to the Tomb," Kit said.

"The ghouls challenged the Chosen," Gyre said. "If there's anything left in the world that can stand up to the Order, that's where it'll be."

He shifted awkwardly. He hadn't meant to be so honest, to tip his hand. But he felt like, of all the people he'd talked to, Kit might truly understand. *Something drove* her *there, didn't it?*

"I worry," Kit said, "that you're going to be disappointed."

"I don't care," Gyre said. "I have to get there. I have to try."

"So you can rescue your sister?"

"I'm not stupid," Gyre muttered. "If the Order saved her, then she's been living with them since she was five years old. They've had plenty of time to get their hooks into her. By now I'm sure she's as bad as Va'aht." He took a deep breath. "Nothing's going to fix my family. I just don't want them to break anyone else's."

There was another long pause, then a shuffling of cloth. After a moment, Gyre felt Kit's hand, her fingers twining through his. She gave him a comforting squeeze.

"It's a good story," she said. Once again, she was close enough that her breath tickled his cheek.

"Sorry," Gyre said. "I didn't mean to—"

"Tell the truth?"

He smiled faintly. "Something like that."

"It's not something you should regret." She pulled away. "I'm going to check if those sentries are still waiting for us."

Gyre nodded, pointlessly. Kit's footsteps padded away, vanishing quickly into the shadows and stillness.

It felt like an eternity before they left the tunnels.

Kit had come back to report that the Legionary was still in place, so they settled in for another round of waiting. This time, she'd volunteered a story about traveling with a scavenger band who'd had their mounts and packs stolen, which turned extremely bawdy very quickly. Gyre was laughing by the time she narrated her triumphant return to town, naked but swaggering, her embarrassed companions scuttling along in her wake.

"Is *any* of that true?" he said when she was finished.

"Some of it. Probably," Kit said. "The good parts."

Topping that would have been difficult, but fortunately they were interrupted by the sound of the Auxies moving out in a storm of shouted orders and recriminations. They waited a few minutes after silence fell, then crept along quietly just in case someone was playing games with them. But the soldiers had really gone. *They must not like sitting around these tunnels any more than we do.*

"Chalk one up for plan B," he muttered to himself as they climbed out of the depths.

"Hmm?" Kit said, leaning on his shoulder from behind.

"Nothing." He shook his head. "Hopefully Yora found a way out, too."

"Hopefully," Kit agreed, but there was a flat sound to the word that Gyre didn't like. "What now?"

"We should stay together until we hear something," Gyre said. "Unless things have gone *very* wrong, we should be safe at my place."

"Oooh." She leaned closer. "Does this mean you trust me now?"

"I'm fairly sure you're not working for Raskos, at least."

"Do I get to know your real name?"

"It's Gyre," Gyre said after a moment's hesitation.

"Gyre." Kit grinned mischievously. "And where do you live, Gyre?"

He took her, back out through the noisome tunnel-slums, past the more respectable district close to the entrance, and finally into the open air via the trapdoor in the old stable. When they reached Lynnia's, Gyre made Kit wait while he circled the building, trying to spot any lookouts. When he was satisfied, they went in through the basement door.

The alchemist was waiting, as Gyre had expected. She spun in her swivel chair to face him as he came in, then froze at the sight of Kit behind him.

"Sorry," Gyre said. "I couldn't think of a good way to warn you."

"Warn me?" Lynnia crossed her arms. "Where the plaguing *fuck* have you been? Nobody knew anything!"

"You heard about the ambush?" Gyre said.

She nodded sourly. "I knew they'd find that place eventually."

"Your back door worked nicely," Gyre said. "But we got stuck hiding in the tunnels when the Auxies came after us. It took this long to get away from them."

"And what is she doing here?" Lynnia turned to Kit. "I assume this is your mysterious benefactor."

"Kitsraea Doomseeker," Kit said with a slight bow. "By your temper, I'm guessing you're Lynnia Sharptongue?"

"Ooooh," the old woman said with a dangerous smile. "Gyre's been telling stories, has he?"

"I have not," Gyre snapped. "And, yes. I thought it would be safer for Kit here until we figure out what tipped off the dux." He hesitated. "Have you heard anything from Yora?"

"Got a note an hour ago," Lynnia admitted. "She and most of the others got away clean. She says the plan is still on schedule."

"That's something," Gyre said.

Kit's expression had gone thoughtful. "I need to send some messages."

Lynnia sniffed. "I imagine you'll also be wanting a bath and a change of clothes."

"And something to eat," Kit said brightly.

The alchemist snorted. "Of course. Be my guest. Since you apparently are." She glanced at Gyre. "Will she be needing the spare bedroom?"

"Yes," Kit said, one eyebrow raised. "For the moment."

"Right." Lynnia shoved the chair back and stood. "Come on, then."

She clomped up the stairs, with Kit just behind her. Gyre rolled his eye, said a silent prayer for safety, and followed.

Chapter 11

The sun also rose late in mountain-shrouded Deepfire, which under
the circumstances was probably for the best. Maya opened her eyes
and groaned.

She lay on the big bed but had apparently twisted sideways during
the night, drawing the sheets around her like a cocoon. The sun coming
in through the bedroom windows felt too bright, even through a layer
of thin curtain, and her throat felt like she'd swallowed a plaguespawn.
After a few seconds frantically fighting her way free of her silken binding, she wormed off the bed and stumbled to the bathroom, halting in
front of the sink as the first wave of the headache hit.

Chosen defend. She closed her eyes, one hand on the Thing, and
focused on breathing. *Ow, ow, ow.*

Eventually, the pain subsided to the point where she could fill a
pitcher with cold water, and she guzzled it greedily. She washed her
face, wincing at the icy cold. It seemed to help, a little.

That was . . . not a good night. For more than one reason. Maya went
back into the bedroom. The letter to Raskos, carefully unfolded and

smoothed, was wedged under her pillow. She'd jammed it there, head swimming, in the hopes that it would be easier to understand in the morning. Now, head pounding, she pulled it out again. The script was awkward, with many corrections where Raskos had made mistakes with the cipher, but the results were at least legible:

Cipher 17568.13
To: Dux Raskos of Deepfire
From: Kyriliarch Nicomidi Thunderclap

Received your last. I grow tired of your delays, and your transparent excuses. You will deliver the Core Analytica as agreed. If you prevaricate further, my agathios, from whose hand you are receiving this, will be given instructions to begin an investigation in Deepfire that will no doubt prove to be very enlightening for the Council. For your sake, I suggest you expedite matters.

Reading it again did not help with her headache, or the churn in her stomach. *What am I supposed to do with this?*

I should tell Beq. Beq, at least, might have some idea what a "Core Analytica" was. Maya remembered the state she'd left Beq in, and winced. *In fact, I should check on her anyway.*

In the sitting room, the servants had left her a silver tray laden with bread, butter, slices of summerfruit, and hard-boiled eggs. There was also a paper-wrapped tablet of quickheal, set neatly on its own china saucer. Maya hesitated before picking it up. Jaedia had always taught her to be frugal with sanctioned arcana—you never knew when you'd be able to resupply, and so using them for anything less than an emergency was a waste. *A hangover probably doesn't count as an emergency.* On the other hand, her own supply was safe in her pack, and their host was the dux himself. *I'm sure he can afford it.*

The waxy, mint-tasting stuff dissolved as she chewed it, and Maya gave a sigh as she felt wonderful numbness spreading back from her throat. In a few moments, her headache had been reduced to a manageable level, and she was able to properly address the food. When it was gone, she felt considerably better. She dressed—she had no option but to put her traveling clothes back on, sweat stains and all—and folded the letter into her pocket. With her haken on her hip, she ventured out into the corridor.

She crossed the hall and knocked on Beq's door. There was a distant *thump* and the sound of running feet. The door finally opened, revealing Beq in one of the palace's silk dressing gowns, her green hair piled inelegantly atop her head, frantically adjusting her spectacles.

"Sorry," Maya said. "I hope I didn't wake you."

Beq shook her head frantically. "No, I've been up. I was getting some reading in."

"Reading?"

"There's quite a nice little library in the sitting room, did you see? I found a history of Deepfire; it's fascinating."

"Oh." Maya hesitated. "I just wanted to see if you were okay."

"Fine!" Beq clicked a dial on her spectacles, and a lens flipped over. "Feeling remarkably good, actually."

"That's . . . good." Maya waited a heartbeat, then shrugged. "Well. If you're okay—"

"It's not—I mean—" Beq shook her head, then stepped out of the doorway. "Do you want to come in?"

"If I'm not interrupting your reading."

Beq gestured Maya to one of the chairs and took the one opposite, pulling her feet up to perch on the edge.

"About . . . last night," Beq said, pushing her spectacles up her nose. "I drank too much. Obviously. I'm sorry."

"It's all right," Maya said. "I think everyone was . . . relaxed."

"I mean I'm sorry you had to take care of me." Beq looked down at her hands. "You seemed like you were enjoying yourself, and then I dragged you away."

"Look, it's *all right*," Maya said. "Honestly."

"But—" At Maya's warning glare, Beq subsided. "Okay. I'm also sorry if I said anything...stupid. You can probably ignore it. I don't have a lot of experience being drunk."

"I gathered that." Truth be told, Maya didn't either; she'd had her share of wine and beer at village festivals, but always under Jaedia's watchful eye. "I don't remember anything too embarrassing."

"That's good," Beq said, looking genuinely relieved. "I'm...I'll be more careful next time."

"And you really feel okay?"

"More or less?" she said. "A little stiff, maybe, but that could be the bed. It's too soft for me."

Some people, Maya thought, rubbing her own still-throbbing head. *Oh well.*

"Listen," Maya said. "I...found something, last night."

"What kind of thing?"

"Something I wasn't supposed to see." Maya's hand tightened on the letter in her pocket. *Here goes nothing.* "I think it's the letter Tanax brought for Raskos."

Beq blinked, and there was a long silence.

"How?" she said after a moment. "It should have been ciphered."

Maya let out a breath. *At least she's not turning me in to Tanax yet.* "Raskos copied out the plaintext. He thought he'd burned it afterward, but he didn't manage to, and I...picked it up."

"That's careless of him." Beq's eyes were bright with curiosity, and Maya relaxed a little further. "Let's see it, then."

Maya unfolded the letter and handed it over, and explained the conversation she'd heard along with it, about the assault on the rebels. Beq frowned, peering closer at the letter.

"It explains what we're doing here, anyway," Maya concluded. "And why Raskos wasn't pleased to see us. We're not here to help him, we're here as a *threat*, or at least Tanax is."

"But that doesn't make sense," Beq said. "Nicomidi is a Kyriliarch. If he wanted something from Raskos..."

"He could order him to hand it over, right?"

"Not...exactly," Beq said, thoughtfully. "It's all a little vague. *Technically*, as a dux, Raskos serves the Republic and the Senate, not the Order. Most of the time, Republic officials will obey the Council as a courtesy, but if Nicomidi really wanted to give an *official* order to Raskos, he'd have to go through the Republic bureaucracy."

Something clicked in Maya's mind, and she felt a chill. "And if he did that, it would be impossible to keep secret. Doing it like this, with a threat, only makes sense if he doesn't want anyone to find out about it."

Beq stared down at the letter with a new tension, as though it were a snake. "You think he's hiding something from the rest of the Council?"

"If he isn't, why would a Council investigation be such a threat?" Maya took the letter back and read it over again. "Have you ever heard of a 'Core Analytica'?"

"Not exactly," Beq said. "Analytica are a kind of ghoul arcana; I know that much. They're associated with some of their larger creations, but nobody really knows what they're for. I know they're supposed to be very rare, though."

Rare, and therefore valuable. Though it couldn't be as simple as that, not for Nicomidi to go to all this trouble.

"Why would Nicomidi want to keep this secret?" Beq said. "He's with the Dogmatics, isn't he? If they knew Raskos was up to something illegal, they ought to be ready to expose him on the spot."

"The only thing I can think of is that he'll get some kind of advantage from it on the Council," Maya said. "My master, Jaedia, works with the Pragmatics. Before I came on this mission, she told me that the Dogmatics might try to do something to sabotage it. Maybe this has something to do with it."

"*My* master told me that arcanists have to stay away from any kind of faction conflict," Beq said unhappily. "Leave that to the centarchs, he said. They can afford to waste their time with nonsense; the rest of us have work to do."

"Sorry," Maya said, suddenly uncomfortable. "I had to talk to someone about this. I didn't think about the position it might put you in—"

"No!" Beq squeaked. "No, I didn't mean—it's fine. I'm glad you... you trust me." She hesitated a moment, then said, "So what are you going to do?"

"I can't tell Tanax," Maya said. "Nicomidi's his master."

"He didn't know what was in the letter," Beq said.

"He'd just say that Nicomidi and the Council have their reasons, and report me for even looking at this," Maya said. "When we get back to the Forge, I can take it to Jaedia and Baselanthus, and they'll know what to do."

"What happened to the original ciphered letter?"

Maya shook her head. "I left it on the table. I figured Raskos would come back for it."

Beq bit her lip. "Without that, this isn't exactly evidence. It could have been written by anyone."

"*Dhak,*" Maya swore. She took a deep breath. "All right. So we need to figure out what's going on, *and* find some kind of proof to take to the Council."

"Or you could just burn the thing and forget you saw it," Beq said quietly. "It's an option."

"I can't," Maya said. "Jaedia warned me that the Dogmatics were up to *something*, and this has to be it. It's something they were going to use to try to hurt her, and I can't let that happen. If I can get evidence of what they're trying, then she can show it to the Council and defend herself." Maya looked down at the letter again, then shoved it in her pocket. "Thank you. I'll figure this out. I don't want to get you any more involved than you already are."

"I—" Beq bit the word off and went silent. Maya cocked her head. "What's wrong?"

"I don't mind... being involved." She took a deep breath, and the words came out in a rush. "I'm supposed to be supporting you, and I know I might not be much good, but I *did* help you fight those smugglers, but if you think I'd slow you down I can—"

"Stop." Maya held up a hand. "You're sure? You might get in trouble, you know."

Beq smiled weakly and shrugged. "I've gotten in trouble before."

"Okay." Maya grinned back, heart beating a little faster at the spark in Beq's eyes. "So what are *we* going to do?"

"We could try to track down this Core Analytica for ourselves," Beq said thoughtfully. "That would lead us to whatever Raskos wants to hide so badly."

"That would mean getting out of the palace," Maya said. "If a scavenger found this thing, someone must know something."

Beq nodded. "We should talk to Varo."

"You think we can trust him?"

She nodded. "He won't go running to Tanax, anyway. And if we're going outside, we'll need his help."

"You're right," Maya said. If anyone could get them outside without being noticed, it was the scout. "So let's talk to him."

"Now? I mean, I guess now." Beq looked down at her robe. "Give me a minute."

She retreated to her bedroom, emerging in her stained travel clothes, hair fraying from its bun. Varo's suite was just beyond Beq's. Maya threw a quick glance at Tanax's door, but it remained closed.

She knocked, and then knocked again, louder. Eventually it was answered, but not by Varo. A tall young man with long silver hair and a delicate goatee, wearing a loose silk dressing gown, looked Maya up and down and then gave a shallow bow. After a moment, Varo appeared behind him.

"Good morning, Agathios," Varo said, yawning. "Do you need something?"

"I just…wanted to ask you something," Maya said, feeling her cheeks flush slightly. "Do you have a minute?"

"Of course." Varo touched his guest's arm, and the man bent close.

They exchanged a few whispers, followed by a kiss that went on long enough that Maya's blush deepened. The young man left, and Varo gestured Maya and Beq inside. His breakfast was on the table, half-eaten, and he sat down with a sigh, sprawling bonelessly in the chair.

"You seem to have had a relaxing night," Maya said carefully.

"The comforts of civilization," Varo said. "In the scouts we learn to enjoy them while we have the chance. My friend, for example—"

"Can I ask you something?" Maya interrupted, not ready to deal with another gruesome anecdote. "Purely hypothetically."

"Oh?" Varo raised an eyebrow and took a slice of summerfruit from the tray. "Go ahead."

"If someone wanted to sneak out of the Spike, how would they do it?"

"What sort of someone?"

Maya hesitated. "Someone like me and Beq, say."

"Ah. *That* sort of hypothetical." Varo popped the fruit into his mouth and chewed thoughtfully.

"You don't have to answer," Maya said. "If you're not comfortable—"

"*Hypothetically,*" Varo broke in, "it doesn't seem like it would be very difficult. Security in this part of the palace is fairly lax, except around Raskos personally, and there's a lot of staff that no one really pays attention to. If you got your hands on a couple of servants' uniforms, I imagine you could walk right out the front door."

"If we're speaking hypothetically," Beq put in, "I might know where there's a laundry."

"What are you going to do about Tanax?" Varo said. "I assume, in this hypothetical, he's not supposed to know you're gone."

"I was hoping you might help with that," Maya said. "If we tell him Beq and I are sick after last night, and staying in our rooms, you might volunteer to check up on us."

"I might." Varo looked between Maya and Beq. "Do I get to know what this is about?"

"It's probably best if you don't," Maya said. "Not that I don't trust

you, but I don't want you to get in any more trouble than you already
might if Tanax catches on. Just tell him we lied to you about it."

Varo pursed his lips and nodded. "Well then. Hypothetically, that
sounds like a plan."

"Okay. What if I told you this wasn't hypothetical after all?"

"*What?*" Varo grinned. "I'm shocked."

It seemed like ages before Tanax knocked at Maya's door. She waited,
counting off the seconds, and then just as he knocked again she said,
"Hello?"

"Maya?" he said. "The dux has sent us another invitation. He wants
us to attend a review of his forces this afternoon, and then tonight
there's a dinner with a few distinguished guests."

"Oh," Maya said. "I'm very sorry to report that Arcanist Bequaria
and I are ... feeling poorly."

"What do you mean?" Tanax said.

"I think we may have ... overindulged last night. Neither of us is as
familiar with this sort of event."

"I see." Maya could hear the smug edge in his voice. "You're certain
it's nothing more serious?"

"Quite certain," Maya said. "I think you should go to the review,
while we rest for a while."

"The dux might be insulted," Tanax said.

"I think he'll be more insulted if I throw up in his lap," Maya said
bluntly.

Tanax paused at that. "I suppose," he said gruffly, "that it can't be
helped. This sort of society *is* new for you, after all."

"Indeed."

"I'll ask the dux to have a few servants check on you—"

"No need for that," Maya said. "Varo has already volunteered. That
way we can ... avoid embarrassment."

"Good thinking," Tanax said. "I will make your excuses to the dux, then. Perhaps by evening you'll be feeling better."

"Hopefully," Maya said. "My apologies, again."

She stood quietly for a while, listening to Tanax's booted footsteps retreating down the hall. When they became inaudible, Maya cautiously opened her door and found Varo and Beq doing the same across the hall.

"I can't believe that worked," Beq said.

"I can," Maya said. "Of *course* the country bumpkin agathios got herself sick with drink the first chance she got at civilized company. It's exactly what he wants to think of me."

"We should move quickly, though," Varo said. "I want to be in position to deflect him when he comes back."

Beq led them to the laundry, a floor down from their rooms. Maya had to fight a smile as the arcanist skulked suspiciously down the corridor, trying to look in all directions at once like the most stereotypical burglar imaginable, while she and Varo strolled casually behind her. Fortunately for all concerned, the place was unoccupied, with big hampers of things to be washed lined up against one wall opposite vats of soapy water. A few minutes' search produced servants' uniforms in approximately the right sizes that weren't too dirty to wear, and they grabbed a few and hurried back upstairs.

"This feels strange," Beq said, turning back and forth in front of the mirror in the bedroom. "Have I got it on right?"

Palace uniform for common servants was a long, dark skirt and undertunic with a white blouse and cap. It was plain enough that Maya hoped they wouldn't stand out once they got into the city proper. She gestured, and Beq spun in a circle.

"Pull your socks up," Maya said. "They don't look quite right, but that'll be closer." They hadn't found any footwear in the laundry, so they were stuck with their own boots. "I'll change; give me a minute."

Beq knelt to tug at her socks, inadvertently exposing quite a lot of well-toned leg in the process. Maya averted her eyes and went into the bathroom, hurriedly putting on her borrowed uniform. Her panoply belt fit snugly underneath, silver mesh pressed against the skin of her midsection, and a strap held her haken against the small of her back. The fit was a little tighter than she would have liked, but she didn't think the weapon's bulge was too obvious.

The most dangerous part was leaving their own rooms. Maya opened the door a crack and made sure the hallway was empty before she stepped outside.

"Try not to *look* like you're sneaking around," she told Beq. "Remember, as far as anyone knows, we belong here."

"Right," Beq said, swallowing hard. "I can do this."

Maya led the way to the nearest corner at a brisk walk, turned at random, and hurried through another couple of hallways before slowing. She gave a casual nod to a pair of footmen as they passed, and as she'd hoped they paid her no attention whatsoever. After a few wrong turns, Maya found a staircase that led to the ground floor, and from there she and Beq could thread their way through the other servants to a door opening onto a gravel drive.

The Spike must have a grand entrance, Maya guessed, but this wasn't it. Several doors opened onto a broad turnaround, liberally dotted with loadbird droppings, and teams of men were unloading wagons and hauling the crates and sacks inside. To Maya's relief, there were a few smaller carriages labeled as cabs. She went up to one of these and found the driver resting with his hat tipped down over his eyes, his loadbird pecking irritably at the gravel.

"Excuse me," Maya said. "How much for a ride into town?"

"Depends where you're going," the driver said, without raising his hat. "One thaler thirty to the West Central."

"I don't...exactly know where I'm going," Maya said, improvising. "Truth be told, I'm new to the city. But my grandmother is ill, and now that I've got an evening off I wanted to see if I could find something that could help her. Do you...have any idea where I might—"

"Tunnel market," the driver said, still not sitting up. "Two thalers ten."

"Oh," Maya said, deflating. The only kind of help a common servant could afford to buy would be *dhak* medicine, so she'd expected a little more reticence. *Maybe he didn't understand me.* "Well, we'd like to go there, then."

"All right." The man pushed his hat up, revealing a craggy, weathered face, and smiled. "Get in."

"So why the sick grandmother story?" Beq said quietly as the carriage rattled along.

"If anyone's going to know anything about the Core Analytica, it's going to be scavengers and *dhak* merchants," Maya said, equally quietly. "I figured this would get us to the right neighborhood, and then we could ask about it." She fingered a leather pouch in her pocket. "Baselanthus gave us plenty of travel money, so we can spread some coins around. That generally makes people friendly."

"Good thinking," Beq said. She shook her head. "I'm hopeless at this stuff. Is this how your master taught you to get information?"

"More or less," Maya said. She didn't add that Jaedia had mostly demonstrated the technique in small towns and villages, and that here Maya was largely making things up as she went along. *Beq's nervous enough as it is.*

Beq, suddenly, was not paying attention. She peered out one window, motioning frantically to Maya. Curious, Maya slid over and looked out, but it took a moment before she understood what she was seeing.

She'd known the palace was called the Spike, but until now she hadn't seen it from the outside. It rose into the air, a spire of dark unmetal, so thin and featureless it was hard to guess at its scale. Only by tracking upward from the base, where merely human architecture gathered around it, did it become obvious that the tip of the spire had to be hundreds of meters in the air. The more mundane palace had accreted around this Elder thing, like barnacles clinging to a wave-battered rock.

"One of the best-preserved and latest examples of Chosen architecture, obviously," Beq said, rapidly dialing through the lenses on her spectacles. "Though the haste of its construction makes it less interesting *artistically*, it's a fascinating study in Chosen methodology under pressure—"

"Why?" Maya asked.

"Why what?" Beq said.

"Why build something like that?" Maya said. "What's it for?"

"It went up at the same time as the Gate here," the arcanist said excitedly, "but obviously the spire isn't necessary just to connect to the Gate network. There's a theory that it's tied somehow to the weapon that made the crater, or else that it's some kind of *sensor* they used during the first purges of what was left of the ghouls. But—"

"We don't know," Maya translated.

The reference point of the Spike made it easy to trace their path around the city. The carriage swung south and west, clear of the sullen glow of the Pit—disappointing Beq, who'd hoped for a better look—and trundled through street after street of square, solid-looking brick buildings. To the north, long rows of smokestacks belched black columns into the pale blue sky.

As they continued west, the mountain above them loomed larger and larger, a slab-sided cliff dwarfing the human construction at its base. Just when it seemed they couldn't go any farther without running into a wall of rock, the road took on a downward slope, passing under a broad stone archway and merging seamlessly into a wide, high-ceilinged tunnel. Maya caught sight of a line of Auxiliaries guarding the arch, but they seemed to be checking traffic only in one direction, from the tunnel into the city, and ignored the cab. The light took on the blue tinge of glowstones, alternating with the flicker of torches and bonfires, and the buildings grew more colorful and haphazard.

"These are real ghoul tunnels." Beq was glued to the window again. "The whole mountain is riddled with them."

"And people *live* down here?" Maya said. Having spent so much of her life in the open, she found it hard to imagine. "Why?"

"You have to be a Republic citizen to live on the surface, or else have a permit, I think," Beq said. "Everything belowground is technically across the border."

Maya felt something twist in her stomach. She'd never left the Republic before, and her first impression of the world outside it was not a happy one. Once her eyes had adjusted to the dimmer light of the underground, she'd started taking in the people, who milled on either side of the street in a steady stream. Most of them were as pale as mushrooms, even their hair white or gray, hunched over as though holding up their heads was too much effort. Men and women in workmen's coveralls moved in large groups, some filthy from a shift just finished at a manufactory, others heading in to replace them.

In and among the workers were the beggars, who were so numerous they'd claimed the entire strip of ground in front of the buildings on either side. A few stood, hurrying up to likely prospects, but most simply sat in sullen silence, a bowl or a hat placed in front of them to catch a few centithalers. They were filthy, and some so horrifyingly thin that their bones stood out from their skin in sharp relief.

Maya had always thought she'd seen poverty. She and Jaedia had spent much of their time in villages where owning more than one metal pot was considered a sign of wealth, or towns where one failed harvest might mean disaster. Places like Bastion had their slums, where the poorest citizens were packed cheek by jowl into tiny apartments and the human waste overwhelmed their rudimentary sanitation. But *this* was something else entirely.

"This is as far as I can take you," the driver called back. "No carriages from here on in. But the market's just another block up—see the colored tents? Walk that way and you'll find what you're looking for."

"Thank you," Maya said, tearing her eyes away from the press of humanity.

She got down from the carriage and handed the man three thaler notes. Beq alighted beside her, and the cabbie whistled to his bird, which somehow managed to get turned around in spite of the crowd. They were in a sort of square, a junction of two tunnels crowded with small booths hawking food or liquor. Beq shuffled in close to Maya's side, nervously, and Maya bent to whisper in her ear.

"You all right?"

"It's just . . . a lot of people." Beq took a deep breath. "I'll be okay."

At least no one seemed to be paying them special attention. Maya started moving in the direction the cabbie had indicated and immediately found she could only make progress by shoving. The locals didn't seem to mind this, and before long she abandoned any pretense at dignity and simply bumped and elbowed her way through the press, checking over her shoulder to make sure Beq stayed with her.

The colored tents the cabbie had mentioned quickly came into sight. They were wedges of tattered cloth that fluttered gaily, like flags, marking the positions of various merchants. Men and women sat on a spread carpet, their wares laid out in front of them, while the crowd milled around and shouted questions.

Maya had seen a similar scene at town fairs across the Republic, but as they neared the first of the sellers she did a double take at the items on display. There were bits of unmetal, crystalline devices both shattered and intact, small globes that pulsed with weird, organic veins, and packets of mysterious powders. *Dhak*, in other words, a carpet full of *dhak*, dangerous relics from the Elder world. In the Republic, any one of the items on display would have been enough to justify arrest by the Auxiliaries. Here, it was just one merchant's wares among many.

Maya had heard that *dhak* was traded openly in the Splinter Kingdoms—Grace was a notorious hub and base for smugglers— but she hadn't expected to find a market for it *here*, on the doorstep of a Republic outpost. She'd been thinking in terms of a back-alley exchange, not a bazaar. *No wonder the cabbie didn't bat an eye when I asked him.*

"Look!" Beq said. "That's a piece of a linear motivator. And I think that one is a lightning conduit, but someone has bent it the wrong way round. And—"

"There's so much of it," Maya muttered.

"Even after four hundred years, this area is one of the richest scavenger sites around," Beq said. "Especially for ghoul arcana, but there's plenty of Chosen relics, too."

"Isn't Raskos supposed to put a stop to all this?"

"We're outside his jurisdiction," Beq said. "I suppose he just has to keep watch at the border." She cocked her head. "My master back at the Forge told me that most of the components we use come from Deep-fire. I didn't understand why until now."

Of course. The Order needed scavenged components so its arcanists could maintain the weapons and armor of the Legions and create sanctioned arcana. *I suppose it has to come from* somewhere. Still, the sight of the bustling market left Maya feeling shaken. *If Tanax were here, he'd pull out his haken right now and try to detain everyone.*

She touched the Thing, feeling its hard, familiar shape, and let out a breath. *Stay on task. We need to find out if anyone knows anything about the Core Analytica.* Her initial plan of just asking around seemed hopelessly naïve now. *But someone must know something—*

"—found it up by Green Crag," the merchant was saying. "There's a skyship wreck there, though it's stripped pretty clean, and some tunnel entrances."

"This definitely isn't from a skyship," Beq said. "I think it's from a hexapod walker. Look, see how heavy the filament is? This had to move some serious weight. And the articulation is wrong for a crane-lift."

Maya blinked and looked down. Left on her own for a moment, Beq had bent to examine the wares on display more closely and apparently fallen naturally into conversation with the proprietor. That merchant, an older woman with silver hair coiled in tight dreadlocks and elaborate earrings, was looking up at the arcanist with a mixture of puzzlement and respect.

"You know your stuff," she said, grabbing another hunk of unmetal and crystal. "What about this? I've never been able to figure that out."

Beq laughed. "Now that one *is* from a skyship. I recognize the design."

"A weapon?" The merchant sounded eager. "Something to make it fly?"

"No, it's part of a toilet." Beq took the piece and turned it upside down. "See the tubes? This is a piece of a water filter."

The merchant looked disappointed for a moment, then grinned. "Keep that to yourself, hey? I still might be able to find a buyer."

"Of course," Beq said. She started and looked back as Maya touched her shoulder. "Oh. Sorry, were you asking me something? I got distracted—"

Maya raised her eyebrows suggestively, jerking her head toward the merchant. Beq frowned in incomprehension, and Maya sighed and took her arm, bending low so the seller could hear.

"My friend had a question for you," she said. "We're looking for something."

"What you see is what I have," the merchant said. "Come back next week; there's a few expeditions due in."

"Have you ever heard of something called a Core Analytica?" Maya said. She pulled a couple of thalers out of her pocket. "I'd be interested in any information you've got."

"A Core Analytica?" The woman frowned. "Just the name. But—" She held out her hand, and Maya handed her the money. "Gero Fork-tongue was talking about it. He'll be at his stall just up the street, the green tent. Pay him a visit; maybe he'll tell you what you need to know."

"Thank you very much."

"Thank *you*," the merchant said to Beq, with a broad smile. She stared down at the thing in her hands and laughed. "A piece of toilet, eh?"

*   *   *

That conversation started a pattern that began to feel very familiar over the next hour. Maya pushed from one stall to the next, with Beq in tow, then let the arcanist start talking shop. Not *every* merchant was as fascinated as Beq by arcana, but with quite a few she formed the instant bond of fellow enthusiasts, which let Maya cut in to ask about the Core Analytica.

"You're really good at this, you know?" Maya said as they left behind yet another vendor. "For someone who says they aren't good with people."

Beq's face was flushed. "I'm just... Talking about arcana is easy."

"Try it next time we're at a party."

"I doubt anyone would be interested."

"You never know."

Maya grinned. Her own skin was feeling a bit warm, partly from the press of the crowd but partly because the two of them had remained arm in arm for some time now. It was just to keep them from being pulled apart, of course, but she couldn't help but feel a thrill whenever Beq's hip bumped hers. *Focus, Maya, or you won't get anywhere.*

"Time for a break," she said, spotting a tavern sign on a building jutting between stalls. "Come on."

There wasn't much to the tavern, once they'd pushed their way inside. A bartender served up cheap clay mugs of wine and beer to patrons at a scattering of tables and chairs. Business was light this early in the day, which was a welcome respite from the crowds outside. Maya ordered two cups of watered wine, tossed down a couple of decithaler coins, and led Beq to the nearest table.

Beq looked down at the mug mistrustfully. "After last night, I'm not sure I'm up for more alcohol."

"Wine's safer than water if you don't know the water's clean," Maya said, sipping from her own cup. "That's what Jaedia taught me. And down here..."

"True." Beq took a drink and made a face. "Eugh."

"Honestly I just needed to get off my feet." Maya shook her head. "And maybe rethink our approach. I'm not sure we're getting anywhere."

"We've only covered about half the stalls," Beq said. "Give it time."

Maya grinned at the arcanist's transparent eagerness to finish examining what the market had to offer. She sipped again and scanned the crowd. Conversation filtered in from neighboring tables, mostly mundane, but a familiar pair of names focused her attention.

"—Yora and Halfmask got raided last night."

"A hundred Auxies, I heard."

"But they got away clean!"

"How do you know?"

"Don't be an idiot. If Rottentooth had caught them, you don't think he'd have told everyone by now?"

The rebels. Or just bandits, depending on whom you asked. *Are they tied to this, or—*

"Do you mind if I sit down?"

Maya blinked and looked around. A short, plump woman in a long coat stood by their table, waiting politely in front of an empty chair. Beq peered at her, twisting dials on the spectacles. The lenses clicked and shifted, and the woman leaned closer.

"Ooh, I've heard about these, but I've never seen one intact!" she said. "Is it true you can see in the dark?"

"A...a little bit," Beq said, unnerved. "One of the lenses has the same intensifier coating used on the Legionary masks, but it washes out most of the color—"

Maya cleared her throat. "I'm sorry, do we know you?"

"Oh! No, you don't. I'm Sarah." She gave a slight bow. "I've been looking for you."

"Can I ask why?" Maya said.

"Because I heard you were asking about the Core Analytica, and you were willing to pay for information. That's true, isn't it?" She smiled. "Word spreads fast in this place."

"It's true," Maya admitted. "And you have something?"

"No, but I know someone who does," Sarah said. "I can take you to him."

"For a price, I assume."

"Just a half thaler. And I'll knock off a decithaler if your friend will let me look at her spectacles."

Beq recoiled protectively. Maya said, "Half a thaler will be fine. Where are we going?"

"It's easier to show than to tell," Sarah said. "Come with me, if you're ready."

Maya looked at Beq, who gave a tiny shrug. *It's the best lead we've got so far.* She pushed her wine away and got up. "Then, let's go."

Sarah, judging by the expert way she elbowed a path through the crowd, was clearly a native of the tunnels, though she looked better-off than most. As they cut through the market, she chattered about the stalls, a running commentary of which Maya caught only snatches.

"...old Perses Ironjaw used to sell there, until he got caught in a blizzard, so now its Polarc. And this is Snipwillow; he loves those little flower-mushrooms you find in ghoul caves sometimes; you can use them—"

"Maya," Beq whispered. "I think someone's following us."

"Who?" Maya said.

"Not sure." Beq adjusted her spectacles and looked over her shoulder. "There's at least three of them, though."

Friends of Sarah's? Maya reached back to touch her haken, just to make sure it was easily accessible. *We'll see.*

Sarah turned down a side street and then went through an arch into a smaller tunnel. This one curved away from the market, branching into a number of other passages. Apart from a few sleeping forms huddled against the wall, these were almost empty of people. One archway was partially collapsed, half-blocked by a chunk of broken rock, and this was where Sarah stopped.

"Can you climb over this?" she said. "It opens up once we're past."

"It doesn't look like anyone lives down there," Maya said.

"It was abandoned after a cave-in," Sarah said. "Which makes it a good place to meet if you don't want to be seen."

Maya glanced behind them, but if there had been someone following, they'd stayed far enough back to be out of sight. She shrugged. "Lead the way, then."

Sarah nodded cheerfully and hoisted herself through the gap left by the fallen stone. Maya followed, with Beq bringing up the rear. As Sarah had promised, beyond that initial squeeze the tunnel opened out, with chunks of broken rock and debris scattered around a larger space, dark except where torchlight filtered in through the archway. Sarah got out a glowstone and shook it to life, beckoning them to follow.

"So who is this person we're going to meet?" Maya said, walking cautiously in the rubble-strewn street. Broken rock mixed with scraps of wood and other more human debris underfoot. "Another arcanist?"

"Funny thing about that," Sarah said. "It's actually me that wanted to talk to you. Although I *am* an arcanist." She hopped up on a large chunk of curved stone and turned to face them. On either side of the rock, another figure loomed out of the darkness, glowstone light gleaming blue on the point of a crossbow. "And I'm really sorry about this, but I'm the one who's going to be asking the questions."

"Look," Sarah said. "I really am sorry about this. If it helps, these two are just a precaution."

Sarah's "precaution" consisted of a wiry older woman and a bald-headed man, both armed with swords and crossbows. After Maya and Beq hadn't shown any sign of immediate resistance, they'd raised their weapons so they weren't exactly pointed *at* the pair, but weren't pointed away from them, either.

Maya thought she could get to her haken before they could shoot. She *might* be able to raise her panoply field in time. *But where does that leave Beq?* She bit her lip and waited.

"So here's the thing," Sarah said. "You've been asking around about the Core Analytica, and I would very much like to know why."

"We just heard a rumor, that's all," Maya said with a glance at Beq. "Seems like everyone's heard of it."

"Everyone's heard of it here because *I* have been asking around," Sarah said. "When two girls nobody's ever seen before started asking the same questions, some of my friends got in touch. So where did you hear this rumor?"

"Just . . . around," Maya said vaguely.

"Around." Sarah shook her head. "Can I tell you what I think?"

Maya eyed the crossbows. "I don't think I can stop you."

"I'm trying to think who might be interested in a rare ghoul arcana, and only one thing makes sense to me." Sarah sat up straighter and grinned. "You two are Order scouts, aren't you?"

Maya tried to school her features. "We'd hardly tell you if we were."

"Of course." Sarah spread her hands. "But it presents me with a bit of a dilemma. You see—"

She paused at the sound of metal scraping on rock from the direction they'd come in, frowning.

"Probably your friends," Beq put in. "The ones you had following us."

"I didn't have anyone following you," Sarah said, her brow furrowing. Then her eyes went wide, and she dove off the rock, at almost the same moment Maya threw herself against Beq.

They crashed to the rocky ground in a tangle, and Maya heard the *snap-hiss* of crossbow bolts passing overhead. Sarah's guards were both down, the woman clutching her throat, the man slumped over a piece of rubble with a pair of bolts in his chest. At the entrance to the tunnel, a half dozen bright lanterns came on, filling the space with crisscrossing beams.

Sarah, who'd dropped behind her boulder, emerged for a moment and hurled something in a high arc. It dropped among the advancing lights and exploded with a *crack* and a burst of thick smoke. More crossbows *twanged*, the bolts zipping past and ricocheting off the rocks with bright sparks. Maya pushed herself up, helped Beq to her feet, and ran for it, ducking behind the nearest boulder. They found themselves across from Sarah, hunkered down as another volley shredded the roiling clouds of smoke and clattered off the stones.

"*Not* friends of yours?" Beq said.

"Auxies," Sarah muttered. "No idea how they found me." She leaned out to look, then jerked back as a bolt sparked off the stone just beside her. "Listen, if you *are* Order, I don't suppose you could—"

Maya shook her head. *Not without pulling out my haken, anyway, and that's a last resort.* Revealing herself would put paid to any chance of getting the information they needed.

"Of course," Sarah said. "Well, in that case I'm open to suggestions."

Maya risked a peek around the boulder. A dozen helmeted Auxiliaries were working their way slowly forward. Reaching out to Sarah's dead guard, Maya grabbed his crossbow and fired into the air. The bolt caromed off the ceiling, the sound making all the Auxiliaries duck for cover. Maya ducked back as they returned fire.

"Is there a back way out of here?" Beq said.

"There is, but I don't think we can get there," Sarah said. "That little surprise was the only one I brought with me."

Inspiration struck, and Maya grinned. "Fortunately, my friend has a little surprise of her own." Beq gave her a quizzical look, and Maya waggled her eyebrows. "Get ready to run."

"What exactly do I have?" Beq whispered, when Maya bent close.

"Just throw something," Maya said. "I'll do the rest."

Understanding spread across Beq's face. She surreptitiously grabbed a chunk of rock, hefted it as though she'd pulled it from her pocket, and tensed. When Maya gave her the nod, she hurled it at the Auxiliaries.

A few crossbow bolts zipped past, but at the sight of something flying toward them, most of the Auxiliaries sensibly dove for cover. Maya reached around to the small of her back, laying a finger against her haken, and drew on *deiat*. Where Beq's stone hit the ground, she summoned a column of flame, liquid fire that blasted out of the rock and splashed off the ceiling in glowing droplets. She kept the temperature low—it wouldn't do to actually sear some unlucky Auxiliary—but the light and smoke were enough to make everyone keep their head down.

"Now!" Maya said.

She surged to her feet, grabbing Beq's arm with one hand, and ran for it. Sarah did the same, dodging between the chunks of rock. She rounded a particularly large boulder, then doubled back. Concealed behind it was a narrow crack in the rock, which in the blue light of Sarah's glowstone revealed itself to be an entrance to a parallel tunnel.

Sarah didn't hesitate in wedging herself through, and Maya and Beq followed. Maya let the fire blink out, and she heard the harsh voices of the Auxiliaries shouting to one another. The sound of boots and crossbow fire faded quickly, though, as they pounded down a narrow, darkened tunnel.

"Wait here," Sarah said quietly. She shoved the glowstone inside her coat, plunging them into near-total darkness. "See if they follow."

For a few tense minutes they stood there in silence. When no lights flickered behind them, Sarah relaxed, producing the glowstone again.

"Probably charged off down the main tunnel after us," she said. "I hope they get lost for days."

"Are you all right?" Maya said to Beq.

"I think so." Beq raised an eyebrow. "Maybe a little singed."

"I'll say," Sarah said. "That was a plaguing impressive alchemical. I don't suppose you want to tell me where you got it?"

"Honestly, I'm not feeling generous right now," Maya said. She looked down at Sarah, who raised her hands apologetically.

"I said I was sorry! When they told me someone was asking questions, I figured bringing a couple of sell-swords along was the smart move." She sighed. "More fool me."

There was an awkward silence.

"So now what?" Beq said.

"I think *we* ask some questions," Maya said. "Starting with this one. You're one of these rebels, aren't you?"

It was a shot in the dark, but an educated one. *With a whole market full of people selling* dhak, *who else would rate the attention of a full squad of Auxiliaries down here?*

"I wouldn't tell you if I was," Sarah said with a slight smile. "But I'm starting to think we might share a mutual interest."

"What exactly would that be?" Maya said.

"Dux Raskos Rottentooth," Sarah said. "Specifically, seeing him get what's coming to him."

"That's . . . not impossible," Maya said. "So what if we do?"

"*If* there were agents of the Order in the area," Sarah said, "and they weren't bought and paid for by the dux, I might advise them to check out the warehouse at the corner of Third Street and Broad Way, on the edge of the manufactory district. I think there's quite a lot there that they might find . . . interesting."

Chapter 12

Yevri's Café had been a fixture of the West Central district for many years. It had been built in a prime spot, a prudent distance from the edge of the Pit but still close enough to bask in the warm, sulfurous air that rose continuously from the depths. But the Pit was always expanding, stone gradually crumbling under its acidic breath, and yesterday's prudent distance was today's teetering on the brink.

More than teetering, actually. At least half of Yevri's building now projected over the edge, cantilevered out on a complex set of struts that had been built up, bit by bit, as the underlying rock fell away. Old Yevri and his sons insisted it was still safe, and most days someone was out there hanging from a rope harness, adding yet more beams and props. There was a morbid betting pool on whether the old man would live long enough to see his beloved café finally topple into the abyss.

In the meantime, the place was pleasantly warm, the food was reasonably priced, and no one looked too closely at suspicious characters. Gyre hadn't had time to apply a fake scar, so he'd resorted to a scarf and a hood, making it obvious he didn't want to be recognized. Yora, when she arrived, had her golden hair gathered in a tight bun under a shapeless hat.

She sat down opposite him at the rough-hewn wooden table, looking somewhat the worse for wear. Her skin was a shade paler than usual, and there were bags under her eyes, as though she hadn't slept since the attack.

"It's good to see you," Gyre said.

"You too," Yora said. "You had us worried."

"The Auxies were persistent," Gyre said. "Everyone else all right?"

Yora shook her head. "We lost three people in the attack, and another couple were badly hurt. The good news is Raskos didn't get anyone alive."

Gyre guiltily bit off what he'd been about to say. He'd barely thought twice about the new faces, the tunnelborn Yora had pulled in for security. "I'm sorry," he managed.

"Sarah's all right. She and Nevin were putting the finishing touches on our way into Raskos' warehouse. But—"

She stopped for a moment as one of Yevri's sons approached, a scowling, blue-haired boy in his teens, who set down two bowls of thick, meaty soup. Yora peered at hers suspiciously.

"House special," Gyre said. "It's good."

She took a bite and gave a little sigh of pleasure. Gyre grinned and picked up his spoon, and for a few moments they gave the food the attention it deserved. The meat was vulpi, tender and juicy, with a thick glistening layer of fat rising to the top. It reminded Gyre of home, though his mother had never cooked anything so heavily spiced.

"You were about to tell me the bad news," he said, when Yora was scraping the bottom of her bowl.

"We've had new information," Yora said. "Raskos is moving the Core Analytica, shipping it out of the city. We think he's finally found a buyer."

"Plague it," Gyre said. "You're sure?"

"Yeah. The information's solid. So it sinks most of our plans, but it's also an opportunity. It looks like they'll be transporting it in a single wagon, with only a couple of guards. The dux doesn't want to draw attention."

"You have to figure he'll have his people watching the route out of the city, though."

"He will. But Nevin and I went over the maps, and we have a plan. He'll be moving it through Sprayfall Tunnel, and we can block the road behind them, cut off any reinforcements."

Gyre frowned. "Getting clear is going to be tough."

"Sarah's on it. She promised me she'd come up with something."

"Right." Gyre went over his mental map of the city, figuring distances. *With a little cover from alchemicals, it could work.* "When?"

"Tomorrow." At his expression, Yora said, "I know, it's not enough time. But this is our only shot. If he gets the thing away, then Kit's out of luck, and we're out fifty thousand thalers." Her expression went stony. "And Harrow and the others died for nothing."

"Then we don't have much choice, do we?" Gyre looked down into his empty soup bowl, then back up at Yora. "I'll let Kit know. Send Lynnia the details for the rendezvous."

"I will," Yora said. "Thanks for the meal."

"You looked like you could use it."

She snorted a laugh and walked away.

When Gyre returned to Lynnia's, the old alchemist met him at the door, stone-faced.

"I'm telling you," she said without preamble. "I won't be responsible."

"Responsible for what?"

"The consequences!"

"What con—"

"Just go talk to her," Lynnia huffed. "And keep your head down."

The alchemist clumped out of the way, and Gyre, puzzled, dropped his coat on a chair and descended the spiral steps to the basement workshop. The air was thick with a purple-gray haze, and one of the stone worktops had been cleared off, then freshly scarred with blast marks. Kit sat in front of it, about to tip a vial of something blue into a bowl of something green.

"Kit?" Gyre coughed, waving the smoke away.

She looked up at him with a grin. "I always thought I might have a talent for alchemy."

Gyre looked at the bowl. "What are you mixing?"

"Dunno."

"What's it going to do?"

"Not sure."

"Is it safe?"

"We'll find out!"

"Maybe put the vial down," Gyre said.

"Oh, relax. Lynnia keeps the dangerous stuff locked up."

"She keeps the *expensive* stuff locked up. It's not the same thing."

"Spoilsport," Kit said. She put the vial down with a sigh and yawned. "Just trying to keep myself entertweeee..."

Gyre crossed the room in time to catch her as she slid off the chair. She flopped against him, giggling, and threw her arms around his neck.

"Spinning," she said happily. "Why're we spinning?"

"I think you've been breathing too much of this stuff."

He lifted her, surprised at how little effort it took. Kit leaned on his shoulder, still giggling, as he backed out of the room and brought her upstairs. On the main floor, Lynnia was in the kitchen, stirring something as she fixed them with a baleful glare.

"Sorry," Gyre said. "I don't think she got into anything really terrible, but you should let it air out a little."

"Serve her right if she blew her fool head off," Lynnia muttered.

"Kaboom!" Kit said happily, then dissolved into another fit of giggles.

Lynnia rolled her eyes. Gyre shifted his grip and took Kit upstairs. Her head was still resting on his shoulder, and the feel of her breath against his neck was distracting. From the sly look in her eye, he suspected she knew it. When he reached his room, he deposited her on the bed, then sat heavily in his chair.

"Ooooh," she said, bouncing a little and making the bed frame creak. "Is this where you take advantage of my helpless state to toss me on the bed and ravish me?"

"Of course not," Gyre said.

"You sure? It's been a long day."

He rolled his eye. " I don't believe you're helpless for a minute."

"You're learning." Kit sat up, her coordination returning abruptly. "This your room? You don't decorate much."

"It's just a place to sleep," Gyre said.

"Nice of Lynnia to put up a notorious rebel," Kit said. "What's she getting out of it? A hot young lover? No need to be shy."

"Lynnia," Gyre said, maintaining his calm with an effort, "has been married twice, both times to women. You're more her type than I am."

"There's a thought. Maybe then she'd let me into the interesting shelves."

"She helps us because she believes in Yora's cause," Gyre said. "Freedom for the tunnelborn."

"And you don't," Kit said. "Does that bother you?"

"Freedom for tunnelborn means hurting the Republic and the Order," Gyre said. "Which means we're on the same side."

"Until something better comes along," Kit said, tapping her chest with a finger.

"Kit—"

"So what did your rebel leader tell you?"

Gyre took a deep breath. "Raskos is moving the Core Analytica."

Kit leaned forward, suddenly all focus. "Is he really?"

"Yora guessed he's found a buyer for it."

"Mmm," Kit said noncommittally.

"She's got a plan. We'll have an opportunity to grab it when they try to get it out of the city."

"I'm sure she does."

Gyre narrowed his eye. "Is there something you want to tell me?"

"Here's the thing," Kit said, crossing her legs underneath her. "I heard from my own sources this morning. After the Auxies crashed our party, I guessed something was fishy, but now I know for certain. Someone in your group is talking to the dux."

"Not possible," Gyre said. "If we had a traitor, we'd all have been caught by now."

"Yora had to bring in new people, didn't she? Do you trust them all?"

"I—" Gyre stopped. He didn't, not like he trusted Sarah and Ibb. "How do you know?"

"It's a little hard to explain. But you understand that this means your 'opportunity' is almost certainly a trap? In fact, I'm reasonably certain they're not moving the Analytica at all. I doubt the dux would risk it, not with the Order in town."

Something tightened in Gyre's chest. "The Order, here?"

"Two centarchs, at least," Kit said. "They're staying at the Spike, for now. Best guess is someone is leaning on the dux."

Gyre shook his head. "Then we have to call everything off. Go to ground until they're gone."

"And if they take the Analytica with them when they go?"

"Your client will just have to take that risk," Gyre said. His scar itched fiercely. "Going up against centarchs is suicide."

"I thought the legendary Halfmask would be more daring," Kit said. "Here's the thing about a trap, though. If you know where it's going to be, you know where it's *not* going to be."

Gyre paused for a moment. "You think the Analytica will still be at the warehouse."

"Got it in one. While the dux and his Order friends are waiting for us to take the bait, we can sneak the prize out from behind their backs."

"That...might be possible," Gyre said. "I'd have to talk to Yora and the others—"

Kit rolled off the bed and leapt to her feet, suddenly exasperated.

"Have you even been listening to me? Yora's organization is *compromised*. If you tell her, Raskos finds out, and we're back to walking into an ambush."

"Then what are you suggesting?"

"*We* steal the Analytica. You and me. No leaks."

"That's . . ." Gyre shook his head. "We'd never get inside."

"Most of the equipment is ready, and I can get the rest. I've been watching Nevin's planning. We can do it."

"We still need to warn the others."

"We can't. Because if we *do*, then our window disappears." Kit crossed the room to stand in front of him, hands clasped behind her back. "You want what I'm offering? This is your shot. Screw it up, and there won't be another."

Gyre looked up into her eyes, alight with mischief, a slight grin on her lips. For a moment he was back in the tunnels, surrounded by bandits, her blaster fire the spark that ignited a sudden flare of steel and blood. *Doomseeker.*

He'd followed her this far. *But—*

"I can't," he said.

"You told me you'd do anything to get to the Tomb," Kit said, her voice quiet and dangerous.

"I've seen precious little evidence that you can actually take me there," Gyre said.

"Ah." Kit regarded him in silence for a moment, then straightened up. "Tell you what. Come with me, and I'll show you something."

Gyre wasn't sure where he'd expected Kit to lead him, but it hadn't been here.

They'd caught a cab together, and Kit had directed the driver north and west, away from the Pit and toward the strip of manufactories and warehouses. The border between the industrial area and the residential part of the city was a ragged wound. A few small brick buildings stood together in isolated outposts where all their fellows had been knocked down to make way for encroaching industry, like the last clumps of trees on a logged-out plain.

Their cabbie deposited them in front of one of these buildings, a simple two-story town house now without its neighbors. A crust of broken bricks on one side showed where another structure had been shorn away. The walls were carved with graffiti, and all the windows had been boarded up long ago.

"Here?" Gyre said.

"Appearances can be deceptive." Kit clapped him encouragingly on the shoulder. "Try to make a good impression."

"Who, exactly, are we meeting? Your clients?"

"You'll see."

She strode up to the front door and rapped. For a moment there was no response, and then Gyre heard the scrape of a bar pulling away, and the door swung very slightly inward. Kit pushed it the rest of the way open, but Gyre could see nothing but a heavy black curtain behind it.

"Come on," Kit said. "It's safe. Probably safe."

She found a seam in the curtain and slipped through. Gyre hesitated for a moment, then followed. The cloth was thick and utterly black, in several layers, folding and whispering around him. When he finally got free of it, he found himself in total darkness. His groping hands encountered Kit, and he kept hold of her shoulder.

"Kitsraea." The voice that came out of the darkness was female, soft and musical, with the precise diction of someone speaking a foreign language. "Welcome back. You decided to take the risk, then."

"It seemed like the best option," Kit said. "This is Gyre, otherwise known as Halfmask."

Gyre's skin prickled, and his scar itched. He ducked his head politely, then realized whoever was speaking couldn't see it in the gloom. "Uh... hello."

"Hello, Gyre," the voice said. "Welcome to you as well, for whatever it's worth. My name is Elariel."

"A little light would be nice," Kit said. "I'm not sure Gyre appreciates what he's gotten into."

"Of course." There was a shuffling sound. "Please don't scream."

A glowstone came on, a very weak one, shedding the faintest blue radiance. It was barely enough to outline the edges of things, but Gyre's eye had had a few moments to adapt to the darkness. He quickly got the impression of a high, cavernous space. While the building looked intact from outside, the interior had been gutted, two stories combined to make a single enormous chamber. Detritus from this deconstruction work was still in evidence, piled against the far wall in a tidy heap.

The space had been filled with arcana. The largest was a delicate-looking filigree of crystals and metal wire that took up much of what had been the second story, wound round with tough-looking vines. Plantlike shapes bloomed from the walls, sprouting crystalline protrusions and webs of leaves that gleamed with a metallic shimmer. Similar objects sprouted from the floor, clustering in a rough semicircle.

Of more immediate concern were the two hulking shapes that waited on either side of Gyre and Kit. They were vaguely humanoid, but at least eight feet high, and put Gyre in mind of the rock-like guardian that had killed Harrow down in the tunnels. These lacked the stony outer layer and were seemingly composed entirely of gleaming black muscle. They stood in complete stillness but nonetheless carried an air of barely contained tension, like springs that would unwind in sudden violence if the pressure was ever released.

But directly in front of him, beside the light, was a figure that put even these out of his mind. Gyre blinked, felt his mouth hanging open, and closed it with an audible *clack*. He swallowed hard, fighting for control of his throat. When he felt he could trust his voice, he spoke.

"You're a ghoul."

Elariel cocked her head. "I admit you're taking it better than I expected."

She was tall, a head taller than Gyre, and by human standards painfully thin. Her arms and legs were thin, too, and longer than a human's. Her spindly appearance was offset by her fur, a thick red-brown coat that covered her completely except for hands, feet, and face. She wore no clothing, and her small breasts were tipped by broad black nipples. Her face seemed more human than the rest of her, with an upturned nose, a broad, expressive mouth, and enormous eyes, pupils so wide they were nearly black from edge to edge. Her ears were long and pointed, sticking well out to the sides of her head and twitching with interest. When she spoke, Gyre saw sharp, feline teeth.

"You…" Gyre turned to Kit. "*This* is your client?"

"More like my handler," Kit said. "The client is still back in the Tomb."

"That's right," Elariel said. Her voice sounded so human it was a shock to hear it again. "I'm just the errand girl."

"You…" Gyre shook his head and squeezed his eye shut for a moment. He could hear his heartbeat roaring in his ears. He took shallow breaths, striving for calm. "The ghouls are all dead."

"I'll be sure to tell everybody when I get home," Elariel said dryly.

"I mean…" Gyre opened his eye and stared at her. "That's what everyone says. What we were always told. Even by the Order."

"We do our best to keep it that way," Elariel said. She glanced at Kit, who cleared her throat.

"You understand the problem now," Kit said. "Just by bringing you here—"

"You can't let me leave." Gyre felt his lips curl in a manic grin. "Not when I might spill the secret."

"It's possible I could convince Naumoriel you don't pose a threat," Elariel said. "But the more you see, the less likely that is. I warned Kitsraea it was a risk."

"I can't get the Analytica without him," Kit said. "This seemed like the quickest way to make him understand. We need to talk to Naumoriel."

"Nau—" Gyre began.

"The client," Kit cut him off, waving a hand. "We're out of choices, El."

The ghoul sniffed, her ears twitching. "I have told you that your use of nicknames would be considered highly insulting—"

"*Elariel.*"

"I will contact my master," she said, her huge eyes flicking to Gyre. "For the boy's sake, I hope you know what you're doing."

The ghoul turned away, bending to touch the semicircle of misshapen arcana. Lights flickered inside the crystalline surfaces, and plantlike tendrils unwound and reshaped themselves into new configurations. The ghoul's wide, spindly fingers danced across the irregular surface.

Just the things in this room would be the biggest find any scavenger's ever had. Gyre looked up at the metal lattice overhead, which was slowly shifting its position. *It's all* alive—

"You okay?" Kit said, leaning close with a conspiratorial air.

"Just a little surprised."

"A little?" She grinned. "You should have seen your face."

"You really did find the Tomb."

"I told you I did, didn't I?"

"Not in so many words."

Kit sniffed. "Well. I didn't deny it, anyway."

"And it's still alive? A whole *city*...like this?"

"Let's put a hold on the questions until we figure out if you're going to survive," Kit said. "El's friendly enough, but Naumoriel is the boss here. If he tells her to kill you, she will." She glanced at the silent, dark-muscled figures. "And don't doubt that she can."

"I don't. What *are* those things?"

"What did I say about questions? Just listen. I'm going to try to convince Naumoriel that I need you to get the Analytica and that he can trust you. You need to help me. If he asks you a question, be honest."

"Is he coming here, or—"

Kit laughed. "Just watch, Halfmask."

After a few moments, Elariel finished what she was doing, and the room was filled with a rising hum. Bits of tendril overhead extended, quivering with effort. In front of Elariel, fat blue sparks crackled from crystal to crystal, then abruptly rose into the air to form a shimmering, shifting curtain of blue light taller than a man. Elariel stepped away as the curtain wavered, then cleared like frost melting from a window. In the empty space where it had been, the image of a ghoul stood, half-transparent and outlined in blue light.

Gyre was hardly an expert on ghouls, but he guessed that this one was much older. His fur was a ratty gray and had fallen out in places, showing fish-belly-pale skin broken by angry red sores. The crown of his head was bald and liver spotted, just like a human's, and one of his eyes was a milky white. Like Elariel, he was naked, but the left-hand side of his chest was covered by a steel plate studded with crystalline protrusions. From underneath the metal, tiny tendrils extended a few centimeters before plunging into the ghoul's flesh.

The arcana that brought his image up from the Tomb evidently enabled him to see them as well. His good eye swept over Kit and Elariel and focused on Gyre at once. His long, gray-tufted ears went stiff, and his voice was cold.

"Who is this?" he snapped.

"The boy called Gyre, Master," Kit said, stepping forward to stand directly in front of the flickering image. "I mentioned him in my last report."

"He has seen too much already." The old ghoul waved a hand. "Dispose of him."

"I need him, Master," Kit said. "The Twilight Order's centarchs are already here. We have only one chance to get the Core Analytica—"

"Because you waited too long!"

"The dux is careful," Kit said.

"I care very little for the *dux*," Naumoriel said, "and not at all for your excuses. You know the price of failure."

"I do." Kit bowed her head. "With Gyre's help, we will have the Analytica in hand tomorrow evening."

"Then why bring him here?"

"It was the only way to ensure his cooperation." Kit stepped aside, letting Naumoriel look at Gyre. "His price for helping us was that I guide him to the Tomb."

To Gyre's surprise, the ghoul laughed at this, his ears twitching. It ended with a cough, and there was a wheeze in Naumoriel's breath when he spoke.

"Bold, boy. Bold."

"I've been called that," Gyre said.

"And quite foolhardy."

"That as well," Gyre said. Kit sniggered.

"I supplied Kitsraea with ample resources to secure the help she needed." Naumoriel cocked his head, ears quivering. "And yet she brings you to see me."

"It wasn't her money I wanted."

"You want to visit the Tomb." He pronounced the word with an ironic twist. "Why? Did you think to plunder our graves?"

"I didn't know the ghouls survived," Gyre admitted.

Naumoriel leaned forward. "And now that you know, do you regret your request?"

"Not at all."

"Why?" Naumoriel's lips split in a cold smile, showing small, sharp teeth. "What do you hope to find?"

"*Be honest*," Kit had said. Gyre took a deep breath.

"Power," he said. "The Twilight Order destroyed my family. My whole life, I've searched for a way to destroy them in turn. But they have the power of the Chosen, and they leave the rest of us nothing. Only the ghouls ever stood up to that power."

"Power. And you thought you'd just come down here and find it?" Naumoriel's grin widened. "That goes beyond bold."

Gyre shrugged.

The old ghoul barked another laugh. "You certainly know how to choose your allies, Kitsraea."

"Thank you, Master," she said, though Gyre wasn't sure it had been a compliment.

"Very well," the old ghoul said to Gyre. "Get me the Core Analytica, and you may bring it to the Tomb." A tiny pink tongue ran across his pointed teeth. "I make no promises as to whether you'll return."

Before Gyre could answer, the image vanished.

Emerging onto the street after the darkness of Elariel's lair was like stepping into a different world. The sun was low in the western sky, but it was still blinding, and Gyre felt half-drunk as he staggered out the door. Kit took his arm in hers.

"Well," she said. "That went better than expected."

"You..." Gyre shook his head. He had a thousand questions, and an unpleasant feeling she wasn't going to answer any of them. "Are *these* your 'contacts'?"

She nodded. "Elariel has spies all over the city. Tiny constructs"— she held her hands a few centimeters apart—"that let her see or hear what they do."

"And she told you that Raskos has an agent in Yora's crew?"

Kit nodded again. "She hasn't been able to catch anyone in the act, but she's seen the reports in the Spike. Enough to be certain." She raised an eyebrow. "So what's it going to be? Are we going to waste our chance, or are we going to get this done ourselves?"

Gyre took a deep breath, cold air flooding his lungs and dispelling some of the fog from his head. It had been less than an hour since he'd gotten into the cab with Kit, but it felt like a lifetime.

The Tomb. What he'd been searching for all these years. The best chance—the *only* chance—at power to match a centarch's. *And it's more than I ever imagined.* He'd hoped to plunder some unknown arcana from a ruin. What a living ghoul city might offer—

I have to get there. He knew, intellectually, that he might simply be hurrying to his death, but there was no fear, only the iron determination that had brought him this far. His scar itched, and at the back of his mind he heard Maya's scream. *I have to.*

Yora. What would she do, if he simply disappeared? *Surely she wouldn't go through with the attack.* The natural assumption, if he and Kit didn't show up at the rendezvous, would be that they'd been captured. In that case, the only logical thing to do would be to call everything off and hunker down.

She wouldn't go through with it. She's too smart for that. He let out his breath. *And once Kit and I have the Analytica, we can hand off the money to Yora and the others.* Whatever happened in the Tomb, Gyre didn't think he'd need a pile of thalers.

This is the only chance I'm going to get.

Kit was watching him curiously. Gyre squared his shoulders and met her gaze.

"We'd better start going over the plan," he said.

Chapter 13

It felt like no time at all passed between the moment Maya's head hit the pillow and the knock that woke her. In truth, she didn't know how long it had been—she and Beq had snuck back into the palace while it was still dark, and now sunlight was streaming in through the window. However much sleep she'd gotten, though, it hadn't been enough.

But we made it. Thinking of last night's adventure made her feel giddy. *We have a lead on Raskos, and what's really going on here.* Now all she had to do was figure out what to do with it.

The knock repeated, politely, and Maya shook off her lassitude and hastily rolled out of bed. She pulled a dressing gown over her shift and hurried to the door, which opened to reveal a liveried footman with her breakfast on a silver platter.

"Thanks," Maya said, a little confused. Yesterday they'd left the food without waking her.

"Agathios Tanax instructed me to say that he needs to speak with you at once," the footman said, bowing again.

"Ah." Maya glanced longingly at the tray, where steam was rising from a thick slab of bread drizzled with butter and chocolate, beside eggs and vulpi fry. She swallowed and put on a brave face. "I'll be with him as soon as I'm dressed."

"Of course." The servant bowed and withdrew.

Maya swore and pulled on her rumpled uniform, pausing only to jam a strip of vulpi into her mouth. She chewed hurriedly as she crossed the corridor to knock on Tanax's door.

"Come in," Tanax said.

To her annoyance, he was sitting at a table, working his way through his own breakfast. She tried not to stare.

"Good morning," he said. "I hope you slept well."

"Not particularly," Maya said. "I need to tell you something."

"You and Beq left the palace last night," Tanax said mildly, cutting a slice of butter-drowned toast.

"I..." Maya stared at him. "You knew?"

"I suspected. You just confirmed it."

Maya swore silently and took a deep breath. "We were never told we were confined to the grounds."

"Some things shouldn't need to be spelled out," Tanax said, and shrugged. "But I understand. Neither of you have been exposed to the temptations of the city. It's only to be expected."

"The—what?"

"You'd hardly be the first agathios to sneak out to a tavern or a brothel. I'll have to include it in my report, but I'll certainly encourage the Council to be understanding."

"A *brothel*?" Maya's hand went to the Thing, a hard lump in her chest. It helped suppress her rising anger. "What exactly do you think we were doing?"

"There's no need to be offended," Tanax said, cutting another piece of toast. "You're at the age—"

"You are *one year* older than me," Maya said.

"*The point* is that I know how to avoid offending our host. This is an important lesson for the two of you."

"*That* is what I need to talk to you about. Our host." Maya paused for a moment, doing her best to regain her calm. "I have reason to believe Dux Raskos is abusing his office and smuggling *dhak*."

There was a long moment of silence.

"That's . . . not possible," Tanax said.

"Why not?" Maya said. "The dux has been eager to keep us in the palace since we arrived. He hasn't asked for our assistance against the rebels, or even mentioned them. He's worried about what might happen if we really started to investigate—"

"*Enough*." Tanax got to his feet. "Have you spoken to anyone else about this?"

"Of course not," Maya said. "I have no idea who we can trust."

"That's something, anyway." The other agathios stepped away from the table and started to pace. "You will say nothing, to anyone. Do you understand?"

"No!" Maya turned to face him as he walked. "What do you mean, say nothing? We need to move *quickly*. The evidence—"

"I have instructions from my master," Tanax said. "Those instructions are very clear."

Of course. If Nicomidi truly was working with Raskos on something illegal, he wouldn't want his agathios getting anywhere near it. *And Tanax certainly isn't going to listen to any accusations against Nicomidi.* Maya chose her words carefully.

"Obviously your master doesn't know the dux is corrupt," Maya said. "That changes the situation."

"I believe my master knows everything relevant about the *situation*," Tanax said. "The dux has responsibilities that are not common knowledge among the public."

"Responsibilities like gathering a warehouse full of unsanctioned arcana to sell to smugglers?"

"You don't know that," Tanax snapped.

"And you're making this up as you go along," Maya said.

Tanax reached the wall and put a hand against it. She got the sense he wanted to hit something, and hoped he would stop restraining himself. *Let him put a hole in the dux's plaster.* Their eyes met for a moment, and she saw a flash of rage before Tanax visibly got himself under control. He swept one hand through his hair, irritably, and looked away.

"I have perfect confidence in my master and his instructions," Tanax said. "When we return to the Forge, you are welcome to take the matter up with him yourself."

"By the time we return to the Forge, we won't have any hard evidence," Maya said.

"If necessary, a full centarch will be sent to investigate—"

There was a knock at the door. Maya stopped, breathing hard. Tanax fixed her with a glare, then said, "Who's there?"

"Agathios Tanax." The voice had the metallic quality of a Legionary helmet. "The dux requests you and your team join him at your earliest convenience."

"Are we due at another party?" Maya said aloud, drawing another glare.

"No, Agathios," the soldier said. "The dux is ready to move against the rebels, and he would like your help."

A quarter of an hour later, the four of them followed the white-armored Legionary into a sparely appointed chamber in yet another section of the palace.

Beq was yawning, which was no surprise. When they'd collected her and Varo in the corridor, she'd caught Maya's furious expression, but with Tanax standing beside her there'd been no chance to talk. Varo, by contrast, looked cheery and well rested and had even found time to clean his uniform.

"Action at last," he said. "Though I suppose you should never wish for action, since it might find you when you're not expecting it. I had a friend—"

"Scout Varo," Tanax said. "This is not the time."

"You're right," Varo said, then caught Maya's eye and muttered, "That's just what *he* said, actually."

Another Legionary waited outside the room, offering a slight bow to the agathia when they arrived. Inside, a large circular table and a few plain wooden chairs were the extent of the furnishings. Raskos stood behind the table, looking distinctly out of place in an Auxiliary uniform. The man beside him seemed more at ease. He was large, with a gray-green beard and a receding hairline. Several more Auxiliaries waited at attention along the wall, spears in hand.

There were several maps of varying scale on the table. The street plan of Deepfire was easy to recognize from the shape of the Pit, with the Spike on one side and the rest of the city huddled close on the other. Pencil marks showed a route to the south and east, along a road that left the close huddle of buildings and rose into the mountains.

"Agathia," Raskos said, with his horrifying black-toothed smile. "Honored guests. Thank you for coming."

"We are at your service," Tanax said, with a bow. Maya only reluctantly followed suit.

"There is a band of especially...persistent criminals that we have been tracking for the past few months. Smugglers and thieves. We have an opportunity to strike a blow against them that you are uniquely suited to exploit," Raskos said. "This is my commander of Auxiliaries, Guria Fairshot. He will explain the details."

"Agathia," Guria said gruffly. He pointed to the map. "We've let the thieves learn that we're moving some valuable arcana from quarantine. We're confident this is a target they won't be able to resist, which means it's a chance to catch them in the open." He frowned. "Unfortunately, they're not stupid. If the shipment is too heavily guarded, they'll call off their attack. An ambush would be hard to conceal from the reconnaissance."

"But the two of you, we can hide in the transport wagon itself," Raskos cut in. He looked immensely pleased with himself. "They will expect a handful of guards and be met instead with a pair of centarchs. I doubt they will even put up a fight."

"We'll need you to prevent their escape," Guria said. "I understand that's within your...abilities." Guria pushed a smaller-scale map forward. "The thieves plan to attack in the Sprayfall Tunnel, at the edge of the city. It's a good choice, tactically—there's nowhere for us to hide a squad closer than the tunnel entrance. But if you can seal the exit behind them, they'll have no retreat."

Maya thought furiously. *It has to be the rebels he's going after. No ordinary band of criminals would be worth the risk of involving us.* She glanced at Tanax, who was nodding approvingly at the map.

"I don't like it," Maya ventured. "What if these thieves bring more firepower than you're expecting?"

"I'm sure we can handle it," Tanax said, looking at her irritably.

"I have every confidence," Raskos said.

"In any event, our backup squads will wait at the tunnel entrance," Guria said. "If needed, they can provide covering fire relatively quickly."

"I said that I'm sure we can handle it," Tanax snapped. "I understand your plan, Dux Raskos. When do you want to proceed?"

"The wagon leaves the palace in an hour," the dux said.

"Then we'll be ready," Tanax said. He didn't look back at Maya and the others.

"Maya," Beq said in a low voice. "These thieves—do you think—"

"Probably," Maya said, looking around carefully.

They stood in a courtyard outside the palace, ringed by a gravel drive. A tall, stout-looking cargo wagon was being loaded with iron-bound chests by a couple of servants, while a groom led two loadbirds to the harness.

"Did you tell him?" Beq said. "About what Sarah told us?"

"I told him," Maya said quietly. "He didn't think it was important."

"Not *important*?" Beq snorted. "That the dux smuggles *dhak*?"

"Nicomidi's told him to help Raskos, so that's what he's going to do. Nicomidi knows best, after all." Maya shook her head. "I swear, to hear Tanax talk, you'd think the man was half-Chosen."

Beq smiled slightly. "I *have* heard you praise your own master from time to time."

"Jaedia's different," Maya said automatically, then laughed with Beq. "Jaedia would never expect me to be mindlessly obedient to a *letter*. She'd understand that situations can change. And if I didn't understand why we were doing something, she'd explain it to me, not just order me to obey." She glanced over at Tanax. "I get the sense that our training may have differed in that respect."

"I think you were lucky," Beq said. "Most of the centarchs I know are bigger on obedience than explanations." She flicked the lens back into place and shook her head. "So what are you going to do?"

"I don't *know*." Maya glanced at the wagon. "I can't refuse to help. Tanax would just go without me, and we'd lose any chance of getting the rebels to work with us." She shook her head. "I need to *talk* to them. If their grudge is really against Raskos, maybe I can convince them I'm on their side."

"Be careful," Beq said. "Tanax is eager to start something, and the rebels may be more dangerous than he thinks. Remember how much *dhak* and arcana we saw out there."

Maya nodded. "I'll be careful."

"Thank you." Beq took a deep breath. "Varo and I will be with the backup, if you need us."

"You be careful, too," Maya said. "Keep one eye on Raskos."

Beq grinned and clicked something on her spectacles—the lenses shifted, making her eyes point in different directions. "Got it covered!"

Maya let out a startled laugh. Beq grinned at her, her cheeks going red, which made her freckles stand out. She brushed absently at her braid, tucking away a few loose green hairs.

"Can you actually see like that?" Maya said.

"Oh, no. It just gives me a headache." Beq snapped the lenses back into place. "But I'll be careful."

"Maya!" Tanax said. "We're ready to move."

Maya held Beq's gaze a moment longer, then turned away, fighting down a rush of blood to her own cheeks. *Not the time, Maya. Not the time.* She took deep breaths as she walked across the courtyard to the wagon.

"I know you disagree with some of my decisions." Tanax gave her a sharp look. "But this is not the time or place for disagreement. Do you understand?"

Maya held her tongue and gave a silent nod.

Tanax climbed up into the rear of the wagon and bent down to offer her his hand. She ignored it, pulling herself up, and sat on one of the iron chests. Tanax sat down opposite her, arms folded across his chest.

"Good fortune!" Raskos called from outside.

The servants closed the back door, leaving them in warm semidarkness. Maya heard the driver whistle, and the loadbirds started forward, the wagon rocking as it rolled out onto the gravel.

As the minutes ticked past and the wagon trundled along, Maya's nerves were jangling. She found her foot tapping and stilled it with an effort. Tanax gave her a withering look.

"These...thieves," Maya said. "It's possible I might have a contact among them."

"You didn't think that was worth mentioning earlier?" Tanax said.

"I'm not certain," Maya said. "And I've already told you I don't trust Raskos."

Tanax snorted. "I'm glad *I* am worthy of your trust."

"Just listen, all right?" Maya took a deep breath. "It's possible I may be able to talk them into coming peacefully. Can we agree that would be a better outcome than a fight?"

"I suppose it is always better for criminals to be seen to face the Republic's justice," Tanax said. "But I don't know if it's likely. I suspect they'll flee once they realize who they're facing."

"I know. If it comes to that…" Maya shook her head. "Just promise you'll give me a chance to talk."

"We'll see," Tanax said. "But I will do my best."

The darkness grew deeper, the fans of sunlight that slipped in between the boards of the wagon disappearing. Tanax sat up straighter.

"We're in the tunnel," he said. He brought up his panoply field, and Maya did the same, pressing a finger against her haken. Her other hand went to the Thing. She could feel her heartbeat through it, fast but strong.

Seconds passed in tense silence.

"How long—" Maya began in a whisper, before the *snap-hiss* of a crossbow cut her off. It was followed by an inhuman squeal, then another shot.

"Stand down," a woman's voice said. "Go for that sword and you're a dead man."

"This is Auxiliary property," the driver said. He sounded frightened.

"We know." Another woman, and this one Maya recognized. *Sarah.* "That's why we're taking it."

"I'm going out," Maya hissed. "Remember, just let me speak to them."

"Until someone makes a move," Tanax muttered, one hand on his haken. "I'll be right behind you."

Maya was already kicking the back door open. She waited for a moment to see if the motion would draw a shot, and when it didn't she hopped down.

"I'm coming around the wagon," she said aloud. "I'd like to talk."

The first woman spoke again. "Move slowly."

"There are two of us," Maya said. She edged out to the side of the wagon, her hand on her haken.

They were in a long, wide tunnel. There were no buildings here, just the road. Ahead, it curved, so there was no sign of the tunnel exit, but the glowing arch of the entrance was visible a hundred meters behind them.

The two loadbirds were dead, sprawled in their harness, crossbow bolts jutting from their sides. The driver, a young man in an Auxie uniform, sat on the box with his hands raised, showing no inclination to go for the weapon at his side.

Beyond the wagon, spread in a rough semicircle, were a dozen men and women. They wore scavenged armor, bits of steel and fragments of unmetal over leather. Most carried crossbows, though Maya saw at least a couple of blaster pistols, and some wore swords or short spears. Sarah was in the first line, a blaster pistol in one hand, looking bulky under mismatched unmetal plate armor. Beside her was a tall, slim woman with long metallic-gold hair and an unmetal spear.

Maya hurried forward and saw Sarah's eyes widen in recognition. Crossbows and blasters tracked her as she came forward, and the tall woman retreated a step, but Sarah held her ground. Maya's voice was low and urgent.

"Please. Don't do anything rash. I need to talk to you."

"He's got a haken!" one of the men said from behind her. "They're plaguing *centarchs*!"

Weapons were raised all around.

"Everyone, please stay calm!" Maya said. "Tanax, you too!"

"You didn't tell me everything," Sarah murmured. She looked up at the tall woman, who kept her eyes on Maya.

"What is going on here?" the woman said. "Sarah, you know these two?"

"Just this one," Sarah said. "I figured her for an Order scout. Apparently I wasn't thinking big enough."

"And were you planning on informing the rest of us?" the woman said, her hand tightening on her spear.

"My name is Maya," Maya said.

"And this is Yora," Sarah said. "She's in charge."

"Please listen," Maya said. "We don't have long. Nobody has to get killed here."

"Not if you get out of the way," Yora said. "Centarch or not, we're taking the Core Analytica."

"The Analytica's not here," Maya said urgently. "This is a trap. Raskos wants Tanax and me to bring you in."

Yora's face hardened, and Sarah paled.

"I knew something was wrong," Sarah said. "Halfmask—"

"Quiet," Yora said.

"Maya!" Tanax said, a dangerous edge in his voice. "What's going on?"

"We're discussing the terms of surrender," Maya said, loud enough for him to hear.

"We're doing nothing of the kind," Yora said.

"Please," Maya said. "Listen to me. Sarah said your grievance is with Raskos, and this is your chance to prove it. I can guarantee your fair treatment. We'll send to the Forge for a centarch to investigate. You can present your evidence."

"The Order has had a decade to curb Raskos' excesses," Yora said. "If they cared, they would have done something before now."

"The Order doesn't *know*." There had to be more to it than that, but Maya was running on instinct and didn't want to complicate the case. "I swear that I will do everything I can to see that justice is done here."

"Maya!" Tanax said again.

"Just *shut up*," Maya shouted back. "Sarah, Yora, please."

"Halfmask wouldn't trust her," Sarah said slowly.

"I told you to shut up about him," Yora said.

"I was going to say I think he'd be wrong." Sarah took a deep breath. "This might work."

"I . . ." Yora's eyes flicked from Maya to Tanax, then to the wagon and back again. For a moment, Maya saw mistrust and hope warring behind her eyes. "I'm not . . ."

Sarah went stiff, looking over Maya's shoulder, then screamed a warning. "*Down!*"

The *crack* of a blaster bolt, in the empty space of the tunnel, was like a bolt of lightning at close range. The shot impacted with a flash bright enough to dazzle and a wash of heat. It caught Sarah high in the chest, punching her off her feet and sending her sprawling to the tunnel floor, bits of white-hot metal spalling away from her makeshift armor.

"You fucking traitorous *plaguepit*," Yora snarled, barely audible over the ringing in Maya's ears. She raised her spear as a half dozen cross-bows went off at once.

No. Maya felt like she was watching herself from a distance. Her panoply stopped two bolts, sending a wave of cold through her, and she drew her haken. The blade ignited, the flood of *deiat* sending familiar pinpricks of energy spreading across her body. Yora was already slashing at her, and Maya parried high, her flaming sword spitting and crackling against the unmetal spear. Before Yora could disengage, Maya kicked her in the stomach, sending her stumbling backward even as the rest of the rebels pressed in.

One older man in the rear had a blaster, and he raised it and fired. Maya interposed her blade, and the bolt of coherent energy twisted into the flaming weapon as though drawn by a magnet, impacting in a shower of sparks. The old rebel looked startled, but his companions had already tossed aside their crossbows and drawn their swords.

No, no, no!

But it was too late.

The first man to reach her feinted high, then thrust low. Maya saw it in time to parry, and his ordinary steel parted easily where it met *deiat*, leaving him holding a stump. He backed away, gaping comically, and Maya spun to one side and chopped the head off a spear as it thrust at her. The first man dug in his pocket and produced a small clay bomb, which he hurled at her just as a third rebel bore in with a knife in each hand.

Maya pulled a thread of *deiat*, sending a narrow bolt of flame to incinerate the alchemical. It burst with a *whoomph*, sending several men toppling. The knife-wielding rebel, a teenage girl, ignored it and came in fast. Maya was hard-pressed to parry, blocking one stroke while the other scored against her panoply. The knives were unmetal, too, holding their own against her haken. Maya took one step back, then another, as the girl pressed in, her face twisted with hatred.

Stop. Please.

"You fucking Order bastard—"

The girl drove in with both knives. Maya hopped back to buy a moment, raised one hand, and incinerated her.

The rebel's curse became a scream of agony as *deiat* roared around her, the concentrated essence of the sun engulfing her in a pillar of fire. Her voice cut off mercifully quickly, and her blackened body toppled, shattering into a drift of ash when it hit the floor.

The rest of the rebels hesitated, but Yora had regained her footing and went back on the offensive. Maya wanted to scream, but she didn't have the breath.

The golden-haired woman was good, her spear spinning and thrusting unpredictably, blocking Maya's ripostes with the unmetal haft. The weapon was nicked and pitted where it had stopped the haken— even unmetal would eventually melt under the power of *deiat*—but Yora skillfully stayed away from a prolonged clinch. Every parry Maya missed sent a wave of cold across her panoply.

She needed a moment to get clear, to blast Yora away, to end this fight, but she didn't have it. Maya fell into the routines Jaedia had drummed into her, the fighting stances and reflexes, her own blade licking out to score Yora's thigh. It burned through leather and flesh, and Yora stumbled for a moment, her onslaught faltering.

"Stop this," Maya gasped. "Help me—"

Something passed across Yora's body in a clean line from shoulder to hip, a distortion in the air like a line of folded space. For an instant, she looked puzzled, brow furrowed as though trying to work something out. Then a long slice of her body simply *disappeared*, flesh twisting in on itself. Blood exploded out of the gap, and the mangled wreckage fell away in two separate pieces.

Tanax stood behind her, breathing hard, the blade of his haken a writhing snarl of impossible geometry. Several rebels lay dead in his wake, carved into pieces that still flickered and distorted where his weapon had cut them.

"Are you all right?" he said.

No. Maya gave a brief, jerky nod. Tanax turned away, avoiding Yora's broken corpse.

"Throw down your weapons and surrender," he said to the survivors. "*Now.*"

Most of them did. One man, the older one with the blaster pistol, started to run instead. Tanax frowned and raised a hand, and Maya felt *deiat* lash out. Space around the fleeing rebel twisted in on itself, folding his body in an impossible contortion with a distant *crunch* and a spray of blood. No one else moved.

"Well," Tanax said. "They made an unfortunate choice."

"They didn't make a choice," Maya said. "We were *talking*, and—"

She looked up at the click of warbird claws. Three riders were approaching from the direction of the city. Two wore the white armor of Legionaries and had blaster rifles slung over their shoulders. Between them rode Raskos Rottentooth.

Raskos. In Maya's mind, a suspicion hardened rapidly into certainty. She turned to face him, her haken still crackling quietly at her side.

"Excellent work, my friends," Raskos said, whistling his bird to a stop and sliding off. "I see my trust in you was not misplaced."

Tanax dismissed the blade of his haken and bowed. Raskos swept past him, the two Legionaries at his side, and picked his way among the corpses. When he reached Sarah, he stopped and prodded her with one boot.

To Maya's surprise, Sarah responded, her words forced through gritted teeth. "Come a little closer, you plaguing *fuck*."

"Now, now." Raskos looked down at her with his horrible smile. "Your rebellion is over. Your leader is dead. Tell me: Where is Halfmask?"

"Check your fucking chamber pot." Sarah struggled up on one elbow. Her other shoulder was a blackened ruin, leather and skin burned to identical black char by the blaster bolt. As she moved, the crust cracked and blood seeped through. "He's too smart for your traps."

Raskos raised his foot, delicately, and pressed it down against her wound. Sarah's jaw locked with the effort of stopping a scream.

"Where," the dux repeated, "is Halfmask?"

"Get off her," Maya said.

Raskos looked over his shoulder and found himself staring at the point of her haken, divine fire boiling a few inches from his nose. His smile faded.

"That woman is a prisoner," Tanax said, coming forward. "She's entitled to medical care."

"Of course." The dux didn't seem amused, but he lowered his foot. Maya didn't budge.

"Your men fired the first shot," she said.

Raskos tried to look at her past the blazing haken. There was sweat on his forehead.

"My men had orders to give support if it looked like either of you was threatened," he said. "For your protection."

"I wasn't threatened," Maya said. "They were going to surrender."

"A difficult judgment to make at a distance, unfortunately," Raskos said.

"*Unfortunately?*" Maya edged her haken closer. "This is what you wanted. A bloodbath, with us as your private executioners."

"I am not sure I like your tone," Raskos said. "Agathios Tanax, please control your *junior* partner."

"Stand down, Maya," Tanax said.

Maya felt blood thundering in her head, and *deiat* pulsing through her body in waves. *It would be so easy.* Close her hand, and Raskos would be consumed in the fire of the sun, just like that poor rebel. Reach forward, and his rotting smile would melt around her haken.

That's what being a centarch is, isn't it? Judgment.

She wasn't a centarch, though. *Not yet.*

"Agathios Tanax," Raskos snapped. "Stop her—"

Maya lowered her haken, the blade flickering and fading.

The dux let out a long breath. "Thank you, Agathios. I understand that emotions can run high in battle—"

Maya had already turned away. She stalked past Tanax, toward the three warbirds. No one realized what she was doing until she grabbed the saddle post of the closest and pulled herself up.

"Maya!" Tanax said. "What are you doing?"

"What we should have done in the first place," Maya said.

She hauled on the reins, and the bird rounded with a squawk. A whistle brought it up to a trot, its long, loping gait quickly reducing Tanax's protests to distant shouts. At the tunnel entrance, she passed a troop of Auxiliaries and caught sight of Beq and Varo among them. None of them had time to do more than gape before she was past.

If we're going to bring Raskos down, Maya thought, leaning over the bird's long neck, *we'll do it properly.*

Chapter 14

Gyre

Fortunately, Nevin had not yet returned to pick up his gear.

The thief had assembled his equipment on the roof of the warehouse opposite Raskos'. Each building was surrounded by a strip of gravel, which made the distance between the two at least ten meters, but it was still the closest convenient spot. Behind a concealing bank of chimneys, the crew had stashed wooden crates full of alchemicals from Lynnia's workshop. There was also a small arcana contraption, something like a wagon wheel made of iridescent unmetal and colorful, faceted crystals.

"What's that for?" Kit said, watching as Gyre sorted through the stuff.

"I thought you'd gone over the plan," Gyre said.

"The broad strokes," Kit said with an unrepentant grin. "So what's that thing?"

"It melts screamerwire," Gyre said. Sarah had explained its basic use, though she'd been light on details. "Once we get to the trapdoor, we activate it and then hope none of the stuff starts a fire."

"Exciting."

"It's the easiest way in." Screamerwire was ugly stuff, as thin and easy to break as a cobweb. True to its name, if it was torn, it would shriek loud enough to deafen anyone nearby. Fortunately for would-be thieves, it was rare and fantastically expensive. *But Raskos can afford the best.* "That's step two, though."

"Right," Kit said, glancing around the chimney at the gap between two buildings. "That first step is a long one."

"It's all here," Gyre said, finishing his checks. "Your eyes ready?"

"Clear as day," Kit said, pupils huge with the effect of nighteye.

"Keep the neutralizer handy. We don't know what it'll look like inside." Gyre picked up the grapple ball, carefully touching only the metal stick, and shouldered the coil of wire-thin alchemical line. "Let's go."

Getting into Raskos' private storehouse was never going to be easy. They'd seen at least two dozen uniformed Auxie guards, on top of the various alchemical and arcana protections. But Raskos' paranoia worked to their benefit, too. Only a handful of senior officers were allowed *inside* the building, which meant that if Gyre's crew got that far unnoticed, they'd be relatively safe.

There were four guards on the roof, walking the edges in two pairs. They carried no lights—presumably they were using nighteye as well—and Gyre had watched them from behind the chimneys until he was sure he had the timing down. Given the size of the building, he had a couple of minutes to slip across, but no longer.

Now he ran for the edge of the roof, Kit following closely behind. The grapple was a simple piece of alchemy—a ball of squishy, gooey stuff that would stick hard to anything it touched, except for a specially treated metal stick. Holding the stick by the free end, Gyre took a running start and whipped the thing around, sending the gooey ball sailing out into the darkness. The alchemical line trailed behind it.

The ball landed on the opposite roof with a soft *splat*. Gyre gave the line a quick tug to confirm it was stuck fast. He spilled a few drops of glue from a tiny container onto the roof tile at his feet, pressed the near end of the line into it, and stood back. The length of alchemical wire now stretched between the two warehouses, straight and taut.

"You're sure you can do this?" he said to Kit. "There's a lot of Auxies down there who are going to be very surprised when you fall on their heads."

Kit snorted. "Watch and learn, Halfmask." She stepped out onto the line with one foot, then another, balancing easily.

"Just don't step on the grapple at the far end," Gyre said, smiling. "We'd have to cut your foot off to get you out."

Kit didn't dignify that with a response. She stepped forward again, a steady walk, the line shifting slightly under her feet. Then she twisted, bending over, and for a heart-stopping moment Gyre thought she was going to fall. Instead, she turned the motion into a tumble, one hand pressing against the line, then the other, executing a perfect cartwheel on a wire-thin bridge over forty meters of darkness.

Plaguing Doomseeker, Gyre thought, but not without a hint of admiration. And, he had to admit, a certain appreciation for the lithe, elegant lines of her body in her well-fitted thief's gear.

When she'd reached the other side, he started across, doing his best to ignore the buzzing sensation at the pit of his stomach. Wire walking wasn't his favorite trick, and he certainly wasn't trying any cartwheels, but he made it.

"Okay," Gyre whispered. "Low and careful to the trapdoor."

There wasn't much cover on the roof, just a few banks of connected chimneys, and Gyre hurried from one to the next as quickly as he could. Kit, padding behind him, was as silent as a cat and just as quick. The trapdoor was a massive thing, iron-banded wood in an iron frame, with no handle on this side.

He activated the anti-screamerwire arcana with a twist and set it down beside the trapdoor, then extracted another couple of vials of Lynnia's genius from his pouch. The first contained an oily substance that would drip through cracks and coat anything it touched. The second was a catalyst that would turn that oil into a vicious acid. Careful application of the pair was an art, but fortunately it was one that he'd had plenty of practice with in his years as Halfmask. Thin wisps of caustic smoke started to rise as he worked.

"Guards coming," Kit whispered from behind him. "Must be shift change."

"Shit." Gyre looked up and saw two figures approaching from the edge of the roof. *Nowhere to hide—*

"Stay here. I'll take care of it."

Kit faded into the shadows, a dark shape that was hard to track even with nighteye. Gyre hunkered down, oil bottle still in hand, watching the pair get closer. It was a man and woman, with spears and pointed helmets. Either they didn't have nighteye themselves, or they'd already neutralized it, because they ought to have seen him by now—

Silent as a specter, Kit rose behind the woman. Something fast and messy happened at her throat, and she collapsed with only a faint gurgle. At the sound of her body hitting the tiles, the man turned quizzically, and Kit surged forward to meet him, driving a dagger up under his jaw. He twitched spastically for a moment, spear clattering away, before she let him drop.

"Better," Kit said, shaking blood off her hand. She bent to wipe it on the Auxie's uniform. "You going to be able to get that open?"

Gyre coughed to cover his momentary hesitation. "Yeah. Give me a minute."

He turned back to his task, shaking his head. *It's not like I haven't killed Auxies.* They were part of the Order and the Republic, after all, just as much as the centarchs or the duxes. But there was something about the utter casualness of Kit's violence that gave him pause. *Don't get soft*, he chided himself. *You've done far worse things to get to the Tomb.* And, if he *did* find the power he wanted, no doubt there would be worse yet to come.

With a final *hiss*, the acid burned through. Gyre jammed a handle mounted on a corkscrew-shaped tine into the wood and gave it a few twists. When Kit rejoined him, crouching at his side, he opened the door.

There was a ladder leading down into a junction of two hallways. Everything was dark and still. Gyre listened for a moment but heard no sign of movement.

"I'll get the bodies," Kit said. Gyre started a little at the thought, but it only made sense. *Hopefully there's no one watching inside. Leaving them out here makes it more likely someone will trip over them and sound the alarm.* His scar itched, and when he went to scratch it, his finger tapped irritably against his mask.

Gyre climbed down, waiting at the bottom of the ladder until Kit returned carrying the dead Auxie woman. She lowered the corpse carefully by the arms until Gyre was able to catch it around the waist. Blood still oozed from the broad gash across the woman's throat, and her blank gaze made Gyre shudder. *Don't. Get. Soft.*

Kit let the other Auxie's body down, and Gyre piled the two corpses against the wall. Kit herself jumped to the ground, eschewing the ladder and landing with catlike grace. With his nighteye, Gyre could see the darker stains spattered across her black clothing.

"From this point, we're going in blind," Gyre said. "Any ideas on how to actually find this stasis web?"

"Given how heavy it is, it'll be on the bottom floor," Kit said. "And it's big enough that they won't have just tucked it in a corner."

Gyre turned in a circle, but one way seemed as good as another. He picked a direction and started walking. This floor of the warehouse was divided into many smaller rooms, all carefully closed and locked. Kit darted ahead of him, checking the doors.

"Think we'll have time to search some of these on the way out?" she said. "Raskos must have a lot of interesting things stored up."

"Let's just get this done," Gyre muttered. Kit gave an exaggerated pout.

As he'd hoped, the corridor led to a stairwell, iron steps corkscrewing downward. Gyre descended carefully, wary of creaks and groans, and was relieved to find that the bulk of the warehouse was a single open space. A network of catwalks ran above it, with circular landings around the massive stone pillars that supported the roof. Below that, the main floor was a jumble.

Even with nighteye, it was hard to get a sense of just what Raskos had been collecting. There were boxes, barrels, and sacks, piles of stones and bricks, but mostly there were bits and pieces of arcana. Long metal tables were covered in smaller artifacts of every possible description, crystalline shapes embedded in dull ceramic or iridescent unmetal, ancient tools with no clear purpose or broken pieces of who knew what. In between were larger objects resting on wooden pallets. Some seemed tantalizingly familiar—an unmetal pod, bigger than a man, with delicate crystal vanes on either side, or a sort of chair with three wheels and a tall protruding spike. Others were just lumps, veined with crystal, complex and incomprehensible.

I had no idea there was so much. A consul's ransom didn't begin to cover it. *What is he keeping it all for?*

"There!" Kit said. Gyre winced at her excited tone, but they seemed to be alone in the warehouse. Following her pointing finger, he saw a misshapen lump of volcanic glass, about the size of a coffin. It looked like a black bedsheet thrown over a stack of rocks, then frozen in place.

"That's it?" Gyre said.

"That is *it*." Kit hurried forward. "It's really fucking here. Plague and fire, I thought for sure..."

She reached a narrow iron stair near the thing and descended, Gyre close on her heels. The objects were arranged with aisles between them, and they came down a few rows over from the stasis web. Rather than find the nearest junction, Kit vaulted over a pile of stones etched with strange patterns, then dodged around the edge of a table spread with dull, broken sunsplinters. Gyre followed more cautiously.

The destabilizer, the black rod they'd found in the ghoul tunnel where Harrow had died, was already in her hand.

"Here we go," Kit muttered. "Here we go here we go." Her free hand was clenched and shaking.

"Is there a trick to it?" Gyre said.

"No," Kit said. "You just jam *this* into *this*"—she pressed the end of the destabilizer against the slick black surface of the stasis web—"like so. And then you wait for a moment."

Light spiderwebbed out along the surface of the stasis web from the point where the two touched, like a crack spreading through glass. There was a low buzz, and the black surface started to dissolve, motes breaking away and drifting into the air like fine ash. Kit tossed the destabilizer carelessly aside, staring at the disappearing surface as though it were all that mattered in the world.

Most of the web was empty, leaving nothing behind once it had finished its dissolution. Then, in the very center, something came into view. Kit let out a long breath and staggered back against Gyre, who put a steadying hand on her shoulder.

"Is that it?" he said.

"That's it." She bent to pick the thing up. "We actually fucking found it."

The Core Analytica, after all that, wasn't much to look at. It was cube-shaped, about the size of a man's head, made of some dark, metallic substance without the sheen of unmetal. At first Gyre thought it was solid, but on closer inspection he saw it was formed of interlocking metal rods, slotted over and around one another to form a three-dimensional grid. The largest of them were as big as his thumb, but through the gaps he could see smaller and smaller grids inside the thing, delicate hair-thin rods, like filigree.

"What does it do?"

"Don't know. Didn't ask." Kit stared at the thing in reverence. "Naumoriel wants it bad, and that's good enough for me."

His hand was still on her shoulder, and he gave her a tentative squeeze. "Then, let's get it back to him."

Kit nodded breathlessly.

Something rumbled, the sound coming in through the walls like distant thunder. The arcana shifted and clattered on their tables. A few windows, set high and narrow like arrow slits in a fortress, momentarily strobed with brilliant light.

"What in the plaguing fuck?" Kit said.

"I think," Gyre said slowly, "that we should get out of here *now*."

A moment later, the front door blew in.

Maya

Maya had learned to ride, of course, but she wouldn't call herself an expert. She'd had a few turns around a yard on a broken-down old warbird, and once Jaedia had let her gallop a swiftbird up and down an empty field, but that was about it.

Fortunately, her current mount was well trained and responded easily to the reins and her half-remembered whistle commands. She clung to the saddle as it raced back into Deepfire, other traffic giving her a wide berth. When she had a moment, she glanced up at the Spike on her right, using the huge building to gauge her progress.

In her breast, rage and shame wrestled back and forth. She saw the light of her power as it consumed the rebel girl, Yora's face as Tanax cut her down, Sarah's muffled scream. Behind them was Jaedia, smiling her sad smile.

Raskos used *us*. Centarchs were supposed to be exemplars, both protecting civilization and demonstrating why it was *worth* protecting. The dux had turned them into his personal assassins.

He's not going to get away with this.

The chimneys of the manufactories loomed ahead of her. It took a few turns to find Third Street and Broad Way, but eventually she reached a broad stone building, entrance blocked off by a high iron fence. Auxiliary guards lined the front, more than she'd seen last night, and there was a carriage parked just inside. For a moment, Maya hesitated.

Jaedia...She touched the Thing, a hard lump in her chest, and her resolve hardened. *Jaedia would find some way to get the truth.*

She whistled the warbird to a halt well short of the gates, dismounted without much grace, and turned to face the line of guards. There were a half dozen of them, with spears and pointed helmets, already watching her in the light of lanterns hanging from the fence. Maya stalked over, *deiat* still threaded into her panoply.

"Open the gate," she said when they moved to bar her way.

"This is private property," said a nervous woman with a sergeant's marks. Maya stopped a few meters from them and drew her haken.

"I am an agathios of the Twilight Order," she said as the blade ignited with a *whoomph*. "I answer to the Council of Kyriarchs. Now, *open the gate* before I open it for you."

The Auxies were edging sideways, out of her path, but the luckless sergeant was stuck. The woman's throat worked nervously.

"I can't...my orders..."

Maya closed her fist. A spear of white-hot fire flashed past the sergeant's head, frizzling her hair and hitting the door where it was secured by a thick iron bar. The center of the bar and a good chunk of the ironwork splashed into liquid metal, which sprayed, sizzling, across the gravel courtyard. The two halves of the gate swung inward with a groan as the remnants of the bar fell away.

The Thing felt hot in Maya's chest. *Deiat* was flowing through her like blood, the power bubbling just below her skin.

"Thank you," she snarled, "for your cooperation."

The sergeant stood stock-still as Maya passed, shoving the broken gate aside. At the far end of the courtyard, another squad of Auxies was forming up. She recognized Guria Fairshot at their head. Each of the dozen men and women had a blaster pistol trained on her. *Raskos must have sent his inner circle to keep his precious treasure safe.*

"Agathios," Guria rumbled. "I didn't think to see you here."

"Get out of my way," Maya said. "In the name of the Twilight Order."

"My instructions come from the dux," Guria said stolidly. "No one is to enter."

"The dux is not a centarch."

"Neither are you," Guria said.

She raised her haken and stepped forward. "Take it up with my master, then."

The blasters followed her. Guria looked uncertain.

"I don't want to hurt you, Agathios."

"I was about to say the same thing," Maya said, taking another step forward.

"Stop—"

An Auxie with a nervous trigger finger robbed Guria of the chance to give the order to shoot. An energy bolt lanced out with a *crack*, followed by a dozen more as the rest followed suit.

A blaster was a simple device, at its core. It held a sunsplinter—a bit of arcana that stored *deiat*—and channeled that power down the barrel in its simplest, most destructive form. Jaedia had taught Maya to respect the weapons. As Chosen arcana, they could be dangerous, even to a centarch, and her panoply would strain to protect her from more than a few hits.

However powerful the bolts were, they were infinitely simpler than even the basic attacks Jaedia had used in their sparring. With plenty of time to prepare her defense, Maya stood in the center of a ring of fire, discs of blazing power shifting and whirling to block the incoming shots faster than the eye could follow. An instant later, she released the trapped energy as a wide burst of divine flame, blasting the Auxies off their feet and sending Guria sprawling against the warehouse doors.

With time to think, she'd done better than that moment in the tunnel. The soldiers might be scorched, but they weren't incinerated. Every lesson Jaedia had ever taught her, all the lectures about careful control, ran through her head as she saw the rebel girl burn to ash once again.

"You can't," Guria croaked as she walked past him. "The dux..."

"Let's see what the dux is so eager to hide," she said. She raised her haken and slashed across the doors, and they fell in flaming pieces around her.

Gyre

Gyre stared down the long aisle of artifacts at the broken doors. With his nighteye still active, the light was painfully bright, a flaming sword like an actinic bar of agony etching itself onto his retina.

"That's a plagued centarch!" Kit hissed, ducking back behind a large, multijointed unmetal crab claw.

"I figured that out," Gyre said. He pressed in beside her, eye streaming. "Now what?"

"If anyone's in here," a young woman's voice called out, "surrender now in the name of the Twilight Order!"

"Raskos must have figured out we were hitting the warehouse," Gyre said.

"How?" Kit snarled, clutching the Analytica to her chest.

"Does it matter? We have to get out of here."

"Shit." Kit's lip twisted. "Shit shit fucking plaguefire." She clutched the thing tighter. "I'm so fucking close. But we'll never get back upstairs now."

"Just…calm down." Gyre took a deep breath. "I've got some alchemicals. That might put her off-balance."

"A blaster can hurt a centarch," Kit said. "Or so I hear. I haven't had the chance to test it myself."

"Okay. You get up to the catwalk. I'll try to stun her. We just need to buy enough time to get clear."

"This was *not* part of the plan," Kit muttered, and then, under her breath: "*Fuck*. Here."

She held out the Core Analytica. Gyre looked at her questioningly.

"It won't fit in my pack," she muttered, "and I'm going to need my hands free. Just…don't let her get it, all right? No matter what. If you want your trip to the Tomb—"

"I got it." Gyre shoved the cube into his pack. "Ready?"

"No," Kit said. She grinned, a little shakily.

Gyre spun out from behind the claw-thing, running down the aisle long enough to catch the centarch's attention, then hopping over a table full of loose coins. He judged the jump wrong and scraped half of them to the floor, where they pinged on the flagstones and rolled away.

That definitely got her attention, at least. He heard footsteps and caught a glimpse of the flaming sword getting closer. He pulled a stunner from his belt pouch, judged the distance carefully, and hurled it over the row of junk, squeezing his eye closed and looking away. It went off with a *whump* and a brilliant light, and almost simultaneously a *crack* of blaster fire came from overhead.

"*Not* going to surrender," the centarch said. She sounded younger than he was. "Okay, then."

Gyre was already moving. Behind him, a pile of bricks blew apart in a wave of flames, and the girl stepped through the wreckage after him. He turned long enough to hurl another alchemical, but a pinpoint blast of fire caught and incinerated it in midair.

"I have some questions for you," she said. "So just stop before someone gets hurt."

Her haken snapped up in time to intercept a blaster bolt, the blinding energy vanishing into the sword. The centarch turned and spotted Kit's dark figure hurrying along the catwalk.

"That's getting really irritating," she said, and raised one hand.

A blast of flame scythed out, and Kit threw herself flat. The burst was aimed not at her but at the catwalk behind her, and a chunk of the wood-and-iron walkway was blown into flaming splinters. As Kit bounded back to her feet, the whole structure started to twist, brackets popping away from the support pillar. Kit rode the still-burning catwalk down, pieces falling away and crashing among the gathered artifacts, raising clouds of dust and smoke.

"Kit!" Gyre shouted as he lost sight of her. He started in that direction, then pulled up short as the blazing haken interposed itself, eye-wateringly bright.

"I said I have some questions for you," the centarch said. Her hair had gotten loose, blowing in the rising heat of the flames, red as blood. "Drop your weapons."

No! Gyre squeezed his good eye shut. *No no* no. For a moment he was eight years old again, watching as Va'aht Thousandcuts casually destroyed his family, took his eye, showed him the truth about the Dawn Republic and the Twilight Order. Republicans might sneer at the subjects of the Splinter Kings, call them slaves under the heels of vicious despots, but as long as the centarchs existed, the people of the Republic were something worse. Ants, to be crushed or brushed aside.

Under his mask, pain lanced through his scar.

No. He let out a breath, heart pounding, and opened his eye. Then he moved, with all the speed and ferocity he'd spent twelve years learning.

Another alchemical bomb slipped into one hand, and he lofted it high over the centarch's head. She reacted as he'd hoped, sending a blast of fire to intercept the thing, and it detonated with a sharp *crack* that staggered them both. In the brief moment of distraction, Gyre drew his blades, long and short. The long blade slashed at the centarch's face, and she had time to bring her haken down to parry.

Steel met *deiat*, and the metal melted away in the fury of the power of creation. But Gyre was already dropping the weapon, fading to the side, his small blade coming up to bury itself in the centarch's belly.

Blue energy flickered around him, and the weapon stopped, an inch from her shirt, as though it had struck solid steel. For a stunned moment, Gyre was still. The centarch whirled to face him, long red hair swinging behind her, and to his watering eye something in her face looked almost familiar.

Then, as the haken came around—

Maya?

Maya

The warehouse was everything she'd imagined and more. Enough unsanctioned arcana to hang Raskos, she was certain. For a moment, staring at all of it, she wasn't sure what to do next.

Movement along one of the aisles answered that question. Two dark-clad figures, hurriedly stowing something away. Her fight with Guria must have warned Raskos' people to try to hide whatever they could. Maya found herself grinning as she strode forward. *Too late.*

Power flowed through her, pulsing with every beat of her heart. The Thing seemed to pulse in time, blood warm. She'd never done anything like this before. Jaedia had taught her to stay in control, to be precise. Now *deiat* seemed to be boiling under her skin, straining to be released. One of Raskos' spies confronted her, and she blew his alchemical tricks away with a wave of flame. When his companion opened fire with a blaster, Maya cut loose with a blast of fire that brought down a wide section of catwalk.

She wanted to laugh as the man in black scurried away from her. She stalked after him, half expecting the ground around her to blaze with the power of her passing. Maya had always known that *deiat* was the raw fire of the sun, the power of creation, but she'd never understood it as powerfully as she did now. She felt like the sun itself given human form, smashing aside any human obstacle with a flick of her finger. She felt like a god.

Raskos' agent hesitated, then came at her again. Maya incinerated his alchemical bomb and parried his first strike, his steel vaporizing in the heat of *deiat*. He slashed at her gut with a dagger, but her panoply caught the blow, and she barely felt the wave of cold from the impact. His hood fell back, revealing a youth not much older than her, with brown skin and dark hair. Most of his face was obscured behind a silver mask, intricately carved in abstract patterns, blocking one eye completely.

Halfmask! It had to be. But Halfmask worked with Yora. *So what in plaguefire is he doing in Raskos' sanctum?*

The power running through her seemed to quench all doubts. Time enough for questions when he was at her mercy. Maya brought her haken around, slamming the butt end into the side of his head. The blow knocked him sprawling to the ground, and the silver mask came free, skittering across the tiles. The man rolled onto his back, edging away, as she once again brought her flaming blade level with his nose.

Under the mask, his face was dominated by an ugly scar, a vertical slash running from his cheek up past his eyebrow, bisecting his ruined left eye. Maya stared, perversely fascinated. The wound seemed...

Something moved, in the deepest of her memories, like a monstrous shark stirring in a placid pond. *Blood.* So much blood, and so many screams—her own throat, torn raw with shrieking—and—

Recognition was so visceral that Maya nearly dropped her haken. The brilliant blade vanished, and she blinked in the sudden darkness. When she tried to speak, her lips seemed to be fused together.

"It...you can't..."

"Maya." He pushed himself up on his elbows. Blood trickled down from his hairline. "It's Maya, isn't it." It wasn't a question.

"Gyre?" She whispered the name. "You're...*here?*"

For a moment, they were silent. Somewhere in the warehouse, flames crackled.

"I wondered if I'd see you again," Gyre said. He sounded weary. "I didn't imagine this, though."

"You're—" Maya shook her head. "*You* are Halfmask? The one the dux is so desperate to get his hands on?"

"And you're his loyal little attack dog," Gyre said.

Maya felt like she'd just startled awake from a doze. All the certainty of moments before drained away. Her free hand went to the Thing and then flinched back, finding the tiny arcana almost too hot to touch.

"I'm not—" she started, then shook her head again. "What are you *doing* here?"

"Here in Deepfire? Or here in Raskos' treasure horde?"

"*Either!*" Maya said. "Why aren't you back at the farm with Mom and Dad?"

"At the *farm?*" Gyre choked out a laugh. "You have no idea, do you? Never thought to check up on us?"

"Agathia aren't allowed contact with their families," Maya said. "I thought after I got my cognomen, I might..."

Staring at Gyre, at his scar, she felt her memory shifting again.

"Of course," Gyre said. "Can't let our brave defenders of the Order be contaminated with *feelings.*" He coughed, and spat blood on the tiles. "Mom and Dad are dead."

"What..."

"Mom died less than a year after they took you," Gyre said. He spoke quickly, as though the words were bubbling up from somewhere dark inside him. "It broke her, what happened. Dad would barely talk to me after that. I left when I was twelve. The next time I came back, he was gone, too. Some illness, the neighbors said."

"I'm...sorry." In truth Maya didn't know how to feel. Her parents were barely memories, vague blurs of love and affection at the dawn of time. "No one told me."

"How could they?" Gyre said. "After the Order kidnapped you, they didn't exactly leave us an address."

"The Order didn't *kidnap* me."

"You didn't want to go."

"I was *five.*" Maya's hand went to the Thing again and found it marginally cooler. "They saved my life."

His good eye narrowed. "You don't remember what happened that day, do you?"

"I..." Maya swallowed, looking down at him. "I remember that you tried to stop them from taking me."

"And do you remember Va'aht Thousandcuts carving out my eye, for the crime of spilling precious Order blood?" His lip twisted in an ugly smile at her hesitation. "I thought not."

"Gyre..." Maya took a deep breath. "I don't know what to say."

He climbed, slowly, to his feet. "You don't need to say anything."

The venom in his tone was enough to stoke her anger again. "I suppose you're going to tell me you became a rebel in order to come and save me?"

"No," Gyre said. "I imagined that. I always knew that by the time I got the chance, the Order would have made you into one of *them*."

"You've been fighting the Republic—killing innocent people, smuggling *dhak*—"

"I haven't killed anyone innocent," Gyre said. "Unless you count Auxies, which I don't. And I've smuggled quickheal, and bone-break potion, and—did you know Dad had a shed full of weevil killers on the farm? That's your *dhak*. I'm sure the weevils will be grateful for your efforts."

"It's not about the fucking weevils." She could see the cavern under Litnin, the children in cages waiting to be torn apart by plaguespawn. "The Order keeps people safe."

"The Order props up thugs like Raskos in the name of keeping all the power to itself," Gyre said. "But I don't expect you to understand."

"I—"

Maya hesitated. There was so much she wanted to explain, but Gyre's anger was a palpable force, hanging in the air between them like a dark curtain. Before she could think of a way around it, there were shouts from outside, new voices. Maya thought she recognized Tanax's.

"Are you going to kill me?" Gyre said.

"Of course not," Maya said. "You're my brother. You—"

"Then I'm leaving," Gyre interrupted, "before Raskos does it for you."

He bent to retrieve his pack. Maya stepped forward and put her foot on it, raising her haken again.

"You know I can't let you just . . . *steal* this," Maya said. "Please, Gyre. You don't have to go. I can protect you."

"I very much doubt that." Gyre stared at the pack for a long time, as though trying to figure something out. Then he sighed and turned away. "I assume you don't have any objections if I take my friend, at least?"

The voices outside were getting louder. Maya bent and picked up the pack herself, then shook her head.

"If you have to go, then go."

"I doubt I'll see you again," he said.

"Gyre—"

He let out a breath. "Goodbye, Maya."

She watched, mutely, as he rounded a corner toward where the catwalk had fallen. For a moment she considered going after him, igniting her haken and forcing him to his knees. *If only he would stay and* listen. She was certain she could explain, cut through whatever poison the years had built up inside him.

Instead, she turned away, letting *deiat* fade from her body. She felt suddenly, unutterably tired.

At the entrance to the warehouse, Tanax was just coming through the broken doors, with Beq and Varo close behind him. Beq caught Maya's eye, frantically, and made a gesture Maya didn't understand. Maya frowned and stopped, dropping the torn pack.

"Agathios Tanax," she said. "I need to report the discovery of a considerable quantity of *dhak* and unsanctioned arcana, which I believe belongs to—"

"*Agathios Maya,*" he grated, and raised his haken. His blade, a shimmering line of folded space, twisted and shivered in front of her eyes. Maya went silent.

"I am seizing you in the name of the Twilight Order," Tanax said, his voice cold. "You will have the opportunity to present evidence in your defense." He took a deep breath. "You stand accused of treason."

Chapter 15

It was good that Kit was so light, because Gyre had to make his exit from the warehouse with her limp body slung over his shoulder, and his legs already felt like rubber beneath him.

For a moment, head still ringing from Maya's blow, he'd been unable to find her amid the wreckage of the catwalk, and he wondered if she'd already run for it. Eventually, though, he spotted the blue of her hair, lying motionless on a broken table among scattered arcana. Stomach churning, Gyre bent beside her. To his relief, she was still breathing, though a cut on her scalp was bleeding badly. When a few prods didn't wake her, he hoisted her up and staggered toward the back of the warehouse. Voices were already audible from the front door.

Fortunately, Maya's arrival had attracted all the guards on the premises. Gyre went out a back door and found the rear of the building unattended.

Traffic was light in the manufactory district at this hour, and he had to walk several blocks before reaching a road busy enough to hope for a cab. A few passed him by, either because they were off for the night

or because they didn't like the look of the scarred man with an unconscious girl on his shoulder. Finally, though, a two-wheeler pulled up.
The driver, a big woman with an enormous shock of frizzy teal hair,
looked down at them with concern.

"You all right, friends?" she said. "You been robbed? Need a lift to
the guard station?"

"Not robbed," Gyre muttered, trying to put a little slur into his
words. "Jus' a good night at the tavern. Little punch-up." He swayed—
no great trick—and gave the driver a sloppy grin. "You should see the
other guys."

She laughed. "Try not to bleed all over the cushions, all right?"

He gave her an address about a block from Lynnia's. It was a risk,
going there, but he'd hardly be the first injured person to stagger up to
the alchemist's doorstep at all hours. *It'll be all right. I think. I hope.* At
this point, he didn't see another option.

Once they were in the cab, Gyre gave Kit a more thorough examina-
tion, wrapping her head in a makeshift bandage torn from his sleeve. A
few other cuts bled shallowly, and the two smallest fingers on her left
hand were definitely broken, with bruises blooming all along that arm.
She must have landed badly. Still, she hadn't cracked her skull, so he
didn't think she was in immediate danger. *Lynnia can take care of her.
Of us.*

He leaned back against the threadbare cushion, heart slamming in
his chest. His pupils were still wide with nighteye, and the neutralizer
was gone with his pack, so every lamp and lantern seemed like a miniature star. Afterimages of that flaming sword danced across his retina,
even when he closed his eye.

Maya. After twelve years.

Fuck.

He hadn't had a plan, when he'd talked to her. The words had just
come tumbling out, the product of a thousand imagined conversations,
a hypothetical argument turned horribly real.

The hard part is that it went about as badly as I expected.

Something at the back of his mind, the part of him that had never grown up, screamed at him that he should have stayed. Talked to her, made her understand. *I wouldn't have gotten the chance.* The notorious rebel Halfmask had a prison cell to look forward to, at best, and more likely quick execution. He doubted that Maya, young as she was, had the authority to change that.

And maybe she wouldn't have wanted to. Just because she'd let him go, in the heat of the moment, didn't mean she would take his side in front of the dux and her fellow centarchs.

She's a centarch. The look in her eyes had been all he needed. The superior glare that said he was beneath contempt, even before she'd recognized him. *I always knew I would never get her back.*

Kit moaned weakly, but her eyes stayed closed.

The cab driver let them out, and Gyre shoved a few thalers into her hands, waving aside her offers to help. Gathering Kit in his arms again, he trudged around the corner and made his way to Lynnia's front door. On the doorstep, he realized he didn't have his key—he hardly ever came in this way, and it had been at the bottom of his pack—but the lights were still on, and Lynnia opened the door to his knock.

"Get inside!" she snapped at the sight of the two of them. "Fool boy. What if someone followed you?"

"Don't think they did," Gyre said. "Auxies are busy."

"I thought you were caught for sure, or dead." Lynnia slammed the door and started pulling the curtains, her bad leg dragging behind her. "What *happened*?"

"What happened?" Gyre blinked. His head was still pounding, and his scar throbbed. "What do you mean?"

"At the *tunnel*, you plaguing moron!"

Gyre frowned. "Nothing happened at the tunnel. Kit and I got... we missed the rendezvous. I thought Yora would call everything off."

"You..." Lynnia stopped, facing the last window, and didn't look around. "Oh, Chosen defend. You don't know, do you?"

Gyre's throat went tight. "Know what?"

"The tunnel was an ambush. Yora's *dead*, Gyre." When she turned to face him, her face was tight with fury. "A lot of the others, too. The rest are in the dux's cells. Sarah's with them, I hear, but they don't expect her to survive."

"Yora's..." Gyre swayed. "She..."

"Where were you?" Lynnia stalked closer. "You didn't even *know*? Gyre, what have you *done*?"

Gyre staggered back against the door, the room spinning around him. Lynnia was saying something, but he couldn't parse it. She hurried forward, taking Kit out of his arms, but made no effort to assist Gyre as his legs gave way and he slipped to the floor.

When he woke, he was in his own bed, and Lynnia was working at his table by the light of a lamp. The nighteye had worn off at last, but his good eye still ached from the abuse, and his scar pulsed with a deep, throbbing pain. He tried to sit up, which set his head spinning again, and he settled back on the pillow with a groan.

"I'd stay put a little while longer," Lynnia said without looking up. "You've got some quickheal in you, but that's quite a bump on your skull."

"I gathered." Gyre found a mug of water on the bedside table, lifted it carefully, and drank. "Is Kit all right?"

"She will be. She was in worse shape. Splinted the fingers and gave her some bone-break potion. It looks like she fell off a plagued roof."

"That's more or less what happened," Gyre said. He paused. "Yora's really..."

His voice trailed off into silence, which stretched on for what felt like an eternity as Lynnia's pen scratched over a ledger book. Eventually the old alchemist sighed and turned her chair around.

"That's the word on the street, and I don't see any reason to doubt it," she said. "Nobody who went to the tunnel with her came back, and some of them are definitely in the dungeons. Raskos proclaimed a great victory over the criminals and smugglers." Her eyes narrowed, gaze pinning him to the bed. "I *also* hear that Raskos' private treasure horde nearly burned down. Some kind of fight there."

Gyre swallowed. "What do you want me to say?"

"You don't need to say anything." Lynnia got to her feet, stretching her bad leg with a wince. "Yora was... Did you know I helped her father, in his stupid little war?"

"She told me that once," Gyre said.

"After he died, those of us who were left felt... responsible for her. I helped her as much as I could."

"I thought you believed in her cause."

"It gets harder to believe in causes when you get old," Lynnia said. "It's all I can do to believe in people. I believed in *you*, Gyre, when you washed up on my doorstep. I introduced you to Yora because I thought you could help each other." Lynnia sucked in a deep breath. "And you left her to die."

"I didn't—" Gyre struggled until he was sitting up, head pounding. "She wasn't supposed to—"

"Save it. Yora always knew you weren't in it to help anyone but yourself and find your plaguing *Tomb*, but I didn't think you'd just cut and run when the time came."

"What makes you think I'd have been able to help Yora if I'd been there?" Gyre shot back, pressing one hand against his ruined eye. Pain spiked in his head. "Maybe I'd just be dead with the rest of them."

"Maybe that would have been better," Lynnia said, voice cracking.

They stared at one another in silence.

"You need to leave the city," the alchemist said quietly.

"How long until Kit is fit to travel?"

"You're not going to abandon her too?" Lynnia snarled. "I suppose you still need her, don't you?"

Gyre tried to keep his voice steady. "Once she can move, we'll leave. You won't see us again."

"Good," Lynnia said. She turned away from him, and a measure of professional detachment returned to her tone. "She should wake up anytime. I'd wait until tomorrow evening to get moving."

"Until tomorrow evening, then." Gyre hesitated, and Lynnia walked away, bad leg dragging. "Thank you, Lynnia."

The alchemist snorted and slammed the door behind her.

Eventually, with the quickheal doing its work, the pounding in Gyre's head subsided. He managed to make it to the washroom at the end of the hall, and after a long piss and the chance to scrub the last of the bloodstains from his face, he felt better.

He found his mind already back at work, planning the next step. *It all depends on where they took the Core Analytica.* From Lynnia's description, it sounded like there had been considerable chaos at the warehouse, and it was just possible no one had realized its importance. *But Maya would have brought my pack back with her, so it's probably in the Spike by now.* That made things harder, but not necessarily impossible—

Halfway down the hall, outside the guest room door, he paused at the sound of sobbing.

The only person who could be in that room was Kit. But the idea of Kit crying—Kitsraea *Doomseeker*—seemed about as likely as taking a stroll to the moon. She'd barely flinched at the charge of an ancient ghoul-construct, and laughed at the prospect of being caught by Raskos' Legionaries.

He hesitated, then rapped at the door.

"I'm still not hungry." It was Kit's voice.

"It's me," Gyre said. "Can I come in?"

There was a long pause. "I suppose."

He opened the door. Kit was sitting up in the spare bed. She wore nothing but a thin shift and a collection of bandages, one wound around her head, another swathing her broken fingers, and several more covering a variety of cuts. Bruises were blooming across the right side of her body, and her eyes were red and puffy.

"You carried me back here?" she said.

Gyre nodded and closed the door behind him.

"I admit I expected to wake up in a prison cell," she said, pulling her knees to her chest under the blanket. "Or not at all. Did you kill that centarch?"

Gyre gave an involuntary laugh. "Not even close."

"Then what happened?"

"She let us go. It's...a long story."

"But she got the Analytica."

Gyre nodded. Kit put her chin on her knees, eyes fixed on the opposite wall. After a moment of silence, Gyre dragged a chair over to the bedside and sat down beside her.

"Lynnia's very angry with us," he said. "With me, really. But she said we can stay here until tomorrow night, and you should be mobile by then. We can try—"

"You don't need to wait for me," Kit said. "Just go."

"I need you," Gyre said. "That hasn't changed. And I think you still need me, if we're going to get the Analytica."

"You don't understand." She turned to face him. "It's over, Gyre."

"Of course it isn't."

"Naumoriel doesn't tolerate failure. After this, he'll cut us loose. Use someone else."

"I'll apologize," Gyre said. "Grovel, if I have to."

"Gyre—"

He got to his feet. "We can't just give up."

"You don't understand."

"You're right, I don't." Gyre turned away. "Stay here. Get some rest."

Kit looked down at the bed and said nothing.

Gyre had a fair few bruises of his own, and his fighting gear was stained with sweat and blood, so he ventured out in civilian clothes and a hooded robe. He didn't bother bringing any weapons. If the ghouls decided they were going to kill him, he wasn't foolish enough to imagine he could change their minds.

Lynnia was working in the basement when he slipped downstairs and out into the city. It was still before noon, and the streets were busy as usual, full of hurrying pedestrians and animals hissing, bellowing, and squawking. It didn't seem fair, somehow, that nothing had changed, that Deepfire went on just as it had before last night. *Before my sister found me. Before someone killed Yora.*

A cabbie was happy to take him back up to the manufactory district, and even happier to wait around once Gyre shoved a stack of thalers at him. He got some odd looks from passing vehicles as he approached the door to the ghouls' hideout. It looked the same as before, windows boarded up, apparently long abandoned.

The closer he got, the less sure he was that this was a good idea. *Maybe Kit is right. Maybe we're better off just getting as far away from here as we can.* They could flee into the Splinter Kingdoms, beyond the reach of the Republic, and . . .

And what? His lip curled in a snarl. *You've been chasing the Tomb for years, Gyre, and this is as close as you've ever gotten.* More to the point, now that he knew the city was full of living ghouls and not just their wreckage, he didn't just need to *find* it to get the power he wanted. *I need them to help me.*

I just have to explain that we're not finished yet. He was already working on a plan to get the Core Analytica out of the Spike. *It just needs a few tweaks. Maybe more than a few. But we'll get there.*

He knocked. No one answered, but the door swung inward, just a fraction. The latch hung limp and broken. Gyre pushed through slowly and closed it behind him before parting the heavy curtains that blocked any hint of light from the outside.

"Hello?" he said. "Elariel?"

Even in total darkness, he could tell something was wrong. Fumbling in his pocket, he produced a glowstone, then hesitated.

"If you're here, say something," he said. "Otherwise I'm lighting this."

Only echoes answered. Gyre gave the stone a sharp rap against his leg, and it started to glow with a soft blue light. The cavernous interior space of the hollowed-out building drank it in, wreathed in long shadows, but it was enough to see that nothing remained of the huge arcana Elariel had been tending. The complicated network of crystal and wire, the plantlike armature, everything was gone. Gyre raised the stone above his head and turned in a circle, then swore, as loud and violent as he knew how.

By the time he returned to Lynnia's, it was late afternoon. A tray with a bowl of soup and some soft bread sat untouched outside the closed door of the guest room. Gyre stepped over it, rapped sharply, and went in without waiting for an answer.

Kit, still in a borrowed shift, was sitting cross-legged on the bed, unwinding a bandage from her arm. She looked up as he came in, and for a moment he expected a sarcastic quip, but she didn't seem to be able to muster the energy.

"They were gone," she said.

"I don't understand," Gyre said. "How could they move all of that in one night?"

"Most of it moves itself, I think." Kit finished peeling off the bandage with a wince.

"You knew they'd just vanish like this?"

"Mmmhmm." She poked the bruise and winced again. "It's what they do. When one pawn fails, throw it away and bring out the next."

"So that's it?" Gyre said.

"That's it." Kit looked up at him. "I told you to leave, didn't I? I'm useless to you now, I promise. I won't even—" She stopped abruptly.

"You won't what?"

"It's not important," Kit said. "You should go."

"Kit. Tell me."

"If you're *that* interested." She sighed and put on a singsong tone. "In about a month, I'll be dead. Six weeks at most. So if you've got some fantasy about you and me, I don't know, becoming partners in crime out in the Splinter Kingdoms, you can give it up."

"You'll be...why?" Gyre's eyes narrowed. "Is it the ghouls? They don't want you to give up their secret—"

"They couldn't care less. Maybe once upon a time they were worried the Order would find out they're still alive, but after this long, who would believe me?"

"So who's going to kill you?"

"Nobody. I'll just...expire. Although, frankly, maybe it would be more poetic to find a cliff somewhere—"

"I don't understand." Gyre took a step closer. "You're—"

"Oh, for Chosen's sake." Kit leaned over and grabbed his wrist, pulling him forward and pressing his palm against her chest. "Feel."

After a moment, Gyre cleared his throat. "Your breasts may be a little on the small side, but that hardly seems *fatal*—"

"Not my lack of tits, moron." She actually smiled, though her eyes were damp with tears. "My heartbeat."

Gyre concentrated a moment on the gentle pulse under his hand. It sped up slightly, and in between the thumps, he felt something else, a soft buzz like there was an insect trapped under Kit's breastbone.

"I told you when I was fifteen, I got some bad news," she said. "I'd been having...spells. Dizziness, nausea. I went to an alchemist, and she told me it was my heart, that it was weak and getting weaker. Within a year or two, it would just...stop. And that would be that." She shrugged. "I asked if there was anyone who could help me, and she told me that I needed a *dhakim*."

"So you went looking for the Tomb," Gyre said.

"I wasn't *looking* for it, exactly. I wasn't in a good place." Kit took a deep breath, and her heart thumped harder against Gyre's hand. "I figured either I'd find something that could save me, down in the dark places, or I'd die trying. The latter seemed more likely."

"But the ghouls helped you."

"Most of them wanted nothing to do with humans. *Naumoriel* helped me, after a fashion. He put a little bit of arcana in there"—she tapped the back of Gyre's hand—"that keeps my heart going. But it needs fuel, and only a ghoul can fill it back up again." She blinked and rubbed her eyes with the back of her hand. "By this time my heart is too weak to manage without it. So in a month or so, it runs out, and then . . . all done. No more Kitsraea."

Gyre sat for a moment, trying to digest that.

"You can take your hand off my tit now," Kit said.

"Sorry." Gyre leaned back. "So you've been working for Naumoriel in exchange for more fuel?"

She nodded. "He had a whole series of things he wanted retrieved, Chosen know why. The Core Analytica was the last, and the hardest to get to. He said . . ." She swallowed. "He said if I got it for him, he'd fix me permanently. I'd be free."

"Do you believe him?"

"Maybe. I don't have much of a choice, do I? Not that it matters now." She flopped back on the bed, staring at the ceiling. "Do you think it hurts to blow your head off with a blaster? It *looks* like it hurts, but I think it'd be over too quick for you to notice."

Gyre looked past her, eyes distant.

"I know what you're thinking," Kit said. "If I'm going to die, why not spend the next six weeks getting absolutely *catastrophically* drunk and fucking anything that's warm and willing? And believe me, I intend to. But I don't know *exactly* when it'll happen, and how disgusting it'll be when it does, and I'd rather not be remembered as the mess someone had to clean up in the back room of a tavern."

"Kit—"

"And can you imagine if it happened while you were, you know, busy? Like one minute someone's fucking your brains out, and then next minute, *GACK*." She put her hands to her throat and stuck out her tongue. "Definitely not an appealing prospect. I don't know if I could live with myself, putting that on someone. I mean, I guess I wouldn't have to, obviously, but—"

"*Kit.*"

"*What?*" Her eyes were tearing up again. "Can we please be *done* with this subject? Better yet, can you just *go*? You're done with me."

"I'm not," Gyre said. "I want you to take me to the Tomb."

Kit snorted. "I told you, the ghouls won't contact me again."

"So? You found it once."

"Not exactly," Kit said. "It was more like I got separated from my crew, and I was wandering alone in some old tunnels, and when I passed out from exhaustion I was close enough that they sent their constructs to bring me in. I couldn't find my way back."

"You know the basic location, which is more than anybody else. We'll find it together."

"I'll draw you a map. I have important drinking and fucking to do."

"Kit—"

"I *failed*, Gyre. Do you have any idea what they'll do to me—to *us*—if we just turn up again?"

"Kill us?"

"Worse," she muttered. "It could be so much worse. You haven't seen that place; you have no idea—"

"I'm willing to risk it, if there's a chance." He cocked his head. "Aren't you supposed to be the Doomseeker?"

"You're serious," she said. "Even if we get there, which we won't, what are you planning to tell Naumoriel? 'Sorry we fucked up, can we have another shot?'"

"More or less. I'll have time to work on the wording."

"You're crazy." Kit sat up, and for a moment her old smile flickered across her face. "And that's *me* saying so."

"I can't go backward," Gyre said. "Not now."

Kit stared at him for a long moment, then burst out laughing.

"Plague it," she said, running a hand through the blue spikes of her hair. "What the fuck. Why not? Tramping through freezing tunnels is as good a way to spend the last few weeks of my life as sitting in a tavern with a bucket of rum and a pretty boy's head between my legs, right? Don't answer that."

Gyre found himself smiling back at her. "I wasn't planning on it."

Chapter 16

Someone had apparently drawn the line at actually throwing Maya into a cell.

Tanax had taken her haken and panoply belt, and she'd been escorted back to the Spike by a quartet of Legionaries. Once there, though, they hadn't taken her to the dungeons. Instead, she'd been marched gently but firmly back to her own room, where two of the white-armored soldiers settled in beside the door as guards. Another, she noticed, was stationed outside to keep an eye on the windows.

Treason. She could see how it might look that way to Tanax. She'd disobeyed his orders and attacked Auxiliaries, and no doubt Raskos had been on hand to explain why his private warehouse was stuffed full of illegal arcana. *But he won't get away with it.* It was obvious that an investigation by an unbiased inspector was called for, and whoever it was wouldn't be fooled by the dux's justifications. *He's not going to wriggle out of this one.*

With *deiat* gone and adrenaline fading from her veins, exhaustion slipped over her like lead chains, but sleep still seemed distant. She found herself walking up and down her too-large suite, replaying the conversation with Gyre, trying to imagine what she could have said to make him understand.

I didn't realize Va'aht hurt him so badly. She'd remembered Gyre standing up to the centarch, and that something had happened afterward, but she hadn't imagined anything like the scar that sliced across her brother's face. *It's no wonder he hates us.* She hadn't seen Va'aht since he'd brought her to the Forge and given her into Baselanthus' care. Now she wondered if that was deliberate, if he was ashamed to face her.

And still, for all the anger she'd seen in Gyre, she couldn't help but think that if he would only *listen*, she could reach him. *If I could sit him down and explain everything. Tell him about my work with Jaedia, how we've helped people.* The threats of plaguespawn and *dhakim* were *real. If the Order doesn't stop them, who will?*

She wished, more than anything, that Jaedia was with her. *She would understand everything.*

From time to time, she caught the sound of conversation outside her door, but not clearly enough to make out the words. No one seemed inclined to come and check on her, in any case. Eventually, she decided to at least *try* to sleep, and to her surprise she barely managed to get her boots off before collapsing into bed. Between blinks, night outside the windows changed into a rosy dawn, and someone was knocking at her door. Maya sat up, head spinning.

"Who's there?" she said.

"It's Beq."

Shit. Maya looked down at herself, still in a rumpled uniform stained with ash, blood, and sweat. "Uh. Wait a minute, would you?"

"Are you all right?" Beq said.

"Fine. Just...hang on."

What she really needed was a bath, but that would have to wait. Maya hurriedly stripped and went over herself with a dampened towel, removing at least the worst of the grime. She paused for a moment at the sight of the Thing in the mirror—the little arcana was surrounded by a ring of angry red flesh, puffy to the touch. It itched.

Another thing to ask Baselanthus about. She shook her head and dressed—thankfully, the palace staff had cleaned her other uniforms—before rushing to the suite door. Beq, framed between the two Legionary guards, was carrying a tray with breakfast, for which Maya was suddenly ravenous.

"Let me put this down," Beq said, depositing the food on the table and closing the door behind her. Then, to Maya's surprise, Beq wrapped her in a tight hug. "Chosen defend, Maya. Are you okay?" She pulled back and put her hand against Maya's forehead. "You're burning up."

"I'm all right," Maya said. She was more aware than she wanted to be of the shape of the other girl's body pressed against her. *Idiot. She's trying to be a friend, something you badly need, and you're thinking about...* that. "Really. A night's sleep helped a lot."

"You must be starved," Beq said. She was also dressed in a fresh uniform and looked considerably better than Maya felt. "Please, eat something."

Maya didn't need more urging than that. She sat down at the table, guzzled water from the pitcher, and started in on the vulpi bacon and toast. Beq sat down opposite her and watched with a faint smile.

"Sorry to eat like a thickhead," Maya said. "I just didn't realize how badly I needed this."

"It's all right," Beq said. "But maybe wait a moment. I have news, and I'd rather not get a face full of half-chewed bacon."

That doesn't sound good. Maya washed down the toast with more water. "Let me hear it."

"Raskos is gone."

"What do you mean, *gone?*"

"No one can find him, as of not long after Tanax put you under arrest. The palace is going mad. Rumor is that he's fled the city because of what you found at the warehouse."

"That plaguing rat," Maya said. She wasn't sure whether to be furious or relieved that she'd been proven right. "So now what?"

"The Forge is putting together a temporary governor and a Legion detachment to keep order." Beq hesitated. "Their messenger said that your arrest stands, though. We're all to report back there today."

"I imagine it will take the Council a while to sort out what happened," Maya said, forcing a note of confidence.

"I hope so," Beq said. She lowered her voice and leaned forward. "There's something strange going on. Varo says that Tanax got a message from the Forge *before* you went to the ambush. He saw him going down to the Gate chamber. But Tanax didn't mention it to anyone."

"He is the *senior* agathios," Maya said. She leaned back, head spinning a little. "No doubt he has many secrets."

"Maybe." Beq glanced around, then shook her head. "Never mind. I'll tell you later."

"Is everything all right?"

"Fine." Beq swallowed. "Well. They've got Sarah in the cells."

"Is she going to live?"

"Maybe. They had to take off her arm." Beq shuddered. "I just... I don't know."

"What happened in the tunnel is on Raskos' head," Maya said. *It has to be.* When she closed her eyes, she saw the rebel burning away into ashes and bones. "And he'll get what he has coming to him."

"What about Nicomidi?" Beq said, very quietly. "If he's involved..."

"The Council will sort it out," Maya said firmly.

Beq gave a weak smile and got to her feet. "Finish your breakfast," she said. "Tanax will send for you before long. It's time to go home."

The Forge had never been *home*, not for Maya, but she couldn't say she was sorry to be seeing the last of Deepfire. The knowledge that Gyre was still out there, somewhere, only made it worse.

When I'm a centarch, maybe I can find him. She could come back here on her own, with no one to question her authority. *Though I don't think Jaedia would approve.*

No point in visiting the farm, though. Maya probed at that thought as she waited, pack at the ready, for Tanax to summon her. *Mom and Dad…* Thinking about them tugged at something in her chest, but it felt distant, as though it belonged to another life. *Does that make me horrible? My parents are dead. Have been dead, for years, and I didn't know.* She felt like she should feel more.

Maya shivered and wiped sweat from her forehead. The Thing itched, and she rubbed at it with the heel of her palm.

I wish Jaedia was here.

Eventually, the door opened. Tanax had washed and changed as well, into his dress uniform instead of his traveling clothes, and he looked every inch the aristocratic young agathios. Maya drew herself up to attention.

"Agathios Maya," he said.

"Agathios Tanax," she replied with a slight bow.

He glanced over his shoulders at the pair of Legionaries, still standing at the ready. "We are returning to the Forge. You will accompany me and be given into the Council's custody."

"I understand," Maya said. "I'm not planning to resist."

"Good." Tanax paused, as though on the point of saying something else, but quickly turned away. "Follow me."

Out in the hall, Beq and Varo joined them, along with another pair of Legionaries. Varo gave Maya an encouraging smile and fell in beside her as they walked.

"Had a friend who was accused of treason once," he said without preamble.

"Why do I feel like this isn't going to be encouraging?"

"The centarch looked into it and found him innocent!" Varo protested. "Said he was free to go."

"That's something."

"It's just that the next night, he got so drunk celebrating that he fell in the swamp and got his—"

Beq sniggered, and Maya rolled her eyes. Even Varo, to everyone's surprise, chuckled.

"I know this has been a...difficult conclusion to our assignment," Tanax said without looking around. "But I have faith in the Council's judgment. Perhaps we will be assigned to work together again someday."

Maya didn't know if he was talking about her, but she found herself thinking of Beq. *This is the end of our assignment.* Presumably, that meant Beq would go back to her workshop duties at the Forge, or be assigned another centarch or agathios to support. Either way, Maya wouldn't see her again unless the duty roster happened to bring them together. *That* thought was more wrenching than she cared to admit.

I have to talk to her. It was, given that Maya was currently under arrest for treason, perhaps not the most rational set of priorities, but it weighed on her mind as they descended the long spiral stairs, moving from the human-designed part of the palace to the ancient architecture of the Chosen. Maybe it was just that she didn't know what to expect from the treason charge, and whatever happened, for the moment it was out of her control. Whereas trying to talk to Beq, to express what she wanted to say—*that you're smart and funny and brave and also I've wanted to kiss you basically since the moment I first saw you*—was all too easy to picture, and no matter how she tried to phrase it in her mind, everything went horribly wrong.

The Gate was waiting for them, as changeless as the Spike itself. Maya felt Tanax send it the activation code, and the archway filled with swirling mist. He stepped aside and gestured for Maya to go first. With a shrug, Maya went through, crossing most of the Republic in an instant, and emerged in the Gate chamber of the Forge.

The last time she and Jaedia had returned, there'd been a single centarch on duty at the door. Now four of them were waiting, in full unmetal armor, with a rank of Legionaries standing behind them, rifles at the ready. Maya pulled up short, too surprised to even read their heraldry.

"Agathios Maya," one of the four said. Her voice buzzed from inside her helmet. "Where is your haken?"

"Tanax has it," Maya said, forgetting formality for a moment. "I'm not going to hurt anyone, I promise—"

"Council orders," the centarch snapped. "Come with us, please."

Maya had always assumed the Forge had jail cells—it had everything else—but she'd never heard of anyone being sent to them. Ordinary criminals were forwarded to the Republic system of justice, and *dhakim* were always swiftly executed.

It turned out that the Forge's prison was just as large and empty as the rest of the fortress. Her captors marched her down a row of open cells, their barred doors removed or rusted away. At the end of the hall, a stairway descended to a deeper level and another set of cells. These were larger and better maintained, carved out of stone and secure with iron doors. Maya expected to stop here, but the centarchs marched her grimly on, down *another* staircase.

This far beneath the mountain, the air was close and oppressive. There were only a few cells on this floor, but the door to each had no window and was plated on both sides in iridescent unmetal. Instead of a lock, there was a complex bit of arcana on the outside, which one of the centarchs touched with a small bit of crystal and wire. When the door swung open, Maya could see that the inside of the cell was plated with unmetal as well, with grills to cover the ventilation and the drains.

This is a cell for centarchs, she realized. Even if she'd somehow managed to smuggle in a haken, carving a way out through all that unmetal would take long enough that someone would surely notice. It made her wonder how often the Order had needed to contain a rogue centarch, down through the centuries. It also made her wonder if she was in bigger trouble than she'd realized. Tripping over her tongue trying to confess her thoughts to Beq suddenly seemed minor.

"Get inside," the centarch said.

"How long am I going to be here?" Maya said. "I need to speak to the Council—Kyriliarch Baselanthus—"

"The Council will deal with you when they see fit," the centarch said. Something in her voice was chilling.

Maya edged into the cell, and the guards slammed the door behind her. She heard the arcana lock click and the sound of retreating footsteps, and then she was alone.

At least the cell didn't have rats. And it was clean, not because anyone had made any special effort to keep it that way, but because filth couldn't be persuaded to stick to unmetal. There was a cold-water tap, a drain for waste, a stool, and a thin mattress. That was all.

Her fever was getting worse, leaving her alternating between chills and sweats. In between, she tried to focus. *If I'd known I was going to be locked up, I would have brought a copy of the* Inheritance. *I could have caught up on my lessons.* That would have made Jaedia happy, at least. Instead, she had only a blank notebook, which had been part of her traveling supplies. She occupied her time writing down an account of everything that had happened since they'd left the Forge. If Tanax was going to file a report, she could at least submit one as well.

She'd only reached her fight against the smugglers in Litnin—the memory of which made her hand shake a little—before she heard voices outside. At first she thought it might be dinner, since her stomach was definitely starting to rumble. Then someone snapped, "Open it," and she recognized Baselanthus' voice.

Her heart leapt, then fell again as the door opened. Baselanthus was there, but he wasn't alone. Nicomidi, Tanax's master, stood behind him, and so did old Prodominus. The same trio who had sent them off on their mission, representing the three factions of the Council of Kyriliarchs—Baselanthus' Pragmatics, Nicomidi's Dogmatics, and

Prodominus' quixotic Revivalists. *This can't be good.* Maya shot to her feet, then bowed deeply.

"Kyriliarchs," she said. "Thank you for seeing me so quickly."

"Agathios," Basel said.

"I want to say that I understand the seriousness of my offense," Maya said, hoping to get in front of the conversation. "I disobeyed Agathios Tanax's orders, and I am willing to accept whatever punishment you think is appropriate. I would like, however, to present some other evidence that might..."

She trailed off as Nicomidi held up a hand. Basel looked worried, and Prodominus' eyes were pitying. Nicomidi, though, looked as smug as a cat.

"While we will review your conduct in Deepfire in due time," Nicomidi said, "it is not the primary issue here."

Maya blinked. "Then...what is?"

"I need you to remain calm, child," Basel said. "Something has gone wrong with Jaedia's mission."

"Gone wrong?" Nicomidi sneered. "She's turned traitor to the Order."

"That's not proven," Basel said. "All we know—"

"Is that she made contact with one of our undercover outposts, which subsequently disappeared," Nicomidi said. "And that our investigators found witnesses who said Jaedia attacked the outpost herself and slaughtered our scouts."

"That's impossible," Maya said. She felt as though she'd been punched in the gut. "It's a mistake. Jaedia wouldn't...I mean..."

She spread her hands, trying to convey the ridiculousness of the notion. *Jaedia* turn against the Order? *It would be easier for this mountain to turn itself upside down.*

"Our investigation is ongoing," Basel said, then sighed. "Unfortunately, what is not in dispute is that Jaedia has not checked in according to plan, nor responded to any messages sent to her by various emergency channels. Therefore—"

"Something's happened to her." Maya took a step forward. "Please. I'll go and find her, and I'll prove to you that none of this makes sense—"

"*Agathios*," Prodominus rumbled. "You may want to pay more heed to your own position."

"Indeed," Nicomidi said with a thin smile. "Jaedia kept you away from the Forge, and any influence apart from hers. Now, we are forced to wonder, was this so you might be indoctrinated into whatever heresy she had concocted?"

"There's no *heresy*," Maya shouted. Her head was spinning again. "Jaedia and I were *helping* people, instead of sitting around here playing at politics."

"Regardless," Nicomidi snapped. "Your reliability is in question. You will be investigated as an accomplice."

"Once again, I must protest," Basel said. "We have no evidence whatsoever that anything Jaedia has done included Maya."

"Only the evidence of common sense," Nicomidi said. "How could her agathios, who accompanied her everywhere, not have been privy to her plans?"

"Assuming this was a plan—" Basel began.

"Your efforts to protect your protégé grow tiresome, Basel," Nicomidi said. "The decision is in the full Council's hands now." He turned, cloak flaring behind him, and stalked out of the cell. Maya stared after him for a moment, then looked at Basel.

"You can't keep me in here," she whispered. "Not if something's happened to Jaedia. *Please.*"

He sighed. "I'm afraid my say in the matter is limited, but I will do everything I can. Perhaps Jaedia will contact us soon with an explanation. But..."

"You know she couldn't do this!"

Basel's eyes were hooded. "I thought I did."

He turned to leave as well. Prodominus, stroking his beard, looked down at Maya and cleared his throat.

"This will not be easy, girl," he said. "Stay strong."

"Please," Maya said.

"The path the Chosen have laid is always a difficult one." And Prodominus, too, turned away.

"You are an interesting experiment, *sha'deia.*"

Maya hung by her wrists from one wall of a brick cistern, pinioned and helpless. Her shoulders were screaming with pain.

This isn't real.

Hollis Plaguetouch regarded her with cold eyes. He'd shed his coat with its high collar, and she could see the black spider clamped on the back of his neck, legs digging into his skin.

This is a dream. Hollis was dead, and Jaedia had rescued her. *Unless* that *was a dream, and I've been here all along...*

"This makes twice that you have stumbled into long-laid plans," Hollis said. "Coincidence? Perhaps."

"You're not Hollis," Maya said.

"No." The legs of the black spider twitched. "Hollis Plaguetouch is dead."

"Who are you? What do you want with me?"

"I don't owe you answers, little *sha'deia.* As to what I want with you, that's the real question, isn't it?" He stepped closer and reached out a finger to touch the Thing in her chest. "Is this experiment worth the vexation you cause me?"

"I'm not your experiment." Maya struggled to pull away from him.

"You've crossed the threshold, haven't you? Yes, I can see it. Poor little *sha'deia.* It must be painful. The world no longer welcomes our kind." He cocked his head, and the black spider twitched again. "Are you the one I've been waiting for all these years?"

"Whoever you are," Maya said, "*whatever* you are, I'm not—"

"We shall see," Hollis interrupted. "Assuming you survive."

His finger traced a circle around the Thing, and in its wake Maya could feel her flesh bubble and *change...*

*   *   *

Maya screamed until she woke up, sweating. She lay on the thin, lumpy mattress, one hand pressed to the Thing. Her skin was unmarred, and the nightmare was fading, but waking was very nearly worse.

She had no idea how long it had been. Only a week, she guessed, but some part of her mind insisted it was months, years, and she had no way to be certain. The cell was lit by a sunlamp whose radiance never wavered. Twice a day (once? three times?) a slot opened in the door and a tray was shoved through with a simple meal—bread, cheese, dried meat. She gnawed at it, from habit more than hunger, and drank water from the tiny basin, pissed into the drain. The rest of the time she spent lying in bed.

The cell became more dreamlike, and the dreams that plagued her whenever she closed her eyes became more like reality. It wasn't only Hollis she saw in her nightmares. She lived the day she'd been taken to the Order, a struggling little girl; only Va'aht turned on her parents after taking Gyre's eye and carved them into bloody chunks. Or it was Jaedia who slaughtered her family, Maya herself doing the killing, her mother begging her to stop as she burned her to ash, Gyre's remaining eye filling with hatred. The nameless rebel girl stepped onto a pyre, dancing as her skin burned away. Beq came to her, in the dark of their tent, and they kissed and fumbled with each other's clothes, until suddenly the other girl's mouth was full of sharp, tearing teeth and her fingers cut like knives.

Eventually—after what felt like an eternity—there came a day when she woke and found her head clear. Her body felt numb, as though she'd jumped into a river swollen with snowmelt. She rolled out of bed, shivering, and took a few moments to gather the strength to stand.

What's wrong with me? She had faint memories of illnesses as a girl, fevers and nightmares like this that no doctor had been able to explain. *That's why Baselanthus gave me the Thing.* She touched the little arcana again and found the swelling around it had subsided. With an effort,

Maya got to her feet. Her legs felt shaky, as though she'd run for hours. It was an effort to squat over the drain, but she managed.

Afterward, her head still feeling clear, she dug her journal out of her pack for the first time since the Kyriliarchs had visited her. She wasn't sure if the report would do her any good, but it was *something. They can't just keep me in here forever. Can they?*

There was a knock at the door, which made her jump. Maya hurriedly stuffed the journal and pen back in her pack, heedless of ink smudges, and sat back on the bed.

"Come in," she said.

The door opened, and Beq stood between the two white-armored guards, a fresh tray of food in her hands. Maya jumped to her feet, then hesitated.

"This is real, right?" Her voice felt scratchy. "I'm not dreaming?"

"I don't think so," Beq said. "But I'm not sure how I'd know."

Beq set the tray of food down and came forward. Maya kept still until Beq's arms were around her, then wrapped the other girl in a tight hug, head pressed against Beq's shoulder.

"If this was a dream," Maya said, her voice muffled, "at this point you'd bite my head off or turn into a vulpi or something."

"That's alarming," Beq said.

"It's been..." Maya found her eyes full of tears and rubbed them on Beq's shirt. "How long have I been down here?"

"A week," Beq said, pulling away slightly. "I tried to get a chance to come sooner, but they told me you were ill. How do you feel?"

"Like I've gone crazy." Maya took a deep breath and wiped her eyes again. "But better today."

"Here, sit down." Beq gestured to the bed, and Maya flopped onto it, while Beq sat cross-legged on the unmetal floor. "I'm glad you're feeling better."

"How did you get them to let you in here?" Maya said.

Beq grinned, idly twisting a dial on her spectacles. "I called in a few favors with the servants. Traded some shifts."

"The Council didn't send you?" When Beq shook her head, Maya said, "Have you heard what they're saying about Jaedia?"

"It's all anyone's talking about," Beq said. "All over the Forge."

"It's a lie," Maya said fiercely. "I know Jaedia better than anyone. She would rather die than turn against the Order."

"You're not the only one who thinks so," Beq said, lowering her voice. She glanced over her shoulder at the guards outside and continued in a whisper. "There's been serious accusations on the Council. The Dogmatics are accusing Baselanthus and the others of plotting against the Order, and the Pragmatics say that Jaedia must have been set up."

"*Obviously* she was set up," Maya said. Her heart pounded in her chest, and her insides felt stretched. She touched the Thing absently. "I have to get out of here. She needs my help."

"I have…" Beq paused, then leaned in even closer, until her forehead rested against Maya's. Startled, Maya froze. Beq's skin was warm against hers, and her lips were almost close enough to kiss. "There's something I have to tell you."

Maya swallowed. "What?"

"I found something. In the Spike, before we left."

"Found what?"

"Correspondence between Nicomidi and Raskos," Beq said. "I think. It's all in cipher, like the letter you found. Tanax had us search Raskos' office after he fled the city, and I…um…took it." She shook her head, forehead rolling against Maya's. " If I handed it over, I was worried Tanax might…misplace it. It was wrong, but I was so mad at him—"

"Can you read them?"

"Not easily. But I checked the archives to see who was allocated those codes in particular. They definitely all came from Nicomidi."

"If Nicomidi was working with Raskos all along—"

"*Shhhh*," Beq said frantically.

There was a long silence.

"So what are you going to do?" Maya said.

"I don't *know*," Beq said. "I *should* burn the things, or find a way to turn them over to the Council. But..." She swallowed. "I want to help you, Maya. It's wrong that they're keeping you in here. Even if you disobeyed Tanax. Raskos was corrupt, and Tanax wasn't going to do anything about it! And—"

"Shhhh." Maya let out a deep breath. "Thank you, Beq."

"I feel stupid," Beq said. "You're the one in a cell for treason, and I come to *you* for help. But I don't know what to do."

"Is there any chance you can decode the letters?"

"It's possible," Beq said. "The codes should be on file in the master archive. It'll take time to track them all down, though."

"That's the first thing we need to do, then," Maya said.

"You don't want me to go to Baselanthus?"

"I'm not sure how much Basel can do," Maya said. "If we know what Nicomidi and Raskos were talking about, we'll have more leverage."

"Okay." Beq pulled away from Maya and took a deep breath. "I'll do it as fast as I can."

"Will you be able to get in and see me again?"

"Not for a while," Beq said. "But I should be able to send a note. I have a friend on the kitchen staff."

Maya perked up. "Could you send me a book?"

"I can try," Beq said. "What do you need?"

"A copy of the *Inheritance*, to begin with."

"Really?" Beq stuck out her tongue. "Haven't you studied it enough? I certainly have."

"The basic rules of the Order are in there," Maya said. "I want to see if there's anything about...treason, I guess, and how the trial might go." She shook her head. "I need to get out of here, one way or another."

"I'll try," Beq said. She got to her feet, looking over her shoulder at the guards. "I'd better go."

"Beq—" Maya stood up, a little too fast. Beq paused, her beautiful eyes too big through her golden spectacles, wisps of green hair escaping her braid. She looked worried and harried and achingly beautiful.

"What?"

"Thank you. You didn't have to do any of this."

"Oh." Beq looked down, flushing a little. "I...when we were on the mission, I thought..."

Maya waited, hardly daring to breathe.

"Never mind," Beq said, her voice rising to a squeak. "I'll be back. As soon as I can. And I'll get those books. If I can. And—"

Maya glanced at the waiting guards, and Beq paused, then nodded fiercely. Maya didn't move until the door closed behind her.

Focus, Maya. She sat down by the meal Beq had brought and ate every scrap, dutifully chewing the too-tough meat. *Get out of here first. Jaedia needs your help.*

Nevertheless, when she fell asleep again, she found her dreams considerably more pleasant.

Days passed. The last of Maya's fever vanished, and her mind felt like her own for the first time since she'd left Deepfire.

A copy of the *Inheritance* arrived with one of Maya's meals, and not long after, a thick tome detailing Council precedents in serious judicial matters involving centarchs, going all the way back to the founding of the Order after the Plague War. Maya finished her report of the events of the mission, then threw herself into reading. It wasn't her favorite activity at the best of times, and the judicial book made for exceptionally slow going, but there wasn't much else to distract her. She took to pacing quickly while she read, trying to work up a sweat, or putting the book on the floor and doing a handstand.

It was the latter exercise she was engaged in when she heard voices outside the door. She held her pose, arms beginning to ache and sweat trickling down her nose, but stopped trying to focus on the technical merits of the argument made by a century-dead Kyriarch and listened. Someone snapped an order, and she heard the stamp of boots. Then the door lock clicked open.

Beq? It didn't seem likely. Maya tensed, then sprang back to her feet, breathing hard. The door opened, and she found herself face-to-face with Nicomidi. The Kyriliarch was alone, without even the usual pair of door guards in sight.

"Agathios," he said with the hint of a smile. "I hope I'm not interrupting."

"Just trying to keep busy," Maya said carelessly. "How can I help you, Kyriliarch?"

He stepped into the room, glancing around curiously. "I'm told your health has recovered."

"It has." In truth, Maya still didn't know what to make of the fever and nightmares. *Shock, maybe.* But they seemed to have passed. "Thank you for asking."

"I have been looking into your case, as you might imagine," Nicomidi said. "And I have reviewed Tanax's reports of your conduct. I am starting to believe that I may have been ... overhasty in my judgment."

Maya hesitated, sensing a trap. "How so?"

"The picture that Tanax paints of you is a young woman dedicated to the highest principles of the Twilight Order." He coughed. "If, perhaps, somewhat impulsive and inclined to disrespect authority. It seems out of character for you to have been involved in a plot with Jaedia against the Order."

"It's out of character for Jaedia, too," Maya said, then frowned. "*Tanax* said that about me?"

"He did. Although you should address him as Centarch Tanax Brokenedge now." Nicomidi gave his thin smile again. "His cognomen ceremony was yesterday."

"Congratulations to him," Maya said, a bit sourly. She knew Brokenedge was an ancient, honorable cognomen, indicating the favor of the Council. "I'm ... glad he speaks well of me."

"He is an honorable young man, and attentive to his duty. He will make an excellent centarch." Nicomidi fixed her with a careful stare. "In any event, his testimony has convinced me that we need not be enemies. I am respected among the Dogmatics. If I were to speak on your behalf, I am certain your release could be arranged."

"I see." Maya hesitated again, then said, "And what would you want from me, in exchange for this favor?"

"I see you grasp the nub of the issue," Nicomidi said. "Your testimony would be...informative to our discussions of Jaedia. You would only need tell the truth, of course."

"Of course," Maya murmured. *I'll bet I would, you snake.* "And if I refuse?"

Nicomidi's smile became more strained. "If you refuse, matters might be more difficult. You could be here for some time."

"You can't hold me forever." Maya put her foot on the thick book of judicial proceedings. "I'll demand a Council hearing, and you don't have any evidence of treason."

Now the smile was gone entirely. "You think you're very clever, don't you?"

"Not really. Just persistent."

"Perhaps you should consider this, then. Council members do not require evidence to, say, make recommendations for postings. Your next assignment could bury you away on the northern frontier, where you will have nothing to do but write reports and check your toes for frostbite. You'll lose your teeth before you get your cognomen."

"If that's the judgment of the Council, then I would accept it." She said it with a straight face, because it seemed to annoy him.

"Or there's your arcanist friend."

"Leave her out of this."

"I hope she's careful in her work. Arcana are dangerous, after all. We don't want any...accidents."

There was a long pause.

"You'd go that far?" Maya said. Her voice was small. "Really?"

"You don't know the stakes you're playing for," Nicomidi said. "Now. Will you be a good girl and tell the Council the truth about Jaedia? Or do we have to go over other potential mishaps?"

Maya looked down at the law book again, then back up at Nicomidi. "I'll speak to the Council."

*   *   *

The next morning, the guards opened the cell door, and one of the Legionaries motioned for Maya to follow. The white-armored soldiers brought her to a residential level that it took her a moment to recognize as her own. They stopped in front of her door, which she'd left only a couple of weeks before.

"Your uniforms have been cleaned," one of the Legionaries said. "Make yourself presentable for the Council."

"How long do I have?" Maya said.

"Why?"

"Because if I'm going to make myself presentable, I need a bath, too."

The soldier consulted with her fellow for a moment, then nodded. "Collect your things. We'll escort you."

Thankfully, with a pair of Legionaries blocking the entrance to the baths, Maya didn't have to worry about anyone wandering in. She took her time, rinsing days of sweat off her skin and out of her hair, then climbing into the hot pool for a soak. *The Council can wait.*

When she was finished, she put on her dress uniform, which had been cleaned and folded as promised. As always, its tailoring felt awkward, but at this point Maya welcomed the discomfort. *Anything to keep my mind off what I'm about to do.*

"Are you ready?" the Legionary said when she emerged. The woman's voice was flat, deadened by her helmet, but Maya swore she could detect a trace of annoyance. She gave the soldier her best smile.

"Absolutely."

They climbed the spiral stair, her two white-armored shadows a half step on either side of her. For the first time since she'd returned, Maya saw other inhabitants of the Forge, servants, arcanists, and agathia hurrying between floors on various errands. They stopped to watch as she passed. It made her wonder what they were saying about her.

A centarch in plain clothes met them at the top of the stairs. She was an older woman, her purple hair going gray and pulled back in a

severe bun. Her cloak was fringed purple-red-orange, and Maya's studies supplied her name: Evinda Stonecutter, one of the most respected
centarchs. Jaedia had said she could have been a Kyriliarch, if she'd
been willing to play politics, but she'd maintained a position of studi-
ous neutrality between the factions.

"Centarch." Maya bowed. "It's an honor."

"Agathios Maya." Evinda looked her over. "The Council will hear
your testimony. You will respond only to questions from the Kyriliarchs, and not otherwise speak. Your answers should be truthful and
succinct. Do you understand?"

"I understand," Maya said. Her heart fluttered in her chest, and her
hand brushed the Thing as Evinda turned away.

The Council chamber was down the hall from Baselanthus' office,
behind a set of double doors elaborately carved with a scene from the
Inheritance—the first centarchs, swearing their oaths to Sif-Nal-Bjaern,
one of the last surviving Chosen. Sif was rendered as an abstract figure,
featureless and aglow with light, but the six men and women who'd
founded the Order were picked out in loving detail.

A pair of Legionary guards nodded to Evinda and pushed the doors
open. Beyond was a broad oval chamber, with the twelve Kyriliarchs of
the Twilight Order seated behind a long, curving table. The opposite
side of the room was lined with chairs, some of which were occupied by
a variety of aides and functionaries. In the center of the room was an
open space, at the focus of the Council's attention, and Maya guessed
this was where she was supposed to stand.

She swallowed hard as Evinda guided her forward. In addition to the
Council, she guessed there were a dozen other centarchs in the room.
Twenty-five of the most dangerous people in the world, the guardians
of civilization, with enough power between them to level cities and topple mountains.

And I'm about to stick my finger right in their eye.

Evinda touched her shoulder, bringing her to a halt. Maya looked
down the line of Kyriliarchs. They were arranged by faction, with

Baselanthus and the five other Pragmatics on the left, and Nicomidi and the four Dogmatics on the right. In the center, facing Maya, sat Prodominus, idly scratching at his beard.

"I have brought Maya, agathios to Centarch Jaedia Suddenstorm, as instructed," Evinda intoned.

"Yes, thank you," Prodominus said. "You may go."

Evinda bowed and backed away. There was a long moment of silence.

"Agathios Maya," Nicomidi said. "As you know, this Council is in the midst of weighing the evidence against your master. We wish to ask you about your experiences with her, and to clarify certain matters in her reports that have been . . . obscured. Answer truthfully, and you have nothing to fear."

Maya knew how that would go, if she let it. Jaedia hadn't always been able to work through proper channels. Like when they'd cornered Hollis Plaguetouch at Bastion, she'd cut corners to get things done, greased palms, avoided notice. Maya had no doubt Nicomidi had assembled a battery of specific questions that, even if she answered honestly, would paint Jaedia as someone who operated outside the Order's rules.

Fucking plague that.

"Are you ready to begin?" Nicomidi said.

Maya took a deep breath.

"No, Kyriliarch."

Nicomidi blinked. A mutter ran through the room. Prodominus raised an eyebrow. Baselanthus, who had been studying something on the table in front of him, looked up suddenly.

"You want to wait, then?" Nicomidi said. "I understand if you are overwhelmed, but the Council's time is valuable—"

"I do not wish to waste the Council's time, Kyriliarch," Maya said. "But I will not be answering your questions. I came before you today to say that I believe I am ready to assume my cognomen immediately."

Nicomidi snorted. "That is hardly for you to decide. Nor is it relevant—"

"If the Council disagrees with me," Maya said, "then I formally challenge the centarchate, as is my right under the codes of the *Inheritance*."

Nicomidi froze. Across the room, the muttered conversations stopped and everyone stared. Everyone except Prodominus. The old Revivalist was hunched over, shoulders shaking, and before anyone could speak he burst into huge, bellowing laughter.

"No one has challenged for their cognomen in a hundred years," Nicomidi snapped, when Prodominus had subsided.

"One hundred and seventeen," Maya said. "And Agathios Canivo was defeated. It has been one hundred and forty-eight years since a challenge was successful."

"You don't need to do this," Basel said. "Maya, please. The Council understands—"

"With respect to the Council," Maya said, "my decision is made, and the challenge has been issued. How do you respond?"

"You don't understand what you're doing," Basel said. "If you lose—"

Maya cut him off again. "If I lose, I give up my status as agathios and any chance of becoming a centarch. I will be confined as the Council sees fit for the rest of my natural life."

She'd flinched on reading that part. But the Order's rules were harsh for a reason—anyone who could touch *deiat*, especially after receiving most of a centarch's training, was far too dangerous to be allowed to roam free.

"I understand the consequences," she went on. "How does the Council respond to my challenge?"

"I..." Basel shook his head, but Nicomidi jumped in angrily.

"I move that the Council contest the challenge," he grated. "I call for a vote at once. All in favor, stand."

The Dogmatics got to their feet all together. The Pragmatics rose one by one, more hesitantly, all except Baselanthus, who looked down at the desk as though he'd lost something there.

"I...abstain," he muttered. "I cannot..."

Prodominus was the last to get on his feet, still wiping his eyes. He grinned at Maya.

"I hope you win, girl," he said. "But I have to see you fight for it."

"That's eleven votes in favor, with one abstention," Nicomidi said. "The Council will contest *Agathios* Maya's assumption of the title of centarch. I volunteer as champion, and—"

"Oh, no," Prodominus said. "That's not what the rules say."

"Correct." Maya forced herself not to smile.

Nicomidi's eyes narrowed. "Then *enlighten us*, Prodominus."

"The code specifies that the centarchate is a chain through the generations that is only as strong as its most recent link," Prodominus said. Maya blinked in surprise—that was practically word for word from the *Inheritance*. "The member most recently raised to their title represents us all."

"In this case," Maya said, "I believe that would be Centarch Tanax Brokenedge. I look forward to facing him in the dueling ring."

Chapter 17

An old saying held that there were only two roads out of Deepfire. Like most old sayings, it wasn't literally correct, but it contained a grain of truth. There were a dozen roads leading south, either passing through tunnels that pierced the edge of the city's crater or switchbacking over the top, but after descending into the foothills they all joined to become the Republic Road. This highway ran through the Splinter Kingdoms of Meltrock and Drail before finally reaching Obstadt, the great entrepôt of the northern Republic. Merchant combines like the Moorcats had made their fortune running caravans along the route, putting up with plaguespawn attacks and the taxes of the Splinter Kings to bring the salvage of Deepfire—and the cheap goods of its manufactories—back to the Republic.

Going north, on the other hand, there truly was only one road. The Hunter's Gap was a notch in the wall of the crater, where part of the mountain the Chosen weapon had blown apart had collapsed into a narrow valley, creating a broad slope of melted, misshapen boulders and bits of twisted glass. Scavengers had cut a crude stairway through the debris, descending from the crater's edge into the valley of the Brink. The tiny river led into the network of valleys and passes that were the only practical way to move around the Shattered Peaks.

Standing at the top of the Gap, wind viciously cold against his face in spite of a thick knit muffler, Gyre looked out at the serried ranks of snowcapped mountains and felt his heart sinking. He told himself they didn't have far to go, all things considered—Kit's ill-fated delve toward the Tomb had started on the flank of a mountain called Snowspear, which he figured they could reach in less than a week.

"Having second thoughts?" Kit said cheerfully, coming up behind him.

"Just contemplating freezing my balls off," Gyre muttered.

"I suppose I've got one up on you there," Kit said. "Come on. It's not much warmer down in the valley, but at least we might get eaten by plaguespawn!"

She pushed past him, trooping down the uneven stone steps that ran back and forth through the scree of broken rock. Kit's slight figure was swathed in so much cloth and leather it was a wonder she could move, with fur-lined trousers and a jacket on top of several other layers, her blue hair concealed under a leather cap, and a wool muffler like Gyre's over her face.

He'd had to provide gear for both of them, naturally, since Kit's funds had disappeared with her ghoul allies. Fortunately, Gyre had a few stashes of thalers for emergencies, and cleaning them out had been just about enough to cover what they needed for their expedition. Between food, tent, bedding, and a selection of useful alchemicals, Gyre's pack was bulging, and Kit's was scarcely lighter.

He'd also replaced his long blade and packed a couple of spares. Kit's banter aside, plaguespawn were no laughing matter this deep in the mountains. One thing they hadn't been able to afford was a spare sunsplinter for Kit's blaster, which had an unknown but probably small number of shots remaining.

In spite of an early start, it took all afternoon just to reach the bottom of the steps. By the time they got to the relatively flat ground of the valley floor, Gyre's knees ached abominably. If Kit was fatigued, though, she didn't show it, hurrying ahead to find the loosely marked path that paralleled the narrow river. Gyre muttered to himself but kept walking.

At least the scenery was spectacular. The valley floor was low enough that it was clear of snow at this time of year, and a narrow belt of stunted trees and tough grass survived by the banks of the river. A few hundred meters to either side, the slopes of the neighboring mountains rose steep and unforgiving, shrouded in white. Streams flowed down to join the Brink at regular intervals, some emerging from the rocks, others tumbling down from on high in streamers of spray. Big brown birds wheeled and called out overhead, and now and then Gyre saw a few goats in the distance.

"See?" Kit said, her breath puffing into steam as she walked. "It's not so bad. There's not even any snow."

"People really live out here?" Gyre had made the ascent to Deepfire safe in the confines of a caravan. Like the majority of the inhabitants, he'd never ventured outside the crater.

"A few," Kit said.

"Why?"

She shrugged. "Scavengers pass through. They've got money, and they need food, booze, and bed warmers. There are worse ways to make a living."

"It's hard to think of many."

"There's this little...not a town, really, but a couple of buildings next to each other. It's not far from Snowspear; we could pass by. They might even remember me."

"Just as long as you didn't kill anyone the last time you came through."

"I don't...think so?" Kit looked at the sky. "Maybe—no, that was farther east. It'll be fine."

Gyre snorted a laugh, and they walked on.

The sun vanished early, hidden behind the mountains to the west, and they walked for a while in the long twilight. Eventually, though, the light drained from the sky, and Kit found them a spot to camp in the lee of a rock outcropping, which would provide defense on two sides and keep them out of the wind.

"Risk a fire?" she said inquiringly.

"What's the risk?"

"They say it attracts plaguespawn," Kit said. "Though I don't think anyone really knows for sure."

"We'll be all right," Gyre said. "Go ahead."

He dug in his pack for the roll of alchemical camp-guards while Kit went to work on the fire. The little things were the standard clay balls of most alchemicals, connected to a fine wire mesh. He unrolled them around their little nook at the distance of a couple of meters. The clay balls were full of explosive powder, enough to make a flash and a loud bang, connected to the wire with a clever mechanism. Once it was set, any pressure would set them off and sound the alarm. As a general security measure, it wasn't ideal, since it was easy enough to step over the wire mesh if you saw it, but plaguespawn weren't smart enough for that.

"You *are* well prepared," Kit said, tending her small pile of twigs as the fire grew. "More of Lynnia's work?"

Gyre nodded. "She's got a temper, but she's the best alchemist in Deepfire." He sighed. "Not that she'll ever work with me again, most likely."

"Ah." Kit shook her head. "It's too bad about Yora. I'd hoped you were right about her calling off the job—"

"I'd rather not talk about it."

Gyre settled down next to the fire, drawing his legs to his chest. He still wondered if there was something he could have done, some way out of the trap. *Warn her, and risk losing everything. Except we lost everything anyway.*

"Fair enough." Kit pushed a larger piece of wood into the flames and sighed pleasantly as the fire rose. "Can I ask you something else, then?"

"Maybe," Gyre said cautiously.

"That centarch," Kit said. "She let us go. And I thought I heard you talking to her."

"You were unconscious."

"I was in and out." Kit cocked her head. "So what happened? Do you know her?"

"In a manner of speaking." Gyre sighed. "It was Maya. My sister."

"You're joking."

"I wish I was." He shook his head. "Or maybe I don't. If it was anyone else, I doubt we'd have gotten out of there alive."

"What did she say? Was she glad to see you?"

"She said…" Gyre paused. "About what you'd expect. What the Twilight Order taught her to believe."

"Was she surprised to find out her brother is a notorious rebel?"

"I think so. She said she doesn't remember what happened the day they took her." Gyre sighed. "I wouldn't blame her for not *wanting* to remember."

"Family," Kit said in a long-suffering tone.

"Do you have any?" Gyre said, genuinely curious.

"Just my mother. She ditched my dad before I was born, and I only saw him a couple of times before he drank himself to death."

"And what does she think of…" Gyre waved vaguely, as though to encompass Kit's entire life.

Kit held up a hand and waggled it so-so. "I ran off when I was ten. Spent the next five years fighting with her by letter. I thought we were through it, and I was planning to visit her, when I found out about…" She tapped her chest. "Since then I haven't been able to figure out what to say."

There was a pause that stretched into an awkward silence. Kit yawned.

"Well," she said. "I'm for bed. Long way to walk tomorrow."

"Yeah," Gyre muttered. But he stared into the campfire for a long time after she'd crawled away, seeing the blinding light of a flaming sword.

They saw their first plaguespawn the following day.

When you lived within the well-guarded borders of the Republic,

Gyre reflected, or in a protected city like Deepfire, you thought of plaguespawn as occasional disasters. Like storms or earthquakes, they could never be banished entirely, but for most people they weren't a pressing risk. And when they did turn up, everyone knew what to do. Gyre had participated in a few plaguespawn hunts as a boy, sticking close to his father and a crowd of other farmers as they cornered some dog-sized monstrosity and beat it to death with clubs and farm tools. And once they'd found it, the threat was *over*, and everyone went home and congratulated themselves on a job well done.

It was easy to forget that most of the world wasn't like that. The Splinter Kingdoms didn't have the manpower of the Republic, or the weapons the Order maintained for the Legions, blaster rifles and unmetal armor. Every city and town had its wall and its watchtowers. Villagers fortified their houses and went armed in the fields. Travelers and traders moved in well-armed groups. And that was in the lowlands—no nation claimed the mazy valleys and narrow passes of the Shattered Peaks, and no army swept the wilds.

The Twilight Order liked to take credit, but Gyre thought the only thing that had saved humanity, after the fall of the Chosen, was the sheer mindless stupidity of the abominations. Plaguespawn wanted only one thing—to find living animals, humans above all, and incorporate their freshly slaughtered flesh into their own twisted bodies. They had no strategy, no sense of caution, not even the simple instincts of an animal. They didn't set ambushes, or try to hide when they were overmatched.

Consequently, Gyre heard the thing coming long before he saw it, a rattling sound of bone on rock. He glanced at Kit, who drew her saber at once. Gyre pulled out his long blade and took a long step away from her, giving her room to fight.

The plaguespawn came into view a moment later, scuttling around a boulder. It was a big one, the size of a pony, with a mismatched collection of a dozen legs rising and falling on either side of its body in weird, synchronized waves. Like all plaguespawn, most of it consisted

of yellow, splintered bones and ropy red muscle, the organic wreckage of several creatures stripped and repurposed by *dhaka*. Bits of its
past prey remained intact—its head was a pair of goats' heads partially
fused together, mouth horribly extended, four horizontal-pupiled eyes
blinking in unison.

It came straight at them, legs rising and falling. Gyre intercepted it,
darting forward to deliver a slash across its snout that left a flap of wet
flesh hanging loose, dripping dark blood. The creature came after him,
goat teeth snapping, and he danced backward, slashing at it whenever
it got too close.

Kit came in behind the thing, delivering a heavy downward cut to
its rear with her longer, heavier blade. Three legs fell away from one
side, twitching spastically on the ground, and the thing staggered off-
balance. It screeched and chattered madly, trying to turn, but Gyre
slammed his long knife into its throat, putting all his weight behind the
blow. As it reared, trying to bite him, Kit reversed her saber and brought
it straight down through the center of the creature's body. Blood gushed
from its underside, and all its legs twitched violently, then went limp.

"Nicely done," Gyre said, putting his foot against the monster's skull
and pulling his knife free. Something *crunched* wetly under his boot.

"I've had a lot of practice," Kit muttered. "At least up here they're
mostly goat. You wouldn't believe how big they can get down in the
tunnels with only bats and rats to eat."

"Did you ever ask your friend Naumoriel why the ghouls created the
plaguing things?"

"He claims they didn't," Kit said. "But trying to get straight answers
out of a ghoul about the war is...challenging. You'll see." She wiped
the blood off her saber on a cloth, then frowned at the rag and tossed it
away. "Assuming we get there. And that they don't kill us immediately
when we do."

"So many wonderful possibilities," Gyre said.

A few more plaguespawn turned up before nightfall, but nothing
nearly so large. The smallest of them could be crushed under a boot or

dispatched with a kick, like twisted rats but with none of a rat's natural intellect or caution. As far as Gyre knew, no one was quite sure where new plaguespawn came from, but the popular theory was that smaller monsters periodically budded from larger ones.

That night they didn't light a fire. Gyre double-checked his alchemical alarms before retiring to the small, single-person tent he carried in his pack, little more than a raised frame to protect his bedroll from wind and rain. Once again, nothing disturbed them, and in the morning they turned away from the valley of the Brink and started climbing into Goatskull Pass.

The pass was barely worthy of the name. Really, it was just a narrow saddle of ground between two mountains, the bottom of a ravine dotted with boulders. It sloped upward, enough that patches of snow appeared on the rocks. Here and there a drift blocked the way, remnants of an avalanche. It was enough to make Gyre glance upward nervously, shading his eye against the glare.

Two days went by as they worked their way along the pass. Here and there, they found evidence that humans had been this way before, a few steps carved into a particularly difficult section or boulders arranged into rough stepping-stones. For the most part, though, they might have been alone in the world, aside from the ever-present plaguespawn. The air grew thinner and colder, and Gyre slept with every blanket he had.

Eventually, Kit had told him, the pass would crest and then start downward into another valley. Before that point, they would branch off, following a narrow shoulder of ground to a hidden tunnel entrance. On the fifth day out of Deepfire, Gyre's legs were burning long before the sun had reached its height. Kit slogged at his side, relentless and uncomplaining, and once again he found himself wondering how so much strength fit in such a slight frame.

"We're going to need to rest soon," Gyre managed as they edged around a boulder and kicked through another patch of snow. Kit looked at him sidelong, and he gasped out a laugh and amended, "*I* am going to have to rest soon."

"Wimp." But she slumped against the boulder eagerly enough, digging her canteen out from under her coat and taking a long swallow. "You should come up here in winter."

"Have you been?"

"No, but I heard stories from a scavenger who tried. And he was short an ear, three fingers, and seven toes, so I'm inclined to believe him."

Gyre snorted and looked upward. The clouds were heavy and low, masking the sun, like when Deepfire's fog pulled in tight. Something brushed his eye, and he blinked.

"Hmm," Kit said. She held out a gloved hand and watched as several fat flakes landed on her palm. "This could be a problem."

It turned out to be more than a problem.

At first they'd pushed straight on, but the clouds grew lower and more threatening and the snowfall intensified as the wind picked up. It wasn't even properly dry snow, either, but a mix of snow and half-melted sleet. Sprays of white whipped down the throat of the pass, picked up by the wind from the slopes of the mountain, and blasted Gyre's face with stinging grit. In no time, he felt like his weight had doubled, inner garments soaked and outer layers crusted with snowfall.

"We have to get out of this!" He had to grab Kit's arm and pull her closer before she could hear. "Find somewhere to put up the tents!"

She shook her head. Her eyes were the only part of her visible under layers of cloth.

"Put them up *where?*" she said.

"Somewhere out of the wind." Gyre looked around desperately for a convenient boulder, but with the darkness and blowing snow, he couldn't see much farther than the end of his arm.

"Got a better idea. Just a little farther."

"What is?"

"'S a cave." Kit had trouble getting her voice out between chattering teeth. "Used it last time. Might even still be some supplies there."

"Are you sure you can find it?"

"Nope!" He couldn't see her smile, but he could hear it, even through the wind. "Come on!"

Each step felt like he was passing further into a nightmare, but Gyre plodded along in Kit's wake. His fingers went from painfully cold to ominously numb, and he wasn't sure he could move his toes inside his boots. The slush was building up on the floor of the pass, and the rocks became slippery underfoot. Kit stumbled several times, and Gyre caught her, hoping like the plague that his own footing would hold.

Just when he was starting to think that Kit couldn't possibly find her own nose in the murk, much less a cave she'd used a year before, she gave a triumphant cry and hurried ahead of him. He followed in her footsteps, boots heavy with wet, clinging snow. She ran up to the rock wall of the pass and, sure enough, there was a gap in it, just wide enough for a person to slide through. Kit shrugged out of her pack, slipped inside, and pulled it after her. Gyre followed suit and found himself in absolute darkness.

"Hang on." Kit struggled for a moment, then produced a glowstone, lighting the cave with a faint blue glow. "Here we are. Told you there'd be something!"

The cave was long and narrow, a crevice stretching a dozen meters into the side of the mountain. At the back of it was a canvas sack, torn apart, and a small pile of twigs and branches.

"I stayed here a couple of days before I went into the tunnels," Kit said, teeth still chattering. "Looks like something's been at my spare clothes, but we can use them as kindling. At least there's firewood."

Fire seemed like an astonishingly good idea. Kit delved into the sack, tearing apart garments that time and animals had reduced to rags, and Gyre arranged some twigs among them. He had to brush off a thick coat of snow to get into his pack and retrieve a firelighter, but the alchemical device threw sparks on the first attempt, and the campfire caught quickly.

"Clothes off," Gyre said, as Kit sighed and sagged against the wall.

She yanked down her scarf and gave him a mischievous grin. "Well, *that's* bold of you."

"To keep warm," Gyre said. "If you stay in your wet things—"

"I *know*," Kit said, laughing. She was already undoing the buttons on her outer jacket. "I have been caught in storms before."

There followed a few minutes of awkward shuffling, working by the light of the fire and the glowstone. Gyre stripped to his underwear, trying to ignore the glimpses of flame-tinged skin he got from Kit as she did the same. By the time he was finished, she was already sitting, a blanket draped around her shoulders.

"Come on," she said, lifting the blanket to pat the space beside her, and incidentally showing him quite a bit of herself in the process. "It's warmer this way."

He couldn't argue with that. Spreading his damp, snow-crusted gear beside the fire, he slipped under the blanket beside her. She leaned against his shoulder, her skin clammy-cold and damp. Gyre let out a deep breath and tried wiggling his toes, which got him a vicious pins-and-needles feeling. *At least they're still there.*

"Bad luck," she muttered. "You don't get many storms this time of year."

"You'd know better than I would," Gyre said. "It hardly ever rains in Deepfire. Something about the draft from the Pit."

"That's convenient." She shuffled sideways, pressing herself closer against him. "Not a lot of mountains where you grew up?"

Gyre snorted. "We had a hill twenty meters high that we thought was the tallest spot in the world. I used to climb the tree on top of it and pretend I could see all the way to Skyreach." Maya hadn't been able to make the climb, he remembered, and he'd been teasing her with the imaginary wonders he could make out from up there. "Really it was just farms and more farms."

"And that was going to be your life?" Kit said. "Mucking out vulpi?"

"And feeding vulpi, and helping birth vulpi, and milking vulpi, and butchering vulpi—" Gyre shrugged. "Pretty much. It was what my father did." He blinked as a bead of sweat rolled past his eye, and extricated one hand to scratch at his scar. "Until the Order came for Maya, it was all I wanted."

Kit was silent for a moment. Her breathing was soft against his shoulder, and he wondered if she'd fallen asleep.

"What if this works?" she said quietly. "What if Naumoriel gives you what you want? Are you going to try to save your sister?"

Gyre closed his eye.

"It's not like that," he said. "Maya is ... She doesn't do things by half measures. You should have seen her as a little girl. If she believes in the Order, she'll fight me to her last breath, brother or not."

"Then what's the point?"

"It's bigger than her and me. It's about ... humanity, I guess. All of us." Gyre sighed. "Maybe it's silly to think about it that way."

"What do you mean?"

"You haven't spent much time in the Republic, have you?"

Kit shook her head.

"The Twilight Order defends the Dawn Republic. That's how it's always been. But they defend us like a suit of iron armor. It might stop a knife, but it weighs you down until you can barely move." He shifted uneasily, and Kit twined her arm through his. The slim curve of her breast pressed against him, and he cleared his throat. "It's not about kids like Maya. Not *just* about that, anyway. The Order tells us what sort of arcana we can use, and they keep anything dangerous for themselves."

"I know all about that," Kit said. "I grew up in Grace. Smuggling stuff into the Republic is the main industry."

"They say it's to protect people from *dhakim*," Gyre said. "But Lynnia's not a *dhakim*, and she gets along fine. My father was the furthest thing from a criminal you'd ever meet, but even he had a shed full of little bits of *dhak* for when our vulpi got sick or our garden was in trouble."

"So you want to bring *dhak* to the Republic?"

"Not ... exactly." Gyre hesitated. "As long as the Order is running things, we're still following the plan the Chosen left for us. While they were around, maybe that was okay; maybe they would have improved everyone's lives. But now? We're not *going* anywhere. In four hundred years since the war, the Republic hasn't gotten anywhere but smaller and poorer and hungrier. And all anyone can do about it is cling tighter to the Order and hope they can save us."

"The Splinter Kingdoms are no better," Kit said. "At least the ones I've visited."

"I don't know the answer," Gyre said. "But the Order isn't it. So I'm going to destroy them."

"Destroy them?" Kit said after a moment. "Destroy the Twilight Order. The centarchs. The heirs of the Chosen."

"The ghouls destroyed the Chosen themselves," Gyre said. He felt simultaneously unburdened and embarrassed. He'd never said all that aloud, not in those terms, not even to Yora or Lynnia. "The Order is only their shadow. That's why I thought . . ."

"I get it." Kit looked up at him, grinning in the shadowy light. "You don't dream small, do you?"

"What about you?" Gyre said defensively. "What were your dreams, before you found out you were . . ."

"Dying?" Kit said brightly. "I just wanted to get rich. I ran away from Mom because she wanted me to take a job sweeping gutters for a few decithalers, and I looked at the old people who'd spent their lives doing that and I thought, no. I'm going to find something better, and I'm going to have some fun doing it." She shrugged, pressed tight against him. "That winter I nearly died of a fever because I didn't have a roof over my head."

"Doomseeker," Gyre said, grinning.

"Back then, it was just stupidity."

She let out a breath, and they fell into a comfortable silence. It was warm under the blankets, and Kit's skin had lost its clammy feel. It was probably time to pull apart and check on the state of their gear, but Gyre couldn't bring himself to suggest it.

"Gyre," Kit said. "Look. I have a . . . a rule."

"Hmm?"

"About people on my expeditions. And what we're allowed to do. I've had some problems, you know? But—this is a little different, right? Us."

Gyre blinked. His mind felt slow and sleepy. "I really don't know what you're talking about."

Kit sighed and paused for a moment. Then she muttered, "Fuck it," and kissed him. Gently, inquisitively at first, waiting to see if he pulled away. When his mouth opened under hers, she leaned harder against him, bare skin pressed against his.

"Are you," Gyre managed between snatched breaths, "teasing me again?"

Kit growled, low in her throat, and kissed him harder. He felt her hand fumbling beneath the blanket until it found his own, and their fingers intertwined. Then she pulled his hand toward her, spread it flat against her stomach, guided it downward. His fingers slipped under the hem of her underthings, through dampened curls of pubic hair. When they found the wet warmth of her, her breath hitched, and she pressed herself tight against him.

"Apparently not," Kit said, and nipped playfully at his ear.

Morning found them curled around one another in the blankets, huddled close to the last embers of the dead fire. Through the narrow entrance to the cave, Gyre could see a slice of pure blue sky, and a slash of sunlight was gradually creeping across the floor.

He pulled himself away from Kit, who groaned at the cold air that infiltrated their nest. She rolled over, wrapping the blanket around herself like a cocoon, and lay facedown.

"Sorry," Gyre said. He started dressing, his things chilly but dry.

"Mmf," Kit said, voice muffled as she spoke directly into the blanket. "Usually I'm the one sneaking away before last night's bad decision wakes up."

"Bad decision?" Gyre said.

"Well." Kit raised her head and watched as he tugged on his trousers. "Maybe not entirely a bad decision."

"I'm honored," Gyre said.

He grabbed some twigs and set about coaxing the fire back to life, while Kit disentangled herself from the blankets. She yawned and stretched, unselfconsciously naked. When she caught him staring, she shot him a grin before shivering and casting about for her clothes.

Gyre boiled water and made tea, which Kit accepted appreciatively. Armed with the steaming cups, they went to the entrance of the cave and squeezed outside. The temperature had dropped overnight, and the wet, stormy air had been transformed into something crystalline and cold. Icicles hung in sheets from every overhanging rock, and the piles of snow were encased in glittering armor.

"That's going to make this an interesting day's walk," Gyre said.

"Fortunately, we don't have far to go," Kit said. "Only a couple of hours to the tunnels."

At Kit's suggestion, they lightened their packs by leaving the tents behind, since they'd soon be underground. *And if we make it to the Tomb, either we'll have the ghouls to help us on the way back, or it won't matter.* Gyre cached the surplus supplies at the back of the cave, then took up his reduced burden and followed Kit back out into the pass.

As he'd predicted, it was tricky going. The footing was treacherous, and every surface was coated in ice, so no handhold was secure. It got worse when the time came to leave the bottom of the pass—a narrow ridge of rock extended off to the left, curving around the flank of the mountain, with a sheer drop on one side and an icy cliff on the other. Gyre, no stranger to heights, felt a flutter in the pit of his stomach when he looked at the prospect.

"Maybe we ought to tie ourselves together?" he offered, as Kit strode ahead onto the lip of rock.

"What, so that if you fall you'll definitely take me down with you?" Kit said, smiling back at him. "No, thanks. Just because I fucked you doesn't mean I'm ready for a suicide pact."

She edged along, one glove trailing against the icy stone, and there was nothing for it but to grit his teeth and follow. They made progress one step at a time, testing the ground ahead for loose stones. Twice massive icicles blocked the way, and they had to pause while Kit hacked at them with her saber until they shattered and tumbled into the abyss.

"I thought you said it wasn't far," Gyre muttered, glancing up at the sun. It was sinking steadily toward the western horizon.

"It isn't," Kit said. "We're just slow. But nearly there."

The tunnel entrance, when they reached it, was hardly recognizable as such. It hadn't been meant as a way in. At some time in the four hundred years since the war, a big chunk of rock had tumbled away from the mountain, exposing a section of ghoul construction like pulling the skin back from a beehive. From the ledge it just looked like a depression in the stone, and it wasn't until Gyre edged around that it became clear the space continued much deeper. Where it was exposed to the elements, the surface was rough and weathered, but after a few meters it took on the unnatural smooth texture of ghoul construction.

"This is it," Kit said unnecessarily. She pulled a glowstone from her pack and lit it, throwing a long shadow behind her.

"How did you find this place?"

"Bits and pieces." She shrugged. "There's a bunch of tunnels that ought to lead in this direction, but they're all blocked, and when I went to look at them the collapses seemed deliberate. As though someone wanted to cut this whole section of the warrens off from the rest. I started asking around about this area, and an old scavenger told me that he'd seen this entrance but never managed to make it up here."

"And based on that you made the trip?"

She raised an eyebrow. "I chased a lot less than that a lot farther. You tried looking for the Tomb by collecting rumors in Deepfire. I went out and dug for it."

"Point taken," Gyre said. "So what should we expect?"

"A whole lot of nothing, at least for a while." Kit shifted her pack across her shoulders. "It's a long way down."

Several hours later, Gyre was starting to understand what she meant. The tunnels were the same broad, circular spaces that he was used to seeing under Deepfire, but where those were cracked and broken by the impact of the weapon that had made the Pit, these were smooth and featureless. Here and there, faded markings on the walls hinted that they might have served some purpose, but whatever had been here was gone. There weren't even any of the rotting wrecks or light-patches that scavengers gathered to render into alchemicals.

As though someone has scraped the place clean, he thought. *Gone out of their way to make this set of tunnels as unappealing as possible. "Go home, humans, nothing to see here..."* His heart beat a little faster.

At first, Kit guided them with confidence, stalking through each junction as though she were following a map drawn on the inside of her eyelids. They went down, always down, winding around and around over ramps and sloping corridors, a crisscrossing, zigzagging path into the heart of the mountain. The air grew close and started to get warmer, and Gyre shrugged out of his heaviest layers.

Eventually, they stopped to rest. Gyre had no idea what time it was outside, but his legs were burning. He drank a carefully measured amount from his canteen—there'd been no running water in the tunnels thus far—and ate from the dried fruit and meat in his pack. There was no question of a fire—down here, there was nothing to burn, except for their own gear.

Kit shrugged out of her pack and went through her own routine, chewing steadily on the tough rations. She set the glowstone down between them and watched Gyre as he swallowed another spare mouthful of water.

"I don't remember the way much past this," Kit said. She kept her voice down. Loud sounds echoed strangely in the long, circular tunnels. "I'd been out a long time before I found this place, and after a while I got a little...frantic."

"I'm amazed you remember this much," Gyre said.

She shrugged. "I've had a lot of practice."

"Well. We just need to keep heading down, and we'll get there eventually, right?"

"Right!" Kit said brightly. "Or we'll reach a dead end, or get stuck in a loop, and get lost and eventually die."

"Very cheery."

"You know me." She set her canteen down and raised her eyebrows. "Well?"

"Well what?" Gyre read her smirk and blinked. "Here?"

She rolled onto her hands and knees and crawled toward him. "You've got something else to keep you busy?"

"There might be plaguespawn," Gyre muttered.

"That's all right," Kit said. "Adds to the thrill."

When they were finished, they both slept for a couple of hours. Gyre found the rest fitful and full of strange, half-mad dreams. If Kit had the same problem, she didn't say, but the third time he woke up he found her dressed and sitting against the wall, staring into the darkness. Gyre shook a glowstone to life, and their eyes met in the half-light. By unspoken consensus, they rose and continued onward.

Now Kit's steps were less sure, and more often than not she seemed to just choose whichever branch tended downward. Before long, the character of the tunnels changed, the simple circular pattern giving way to broader, less regular caverns. It had a less constructed feel, though the floor was still smooth and level, as though they were natural caves that the ghouls had repurposed to their own ends. Gyre guessed some crevices must reach the surface, since some of the chambers were dense with bats, the creatures nesting upside down on the ceiling; the floor was thick with guano and skeletons.

Even here there were plaguespawn, though fortunately they were all small, mad little things, like a dozen bats rolled into an awkward ball the size of a melon. Kit split one in half with her saber, and Gyre pinned another with his long knife and crushed it with his boot. They glanced at one another and continued on in silence. They'd barely spoken for hours.

Beyond the bats, another long, twisting corridor turned down, running in a descending spiral like a giant corkscrew. Gyre gave Kit a questioning look, and she only shrugged. They followed it anyway, walking for at least an hour, as the temperature rose and Gyre's ears popped.

It finally ended in another natural-looking cave. Directly across from where they came in, another tunnel entrance gaped, descending into darkness. The center of the cavern, though, was broken by a ragged-edged crevasse, like the Pit in miniature. Gyre and Kit stood by the edge of it in silence. Kit kicked a stone in, and they listened to it rattle and ping as it descended, long after it had passed out of sight.

"I take it you don't remember this?" Gyre asked.

Kit shook her head, eying the gap speculatively. "We have to backtrack."

"All the way up that ramp?"

"Unless you have a bridge handy."

Gyre considered for a moment. "I may have...something. Give me a minute."

He shrugged off his pack and rooted around in it, opening the leather case at the bottom where he kept Lynnia's alchemicals. There was a bottle of thick black sludge, a tiny thing only the size of the end of Gyre's pinky. With some effort, he undid the stopper, and recoiled at the acrid smell.

"Yuck," Kit said.

"Pretty sure she makes this by boiling lizards." Gyre tried not to breathe as he tipped a fat drop of the black stuff into the center of his palm. Working quickly, he restoppered the bottle, stowed it, then pressed his hands together, spreading the black goo around. After a few moments, he tried pulling them apart, and found them stuck fast. "Perfect."

"You glued your hands together?" Kit said. "I'm overcome by your brilliance, Halfmask."

"Just watch." Gently, he opened his palms, applying force from the side, and the black goo separated reluctantly. Both hands were covered in the stuff. "Scuttlerskin, she calls it. After the little lizards. Sticks hard in one direction but not the other."

"That's strange," Kit said. "How does it know which is which?"

"Don't ask me." Gyre shrugged. "Tie that rope around my waist."

Kit retrieved the coil of alchemical line, light and strong, and expertly knotted one end around Gyre. She looked at the rest of it dubiously. "If you fall, I'm not heavy enough to hold you up."

"Hopefully that won't be a problem." Gyre backed up to the bottom of the ramp, careful to keep his hands from touching his clothes. "Here goes."

He'd been half hoping Kit would try to talk him out of it, but she only stepped out of the way, with a look that seemed almost admiring. Gyre focused on the opposite side of the crevasse and started to run. Halfway across the room, the pit loomed wider with every step, and his plan suddenly looked very bad indeed. By then it was too late, though, and there was nothing he could do but keep running and try not to miss the jump. He planted his boot on the lip of the rock and put everything he had into a horizontal leap, arms stretching ahead of him, reaching for the other side.

For a moment, he thought he would make it. Then gravity caught up to him, and he was falling into the darkness.

A second later, he impacted the opposite wall of the crevice, hard enough to take his breath away. His boots scrabbled at the rock, desperate for purchase, but his scuttlerskin-coated hands stuck fast. The sudden weight nearly jerked his shoulders out of their sockets, but it kept him clinging to the wall long enough to find a foothold with one toe. He hung there, chest aching where it had struck the wall, sharp pains shooting out from his shoulders. *Why did I think this was a good idea?*

"You still alive?" Kit called from out of sight.

"Ow," Gyre called back.

"Oh good."

He started to climb, slowly and carefully. Fortunately, he'd practiced with scuttlerskin a few times back in Deepfire. The trick was to be very aware of the direction of the weight on your hands. Straight backward, or toward the ground, and it was strong enough that you could hang from your fingertips. Pull sideways, and it gave way, with unpleasant consequences if you weren't expecting it. Move carefully, though, and you could climb anything.

The edge of the cliff seemed a very long way above. Gyre resolved not to look at it, and pulled himself up, hand over hand. Peel one palm away, lift himself on the one that was still stuck, attach the other, repeat. Sweat dripped into his eyes, and he fought the urge to scratch his scar. *Bad enough to fall to my death without also having my hand glued to my face.*

Eventually, his groping palm found empty air, and he had a moment of panic before he managed to slap it down on the floor, past the top of the crevice. Another heave got him over the edge, and he rolled over, hands held out and away from his body. From the other side of the gap, he could hear Kit's polite applause.

"That," she called over to him, "might be the stupidest thing I've ever seen someone try. And believe me when I say you're up against some strong competition in that category."

"My arms are inclined to agree with you," Gyre said.

"And they call *me* Doomseeker."

"Can you get across the rope?"

"Oh, sure. Just keep that end set."

Gyre took the slack rope, a long loop of which now hung in the pit, and stuck it in place by jamming his hand against the floor. Kit pulled the line taut, used another alchemical to stick her end in place, and gathered up both packs. She trotted lightly across, as easily as if it were a city sidewalk.

"I really hope this is the right way," Kit said. "It'd be a shame to waste a performance like that."

"There's more scuttlerskin," Gyre said. "You can try it next time." He peeled his hand up, carefully, then looked speculatively at the pack.

"You'd better do this. Find the little white bottle, would you? It's the solvent that takes this stuff off."

Kit found what he needed and looked at it speculatively. "Seems like I should ask for a ransom."

"Kit…"

"I mean, if I dropped this over the cliff by accident, you'd be in a tight spot, wouldn't you?"

He waved his hands in her direction. "Hand it over or I'm going to stick myself to you somewhere very inconvenient."

"Promises," Kit said, laughing.

Beyond the crevice, the tunnels changed again, in a way that made Gyre's heart race.

The farther they got, the more they looked… alive. Like the tunnel where they'd found the destabilizer, it seemed as though the four hundred years of decay that had afflicted every other ghoul ruin had never touched this place. The smooth but natural rock was replaced by something dingy green and slightly soft to the touch, with a warmth that made Gyre suspect it was insulation. Markings appeared, incomprehensible glyphs that were still sharp-edged and clear, as though they'd been painted days before.

Eventually, circles of light became visible on the ceiling as they approached, flickering gently to life with a soft blue-white glow. It wasn't bright, but it was enough to see by. Each time one of them came on, Gyre felt like it was escorting him along the path.

The Tomb. This had to be it, just as Kit had promised. *Not a ruin. A living ghoul city.*

Kit, by contrast, seemed to get jumpier the deeper they went. Each flicker of light made her twitch, and her hand was never far from the blaster at her side.

"Something wrong?" Gyre said, when they reached yet another junction.

"Shhh," Kit said. "This isn't right."

Gyre lowered his voice to a whisper. "What?"

"*This.*" She gestured at the walls, the lights. "We're getting close to the Tomb."

"That's the idea."

"It's not just a place you wander into! If this is the way in, then there'll be—"

Something hit the floor nearby with a heavy stone-on-stone *thud*.

"Guards," Kit finished. Her blaster pistol was already in her hand.

A massive shape loomed in one of the adjoining corridors. Gyre recognized the humanoid outline of a ghoul construct, like those he'd seen escorting Elariel, though this one was larger and covered in a layer of stone armor. Gaps at the joints showed the rippling muscle underneath, like the body of a plaguespawn but refined and perfected. It paused for a moment, looking them over—though it had no eyes that Gyre could see, no features on its blank stone faceplate—then lumbered forward. For all its weight, it was shockingly fast.

"Get its attention!" Gyre hissed, tossing his pack on the floor and yanking it open.

"I think we have it already," Kit growled. But she dropped her own pack and started running across the floor of the tunnel. When the construct didn't follow, she skidded to a halt, took careful aim with her blaster, and fired.

The *crack* of the bolt echoed painfully in the tight space, and Gyre had to put a hand over his dark-adapted eye. Instead of a detonation, though, the blast splashed harmlessly just before impact, shimmering energy briefly surrounding the construct. The thing turned toward Kit, and she encouraged it with another shot, which was similarly deflected. The floor shook as the construct started to run toward her, huge stone-armored fists at its sides.

"Gyre," Kit shouted, backing away. "Maybe hurry it up?"

"Working on it," Gyre muttered. He extracted the largest clay sphere from his satchel and spread liquid from another bottle across it. The stuff foamed on exposure to air, expanding into a ball of sticky goo. Pushing the rest of the alchemicals aside, Gyre ran after the creature. "Try to get it to hold still!"

"How—" Kit jumped aside as one huge fist pistoned down, hitting the floor hard enough to send chips of stone flying. "—the fuck—" She ducked as the thing's other hand whistled overhead. "—am I supposed to get it to hold still?!"

"Just like that," Gyre said. The construct had stopped running, concentrating on trying to hit the elusive target at its feet.

Gyre went into a sprint—his legs reminded him that he had not been kind to them recently—and caught up to it from behind, planting the alchemical against the small of the construct's back. The foam stuck it in place, and Gyre dodged around the thing's feet as it spun, groping for him. He got past it and grabbed Kit, bowling her over and sending both of them to the ground in a painful roll across the stone. As soon as they came to a stop, Gyre jammed his hands against his ears, and Kit did the same.

An instant later, the bomb went off with a noise like the end of the world. Gyre's teeth slammed together hard enough to hurt, with every bone in his body vibrating in sympathy. A wave of boiling heat washed over them, mercifully brief, followed by a rain of small stones and a smothering curtain of dust.

Kit was saying something, her mouth opening and closing in apparent silence. Gyre dropped his hands, and his ears popped. "What?"

"I said, you were carrying *that* in your pack all this time?" Kit's voice was audible as if from a great distance.

"It was the biggest Lynnia had," Gyre said. His own words sounded weirdly muted. "I thought we might run into something like this."

"Remind me to take cover next time you trip," Kit said.

She pulled herself out from under him and clambered to her feet. The corridor still boiled with dust, but where the construct had been standing there was now nothing but a shallow crater. Pieces of its stone carapace and shreds of organic debris littered the edges.

"Wasn't sure that was going to work," Gyre said, flexing his jaw. His ears popped again. "Your blaster didn't bother it."

"That's different," Kit said. She examined the detritus admiringly. "The ghouls have a sort of shield that absorbs *deiat* until it burns out. But plain old explosives apparently work just fine." She turned back to him and held out a hand. "You all right?"

"More or less." She pulled him to his feet, and he winced. "Sorry for using you as bait."

"Eh." She waved a hand dismissively. "I'm used to it."

"So now what?"

"Keep heading down." Kit picked her way around the edge of the crater and scooped up her pack. "And hope that—"

She stopped, and Gyre nearly cannoned into her.

"Hope that what?" he said.

"How many more of those bombs have you got?" Kit said. "Just for information's sake."

"None," Gyre said. "That was all Lynnia had on hand. I've got some smaller crackers, but—"

"Then," Kit interrupted, "I think it's time to run."

Gyre looked down. His numbed ears couldn't hear much, but he felt a buzz through the soles of his feet. On the floor, tiny pebbles rattled and jumped to the echoing tread of many oncoming footsteps.

They ran, down into the dark.

To this point, Gyre had been doing his best to keep track of the route in his mind, so that they could backtrack at least a little ways if they ran into a dead end. Now any hope of that was abandoned. He sprinted down one curving corridor after another, Kit just behind him. When he came to a branching, he chose whichever tunnel wasn't already thick with the rumbling tread of constructs.

"They're herding us," Kit gasped out between breaths.

Gyre nodded, too winded to speak. *Not that there's anything we can do about it.*

A stitch stabbed in his side like a dagger, and his pack dragged at his shoulders. Light-patches blinked on ahead of them and went out once they'd passed, corridor after corridor, the endless web of tunnels stretching down and down. His knees screamed with every step.

They came to a four-way junction, a pool of light with darkness all around. Ahead and to the right, distant shapes moved, and footsteps were still closing in from behind.

Left it is, then. Gyre ran down another curving corridor and skidded to a halt in a small circular room. A light-patch on the ceiling flickered on, revealing no other exits. Except—

There was an opening on the rear wall. Not a passageway, just a hole in the rock, barely big enough for Gyre to crawl through. It was lined, not with stone, but with something soft and wet that glistened in the faint light. It looked distressingly *alive*, and as he watched, the edges of the aperture contracted in a fit of peristaltic motion, the wave running down the narrow chute and out of sight.

"Yuck," Kit said.

"No idea what that is?" Gyre said. They approached the strange opening, the pounding of footsteps behind getting louder.

"Nothing I saw the last time I was here," Kit said. "On the other hand, I was unconscious when they brought me into the city."

"You think this might be an *entrance*?" Gyre said. "It looks like..." Words failed him.

"It looks like the inside of someone's throat, after you cut their head off," Kit said.

"Thank you for that image," Gyre muttered. "So what are the odds it leads to a stomach?"

Two constructs appeared in the doorway. They looked more dangerous than the one Gyre had destroyed, their carapaces spiked and gleaming with sharp metal tines.

"Does it really matter?" Kit said. She took a deep breath.

"You're not seriously—" Gyre began.

But she was. She hurled herself forward, arms outstretched. In an instant she was gone, carried down the slimy passage on a wave of muscular contraction. Gyre could have sworn he heard her shouting excitedly, like a child on a slide.

"So many bad ideas today," Gyre muttered, and followed.

Chapter 18

They let Maya sleep in her own room, which she hadn't expected.

She wasn't free, by any means. She didn't have her haken back, and two Legionaries waited just outside the door. But challenging the centarchate apparently afforded her a bit of formal status, at least until the challenge was resolved.

Practically the moment she'd left the Council chamber, she'd felt the adrenaline draining out of her, replaced with wobbly-legged fatigue. By the time she got to her own chamber, it was all she could do to collapse into bed. But sleep eluded her for some time, as the day's events replayed themselves in her mind. Eventually, she must have passed out, because when she sat bolt upright, heart pounding, the gradual dimming of the Forge's sunlamps told her it was early evening.

Maya put her hand on the Thing and made herself breathe, feeling the muscles in her chest work, the blood rushing through her veins. Jaedia had tried to teach her to clear her mind, to focus on the rhythms of her body as a way of maintaining her calm. It was not something Maya had ever been very good at.

Jaedia. I'm coming. She felt better now that her feet were planted on a new path. It might be treacherous, but it was a way forward. *All I have to do is keep moving.*

Here and now, that meant beating Tanax in the dueling ring.

When her pulse no longer roared in her ears, she got up and went to the door. Two blank-masked Legionaries waited outside, and Maya asked if she could have some dinner. One of them nodded and went to summon a servant. The food, when it arrived, was plentiful, roast chicken and thick soup and some of the doughy dumplings Marn liked so much.

Marn! A stab of guilt went through her. *I never even* asked *what happened to Marn.* As far as she knew, he'd gone with Jaedia on her mission. *Which still doesn't make sense.* Had he made it home, or... *Jaedia couldn't have killed him. Not her own agathios.* She shook her head, swallowing hard. *Chosen defend, none of this makes any sense. I hope he's all right.*

There was a soft knock at the door. "Yes?" Maya said.

"It's Beq."

"Beq!" She pushed her tray aside and scrambled across the room. She'd been ready to throw her arms around the arcanist, but Beq stood awkwardly between the two flanking Legionaries, and Maya paused. "Is it all right if she comes in?"

One of the soldiers nodded. Maya gestured Beq inside and closed the door behind her. *Then* she hugged her, as Beq exhaled and relaxed.

"You—" Beq said, as Maya pulled away. She paused, started again. "I heard what happened with the Council."

"You think I'm crazy," Maya said.

"No one *challenges* to get their cognomen, not anymore." Beq shook her head. "I didn't even know you still could."

"It's in the rules," Maya said. "Never been changed. That used to be the only way to become a centarch. Back then there were more candidates than haken, so—" She trailed off. "Sorry. I did a lot of reading in my cell."

"I gathered." Beq smiled. "Usually it's *me* getting excited about ancient history."

Maya laughed out loud. She offered Beq the chair and sat down on the bed, unable to stop herself from fidgeting with the covers.

"Have you seen Varo?" Maya said. "They haven't accused him of anything, have they?" She felt a stab of guilt for not asking earlier.

"Not officially," Beq said. "But the Council was quick to send him on another assignment. He's somewhere in the south now, I think."

Maya nodded, then took a deep breath.

"And have you...made any progress?" she said. "On what you... found."

"I think we should be safe to talk in here," Beq said. "And, yes, a little. It turns out there are a few different codes, and I've found at least two in the master archive."

"And Nicomidi was working with Raskos," Maya said, leaning forward eagerly.

"Maybe. He writes carefully, even in code." Beq frowned. "Why are you so sure?"

Maya's eyes flicked to the door, and she lowered her voice. "Nicomidi came to me in the cell. He wanted me to give evidence to the Council against Jaedia. Offered to get me off the hook. When I wouldn't do it, he threatened you."

"Threatened *me*?" Beq squeaked. "Why?"

"I don't think he knows what you're working on," Maya said. "He just knows that we're friends, and he thought it would motivate me." She found her hands clenching into fists. "A member of the *Council* threatened to murder an Order arcanist. This is the fucking Republic, not some Splinter King's court. We don't *assassinate* people."

"Can you tell the rest of the Council?"

"He'd just deny it," Maya said. "But if you can prove he was part of Raskos' corruption, they won't be able to ignore *that*."

"Assuming he *is* part of it."

"He must be. Why else would he go this far? Sending us to Deepfire, and then trying to keep me from looking into what happened to Jaedia—"

"Wait," Beq said. "You think he was involved in that too?"

"I don't *know*." Maya flopped back on the bed and closed her eyes. "It all has to be connected, but I don't see quite how. But we can find out. We *have* to find out. And I'll find Jaedia, and...and Marn, and..."

She trailed off, and there was a long silence. Beq fiddled with her spectacles, lenses shifting and whirring.

"You're sure the Council will act?" she said. "Nicomidi's a Kyriliarch. And the Dogmatics will say it's a Pragmatic plot."

"They *have* to do something if we have proof," Maya said. "If we give up on that, we might as well give up on the Order altogether."

"I'll find the rest of the codes," Beq said.

"Thank you," Maya said. She raised her head. "You'll be careful?"

Beq nodded. She lapsed into silence again, hands pressed together in her lap. Maya sat up, blood rushing to her head and making it spin. "What's wrong?"

"I..." Beq swallowed and took a deep breath. "You'll beat him, won't you?"

"Tanax?" When Beq nodded, Maya put on her best grin. "Of course."

"Don't just...laugh it off," Beq said. "I don't know how you centarchs measure one another, but I saw what he did in the tunnel. He's..."

"He's dangerous," Maya said gently. She got off the bed and knelt in front of Beq. "I know. But it's a duel, not a fight to the death. We'll wear panoply belts."

"But if you lose, you'll be sent away," Beq said. "That's what the master arcanist told me. If you challenge the centarchate and lose, you forfeit any chance of ever becoming a centarch, and the Order will bury you away in the middle of nowhere. For the rest of your life."

"Probably," Maya said. "It's up to the Council, and there's not a lot of recent precedent. But they can't have people who can access *deiat* running around loose."

"I don't care about the *reasons*," Beq said abruptly. She took a deep breath and swallowed hard. "I would never see you again."

"I..." Maya found her own throat thick. She managed a quick nod.

"That would make me . . . very unhappy," Beq said. "I was sitting in my room thinking about it, and I realized just how unhappy. I think I would . . . I don't know."

"Beq . . ."

"Ever since we got back, I just . . ." Beq shook her head. "I kept thinking about . . . that. And other things. And then it felt like I was going around in circles and I didn't know how to stop and I couldn't sleep and can I please kiss you?"

"I . . . um." Maya felt her cheeks start to burn as her brain caught up with her ears, and her own voice sounded distant. "Uh. Yes?"

Beq leaned forward, and Maya rose to meet her. Their lips met, and for a moment Maya was frozen, not sure what to do next. She could feel every tiny movement of Beq's tongue, the hot tickle of the other girl's breath against her face, the press of Beq's golden spectacles against the bridge of her nose. One of Beq's hands had landed on Maya's shoulder, and that slight contact sent a crackle through her like *deiat*.

"I don't. Um." Beq pulled back, slightly. "Know what I'm doing. I've never kissed anyone before." Her throat worked as she swallowed. "I never thought I would want to."

"I wanted to kiss you the day we met," Maya said.

"Oh." Beq seemed genuinely nonplussed. "Really?"

"Really." Maya shook her head. "I don't know what I'm doing either."

"We could. Um. Try again."

They tried again. And again, and again. Maya felt a deep, sweet ache rising inside her, and more than anything she wanted to feel Beq's fingers against her bare skin. Beq's hand was still on her shoulder, and Maya let her own hand land on the other girl's knee, fingers brushing her trousers as she leaned into the kiss—

Beq pulled back abruptly and got to her feet so fast that Maya had to scramble out of the way.

"Sorry," Maya said. "Did I—"

"Sorry," Beq said at the same moment. "I'm sorry, I just—"

They lapsed into a deeply embarrassed silence.

"I didn't mean to...startle you," Maya said. "If I did anything—"

"No, it's not that. I mean. It's not..." Beq swallowed again. "I just need to...think."

"That's fine." Maya drew in a long breath, blew it out, trying for calm. Seeing the expression on Beq's face, she got to her feet. "It's *fine*, Beq."

"I'm sorry for making things...complicated." Beq shook her head, and tears glittered in her eyes. "I should go."

Maya wanted badly to grab her hand but guessed that would make things worse. "Beq. Look at me." When the other girl met her gaze, eyes huge through her spectacles, Maya spoke carefully. "Thank you. For the kiss. It was something I wanted...pretty badly. And you have nothing to apologize for."

"Okay," Beq said in a small voice.

"I'm going to beat him," Maya said. "When I do, I'll be a centarch, with a centarch's authority. The Council doesn't have enough evidence to lock up a full centarch, and I'll be able to choose my own assignments. I'm going to follow Jaedia and find out what happened. I hope you'll come with me."

"Of course," Beq said. She pushed up her spectacles and wiped her eyes.

"In which case," Maya said, "we'll have plenty of time to...talk about this. After you've thought about it."

"Okay." Beq's voice sounded stronger. "Thank you."

"Go get some rest."

"You too," Beq said.

She paused, awkwardly, as the Legionaries opened the door. Then, catching Maya's eye one last time, she shuffled out. The guards closed the door behind her, and Maya was again alone.

Chosen fucking defend. She fell back on the bed, head still spinning. *She kissed me.* For a moment, all her other problems seemed far away. *She really kissed me.*

Now all I have to do is win.

*   *   *

The Forge's dueling ground, like the rest of the fortress, had been built to a titanic scale to accommodate a golden age that had never come. The arena was an oval ring several hundred meters across, floored with sand. Dozens of huge rough-cut stone pillars were strewn around it, leaving a clear space in the very center. Given the rarity of formal duels between centarchs, the place saw more use as a training field, and the stones were scorched, chipped, and twisted in a mute testament to the eager agathia who'd sparred here.

A ring of seats surrounded the arena, protected from any stray energy by a wall of unmetal-laced glass. They were already filling up when Maya and her guards arrived, centarchs in their colored cloaks claiming the best view in the center, with the drabber figures of scouts, arcanists, quartermasters, and servants settling in around them. *It looks like the whole Order turned out.* Maya hadn't imagined there *were* so many people in the Forge.

Beq would be down there, somewhere. The thought of her sent a thrill through Maya, which she tried hard to banish. *Win first. Sort out your love life later.*

They'd arrived on the highest level, a spectator's balcony that overhung the seats. The two Legionaries waited patiently by the stairs as Maya looked over the arena, trying to fix in her mind the positions of all the stone pillars. When the height started making her a little dizzy, she returned to them, and they took her back to the stairs. They switchbacked through several more landings, past the tunnels that led to the seats, and finally reached an archway guarded by another pair of soldiers. Maya guessed they were now level with the floor of the arena.

The guards motioned for her to stop. After a moment, Evinda Stonecutter emerged from the doorway, recognizable only by the colored fringe on her cloak. She was fully armored, haken on her hip, face concealed behind an unmetal helmet.

"Centarch." Maya bowed.

"Agathios-Challenger Maya," Evinda said, painfully correct as ever. "In the name of the Council, I offer you this final opportunity to retract your challenge, without prejudice."

Not much chance of that. While the Council as a whole might prefer to avoid this, if she backed down she'd be entirely in Nicomidi's power. As an agathios without a master, she had few formal rights. If she became a centarch, his ability to move against her would be much reduced.

"Thank you, Centarch. But I maintain my challenge."

Evinda grunted, then paused. "I cannot approve of your action," she said eventually. "It goes against tradition. But I must admire your courage."

"Thank you, Centarch."

"Your haken and panoply belt are waiting in the preparation area. Understand that they are being returned to you only for the duel, and no other purpose. If you are so lost to honor as to try to escape, I will be waiting." Her hand brushed her haken.

"I understand, Centarch. I don't plan to run away."

The older woman nodded, then stepped out of Maya's path. "You may proceed."

The guards stayed behind as Maya walked into the tunnel. It entered a broader space, half changing room and half armory. There were benches and a small table, and racks full of equipment of all sorts—swords, axes, pole-arms, armor. Another door let out into the arena itself.

Tanax—Centarch Tanax Brokenedge now—sat on one of the benches, legs crossed, eyes closed as though lost in thought. He already wore his haken at his side, and the silvery length of a panoply belt was wound around his midsection over loose, informal fighting clothes. Maya's own haken lay on the table, with her panoply belt beside it.

"Hello," Maya said. Then paused, cleared her throat, and started again. "Greetings, Centarch."

Tanax opened his eyes and inclined his head. "Agathios-Challenger."

"Congratulations on your cognomen."

"Thank you."

Maya's mouth was suddenly dry. She felt a stab of sympathy for Tanax, who hadn't asked for his role in this drama. While the stakes were not as high for him, losing the duel on behalf of the centarchate would still shame him greatly, and no doubt cost him Nicomidi's good opinion.

"I wanted to say—" she began, but Tanax cut her off.

"You don't have to do this," he said.

She blinked. "What?"

"I know we have…had our differences. I hope you understand I was obeying orders when I brought you in. And while you deserve some punishment for your insubordination, I think…" He took a deep breath. "It's possible my master has acted too harshly."

"Possible," Maya deadpanned.

"You know I have always tried to behave correctly. If you are willing to call off this foolish challenge, I swear I will petition my master and the Council on your behalf."

"You're too late," Maya said. "Centarch Evinda already gave me my last chance outside."

"Maya—"

"Besides," she went on, "in your 'correct behavior,' have you ever considered the possibility that I was right? First about Raskos' corruption, and now about Jaedia."

"My master says—"

"Your *master* is up to his neck in it," Maya snapped. "Right next to Raskos."

"That's enough." Tanax shot to his feet. "It's one thing to defend yourself. To suggest that a Kyriliarch of the Council could be involved in base corruption is absurd. Do you seriously think that someone like Nicomidi would betray the Order for *coin*?"

In her own mind, Maya had to admit it seemed unlikely. But her anger was at a rolling boil, and she wasn't about to tamp it down.

"You can try to ignore it for now," Maya said. "But once we're finished here, I'll drag the Council's noses through the shit myself, if I have to. They'll smell it eventually."

Tanax quivered, teeth clenched, and took a deep breath as he mastered himself. When he spoke, his voice was calm.

"You would make a good centarch someday, Maya. I don't want to hurt you."

"Really?" Maya snatched up her haken and belt. "I'm not sure I can return the sentiment."

They walked out together, through the forest of battered pillars, to the very center of the arena.

Maya tugged at her panoply belt, which still felt a bit off. In truth it didn't matter whether it fit or not, but she was nervous, and trying hard not to touch the Thing for reassurance with half the Order watching. From the floor of the arena, she couldn't make out individual faces, but the colored robes of the Council were clearly visible.

A small unmetal circle, set into the sand, marked the exact center of the dueling ground. Maya took her place on one side of it, and Tanax walked to the other side, turning to face her. For the moment, he kept his hand away from his haken, and she did likewise. She searched his face—dark-skinned, features hawk-like and aristocratic, lips pressed together and tight with suppressed anger.

She wished she'd insisted on sparring with him, sometime during the mission. She'd seen his power at work, the strange twisting of space that rent matter apart, but that wasn't the same as going up against it. At a deep level, the power all centarchs wielded was the same, and duels were trials of *deiat* against *deiat*, blade to blade and mind to mind, regardless of how that power manifested. At the same time, though, each centarch materialized that power in a different form, and that inclined their fighting style in certain directions. Jaedia, for example, had always been far more mobile than Maya, her body as slippery and nimble as one of her breezes, preferring to evade an attack rather than meet it head-on.

Maya guessed that this would not be Tanax's technique. What she'd seen of his power was brutally straightforward, though his sheer strength was impressive. *We'll see.*

"Agathios-Challenger Maya." Prodominus' voice echoed down to them, boosted by some arcana device until it rang through the arena. "Centarch Tanax Brokenedge. The Council has voted me authority to oversee this duel. Raise your arm if you have any objections."

Maya didn't move. Neither did Tanax.

"On my command 'draw,' you will draw and ignite your weapons," the old Kyriliarch went on. "On my command 'fight,' the duel will commence. It will continue until one of you surrenders or is unable to continue. On my command 'stop,' you will cease fighting *immediately.*"

Sweat prickled across Maya's forehead. Tanax's hand clenched into a fist, then loosened.

"Very well," Prodominus boomed. "Draw."

Maya took hold of her haken, opening herself to *deiat*. The power ran through her, first in pinpricks of energy throughout her body, then as a steady flow. It felt like a mug of water after a week of thirst. In the years since Jaedia had given her her haken, Maya had never gone without touching its power for this long, and as it flooded into her she realized how hollow she'd felt without it.

She pushed a thread of the burgeoning energy into her panoply belt and felt its field activate, tinting her vision with the usual hint of blue. Raising her haken, she let *deiat* flow into it, and its flaming blade materialized with a *whoomph*. Across the circle, Tanax lifted his own blade, and a narrow line of space twisted and writhed, distorting everything behind it. It emitted a faint drone, like a swarm of bees.

"Fight!" Prodominus shouted.

Maya flung out her free hand before the Kyriliarch's voice had faded, and a burst of fire slammed across the space between them. It hit Tanax hard enough to knock him off his feet, sending him sliding across the sand, and she saw the sparking blue aura of his panoply flare.

But her opponent recovered impressively quickly. He rolled onto his knees, throwing up a shield of warped space around himself that deflected the flames like a breakwater. Maya closed her hand, and the stream of fire vanished. Tanax got to his feet behind his aura of paradoxical geometry, breathing hard.

"Feel free to yield," Maya said. "I don't want to hurt you."

He growled a curse, and the real battle began.

Tendrils of *deiat* reached out, slicing through the space all around her like a blooming flower with Tanax at the center. She could see them as shimmers in the air, bits of twisted space like the ripples rising from a hot stone, but it was easier to *feel* them resonating with her connection to *deiat*. She channeled power through her haken and slammed her own energy against them. Fire bloomed all around her, motes of energy devouring one another and being devoured in turn.

Bit by bit, Maya's grin faded. *He's plaguing* good. Not as good as Jaedia, who made the whole affair look effortless, but he wove *deiat* with speed and efficiency, sending little dust devils of twisted space spinning across the floor, then sweeping a broad wave of distortion that forced her to block in a wide arc. When she struck back, he withdrew, leaving her wasting her energy against emptiness while he attacked elsewhere. Within a few moments, she was focused entirely on defense, and she could tell it wasn't going to work for long. Waves of ripping, twisting space came closer and closer.

The next time he lashed out, Maya dodged instead of blocking, letting the energy slash past. That bought her a second to launch an assault of her own, throwing curving lines of flame in his direction. He deflected them, but she sprinted forward as he moved, coming at him with haken swinging.

He parried, and flame spat and crackled against the weird buzzing of his twisted blade. Maya disengaged, slipping around his guard and pressing in, and Tanax had to give ground. His power curved in against her from all sides, but Maya wove a nimble shield of flame to block. He was slower, off-balance, splitting his attention between trying to slip past her defenses and keeping her blazing haken away. She hammered him relentlessly, and he backed up another step, then another.

Stay close. Her swordwork was better than his; she could *feel* it, feel the desperation behind his parries. *Let him get clear and he can wear me down. Keep it close and I can win.*

Tanax apparently had come to the same conclusion. He hopped backward, momentarily out of range, and reached out with his free hand. Maya readied a block, but his wave of energy slashed out sideways, into one of the stone pillars. A chunk of granite broke free, falling toward her, and Tanax's power lashed out and shattered it into a hundred razor shards plummeting toward her.

Stopping them with *deiat* would only mean spattering herself with molten rock, so Maya bulled forward, trusting to her panoply. Blue energy flared around her, and she felt a wave of cold, but it passed in moments. She caught sight of Tanax slipping around the pillar and hurried after him, incinerating a distortion wave he left in his wake. Her own power lashed out, touching the ground behind him and raising a wall of flame. He danced away from it and pressed his attack against her, blade swinging. Maya parried and took a step back, their crossed haken crackling and sparking.

Tanax's eyes went suddenly wide. He stepped back from the clinch, mouthing something Maya couldn't hear. His free hand went to his face, and Maya automatically followed suit, feeling something hot and wet on her skin.

Blood. There was a long cut running along her cheek. *One of the rocks must have gotten me.* It wasn't deep, and she'd barely felt a sting, but—

The panoply. It had flared, she was certain. She ran her mind along the stream of *deiat* she was feeding it. *But if it was working, it wouldn't have let anything cut me—*

Which meant that it wasn't working.

Which meant that if he caught her with that haken, it wouldn't be a rush of cold and a brief spell of unconsciousness. She would end up like

Yora and the other rebels, carved into fragments by a blade of twisted space, bleeding from wounds still ragged with distorted echoes.

Fuck. Maya was suddenly aware of her heart racing, the sweat pouring down her cheeks, soaking her shirt, trickling past the Thing between her breasts. *Fuck fuck plaguing* fuck.

Tanax's voice was still inaudible over the roar of her own flames, but she caught the word he mouthed at her. "Yield."

If my panoply isn't working, it's not an accident. Call off the duel now, and there was no guarantee she'd get another chance. *Not when they're willing to go this far.* If she'd been less careful stopping Tanax's attacks, she could easily have died already.

She fixed Tanax's gaze and shook her head. Then, as his eyes widened, she charged.

He met her with a flurry of parries, blocking every strike, backing away.

"Maya, please," he said over the crackle and buzz of their weapons. "You'll get yourself killed. *Yield.*"

"You *yield*," Maya snarled, slamming her haken down. Tanax retreated another step, found his back to a pillar, and hastily parried. Maya pressed down with all her weight, forcing the paired weapons toward his face.

"I can't," Tanax gasped. "Master Nicomidi…he told me…"

"I can guess." Maya thrust her free hand toward his stomach, fire gathering around it to form a blazing gauntlet. Tanax spun a shield of twisting force just in time, and her blow slammed against it. They stayed there for a long moment, locked together, two streams of *deiat* thrashing against each other like roaring beasts.

"I can't…go easy," Tanax gasped. "If you don't…yield…I have to…"

"Do what you fucking like," Maya grunted.

Tanax swallowed. He reached out to the ground below them, and sand exploded upward in a gritty geyser that drove Maya back, letting him spin away. Half-blind, she wiped at her eyes even as she charged after him, relying on her sense of *deiat* to feel his assault. Tanax ran, darting between the pillars, launching attacks over his shoulder as she pounded doggedly after him.

Stay close. She forced herself to move, though all she wanted to do was turn away and find somewhere to hide. *Keep on him.* She'd never been so *aware* of her body, in all its horrible fragility, soft skin and brittle bones, a bag of guts and muscles that stood about as much chance against the raw power of creation as—

As that girl. Behind her eyes, the rebel charred once again into a lifeless skeleton, and Yora fell in two pieces. *Plague plague plaguing* fuck *what in the name of the Chosen am I doing*—

She missed a block and threw herself to the ground just in time. A wave of rippling space slashed over her head, impacting a pillar behind her, blasting a crater in solid rock. Tanax skidded to a halt in a spray of sand.

"Maya, *please*—" His voice was hoarse.

Maya bounced back to her feet, breathing hard, bolts of flame lashing toward him. Tanax blocked and kept running, and Maya pounded after. Space boiled in his wake, ripples and twists of impossible geometry floating around her like dandelion seeds, then falling inward. Intercepting them took more and more of her attention, and Tanax got farther and farther ahead, darting through the maze of pillars.

He knows I can take him blade to blade. She wanted to scream with frustration. *This isn't going to work.* Her legs already felt leaden, and she wasn't going to be able to run him down, not with his power lashing at her from every direction. *Sooner or later, he'll get through, and*—

She cut off that thought, abruptly, and came to a halt in the shadow of a pillar. Tanax paused as well, keeping a safe distance and concentrating on the threads of *deiat* that boiled all around him. Maya's defenses retreated closer and closer, a shell of flame that contracted by the moment.

She raised her free hand and drew hard on her connection to *deiat*.

Diverting power meant her defense weakened even faster, but she persisted, gathering energy for a single, colossal blow. She saw Tanax frown, and his attack slowed as he gathered power to counter. She imagined his confusion—an attack like this was wasteful, easy to see coming, trivial to deflect. She raised her hand, and a shield already shimmered in front of him.

Grinning savagely, Maya turned, shifting her aim. The energy she'd gathered lanced out as a single coherent beam of light, the backwash strong enough to kick the sand at her feet into a raging cyclone. It blasted across the arena, missed Tanax by a meter, and impacted on the stone pillar behind him. As the light faded, a thunderclap rolled out in its wake.

Tanax raised his haken, hesitated. Looked up.

The lance of pure energy had blown a hole in the stone pillar the size of a wagon wheel, sending the rock in molten spatters across the sand. Maya had judged her aim carefully, shearing away the stone on the side closer to Tanax. It started to tip, stone cracking with a sound like a blaster bolt, slowly at first but with unstoppable momentum.

It was falling behind him, blocking off his retreat, unless he wanted to test his panoply against a thousand tons of granite. Tanax turned back to Maya to find her charging straight at him, haken leveled like a spear.

Get close. A hundred wisps of twisted space raced toward her, threads of *deiat* blooming all around him. Maya focused her power in front of her, a wave of fire that cleared her path, and ignored the rest. Tanax adjusted, flinging waves and ripping tendrils of energy, too many and too fast, desperate to make her back off and resume the long-range battle he was sure to win.

Maya refused. She kept coming, twisting aside to avoid his attacks as Jaedia would have done, not meeting him force for force but letting his power flow past her. Behind him, the huge stone pillar hit the ground with a *crunch*, and a wave of dust and sand engulfed them both. Maya closed her eyes against it, navigating by *deiat* alone, feeling the energy flowing through Tanax and the concentrated power of his haken.

A line of power touched her hip, space warping to snag and tear, ripping away a chunk of flesh. Another caressed her left arm, shredding her skin like a wood saw. Pain hammered at the edge of her consciousness, but she kept moving. *Almost there.* Tanax was right in front of her, haken raised, blinded by flying grit. At that moment, it was the easiest thing in the world to duck, letting his blade swing over her head, and pivot on one foot with all the momentum of her charge. Her flaming sword caught him high in the chest, drawing a titanic burst of power from his panoply belt as the blow picked him up and tossed him against the broken pillar.

He vanished from her sight, his connection to *deiat* snuffed out. Maya opened her eyes in time to see him slump forward, falling on his face to lie motionless on the sand. She stood in the center of a whirlwind of dust, bleeding freely from arm and hip, her skin slick with sweat. At the center of her chest, she could feel the Thing humming to itself, resonating with her power. The flames of her haken roiled and crackled.

As the roar of her own pulse in her ears faded, she could hear the cheering of the crowd.

Slowly, Maya focused on the seats high above the arena. The Order was on its collective feet, the arcanists and the servants and the quartermasters, all shouting their approval. The centarchs were more reserved, as befitted their station, but their applause added to the storm of noise.

Pain rose around Maya, threatening to engulf her. Blood pattered to the sand beside her at a frightening rate. Her legs threatened to give way, but she forced herself to stay on her feet. She let her haken's blade vanish and tossed it to one side. From the arena entrance she could see Evinda approaching with a gang of servants. *I hope they brought a healer.*

Above the arena, two things caught her eye. One was Beq, pushing forward to the very front, marked out by her golden spectacles. Maya gave her a weak wave, and her heart flopped as Beq waved back.

The other was the Council. Prodominus was on his feet, applauding and whistling through his teeth, and after a moment Baselanthus joined him. The rest had their heads bent together, in urgent discussion. Except for Nicomidi. Nicomidi was—

Gone.

Chapter 19

Gyre opened his eye and found himself in complete darkness. When he tried to move, his right arm didn't respond, as though it was bound tightly against him, and something restrained his legs. His left hand flailed weakly across his body, and he felt his breath quicken in panic.

Focus. Calm. He gritted his teeth. He remembered—falling, and pain—

"Oh, you're awake." A pleasant voice, familiar. Gyre tried to clear his throat and coughed.

"E...Elariel?"

"Nice to meet you again," the ghoul said politely. He heard her moving around, felt something brush against him. "You were in better shape last time."

"Why can't I see?" Gyre said.

"Ah, yes. Hold still."

It took considerable effort for Gyre to keep himself calm enough to obey. He felt the ghoul bending over him, the warmth of her breath on his face, and then her fingers touched the skin around his good eye. He suppressed the urge to jerk away, clenching his jaw so hard his teeth ached. Something cool and wet dripped into his eye, and he blinked involuntarily. Elariel let go and moved away.

"This is similar to what you humans call 'nighteye,'" she said. "But considerably more effective. Don't light any fires before it wears off, or you may blind yourself."

Whatever the stuff was, it worked quickly. Gyre blinked again and found the room fading into view in spite of the lack of any light.

He lay on a table in a small chamber. The only other furnishing was a tall stool on which Elariel sat, legs primly crossed, hands on her knee. Her long, expressive ears were raised, and her huge eyes, nearly all pupil, regarded him calmly.

"Where am I?" Gyre said, though he could think of only one possible answer. His breath caught.

"The city you humans call the Tomb," Elariel said. "We call it"—she made a rolling, whistling sound he couldn't hope to replicate, and went on—"which in your language translates to something like Refuge."

The Tomb. Gyre looked around the windowless chamber. *Refuge. The last city of the ghouls.*

I made it.

"What happened to me?" He tried to sit up but couldn't manage it, his right arm still restrained. "Where's Kit?"

"Kitsraea is being tended to," Elariel said. "As to what happened, the two of you jumped into a rock ingestor."

"A...what?"

"A construct designed to reduce solid granite to rock slurry and deliver it to the city for use in construction." There was a slight smile on her face, and her ears twitched. "Needless to say, you were injured in the attempt. It was a most unexpected move."

"We were running low on options at the time," Gyre said. "At least it worked."

"We were forced to extract you before you reached the liquefaction pool," Elariel said.

"Thanks," Gyre muttered.

"No thanks are necessary," she said. "Your digested remains would have ruined a perfectly good batch of building material."

Now there was *definitely* a smile on the ghoul's face. Gyre leaned back on the table, which was pleasantly spongy in texture.

"What's wrong with my arm?" he said.

"It was broken in three places," Elariel said, getting off her stool. "I fixed it in place to keep you from injuring yourself further. Do you feel any pain?"

"Not really," Gyre said, propping himself up again on his other hand. He noticed for the first time that he was nearly naked, with no shirt and only a pair of short, loose trousers. Elariel, of course, wore no clothing at all, and Gyre wondered if that was normal for ghouls. "It just won't move."

He tried again and peered a little closer. His right arm was pressed tight against his side, and there was something strange—

His gorge suddenly rose. His arm wasn't pressed against his side; it was *fused* to it, skin stretching unbroken from limb to torso. *Plaguing fuck!*

"Give me a moment."

Elariel stood at his side, and her hands touched him, fingers running along the join. As Gyre watched, his skin *split*, painlessly, separating his arm from his body again. Bands of fresh pink were wound around his biceps and wrist, presumably where he'd been . . . repaired.

Dhaka. The life-magic of which the ghouls had been the foremost masters. For all that he'd come to the Tomb looking for their power, actually seeing it—feeling it used on his own flesh—roiled his stomach. There was no visible sign of the power, just Elariel running her fine-furred hands up and down Gyre's body, pressing and testing. When she found a stray flap of skin, she touched it, and it retreated obediently. Gyre flexed his arm, and she nodded approval.

"How long have I been down here?"

"Three days now," Elariel said. "Your legs were damaged, too, so you may feel some aches for another day, I think."

Three days. Quickheal and bone-break potion—though they were *dhak* by Order standards—had never worked *that* fast.

"And Kit?" Gyre said.

"She should be awake before tomorrow."

Okay. He sat up and met the ghoul's gaze. She retreated a step, her smile fading, and her long ears drooped. *Time for the real question.*

"So why are we still alive?"

Elariel looked at him for a moment, saying nothing.

"You must kill anyone who stumbles into your Refuge, or it wouldn't remain secret," Gyre pressed.

"No one 'stumbles in.' We have had four hundred years to conceal ourselves." Elariel sighed, her fur rippling. "But you are correct. If the Geraia knew you were here, they would have you killed at once."

"They're your leaders?"

She nodded. "The oldest and wisest among us." Gyre was certain he detected a sarcastic spin on the words. "The heads of all the families who remain in Refuge. They decide any matters that affect the city."

"And you're hiding us from them?"

"We are...delaying our report." Elariel cocked her head. "My master says we need to discover what you know. He commanded me to heal you so you could speak to him."

"Ah." Gyre shifted to the edge of the table and stretched his legs. "I suppose I should thank him."

"I would...wait." Elariel's ears drooped again. "He may decide the best way to obtain the information he needs would be to render it from your living brain."

There was an uncomfortable silence.

"Or he may not!" Elariel said, with a forced smile. "He is unpredictable. But now that you're awake, you will have to go and see him."

*   *   *

The state of Gyre's clothes gave him some idea of what the rock ingestor had done to his body. They were practically shredded, ripped and
torn as though they'd gone through a spiked mangle. When he asked
Elariel if the ghouls had anything that might serve, she shook her head.

"I fashioned those"—she indicated the shorts he was wearing—
"when I remembered how odd you humans get about your coverings.
Are they insufficient?"

Gyre assured her they were perfectly adequate. They were a little
large for him, but he managed to retrieve a mostly intact belt from the
wreck of his gear. In the process, he investigated the remains of his
pack, but his stash of alchemicals had either been confiscated by the
ghouls or destroyed by the journey. Both his knives were missing as
well.

Not that it matters. Gyre had no illusions that he would be able to
fight his way out of the Tomb, if it came to that. Elariel had escorted
him out of the room he'd awoken in, and just on the short trip to where
she'd stored his gear he'd seen a dozen constructs. They weren't the
spiked, stone-lined guardians from up above, but many of them were
large and powerful-looking, and presumably more martial versions
weren't far away.

Not all the constructs were humanoid, either. Smaller things trotted
on four legs or hopped like rabbits, and even tinier varieties hummed
through the air on delicate, multicolored wings. They all had a similar look, their bodies built of striated black muscle laid over metallic
bones that poked through at the joints, like anatomy models no one
had bothered providing with skin. Some had specialized limbs, sporting knives or hammers or more complicated tools whose function Gyre
couldn't begin to guess.

The complex they were in seemed to be mostly small rooms set off of
long, winding corridors. The floor was covered in gray-green stuff that

he initially thought was carpet but on closer inspection turned out to be some kind of plant, sprouting myriad fine, hairlike stalks that were soft on his bare feet. The walls were smooth, polished stone, and every so often light-patches gleamed on the ceiling, bright to his adjusted eyes but probably invisible to a normal human.

Doors were oval metal slabs, and they opened themselves at a tap from Elariel. Gyre nearly jumped the first time this happened, but when they went inside the room, he saw the door itself was a construct, with hinges of black muscle.

The Tomb. It was overwhelming, and Gyre tried to discipline his thoughts. *Call it Refuge.* He wondered how far underground they were. The air felt fresh, not too warm or cold. *No wonder the ghouls don't bother with clothes.*

"How many of your people live here?" Gyre said as they walked.

"Oh, hundreds," Elariel said. "Hardly a city by your human standards, I know. But we live longer than you do."

"And—"

"We had a conversation once before, didn't we, about how the less you knew the safer you'd be? Perhaps you should keep your questions to yourself."

"Just this one, then," Gyre said, hurrying a little to keep up. "What does Naumoriel want with me? It can't be coincidence that the only two ghouls Kit and I know are the two that found us here."

"No coincidence," Elariel said. "My master is"—her lips worked briefly as she translated—"Sovereign of the Exterior, you would say? King of the Outside, maybe. His assigned area of responsibility is everything that lies beyond the boundaries of Refuge."

"That sounds like an important job."

"Most of the Geraia would rather tear out their own fur than go near it. It carries very low...mmm, you might say 'social standing,' but it's more complicated than that." Elariel's ears twitched in a manner that Gyre was starting to recognize as something like a chuckle. "My master is considered strange, by our standards. Possibly insane."

"Wonderful," Gyre muttered.

"Monitoring the boundaries of the city is among his tasks, naturally. So he was the one who noticed your approach."

"Along with... whatever you were doing before?"

Elariel blinked, and her ears drooped. "Yes. Of course." She tapped another door. "In here."

The door, swinging open of its own accord, revealed only a very small room shaped a bit like an egg, big enough for three or four people to stand uncomfortably close together. Gyre looked at Elariel curiously, and she gave him a mischievous grin.

"Just get in." Her ears twitched again.

Gyre stepped over the threshold, cautiously. Elariel followed, then turned around to face the way they'd come, tapping the door to close it and then stroking a complicated gesture on its surface. A moment later, the bottom dropped out of Gyre's gut as the whole tiny room began to rise.

"It's a—" Elariel said something in the ghoul language, ears twitching wildly. "A lifter. It's just taking us to the top of the tower."

"You might have warned me," Gyre said.

"I might." Elariel's lip quirked.

A few moments passed in silence, and the feeling of acceleration faded. The door opened again, now facing a small antechamber, blocked off from the lifter by a spray of what looked like the fronds of ferns, stretching from floor to ceiling.

Elariel said something in her own language, then added, "I have brought the human Gyre."

Naumoriel's rumbling voice came from beyond the ferns. "Leave him. Attend to the other until I summon you."

Elariel answered with a liquid warble, then stepped back into the lifter. Her ears were drooping again, but she managed a half-hearted smile.

"Good luck," she whispered, before the door closed.

"Gyre," Naumoriel said. "Come here."

Gyre hesitated, but there didn't seem to be anything to be gained by refusing. He found a gap in the ferns and pushed his way through, into a larger room beyond.

It was a big, circular space, floored with the same carpet-like plant. One wall was taken up by what looked at first like panels of pure darkness. Even with the nighteye, it took Gyre a moment to realize he was looking at windows, and even longer for any details to resolve. He got the sense of vast shapes, tall and slender, marching back into the darkness in irregular ranks. Here and there, tiny pinpricks of light gleamed, barely bright enough to throw shadows. There was a sense of motion, though it was too dark and distant to make out details, like looking into the teeming mass of an anthill.

"So, boy," Naumoriel said. "You have found your 'Tomb.' What do you think of it?"

The old ghoul sat in a chair by the window. Or not a chair, Gyre realized as he turned, but a chair-shaped construct, moving precisely on eight jointed, spindly legs. It rotated to face him and glided forward, keeping absolutely level, so that its occupant was not disturbed. The room around him was full of odd structures, tables with multiple levels and complicated armatures, standing columns of crystal-strewn stone that could have been art projects or unknown arcana. The cluttered space put him in mind of Lynnia's workshop.

"It's not what I expected," Gyre said honestly.

Naumoriel's chair stalked closer. The old ghoul's gray fur was patchy, but his huge eyes were disconcertingly intense in person. The plate that covered part of his chest shifted as he breathed, the tendrils connecting it to his flesh pulsing in unison.

"You expected a ruin you could loot," Naumoriel said. "It's all your kind have ever been good for, picking at the leavings of your betters."

Gyre inclined his head in acknowledgment. Naumoriel snorted.

"And yet you knew better," he said. "Kit must have warned you what would happen if you found us."

"She did," Gyre said. "But she came here and was allowed to return alive."

"Under unique circumstances."

"I thought I would take the risk."

"Why?" Naumoriel gestured upward. "Going through the sun-lovers' trash wasn't enough for you?"

Gyre hesitated under the gaze of those dark eyes. Whatever he said, it would be a gamble. *But just being here is a gamble, and everything's already on the table. Might as well raise the stakes.*

"Because I want to destroy them," he said. "The Republic, the Order. I want to break them once and for all."

Naumoriel cocked his head, waiting.

"The Order did this." Gyre tapped his ruined eye. "They destroyed my family. They dragged my sister away and turned her into one of their soldiers. When I started, that was enough for me to hate them, but it's worse than that. In the name of keeping humanity safe, they put their boot on anyone trying to make a better life. We have bound our-selves to a corpse, and the Twilight Order is the shackles." Gyre spread his hands. "I want to set humanity free."

"Bold words," Naumoriel mused. "But Elariel tells me a single one of their centarchs sent you scurrying for cover."

"Of course," Gyre said. "The Order claims the moral high ground, but behind all their pious bleating are the centarchs and the Legions. The Chosen are gone, but as long as their heirs hold their weapons over the rest of us, who can stand up to them?" Genuine anger crept into his voice. "They say they have the *right* to rule, out of a duty to keep the rest of us safe. As though we were children, inferior, just because we weren't born with whatever special trick that lets the centarchs touch *deiat.*"

Naumoriel remained silent, waiting. Gyre took a deep breath.

"I went looking for the Tomb because I thought there might be some-thing here that would tip the balance in favor of ordinary humans," he said. "The stories of the war say that only the Chosen could use *deiat*, but anyone could learn *dhaka.* I thought…" He shook his head. "Instead of the Tomb, I found Refuge, but my goal hasn't changed."

"Oh, how young you are." A very slight smile crept across the old ghoul's face, showing a line of pointed teeth. "And how ignorant of the true history of things. But now that you know our secrets are not simply lying around for the taking, what makes you think we have any use for you or your plans?"

"You must hate the Order, too," Gyre said. "After what you did to the Chosen, the war—"

"*Lies*," Naumoriel spat, suddenly rigid with fury. "The sun-lovers struck first, as they always did. My people wanted nothing but to be left in peace."

"I believe you," Gyre said. "All we know of the war comes from the Order. But there are stories of hunts and purges of your kind, even as the Chosen dwindled. At Deepfire—"

"They found our defenders too brave, our power too formidable," Naumoriel said. His eyes got a faraway look, as though they were looking through the walls to the distant city. "But they dared not simply leave us be. Instead they broke the mountain around us and killed more of my people in one night than survive in the world today. And then they sent their slaves to hunt the cowering remnants through their own tunnels. The *Chosen*."

"Elariel told me most of your people aren't interested in anything happening outside Refuge," Gyre said, watching the old ghoul carefully. He felt as though he were inching across thin ice, with a bottomless cold depth beneath him. "But you're different, aren't you? You sent Kit out into the world for a reason."

"Don't presume to know me, *boy*." Naumoriel's chair lurched sideways, turning abruptly. "I have little use for your kind at the best of times. You and Kitsraea have already failed me once."

"If it's the Core Analytica you need, I can get it for you. Give me the power to confront the Order, and I will do whatever you require."

"*Give* you the power." Naumoriel sneered. "How much would you sacrifice for it, human?"

"I've spent years searching for this place," Gyre said. "I came here, knowing it would probably mean my death. I abandoned my life in

Deepfire, whatever security I had." He closed his eyes and saw Yora's face. Sarah's, Harrow's. "I let my friends die."

Naumoriel beckoned with one hand, and Gyre hurried after him as the animated chair stalked across the room. It came to a halt beside a long, low table, almost like a bed. It had neatly rolled strips of silvery cloth attached to it, and Gyre took a moment to recognize them as restraints.

"And if I were to tell you that is not enough?" Naumoriel said. His voice was quiet.

"Then I would say," Gyre said, struggling to keep his voice steady, "that I would be prepared to offer whatever was required."

There was a long silence.

"We shall see, human." The old ghoul leaned forward and stroked the table. With a clicking, whirring sound, insect-like limbs spidered out from underneath it, unfolding in a horrible ballet of steel and dark, pulsing muscle. They were tipped with spikes, and grippers, and exquisite little knives in a hundred varieties. Naumoriel looked at them like a doting father at his children. "We shall see."

Chapter 20

"A gathios-Challenger Maya." Prodominus' voice was clearly audible in the hall. "Present yourself to the Council."

Maya looked at Evinda, who was once again on watch outside the Council's door. The old centarch gave her a nod and stepped aside, and Maya bowed deeply in return. For a moment, she thought she caught a hint of a smile on Evinda's stern face.

Taking a deep breath, Maya straightened her formal uniform, touched the Thing for reassurance, and opened the door. Inside, the Council sat as before, except that the edges of the chamber were much more crowded with aides and onlookers. Everyone who could contrive an excuse to be here, Maya guessed, had packed themselves in along the walls to see what happened to the upstart agathios who had challenged the centarchate.

And, of course, one of the twelve chairs was empty.

"Kyriliarchs," Maya said, when she reached the center of the chamber. She bowed again, and waited.

"You have challenged the centarchate, as tradition allows," Prodominus said. "And in accordance with tradition, the centarchate has answered. The ancient forms have been followed."

From the Dogmatic wing of the Council, two Kyriliarchs started saying something in low voices. A buzz ran through the onlookers, then cut off when Prodominus raised one hand.

"Your duel with Centarch Tanax Brokenedge was most impressive," Prodominus said. "There were, however, some…irregularities."

Maya tried to keep herself under control, but her chest went tight. In spite of generous doses of quickheal and the care of the Forge healers, the gouge on her hip still hurt when she walked, and she held her arm stiffly at her side. *Irregularities.*

"Some of my colleagues have asked whether the result of the duel should be accepted," Prodominus said, glancing at the Dogmatic wing. "They question whether Centarch Tanax, once he knew your panoply belt had failed, could have fought at full strength."

"He offered me the chance to yield," Maya said. "I refused, and accepted the consequences."

"Even so—" a woman on the Dogmatic side began.

Prodominus held up his silencing hand again. "The Council questioned Centarch Tanax fully as to his state of mind at the time."

"And he said he was holding back?" Maya felt her fury boiling over. *Of course.* "Don't you think—"

"Centarch Tanax," Prodominus interrupted, "confirmed that he fought to the best of his ability, as was his duty to the centarchate, in spite of your vulnerability. He asked that the result of the duel stand."

The Dogmatic woman crossed her arms, disgruntled, and her companions looked equally unhappy. On the Pragmatic wing, there were quiet smiles.

Maya prickled uncomfortably, her triumph soured by the frustrating feeling of being in Tanax's debt. *No. I shouldn't owe him for doing the right thing.* The exhausting part, she reflected, was that he would probably agree.

"Therefore, as dictated in the founding rules of the Twilight Order and the *Inheritance*, the Council recognizes your skill and courage," Prodominus went on. "You are hereby granted the rank of Centarch of the Order."

I'm... Maya blinked. *That's it? Just like that?*

Everyone was staring at her, and she realized she was supposed to speak. Maya coughed.

"Thank you, Kyriliarch. I am honored by the Order's trust."

Prodominus continued. "As you know, tradition dictates that new centarchs receive a cognomen from their masters. With Centarch Jaedia's absence, that duty falls to us."

Maya tensed again, waiting for the Council to stick in the knife. A highly respected agathios would receive a cognomen held by many centarchs before them, the more prestigious the better. One who was in disfavor might get a 'virgin' name, with no prior lineage. She could guess which of the two someone who had challenged the Council was more likely to receive, without a master to speak for her.

To her surprise, though, Prodominus fell silent, and Baselanthus spoke up.

"Jaedia was my own agathios. In spite of what she stands accused of, I have always believed in her. She told me what cognomen she intended to grant Maya, on the completion of her training, and I shall honor her wishes." He cleared his throat. "The Council names you Centarch Maya Burningblade."

Burningblade. At first Maya thought she'd misheard, especially since the murmur around the edges of the room swelled to a quiet roar as soon as Baselanthus fell silent. The name was on everyone's lips. *Burningblade.*

It was not a virgin cognomen. Far from it. Gaesta Burningblade had been one of the twelve centarchs first given their haken by the Chosen themselves, the distant ancestors of the Kyriliarchs. It had been granted many times in the past four hundred years, always to centarchs whose power manifested as Maya's did—in the pure fire of the sun. None of its bearers had failed to do the name honor.

Jaedia wanted that for me. For a moment, her throat was too thick to respond. Finally, she managed a small voice, which went mostly unheard among the rising tumult.

"I am...honored, Kyriliarch."

After that, the Dogmatic members of the Council had left, stiff-necked, while everyone else seemed to want to congratulate Maya. She shook hands, numbly, with some of the most respected and powerful members of the Order, too shocked to note their colors or remember their names. Someone clapped her on the shoulder, which sent a jolt of pain through her arm, and she doubled over. Distantly, she heard someone saying that the new centarch was tired and needed rest. An arm slipped through hers—on her good side—and she found herself pulled toward the door.

Only when she was out in the corridor did she manage to straighten up. Baselanthus looked down at her, eyes twinkling.

"You seemed like you needed rescue, my dear," he said.

"Chosen defend me," Maya said. "Thank you. And...for what you said—"

"As to that," the old man said firmly, "we should speak in private. Do you think you have the strength?"

Maya nodded. Basel let go of her arm and led the way down the hall to his office. He settled in behind his desk, among the collection of strange arcana, and Maya closed the heavy door behind her. With the sound of conversation from the hall cut off, she relaxed a fraction.

"You seem surprised at how things worked out," Basel said.

"I...expected more..."

"Resistance?"

"Yes, Kyriliarch."

"Oh, no need for that. Not in here, at least. I was always Basel to Jaedia." He waved at the chairs opposite his desk. "Sit, if you like. I know your hip pains you."

"Thank you, K—Basel." Maya took the seat opposite him with relief.

"If Nicomidi had not decamped so suddenly, I daresay you would have had more of a fight on your hands. As it is, the Dogmatics found the wind quite taken out of their sails and declined to make an issue of it after we heard Tanax's testimony."

"It just feels very...sudden."

"Under normal circumstances, there's a bit more pomp. A ceremony and a reception. But things being as they are, we thought it best to move quickly." He fixed her with a sharp gaze. "I imagine it is your intention to go after Jaedia as soon as possible."

Maya nodded vigorously. "Whatever information the Council has must be wrong. Jaedia would never betray the Order; you know that. I suspect she has been deliberately set up."

"I have never been one to construct conspiracies," Basel said. "But with Nicomidi's flight, it does look a bit more plausible. The Council is pursuing its own investigation, of course. I don't suppose I can convince you to wait?"

"No. Jaedia may need my help."

"I thought not. As you are a centarch now, and no one is pressing the accusations against you, I have no authority to stop you. And perhaps it is for the best. The Council is...divided."

"Do we know where Nicomidi went?"

Basel shook his head. "Only that he was in a hurry. He left the arena as soon as your duel ended, visited his office, and then went straight to the Gate chamber before anyone could think to stop him. No one seems to have any idea why, not even his colleagues."

"If he was the one framing Jaedia—"

"He might have been worried that would come out," Basel said. "Though the odds of the Council finding evidence to punish a Kyriliarch seem small. But even then, it only pushes the question back a step. Why frame Jaedia at all? What does he have to gain? A minor injury to the Pragmatics and myself doesn't seem worth the risk."

"I don't know," Maya said. "But I plan to find out. If I see Nicomidi—"

"If you see him, I advise you to stay well away." Baselanthus leaned forward. "Do not become overconfident, Maya. Nicomidi Thunderclap is most assuredly not Tanax. In due course, the Council will authorize a group of centarchs to hunt him down, if he has truly abandoned us."

"I'm going to find Jaedia," Maya said. "Well, and Marn, I suppose. That's all."

"I understand. And I wish you the best of luck." He sighed. "As much as I am bound by the Council and its politics, please don't think that I love Jaedia any less for it."

"I don't." Maya swallowed. "What you said, about my cognomen . . ."

"Jaedia requested it for you," Basel said. "She told me you were going to be the greatest centarch since our founding. Maybe the greatest ever. Bearing the name of our greatest fire-wielder seemed appropriate." He chuckled. "You can thank Nicomidi, in a way. If not for the state of disarray he put the Dogmatics in, I have no doubt they would have fought to prevent us from giving you such an honor."

"I . . ." Maya looked down at her hands. "I will do my best to live up to it."

"I know you will, my dear." Basel leaned back in his chair. "Now go and get some rest."

Maya did, indeed, feel wrung out. She got to her feet, bowed respectfully, and went to the door.

"Oh, one more thing," Basel said. "I read Tanax's report from Deepfire. He described your performance at the warehouse as extraordinary."

"I . . ." Maya hesitated. "I lost control of myself. Jaedia would have scolded me."

"Quite possibly," Basel murmured. "Can I ask if you experienced any aftereffects? In particular . . ." He tapped his chest, just where the Thing was on Maya.

"I . . . think so," Maya said, frowning. "It felt . . . hot, and the skin around it was inflamed. Then, after I returned, I collapsed for days."

She described her brief period of delirium in the cell. "I thought it was the shock of hearing about Jaedia. Do you think they're related?"

"It's...possible." Basel frowned. "The arcana in question is largely untested. We had some concern that it would react if you channeled *deiat* too powerfully for too long. Without experiments, I'm afraid we can't know for sure."

Maya touched the Thing, the hard knot of it firm against her fingers. "Do you need to examine it?"

"Not at the moment," Basel said. "Just be cautious, and try not to stretch your limits. When you return with Jaedia, we will see what we can discover."

"I understand," Maya said. She bowed again. "Thank you, Kyriliarch."

"Good luck, Centarch," Basel murmured as she slipped out the door.

It was barely midafternoon, but the prospect of collapsing into bed seemed more and more attractive as Maya made her way down the interminable stairs and back to her own room. Her feet were dragging as she thumbed the latch, and she was trying to decide whether she had energy to change out of her formal tunic when she realized Beq was sitting in her chair. The sight of her sent a bolt of energy running up Maya's spine, banishing her fatigue, even as the pained expression Beq wore set something twisting in her gut.

"Um," Maya managed, letting the door close behind her. "Hi."

"They wouldn't let me in to see you," Beq said. The light caught her spectacles and turned them into flat white disks.

"The healers...were very thorough." Maya shifted her arm and winced. "And until just now I was still under Council restraint."

"And now?" Beq said.

"I'm a centarch," Maya said. Stating it like that, so simply, made her feel...strange.

"You won," Beq said. Her voice was still flat.

"I won." Maya took a hesitant step forward. "Beq, are you all right?"

"You..." Beq shot up from the chair and crossed the room to meet her. Her face was a mask of rage, and her eyes were full of tears. "You... *idiot*." That clearly did little to relieve her feelings, and she went looking for harsher language. "You stupid plaguing *fuck*. You crazy *fucking* plaguepit."

"Beq—"

"You could have *died*." Beq squared off across from Maya, hands clenched into fists, shaking with rage. "I saw what happened. When you realized your panoply wasn't working. You could have stopped the duel."

"I thought..." Maya took a deep breath. "I wasn't sure if they would let me start it again if I did. Panoplies don't just *fail*—"

"You think *I* don't know that? Which one of us is the fucking arcanist?" Having gotten onto a good swearing streak, Beq seemed determined to continue. "Someone was trying to kill you, and you found out, and you decided to just... let them have a shot?"

"I didn't see much other choice." Maya scratched the back of her neck, embarrassed. "I was a little busy at the time."

"Chosen fucking defend, Maya." Beq sucked in a breath. "I have never been so scared in my life. Watching you charge Tanax, and every second thinking this is going to be the moment where you get ripped into bloody chunks. I just... I couldn't move. Couldn't even close my eyes."

"I'm sorry."

"You'd better be sorry." Beq stepped forward and wrapped her arms around Maya, pressing her face into Maya's shoulder. Her spectacles dug painfully into Maya's skin, but Maya didn't complain. "If you do something that fucking stupid and get yourself killed, I'm never speaking to you again."

Maya didn't think it was the moment to point out the inherent contradiction there. Beq sniffed, pulled off her spectacles, and pressed her face against Maya's uniform. Maya gently hugged her back.

"It's all right," she whispered as Beq's frame shook with sobs. "I'm all right."

"You won," Beq murmured after a while.

"I won."

"Now what?"

"Now I go and find Jaedia. She needs my help."

"I'm coming with you." Beq's muffled voice was fierce.

"Of course you are," Maya said, hugging her a little tighter. "I need you."

"Okay." Beq released her hold, slowly, and pulled away. She wiped her reddened eyes and fumbled her spectacles back on, blinking. "Okay. As long as we're clear on that."

"As a centarch I can choose my own support personnel," Maya said. "Not that I would make you come if you didn't want to, of course. But you can travel with me as long as you like, and there's nothing the Order can do about it."

"That's...good." Beq sniffed. "I'm sorry I called you a crazy plaguepit."

"It's all right," Maya said. "I probably deserved it."

"I need to sit down."

Maya guided Beq to the chair and poured them each a mug of water. She took a seat on the bed, facing Beq.

"We have to leave as soon as we can," Maya said. "I don't know where Jaedia is now, but the longer we wait, the harder she'll be to find. And the worse trouble she might be in. Can you be ready by tomorrow?"

Beq nodded. "I just need a few hours to gather my gear. And I'm nearly finished decoding Nicomidi's messages to Raskos. It's going a lot faster now that I don't have to worry about him spotting me in the archives."

"Is there anything useful there? Basel agrees he must have been involved with whatever happened to Jaedia, but we still don't know *why*."

"I'm not certain," Beq said. "Nicomidi and Raskos were definitely working together. He's coy about it in the messages, but I *think* Nicomidi had Raskos on the lookout for particular pieces of arcana."

"That makes sense," Maya said. She remembered the horde in Raskos' warehouse. "Raskos certainly seemed to have his fingers in everything. But what was Nicomidi getting out of it? Money? What would that get him that he couldn't already have?"

"Nicomidi was insistent that some finds be kept secret from the Council."

Maya nodded slowly. "That seems...more plausible, at least. You said the Core Analytica was probably ghoul arcana—I can't imagine the Council would let him keep that around. But I don't understand what he was going to *do* with it. And I still don't see a connection with Jaedia."

"Maybe there isn't one?" Beq suggested. "Maybe that part is just ordinary Order politics."

"It seems unlikely. Even Basel was surprised at how far Nicomidi was willing to go. It's beyond the usual Council sniping." Maya shook her head. "It doesn't matter for now. We have to find Jaedia. Everything else comes after."

"Right." Beq gave a firm nod. "Do we know where we're going to start?"

"Grace," Maya said. "Basel promised to send the files with details on where Jaedia was last seen."

"Grace?" Beq's voice was a squeak. "Really?"

"Is that a problem?" Maya said. She didn't know much about the notorious Splinter Kingdom city, other than that it was famous as a smugglers' market.

"Oh no." Beq grinned. "I've just always wanted to see it for myself."

"It's a long way from the nearest Gate, unfortunately," Maya said. "A couple of weeks or more by wagon. We'll need to join up with a caravan at Uqaris, near the border."

Beq nodded and got to her feet. "I should start getting ready. I'll need to make a list for the quartermasters."

"Me too." *But...*

Maya swallowed the last of her water and set the mug aside. As Beq turned to the door, Maya rose abruptly. Her heart thumped loud enough that she was sure Beq could hear it.

"Wait a minute."

Beq hesitated, then half turned. "Is something wrong?"

"I just..." Maya swallowed. Forcing the next few words out was nearly as hard as charging Tanax head-on without a panoply. "I want us to be clear on something."

"I should really..." Beq murmured. At the look on Maya's face, though, she trailed off and took a deep breath. "Okay."

"You kissed me," Maya said. Her hand came up automatically to brush the Thing. "I kissed you. We kissed each other. Whichever."

"We...did." Beq's freckled cheeks were flushing.

"And then you..."

"Ran away." Beq's hands twisted the hem of her shirt between them. "I know."

"You don't need to explain." Maya closed her eyes. "I just want to know if...if you would be interested in kissing me again. At some point. When you're ready."

Silence. Maya waited, trembling, not daring to open her eyes and look at Beq's face.

She nearly started at the feel of hot breath against her cheek. Then Beq's lips pressed against hers, hesitantly. Maya stood stock-still, frozen, until Beq pulled away.

"Oh," she said. When she opened her eyes, Beq was already facing the door. "Okay."

"Okay."

"I'll see you." Maya's brain didn't seem to be working quite right. "Tomorrow."

"Tomorrow."

Beq moved forward, mechanically, and nearly bumped into the door when she missed the latch. She grabbed it at the last minute, swung around it like they were partners in a dance, and stumbled out into the corridor. Maya could hear her drunken footsteps receding into the distance.

Okay. Maya touched her lips, which still tingled from the contact. *Okay.*

Jaedia should have been at the top of her mind. Her mentor was in danger. Maybe hurt, captured. *Not* dead. Maya refused to even think that, refused to admit the possibility that she wouldn't arrive in time. But she felt that she should be going into her rescue mission with nothing on her mind but worry for Jaedia (and Marn, when she remembered him) and grim determination.

And she could summon those emotions, when she tried. When she wasn't trying, though, her mind...wandered.

Two weeks on the road. The Gate wasn't far from Uqaris, on the border between the Republic and the Kingdom of Grace, but it was a long, slow trip north, even along the old Chosen road to the kingdom's eponymous capital. Two weeks' riding on the back of a wagon as the loadbirds plodded along, keeping watch for plaguespawn, concealing her true identity. Two weeks sharing a tent at nights with the most beautiful girl in the world, with whom she'd reached an agreement that they wanted to further investigate this kissing business.

It was this last thought that had made it hard to sleep. Maya wondered if she was the only centarch of the Twilight Order to spend the night before her first mission masturbating until she was sore. On reflection, she decided, probably not.

Now she stood in the Gate chamber, going through her pack one more time as she waited for Beq. The three arched Gates were empty and silent, but she could still feel the potential of them, the power awaiting her commands through *deiat*. An armored centarch guarded the door, as always, with two Legionaries flanking him. Maya felt his eyes on her, though it was impossible to tell if under his helm he was really watching or not.

Focus. She touched the Thing, trying to calm herself, and looked down at her open pack. It was stuffed to bursting, tools and food fitted intricately into the available space in a way she'd never be able to replicate. Fortunately, as her supplies were used up, it made more space—

"Maya?"

Her head snapped up, adrenaline flooding into her veins at once. Tanax stood a little ways off, posture formal as always, his expression uncomfortable. He cleared his throat.

"My apologies," he said. "Centarch Maya Burningblade, I should say."

"Centarch Tanax Brokenedge." Maya forced herself to meet his gaze. Her hand itched to go to her haken, which hung once again in its usual place on her hip. She kept it still with an effort. "I didn't expect to see you before I left."

"You're certainly moving quickly. The tailors can't keep up." He gave a weak smile at the joke; they both still wore the uniforms they'd had as agathia. "I wanted to offer my congratulations."

"Thank you," Maya said stiffly. She hesitated for a moment and then forced herself to add, "And thank you for what you told the Council."

"I only told them the truth."

"I know," Maya said. "But you didn't have to."

Tanax was silent, and Maya had no idea what to say.

"I would have killed you," he began, haltingly. "On the arena floor. You came at me, and I knew your panoply was broken, and I would have killed you if I could. My master had told me . . . that I had to win. That you were a traitor." He swallowed. "It was a lie. Everything he told me was a lie. He was . . ."

Maya felt a pang of sympathy. "You weren't the only one he lied to."

"I wish I'd had the chance to talk to him before he left. I just want to ask him . . ." Tanax shook his head. "Many things, I suppose. But I'm not sure what I expect him to say."

"You were doing your duty as a centarch," Maya said. "I don't hold it against you."

"I was doing as I was ordered," Tanax said. "That is not the same as my duty." He paused again, then spoke all in a rush. "I want to come with you."

"To come *with* me?" Maya repeated, shocked. "Why?"

"My master was determined to destroy Jaedia, I know that much," Tanax said. "Willing or not, I helped him. I would like to...try to make amends for that. For him."

"You're not responsible for Nicomidi," Maya said. "No one is suggesting you are."

"I know," Tanax said. "But this is the right thing to do."

Maya glared, and Tanax looked away awkwardly.

"I would also like to know *why* my master did what he did," Tanax said. "Even if I cannot undo it. It's...hard, not understanding. Figuring out what he was trying to accomplish by framing Jaedia seems like a good first step."

"I'm not concerned with figuring out Nicomidi," Maya said. "I just want to help Jaedia."

"I know. I won't get in the way, I swear by the Chosen."

She gritted her teeth. "This is my mission. My command. You accept that, or stay behind. Is that clear?"

"Perfectly," Tanax said, nodding eagerly. "I will accept your orders."

Maya chewed her lip. She didn't doubt Tanax when he said he tried to do what he thought was right; whatever treason Nicomidi had been involved in, she didn't think he'd known about it. Part of her wanted to shove him away, this young man who'd arrested her, nearly killed her.

But having another centarch along would be an asset; there was no doubt about that. Especially if there *was* more to Nicomidi's pursuit of Jaedia, and they ran into the disgraced Kyriarch himself. Maya didn't know if she and Tanax together were capable of taking Nicomidi on, but she wasn't foolish enough to imagine she could do it alone.

"Tent," she muttered.

"What?"

"You've got your own tent?" She took a deep breath. "Beq and I are sharing, but ours is only big enough for two."

"I have my own." Tanax ventured a smile. "Thank you, Maya. You won't regret this."

"I'm regretting it already," Maya said as the big door opened and Beq came in. "Now, let's get moving."

Chapter 21

The basement door was exactly where it had been. Gyre pushed it upward with care and pulled himself up into Lynnia's workshop.

The alchemist was hunched over her workbench, perched on the edge of her chair, just where he'd seen her so many times before. Gyre prudently waited until she'd set her mortar and pestle aside before he cleared his throat.

Lynnia spun in her chair, speed belying her age, snatching a clay alchemical off the desk and raising it over her head. She blinked, eyes adjusting.

"Who's there?" she said. "Make a move and I'll blow us both to the Chosen's side."

"I'm not sure there's a need to go that far," Gyre said. "If you don't want people coming in through the back door, you should put a lock on it."

Lynnia's mouth fell open. Setting the alchemical down, she picked up a glowstone and shook it to life.

"Gyre?" she said. "Chosen defend. I thought you were dead."

"You and almost everyone else in the city," Gyre said, standing up. "I'd like to keep it that way, if I can."

Lynnia got to her feet, raising the glowstone as she shuffled toward him. "I told you never to come back here."

"I know. I'm sorry."

"You still working with that Kitsraea?"

Gyre nodded, and Lynnia gave a snort.

"Vile little thing, even if she is nice to look at," the alchemist said. "You'd be better off rid of her, and—" She paused, sucked in her breath. "What happened to your eye?"

"Ah." Gyre scratched at the ridge of scars around his left eye socket, the neat new incisions overlaying the childhood wound. It still felt so strange. "I found a replacement."

"Is it—" Lynnia leaned closer. "That's not just some marble. Does it *work*? Gyre, where did you—"

"Please," Gyre said, retreating a little. "There are a lot of questions I can't answer."

"Of course," Lynnia said. "You and that mad little girl fuck off for parts unknown after turning the city upside down, and then you turn up with a new silver eye in your head. Why would we have any questions?" She turned away, bad leg dragging. "Why did you come here, if you knew I wouldn't have you?"

"I need to talk to Sarah. I know she's staying with you."

"Sarah?" Lynnia spun around, suddenly full of fury. "You don't think you've done enough for Sarah already?"

"I just want to talk."

"Well." Lynnia huffed. "I'll tell her you're here. Whether she'll see you, I don't know." Lynnia paused at the foot of the stair. "You might as well come up to the parlor. Make it easier to pitch you out the door."

Gyre smiled to himself and followed her up the tight, winding steps. Entering Lynnia's parlor felt like stepping into the distant past, for all that it had barely been a few months since Kit's note had upended his life. The stolid respectability of it—lace cushions, neat dark curtains, polished wooden furniture—felt like a foreign country.

He settled himself in one of the overstuffed armchairs and waited. Eventually there were footsteps on the main stairs. Sarah moved slowly, as though uncertain of her balance, and Lynnia hovered close behind her.

"I'll make you some tea, dear," Lynnia said when they reached the bottom. "Try not to strain yourself."

"Thank you, Lynnia," Sarah said.

She made her way to the other armchair and threw herself into it with a sigh. Gyre couldn't help but wince at the sight of her. Her left arm was gone, barely even a stump remaining at the shoulder, and the wound still thickly swathed in gauze. The left side of her face and what he could see of her neck were covered with angry red welts where sparks from the blaster bolt had landed, already hardening into shiny, coin-shaped scars. She'd lost considerable weight, and her skin hung loose on her bones.

For all that, though, she smiled when she saw him, eyes alight. "Gyre! It's so good to see you. We all thought—"

"That I was dead? Lynnia was saying." Gyre smiled back. "It's good to see you too. When I left, you were still with the healers in the Spike. You're looking—"

"Like shit?" Sarah laughed. "You don't have to pretend; I can use a mirror. It's better than it was a week ago." She looked down at herself. "Apparently the armor I was wearing saved my life, even if the surgeon did have to spend hours picking bits of broken metal out of my tit. Trade-offs, I guess."

"I'm sorry," Gyre said.

"Why? You didn't shoot me." She caught Gyre's look and leaned forward. "Listen. What happened to us isn't your fault. It was the risk we all ran, and we knew it. I know that you think you could have helped if you'd been there, but those were *centarchs* that ambushed us. Probably you'd just be dead too."

I could have warned you. Gyre swallowed and forced himself to nod. Sarah watched him curiously, then abruptly sat up straight.

"Chosen defend, Gyre, your eye! What happened?"

"Ah." Gyre brushed his hand over the scars, feeling the hard lump of metal in the abused socket. "It's a long story—"

But Sarah was already out of her chair, coming closer and waving her hand from side to side.

"It *focuses*!" she said, and laughed with delight. "You can see, can't you? I've never heard of arcana like this. Where did you—"

Gyre held up a hand. "I can't tell you much. Anything, really."

"Just a hint?"

"Sorry."

She looked at him quizzically for a moment, then shrugged. The movement seemed to pain her, and she wobbled as she made her way back to her chair.

"Well," she said, "if you came hoping to get the crew back together, you're going to be disappointed. I'm about all that's left."

"What about Ibb?"

"Gone straight and playing the good husband and father, from what I hear. I don't blame him. He has more to lose than the rest of us."

"Has the Republic come after you?"

She shook her head. "After Raskos fled the city, a bunch of Order people turned up and started going through his records. Whatever they found must have been pretty bad, because they declared a general amnesty. That's why I'm here instead of rotting in some cell in the Spike." She scratched idly at the gauze on her stump. "There's a Legionary commander in charge now, until the Senate appoints a new dux. Some of Yora's people have been petitioning for more rights for the manufactory workers, and it sounds like something might come of it."

"That's a start, anyway. Yora would have been glad to hear it."

"Probably." Sarah regarded him curiously. "So why *are* you here, Gyre? You know it isn't safe, amnesty or not."

"I need your help."

"*My* help? What are you doing that a one-armed arcanist would be so useful?"

"One-armed or not, there's no one better that I trust. I have a job to do, and I need some equipment."

She made a pained sound. "I could give you a few names—"

"I think it's got to be a custom build," he said. "A tricky one."

"I'm listening," Sarah said.

"Explosives," Gyre said. "Big ones. Lynnia can provide that part, but the timing is very sensitive."

"Her fuses are the best, you know that. Accurate to maybe a quarter of a second. You're not going to do any better."

"I need something more...flexible. A bomb I can set off remotely. Three of them, actually."

"Ah." Sarah raised her eyebrows. "Which means the triggers have to be arcana."

"Is it possible?"

"Probably," she admitted. "There are plenty of arcana devices that send a signal from one place to another. It's just a matter of modifying some so they'll set off the bomb."

"Then you can do it."

"Maybe." She looked at her right hand, then at her stump. "I can try. But getting the devices is going to be expensive."

"I figured." Gyre lifted his satchel onto his lap and opened it. Stacks of neatly wrapped thaler notes were piled inside. Sarah's eyebrows went up even farther. "Will ten thousand be enough to buy what you need?"

"It should be," Sarah said.

"Good. The rest is for you." Gyre closed the satchel and set it at her feet. "Fifty thousand thalers."

There was a long pause.

"If I asked where you got that kind of money—" Sarah began.

"I would say that I can't tell you," Gyre said, smiling slightly.

"Though I can't help but think of Kit's mysterious client, who also seemed to have cash to burn." Sarah nudged the satchel with her foot. "I told you I don't blame you, Gyre. You don't have to buy my forgiveness."

"What about Yora's?" Gyre said quietly.

"Yora would…understand." Sarah looked uncomfortable. "Probably."

"I don't suppose it matters." Gyre let out a breath. "Take it. Help the tunnelborn; don't let the shelters close. Keep plenty for yourself, too."

"I should probably argue." Sarah lifted the satchel and peered inside. "But I won't."

"How long will it take?"

"A couple of days," Sarah said. "I'll start as soon as I can."

"I'll see you then," Gyre said. He got to his feet. "Thank you, Sarah."

"Good luck, Halfmask." She grinned. "I suppose we can't call you that anymore, can we? Maybe it's time you had a proper cognomen."

"I fought like the plague to keep anyone from sticking one on me," Gyre said. "They were always Gyre Lackeye or Gyre Scarface or something awful like that."

"Gyre Silvereye, then? I like the sound of it."

"I'll think about it."

Gyre gave her a shallow bow and slipped into the kitchen. Lynnia was waiting by the stove, two mugs of tea in front of her.

"Fifty thousand thalers," the alchemist said, her voice flat. "That won't buy the girl a new arm, you know. Or bring Yora back."

"I know. But it's the best I can do."

"That's enough for her to get away from"—she waved vaguely—"this sort of thing. Stay on the right side of the authorities."

"I hope so."

"So after this, you stay away, understand me? From both of us."

"I understand," Gyre said. "After this, you'll never see me again."

The inn Gyre and Kit were staying at was aboveground, but only just, part of the narrow strip of buildings right up against the edge of the crater, clustered where the main avenues dove into the earth. It was named, for reasons lost to history, the Mushroom's Daughter, and it was tucked away at the back of a twisting alley lined with cheap stables, cheaper cookshops, and a few ramshackle dwellings.

Not the best part of town, certainly, and not a place where city authorities bothered with streetlamps. The sun had slipped behind the western mountains by the time Gyre returned, and the shadows had reached out across the street to swathe the cobbles in darkness. Up above, the tips of the Shattered Peaks still gleamed yellow-gold in the last of the sun.

Gyre Silvereye. It definitely had a good sound to it. *Better than Gyre Lackeye, anyway.*

He wondered what Sarah would say if he told her that being able to *see* was the least of what the new eye could do. He no longer needed nighteye, for example—in spite of the darkness of the alley, if he closed his real eye he could see as though it were broad daylight. But the true power of the thing went beyond that, or so Naumoriel had promised.

Gyre focused his mind, as the old ghoul had instructed, concentrating his attention on the second implant, which sat under another fresh incision by the base of his skull, below his left ear. He could only just feel it with his finger, and once the cut faded there'd be no outward sign of it. When he gave it his full attention, however, it grew warm, and after a second something shifted with a *click* he could feel through his skull. His eye gave a *whirr*, and the world changed.

Everything seemed . . . slow, suddenly. Almost weightless. And objects weren't simply themselves anymore, but were surrounded by a dense cloud of translucent duplicates stretching in the direction they were moving. These were *possibilities*, Naumoriel had told him, the shadow a moving object cast into the future. Where it would be one second, two seconds, three seconds from now. What would happen if it turned, collided, bounced.

At first it had given him no more than a splitting headache. But he'd practiced, as the old ghoul had instructed, and slowly he'd been able to make sense of the crowded shadow-world. Now he bent, picked up a stone, and flicked it into the air, watching its shadows race ahead of it to trace out a perfect parabola. He hurled a second pebble sideways, its path ricocheting off the front of a shuttered stable before precisely intersecting the first rock as it came down. He watched it happen, shadows growing more solid until the two stones came together with a *click* and fell back to the cobbles.

If all else fails, at least I can make my living in a circus. Just not for very long. On his right hip, he wore the energy bottle, and he could feel it growing warm, too, as its power crackled through his body to fuel his new abilities. On his other hip, in its leather sheath, Naumoriel's final gift seemed to hum with anticipation.

Gyre let his concentration lapse, and the world of shadow and possibility faded away. His pulse pounded in his ears, and his head throbbed, but not as badly as it had after his earliest practices. He paused for a moment, breathing deep, until the pain subsided a little, then turned the last corner and headed for the Mushroom's Daughter.

The inn was marked by a sign showing a busty young woman wearing a red-and-white mushroom cap and very little else. Light streamed out from its windows, and smoke gushed from several chimneys. As he got closer, he heard voices emerging as well, belting out an old scavenger's song in not-very-good unison:

First time down she didn't know what she'd find
Second time down she thought she'd lose her mind
Third time down she took me by the hand
Fourth time down she told me I was grand
Show me the way, tunnel girl, show me the way
Down to your secret tunnel

It continued, in much the same vein and at about the same level of subtlety. Gyre did his best to wipe the grimace from his face before he pushed through the curtained doorway.

The common room, facing the street, was packed with people, the warmth of so many bodies making Gyre instantly break out in sweat. It smelled of the press of humanity, and also of piss and spilled beer. The tables had been pushed to the sides of the room, and the crowd ringed a clear space wide enough for a dozen people to dance while the rest of the room kept up the tune.

A couple of dancers stumbled off, arm in arm, both covered in sweat. Behind Gyre, a young woman dragged a hesitating young man onto the floor, with roars of laughter and approval from the crowd. Someone emptied a drink over the boy's head, which stunned him long enough that the girl pulled him away from the safety of the press and started turning him around and around. The next verse was already well along, detailing the adventures of a scavenger boy and the improbable long, hard objects he insisted on bringing on his expeditions.

Kit was dancing. Of course she was. She seemed particularly popular, spinning from one partner to the next, pressed close against a portly woman and then passed off to a gangly boy who nearly lost his feet trying to keep up with her. She'd lost her shirt somewhere and wore only her trousers and a cloth wrap around her chest, her blue hair damp and floppy with sweat. Every time she passed close to the bar, someone held out a clay mug, and she took a long pull and handed it back without missing a beat.

Show me your pack, tunnel boy, show me your pack, the chorus went. *What're you bringing down?*

There was a moment of confusion, since there were at least a hundred verses to the song and a dozen different people had different ideas of which came next. Gyre took the opportunity to slip to the edge of the dance floor and take Kit by the arm, just as she snatched another mug from a waving girl in the crowd.

"Heya," she said, trying to drink and getting maybe half of it in her mouth. By the way she wobbled, she'd had more success earlier in the night. "Where you been? You're missing the fun."

"I can see that," Gyre said. "You seem very popular."

"At first everyone was just sitting around being boring," Kit said. "But when I told 'em drinks were on me until dawn, they livened up. And—" She looked around the packed crowd. "I think people brought their friends?"

"I thought," Gyre said, as quietly as he could given the continued attempts at song, "that we agreed to keep a low profile."

"Relax." Kit patted him confidently on the shoulder. "Raskos skipped town, and your *sister*'s gone too. Nobody's looking for us."

"That we know of. We're still—"

"You *really* need to learn to have fun." Kit gave him a sloppy grin and gestured at the party. "See? This is fun. Fuuuuuuuun." She wobbled dizzily. "I need a drink."

"Okay." Gyre tightened his grip on her arm. "Come on. Time for bed."

"What're you on about?" Kit lurched away from him, tugging hard. "Let go of me."

"Kit—"

"Hey." A large woman, a head taller than Kit, loomed behind her and draped an arm over her shoulders. "This a problem?"

"Nope," Kit said, eyes not leaving Gyre. "Not a problem. Right?"

Gyre let go. Kit looked up at the woman, stood on her tiptoes, and kissed her, awkwardly but enthusiastically. Eventually Kit stumbled back a step, giggling.

"Get me another drink, would you?" she said, and the woman grinned and pushed into the crowd. Kit turned back to Gyre.

"Don't give me that look," she said.

"What look?"

"I am not coming to bed, and I am definitely not coming to *your* bed." She set her jaw. "I may have had a . . . a moment of weakness when we were freezing to death—"

"—and in the tunnel—" Gyre muttered.

"—but that doesn't mean we're . . . whatever you think we are. You don't own me."

"I wouldn't suggest I did," Gyre said. "But we're *partners* on this job—"

"And I'll be ready. You just make sure you are too." She leaned in closer. "You sure you don't want a drink? You need to loosen up."

"I'll be fine." Gyre took a deep breath and immediately regretted it. "Enjoy the dance."

"I plan to."

He turned away, pushing through the crowd until he reached the stairs. It was darker here, which apparently made it the venue of choice for couples who couldn't keep their hands off one another long enough to make it to a room. Gyre edged past two young men in a complicated tangle of limbs and kisses, stepped over a stray pair of trousers, and climbed to the second floor, where several hallways of rooms extended to the back of the inn, up against the rock. The sounds of those who *had* managed to make it to a room followed him as he trudged along the corridor.

It wasn't as though they were short of funds. Naumoriel seemed to be able to produce thalers in almost unlimited amounts, and the old ghoul hadn't batted an eye when Gyre had asked for sixty thousand. What he'd given Kit for traveling expenses would cover buying drinks for the whole inn every night for a month. *But it's still a risk to draw attention like this.*

Something had been off about Kit since they'd left the Tomb. He didn't know how she'd spent her time there, though at least the ghouls had refueled the arcana that kept her heart beating. *Maybe that's what's gotten to her.* The sudden release of tension might be a shock, he supposed. But something was off between them, and they'd barely talked on the trip back up the valley to Deepfire.

He was surprised to discover how much that bothered him. Gyre closed the door to his small room and sat down on the bed, trying to quiet his mind. *It makes no difference to me how much she drinks or who she fucks,* he told himself. *As long as she's there when I need her. That's all I'm worried about.*

Right.

*   *   *

"There will be pain," the old ghoul had said.

Gyre considered himself inured to pain. He'd been shot, stabbed, broken. Had his eye cut out by an enraged centarch. But Naumoriel had taught him he didn't know what pain meant.

He couldn't move. There were restraints on the table, but they were unnecessary—Naumoriel's magic, the soft breath of *dhaka*, had simply turned off Gyre's control of his body. Why he couldn't turn off the pain as well, Gyre had no idea. Maybe the old ghoul was just a sadist.

"The threads wrap around your bones," Naumoriel said. "It is no use being able to see what is coming but not to be able to respond, you understand?" The ghoul gave a toothy smile. "Of course you do."

Gyre could, of course, say nothing. But he could feel. One of the table-construct's narrower limbs was bent over the crook of his elbow, carrying a spool of fine silver wire. A blade had made a narrow cut in the tender skin there, and the wire had *wriggled* of its own accord, one end plunging into the bleeding wound like an eager maggot. Searing agony marked its path as it burrowed through his flesh, down through skin and muscles, until it reached the bone.

"You are fortunate," Naumoriel said, through the haze of blinding pain. "In the days of the war, our methods were cruder. The gifts we gave to those who fought at our side were...less subtle." The ghoul looked down at Gyre, blurry through the tears that filled his eye. "Oh yes. Your kind fought beside us. Those who were brave enough to turn against their masters. Those who wanted a better world. I imagine your Order doesn't speak of such things.

"All we wanted was to be left in peace. Not so dangerous, you would think. But oh no. That was not enough for the lords of the world, the wielders of the fire of creation. They had to have obeisance. It was only their due, they told us. Were they not the Chosen? *Chosen*, pfah." Naumoriel coughed, a tearing sound that rattled deep in his chest. "They feared us. The masters of divine fire feared our power, because it comes from *within*. Anyone can wield it. Even humans can learn. *Dhaka* is the birthright of all who live and breathe. And so the *Chosen* wanted it destroyed. Wanted *us* destroyed." He gave a hollow chuckle. "See how well they have fared, with all their power."

Gyre wanted to scream but could not. The worm reached his wrist and mercifully stopped, leaving a spiraling tunnel of slowly dulling pain in its wake. Naumoriel roused from his reverie, passing his spotted, gnarled hand over Gyre's skin, nodding approval.

"Very good," he said. "Very good. You are strong, for a human." He brushed a finger against the table-construct, and its limbs whirred. Naumoriel poked with one long, ragged fingernail at the tender pads of Gyre's palm. "The hand next, I think..."

Gyre awoke with a mouthful of blood from where he'd bitten his tongue, his teeth clenched against a shriek that seemed determined to work its way out from somewhere deep in his chest. He could feel the wire running through his body, wrapping his skull and spiraling along every bone, a set of blazing threads that seemed to be cooking him from the inside. His new eye was a mass of agony, ghost-memories of the whirring blades of Naumoriel's construct slicing through flesh and bone.

It's over, he told himself, breathing hard and fast. *It's over, it's over, you lived through it, it's finished*. The old ghoul had told them there would be a price, and he'd paid it. *It's only a dream, and the memory of pain*.

Slowly, too slowly, the pain faded. Gyre relaxed, the muscles in his jaw aching. He lay on the bed, a shuddering, sweaty mess. His right eye saw the room in darkness, the rafters above only a suggestion of deeper shadow, but his silver eye laid over that a clean, clear image, bright as day. He could see the cobwebs in the corners and count the desiccated flies trapped there.

It was still before dawn, but there was no chance of any more sleep.

Not with Naumoriel waiting in his dreams, with his whirring blades and his silver wire, his endless ranting about the war. Gyre rolled out of bed, stripped off his sweat-sodden clothes, and dressed in fresh things from his pack.

The corridor was quiet. *Not many early risers after last night, I imagine.* A woman, wearing nothing but a ratty pair of trousers, lay snoring on the landing, still curled around a bottle of something. Gyre stepped over her, then paused by the door to Kit's room. It stood slightly open, and he shifted, peeking through the crack. *Just to check that she's all right.*

She lay on the bed, facedown, a line of drool soaking the sheet by the corner of her mouth. To Gyre's mild surprise, she was alone. *Not that it matters to me, one way or the other.* He turned away and hurried to the stairs and down into the common room, where several harassed-looking servants were clearing away the remains of the night's festivities. An older woman sat behind the bar, shouting unhelpful advice.

"Excuse me," Gyre said, all smiles, letting his old rural accent return. "I have a good friend who works for a grocer that makes deliveries to the Spike. He told me that I might be able to get a position with them, but I can't seem to find the place." He waved his hands helplessly. "This city is a maze."

"There's a dozen grocers that serve the Spike," the woman said. "You know which one your friend's at?"

"I don't have the proprietor's name," Gyre said. He dug in his pocket and produced a couple of decithaler coins. "Maybe you could just point me to the closest? I'm sure I'm in the right neighborhood..."

Two nights later, everything was in place.

Gyre was in the driver's seat of a small wagon pulled by a pair of loadbirds. The name "M. Snadbury, Master Grocer" was rather grandly stenciled on the side in jolly blue letters, and the packet of papers in Gyre's pocket confirmed that he was to deliver a load of mixed fruits to the palace kitchens. All this was quite genuine—M. Snadbury's regular driver had been happy to accept the last-minute change of assignments, especially as it had come with a stack of thalers to make up for his time.

Kit lounged on the seat beside him, looking absolutely untroubled by the enormous volume of alcohol she'd downed over the past couple of days. She wore an ugly brown coat and leather cap, with her fighting blacks underneath. Gyre was in similar garb, plus a large brown satchel containing a selection of interesting gear.

They'd rounded the southern end of the Pit and joined a queue of carriages and wagons approaching the palace. Most deliveries came in the morning, but the grocer had received an emergency order to replace another shipment that had gone rotten. *All the better for us.* Gyre closed his eyes and tried to visualize the grounds, based on the crude map Kit had drawn for him. *Main drive, delivery drive, the servants' entrances. The storehouse.*

"You're sure they're not keeping the Core Analytica somewhere more secure?" Gyre asked.

"Not unless they've moved it in the last couple of days," Kit said, and yawned. "Elariel's constructs confirmed they took it there. And I don't see any reason why they would move it; they don't know what it is."

"*We* don't know what it is."

"I mean they don't know it's important. They cleared out the storehouse to keep all the crap they pulled out of Raskos' stash before they can drag it back to Order headquarters and . . . burn it, or whatever they do with 'unsanctioned arcana.'" Kit snorted. "Such a waste of good scavenging."

"If you're wrong, this is all going to be worse than useless," Gyre said. "We won't get an easy shot at them again."

"Unless you have a way to get past a locked steel door *without* anyone noticing, we'll have to take the risk." Kit sat up straighter and dusted off her coat. "But it'll be there." She eyed him sidelong. "Starting to worry now that we're in the same boat?"

Gyre snorted, but she had a point. Though he wouldn't actually *die* without regular infusions of *dhaka* energy, as Kit would, using his new eye and the advantages it offered depended on a steady supply of energy bottles. Elariel had told him that his own body's energy would refill them, but only very slowly, like trying to fill a canteen with condensation from the side of a glass. Only a master of *dhaka* could provide the energy in bulk.

"Worrying about getting cut to pieces by a dozen Legionaries is quite enough for me, thanks," Gyre said.

"Pfeh," Kit said. "Maybe we'll have to hide in another closet."

"Given the way your breath smells at the moment, I'd take being cut to pieces."

Kit puffed into her cupped hands, sniffed, and wrinkled her nose. "Point."

They were nearing the point where the servants' drive curved away from the main drive, the former curling around the back of the palace, the latter heading off through the gardens to the elegant front entrance. Gyre whistled to the team and tugged on the reins, and they veered to the right, leaving the line of cabs and expensive carriages. Their borrowed wagon rattled over the gravel, eventually pulling into a broad oval space where several other wagons were already parked. Gyre put his at the end of the line, as far as possible from the doors.

A woman in a butler's uniform trudged over to them, clearly irritated at being made to walk so far. Gyre handed her the papers, and she squinted at them, then sighed.

"You're early," she said. "It says ten o' clock here, doesn't it? We won't have staff free to unload you for a couple of hours."

"Sorry 'bout that," Gyre said. "Best I could do. We'll wait. Figured I'd find somewhere quiet and have a bit of a nap, eh?"

The butler gave him the look of someone who was working herself to the bone while other people slacked off.

"Just be here at ten," she said. "We'll need the space, so you'll have to shift as soon as you're unloaded."

"As you say, sir." Gyre touched his cap. "Sorry to be trouble."

The butler turned and stalked back to the kitchen door. Kit glanced curiously at Gyre.

"Is that why you insisted we come early?" she said. "So there wouldn't be people around?"

"We can't have them searching the wagon," Gyre said, looking back at the crates of fruit. "Why, do you object?"

"No," Kit said. "I just thought you were a little bit harder than that."

She hopped down off the box. Gyre stared after her, then shook his head.

Harder? He got down as well and grabbed his satchel. *Maybe. The palace servants work for the Order, just as much as the Auxies do, I suppose.* Still, he had to admit that the idea of slaughtering a bunch of unarmed cooks and porters stuck in his throat. Kit, he guessed, would have no such inhibitions.

He hurried a little bit to catch up to her as she strode confidently toward the back corner of the gravel lot, where there was a small gate in a line of shrubbery. It wasn't locked, just latched, and it let onto a more utilitarian section of the palace gardens, neat lines of herbs and other kitchen plants hidden by the shrubs from visitors. It smelled like a spice shop, and Gyre stifled a sneeze.

"The storehouse is—there." Kit scanned and pointed. Gyre could make out a peaked roof, past several more hedges. She kept turning and pointed farther back, at a bend in the outer wall. "And that's our escape route."

"Looks like the back gardens are empty for the evening," Gyre said. "But let's try not to startle anyone yet."

Kit, who'd been about to doff her concealing brown coat, pulled it back on grumpily. Gyre led the way to another gate, which let into an adjoining garden. They passed through flower beds and a row of eye-watering compost heaps, eventually emerging into a dirt lane that led back toward the kitchen doors. On the other side of it was the storehouse, a solid brick building with a slate roof. The entrance was around the corner. Under normal circumstances, Gyre imagined the place was used for gardening supplies and probably wasn't even locked. Now that it had been pressed into service to store dangerous unsanctioned arcana, there would certainly be guards.

"Okay." Gyre untied the satchel and set it between them. "No blasters unless you have to. Hopefully in the commotion nobody will notice us."

"Yeah, yeah."

Kit's face lit up with glee as she shrugged out of her coat. Her weapons were in the satchel, and she rapidly equipped herself with saber, blaster pistol, and an alarming number of knives.

Gyre retrieved his own sword, the hilt tingling under his fingers, and the pack with spare energy bottles. Another small pack full of alchemicals hung beside it, along with a small folding crossbow. Last but not least was the arcana trigger Sarah had given him. It was a square of unmetal about the size of a sheet of paper, half an inch thick and rounded at the edges. On the face were a dozen depressions, three of which were filled by hexagonal crystals.

What this bit of Chosen arcana had been originally, Gyre had no idea, but Sarah's tweaks had transformed it into a weapon. A metal grille, crude compared to the smooth perfection of Chosen work, had been fitted over the three crystals to keep anyone from touching them accidentally. Sarah had showed him how to unlatch it and press the trigger with his thumb.

"You're sure it'll work?" he'd asked her.

"Of course not." She'd rolled her eyes at him. "I can't exactly test it, can I? I know that when you press the crystal, the trigger part makes a spark big enough to light a fuse. Other than that, we just have to hope."

Now Gyre stared at the thing for a moment, then tucked it into his belt. *It'll work. Sarah knows what she's doing.*

"Ready?" Kit said, bouncing eagerly on the balls of her feet. The prospect of action seemed to have restored her darkened spirits.

Gyre picked up the crossbow, slotted a bolt, and cocked it with an effort. "Ready."

Kit skipped ahead, pausing at the corner of the hedge. Gyre followed more cautiously, and she straightened up and whispered to him.

"Four guards. Auxies."

Gyre grimaced. That was more than he'd hoped, but it made sense. "Too many to take without someone shouting for help."

"Time for the distraction, then." Kit's grin was feral. "Do it."

Gyre knelt in the dirt and pulled out the trigger. He undid the latch on the grille, flipped it up, and hesitated only briefly before pressing his finger against the first crystal.

There was a delay of perhaps a second. Then a spectacular *boom* shattered the quiet of the palace grounds. Even this far away, Gyre felt the blast as a *thump* in his chest and a shiver running through his shoes. Whatever Lynnia had put into the bomb, it had been a monster. He imagined bits of wagon and toasted fruit blasted high into the air, raining down across the drive and spattering the palace. After a few seconds more, a thick column of black smoke developed, rising lazily into the sky.

Shouts and screams echoed across the grounds almost immediately. Every guard in the palace, Gyre guessed, was heading to the scene of what could only be some kind of assault on the grounds. *Perfect.*

"They're staying put," Kit said. "Smart. On three. One. Two."

Gyre snatched up his crossbow and stepped out from behind the hedge as Kit mouthed, "Three." He spotted the four Auxies standing in front of the red-painted double doors, shifting nervously. Their sergeant was an older woman, weather-beaten and tough-looking, and he sighted on her and pulled the trigger as her mouth opened to form a shout. Gyre wasn't an expert shot, but the range was short. The bolt caught her high in the chest, punching through the cheap steel of her breastplate and knocking her off her feet.

Kit had a thin blade in each hand and sent one whipping in a fast arc at the Auxie on the right. It sank into his throat, and he dropped his spear and clutched the wound, staggering backward. The man next to him threw himself to the ground, and Kit's second knife passed just over his head, burying itself in the storehouse door.

She was already halfway across the distance between them, saber drawn. The Auxie still on his feet gave a hoarse cry, lowering his spear to spit Kit as though she were a charging warbird. She slipped lithely aside, dodging the point, and was on him before he could drop the long weapon and draw his sword. Her saber found his throat, and blood fountained spectacularly.

The man who'd ducked Kit's second knife was pushing himself back to his feet when Gyre's reloaded crossbow twanged again, the bolt catching him in the side. He rolled over, clutching at the wound, until Kit came up behind him and slashed his throat.

"Nicely done," she said to Gyre as she bent to finish the badly wounded sergeant. The woman shuddered and stilled. "Didn't even have to draw your pretty new sword."

"I'm hoping to save that until I need it," Gyre said. Not least, he had to admit to himself, because he wasn't sure how well he'd be able to fight with Naumoriel's gift. "The door going to be a problem?"

Kit glanced at it and scoffed. "Give me . . . sixteen seconds." She sheathed her bloodied saber and drew a set of lockpicks from a pouch, bending down to reach under the heavy iron padlock. A moment later, it popped open with a *clack*, and she grinned back at him. "Well? Did I make it?"

"Was I actually supposed to keep count?"

"Of course!" Kit looked offended. "You'll never improve if you don't take every opportunity to challenge yourself." She hauled on the door, which swung outward a bit, then stopped. Kit frowned, then kicked one of the dead Auxies out of the way.

The inside of the storehouse was a mess. It looked like they'd taken half of what had been carefully arranged in Raskos' warehouse and simply dumped it in a pile. Precious arcana was mounded in with worthless junk, bits and pieces of the ancient Chosen Empire and the ghouls all jumbled together. Kit gave a heartfelt sigh at the sight of it, and even Gyre felt a twinge. *If Yora could have gotten to this, we'd all have been set for life.*

"You find the Analytica; I'll move the bodies," Gyre said. "Hurry."

Kit nodded and dashed into the mess, shaking a glowstone and filling the building with blue light. Gyre grabbed one of the corpses under the arms and pulled it inside, trying not to cover himself in blood. If anyone wandered by, missing guards *might* attract attention, but dead ones *certainly* would, and he figured it was better to get them out of sight. He'd shifted three of them and gone back for the sergeant when movement from the direction of the palace caught his eye.

"Shit." Gyre ducked into the shadow of the hedge and hissed into the storehouse. "Kit! Legionaries coming!"

"Coming here?" Kit called back.

"Not sure."

Gyre watched the pair of white-armored figures moving down the garden path. They didn't seem to be in a hurry, as they might have been if they'd heard the fight. *No way they caught that with everyone shouting from the explosion.* Which meant these two weren't *necessarily* heading their way . . .

Come on, plague it, go somewhere else. His urgent wish went unanswered, and the two Legionaries kept coming. *Someone must have ordered them to make sure this part of the gardens is secure.*

"Kit?" Gyre said. "Tell me you found it."

"Not yet," Kit said. "Do you know how much stuff is in here?"

Ah, fucking plaguefire. The Legionaries were moments from turning the corner. Gyre put his hand on his sword and tried not to think about what happened the last time he took on one of the Republic's elites. *No other options. Naumoriel, I hope all this works . . .*

He stepped out from behind the hedge, crossbow first, and fired. The bolt hit the leading Legionary in the chest plate, glanced off his unmetal armor, and whined away. It had the effect of staggering him for a moment, which gave Gyre a chance to engage the second soldier alone. He tossed the crossbow away, drew his silvery ghoul-made sword, and forced his mind down the channels Naumoriel had taught him.

The energy bottle at his side warmed, and the world slowed around him, objects splintering into clouds of shadows. The Legionary came at him, raising her unmetal blade, and a dozen duplicates of the weapon hovered in front of her, possible paths that her attack might take. As she swung, some of the ghosts faded, and one rapidly became solid, thick with momentum. Gyre stepped aside, his movement feeling floaty and weightless, and aimed a cut at her helmet. The blow didn't penetrate the unmetal, of course, but it snapped her head back and sent her staggering away.

The other Legionary had his blaster rifle up, bringing it to bear. As Gyre concentrated on the weapon, lines of light lanced out from it, forecasting the path the bolt would take. The Legionary's finger tightened on the trigger, and Gyre just had time to interpose his sword and hope like the plague.

Even with his heightened perception, the blaster bolt was too fast to track, a burst of white light with a *crack* like a thunderclap. He flinched instinctively, but the energy was already dissipating, splashing into nothingness around Gyre's blade. The energy bottle grew even warmer—Naumoriel had warned him that this defense, similar to the one that protected ghoul constructs, burned power prodigiously. But the Legionary's shock was obvious. Before he could recover, Gyre snatched an alchemical from the pouch at his side and hurled it in a perfect trajectory that burst against the soldier's mask in a shattering concussion. He stumbled drunkenly, tripped, and fell.

His first opponent came back in, her shield raised, sword probing toward his ribs. Gyre faded to his left, meeting her crosscut with his own blade, and the ghoul weapon shivered and whined as it scraped against the unmetal. The soldier disengaged and slashed high, bringing her shield around to block his counterstroke, but the shadows speeding ahead of her attack let Gyre duck neatly under the blow. He angled his sword up and thrust into her armpit, where the overlapping insectoid armor had a gap, and it sliced easily through the resilk and leather underneath. After a frozen moment of shock, Gyre stepped away, silver blade bloody to half its length, and the Legionary collapsed with a clatter of unmetal.

Gyre let his concentration slip, and the shadow-world fell away. Pain pounded in his temples and all around his new eye. He glanced down at the energy bottle—a simple metallic cylinder with a thin line of inlaid crystal around its circumference—and saw that its soft glow had dimmed considerably.

Kit hit him from behind, wrapping both arms around him and nearly lifting him off the ground in her excitement.

"That was *amazing*!" She bounced against him, staring down at the fallen Legionaries. "Chosen defend—well, I mean, obviously not—I've never seen anyone move like that. You were—and you just—"

"Kit!" Gyre tore free of her grip. "Did you find it?"

"Of course I found it!" Kit opened her pack to display the metallic gleam of the Core Analytica.

"Then, let's get out of here."

He glanced at the two soldiers—the woman lay unmoving, but the other one was feebly struggling to rise. Gyre sheathed his sword and reached for the trigger arcana, only to find Kit pressing against him again, rising to her toes to kiss him with desperate energy. It was a moment before Gyre found the presence to pull away.

"I thought we weren't...whatever I thought we were," he said. "What happened to a moment of weakness?"

"Fighting makes me horny," Kit said. "So do explosions. Do it!"

Doomseeker. Gyre suppressed a sigh and flipped up the metal grille, pressing his finger against the second crystal. Moments later, another bomb went off with a *crump* and plume of smoke and dust. A section of the garden's outer wall vanished in the haze.

"And there's our exit." Kit looked in the storehouse, then at the two Legionaries with their armor and blaster rifles, and heaved a sigh of her own. "If only we could carry more of this stuff."

"We don't need the money," Gyre reminded her as they ran toward the billowing smoke.

"I know," she said, giving him a bright grin. "But it's the principle of the thing."

Chapter 22

I t had been the most frustrating two weeks of Maya's life.

She'd known, from the moment she explained to Beq that Tanax would be coming with them, that his presence would make things difficult. While Tanax himself had been scrupulously correct in accepting Maya's authority, Beq stiffened up automatically in his presence. Maya wasn't able to find any time alone with her during the first day's walk, and by evening they'd reached Uqaris, a dusty little city that had grown up around the Auxiliary garrison for this section of the border.

They'd been fortunate in their timing, and a caravan was leaving for Grace the following morning. The caravan master, an expansive, portly woman named Kerchwite with a magnificent thatch of green beard, was happy to accept Maya's thalers and offer the three of them a place among her party. Maya had expected a string of small wagons, like the one she and Jaedia had traveled in, but Kerchwite's were six-wheeled monsters pulled by four thickheads apiece, practically rolling houses. When night fell, she and her caravanners erected large, comfortable tents, in which she'd generously offered Maya and her companions a spot. Maya couldn't think of a good reason to refuse, and so they spent every night among laughing, drinking merchants, listening to stories and bawdy songs and with no privacy whatsoever.

It would have been less frustrating if there had been anything to *do*. After all, Maya had reminded herself, they were out here to find Jaedia, not so Maya could sneak in time with her crush. But Kerchwite's guards and their dogs had the plaguespawn threat well in hand, butchering the small monsters that were drawn to the caravan. They didn't need her help, and in any event Maya wasn't sure how much use she could be without revealing herself as a centarch.

In the evenings, Tanax stayed aloof from the rest of the merchants and guards. Maya tried to fit in—Jaedia had once told her a centarch ought to be able to make herself at home in any company—but the sight of Beq sitting in silence at the edge of the tent drew her away again. When she went to keep Beq company, though, neither of them seemed to have much to say among the shouting and dicing. And so two weeks passed in relative comfort but considerable awkwardness, as the caravan wound its slow way across the plain.

The land near the border with the Kingdom of Grace—called the Red Kingdom by the locals, after the colors worn by its soldiers—was flat and grassy, watered by small, meandering streams. It was grazing country, speckled with cows and dotted by small homesteads. These buildings were ringed by defensive walls, and the herds they passed were guarded by well-armed riders. Each watchman was another reminder that they were beyond the boundaries of the Republic and the cordon of safety that the Legions' sweeps and watch posts provided. Out here plaguespawn attacks were as constant and unavoidable as the rain or the wind.

The city of Grace itself lay on the other side of a range of low hills, jutting up from the flat land like lumpy pillows shoved under a bedsheet. The caravan followed the old Chosen road, a perfectly flat stretch of spongy stone, crumbling at the edges. When it reached the hills, it deigned to divert from its straight-line path to swing through a narrow gap between two large prominences. They took some time to traverse an old cut, where a chunk of one hillside had been sliced back to make room for the road; four hundred years of rain and snow had brought falls of rock encroaching on the path, and they were forced to unhitch the thickheads and use them to clear a fresh spill out of the way. Nevertheless, on the thirteenth day out of Uqaris, they crossed the spine of the hills and found themselves descending a gentle slope, with a good view of the valley beyond.

Beq, on cresting the ridge, raced to the edge of the road with an excited squeak. She scrambled up a large rock and started clicking the dials on her spectacles. For a moment Maya, hurrying after her, couldn't quite parse what she was seeing. There was a city, a loose grid of streets and buildings, closed off by a wall on three sides. On the fourth side, an enormous *thing* stretched out of the ground, a cliff face leaning dangerously outward over the city—

Then her mind sorted the dirt and trees from the smooth, clean lines of unmetal, and she knew what she was looking at. Even half-buried in the earth, the silhouette of a Chosen skyfortress was unmistakable. There were drawings of them in her copy of the *Inheritance*, floating amid fleets of lesser skyships like cloud-bound whales. A skyfortress looked like a flattened teardrop or the business end of a spade, rounded at the back and coming to a point at the bow. All the workings and weapons were inside the unmetal hull, leaving the outside a smooth, unbroken curve of brilliant white.

This skyfortress had driven itself into the ground, bow-first, at about a forty-five-degree angle. Maya could only imagine what it must have been like on the day it fell, because the thing had hit hard enough to punch through the soil and into the valley's bedrock. Four hundred years later, it remained where it had fallen, jutting out of the earth and trees that had filled in around it. The stern hung in the air, hundreds of meters above the streets of the city.

Looking closer, Maya could see that the skyfortress's lines were not entirely intact. In places the unmetal skin had broken, peeling outward like the petals of a flower. She glanced at Beq, who was still staring fixedly at the thing.

"Isn't it beautiful?" Beq said. "There isn't a skyfortress in the whole Republic that's so well preserved. The *Harmony in Judgment* lost its whole stern section, so it's only the bow that's in the city square in Carvoria. And of course *Faith*, *Certainty*, and *Generosity* were lost over the sea in the Last Contact. They say *Purpose* is somewhere on the other side of the Shattered Peaks, but no one knows exactly where."

"I…uh…did not know that," Maya said, glad to see Beq coming out of her funk. "Do you know a lot about this one?"

She nodded eagerly. "It was called *Grace in Execution*—they named the city after it. Its last captain was Ghaea-Ven-Tilophani, and she brought the ship down herself. They'd been boarded by ghouls and plaguespawn, and there were barely enough Chosen aboard to keep the ship in the air. This was late in the war. *Grace* was the last skyfortress, you know, the last of the eight to fall."

"What damaged it, where the skin is broken?"

"Nobody really knows!" Beq sounded *excited* about this lack of knowledge. "It has to be *deiat*, obviously, only *deiat* can damage unmetal, so it was probably one of the mechanisms inside the ship failing. There's a lot more damage around the bow, where it's buried. I hear there are even tunnels that lead inside. Grace got its start as a center of arcana selling off pieces of the ship, and Centarch Garinus Bloodbane led an expedition here in 268 to gather up all the most dangerous relics and bring them back to the Forge. Scavengers have stripped the rest by now." She paused for breath, then pushed her spectacles back and glanced at Maya. "Sorry. I'm talking too much, aren't I? Sorry."

"You don't have to be sorry," Maya said gently. She grinned at Beq, then turned back to the view. "I knew there was a wreck here; I just didn't think it would be so…" She gestured lamely. "Big."

Beq was about to respond with some facts about the dimensions of the skyfortress, Maya was certain, but Kerchwite shouted to them from the road. "Keep moving, you two! You can get a closer look tonight."

As they continued downward, Maya realized that the scale of the thing had tricked her once again. The sheer size of the skyfortress made distance hard to judge. There was still most of a day's travel between the edge of the valley and the city wall, and the whole time *Grace in Execution*'s broken frame loomed larger and larger. By the time they were on the flats, following a packed-dirt road away from the Chosen highway, the wreck looked more like a mountain than a ship, its huge shadow sliding across the valley floor to provide a preview of night.

The city that huddled against it was decidedly less impressive. The wall was a human-built thing of mortared stone, only four meters high, and already crumbling in places. It seemed to be intended less for defense and more to channel people to a few well-guarded crossing places, so the queen's tax collectors could take their due. Traffic was brisk, carts loaded with food mixing with larger wagons like the caravan's, carrying manufactured goods from the Republic. Loadbirds, thickheads, and other beasts of burden squawked, rattled, and hissed at one another. Guards on warbirds with lances and red tabards passed by at regular intervals, halting to sort out disputes between rival carters.

Maya endured an exuberant hug goodbye from Kerchwite, which both Beq and Tanax emphatically waved off. The three of them collected their packs from the caravan's wagons and hiked past the queue of farmers and merchants to a smaller gate for those on foot. The armored soldier waiting beside it gave them only a cursory look before waving them onward, under the arched gateway and into the city.

Immediately beyond the wall was a broad, muddy square, packed full of makeshift market stalls. Wares were spread on portable tables, arranged in the backs of carts, or simply laid on blankets on the ground, their owners standing nearby to shout to the crowds and keep an eye out for pickpockets. It was a familiar sight for Maya—she'd been to any number of market days, in cities much larger than Grace—but Tanax looked overwhelmed by the sheer chaos.

"Doesn't Skyreach have a market?" Maya said, raising her voice to be heard.

"Of course it does," Tanax said, a bit wide-eyed. "It's just a little bit more ... orderly."

Another difference, they soon discovered, was in the kind of goods available. There was food, of course, and the usual things any city needed—leatherwork, masonry, smithing, medicine, and so on. But here in Grace, it all seemed like a sideshow beside the city's economic heart: the trade in alchemical products and arcana. Maya had thought the market in Deepfire was vast, but this was on another scale entirely, and far more permanent-looking. Staples like quickheal, bone-break potion, firestarters, and glowstones were everywhere, but that was only the start. There were bombs and torches, powders and philters, stoppered bottles roiling with colored gases and greasy tonics promising the impossible. Maya doubted half of it was real, but that didn't seem to discourage the sellers from shouting over one another about the fantastic benefits of this or that elixir.

"*Dhak*," Tanax muttered, setting his jaw. "A whole market full of *dhak*. Chosen defend us."

"It can't be that dangerous," Beq said. The lenses in her spectacles clicked and whirred rapidly as she zoomed in on one interesting tidbit after another. "The city's still standing."

"That doesn't tell you how many people have been killed by contaminated medicine," Tanax said. "Or sacrificed by *dhakim*. Life is cheap in the Splinter Kingdoms." His lips tightened. "We ought to have burned this place to the ground decades ago."

Maya shook her head silently. Nicomidi's flight might have made Tanax question his place, but apparently it hadn't shaken his Dogmatic sympathies. His face only grew more thunderous as they made their way through the market, to a section where the stalls were watched by armed and armored men. The merchandise was displayed in locked cases fronted by iron bars as well, a necessary precaution when a sneak thief could slip thousands of thalers into a pocket. The goods on offer ranged from broken junk—bits of unmetal, cracked crystals—through rare but comprehensible devices like rockcrackers and blaster rifles, all the way to apparently complete but utterly incomprehensible machines. The latter drew Beq like a fly to honey, and Maya was forced to take hold of her arm and pilot her away from one crystal-and-glass mechanism after another.

"That one is a flight motivator," she muttered. "And *that* one looks like the amplifier from a relay node, but the bottom part is different. Maybe..." She trailed off into incomprehensible jargon.

Maya exchanged a look with Tanax, who frowned.

"It's a miracle they haven't blown themselves up yet," he said. "No good comes of meddling with unsanctioned arcana."

"Without Chosen or centarchs to power them, most of this stuff isn't going to do much," Beq said. "And sunsplinters are apparently hard to come by."

She nodded at a table where several dozen of the small hemispherical jewels were laid out. None of them had the warm, healthy glow of a fully charged stone. Most barely flickered, and a few shone fitfully. Maya's eyebrows went up when she saw the prices. A splinter that might power a blaster pistol for a few shots sold for enough money to keep a family fed for a year.

"You could always charge a few if we run out of cash," Beq said with a weak smile. Maya chuckled, but Tanax only scowled.

"All right," Maya said, catching his eye and lowering her voice. "We're here to find Jaedia, not clean up the trade in unsanctioned arcana."

"Right." Tanax let out a breath. "So where do we start?"

"I have the location of the Order safe house," Maya said.

"The one that Jaedia supposedly destroyed?" Beq said.

Maya nodded. "I thought we could take a look for ourselves. What's left of the Order team in Grace has a new base, but Basel thought they might have someone on watch. If they do, we'll make contact and get their help."

It felt odd, saying that. Maya was used to *petitioning* for assistance from the Order. But she was a centarch now—*even if I still don't have a proper uniform*—which meant that any Order agent was obligated to drop everything to assist her.

"That seems like a reasonable plan," Tanax said. "How do we get to this safe house?"

Maya opened her mouth to answer, looked around the teeming market, and paused.

Grace lacked signposts or any other way of identifying its twisted warren of streets. Maya doubted that half of them *had* names. The roads were also too narrow for wheeled vehicles, so there were no cabs. Instead, palanquins were everywhere, little wooden huts on long poles carried by two, four, or six bearers. For a few thalers, they hired one of the larger models to bring them to the site of the Order's old safe house, which turned out to be most of the way across the city. The confines of the palanquin were close and dim, with gauzy curtains shielding them from the streets outside, and the ride was bumpy and uneven. Beq looked like she was going to be ill, and Maya patted her sympathetically on the shoulder.

"This is what happens," Tanax said, "when you don't have a proper authority in charge."

"They have a queen," Maya said. "That's an authority."

"She's apparently not interested in street planning." The palanquin gave a bump, which made them all lurch. "Or leveling the ground. Or cobblestones."

"The current queen of Grace is only fifteen," Beq said. "There was a regency council at first, but her uncle tried to take the throne for himself, and she had him strangled. After that—" The vehicle lurched again, and she cut off, looking green.

Finally, they came to a halt and the bearers lowered the palanquin. Beq hurried out with unseemly haste. Maya paid—Basel had arranged for travel funds, most of which were stashed deep in her pack—and waited while they trooped away. They were left alone on a wide dirt road, fronted on either side by wide two-story buildings made of red brick, with sloping slate roofs and heavy shutters on their windows. From the look of it, they were mostly residences, and Maya guessed this was a wealthier part of town.

Their destination was obvious. A little ways along the road, one of the buildings was in shambles. The door hung open, dangling by a single hinge, and several windows on the bottom floor were broken. At one corner, part of the roof had collapsed, and there were marks of fire on the surrounding walls.

"I guess this is the place," Tanax said, looking it up and down. "Do we know how many people were here when it happened?"

"Nine," Maya said numbly. Basel had let her read the report. "Nobody made it out."

Beq fiddled nervously with her spectacles, lenses flipping and whirring.

Maya gritted her teeth and stalked up to the building. The front door had been broken open by a single enormous blow, cracking the hardwood planks. Inside, much of the ground floor had been used as a common room by the agents stationed here, with several tables, a bookcase full of ledgers, and a small kitchen. Whoever had attacked the place—Maya refused to admit the possibility that it had been Jaedia, even in her own mind—had broken everything that came easily to hand. The stones of one fireplace had been torn apart, which had presumably started the fire, and that corner of the house was blackened and charred. There were vast brown stains spilled across the floorboards. Maya could easily imagine where they'd come from.

Something's wrong. Maya took a few steps forward, leaving the other two in the doorway, and knelt to examine the remains of a table. She held up a broken leg for inspection and frowned.

"This is smashed," she said, waving it in their direction. "Look, the end is splintered."

Tanax raised an eyebrow. "Is that important?"

"You've never seen Jaedia fight?" When he shook his head, Maya went on. "She uses blades of wind. Very thin, very sharp. I've seen her dissect a leaf in midair and barely disturb its fall. The cuts are always clean."

"Maybe she was angry?" Tanax said.

"Jaedia doesn't get angry," Maya said. "And...here." She picked up part of a tabletop. "See this cut?" It looked like someone had gouged a long line with a chisel.

"It's ragged," Beq agreed, lenses clicking as she bent to examine it. "Like someone ripped at it."

"That's not much in the way of evidence," Tanax said. "Jaedia might not have been alone."

"She was alone," a woman's voice said, behind them.

Maya turned, hand automatically reaching for the haken concealed at the small of her back. She stopped with a conscious effort and glanced at Tanax, who'd dropped into a fighting crouch. He grimaced and straightened.

The woman leaning on the doorway was tall and lean, with long copper hair pulled into a twisted ponytail and very dark skin. She wore scavenger's leathers and a sword, her features weathered by the elements. Her bright yellow eyes were wary, but she didn't seem surprised to see them.

"Did you, um, live here?" Maya said.

"Am I an Order agent like you three, you mean?" The woman gave them a humorless smile. "You're new to covert work, aren't you?"

"You might say that." Maya straightened up. "I'm Centarch Maya Burningblade. This is Centarch Tanax Brokenedge and Arcanist Bequaria."

The woman pushed herself lazily off the doorframe and offered a half-hearted salute. "Scout Faressa. The Grace outpost is at your service, Centarch." She slumped back into her relaxed posture. "What's left of it, anyway."

"You said Jaedia was alone," Maya said. "How do you know? Were you here when the attack happened? I was told there were no survivors."

"There were no survivors in the safe house," Faressa said. "I was on sentry duty down the road. There's a rooftop that has a good view of the approaches. I spotted Jaedia on her way in and signaled ahead to the house to tell them she was coming." Her lips twisted. "She'd visited several times in the past couple of weeks, so I didn't think it was unusual. Next thing I know, the place is on fire. By the time I got back here, Jaedia was gone."

"No one in the house survived long enough to say what had happened?" Tanax asked.

"She didn't leave them in any condition to," Faressa said. "My husband was here. He was an arcanist. I found most of him about where you're standing"—she pointed, then swung her hand to one side—"and his head and one shoulder over there. The rest were...similar."

There was an awkward silence. Maya swallowed.

"I'm sorry."

"It's the risks of the service," Faressa said. "Giving our lives for humanity and all that. But getting torn apart by one of our own centarchs wasn't the way either of us expected to go."

"I don't..." Maya stopped. She wanted to say that Faressa hadn't actually *seen* the attack, that it hadn't necessarily been Jaedia, but the tight lines of the scout's face made her think better of it. She cleared her throat. "How many others survived?"

"Three of us scouts. We've been poking around as best we can, but there's not much to find." She frowned. "I told the Kyriliarch all of this when he got here. Are you three supposed to be his backup?"

"Kyriliarch?" A chill went down Maya's spine, and her hand brushed the Thing. "*Which* Kyriliarch?"

"Nicomidi." The scout's frown deepened. "What's going on?"

"When was he here?" Maya said. "And what—"

Faressa shook her head. "Strict orders, on Council authority. He told me all this was being investigated by the Kyriliarchs personally." Her expression went sour. "I've probably already said too much. If you're not backing Nicomidi up, what are you doing here?"

"Kyriliarch Nicomidi fled the Forge after accusations of treason," Maya said. "By now he's been stripped of his Council seat."

"That's—" Faressa shook her head. "That's quite a story." She glanced at Tanax. "You support this?"

"I do," Tanax said.

The scout looked at Beq, but the arcanist's attention had wandered, and she was examining some of the debris close-up with her lenses. Faressa shifted uncomfortably and looked back at Maya.

"You don't happen to have any documentation of this, do you?" she said. "I haven't had any messages from the Forge."

"You wouldn't have," Maya said. "We left the day after it happened."

"Nicomidi must have taken a swiftbird across the plain," Tanax said. "That'd gain him three, maybe four days, if he was willing to risk having to fight plaguespawn."

"That's a serious risk," Faressa said. "If the queen's people got word there was a centarch in her territory, it'd be plaguefire for all of us. What's so important that he'd come *here*?"

"I don't know," Maya admitted. "I don't understand what he's aiming for."

"But you've come after him anyway?"

"We're not following him; we're following Jaedia," Maya said with a glance at Tanax.

"And Nicomidi expressly instructed me to say nothing about Jaedia's activities here to anyone without a Council warrant," Faressa said. "Well, this is a fucking brilliant situation all around."

"Whatever orders Nicomidi gave are invalid," Tanax said. "He has no authority."

"Assuming you two are telling the truth," Faressa said, straightening up. "If you're lying, and *he's* not, then helping you might be betraying the Order."

"We're not—" Maya cut off, frustrated. "I just need to find Jaedia. The rest of this can be straightened out later."

"We could send someone back to the Forge for a Council warrant," Tanax said.

"And wait here for a month?" Maya shook her head.

"What's your hurry?" Faressa said. "One of the boys here your brother or something? That eager to get revenge?"

"I'm not..." Maya took a deep breath. "Jaedia was—*is*—my master. I know her better than anyone, and she would never do this. I'm certain she didn't kill your husband."

"*Somebody* fucking killed him," Faressa growled.

"I know. I'm not sure if Jaedia's been...captured, or replaced somehow or...*something*. But I have to find her. Please."

"Shit." Faressa chewed her lip. "How am I supposed to—"

"It wasn't Jaedia." Beq, on her knees, looked up. Her pupil was a huge black dot filling the entirety of one lens. When everyone turned to stare at her, she blinked and wilted a little. "At least, it wasn't only Jaedia. There's all kinds of damage here."

"It only takes one centarch to cause a plaguing lot of damage," Faressa said.

"I know," Beq said, "but there's different *kinds*. Look at this." She pointed to the scorched, tumbled stones of the fireplace. "See the central burst point and halo of spark burns? That's a blaster bolt. Why would a centarch need a blaster?"

"Maybe she was feeling lazy," Faressa snapped.

"There's more." Beq crawled across the floor on hands and knees and found a spot where the floorboards were stained nearly black. "This isn't a burn. It's blood."

"Of course it's blood," the scout said. "The whole damn place was practically—"

"Not *human* blood," Beq said. She pried at the wood, and part of it crumbled under her fingernails. "It's corroded, look. That's blood from a plaguespawn."

"Plaguespawn?" Faressa looked uncertain. "They couldn't get so far inside the walls without starting a riot. And plaguespawn don't use blasters."

"*Dhakim* do," Maya said. "And a *dhakim* could keep his plaguespawn on a leash, hide them somehow." She looked from Beq to Tanax. "You remember the gang in Litnin. They had the things in crates like dogs."

"A *dhakim*." Faressa shook her head. "I know the Forge likes to imagine *dhakim* everywhere, but they're rarer than a clean vulpi. You really think there's a cult here in Grace?"

"It's the only thing that makes sense," Maya said. "Jaedia must have come here to investigate them and gotten trapped somehow. Then they found out about this place and attacked."

"Fucking plaguefire. If I end up locked in a cell over this..." Faressa took a deep breath. "All right. Listen. That fits. I met with Jaedia a couple of times before... all this, and she asked for information on a group of smugglers bringing arcana and *dhak* into the Republic. They're a really nasty bunch, and there's always been rumors that they've got a *dhakim* for a leader. A guy named Cyrtak, though nobody knows much about him. The last time we saw each other, I had a line on a place they might be meeting, and Jaedia was going to take a look."

"Where?" Maya said.

"I'll have to show you the entrance. It's in the caves under the sky-fortress." She hesitated. "That's dangerous territory."

"Just show us the way, and we'll handle it from there," Maya said. "I know you have other responsibilities."

The scout nodded, relieved. "All right. Meet me at the old Chosen temple, just after dark. Any bearer will know how to get there."

More palanquins. Maya suppressed a shudder. "We will. Thank you, Faressa."

"Yeah. I just hope I'm not making a big mistake." She shook her head. "I'd better go let the others know where I'm going."

"One more thing," Maya said, conscience prickling. "Did Jaedia ever have anyone with her? A boy a little bit younger than me?"

"Not that I saw," Faressa said. "But we only met here at the safe house. She had a room somewhere else, as far as I know."

Faressa gave another salute, a little more seriously this time, and slipped out through the broken doorway. Maya heaved a sigh, then turned to Beq.

"That was *great*," she said, grabbing the arcanist's hands. Beq colored slightly, glancing at Tanax. "I didn't think she was going to help us without a note from the Council. Thank you, Beq."

"It's. Um. Just the sort of thing they teach us?" Beq grinned back cautiously. "I'm glad it wasn't Jaedia."

"We don't know if it was Jaedia," Tanax said, looking down at the spot of plaguespawn blood. "Faressa still saw her."

"I told you, Jaedia would never—"

"I know," Tanax said. "But if we're dealing with an actual *dhakim* here, we have to consider all sorts of ugly possibilities. They say that *dhaka* can alter someone's mind."

For a moment, Maya was back in a basement under Bastion, facing Hollis Plaguetouch. *"Fortunately, your cooperation is not necessary. I can change-change you until you want to tell me. Memory and desire are only matters of the flesh-flesh, after all."* She put her hand on the Thing and took a deep breath, searching for calm.

"The *ghouls* are supposed to be able to alter minds with *dhaka*," Maya said. "I've never heard of a human *dhakim* doing it."

"There's a great deal we don't know about *dhaka*," Tanax said. "We still have to face the possibility that Jaedia is working with the enemies of the Order. Willingly or not."

"If she is, then we'll take this *dhakim* alive," Maya said. "And then whatever he did, he'll *un*do."

"And if he refuses?"

Maya's fists tightened. "Then I'll convince him."

Even after dark, the heat lingered, radiating from red bricks that had spent all day baking in the sun. Another palanquin took Maya, Beq, and Tanax to the old Chosen temple, after some discussion with the driver and a few extra thalers. As they moved north and west through the narrow, twisting streets, away from the gate and the markets and toward the looming bulk of the crashed skyfortress, it became clear why the extra payment had been required—this was the poor part of town, condemned to permanent darkness much of the year by *Grace in Execution*'s shadow, and there was no chance of a fare on the way back. Ramshackle dwellings lined both sides of every alley, pressed three or four stories high with no planning or organization. One building had partially collapsed, stabilized only by the hurried addition of several long beams braced against a neighbor, and someone was building a fresh shack on top of it.

"I don't understand these Splinter Kingdom people," Tanax muttered, holding back the curtain to peer out the window.

"They're poor." Maya watched the thin, hard-faced people on the side of the road. "What else is there to understand?"

"But why live *here*?" Tanax said. "I'm not going to pretend Skyreach doesn't have its bad neighborhoods, but even the lowest laborers live better than *this*. If this is what their vaunted freedom looks like, why not come back to the Republic?"

"You think they get a choice?" Maya said. "It was the nobles and merchants who broke away, not servants and beggars." She thought of the tunnelborn, back in Deepfire. "And now the Republic isn't eager to let their children become citizens."

"It was the mill workers who started the Khirkhaz Commune," Beq volunteered.

"And see what that's gotten them," Tanax said.

The palanquin shifted, coming to a halt, and Maya pulled the curtain to look out her window. "I think we're here."

"Thank the Chosen," Beq muttered.

The palanquin and its bearers trooped away, leaving the three of them in a large open area. In the middle of the roughly circular space were the remains of a rectangular building. It was stone, crude and unmortared, with gaps where neighbors had helped themselves to free building materials. Somehow, the walls were still standing, enclosing a couple of rooms. There was no roof—they were so close to the sky-fortress that its sloping unmetal skin was barely twenty meters over-head, and Maya imagined the ground here never saw rain. A single arched doorway stood open, and the space inside was dark.

"This is old," Beq said, lenses flipping and whirring. "See the inscription over the arch? 'May Their power shelter us until Their return.'"

"Not many still praying for that," Tanax said.

Maya thought of Prodominus and his handful of Revivalists back at the Forge, keeping the dream of the Chosen's return alive. Cults worshipping the Chosen and praying that they come back and rescue humanity from the new world had been common in the first century after the Plague, but they'd waned since. After four hundred years, the old temples were almost all abandoned, though the fact that this one hadn't been torn down attested to the superstitious awe that still clung to them.

A shadow moved inside the archway, and Faressa appeared from the darkness. She beckoned them forward.

"Best get under cover," the scout said. "There are eyes all through these slums."

"Whose eyes?" Tanax said as they passed into the shadowy quiet of the old temple.

"Smugglers, mostly," Faressa said. "The gangs are always fighting each other for routes and suppliers. The queen turns a blind eye as long as she gets her cut, so it can become a free-for-all."

She shook a glowstone and by its blue light led them into the back room. The temple was empty except for bits of shattered glass and clay, any furnishings long gone. Faressa walked around, occasionally stamping down hard, until she found a spot where her boot made a hollow wooden sound. A few moments' work uncovered a trapdoor, concealed under ragged cloth and rocks. It swung up on well-oiled hinges, revealing a ladder into a dark tunnel.

"Here," the scout said, handing Maya a scrap of paper. It was a crude map, with tunnels and chambers sketched in pencil. "That's the best information I have, and the same directions I gave Jaedia. It's a maze down there, so be careful."

"Thank you," Maya said. She handed the map to Beq, who examined it under her lenses. "When we get back, how can we find you?"

"Ask at the Butchered Hart inn, near the market. Any of the servers can get me a message." Faressa hesitated. "I hope you're right about Jaedia. That she...wasn't herself. I didn't know her well, but she always seemed...kind."

"We'll find her," Maya promised. "Along with whoever was really behind this attack."

"Good luck." The scout handed Maya the glowstone and stepped aside.

It wasn't a long descent, just a few meters under the earth. The tunnel was narrow and claustrophobic, nothing like the broad, smooth ghoul passages Maya had seen in Deepfire. She hung her haken from her hip, for easy access, and brushed her hand against the Thing. Tanax climbed down behind her, and Beq followed, still peering at the map.

"This takes us directly under the skyfortress," Beq said excitedly.

"Wonderful." Tanax cast a wary eye upward. "It's not going to come crashing down on our heads, you don't think?"

"It's been there for four hundred years; I think it'll stand for another day," Maya said. "Beq, stay behind me and navigate. Tanax, keep your eyes open."

It was the kind of command Maya would have given Marn, but Tanax fell in without a murmur of protest. It was a stark contrast to the arrogance of his behavior in Deepfire. *What Nicomidi did must have really shaken him.*

Maya held the glowstone high as they advanced, illuminating a long stretch of passage, with side corridors like black holes in the walls. Beq kept her eyes on the map, counting turns under her breath. As they moved forward, the buzz of city noise filtering down from overhead grew quieter, until they walked in total silence.

"I think..." Beq stopped, grinning, and pointed to a dark shape sticking out of the wall. "Yes! Here, look." She tapped the protrusion, scraping off a dark patina to reveal the iridescent white gleam of unmetal. "This is the outer hull! We're going inside the skyfortress."

Tanax examined the jagged edge of the hull fragment. "It doesn't look like it's in great shape."

"Presumably the forward sections took the brunt of the damage when it hit the ground," Beq said, looking back at the map. "And of course it's been four hundred years."

"We're here to find Jaedia, not go scavenging," Maya reminded them. "Stay alert."

They moved on. The tunnel grew taller and wider, expanding periodically into large, irregular rooms with more tunnels leading out of them. At times they saw parts of the skyfortress, floors canted at a forty-five-degree angle. Everything beyond the bare walls had been stripped by hopeful scavengers long ago.

"Some of these tunnels lead *up*," Beq said. "Into the heart of the skyfortress. Supposedly it's all been sealed off by the Order expeditions, but the scavengers must still be trying to find a way in."

"Is that where we're going?" Maya said.

Beq shook her head. "The place Faressa marked is just ahead. Looks like a big chamber, with...pillars, maybe? She's not much of an artist."

Up ahead, a hatchway from *Grace in Execution* had once been intact, dogged with an unmetal hatch. The barrier now lay in blackened pieces on the ground, showing the characteristic burns of blaster fire. Repeated blaster bolts were a slow and expensive way of breaking through unmetal, but about the only method available if you weren't a centarch. Maya picked her way across the fragments and clambered through the ragged gap into a much larger room, the ceiling rising several meters over her head. Long, dark shapes hung down in a regular pattern, some reaching the floor, others ending a meter or so above it.

Not pillars. Cables. The things were massive, thicker than Maya's arm, and there were dozens of them, with cut lengths strewn across the ground. Where they were severed, they ended in a spray of fine silver wire. Maya tried to picture what the place had looked like when the skyfortress was aloft, and what purpose it had served.

"Wow," Beq breathed, turning in a slow circle. "This is . . . wow."

"I don't like it," Tanax said. "Too much cover."

Maya had to admit he had a point. The forest of hanging cables made it hard to see the limits of the room. She stepped forward cautiously, then stopped as something moved in her peripheral vision. A cable was swaying slightly, several rows away.

"What do we look for, now that we're here?" Beq said.

"Anything useful. This was the base of the smugglers Jaedia was investigating."

"Given the lack of guards, I'd say they've moved on by now," Tanax said.

"They'll have left some kind of evidence," Maya said. "We'll search the whole place if we have to."

She held up the glowstone, and the shadows of the cables twisted wildly against the walls. Then, distantly, she heard a moan.

"Someone's here," she hissed, putting her hand over the stone and plunging them into darkness.

"Not much point in hiding *now*," Tanax said. "We've already announced ourselves."

Maya scowled at him while he couldn't see, then brought out the glowstone again. There were dark shapes ahead and she started pushing forward, one hand on her haken. The heavy cables she bumped swung like metronomes in her wake. The moan repeated, louder now.

"Maya," Beq hissed. "Something's behind us."

"Where?" Tanax said.

Beq turned, lenses flipping wildly on her spectacles. "Don't know— I can't *see*—"

Maya pushed the last of the cables aside and broke into a clear space. At the same time, the smell of filth and rotting meat assaulted her, and she nearly gagged.

Ahead of her was a shallow pit, half-full of a mass of garbage— fragments of bones, chunks of meat, entrails and organs, all stirred together and rotting into black sludge. On the other side of the pit, a stretch of much-trodden dirt was strewn with chains, empty manacles, and small piles of torn rags. A single figure lay on its side, hands fastened behind its back, moaning faintly.

What in the name of the Chosen—Whatever it was, it was nothing good, and Maya's haken was already in her hand. She summoned the blade, fire igniting with a *whoomph* and the pinprick warmth of *deiat* spreading through her body. Her panoply bloomed—this time, she and Beq had tested the belt themselves—and surrounded her with its faint blue tinge.

"...Maya?" The figure raised its head, trying to look at her through the light of the flaming sword. "Maya!"

He was unrecognizable, but Maya knew the voice. "Marn?!"

"Maya, run!" He sat up, chains clanking. "It's a trap—"

Blasters cracked and spat fire.

Tanax had drawn his haken at the same time as Maya and taken up a position on the other side of Beq. A dozen bolts of raw *deiat* flashed across the room, but the blades of the two centarchs were a blur. Maya could feel the energy coming, drawing her weapon into position like one magnet pulling another, and she surrendered to the motion, letting the blasts vanish harmlessly against the greater flame of her blade.

By the light of her weapon, Maya could see shapes moving through the forest of cables. Some were humanoid, but others were not, loping awkwardly on asymmetrical legs. *Plaguespawn.*

Marn dove to the ground, curling in on himself. Maya glanced at Tanax and Beq, making a fast tactical assessment. *We need something to put our backs against.*

"Beq, get to Marn," she said, pointing. "Tanax, cut through to the left. I'll take the right and meet you over there."

"Got it," Tanax said, and spun away, the twisted space of his blade humming. Beq's eyes were wide behind her spectacles, but she gave a quick nod, put her head down, and started to run.

She'd be an easy target for the blasters when she stopped to help Marn. *Which means it's up to me to get their attention.* Maya gave a shout and charged.

Cables slapped and bumped all around her. She aimed for the center of the oncoming line of men and plaguespawn, haken dancing to deflect more blaster fire. A bolt exploded against a cable, severing it in a massive shower of sparks. Maya's off hand snapped out, sending blasts of flame whipping toward the opponents she could see only as darting shadows.

The plaguespawn closed around her, and from the pack-like way they moved she could tell they had the will of a *dhakim* behind them. The smallest, fastest monsters reached her first, dog-sized creatures of jutting bone and rippling black muscle, and they leapt at her with no thought for their own safety. Maya cut one clean in half, sidestepped another, then staggered as a third hit her and flared her panoply in a wash of cold. She made a half circle with her free hand, and a wall of flame sprang up to her left, catching three of the things and turning them into twitching pyres. She pressed forward, slashing to clear cables out of her path, letting fire drip onto the floor in tiny seedlike chunks.

Another plaguespawn rose in front of her and died, but the rest were closing from behind, a hissing, squelching mass. When they were over her fire-seeds, Maya released her grip, and the tiny things bloomed in concussive flowers of flame. The trap that had failed against Jaedia tore through the plaguespawn, sending bits of muscle and bone spraying wetly around her. Another volley of blaster bolts came at her, and she stopped them all, moving with unconscious grace. She could feel the Thing growing warm in her chest, standing out against the waves of cold from her panoply.

Maya took an instant to look over her shoulder. She'd come halfway around the pit, and as planned she and Tanax seemed to have attracted the attention of their assailants, letting Beq skirt the edge of the mass of rot and reach Marn. Maya turned, heading in their direction, and across the pit she could see the twists and ripples of space that said Tanax was doing likewise.

Two more plaguespawn came at her, a pair of larger monsters as big as loadbirds. One had no legs and writhed forward like a worm, with a dozen disturbingly human arms surrounding a maw jagged with splintered bones in place of teeth. The other was a crab-like thing whose oval body rolled and turned inside dozens of too-long limbs, waves of muscle rippling along their length. Eyes of every color looked down at her and blinked in unison.

Maya sent a wash of flame toward them, buying time as she backpedaled. They bulled through it, unfazed, and split up, the worm going right and the crab slipping to the left. Maya concentrated and sent a lance of more potent fire at the multilegged creature, but it adroitly moved its body out of the way, sacrificing only a few lengths of leg. At the same time, the worm closed with shocking speed, its arms reaching out for her. Maya spun away, slashing, and a woman's delicate hand and forearm went flying. She sent another wave of fire at the worm, and it took light, burning from maw to tail. Even still, it kept coming, and Maya found herself rapidly backing toward the pit.

A blaster bolt slammed over her shoulder, white-hot, and blew apart the top of the worm's head. It reared up, screaming like an angry cat, and another bolt hit it lower down, leaving a crater that wept black fluid. Maya left the thing thrashing in the dirt and charged the crab, letting its arms curve around her as she hacked toward its central body. She felt its claws scraping at her panoply, drawing flares of blue and draining her energy, but before it could close its arms around her she reached the oval mass of eyes and cut it in half. The plaguespawn's limbs twitched and shuddered wildly, and Maya spun free, dancing past the dying worm and reaching the other side of the pit.

Beq was waiting there, on one knee with her blaster pistol in both hands, all her lenses extended and capped with smoked glass. Maya grinned at her, and she smiled back. Beyond her, Marn was on hands and knees, free of his chains. He'd been down here a long time, Maya realized—his hair was long and stringy, and through his ragged clothes she could see the shape of his ribs.

Another plaguespawn, this one nearly as big as a bear, loomed out of the forest of cables on the other side of the pit. It reared for a moment, roaring, then came apart in a half dozen chunks. Tanax turned away from its remains and retreated in their direction, blocking more blaster fire with his twisted-space haken. Maya's own blade snapped up to intercept incoming shots, while Beq fired back from just behind her. The shadowy figures were advancing, and she saw at least one of them go down. She closed her off hand, and a pillar of flame engulfed another, but there were at least a dozen more, and she felt her power ebbing. The Thing was a hot coal in her chest.

Abruptly, the cacophony of blaster bolts and *deiat* halted, leaving only the crackle of Maya's blade and the buzz of Tanax's. Their attackers were spread in a rough semicircle on the other side of the pit, among the last of the cables, with a few more dog-sized plaguespawn at their sides. Directly across the pit from her, a big man stepped out of the shadows. He wore scavengers' leathers, augmented with bits and pieces of broken arcana and fragments of unmetal plate, and a long, heavy coat that swirled about his ankles.

"Cyrtak," Marn gasped out. His breathing was wet and raspy. "Careful. He's—"

"—a *dhakim*," Maya said. "I gathered."

Cyrtak looked at them, head cocked. His eyes focused on Maya, and he seemed almost disappointed.

"Take the girl alive," he said. "Kill the others, and the bait."

"Come and try," Tanax said. Twisted geometry whirled around him like a rippling hurricane.

The attackers hesitated. As Maya had intended, she and Tanax now had a wall behind them, and she was confident they could deflect their blaster fire while Beq picked them off. *The big plaguespawn are all down, too. We can take them.* She tried to inject arrogant confidence into her voice.

"Cyrtak," she shouted. "I am detaining you in the name of the Twilight Order. Come quietly and you will have an opportunity to present a defense."

He barked an astonished laugh.

"The rest of you," Maya said, "are free to go, if you drop your weapons *now*."

A murmur ran through the attackers. Cyrtak looked around, eyes narrowing.

"You pack of fucking cowards," he said. "Fine. I'll take them myself."

He thrust out a hand, palm down. In the pit, the miasma of rotting flesh and bone quivered.

Beq lined up a shot and pulled the trigger, but a tendril of black goo flung itself upward, intercepting the blaster bolt in an explosion of slime. A moment later, the whole mass was heaving itself upward, a gelatinous blob of deliquescing meat, studded with chunks of bone and skeins of gut. It hurled itself up the side of the pit, splitting into a dozen tendrils as it reached for the two centarchs.

Maya and Tanax blasted it simultaneously, a wave of flame and a blade of twisted space slashing into the thing from opposite sides. The fire charred its surface for a moment, and the blade slashed it apart, but it kept coming, burns sloughing away and wounds closing with a gloop. Each tendril split and split again, until a mass of finger-thick ropes were coiling around Maya. She slashed desperately, but each tentacle she severed simply fell back into the central mass and spread outward anew.

Tanax gave a shout of surprise as the tendrils closed around his legs, lifting him off the ground. Black rot splashed and sprayed as he flayed the thing with blades of *deiat* to no avail. Beq fired her blaster until the creeping rot grabbed her hands, dragging her forward toward the bulk of the blob.

It's not a plaguespawn. Monstrous as they were, those creatures had bones and muscles like any other living thing and could be destroyed by cuts or burns. *Cyrtak is using* dhaka *to...animate this thing.* She'd never heard of anything like it. *So if it isn't alive, how do we kill it?*

"Maya!" Beq's voice rose to a scream as a wave of foul-smelling stuff boiled around her, holding her arms pinioned and running up her legs. "Maya, *help!*"

Maya pushed toward her, slashing and cursing. Blasts of flame made the vile stuff retreat, but only momentarily, and she didn't dare direct them too close to Beq. Black tentacles grabbed at her ankles, dragging her backward, and a scream ripped from her own throat as the wave of gory darkness rose ever higher.

All at once, the world *shifted* around her, space folding in on itself in a neat circle. *Tanax's power.* The goo vaporized, falling away, and for a moment Maya was free. She started toward Beq, whose head and shoulders were all that remained visible.

"The *dhakim!*" Tanax shouted, stopping her in her tracks. He was upside down, a meter off the ground, haken flailing. "Maya, get the fucking *dhakim!*"

Plaguefire. He was right, but turning away from Beq was harder than anything Maya had ever had to do. She screamed a curse as she ran into the pit, sending a wave of fire in front of her to drive the rotting mass from her path. In a moment she was past it, pounding along the packed earth, haken blazing as she closed on Cyrtak.

A half dozen smugglers were between her and the pirate leader, blasters leveled. Maya let her haken move on its own, soaking up the bolts. The closest smuggler, a big woman with a vividly blond spike of hair, gave a wild cry as Maya got within arm's length. She shoved her blaster forward, directly in Maya's face. A brave move, Maya acknowledged. She ducked, then came back with a rising stroke that removed the woman's arm cleanly at the shoulder. The next man came at her with a curved sword, which melted into glowing liquid at Maya's parry. She ran him through, tossed him aside, and blasted the next smuggler with a bolt of fire that sent him sprawling backward in a blazing inferno. The rest of her opponents were already scrambling away, leaving her face-to-face with Cyrtak.

"Let them go *now*," Maya growled.

The *dhakim* only laughed. He gripped his right arm with his left hand, and his biceps writhed and twisted, leather splitting as his limb unfolded into two long, twisting whips of flesh and bone. They curved toward Maya, and her parry sent one of them spinning away, but the other lashed her panoply hard enough to make her stagger. Cyrtak's other arm hardened into a long, bone-edged blade, and he came at her in a whirl, whip and sword together. Maya stood her ground, letting her overextended panoply take one more blow as she aimed a counterstrike at his shoulder. Her hold on *deiat* flickered, and her vision grayed at the edges, but she carved his whip-arm away. Her next parry shattered the bone-blade, and she kicked him in the stomach, driving him backward. Another slash took one of his legs at the knee, and Cyrtak fell backward. Maya planted her boot on his chest and leveled her haken at his throat.

"Let them go," she repeated. "And tell me what you did to Jaedia."

"What *I* did to Jaedia?" The big man laughed, fast and insane. The skin of his face seemed to boil, bubbles forming, tiny scraps tearing free into miniature tendrils that reached up toward Maya. "It was Jaedia who brought us here. She told us to wait for you. She's so eager to see you again." His lips split, and his tongue distorted as though he'd swallowed a snake. "Mayaaaaaa—"

Maya closed her fist, and flame engulfed the struggling *dhakim*, hot enough to char flesh and bone. It whipped around her as he blackened, his body still shifting and changing. Finally he collapsed, leaving only a patina of ash and twisted bones behind, his ribs cracking like twigs under the weight of her boot.

Beq. Maya turned away and sagged with relief at the sight of Beq and Tanax sitting in the dirt, surrounded by quiescent globs of black ooze. Behind them, Marn was pressed against the wall, eyes very wide. Cyrtak's remaining smugglers had taken the opportunity to run for it, and they were alone in the smoke-filled chamber.

Jaedia... Maya turned to look at Cyrtak, now little more than a misshapen skull. Her hand touched the Thing, and she yanked it away immediately—the little arcana was hot enough to scorch her shirt and blister her finger. Maya swallowed and let her haken blade fade away.

"Maya?" Beq was on her feet, scrambling across the vile pit. "Are you all right?"

"'M just…" Maya mumbled, and shook her head. "Tired."

She didn't even remember hitting the floor.

When she awoke, they were still in the tunnels, though thankfully no longer in that charnel house of a smuggler's lair. Instead, she found herself propped against the unmetal wall of a smaller chamber, with Beq and Marn sitting anxiously beside her. Tanax, waiting at the corridor entrance with his hand on his haken, looked over his shoulder as Maya groaned.

"Maya," Beq said, leaning forward. She was coated in gobbets of black goop, mixed with larger bits of rotting flesh. Maya's sense of smell had thankfully shut down long ago. "Maya, can you hear me?"

Maya nodded dully. Marn handed her a canteen, and she drank until it was empty.

"Are you hurt anywhere?" Beq said urgently. "We didn't want to move you too much."

"I think…not." Maya shook her head. She felt exhausted, with the hollowed-out sensation that came with overuse of *deiat*, but the only actual pain was in her chest, around the Thing. It felt as though the arcana had been replaced with a hive of stinging wasps. "Drew too much power. Give me a minute."

"As soon as you can walk, we should get out of here," Tanax said. "We don't know when those Chosen-damned smugglers will come back."

"They won't," Marn said. His cheeks were hollow, and his filthy hair hung around his head, but his eyes were still bright. "Cyrtak was the one who brought them here. The rest followed him because he could pay."

"Are you all right?" Maya said, sitting up a little straighter. "How long have they had you?"

"I don't know," Marn said. "A long time. They kept me there while they brought in other prisoners and... used them to create those things. Cyrtak told me he was looking forward to what he could build out of me." He hunched in on himself a little, shuddering. "I'm glad you killed him."

"We're all glad you killed him," Beq said fervently, trying and failing to clean her spectacles with her already filthy shirt.

"Marn." Maya touched his shoulder gingerly. "What happened to Jaedia?"

"Jaedia..." The light in Marn's eyes faded. "She brought me here. Gave me to them."

"*What?*" Maya shook her head weakly. "She would never. You know her."

"I..." He swallowed. "Maybe you're right. Maybe it... wasn't her. It seemed... I don't know." He shook his head. "She left me in the inn when she first arrived. After a few days, she came back and told me to come with her, and we went into the tunnels. Cyrtak chained me up, and Jaedia told him to keep me around until you got here. I was... bait, I guess." He blinked rapidly. "I tried to warn you."

"You did well," Maya said, squeezing his shoulder. "But where's Jaedia now?"

"Gone. Out of the city. I heard her talking with Cyrtak. She was going ahead with Nicomidi, now that he'd arrived, and Cyrtak was supposed to follow once he'd taken you."

"Wait." Tanax turned away from the tunnel and stalked over. "Jaedia left *with Nicomidi*?"

"I didn't see him," Marn said. "But that's what she told Cyrtak. She gave him instructions on how to find them."

"Do you remember the instructions?" Maya said.

"I memorized them," Marn said. "I thought... maybe they'd help you. When you came."

"You..." Maya grinned at him, tears welling in her eyes. "I'm sorry I couldn't come sooner. I'm sorry..."

"You saved me," Marn said, smiling back. "I knew you would."

Midnight had come and gone by the time Maya finally got the chance to sit down, every fiber of her being limp with fatigue.

Fortunately, Grace was the sort of city where there were rooms and services available at any hour. Faressa had been waiting at the tunnel exit, and she'd nearly fainted at the smell coming off them. At her insistence, they'd stripped to their underwear, and she'd hurried off and procured cheap, ill-fitting coveralls for them while Maya piled their soiled uniforms together and incinerated them with a touch of *deiat*.

Marn had started coughing halfway through the trek, deep, wet-sounding retches that doubled him over. Faressa had agreed to take him under her care and to send him back to the Forge at the first opportunity. Marn had tried to argue that he should stay with Maya, but his protests were half-hearted, and he'd eventually agreed.

The scout arranged rooms at an upscale inn for the rest of them. Maya suspected it was at least partly a brothel, since the well-dressed woman in the front hall was unfazed at a party of guests staggering in in the small hours and there seemed to be a lot of good-looking servants hanging around without very much to do. Regardless, it was clean and well furnished and, most important, offered private baths. Burning her clothes had done nothing to get the stench of rot out of her hair and skin, and Maya wasn't far from setting *herself* on fire.

Not long after they'd settled in, a handsome young man had knocked on her door with a tray of pleasant-smelling soaps and washes. She'd waved off his offer to apply them himself and retreated to the washroom once other servants had filled the iron tub with pails of steaming water. Fancy or not, the inn fell short of the accommodations at the Spike, but after two weeks on the road and the chaos of the night, it felt like unutterable decadence. Before climbing in the tub,

Maya spent half an hour scrubbing at herself until her skin was red and sore, then rinsing and rerinsing her hair. Feeling tolerably clean at last, she slipped into the near-scalding water, gritting her teeth at the spike of pain as it lapped at the swollen skin around the Thing.

She prodded the little arcana idly as she soaked. It had gotten hot enough that it had left a blister on her finger when she'd touched it, but where it was actually embedded in her flesh it didn't seem to have burned her at all. The flesh was puffy, as though swollen from bruising, but the skin was unbroken.

I need to talk to Basel about it. He would know something. *After I find Jaedia. After all of . . . this.* Her mind shied away, and she yawned, slipping farther into the tub and sending the water sloshing.

The next she knew, the water had gone tepid, and a knock at the door had her sitting bolt upright. A wave of bathwater went over the side of the tub and wet the washroom rug. Maya hurriedly hoisted herself out of the bath and shrugged into the fluffy bathrobe the inn's servants had left hanging on the door.

"Who's there?" she said. "I've got plenty of soap—"

"It's Beq."

"Oh." Maya looked down at herself, suddenly fully awake. Her skin was shriveled like dried fruit, and her hair hung in a limp rattail, but there was nothing to be done about either at a moment's notice. She hurried back into the main room to unlock the door. "Come in. Sorry, I was in the bath."

"Me too," Beq said. She'd evidently had more time to clean up afterward, because her long green hair was neatly braided, and she wore her spare uniform, slightly rumpled from days at the bottom of a pack. "Chosen defend, I thought I'd never get that stuff off me." She sniffed at her arm and shuddered. "I can still smell it."

"All I can smell is floral . . . stuff," Maya said. "So I think you're all right."

"Do you mind if I come in?" Beq fiddled awkwardly with the dial on her spectacles, one lens flipping back and forth. "I know it's late. I just..."

"I think I'm still too keyed up to sleep," Maya lied, stepping aside.

"Me too." Beq closed the door behind her. "Nice décor. My room has a sort of nautical theme. Lots of mermaids."

Maya hadn't taken the time to look around much. Her room was large, but much of it was dominated by a wide, fluffy bed, with only a small table and a couple of chairs pressed into one corner. The motif seemed to be hunting, with paintings of people on horseback riding merrily across the countryside, presumably in pursuit of something inoffensive.

"I might prefer the mermaids," Maya said. "Sit, if you like."

Beq glanced at the bed, which made Maya's heartbeat kick up a step, then went to the table and pulled out one of the chairs. Maya took the other and poured them water. For a moment they looked at each other, Beq's eyes huge behind her lenses.

"You saved my life," Beq said. "Again."

"And you saved mine. Again." Maya grinned. "I think we don't need to keep score, do we?"

"Probably not. That... thing." Beq shuddered. "Have you ever seen anything like it?"

Maya shook her head. "Not even close. I thought plaguespawn were bad enough."

"Still. You won."

"*We* won. I couldn't have done it without you. Both of you," honesty made her add. "Tanax kept his head when I got distracted."

"And now we go after Jaedia?"

Maya nodded. "She's not too far ahead of us. And if she expected Cyrtak to catch up, she can't be moving too quickly."

"We still don't know where she's going."

"There's a lot of things we don't know," Maya said. "But we'll find out. Whatever Cyrtak did to her..."

"You think it was him?" Beq said, finger tapping nervously against her mug. "That he was behind all of this?"

"He was a *dhakim*. If not him, then who?" *And now that he's dead, will anyone be able to fix Jaedia?* Maya took a long swallow of water and tried to banish the thought.

"And what about Nicomidi? Where does he fit in?"

"I don't know," Maya admitted. "Maybe we'll get the chance to ask him."

"It's..." Beq sighed. "I wish I could be...more helpful. Understanding things is supposed to be my job."

"Beq." Maya put her hand across the table, fingertips on Beq's knuckles. Even this faint contact sent shivers up her arm. "I wouldn't be here without you. You talked Faressa into helping us, you shot that plaguespawn off my back—"

"You could have managed," Beq said, faintly.

"I trust you with my life," Maya said. "Obviously. And it's because you're clearly worthy of it."

"Oh." Beq looked down at her hand. "Thank you."

There was a long pause.

"When you told me Tanax was coming," Beq said quietly, "I think I was angry."

"You were?"

"I don't...get angry very often. And I knew it was stupid. But I kept thinking that you had another centarch to help you now, so you wouldn't need me." Beq swallowed. "And that's so utterly selfish, I know, because you're out here trying to help Jaedia, and all I can think about is—"

"Please," Maya said. "It's all right. Tanax is...Tanax." She shook her head. "He may not be quite the plaguing asshole I thought he was, but he's still not easy to get along with. And I will always need you."

Beq nodded, blinked, and shifted in her chair. Maya got the sense she was trying to work up to something.

"I wanted to talk to you," Beq managed eventually.

"You're doing that," Maya said. "So far, so good."

Beq gave a weak smile. "About...that night. Before you fought Tanax."

"Okay."

"I kissed you."

"You did."

"And I ran away."

"I wouldn't say *ran*—"

"And then we talked about it, afterward, but we haven't...had much time since then."

"Yeah."

Beq took a deep breath. "Can I tell you something that probably makes me insane?"

"Um. If you want?"

"When we were down in the tunnel, and that *thing* was all over me, and it was trying to get in my nose and mouth and—" She shuddered again. "I thought I was going to die. And all I could think about was... why did I run away?"

"Really?"

"I told you it made me insane, right?" Beq pulled her hand away from Maya and hugged herself. "When we didn't die after all, I promised myself I would come and talk to you. Only now I'm doing it and I still feel crazy and I'm kind of wishing I'd chickened out and gone to bed—"

"Beq!" Maya said, laughing.

"It's not fair!" Beq glared at her. "You know what you're doing. I hadn't even *thought* about...that sort of thing, until—"

"Wait," Maya said. "Who says *I* know what I'm doing?"

"You're a centarch," Beq said. "And you spent years traveling around the Republic."

"With my master," Maya said. "Who is the next thing to my mother."

"But you..." Beq hesitated, looking down again. "You seemed to know what you wanted."

"I mean." Maya felt her cheeks growing hot and was glad her darker complexion didn't show a flush the way Beq's did. "I'm not going to say I haven't…imagined things. When I'm by myself. You know. But I don't have any, um. *Practical* experience."

"Oh." Beq sat quietly for a moment, digesting that. "You…imagined things."

Maya wanted to bury her head in her hands. "Yes."

"With me?"

"Y…yes."

"And then you—"

Maya drew her knees up, hiding her face from Beq's gaze, and gave a tiny nod.

"Oh," Beq said again. Her breath seemed to come very fast, and Maya felt her own heart hammering. "I didn't—I wouldn't even know what to imagine."

Maya sucked in a breath, but when she spoke, her voice was barely a whisper.

"Do you. Um." She paused and gathered her strength. "Do you want me to show you?"

And then, somewhat later, an awful thought struck Maya like a thunderbolt. She pulled her lips away from Beq's and sat up, very abruptly.

Beq lay on the bed, green hair coiled beside her, hands on Maya's flanks. Maya had undone the buttons on her uniform shirt and pulled it open, revealing the mesmerizing sweep of her collarbone and the inner slopes of her breasts, dusted with freckles like her cheeks. Maya was above her, on hands and knees, breathing like she'd just finished a sparring match.

"What's wrong?" Beq said. "Did I do something—"

"No, no, no," Maya said. "Sorry. It's not you. I just." She swallowed. "I realize there's something I need to show you." She reached, hesitantly, for the front of her bathrobe.

"Um. Is it breasts?" Beq glanced down at herself. "Because I know I'm not *experienced*, but I don't think that would be such a surprise."

"No, it's not breasts," Maya said. "I mean, it is, I have those, but... listen. You can't tell anyone about this. Not *anyone*."

"I'm very confused," Beq said, sitting up on her elbows.

"Just promise me."

"All right."

Maya took a deep breath and pulled open the bathrobe, letting it fall to her waist. She felt suddenly, horribly vulnerable—not for her skin, but for the Thing, which was dug in above her breastbone like a crystal-encrusted tick.

"Oh," Beq said. And then, "*Oh*. The arcana." Her eyes narrowed behind her lenses. "Is it—stuck there?"

"It's... embedded. Like part of my body." Maya took Beq's hand and brought it up to brush against the Thing. Beq hesitated, then explored the little arcana with her fingers, poking gently at the puffy flesh around it.

"How long have you had it?" Beq said. "Where did it come from?"

"Since I was about five, I think," Maya said. "Not long after the Order took me in. I used to get... sick, all the time. I don't remember it well, but they tell me I'd have fevers, coughs, and nothing the doctors could do would help. It was getting worse, and my parents worried I was going to die. After the Order came for me, Baselanthus examined me himself. He said I had a... a kind of continuous illness, I guess. I've never really understood it. But it *would* have killed me, for certain. To keep that from happening, he gave me this." She tapped one of the crystals. "I call it the Thing. Basel and Jaedia know about it—and Marn, I guess—but no one else. And I'm not supposed to tell anyone."

"I can see why not," Beq said. Her fingers circled the Thing, raising goose bumps on Maya's sensitive skin. "Obviously, if Baselanthus did it, it must be all right, but melding arcana and flesh is usually only possible with *dhaka*. If Tanax and his Dogmatic friends saw this, they might call you a heretic."

"Fortunately," Maya said tartly, "the chance of Tanax seeing it is low."

"Do you know how it works?" Beq tweaked a dial on her lenses. "Does it have an internal power source? Have you ever tried feeding it external power? Are any of the crystals sensitive to—"

"Beq," Maya said.

Beq blinked. "What?"

Maya gestured. At the two of them, the bed, her bare chest. "Do you think you could be a *little* less of an arcanist for just a few minutes?"

"Sorry."

"Don't apologize." Maya bent back down for a kiss, her breasts brushing against Beq's. "Just... try not to get distracted."

And then, later still, a faint gasp.

"Maya."

"Mmm."

"Have you tried a standard Darkwatcher diagnostic sequence to see—"

"*Beq.*"

"I'm sorry! But I think—" And then, as Maya did something with her fingers: "Oh. I'll just... um... try it out... ah... later."

"Good."

Chapter 23

Getting into the ghoul city of Refuge, it turned out, was a great deal easier when you didn't try to climb through a rock ingestor. Kit led them through the tunnels under Deepfire to one of a hundred disused, dead-end sections, and Gyre watched in mild surprise as a passage that looked like it had been totally blocked by a cave-in cleared itself in seconds. Small, crab-like constructs embedded in the boulders extended legs and hauled themselves out of the way, leaving a perfectly serviceable tunnel extending on into the darkness. Another construct waited just beyond, with seats like a carriage on the back of a spidery collection of legs.

"Let me guess," Gyre said. "We *ride* that thing?"

Kit nodded delightedly. "It's a long way to Refuge. That's part of how they keep the city secure—there are a lot of tunnels under these mountains, with a lot of exits, and the constructs are constantly filling them in and digging new ones. So if you don't have a proper mount, you'd just get lost down here."

"Such trusting people, the ghouls," Gyre said. He grabbed the side of the carriage-thing and hauled himself in, while Kit leapt up lightly beside him. Behind them, the crab-constructs were reassembling the pile of tumbled boulders.

Once they were settled, the carriage-construct started moving, its legs shifting with a smooth interlocking motion that conveyed barely a shudder to its passengers. It accelerated slowly but continuously, and within a few minutes they were moving through the tunnel at a shocking rate of speed, the walls a blur on either side and their mount's legs rippling in a rolling gallop. Kit gave a delighted shout and threw her arms in the air.

"I love this part," she confided.

"Until the damn thing runs into a wall and smashes us to paste," Gyre said, trying hard to relax his grip on the arms of his seat.

"That's half the fun!"

Gyre settled for clutching his pack instead. After the fight at the Spike, they'd had to go to ground, so it was stuffed with only the bare essentials. Two extra energy bottles—the one at his side was nearly empty now, with only the faintest glow in its crystal—his pouch of alchemicals, the remote trigger, and the single remaining bomb, a rough cylinder of lumpy clay. And, of course, the Core Analytica, cube-shaped and made of interlocking metal rods, which shifted with a smooth, oily motion whenever he touched it. *I just hope we haven't damaged the damn thing.*

The wind of their passage made conversation impossible, so Gyre closed his eyes—*still strange, having two to close!*—and tried to relax. To his surprise, he managed a light doze, and when he woke it was because the carriage-thing was slowing. The tunnel was the same as ever, round and smooth-walled, dark enough that his natural eye could see nothing at all. His silver eye saw the gray shapes of more constructs waiting for them, and he recognized the multilegged chair that held Naumoriel.

Elariel was there, too, standing between two spiky soldier-constructs. She looked nervous, in Gyre's admittedly limited experience reading ghoul emotions: her long ears flat against her head, her fur rippling. Naumoriel, on the other hand, leaned forward in his chair.

"Hello, Kitsraea. Gyre." Elariel stepped forward as the carriage-thing came to a halt. "I'm glad you've returned safely."

"Do you have it?" Naumoriel said. "The Analytica?"

Gyre glanced at Kit, who raised her eyebrows and gestured him on. He hopped off the carriage-construct and opened his pack, producing the intricate cube. Naumoriel held out his wizened hands, and Gyre passed the thing over for inspection.

"Yes," the old ghoul breathed. "Oh yes. Valthiel's greatest work. Seventeen iterations deep." His mouth hung slightly open, tongue running over small, sharp teeth. "There has never been anything like it in the history of the world." His voice fell to a whisper. "The power under the mountain will be mine at last."

"Which means," Kit said, stepping forward, "we did what you wanted."

Naumoriel looked down at her, and his face hardened. "After begging for a second chance."

"You owe us. You owe *me*." She tapped her chest. "I want this thing fixed, remember?"

"I remember perfectly," Naumoriel snapped. "You want to live out your pathetic human life span, and Gyre desires the power to destroy the Twilight Order." He turned to Gyre. "What do you think of your taste of power, boy?"

"It's impressive," Gyre said, touching the hilt of his silver sword. "But it's just a taste."

"So impatient." Naumoriel clicked his tongue, ears twitching with mirth. "But there is one more task to perform, my human...friends. This"—he raised the Analytica—"must be brought to its...proper place. You will help me with this, and then everything you desire will be yours."

"Help you?" Kit said. "You're coming with us?"

"Indeed I am," the old ghoul said with a toothy grin. "This is the last step on the path I have followed since I was a child. I intend to be there at the end."

Elariel conducted them to their rooms—either the same chambers as before, or others near identical—and advised them to get some sleep. Gyre expected to have trouble with this, since the last time he'd been in this chamber had been just after Naumoriel had slowly disassembled him and put him back together, and his main memory was waking over and over to mind-shattering pain. Even so, exhaustion was a powerful motivator. The fight in the Spike had taken something out of him, more than just physically. *We did it. We really did it. And now...what?* He wanted to talk to Kit, but she'd retired to her own room immediately and firmly closed the door.

A construct woke him later—how long, in this sunless world, he had no idea—with a gentle tap at the door. The little thing scuttled away, leaving behind folded, clean clothes and an energy bottle with a bright white glow. The ghouls didn't wash, as far as Gyre could tell, so he cleaned himself as best he could in the basin before dressing and settled down to wait.

It wasn't long before Elariel appeared, with Kit trailing behind her.

"Are you prepared for your journey?" the ghoul said.

"I suppose," Gyre said. "I don't know where we're going. And I haven't got food or water or any other supplies."

"Naumoriel has accounted for your needs," Elariel said. "Come with me."

"Yeah, Gyre," Kit said. "Of course Naumoriel has accounted for our needs. Let's go."

Gyre shot her a look, and she smirked. Under Elariel's wide-eyed gaze, he didn't want to say anything further, so he merely fell in behind the two of them. They followed another identical-looking passage back to the large tunnel, where the rest of the expedition was waiting.

There were the now-familiar soldier-constructs, a double rank of them, twenty in all. Another five larger versions, still humanoid but at least two and a half meters tall, and a pair of what Gyre guessed were cargo haulers, flat platforms with legs not unlike the carriage they'd ridden. Largest of all, though, was a thing like an enormous spider-crab, eight-legged, with two large, clawed arms and two smaller limbs curled in close to its ovoid body. It was easily twice Gyre's height, and the egg-shaped central core of it was bigger than he was. The reason for this became clear a moment later, when the top of the egg, made of smooth, dark stuff like smoked glass, hinged upward. Naumoriel sat cocooned in the thing, resting in a padded chair, banks of crystalline, incomprehensible controls all around him.

The monstrous thing was like his chair, Gyre realized, only on a massive scale. *Built for war*, he decided, looking at the gleaming, razor-sharp claws of the large arms. *So who are we going to be fighting?*

"Everything is prepared," the old ghoul said. "Humans, are you fit to play your part?"

"You haven't told us what our part is," Gyre said.

"You have proven to be skilled and resourceful," Naumoriel said. "Our destination is a valley deep in the Shattered Peaks, known only to a few. We will certainly encounter the creatures you call plaguespawn. And, given your earlier failure, it is just possible that the Twilight Order will attempt to interfere as well. You will assist in the event of either contingency."

"Sounds great," Kit said. "Let's get to it."

What is she playing at? Gyre tried to catch Kit's eye, but she wouldn't meet his gaze. He hesitated, then nodded his assent. *It's not as though I have much of a choice.*

"Elariel," the old ghoul said. "You understand your duty."

She inclined her head. "I do."

"Then take care of my city," Naumoriel said. "Until I . . . return."

The canopy of his massive construct swung closed. At some silent command, the soldier-constructs started their march, with the others following behind in perfect time.

"I wish you good luck," Elariel said. She hesitated, ears drooping, then turned away.

For most of a day, they followed a curving tunnel, walking in near-total darkness. It was enough to make Gyre miss the carriage-construct. Eventually, their path turned upward, and after a leg-cramping hour or two, they reached a set of massive doors. These slid open at Naumoriel's approach, letting in late afternoon sunlight.

They emerged onto the side of a mountain, sloping down to a narrow river valley. Scrub grass clung in patches to a rocky landscape, but at least they were well below the snow line. The door ground closed behind them, outward surface worked to resemble the stone all around it.

"Do you have any idea where we are?" Gyre said to Kit, looking up at the unfamiliar peaks all around them.

"Nope!" she said cheerfully. "Does it matter?"

"Not really, I suppose." He raised his voice. "How far are we going?"

Naumoriel's voice, slightly distorted, echoed from his towering construct. "Four days' walk, given your human frailties. We follow this valley until it meets up with another, then turn upstream and follow the river to its source." His construct extended a leg, testing the slope, then started its smooth glide forward. "Come. It will be safer to travel by day."

Why? Gyre wondered as they tramped along in the huge thing's wake. *What could he be worried about?* He was hard-pressed to imagine a plaguespawn big enough to challenge even one of the ghoul constructs, let alone a whole squadron of them. And he couldn't see any signs of habitation in this valley, human or otherwise.

They stopped by the side of the stream as twilight was fading from the sky. Naumoriel's construct planted itself next to the water, along with the two cargo carriers, while the rest fanned out to man a wide perimeter. *It certainly beats a few trip wires.* To his surprise, Naumoriel's construct opened up, and its two smaller arms reached down with many-tentacled grips to lift the old ghoul out and deposit him gently on the sandy riverbank.

"I thought you'd be spending the night in that thing," Kit said.

"I will," Naumoriel said. His huge eyes scanned the darkness, ears erect and searching. "But it has been a long time since I was above-ground. I find that I desire... reflection."

"Fair enough." Kit looked back at Gyre. "Shall we see what Elariel packed us to eat?"

She's up to something. He watched Kit suspiciously as she rummaged through the strapped-down packages on the cargo constructs. *But what is it?* With Naumoriel sitting a few feet away, he could hardly ask. Instead, he helped her inventory the supplies. The old ghoul had to instruct them which of the several tightly wrapped bundles was food—it turned out to be boxes of small dried pellets, which according to Naumoriel were some sort of nutritious fungus. Adding water made them balloon to the size of small oranges, and they had a salty flavor and a slightly slimy texture a bit like raw fish. All in all, Gyre concluded, he'd eaten worse, though he imagined a steady diet of the things would get old.

Naumoriel ate a few of the fungus balls and drank from a bulky canteen. He trailed his fingertips in the water of the stream, letting his claws carve lines in the flowing water. Gyre had never seen him in such a contemplative mood, and he decided to take advantage of it, while Kit rummaged to see what sort of sleeping arrangements the ghouls had provided.

"May I ask you something?" Gyre said politely.

"I suppose," Naumoriel said.

"Elariel. You two seem... close. Is she your daughter?"

"Daughter?" The old ghoul's lips spread in a toothy grin, and his ears twitched. "She is family, but my daughters are all long dead. You would say she is my great-granddaughter."

"Great—" Gyre raised his eyebrow. "I see."

"You wish to ask how old I am," Naumoriel said.

"Honestly I don't have any idea how long ghouls live," Gyre said. "You look older than Elariel, is the best I could manage."

"I doubt Elariel has many more years than you do," Naumoriel said. "Whereas I was born...I suppose our calendar would mean little to you. It was the eighth year before the war began."

Before the war? That made Naumoriel over four hundred years old. "Then you remember the war. The Chosen."

"Of course I remember." The ghoul's eyes narrowed. "I was a child, but I remember. The sun-lovers chased us from their world, *this* world, above the earth, but that wasn't enough for them. They cracked our mountains like eggs to get to us. The tunnels flowed with their fire. They sent your kind, their slaves, to root us out. However many we slaughtered, there were always more." He stared, unseeing, into the darkness. "I remember moving from one city to another, always just ahead of the fire. Knowing that all who hadn't fled in time, everyone we'd left behind, had perished at the hands of the *Chosen*."

"Wow," Kit said, over Gyre's shoulder. "No wonder your people unleashed the Plague."

Naumoriel's head snapped around, and his smile faded. "Do not speak of what you have no means to understand, *girl*." He waved a hand, and the big construct's tentacular arms stretched down to lift him up into their embrace. "We leave at first light."

"Come on," Kit said, "let's get the tents up."

The ghouls, it turned out, had provided two neat little tents, made of some shiny material lighter than cloth but as waterproof as oiled leather. No sooner had they driven the pegs into the earth than Kit dove inside hers and buttoned the flap. Gyre stared after her for a moment, then sighed and went back for a few more fungus balls.

In spite of the long walk, some instinct kept him from falling asleep. He lay on his back and stared upward, silver eye showing him the ceiling in perfect clarity. After perhaps an hour, he heard shuffling outside and then a rustle at the tent flap.

Kit pushed her way in, wrapped in one of the warm, lightweight blankets the ghouls had provided. She wormed her way up beside him and propped herself on one elbow.

"Hi," she said breathlessly.

"Hi yourself," Gyre said. "What's the matter, are you cold again?"

"Not really."

"Nightmares, then?"

"Sometimes." Kit sat up, her head nearly brushing the ceiling, and disentangled herself from the blanket. She was naked underneath. "But not tonight."

She bent down and kissed him, fast and hungry. Her hand spidered across his chest, slipped down to his waist, and expertly popped the button on his trousers. Before it could plunge beneath them, he caught her by the wrist, and she pulled away a fraction.

"What?" she said.

"Is this another . . . what did you call it? Moment of weakness?"

"I mean. Probably. So?" A sly tone entered her voice. "Sorry, did that hurt your poor little pride? Here, let me make it better." She grabbed for his cock, and he yanked her hand away. "Ow!"

"Kit," Gyre said, letting go. "What are you doing?"

"I *thought* I was coming over for a quick fuck. Maybe to be followed by a longer fuck."

"I mean . . . all of this. The way you've been talking to Naumoriel." Gyre sat up himself. "You didn't raise any objection when he refused to fix your heart until after this new mission."

"Do we really have to talk about this now?" Kit said. "It's been a long day and I think I am actually *dripping*, so if we could just—"

"*Kit.*"

"Fine!" She threw her hands in the air and drew her knees up to her chin. "I was going to talk to you later anyway. I just wanted to make sure *he* was asleep out there. I have no idea how much he can hear."

"What don't you want Naumoriel to hear?"

"That I'm onto him, obviously." She pulled her legs in a little tighter.

"He's never going to fix my heart. Of course he's not. And he's never going to give you what you want. Either we die getting him to whatever he's looking for, or he's going to keep us on his leash forever." She shook her head. "Or else, once he has his 'power under the mountain,' he'll toss us aside like yesterday's breakfast and leave us to rot. You know he will."

"The thought has occurred to me," Gyre said. "But I always knew that was a risk of looking for the Tomb."

"*You* chose to risk your life trying to turn the world upside down. I'm just trying to fucking stay alive until my next birthday, all right? Forgive me if I don't like the idea of being dropped on a dung heap to wait for my personal hourglass to run out of sand."

"I don't like it much either," Gyre said. "But what's the alternative? You said yourself we're dependent on the ghouls."

"On the *ghouls*," Kit said. "Not on Naumoriel."

There was a pregnant pause.

"Think about it," Kit went on. Her voice was low and fast. "Naumoriel isn't popular among his people, right? He's practically an exile. And he said that dealing with us wasn't something their leaders would approve of. If his project were to go wrong out here, well... who would know, apart from the two of us?"

"That's..." Gyre paused. "That still doesn't solve your problem."

"It does if *we* find this 'power' and take it for ourselves," Kit said.

"We don't even know what it is," Gyre said.

"We know it must be something spectacular," Kit countered. "You've seen what the ghouls can do *already*. What goes far enough beyond that for Naumoriel to risk everything—his own life, even?"

"And you're assuming it'll be something we can use—"

"We don't have to use it. Whatever it is, we just offer to sell it to the rest of the ghouls. Make our bargain over again, only *this* time we'll have the whip hand. That ought to be enough to be worth a little *dhaka* to fix me up. And for you—what would you need, to destroy the Order? An army of those construct things, maybe?"

"Maybe," Gyre muttered. "It's a plaguing big risk. There's so much we don't know."

"I think it's not as much of a risk as letting Naumoriel get what he wants and trusting to his gratitude afterward," Kit said.

Gyre gave a slow nod. "So what are you planning?"

"I'm playing it by ear for the moment. The more we can get Naumoriel to tell us about where we're going, the better. Aside from that, we wait for an opportunity." She grinned in the darkness. "I just wanted to get us on the same page first."

"I may have an idea," Gyre said. "At least it'll be... a little insurance. If he gets out of his construct again tomorrow, see if you can get him talking."

"I'll do my best. He seems to like you better than he ever liked me. Probably because you've both got cocks." She shrugged. "Or I assume he does. Do ghouls fuck like regular people, do you think?"

"I have no idea," Gyre said.

"Elariel has tits, anyway. I should have asked her while I had the chance." Kit looked thoughtful. "That'd be... I mean, all that fur, right?"

"Kit," Gyre said again.

"Plaguefire, I know I'm horny when I start thinking about ghoul snatch," Kit said. "Do you still want to fuck?"

"What you said, back in the tavern."

"Are you *still* thinking about that?" Kit said, with a theatrical sigh. "What is this, you won't give it up until I whisper 'I love you' in your ear?"

"I want to be sure where I stand."

"Argh!" Kit rubbed her hands frantically through her spiky blue hair. "All *right*. I shouldn't have said that. I'm sorry! Is that good enough?"

"I don't need an apology," Gyre said. "I just want to know... what you think, I guess."

"What I *think* is that my life has not done a great deal to prepare me for the experience of maybe giving a little bit of a shit about someone, okay? So maybe I'm not the best at dealing with it. And after what happened to you in the Tomb..." She hesitated. "I thought you might blame me. For, you know. Getting your eye socket ripped open and days of shrieking agony."

"I was the one who made you take me there."

"Yeah, well, people aren't always rational about that sort of thing." She took a deep breath. "I didn't actually fuck anyone at the tavern, if that matters to you. I may have made out with the blacksmith girl a little; I'm not sure, I was pretty drunk. But I'm ninety percent certain that was all." She cocked her head and waggled one hand. "Well. Eighty percent."

"You were right, though. I don't own you."

"Of course not. But if we're going to be the kind of partners who spend time naked together, you know. There should probably be some ground rules." Kit let out a deep breath. "Okay. Done with the feelings-talk. Can we *please* just f—"

Gyre cut her off by pressing his lips to hers. Kit fell over with a delighted squeak, her hands already tugging at his trousers.

Sometime after, Gyre lay on his back, staring at the roof of the tent. Kit was nestled beside him, naked and warm, her breaths slow and peaceful.

What am I doing here?

He could follow the steps that had brought him to this place in his mind. Maya's abduction, his mother's death, the hard years on the road as he'd searched for anything that offered a scrap of hope that the Order might not be all-powerful. Deepfire, Yora and the rest, his pursuit of the Tomb, and finally Kit. *And now I'm following a mad old ghoul in pursuit of a power I don't even understand.*

You found what you were looking for. Yora's voice echoed through his thoughts. *Was it worth it?*

Kit never seemed troubled by the people who got hurt because they got in her way. The Auxies, the bandits, Harrow and all the rest. Gyre didn't fool himself that she'd mourn him, if the occasion arose. And when his rage burned brightest—when he looked Maya in the face and heard her spout the Order's lies—he could almost make himself that cold. It was only afterward that doubt stole in.

Is it worth it?

He turned his head to look at Kit, outlined in perfect clarity through the darkness by his silver eye. She shifted, curling up tighter, as though she sensed his regard.

She's right about Naumoriel. The old ghoul was using them. *But he's the only thread I have, the only connection to the power I need.* He'd had a taste of it now. Defeating the pair of Legionaries had been a start, and he couldn't pretend it hadn't been satisfying. *But it's only a start.*

Is it worth it? Yora echoed.

All through the next day, they descended, following the river.

Try as he might, Gyre still couldn't put names to any of the mountains that surrounded them. The Shattered Peaks was a vast range, and he knew there were whole sections that had never been settled by the ghouls, and thus never attracted the attention of the Chosen or the scavengers who followed them. It was entirely possible that he and Kit were the first humans to set eyes on this valley, at least since the days when skyships passed overhead.

Then again, they were headed *somewhere*, which meant that the place wasn't as free of ghoul settlement as it first appeared.

Inevitably, a few plaguespawn found them, drawn by the steady tromp of the constructs' march. Compared to the ghouls' creations, they were ramshackle, awkward things, organic material haphazardly repurposed into a new form with no coherent plan, no elegance or efficiency. By contrast, the constructs were marvels, the black muscle under their spiked exteriors making their movements fast and lethal. When they engaged the plaguespawn, the difference was clear—the interlopers were smashed aside with casual ease, their stolen forms pulped by stony fists and left as smears of black blood on the rocks. *If Naumoriel thinks that Kit and I are going to be more effective than* that, *he's going to be very disappointed.*

That evening, as Gyre pitched their tents, the ghoul was again gently lifted out of his war-construct and set by the side of the stream. There was something different about Naumoriel out here, Gyre thought. He seemed almost melancholy, a far cry from his manic rants back in Refuge.

He doesn't expect to come back from this, Gyre realized with sudden clarity. He had no idea how long most ghouls lived, but clearly Naumoriel was pushing the upper limit. *Whatever power he's looking for, he doesn't expect to survive using it.*

"Can I ask you something?" Kit said, plopping herself down happily beside Naumoriel. The old ghoul looked at her and heaved a very human sigh.

"If you must," he said.

Please don't be about ghoul fucking, Gyre thought.

"Why me?" Kit said. "You could have killed me, when I wandered near Refuge the first time. You could have just left me alone, even, and I would have died in those tunnels."

"Indeed," the ghoul said. "It was my duty to do just that. The Geraia entrusted me with the defense of the city, so they can go on with their self-involved debating and debauchery and never consider the outside world."

"So why, then?"

"Because the outside world will not ignore *us* forever." He looked down at her, eyes hooded. "And because the war is not over."

"Against the Chosen, you mean? Because the Twilight Order is still fighting? Is that why you need this power?"

Naumoriel's ears waggled with amusement. "Your digging for information is transparent, human."

"Yeah." Kit ruffled her hair. "Subtlety was never my strong suit."

"There is much that is hidden, even from me. Over the years I have discovered...hints. With the power that sleeps under the mountain, I will find the truth. That is all you need to know."

As they spoke, Gyre was working. He finished with the tents, then took out his own pack, digging down to the very bottom and removing the thick clay cylinder. Trying hard for nonchalance, he tucked it under his arm and wandered toward the old ghoul's war-construct, which stood motionless with its canopy open.

He glanced over his shoulder. Naumoriel was still staring at the river, ignoring Kit's chattered questions. Gyre stepped closer to the construct, which was hunched on its legs far enough that he could see into its central cavity. His hasty recollection had been correct—there was a space behind the ghoul's padded seat, big enough to fit the bomb. Naumoriel, Gyre guessed, was unlikely to find it—from the look of things, he didn't move about the construct much.

For a moment, Gyre hesitated. He watched Naumoriel sitting with Kit and felt a stab of guilt. *He hasn't betrayed us yet. Maybe he never will.* He repeated again the list of all those who'd already sacrificed to build the road to the power Gyre wanted. Yora and Harrow, Chosen knew how many others. Sarah, mangled and burned. *Maya, turned into a willing slave.* He touched his face, the new scars laid over the old around his silver eye. *Me.*

Is it worth it?

In one quick movement, he leaned over, lowered the bomb to the floor of the construct, and wedged it in place. He quickly stepped away, and waited a few seconds before looking at Naumoriel. The old ghoul gave no sign he'd noticed, still staring down the river.

Maybe we won't need it. Maybe Naumoriel would fulfill his side of the bargain. *But if not, then at least we'll have an option.*

Late that evening, when Kit slipped into his tent, he told her what he'd done. She kissed him and called him brilliant before she went for his trousers again. After an enthusiastic interval, she fell asleep by his side, nestled in the crook of his arm. She looked younger when she was sleeping, without the swagger and the cocky smile, pale skin smooth and broken by a dozen small scars, body lithe and muscled, with only the barest hint of breasts and curves. He worked his fingers into her short blue hair, and she grumbled and shifted in her sleep.

The kind of partners who spend time naked together. Gyre smiled at her description. *Is that what we are?*

Eventually, he fell asleep. In the morning, Naumoriel led them past the junction of the nameless river with another, and they clambered over a field of rocks to enter a valley, now moving upstream. Not long after, it became clear to Gyre that their real journey had only just started.

"Duck!" Kit shouted.

Gyre threw himself flat. A blaster bolt crackled overhead, detonating against a looming plaguespawn the size of a bear. The explosion tore off a long limb, halfway between an arm and a tentacle, which held one of the soldier-constructs in a death grip. Another pair of constructs hacked at the thing from behind, severing enough of its many legs that it toppled sideways with a wet-sounding bellow.

One down. There had been two of the giants in the horde of bone-and-muscle monstrosities, standing out among their smaller brethren like boulders in a sea of pebbles. Gyre had never seen a plaguespawn that large, nor had he ever heard of the things attacking in vast packs. Since they'd passed into the hidden valley, all the usual rules had apparently gone out the window.

This stretch of riverbank was a mass of struggling constructs and plaguespawn, two sets of inhuman creatures animated by *dhaka* striving to tear each other to pieces. The constructs were bigger and stronger, with stone-and-metal plating covered in spikes and blades, and individually they were more than a match for the haphazard monsters. But there were so *many* plaguespawn, dozens of smaller creatures backed up by a few of the larger varieties, including these latest monsters taller than Gyre. Four times so far the wave of fleshy things had descended on them, and four times they'd fought their way free, but the constructs were falling one by one, pulled down like lions fighting packs of dogs.

This fifth attack was the worst yet. At first, Gyre had barely had to draw his sword. Now he and Kit fought for their lives alongside Naumoriel and his inhuman creations.

Naumoriel himself, in his enormous war-construct, grappled with the second giant plaguespawn. One of his claw-arms had sliced deep into its body, but the thing had thrown several other limbs around it, and the ghoul couldn't get free. His other claw snapped and dodged, keeping back a dozen reaching tendrils trying to pry open his canopy.

Fucking plaguefire. Gyre concentrated and felt the *click* from his skull. The energy bottle at his side grew warm, and the struggling constructs were wreathed in layers of shadow. The silver sword buzzed in his hand, and he sprinted toward Naumoriel with long, loping strides.

There were a dozen smaller plaguespawn separating them. A construct was dogpiled under three of them, struggling to rise. Gyre fell on them like a whirlwind, his sword lashing out on neatly plotted trajectories to intersect the monsters' makeshift bodies with maximum violence. One of the three came apart at one blow, separated into two shuddering halves, and the second lurched away missing most of its inside-out head. The third swung at him with broad claws, but Gyre felt like he had all the time in the world to duck under them, shadows passing over his head. He thrust his sword up into the thing's guts, then twisted it to let stolen viscera gush out.

More of them came at him, two or three together, working side by side with unnatural coordination. Only his speed and the shadows projected by his silver eye kept him safe, while the ghoul blade he wielded was sharper and lighter than it had any right to be. He left wreckage in his wake as he closed in on the remaining giant.

One of the larger stone-constructs stumbled in front of him, crushing a struggling plaguespawn between its outstretched hands. Gyre swarmed up it, gripping its rocky surface with his free hand and pulling himself onto its shoulders. From there, without pausing, he leapt for the plaguespawn's back, sword outthrust to make a handhold. For a moment he hung there, the thing's muscle shifting and rubbery under his fingers. Then he started to climb, boots slipping, using his sword to brace himself. By the time he got to the top of the thing, its tentacles were reaching for him. He dropped into a crouch and intercepted them, one by one, drawing a neat line across their shadow-path and sending them spinning away.

Free of the need to defend itself, Naumoriel's construct gathered its strength and went on the offensive, giving the plaguespawn a shove that nearly sent Gyre toppling off. As it staggered, the construct thrust its other clawed arm into the core of the thing, blades cutting into a massive clutch of eyes. Black blood gushed forth, and the plaguespawn weaved drunkenly, its legs spasming. Gyre jumped clear, hit the ground in a roll, and popped back up, looking for his next opponent, only to find none remaining.

"Kit!" He looked around for the familiar shock of blue hair. "Kit, are you all right?"

Finally he spotted her, one arm waving to him from the other side of a downed construct. Gyre sheathed his sword and switched off his augmented perception with a *click*. A glance at his energy bottle showed that it was nearly empty—he'd brought four with him, and this was the second he'd exhausted in these fights.

He found Kit with her saber laid across her knees, back to the construct's mutilated body, breathing hard. She was covered in blood, both black and alarmingly red, the latter coming from a slash across her midsection and another on her biceps.

"Chosen defend," Gyre said, kneeling to help her. "Can you stand?"

"Yeah." She waved her free hand vaguely, panting. "Not as bad as it looks. Just. Winded." She touched her stomach and winced, her fingers coming away sticky. "Ow."

"Hang on." Gyre bent closer, peering at the wound. "That needs stitching and quickheal, at least."

"Not sure our taskmaster will give us the time." Kit nodded at Naumoriel's war-construct, which had shaken itself free of the dying plaguespawn. Other constructs, in obedience to his silent instructions, were forming up, ready to continue the march.

"Plague that." Gyre took Kit's hand and pulled her to her feet, sending a fresh wash of blood into her already sodden shirt. They walked together over to Naumoriel. "Hey!" Gyre said.

"Humans," Naumoriel's distorted voice answered. "We proceed up the valley."

"Kit's hurt," Gyre said. "She needs to rest. Plague, *I* need to rest."

"We have no time." One smaller arm waved at the assembled constructs. There were less than a dozen left. "Our forces are depleted. The plaguespawn will return. We must reach the head of the valley. If she cannot continue, leave her."

"No," Gyre said. "She comes with us. You promised you'd help her, once we finish this."

"If we delay, none of us will survive."

Gyre thought of the remote trigger, buried in his pack, and gritted his teeth. "Then, do something about it!"

The canopy opened. The construct's two smaller arms reached in and brought Naumoriel down to ground level, holding him face-to-face with Gyre.

"There is a limit," the old ghoul said, "to the insolence I will tolerate from your kind."

"You're welcome to leave me behind, too," Gyre said. "But you won't, will you?" He tapped the brow above his silver eye. "You gave me this because you knew we'd need it to get here."

"Do not overestimate your importance. I was merely determined to make use of every available resource." He sighed. "However, given our depleted state, I cannot deny your contribution. Here."

He extended a hand and placed it on Kit's forehead. She gasped, and Gyre watched the long cut on her stomach knot and close, as though it had never been. Naumoriel withdrew, and the construct's tentacles lifted him up again.

"Conserve your energy as much as you can," the ghoul said. "I do not have much left to spare if you run low."

"I will." Gyre inclined his head. "Thank you."

"We proceed." Naumoriel looked up the valley, then over his shoulder. "We are nearly there, but we do not have much time."

As his canopy resealed and the war-construct stalked off, Gyre bent beside Kit. "Doing all right?"

"Yeah." She pressed her hand to her stomach. "That was . . . weird." She looked up at him and swallowed. "Thanks. You could have let him leave me."

"Partners, right?"

"Right." Kit grinned. "Nearly there, he said?"

"Let's hope."

This valley was much like the other, scrub grass and small trees, but there was no sign of any goats or rabbits, no animals larger than an insect. That was hardly a mystery, though, given the plaguespawn. The ground sloped steadily upward, sometimes in rocky patches they had to scramble past, which the ghoul constructs handled with surprising agility.

They skirted an outcrop of boulders, where the valley's little stream burbled into a broad pool, and found themselves looking at a flat wall of rock, perhaps a half kilometer off across a stretch of scrub grass. Above it, a mountain rose steeply to a jagged, snowcapped peak.

"There it is." Even distorted by his construct, Gyre could hear the satisfaction in Naumoriel's voice. "At last."

"It, um. Doesn't look like much," Kit said.

"There is a door into the mountain," Naumoriel said. "I will open it."

"I think you should hurry," Gyre said, looking over his shoulder.

Plaguespawn crowded the valley behind them. There were dozens, *hundreds* of the twisted things, in every possible size and shape, bones and muscles and eyes combined at the whim of a mad sculptor and brought to horrifying, shuddering life. The largest of the beasts glided through the swarm, the others parting around them like a silent wake. Gyre counted two—three—*five* of them, each the size of Naumoriel's war-construct, walking on multiple legs with long, twisted arms wrapped in skeins of bone armor.

"We can't fight that," Gyre said.

"We do not have to," Naumoriel said. He still sounded calm. "We only have to reach the door. Now, run."

Gyre met Kit's eyes, and they ran.

The war-construct was slow to accelerate, but it gradually picked up speed, legs moving in a blur as it stomped through the grass. Gyre put his head down, arms pumping, but he felt the upward slope cutting into his pace. Kit darted ahead of him, lighter on her feet. The remaining constructs brought up the rear.

The plaguespawn came after them like a horde of locusts. The fastest took the lead, bounding like wolves. Teeth clattered and gnashed, and claws of splintered bone unfolded. Four of Naumoriel's constructs peeled off and threw themselves in the path of the leading monsters, smashing the lightly built plaguespawn to bits, but the lead wave simply parted around them to continue the pursuit. A few moments later, one of the giants arrived, its huge claws cracking rock and metal to tear the constructs asunder.

Halfway there. Gyre was falling behind, Naumoriel's construct surging ahead like a runaway wagon, Kit hard on its heels. He concentrated, and with a *click* in his skull the world went slow and shadowy. His steps became leaps, as though gravity had gotten lazy.

Another seven constructs turned and planted themselves in the path of the plaguespawn, leaving only a pair beside Naumoriel. The war-construct had nearly reached the wall, and it planted its legs stiffly and slewed to a halt less than a meter from the rock. Its tentacle-arm brought up a small, flat-ended device that Gyre recognized as a ghoul code-key, like the one Kit had used to open the way to the destabilizer. Naumoriel pressed the thing against the wall, and something deep inside shuddered to life. The ground shook under Gyre's feet.

Slowly—too slowly—the rock began to part. Kit turned and started firing her blaster at plaguespawn only moments behind them, blowing three of them apart before her sunsplinter went dry and the weapon emitted only a thin whine. Gyre drew his sword, watching the shadow-paths of the coursing monsters multiplying like a wave.

"Inside!" Naumoriel bellowed. He'd turned his war-construct around, swinging its massive claws in horizontal arcs that sent the broken bodies of plaguespawn tumbling. "Now!"

Kit needed no urging. She holstered her blaster and ran for it, darting between the legs of the war-construct and through the gap in the rock. Gyre went after her, ducking under the swipe of a claw as it left shadow-trails across his vision. It was dark beyond the door, but his silver eye showed him a vast, high-ceilinged space, and—

He was on his knees. *What?* There was a *click*, and the world of shadow-lines faded. Then the vision from his silver eye went black, leaving him with only the thin line of daylight from the doors behind them.

"Gyre?" Kit skidded to a halt. "Gyre, what's wrong?"

I...I can't... He couldn't move, as though his limbs were lined with lead. Couldn't speak. Unconsciousness beckoned, like a deep, black sea.

"Naumoriel!" Kit said.

Dimly, Gyre saw the war-construct back through the door. With a grinding crunch, the rock face abruptly reversed its motion, the huge slabs sliding closed again. Naumoriel's claws smashed the plaguespawn that threw themselves at the gap, driving them back, and his two surviving constructs handled anything that got past their master. A moment later, the doors closed, with a spurt of black blood from the desperate plaguespawn caught in the gap.

"Naumoriel!" Kit shouted. "Something's wrong with Gyre!"

"I expect his energy bottle is exhausted," the ghoul said as his war-construct turned delicately about. "Replace it."

Gyre fought for consciousness as Kit rummaged in his pack. He felt her pull the bottle away from his side and fasten another to the strap on his belt. As soon as it was close enough to his skin, it grew warm, and he could feel power flowing into him. His silver eye flickered to life again, pushing back the darkness.

"Gyre?" Kit said, standing back. "Are you okay?"

Gyre tried to speak and nearly vomited. He swallowed hard, nodded, and pushed himself to his feet, swaying a little.

"I'm…" He swallowed again. "All right. I should have switched that out earlier."

"I didn't realize it would hit you so badly," Kit said, handing him the exhausted bottle. Its glow was totally dead.

"Neither did I," Gyre said. "Remind me not to do that again." He took a long breath, stomach settling. "Are you okay?"

"So far." She rummaged in her pouch and came up with a vial of nighteye, adding a drop to each of her eyes. After blinking for a moment, she stared around with huge, dark pupils. "Wow. This place is…big."

"It is unique," Naumoriel said. "We had never attempted anything like it before, and certainly nothing like it has been constructed since." The canopy of his war-construct popped open, and he took a deep breath of the cold, dusty air. His undistorted voice echoed from the distant walls. "Welcome to the Leviathan's Womb."

Chapter 24

Maya had never traveled into the Shattered Peak mountains, except for her brief foray to Deepfire, but from everything she'd heard she expected it to be a difficult and dangerous affair. They'd agreed that speed was of the essence, so she'd used the bulk of her travel funds to buy three swiftbirds in Grace, and stocked up on supplies and maps to supplement Marn's mumbled directions. Unlike the crossing from Uqaris, once they were away from Grace, the land was sparsely populated, so she and Tanax could protect the party from plaguespawn without risking exposure as centarchs. When they'd ridden out through Grace's considerably less busy northern gate, just skirting the unmetal hull of *Grace in Execution*, Maya had prepared herself for a rigorous trip.

Instead, if anything, the journey had become more pleasant as they went along. The foothills of the mountains rose rapidly north of Grace, and they left the stifling heat of the plains behind. Maya's swiftbird was a friendly, biddable creature named Blackbar for the color of her tail feathers, and her long, loping pace devoured the distance and coped easily with the rocky ground. Contrary to their name, swiftbirds were slower than a warbird over short distances, but they had much greater endurance, and Blackbar seemed to be able to maintain her steady stride indefinitely.

With the maps and a little guesswork, Maya surmised it was a five-day ride to the place Marn had specified, the foot of a tiny nameless valley at the bottom of a jagged mountain called Cracktooth. Away from the main passes, the map grew vague, but according to Marn all they had to do was find the outlet of a certain stream and follow it as it wound its way upward. Finding the *right* stream, in a mountain range full of little creeks fed by snowmelt, might be a challenge, but Maya was determined to try.

In any event, that was for the fifth day. Until then, they rode quietly up wooded hillsides, following animal tracks or bare ridges where they could, and pushing through the forest when there was no other way. It never grew so dense that they were really troubled, nor steep enough that it bothered the birds, and if there were plaguespawn in the area they didn't show themselves. The latter, in fact, became almost eerie—Maya had done most of her traveling in the Republic, but based on everything she'd read and heard, they should have encountered at least a *few* of the awful creatures. When she mentioned it to Tanax, he only shrugged.

"Maybe they all migrate down toward Grace," he offered, "where there are more humans to eat? Or maybe someone came through and hunted them out recently."

However safe the woods seemed, they still used Tanax's watch charm whenever they camped, relying on the little device to give warning if their luck ran out. Maya cooked vulpi bacon and griddle cakes over a campfire while Beq and Tanax erected the tents. With mountains to the west, sunset came early, and they went to sleep as the first stars twinkled overhead.

Tanax went to sleep, in any event. Maya and Beq experimented, gently. The reality of it—skin against skin, soft gasps in the dark, the little whining noise Beq made in the back of her throat when she neared her peak—was different from Maya's nocturnal fantasies, slower and more complicated but infinitely sweeter. Falling asleep with the warm weight of Beq in her arms made her wish, full of guilt, that the journey would never end.

We need to help Jaedia, Maya told herself firmly. *We'll bring her back to the Forge and tell everyone what happened. And then Beq and I can... go on together.* She wasn't sure exactly what form that would take, but she had never wanted any future more.

Blearily, Maya reached for her canteen, and swore very quietly when she found it empty.

It was well after dark, and Beq lay beside her, sound asleep. Maya extricated herself, carefully, and crawled to the tent flap. The moon was high, and she blinked in the silver light, skin pebbling in the cool mountain air.

They'd camped beside a stream, and Maya shuffled over to it, empty canteen in hand. She was surprised to find Tanax sitting cross-legged on a nearby rock, looking up at the stars wheeling over the darkened mountains. Maya cleared her throat.

"Is something wrong?" she said.

"Just having trouble sleeping," Tanax said.

"Bad dreams?"

"More like... regrets." Tanax leaned back and sighed. "I keep thinking I should have seen through Nicomidi long before this. If I'd only noticed..."

"You were obeying your master's orders." Maya knelt by the stream and let water glug into her canteen. "Nobody can fault you for that."

"I was his *agathios*. I knew him as well as anyone did. I think back to things he did, things he said, and try to figure out... why, I suppose."

"And?" Maya straightened up.

"And I still don't understand," Tanax said. "Nicomidi was... distant. Stern, maybe. Uncompromising. But what he taught me, to always act in accordance with the principles of the Order, he lived that himself. He thought the Pragmatics were wrong, but he never talked about them like the enemy." Tanax did his best to mask it, but Maya could hear the pain in his voice. "If you'd asked me a month ago, I would have said there was no one less likely to betray the Order."

"I'm sorry," Maya said quietly.

"We'll find him, if he's with Jaedia," Tanax said. "And when we do, he's going to explain to me exactly what he was thinking. I have to... understand, at least. Or else..." He shrugged. "That's why I had to come with you. It seemed like the best chance of getting an answer."

"I think the Council would like some answers, too," Maya said. "Personally, I'll be happy as long as we get Jaedia back."

"Of course," Tanax said. "I won't lose sight of that, I promise."

He paused as Maya turned back to her tent, then spoke up again.

"You and Arcanist Bequaria, eh?"

"So?" Maya challenged. "Are you planning another lecture on Order propriety?"

"When did I lecture you on Order propriety?"

"In Deepfire, you accused us of sneaking out to a brothel."

"I did, didn't I?" Tanax shook his head. "I was..."

"Being an ass?" Maya suggested.

"I was going to say 'unkind.'" He sighed. "Worse than that. I was acting exactly as my master had taught me to act: completely certain of my own moral superiority. He'd told me that you'd been sent by the Pragmatics to ruin the mission, and I was so sure..." He shook his head again. "I'm not sure of anything anymore."

"If it helps, Jaedia told me the same thing about you. Nobody's infallible."

"I suppose not." Tanax gave a dark chuckle and climbed to his feet, stretching. "I should try to sleep. We must be getting close."

"Yes," Maya acknowledged. "Almost there."

"Are you sure this is it?" Tanax said.

Maya shaded her eyes and looked at the little stream, which descended from a cluster of rocks to join with a slightly larger creek and continue winding out of the mountains. The valley stretching up behind it, narrow and stony, looked like a hundred others they'd passed.

"No," Maya said honestly. "But if Marn's directions are right, this is the most likely spot." She sighed. "I wish we had some sign Jaedia came this way. We should have nearly caught up to her by now."

Beq twisted the dials on her spectacles, looking at the mountain that overshadowed the valley like a blue-white bank of grounded cloud. "It doesn't look like it goes too far, anyway," she said. "If we don't find anything, we can backtrack without losing more than a day." She glanced wistfully at their mounts, which were tethered to a scraggly tree a little ways off, pecking at the sparse grass. "We'll have to leave the birds, though. They'd never get through those rocks."

"We'll leave the tents and heavy gear with them," Maya decided. "If we're in the wrong place, we can be back here by nightfall."

"Assuming our luck with plaguespawn continues," Tanax said.

Swiftbirds were big and mean enough to handle a small plaguespawn, but a large one might scatter them, and there was no telling if they'd find their way back. Maya frowned, but there was nothing for it. "We'll have to take the risk. Worse comes to worst, we won't starve before we can walk back to Grace."

Tanax pondered a moment, then nodded agreement. They divested themselves of their heavy packs, leaving them in a pile beside the birds under a staked-down blanket. Maya broke open a bag of feed and scattered it on the ground in front of Blackbar and the other two, and soon they were pecking contentedly. She checked her gear—panoply belt, haken, a small pack with a few emergency supplies—and took a long breath of cool mountain air.

Here we are. Hopefully. Jaedia could be just ahead, along with Nicomidi and Chosen knew what else. Maya stared up the rock slope, mind racing, then gave a start as Beq slipped a hand into hers.

"We'll find her," Beq said quietly.

"Yeah." Maya squeezed her fingers. "Thanks."

After a short scramble, the valley leveled out into a steady uphill trudge broken by a few stretches of tumbled rocks. The sun climbed as they walked, but the air stayed cool. Everything was still and silent—so silent, in fact, that Maya started to worry. They'd surprised the occasional mountain goat or rabbit pretty regularly throughout their journey, but here—

"Plaguespawn!" Tanax hissed, hand dropping to his haken.

"Where?" Maya said.

"There!" Beq pointed, twisting the dials of her lenses.

Maya caught the flash of motion. A dark, asymmetrical shape loped over the ground a few hundred meters ahead, two long, canine heads rimmed with broken bones. But it was sprinting *away*, not charging them. As she watched, it disappeared over the rocks.

"That's...odd," she said.

"It must have been chasing something else," Tanax muttered. "An animal, maybe."

"Plaguespawn prefer humans to animals," Beq said.

"Which means we may not be alone out here," Maya said.

"You think it was going after Jaedia and Nicomidi?" Tanax said.

Maya shrugged. "If so, they can handle a few plaguespawn."

It wasn't long after that they started hearing thunder, rippling *booms* echoing down the valley. Maya squinted and thought she could see flashes reflecting off the rocks.

"That could be Nicomidi," Tanax said. The Kyriliarch's cognomen, Maya recalled, was Thunderclap.

"It sounds...too regular," Beq said, peering ahead. "Like blaster fire."

"Centarchs don't need blasters," Maya said. Uncertainty fluttered in her chest. "Let's hurry."

The booms eventually stopped, but by then there was no longer any doubt what was happening ahead of them. They passed the first battleground, strewn with plaguespawn corpses. Some of the monsters had been shattered by blaster bolts, others cut and torn with raw force. Maya didn't think any of them bore the clean-edged cuts she would have expected if Jaedia had unleashed her powers.

"What in the name of the Chosen is going *on*?" Tanax said. "I've never *heard* of this many plaguespawn in one place. And look at the size of that one!" He kicked the flank of a bear-sized monstrosity, limbs slackened in death. It looked as through it had been torn apart by another beast on the same scale.

"Some of these are strange, too," Beq said. She prodded another corpse carefully. "Look. No blood, and it's covered in... rock, I think?"

"*Dhakim*," Maya muttered. "I knew Cyrtak wasn't at the center of this. There must be another one directing the plaguespawn."

"How powerful does a *dhakim* need to be to pull together this many?" Tanax said.

"That depends on a lot of factors," Beq said. "It's not even clear if a *dhakim*'s reach scales linearly with some kind of overall ability, or if—"

"We have no idea, you mean," Tanax interrupted.

"Basically." Beq swallowed. "But if you want my guess—"

"Stronger than Cyrtak," Maya said. "A lot stronger."

They pushed on, past more places where bodies of plaguespawn had piled up in drifts. Whoever the monsters were fighting, they were certainly giving a good account of themselves. *It has to be Jaedia and Nicomidi, doesn't it? Only a centarch could kill this many plaguespawn.* But Cyrtak had said Jaedia was working *with* the *dhakim*. Maya ran her fingers through her hair in frustration, gritted her teeth, and kept climbing. Midday came and went, but no one suggested turning back. Whatever was happening in this remote valley, it was clearly the place they'd come to find.

The mountain, Cracktooth, loomed ever larger. It did look a bit like a broken tooth, with a gentler slope on the far side but a sheer cliff on the face abutting the valley, rising to a rectangular summit. Passing another drift of plaguespawn, Maya spotted a rock formation that blocked half the valley, with the little stream curling around its base. She was about to suggest they climb it for a better view when Beq darted forward, adjusting her spectacles.

"There's someone up there!" she said. "Two people, I think." She shook her head. "They're behind the rocks now, but I'm sure I saw them." She glanced at Maya, who nodded and looked at Tanax. Then, together, they broke into a run.

A narrow path led up the side of the rocky outcrop, opening onto a wide, relatively flat space atop it. As Maya had predicted, it gave an excellent view of most of the valley, across a broad plain of scrub grass, to the face of the mountain.

The sight of the plain took her breath away. It was *covered* with plaguespawn, hundreds of them, maybe thousands, a sea of raw, rippling muscles and shattered bone, misshapen monstrosities in every possible variety. A half dozen of the twisted giants were at the forefront, against the wall of rock, staring at a single spot where the grass was buried under a pile of plaguespawn corpses. Maya realized that *every* plaguespawn in that vast swarm was doing the same, focused as rigidly as soldiers on parade. As though they were all part of one vast creature, and whatever was there had its undivided attention.

It took Maya a moment to drag her gaze away from the plaguespawn army and focus on the two human figures standing by the edge of the rock outcrop, also looking down into the field. There was a man and a woman, wearing fur-lined leather mountain coats, each carrying a haken on one hip. Beneath the woman's hood, Maya saw the familiar green of Jaedia's hair, lighter than Beq's.

Jaedia and Nicomidi. Standing side by side, without a care in the world, as if they weren't enemies. Maya put one hand on her haken and drew on *deiat*, threading it into her panoply. She could sense Tanax doing likewise, and Nicomidi must have felt it as well, because he turned to face them, taking hold of his own weapon. Jaedia didn't move.

The Kyriliarch seemed to have aged a decade since Maya had last seen him, his thin face worn and unshaven, his eyes deep set with fatigue. A variety of emotions flitted across his features when he saw them—surprise, anger, and finally resignation. The smile he put on when he stepped forward was unconvincing.

"Well, Jaedia, you were right," he said. "Your agathios has come to find us at last. But she brought some unexpected company."

Jaedia remained still, facing the mass of plaguespawn. Tanax took a step forward.

"The Council has declared her an agathios no longer," he said. "She is Centarch Maya Burningblade, as I am Centarch Tanax Brokenedge."

"Of course they have," Nicomidi said. "Without me, I'm sure Baselanthus the coward and Prodominus the dotard have had things all their own way." He strolled forward. "I expected this stupidity from Maya, Tanax, but not from you. What are you doing here?"

"What am *I* doing here?" Tanax shook his head. "You were the one who taught me that loyalty to the Order comes before any other considerations. How could you just throw that away?"

"I'm sorry you were such a poor student," Nicomidi said. "Our loyalty isn't to the Order. It is to the *ideals* of the Order, to the *Inheritance*. Above all, to the Chosen, who have always guided our steps."

Maya tore her eyes away from Jaedia's still form and focused on Nicomidi. "The Chosen are dead and gone."

"That is where you're wrong," Nicomidi said. "They live, hidden from mortal sight. Waiting only for us to make the preparations for their glorious return."

"People have been searching for any hint of the Chosen for centuries," Beq said, stepping up behind Maya. "They've never found anything. How do you know they're still alive?"

"Because," Nicomidi said, spreading his arms, "they speak to me." He gestured over his shoulder. "This place, this mountain, is the last stronghold of the ghouls. The last remnant of their power. Once it is destroyed, the way will be clear at last for the return of our masters. The Republic and the Order have served their purpose. Now we will return to a golden age."

"He's mad," Beq muttered.

"He's a Kyriliarch," Maya said. "Be careful."

Tanax, ignoring her, took another step forward, putting him face-to-face with his former master. "I need the truth," he grated. "Did you try to make me kill Maya, in the arena?"

"What if I did?" Nicomidi looked at Maya, and his lip curled. "She was a danger to the plan."

"There was . . . no honor in that." Tanax took a deep breath. "Kyriliarch Nicomidi, you have committed treason against the Twilight Order. I am detaining you in the name of—"

"I should have known better," Nicomidi snarled, "than to argue with *children*."

He drew his haken and attacked in the same smooth motion, a single sideways cut so fast the eye could barely follow. His blade, a blue-gray ripple in the air, slashed across Tanax's chest, and an ear-splitting *boom* rang out, fading away to a rumble like distant thunder. Tanax's panoply flared, blue-white and too bright to look at, but the force of the blow still picked him up and sent him tumbling across the rock.

Maya snatched her own haken from her side, blade igniting with a crackle. "Beq!" she said. "Help Tanax!"

"Throw down the weapon, *Centarch*, and I won't have to hurt you." Nicomidi returned his haken to his side, bending his knees into an expectant crouch. "For reasons I don't understand, your master wants you alive."

"Jaedia," Maya said. "Stop this. Please."

Jaedia, still looking down at the plaguespawn, did not respond.

"He's all right," Beq said, coming up behind Maya again. "The panoply held."

"All right," Maya said. "Ready?"

Beq gave a tight nod.

"I am a Kyriliarch of the Council," Nicomidi said. "Do you really intend to measure your power against mine?"

In answer, Maya blasted him with a wash of flame.

Nicomidi snarled. A shield of rippling energy hung in front of him for a moment, and then he was coming forward at a run. Wild ripples of twisted air detonated around Maya, blasting her with ear-splitting sound from every direction. Beq screamed, nearly inaudible in the tumult. It was all Maya could do to focus in time to see Nicomidi draw his haken, his strike as fast as thought, cutting across his body. Her own blade was clumsy by comparison, moving to parry far too late, and in desperation she threw herself backward. She cannoned into Beq and sent them both stumbling to the rock. Nicomidi skidded to a halt, straightened up, and returned his haken to his side.

"I'm impressed," he said. "You're not bad. In another thirty years, you might be a match for me." Smiling, he sank into a crouch again. "However."

Chosen defend, he's fast. That single strike, too powerful to stop, too quick to parry. *Thunderclap.* His cognomen suddenly made grim sense.

"Maya," Beq hissed as Maya pushed herself up. "I'll distract him."

Maya gave a tiny nod, levered herself back up, and reignited her haken. Nicomidi sank deeper into his crouch, shifting on the balls of his feet. Before he could move, Beq suddenly rolled onto her stomach, sighting down the barrel of her blaster. The *crack* of the bolt rang in Maya's ears. Nicomidi snatched his haken and intercepted it, then blocked another. By then Maya was already moving.

The Kyriliarch brought his haken around, stopping her downward cut, and lashed out with *deiat*. Maya countered, twisting lines of fire breaking up his sonic bombs as they formed, strikes and counterstrikes surrounding them like a duel of multiheaded snakes as blade slammed against blade. Maya pushed Nicomidi backward, putting all her strength into the blows, not giving him time to recover. His speed was astonishing, but she found that his footwork was weak, his parries predictable. A grin spread across her face. *You've been winning too many fights with that first strike.*

Nicomidi's expression darkened into a scowl as he retreated, searching for a chance to counterattack and not finding it. His *deiat* tendrils retreated for a moment, and Maya hesitated, suspecting a trap. Nicomidi used that chance to leap backward, lashing out at the rock at his feet. A blast of twisted air detonated, strong enough to shatter the stone and send splinters spraying in all directions. Maya's panoply flared, and she heard Beq grunt. Before Maya could recover, Nicomidi had turned in Beq's direction, sending a rolling wave of detonations toward her. Maya reached out desperately, throwing fire, but not fast enough—

The blasts stopped, blocked by a wall of eye-twisting folds in space. Tanax, breathing hard, stood over Beq, his distorted blade in hand.

"You are going to drop your weapon," he said, stepping forward. "And you are going to tell us everything. About Raskos, about Jaedia, about your plans and what you think you heard from the Chosen. *Everything.*"

"You arrogant little *plaguepit*," Nicomidi spat. "You have no idea what you're interfering with."

Maya looked to Beq, who'd rolled onto her side. She was speckled with blood all over, with a large patch on her thigh, and she had her hands pressed against the wound. When Maya's eyes found hers, though, Beq gave a fierce nod. Maya raised her haken and stepped up beside Tanax.

"Fine, then," Nicomidi said. "Come and die."

They attacked. The Kyriliarch's speed was unearthly, his weapon shifting from side to side like a snowflake on the wind, but it wasn't enough. Maya and Tanax moved automatically to either side of him, without a word exchanged, forcing Nicomidi to retreat or be surrounded. He lashed out with *deiat*, and they parried and pushed back, bursts of flame and twisted space pressing rapidly inward against a line of crackling concussions. Nicomidi's panoply started to flare in blue-white bursts as one of Maya's blows scored, then one of Tanax's. A blast of flame slipped through his defenses and caught him full in the face, and when the searing light faded, the Kyriliarch was on his knees.

"Jaedia!" His voice was hoarse. "Will you *control* your fucking student if you want her so badly?"

And then, at last, Jaedia turned. Maya's throat went thick at the sight of her face, framed by the fur-lined hood, calm as ever, wearing a slight smile. She came forward, stepping lightly, not reaching for the haken at her side.

"You seem to be in difficulty," she said to Nicomidi in her lilting, musical accent.

"We cannot fail," Nicomidi grated. "Not here. Not when we're so close."

"I agree." Jaedia caught Maya's eye and winked. Maya fought a desperate grin. *She's on our side, this has all been some plan, we found her in time—*

"Then *do something*," the Kyriliarch shouted.

Jaedia stepped up beside Nicomidi, laid one gentle hand against his cheek, and turned him inside out.

He barely had time to scream. His skin split wide open, bones *cracking* audibly, as his body twisted in ways it was never meant to. His viscera dropped away, making a bloody puddle on the rocks, and his muscles wove and knotted themselves into new patterns. Limbs, with broken ribs protruding from them like spikes. *Plaguespawn.*

"I'm afraid his company has grown-*grown* quite tiresome lately," Jaedia said. Her voice was pleasant, but with a strange tic, as a word repeated in a different tone as though someone had stitched two parts of a sentence together. Maya's mind went back to a basement under Bastion, a lifetime ago. The realization must have showed on her face, because Jaedia smiled and pulled down her hood. Something *squirmed* at the back of her neck, a black spider with its legs wrapped around her throat and its fangs buried in her flesh. "I told you we'd meet-*meet* again, little *sha'deia.*"

"Maya?" Tanax said, staring at the pulsing, bloody thing that had been his master. "What the *fuck* is going on?"

"That's not Jaedia," Maya said, retreating a step.

"To be more precise, it is Jaedia's body-*body.*" Jaedia stepped forward, her head moving with a sudden jerk as she looked from one of them to the other. "Jaedia's mind, Jaedia's mem-*memories.* Jaedia is just no longer in charge."

"Who *are* you?" Maya whispered.

"*I* am nothing. A copy. An instrument." Jaedia put her hand on the fleshy mess at her feet and stroked it lovingly. "A better question is, who are *you*?"

"If you have Jaedia's memories, you know that," Maya said.

"Ah, but do you?" Jaedia smiled wider. "You-*you* have no idea of the trouble you've caused, little *sha'deia*, or the lengths I've had to go to keep-*keep* you alive when you insist on sticking your nose where it doesn't belong. And you *do* like to interfere, don't you? In Bastion you forced me to ruin a perfectly good body. In Deepfire you kept the Core Analytica out of my hands. You can't leave-*leave* well enough alone."

"What is a *sha'deia*?" Tanax said. "Why would you want to keep her alive?"

"She is an experiment," Jaedia said. She tapped her chest, and Maya followed suit automatically with her free hand, feeling the hard lump of the Thing. Something flickered in her mind, shredded flashes of a dream, and her eyes widened. Jaedia went on. "An experiment that has-*has* not yet produced a result, and preserving that has some value. However. I think-*think* it has reached the end of its usefulness."

All at once, the mass of muscle and bone that had been Nicomidi twisted and *sprang*, long tentacular limbs hurling it up toward Jaedia. It opened, more bones cracking, and wrapped itself around her torso like a suit of armor, two extra arms of coiled meat extending from her shoulders. Blood sprayed and spattered, coating Jaedia's clothing in crimson.

Tanax brought up his hand, sending a wave of twisted, shredding force at the Jaedia-thing. She spun lithely aside, and one long tentacle stretched. He slashed down at it with his haken, and it wove out of the way of the blade, rippling muscle whipping it into his stomach in a blow strong enough to send him spinning away and rolling back over the stones.

Maya raised her haken and charged, and another tentacle lashed out at her. She ducked under the blow, blood spattering her hair, and carved through the thing, closing with Jaedia. Her mentor, still grinning, shifted and lashed out at Beq with a second tendril. Maya checked her attack and threw herself sideways, haken cutting down to sever that limb too, but the tentacle reversed course and slammed into her, making her panoply flare. She coughed, winded, and reached out with *deiat*, fire blooming around her in a tight spiral. Flesh crackled and charred, but not fast enough—the groping tips of the tendril wrapped around her right hand, prying her fingers apart and prizing the haken from her grip. With a flick, they tossed it away, and the flames winked out.

"This is the problem with you-*you* centarchs," Jaedia said. Her tentacle lifted Maya by her wrist before her, the tips of her toes dangling inches off the ground. "Your strength, ultimately, comes-*comes* from the outside. For all your power-*power*, it leaves you vulnerable." Jaedia brought Maya up to her, face-to-face, and raised her real arm to touch her cheek. "I learned that more than four hundred years ago."

"Jaedia." Maya's voice was a croak. "Don't . . . do this. Please."

"Oh, dear. Begging for your old-*old* master. How tragic." Jaedia ran her finger down Maya's cheek, and Maya could feel the muscles jumping and twitching in its wake, as though eager to rip themselves away from the bone. "Perhaps next you'll cry for your mother." She shook her head. "This experiment has gone-*gone* on long enough. You are not the one I am looking for."

"Jaedia." Maya stared at the bright green eyes. "Please. Stop this."

"I told you to *give up*," Jaedia said. She pressed her hand against Maya's temple. "I was going to stop your heart first, out of respect. But now I think I'll keep you alive while I . . . repurpose you."

Please. Maya had no more breath, but her lips formed the word.

Jaedia held her palm against Maya's skull, and a long moment passed. Slowly, the vicious smile faded from her lips.

"No-*no*," she muttered. Her head jerked one way, then the other. "Not-*not*-NOT possible."

The tendril holding Maya's arm peeled back, opening like a flower. She hit the ground in a crouch, gasping for breath, right shoulder screaming with pain.

"No*nonono*," the Jaedia-thing snarled. Her flesh-tentacles writhed wildly. "*I* am in control. I am *always* in control. I—"

"Maya!" Beq's voice.

From the corner of her eye, something came flying toward her, and Maya reached out with her good arm, snatching her haken out of the air. Jaedia's eyes went very wide, and the tendrils reached, but fire was already blooming around Maya, pushing them away. Maya surged to her feet and brought her hand around to the back of her mentor's neck. She felt the hard shell of the black spider under her fingers.

"*Sha'deia*," Jaedia gasped. "Maybe you *are* the one—"

Maya focused a burst of flame, as small and hot as she could make it, tearing through the monstrous thing in a blaze of focused plasma. Jaedia dropped at once, like all her bones had been removed. The horrible flesh-armor with its tentacles collapsed around her, disintegrating into twisted meat and shattered bones. Maya landed on her knees, coughing and struggling for breath.

"Jaedia!" Maya tossed her haken aside and scrambled forward, heedless of the slick of blood and torn flesh. Jaedia lay amid the ruins, her breathing ragged. As Maya reached her, she gave a scream, arched her back for a strained moment, then fell limp.

No no no no. Maya fell to her knees beside her mentor. *Not now. Not after all this.* She pulled Jaedia toward her, resting her head across Maya's stained lap. Blood ran from the back of Jaedia's neck where the spider had bitten her, a steady trickle of crimson. Her breath rattled harshly in her chest, and her eyes were closed.

"Jaedia," Maya said frantically. "Jaedia, *please*."

Her mentor's soft green eyes opened, focusing slowly. "M... Maya?"

"I'm here," Maya said. "I found you. You're going to be all right."

"I..." Jaedia's features tensed as a wave of pain ran through her. "I couldn't. Let him hurt you. Not you."

"I know," Maya said. Her throat was thick. "You beat him."

"I... I killed..." Her eyes filled with tears.

"It wasn't you. I'll explain everything to Basel." Maya furiously wiped her own eyes, spreading gore across her face. "We'll get you back to the Forge and figure everything out."

"Marn," Jaedia whispered. "I left him."

"He's all right," Maya said. "I found him."

"Good," Jaedia said, then stiffened again. Her breath escaped her with a sigh. "That's...good."

"Please don't die." Maya's voice was a whisper. "Not now. I need you."

"Maya." Jaedia swallowed. "Listen to me. The mountain."

"W...what?"

"Under the mountain." Jaedia jerked again. "There is—power. The ghouls—"

"The *ghouls*?" Maya said. "I don't understand. Is it a ruin?"

"The ghouls are *here*," Jaedia gasped out. "If they...reach it... everything will fall. Order. Republic. *Everything*." Her hand came up, catching Maya's arm in a death grip. "You have to stop them."

"But..."

"*Stop. Them.*" Jaedia could barely force the words out. "Please."

"Don't do this," Maya said. "Don't put this on me like you're going to die. Jaedia!"

Jaedia's back arched again, her body as taut as a bowstring. Her eyes showed only whites.

No. Maya's hand scrabbled in the wet ruin until she found her haken. *Deiat* bloomed inside her. *You can't.* She pulled at the flow of power, the fire of creation, until it crackled through her body like a tempest of flame. The Thing went from skin-warm to white-hot in moments, and a curl of smoke rose from where it scorched her shirt. *You* can't. *You can't die.*

A voice echoed in her mind. Her own voice, but not, full of such authority that to disobey it was unthinkable.

I will not allow it.

Pinpricks of warmth, all over her skin, grew in intensity to match the Thing's blaze. Maya, suffused with the power of the sun, looked down at Jaedia's body, and she *saw*. The poison the spider had left behind, its petty revenge, caustic venom tearing Jaedia apart from the inside, like black worms writhing through her veins. Maya focused, and the worms *burned*, strings of fire too small to see with the naked eye running through Jaedia like the tide. A hundred, a thousand, a million tiny shreds of divine fire. Too many. *No one can do this*, Maya thought, and she felt herself wobble atop the torrent of power.

You can, little sha'deia. Something was watching her, something distant and vast and cold. *Oh, you can.*

I will see you again. Soon…

The last of the black poison burned away. Maya let *deiat* slip from her fingers, and the world slipped away with it, burying her in darkness.

"Maya!" Someone was tapping her cheek. "Maya, please wake up."

"We can't carry both of them." Tanax's voice, more distant.

"Maya!" Beq.

Maya opened her eyes and saw Beq's face inches from her own, melting with relief. "She's awake!"

"I…" Maya coughed. "Jaedia!"

"She's alive," Beq said. "I don't know what you did, Maya, but it was *amazing*. You were *glowing*, and then Jaedia was glowing too, and—"

"We can explain things later," Tanax said. "We need to get out of here *now*."

"What's happening?" Maya sat up, a little too quickly, and the world spun around her. Beq gave her a hand, and she got gently to her feet. When she saw, she felt the bottom drop out of her stomach. "Oh."

The army of plaguespawn was coming apart. Whatever will had held them in place had died with the black spider, and in its wake had come madness even worse than what was normal for plaguespawn. The creatures were attacking at random, tearing mindlessly at one another with teeth and claws, the giants scything through dozens of their smaller brethren with enormous talons. The whole head of the valley was a boiling, vicious melee.

At the edge of the crowd, monsters were breaking away from the pack in all directions, including directly toward the rock face on which Maya and the others stood. None had yet found their way up the narrow path leading to the top, but it was only a matter of time.

"We have to get away," Tanax said. "Back down the valley." His voice was grim, and Maya could see why.

"We'll never make it," Maya said. "Not with that many of them behind us."

"If we stay here, they'll surround us," Tanax shot back. "Better a small chance than none at all."

"I'm not sure how far I can run," Beq said matter-of-factly. She had a bandage tied around the wound in her leg, but blood was already soaking through. Only the rapid working of her throat betrayed her fear. "And someone has to carry Jaedia."

"We'll never make it," Maya repeated.

"Do you have a better idea?" Tanax snapped.

"Under the mountain," Jaedia had said. Maya looked at the flat cliff face, the spot where the rock was stained with plaguespawn blood, and suddenly understood. "Down there. There's a way inside."

"Inside?" Beq said. "Like into a ghoul tunnel?"

"Something like that," Maya said.

"You have no way of knowing that," Tanax said.

"Jaedia told me." Maya picked up her haken. "She gave me a job to do, and I'm going to finish it."

"You—" Tanax shook his head and glanced at Beq, who shrugged.

"You're the one who wanted to join her expedition," she said.

There was a long pause.

"All right," Tanax said, looking down at the melee. "If we move quickly and don't stop, we should be able to keep them off us. I'll carry Jaedia." He looked up at Maya. "What's this job?"

"Saving the Order and the Republic," Maya said.

"Oh," Beq said. "Is that all?"

Chapter 25

Gyre

"Leviathan's Womb?" Kit said. "What's a Leviathan's Womb?"

"You will understand when you see," Naumoriel said, closing the canopy of his war-construct. "Come."

The huge thing spidered over the dusty stone floor, and Gyre, Kit, and the two remaining soldier-constructs followed in its wake. They passed down a short corridor lined with more constructs, low-slung, six-legged, insectoid things of metal and black muscle. Kit eyed them with distrust.

"These guys weren't willing to come help us outside?" she said.

"They are not yet active," Naumoriel said. "The constructs here are . . . different. Without the Core Analytica, they are incomplete."

"A construct army?" Kit said skeptically. "Is that the power you've come to find?"

Naumoriel said nothing.

Gyre had expected the whole mountain to be a maze of tunnels, like

Refuge or the ruins under Deepfire. Instead, after only a few minutes, they came up into a much larger space. *Much* larger, he realized, as he stared around it. Even his silver eye couldn't make out the ceiling or the far walls. *They must have hollowed out half the mountain.* They stood on a long walkway, a smooth rock wall to their right, while to their left and ahead of them was...

The *scale* of it was hard to grasp. A metal plate, stretching below the level of the walkway and up over Gyre's head. A narrow seam, and then another plate, and another, on and on. Like a building, a *fortress*, the Spike laid on its side. Gyre was about to ask why the ghouls would build their fortification *here* when he spotted the curving, jointed shapes in the distance, like...

Legs?

His mouth fell open and stayed there.

It's a construct. Something like Naumoriel's war-construct, armored in steel, but vast beyond imagining. The size of a *city*. A mountain.

"Leviathan," he whispered.

"Indeed," Naumoriel said. He'd opened his canopy again, leaning forward to look at the awesome thing with his huge, rheumy eyes. "The greatest project ever created by my kind. The pinnacle of our mastery of *dhaka*, our power. It has slept here, undisturbed, for four hundred years."

"This...this is what you've been looking for?" said Kit. For once, even she didn't have a sarcastic remark.

"Of course," Naumoriel said. "My father led the team that created it. It was designed to assault the Chosen in the heart of their power, to crush their precious city and bring their empire to ruin."

"What happened?" Gyre said. "Why is it still here?"

"My father was betrayed," the old ghoul snapped. "Before the Core Analytica could be completed, he was brought down by those who wanted to hide instead of fight. Those who thought it better to cower in the earth while our children were burned like vermin than to strike back and inflict the same pain on our destroyers.

He took a deep breath, something in his chest rattling wetly. "And since then, I have worked to bring it to life. Scavenged what I needed from the rubble of our empire. It was built to fight the Chosen at their height. Once it is activated, nothing in this fallen world will be capable of stopping it." He looked down at Kit. "It hosts a swarm of constructs, all controlled by the Core Analytica, to gather organic material from the land around it, and so it can power itself indefinitely. It is perfection, and all that remains is to deliver the last piece."

Gyre tried to catch Kit's eye, but she kept looking at Naumoriel with a disingenuous grin.

"So," she said. "What happens now?"

Naumoriel pulled his canopy closed again. The war-construct started forward, toward the end of the—*dock*, Gyre realized; that was the best analogy. Ahead, there was a tower, stretching up into the darkness and connected to a bridge that arched over to the top of the vast construct. The pair of constructs that had flanked them doubled back, toward the archway where they'd come in.

"I will install the Core Analytica," Naumoriel said. His tentacle-arm flourished the code-key that had opened the door. "Once it is in place, this key will mark me as the Leviathan's master. It will obey only me."

"I see." And now she *did* look at Gyre, and raise her eyebrows suggestively.

"And us?" Gyre said. "The things you promised us?"

"Elariel will provide Kitsraea's cure when you return to Refuge," Naumoriel said dismissively. "As for you, boy, Leviathan and I will grant your desire ourselves. The end of the Republic and the Order, and the final destruction of all the works of the sun-lovers." He reached the base of the tower, and one tendril stroked its surface. "You only need to watch."

There was a *boom*, echoing out of the tunnel behind them, and a puff of dust emerged from the arch. Gyre half turned, frowning, and saw the two soldier-constructs moving into the murk, blades gleaming. In that moment, the base of the tower opened, revealing a chamber barely big enough for Naumoriel's war-construct. He stepped forward, and the doors began to close behind him.

"The Order comes," he said. "You must delay them until my preparations are complete."

"Wait just a fucking—" Kit began, but the door closed on her words. Gyre heard a whirr as the lifter chamber sped upward, toward the top of the tower, where the bridge connected it to Leviathan.

"*Plaguefire*," Kit swore, skidding to a halt at the doors. She pressed her fingers to the metal, searching for the seam. "I have to get this fucking thing open."

"I can set off the bomb," Gyre said, moving to shrug off his pack to find the detonator. "Stop him."

"No!" Kit said, turning to him and grabbing him by the shoulder. "No. Not until Naumoriel finishes installing the Core Analytica. Don't you get it?" She gestured at the hulking shape of Leviathan, eyes gleaming. "This is *exactly* what we wanted, Gyre. Can you imagine if *we* were in control of that thing? Forget selling it to Refuge. They'll fix me, or we'll crush them underfoot. And the Order? You can take the Forge to pieces. This is *it*. This is what I've been looking for my whole life." She gulped for breath. "All we have to do is get there."

Gyre was about to protest that she hadn't *known* about it until five minutes ago, but the desperate look on her face stopped him. He glanced over his shoulder, where the sounds of combat echoed from the archway.

"Just hold them off," Kit said. She put her hand on his face, cupping his silver eye. "You can do it, can't you? Give me enough time to get these doors open, and we'll take that key off Naumoriel and blow him to the Chosen."

She raised herself onto her toes to kiss him, arms wrapping around the small of his back. Gyre leaned into the kiss, feeling the hot, bright spark of her pressed against him.

"I'll do what I can," Gyre said when he pulled away. Kit grinned, like a kid with a plate full of cookies, and turned back to the door. Gyre loosened the silver sword in its scabbard and ran back along the dock.

Shapes were struggling and clashing in the dust, the murk periodically illuminated by a flare of brilliant fire. One of the soldier-constructs came staggering out of the cloud, missing one arm at the shoulder and with its faceless head slashed to pieces. A young man strode after it. He was covered head to toe in gore, his traveling leathers sodden and caked with it; dried blood smeared his face. He wielded a haken, its blade a line of shimmering distortion, doing odd things to the eye.

A centarch, not much older than Maya. As Gyre watched, he extended his off hand, and waves of twisted space snapped out. They vanished when they hit the construct, splashing harmlessly into nothingness, and the centarch clicked his tongue in disapproval as the thing swung its remaining arm at him. He ducked, but one of the bladed protrusions on the construct's arm caught him on the shoulder. Instead of leaving a cut, blue energy flared, stopping the blow. The centarch surged upward, his distorted weapon slicing the construct from armpit to shoulder, and it fell in two pieces in a welter of black blood.

The boy looked up and saw Gyre. His eyes narrowed.

"Who are you supposed to be?" he said.

"Gyre Silvereye," Gyre said, with more bravado than he felt. He resisted the urge to look back at Kit.

"And I am *Centarch* Tanax Brokenedge," the centarch said, stepping over the broken body of the construct. "Now, drop your weapons and get out of my way."

Gyre took a deep breath and drew his silver sword. With a *click* at the base of his skull, the world splintered into shadows.

"I see," Tanax said, gravely. He raised his haken to a guard position. "As you wish, then."

Before Gyre could take a step forward, the centarch's free hand shot out, summoning a wave of twisting, boiling energy. Gyre held his ground, silver sword extended, and he felt it part around him as it had parted around the construct. The energy bottle at his side grew warmer as Naumoriel's augmentations deflected the *deiat*. Tanax's eyes narrowed.

Gyre didn't intend to give him time to puzzle it out. He charged, coming in high. Tanax responded contemptuously, sidestepping and extending his own weapon. Gyre saw the blow coming, shadow-haken hardening into reality, and he twisted to let it slide by. At the same time, his silver sword came close enough to nick the centarch's sleeve. Energy crackled along the silver blade, as though earthing itself, but the blue-white shield did not appear. Fresh blood bloomed. Tanax spun away, recovering opposite Gyre and glancing at the wound.

"You have some…interesting abilities," Tanax said. "Once you're in chains, I'll have you explain them to me. At length."

Gyre felt a grin spreading across his face. "Come and get me, then."

Now it was Tanax's turn to charge, low and fast. Gyre brought his blade down to meet the haken, twisted space scraping against ghoul silver with a high, shivery whine. Tanax disengaged and came in again, and Gyre parried, feinted, and left another line of fresh blood on the centarch's leg. Their two blades flickered, meeting over and over, but the shadows playing out in Gyre's silver eye kept him half a step ahead, and that was enough.

He felt exultant as his opponent's expression shifted, going from arrogance to fierce, desperate concentration. A centarch, the elite of the Twilight Order, inheritors of the power of the Chosen and all the rest—*and he's not good enough.* Of everything Naumoriel had promised him, Gyre realized, *this* was what he had longed for most of all. He felt like he could reach into his own past, find Va'aht Thousandcuts, and with the power of eye and blade tear him to pieces. As they clashed and whirled, Gyre found himself laughing.

"Who *are* you?" Tanax grated through gritted teeth.

He threw out his free hand, sending distorted waves to either side of Gyre, ripping up the ground to box him in. Gyre retreated, reaching into his pack and working by feel. When Tanax lunged, he slipped to one side, leading with his blade to disperse the *deiat* in his path. The centarch turned, haken raised to guard against a counterattack, but Gyre kept moving, opening the distance. Tanax frowned, then looked down. There was a fist-sized clay sphere at his feet, and in that moment the little fuse burned away.

The blast sent a shivering concussion across the dock and raised another cloud of dust. Gyre skidded to a halt and spotted the prone figure of the centarch lying beside the fresh crater, haken dark and silent next to him. *One down.* He glanced at the energy bottle at his side. The glow had dimmed, but he had a few minutes. *One spare left.* He forced himself to breathe. *I can do this.*

A bar of brilliant flame became visible beside the fallen centarch. A moment later, Maya strode into view, dust roiling around her.

Maya

It had been easier than Maya had expected to reach the cliff face. Whatever drove the plaguespawn to tear at one another overrode even their normal desire for human flesh, and only a few had tried to confront the two centarchs. Twisted space and boiling flames cleared this handful from their path, and they arrived in the lee of the mountain. Tanax, with Jaedia slung over his back, was panting, and Beq's face was tight with pain, her leg now bleeding freely.

"How do we get in?" Beq said. "I don't see any controls."

"The simple way," Maya said, and raised her haken to the stone. Four quick slashes later, and a block about her height fell inward, collapsing with a *boom* and a cloud of dust, revealing a dark passage beyond. "Let's go."

None of the plaguespawn seemed inclined to follow them, but Maya and Tanax propped the broken piece of stone in the opening anyway. They settled Jaedia against one wall, and Beq sat down beside her. Maya looked between them, and her feelings must have been clear on her face, because Beq gave a weary sigh.

"Go," she said. "Jaedia asked you to, didn't she? We'll be all right."

"You're sure?" Maya said, wavering. "Your leg—"

"Nothing a bandage and quickheal won't fix," Beq said, twisting the knob on her lenses. "It's the Republic and the Order at stake, right? Go." She smiled weakly. "But come back, okay?"

"I will." Maya bent down and kissed her. Her lips tasted of blood and dust. When she straightened up, Tanax was looking at her.

"Are you coming?" Maya said doubtfully. Tanax was clearly exhausted, wobbling on his feet like he was punch-drunk. The blows his panoply had taken must have been draining.

"As far as I can," he said. "If you believe that the Order is at stake, don't hesitate to leave me behind if you must."

Slowly, Maya nodded. She checked her haken and her panoply, then followed the tunnel up into the darkness, Tanax keeping pace by her side.

Dust still billowed around them from where they'd cut their way into the tunnel. Maya touched her haken and created a small sphere of light, but it still only showed a little ways ahead, as though they were walking into a fogbank.

"This place has been quiet for a very long time," Tanax said. "Do you think—"

Two figures lurched suddenly out of the murk. Maya recognized them as the strange plaguespawn whose corpses they'd seen earlier—human in shape, underlying muscle black instead of red, with metal skins instead of splintered bone. They looked—better constructed, somehow, than the usual nightmare amalgamations of human and animal parts, as though someone had put them together deliberately instead of simply pressing fresh bits in whenever they could be had. Barbs and blades gleamed all across their metal armor.

Maya raised a hand and sent a wave of fire at the first one. The flames reached it but broke across its surface, withering into nothingness. She glanced at Tanax.

"That's new," she said.

He raised his haken, the twisted blade forming. "Let's see how they like being cut to pieces, then."

Tanax charged, meeting the second monster head-on, ducking the swing of its bladed fist and slashing up and across its blank faceplate. Part of its head fell away, and it staggered back a few steps but quickly recovered. The other plaguespawn turned to attack Tanax from behind, and Maya ignited her own haken and drove it through the thing's midsection. The creatures might not have looked like plaguespawn, but they bled the same, thick black gore gouting from the wound. It spun, both arms reaching for her in a bear hug, and Maya danced back out of range.

The monster was smarter than it had any right to be, too. It used the greater reach of its long arms to keep her at bay, as though it were playing for time. Maya chopped a dozen small pieces out of each limb but couldn't land a killing blow, and in the meantime Tanax and the second monster had vanished up the ramp and into the billowing dust. Frustrated, she feinted to one side, then bulled forward, letting metal blades scrape against her panoply field as she pivoted on one foot and brought her haken around in a horizontal arc. Blood *hissed* and charred in the flames, and the strange plaguespawn fell into two pieces, bisected at the waist. Even then, it kept struggling, and Maya skirted its remains as she hurried onward. She was breathing hard, the chill of drained energy from her panoply fading only gradually.

The ramp opened onto a flat surface, but she was still lost in the dust. Up ahead, she heard Tanax shouting, and then a *boom* and a brilliant flash, brighter than a blaster bolt. *That* wasn't something she'd ever seen from Tanax's powers, and she broke into a run, emerging from the dust cloud and skidding to a halt as she tried to take in the vast chamber.

There was a... thing, only barely visible in the gloom, the light from her blade glinting off metal plates running high overhead and far back out of sight. In the gaps, she could see striated black muscle, like what ran beneath the skin of the plaguespawn she'd just defeated. This was clearly something similar, but—

The size *of it.* She couldn't see far enough to get her head around it. The closest part, a vast curve, resolved into a *limb* big enough to crush a good-sized house underfoot. *Chosen defend, it must be the size of a city!*

"*The ghouls are here,*" Jaedia had said, and talked about a power that could destroy the Republic. *This thing must be a ghoul weapon.* Their answer to a Chosen skyfortress, maybe, a plaguespawn big enough to break mountains. *And someone wants to* wake it up?

A moment later, the eddying dust swirled away, and she saw the crater in the stone floor, with Tanax's limp body lying beside it. Standing over him, a silver sword in one hand, was—

Gyre?

He looked different than when she'd last seen him. Leaner, more dangerous, unruly dark hair grown long enough to curl at the ends. But when the light of her haken fell on his face, there was no doubt it was him. Pale, shiny scars stood out against his brown skin, overlaying the old wound that had taken his eye. Now something *glowed* in the depth of the socket, a silver orb shining from within with an eerie green light.

Watching him stare down at Tanax, Maya felt a sudden surge of guilt. *I let him go. Because he was my brother. I knew he was a rebel, that he'd killed Auxiliaries, that he hated the Order and the Republic, and I let him go. And now...* Now he was here, with this monstrous *thing*, and she had no idea how badly Tanax was hurt. Her heart triple-thumped, and she touched the Thing with her free hand. It had cooled and was just a hard lump under her fingers.

Tanax is probably all right, Maya told herself. His panoply would have absorbed the attack, even if it rendered him unconscious. *And I won't make the same mistake again.*

Gyre looked up and saw her. Something about his expression, in the moment of recognition, tore at her heart, but she pushed it down ruthlessly.

"Maya," he said. His voice was thick.

"I should have known." Maya stepped forward, haken raised, flames crackling in front of her. "You as good as told me you were a traitor to humanity. I should have..." She shook her head.

His expression hardened. "Should have what? Killed me? Thrown me in in a cell? Probably." He sidestepped away from the crater and

Tanax, and Maya moved to match him, beginning a slow circle. "That's what a good Order slave would have done, isn't it? Judge, jury, and executioner all in one." He extended his silver blade like an accusing finger. "What gives you the right?"

"We are carrying out the duty left to us by the Chosen," Maya said. "It's not a *right*. It's a responsibility."

"You're the enforcers for a gang of corpses," Gyre said. "Dogs keeping the flock in line, even though the shepherds are dead and gone."

Maya raised her hand and smothered him with a gout of flame. Not hard or hot enough to kill—she wasn't ready for that, even now—but it ought to have blown him off his feet. Instead, when the fire cleared, Gyre was unmoved, silver sword extended without a tremble.

"Of course," he said. "That's the Order's answer to everything, isn't it? Just burn it, break it, smash it until it can't talk back anymore." He slashed his blade, real eye blazing, silver eye still glowing that eerie green. "You know, I never met a Chosen. Maybe they really did deserve to run the world. Maybe they were better than us—smarter, more moral, *superior*. But you centarchs are only human, with a little fizz in your blood. Just because you can kill anyone who disagrees, that means you have the right to rule?"

Maya thought of Nicomidi, glaring down at her in her cell, casually threatening to have Beq killed. The rest of the Council, broken into warring camps, willing to turn a blind eye to anything that hurt their political enemies. Raskos Rottentooth, representing the Republic and the Order, feeding off the misery of thousands to stuff his coffers. She took a deep breath.

"We're all only human," she said. "Centarchs as much as anyone. But the centarchs aren't the Twilight Order, and neither are the Auxiliaries or the duxes. The Order is a *principle*. That those with power should defend those without."

"Defend them by swaddling them. Keeping them like infants, without any way to defend themselves, because that might mean they can stand up to you."

"And what exactly are you offering?" Maya shouted, gesturing with her haken at the vast bulk of the monstrous plaguespawn. "*That?*"

"*That* is the power to overturn the order of the world," Gyre said. But there was a moment of hesitation in his voice; she was certain of it.

"Please, Gyre. Stop this."

"Take your friend and walk away." Gyre glared at her, but something shifted in his mismatched eyes. "I don't want to hurt you."

Maya gritted her teeth. "You won't."

She charged, and Gyre stood to receive her. Silver blade met blazing haken, and to Maya's shock Gyre's weapon stood up to the test, halting her blow inches from his face. He slipped away, disengaged, shockingly fast, and she had to parry as she fell back. Sparks flew and crackled whenever the weapons met, falling in showers around them. Maya gave ground, tried a riposte, but Gyre seemed to know where her sword was going before she did. He sidestepped, and his blade licked out, touching her shoulder. She waited for the panoply flare, the wave of cold, but it didn't come—instead there was a *crackle* of discharging energy, and the point of the silver sword bit through her coat with a spike of pain. Maya jumped back, putting a hand to the wound, and it came away covered in fresh blood.

Gyre waited, sword ready. He inclined his head. "Like I said. I don't want to hurt you."

Maya felt her heart lurch and sought for calm.

Arcana. He'd found something, scavenging in the dark places under Deepfire. *That eye, that sword.* Apparently it could break a panoply and deflect *deiat. Ghoul arcana. It must be. But it has to have limits.*

She glanced again at the titanic plaguespawn, and her resolve hardened. *I can't let anyone bring* that *into the world. Not even my brother.*

Maya shifted her grip on her haken and attacked.

This time she moved cautiously, drawing on every lesson in swordsmanship Jaedia had ever drilled into her. Her mentor had insisted that she practice, blade against blade. Maya heard her voice, that lilting, musical accent, as haken and sword clashed again.

"Most centarchs rely too much on their panoply. It's a useful tool, but it can be a crutch. You need to be good enough to fight without one..."

She'd done that once already, hazarding her bare skin against Tanax's twisting *deiat* power. Whatever arcana Gyre had found, he had only a sword.

Sparks exploded outward as they came together, clashed, and broke apart. Gyre was *fast*, and his accuracy was uncanny. Sometimes it was all Maya could do to match him. But she was *better*, trickier. Jaedia's lessons ran through her, the haken feeling like an extension of her arm, flexing and striking and drawing back with a fluidity that Gyre couldn't match. He nicked her again, on the leg, came close to landing a strike on her side. But she twisted out of the way and slammed home a counterattack he barely parried. She pressed him, not letting up. His blade wove a cage of silver and sparks around him, but he started to give ground, step-by-step.

There was another difference between them. The power of *deiat* roared through Maya, driving her onward, filling her with the limitless fire of the sun. Whatever force animated Gyre's arcana came from within. And that meant it would run out.

Maya gave a savage grin. *Ghoul weapons are no match for the might of the Chosen.*

The green glow in Gyre's false eye flickered, dimmed. His movements faltered, just for a moment, and Maya pounced. She thrust, a simple attack, and he avoided it as she expected, slipping to one side. At the last moment, her haken twisted, catching his blade in a bind, and with an expert flip of her wrist she tore it from his grasp. The silver sword landed with a *clang* and skittered across the stones, and Gyre fell to his knees, her haken leveled at his throat. The green in his eye dimmed again, and he gasped for breath.

"I don't want to hurt you either," Maya said quietly. "You're my big brother. You always protected me."

"Not always," Gyre said. Sweat dripped from his forehead. "Not when it mattered."

"Why, Gyre? Why go this far? This is monstrous; you have to know that."

"The Order took everything from me," Gyre said. "They took my eye. They took my family." He looked up at her, real eye thick with tears. "They took my little sister, and they turned her into *you*."

For a long moment, Maya didn't know what to say. Then, finally, it came to her, the words that would fix everything, that would bring her brother home again.

She opened her mouth to speak, and searing pain lanced through her.

Chapter 26

"They took my little sister," Gyre said, "and they turned her into *you.*"

He looked up at Maya. His little sister, gap-toothed and grinning, begging for apple pudding. A powerful young woman standing in front of him, sheathed in dried blood, her brilliant red hair hanging limp with sweat, breathing hard. And, between them, a bar of white fire, like a broken shard of the sun.

His words had hurt her, he could see it in her face. She'd never been any good at hiding her feelings. He'd meant them to hurt, his hand still stinging where she'd disarmed him. He was on his knees in front of her, in spite of all he'd sacrificed, everyone he'd left broken and damaged in his wake, in spite of *everything*. Words didn't matter, because she was strong and he was weak. But it was all he had, and he dredged for what he thought would hurt her most.

I'm sorry. He wanted to say it, but his lips wouldn't move. He could have apologized to his sister. *But not to a centarch.* His body felt heavy, slow, as the energy bottle at his side gave up the last dregs of its power.

Maya looked down at him, gave a sudden smile, and then stiffened. The point of Gyre's silver sword, crimson with blood and crackling with energy, emerged from her stomach. Maya blinked, eyes going very wide, and her haken slipped from her fingers, blade vanishing as it hit the stones. She followed it a moment later, collapsing first to her knees, then toppling sideways, red hair splayed out around her. The hilt of the silver sword stood out from her back. Behind her, Kit straightened up and smiled.

Gyre wanted to scream, but he didn't have the strength.

"Sorry I took so long," Kit said. "Had to pick my moment." She looked down at Maya. "This is her, isn't it? Your sister."

Gyre tried to move and nearly fell over, catching himself on his hands and knees. *The energy bottle.* Blocking so much *deiat* had drained it, drained *him*. He fumbled in his pack with one hand, searching for his last spare.

"You're looking for this, I imagine." Kit held up the bottle in one hand. In the other, she had the remote trigger for the bomb he'd put in Naumoriel's war-construct. "I'm sorry about this, Gyre, I really am."

"W…" Gyre's mind felt blank. He tried to raise his head and instead found himself meeting Maya's gaze, empty and staring. "What…are you…"

"I really do like you, Gyre." Kit set the energy bottle down carefully, well outside his reach. "I promise I'll come and collect you on my way out. But Naumoriel was very clear that the Leviathan can only have one master, and it has to be me." She bent over and kissed his cheek. "Just rest here for a minute. I'll go blow up the old ghoul and collect my prize, and then we'll be on our way, yeah?" She leaned a little closer and whispered in his ear. "And if you thought fighting our way out of the *Spike* made me horny…well." Kit straightened up, smiling brightly. "See you soon!"

Her footsteps receded. Gyre's legs gave way, and he slid down onto his belly. The energy bottle sat tauntingly on the floor, meters away. For all the strength he had left to him, it might as well have been on the moon. He stretched out an arm, straining, but even that brief effort was too much. The vision from his silver eye winked out, and shortly after the real one followed.

Gyre woke with a splitting headache and a need to vomit. He managed to roll over before his stomach had its way, spewing a thin stream of bile onto the rock. Gyre turned away from it, gasping, and lay on his back breathing hard.

He could see. Through *both* eyes. His hand went to his side and found an energy bottle, warm and humming with power. Strength was already returning to his limbs.

"Good," said a weak voice. "I hoped that would work."

Gyre sat up, ignoring the pounding in his head. Maya lay on her side across from him, propped on one elbow. The silver sword was on the ground behind her, trailing a slick of crimson. She'd wound a strip of cloth around her middle, but blood was already soaking through. As he watched, her arm gave way, and he lunged forward to catch her before her head hit the stone. He lowered her to the ground gently, and she smiled up at him.

"What are you so upset about, big brother?" she said. "You were trying to kill me a minute ago."

Gyre's throat felt like it had swollen shut. A sob wracked him, doubling him over, and tears ran down his cheeks and dripped off his chin onto Maya's forehead. She brought one hand up to wipe them away, the other pressed against the wound in her stomach.

"Gyre," she said. "Gyre, please. Listen to me." When he swallowed hard and looked down at her again, she opened her mouth and stuck out her tongue at him. He saw the chewed mess of a couple of waxy quickheal tablets. "Emergency supplies. Should be enough to stop the bleeding. Beq has other things. I'm not going to die." She swallowed, and for a moment her brave smile faltered. "Probably. Maybe." Maya hesitated. "Unless you kill me."

"I can't," Gyre said. "You know I can't. You're..." His throat felt choked again, this time with everything he wanted to say, as though it were all trying to escape at once. "My little sister."

"You have to stop them." Maya turned to look at the huge shape of Leviathan. "That woman, and whoever else is up there. You can't let them use that thing."

"I..." Gyre paused, looking down at her, and found himself smiling. "That's not fair."

"I know you hate us. The Order. The Republic. And we're... not perfect." Maya turned back to him. "But the answer can't be to destroy what little humanity has left. You have to see that. Whatever you believe about us, there has to be a better way." She swallowed and looked pained. "That kind of power... is best left sleeping."

"It may be too late," Gyre muttered.

"Try. Please." Maya closed her eyes. "I think... I'm going... to pass out now. Beq is... at the bottom of the tunnel. Call to her. She'll... help us. You..." She let out a shuddering breath. "You know what you need to do."

"I..." Gyre shook his head. "Maya?"

She didn't respond. Heart pounding, he bent over to check her breathing and found it shallow but steady.

Painfully, Gyre got to his feet. Leaving Maya where she lay, he walked back to the arched doorway. He felt like he was moving in a dream. At the top of the ramp, among the destroyed constructs, he cupped his hands to his mouth and shouted.

"Beq!" His voice echoed off the stone. "Can you hear me?"

Silence for a moment. Then a voice called back, "Who's there?"

"Maya's up here," Gyre said. "And her friend. They're alive, but they need help."

"*What?*" Beq said. "Who are you—"

There wasn't time for more. Gyre turned and jogged back along the dock. He scooped up the silver sword, still sticky with his sister's blood, and returned it to its sheath. The fatigue and cramps were burning away in the stream of fresh power, and he felt light again, though a lingering weariness in his bones warned him there would be a price to pay. *And there's no spare bottle, this time.*

The tower with the lifter in it was just ahead, and Kit had left the door open. Gyre stepped into the tiny chamber, and it started upward at once, accelerating smoothly until it reached the bridge over the top of Leviathan. This was a long, curving walkway, and Gyre pounded down it at a run. Beneath his feet, he knew, were the vast plates of the construct's back.

The bridge ended in a short ramp downward to a broad steel plain. It was impossible not to think of the plating as a deck, as though Leviathan were a ship or a skyfortress instead of a muscular creature animated by *dhaka*. Spurs protruded from it, huge flanges like the spiked ends of vertebrae, armored in steel, running in two parallel rows. Between them, some distance away, he could see the hulking shape of Naumoriel's war-construct, with the tiny figure of Kit kneeling in front of it.

Gyre crept down the ramp, taking cover behind one of the lines of spurs. He moved forward, watching through the gaps, until he was close enough to hear. There was a hole in the deck between the ghoul and the human, a deep, square pit, and around the edges something moved. Constructs, Gyre realized, a swarm of the little spiderlike things they'd seen inert in the complex, now animate and in furious motion. They crawled in and out of the pit, carrying bits and pieces both metal and organic—plates, cylinders, bones, and strips of meat. *Spare parts?*

"And the Order?" Naumoriel was saying, his voice distorted by the construct.

"Dealt with," Kit said. "Though Gyre was injured. I left him below."

"Good." Naumoriel waved a clawed limb. "As you can see, the Core Analytica is in place. Leviathan's swarm has awoken. We stand above the primary motivators, and once the swarm has repaired them, Leviathan will be ready." He waved his smaller limb, still carrying the code-key. "And then the world will tremble."

"It certainly will," Kit said, grinning. "But that means I don't need you anymore."

She raised the tablet, flipping up the grille and pressing her thumb against the crystal switch. Gyre flattened himself against the metal spur, waiting for the blast. A heartbeat, then two. Nothing.

Kit looked up in time to see Naumoriel's huge claw impale her.

It took her in the stomach, lifting her entirely off the ground, so she hung bleeding from the arm of his war-construct. Her hands scrabbled along the smooth surface of it, and she coughed, blood spraying from her lips. Her dangling legs kicked frantically.

"I imagine you're looking for this." One of Naumoriel's smaller limbs snaked over, holding a familiar clay cylinder, scored on one side where the ghoul had cut into it. "I found it at once, of course. Poor fool. Did you really think this would work?"

He dropped the bomb to the deck. Kit could only cough again in answer, blood drooling down her chin.

"I should have killed you on the spot, of course. But I reasoned you might still be useful to help reach this place, and so it has proved." The war-construct moved forward, and Naumoriel tossed the code-key aside and ground it under a steel foot. "Not that I would ever trust you with all my secrets, of course. There is no master key to Leviathan. My father was far beyond such crude methods."

One of the spurs, just beside the pit, started to open, the sides folding outward. Inside the cavity thus revealed was a metal chair, set in a complex web of silver wire and gleaming crystal. Naumoriel came to a halt beside it.

"For all its power, the Core Analytica cannot control Leviathan alone," Naumoriel said. "Only a living mind can do that. *That* is what I have lived for, since I learned the truth of what my father had created. I will shed this flimsy body and become a *god*, a titan of steel and its attendant swarm. And I have you to thank, Kitsraea. I would never have found all the pieces without you."

Naumoriel's claw twitched, casting Kit aside as a man might flick a bit of grit from his collar. She hit a nearby spur with bone-cracking force and slid down it in a long streak of blood, lying limp and motionless at the bottom. The war-construct knelt, and the canopy swung open, limbs turning inward to lift the old ghoul out of his seat.

Gyre slipped out from behind his spur as soon as the ghoul turned the other way. The bomb had rolled across the deck, and he snatched it up. Turning the cylinder over, he found where Naumoriel had cut the fuse. It was easy enough to reconnect, and he tossed it over the heads of the little constructs and down the hole. *The primary motivators sound important. Let's hope.* Moving as quietly as he could, he skirted Naumoriel and slipped to Kit's side.

She lay slumped against the metal spur, one arm obviously broken, glistening bits of torn gut visible through the huge rent in her stomach. Her chin was coated in blood, but her eyes were open, and as he knelt beside her, she stirred enough to look at him. Her lips curled in a smile.

"Can't...keep...you down, eh?" Her words were the barest whisper.

"Try to hold on," he said, grabbing the remote trigger from her limp hand.

Kit laughed, a horrible sound that brought another gout of blood from her lips. "Fuck. You." She leaned her head back against the metal. "Just...kill me. For...old times'...sake." Her hands moved against her stomach, squishing wetly. "This...really fucking hurts."

The war-construct shifted with a whirr, tentacles holding Naumoriel halfway to the arcana-shrouded chair. The old ghoul was looking right at them, and Gyre slowly straightened up.

"Fine," Kit said, her voice fading. "Have it. Your way. Slow and painful...it is."

"Boy," Naumoriel said. "What do you think you are doing?"

"Putting a stop to this," Gyre said.

"Too late for that," the old ghoul said, ears quivering. "Besides, I'm only going to grant you what you wanted. The destruction of the Order and the Republic."

"I've been thinking about that," Gyre said. "It's no good if everything else is destroyed as well."

Naumoriel's lips split in a grin, showing pointed teeth. "In that case," he said, "you should have bargained more carefully, *human.*"

"I'd like to renegotiate," Gyre said. He flipped the grille up and pressed his thumb to the crystal switch.

The ghoul barked a laugh, ears twitching. "You ignorant wretch. Apparently you haven't been paying atten—"

There was a low rumble, a buzz through the metal into the soles of Gyre's feet. Moments later a pillar of smoke erupted from the hole in the deck, followed by a tongue of flame that blasted a dozen of the small constructs into the air. Another explosion followed, and then another, marching backward through Leviathan's vast bulk. The deck *shifted* underneath them, canting as the entire enormous construct lurched drunkenly to one side. With a crash like a mountain coming to pieces, it hit the far wall, sliding down it in a scream of tortured metal until it finally stuck.

Gyre lost his footing, rolling across the deck. Across from him, Naumoriel's war-construct staggered for balance on its multiple legs, the ghoul swinging wildly from the tentacle-limbs. It slammed its still-open canopy against the nearby spur, and the smooth black stuff shattered, shards cascading down over Naumoriel and the deck.

"You...*pestilent*...*human!*" the ghoul screamed, as Leviathan finally rumbled to a halt. The deck remained tilted, and the small constructs skittered wildly across it, like a mound of ants after their hill has been kicked over. The arms of Naumoriel's construct lifted him back into his seat, under the shattered remains of the canopy. Fragments of it had cut the old ghoul, and crimson stains matted his fur. "Do you know what you've *done?*"

"Not *precisely*," Gyre said, tossing the trigger away. "But I think I have a general idea."

"You think you've won. You pathetic little *worm*. I fixed Leviathan once, and I can do it again, after my mind is transferred into the Core Analytica." The war-construct stepped forward, claw-limbs extending. "But *first* I am going to take great pleasure in *ripping you to shreds*."

Gyre let out a breath and concentrated. In the back of his skull, something went *click*.

I don't have long. If he burned too much energy this time, there would be no getting back up. *So let's make this quick.* He pushed off, moving in long, floating leaps, running for the construct.

Naumoriel reached for him. The tentacle-arms were faster, splitting at the ends to truss him up like a vulpi for slaughter, but his silver eye projected shadow-lines ahead of them, and Gyre watched where they converged. He stepped around the spot, swinging his blade up, and it slashed through the thin metal skin and into the dark muscle beneath. A length of tentacle flopped to the deck, the severed ends gushing black blood.

The thing's two larger arms barred his path, claws open. Gyre pulled up short, judging his moment. Then, as Naumoriel reached forward, he jumped.

The claw-arm passed beneath him, preceded by its wave of shadows. Gyre pulled in his legs and landed, with perfect precision, just behind the leading claw, balancing on the limb as it shifted underneath him. The second claw swung around, trying to knock him off like a man swatting a fly, and Gyre jumped again. This time he made it as far as the ovoid central body, grabbing the rim where the canopy had once fit and yanking himself up.

Naumoriel straightened in his seat, snarling with bloodstained fangs. His eyes narrowed as Gyre unsheathed his silver sword.

"I should have known," he muttered. "Should have known better than to give a morsel of power to *your* kind. You have always been our enemy, just as much as the sun-lovers." He grinned, shifting his hands against the controls, and the claw-arms rose behind Gyre. "You have no idea what's coming for you."

The claws twisted, reaching for him. Gyre extended his sword, a single neat thrust that took the ghoul through the heart. Naumoriel clawed at the blade for a moment, spitting defiance, then sagged. The war-construct shuddered to a halt, claws open and extended a half meter from Gyre's back.

Gyre slipped under them and jumped to the deck, stumbling slightly on the unexpected slope. He let the shadow-world fade with a *click* and checked the energy bottle at his side. It still had a healthy glow—not much fighting time, but enough to keep him moving for a while. Sheathing his sword, he ran to where Kit lay against the spur. She'd slid sideways when Leviathan shifted, smearing blood in her wake.

"Kit," Gyre said, kneeling beside her. "Kit!"

Her eyes fluttered open. "If you're not going to kill me, can't you let me die in peace?"

"I have an idea," Gyre said.

"There's no more ideas, Gyre." Kit closed her eyes again, and her voice grew fainter. "No more plans. No more chances. I've been gambling with my life ever since that old man sat down across from me. I finally lost, is all." She shuddered and coughed, spraying blood. "I just wish I'd worried a little less about my heart."

"Kit..."

"Hold my hand," Kit said, very quietly. "Please? It won't be long."

Gyre took her hand, squeezed it tight, then let go. He knelt, slipping both arms under her, and lifted her off the deck. Blood squished, and something wet and sticky slid from Kit's midsection and hit the ground with a *plop*.

"That *fucking* hurts," Kit whimpered. "What...are you doing, you...utter...fucking..."

Her eyes rolled back, and her head lolled against his shoulder. Gyre staggered forward, toward the folded-open spur and its arcana-encrusted chair.

"Gambling," he told her under his breath.

Epilogue

Maya

"I can ride," Maya protested. "As long as we go gently."

"We're going down a *mountain*," Beq said. "What part of that is gentle?"

"It might be better than this…thing," Tanax said, indicating the travois he was fashioning out of the poles and canvas from one of their tents. "It's going to be bumpy."

"Not too bumpy, I hope," Maya said, looking down at Jaedia's limp body. "I don't want to have to explain to her why she woke up with two broken arms."

"She'll be all right," Beq said, taking Maya by the hand.

They stood at the base of the valley, where they'd left the three swift-birds. Tanax, as Maya had hoped, had been shielded by his panoply, and he'd awoken after a few hours. After some quickheal, Beq was walking, albeit with a limp. As for Maya herself, Beq had wrapped the through-and-through wound tight enough to make it hard to breathe, given her all the quickheal she could stomach, and proclaimed her intention to drag her to every alchemical healer in Grace, sanctioned or not. For the moment, she could move, though with considerable pain, and that would have to be enough.

Jaedia showed no outward signs of injury, aside from the small punctures at the back of her neck, and her breathing and pulse were steady. But she also showed no signs of waking up, and Maya worried. *The faster we get her back to the Forge, the better.* She winced at a spike of pain. *I suppose that goes for me, too.*

None of them would have made it out of the valley under their own power. The big, spider-legged things—not plaguespawn, Gyre had said, but "constructs"—had carried them, with surprising gentleness, down the rocky slopes. Now they waited a little ways off, with Gyre standing among them. Maya looked at him, then over at Beq.

"We have a lot to do when we get back," she said, apropos of nothing. "Find out who Nicomidi was working with besides Raskos, and figure out what in the plague he meant by 'hearing the Chosen.' And that black spider-thing—" Maya shivered. "I think Baselanthus knows more than he's telling. And—"

"Go talk to him," Beq said, smiling slightly.

Maya sighed and winced again. Even that hurt. Moving slowly and carefully, she left the birds behind and climbed the slight rise to where Gyre was waiting. He crossed his arms as she approached, and Maya fought the urge to touch the Thing for calm.

"So," she said.

"So." Gyre hesitated. "You're going to be all right?"

"Beq thinks so. I'm lucky, apparently." Maya gave a careful shrug. "Or your girlfriend was trying to keep me alive."

"Her name was Kit," Gyre said. "And I seriously doubt that, to be honest."

"Was?"

Gyre closed his eyes for a moment and nodded.

"I'm sorry," Maya said, then thought about that for a moment. "I mean. I guess."

"I'm sorry she stabbed you."

They lapsed into silence again.

"You could have had your constructs kill us," Maya said. "Two help-less centarchs. It must have been tempting."

"A little," Gyre said.

"You told me you'd do anything to destroy the Order."

"I will. Someday." He shook his head. "But it has been brought to my attention that I need to think a little bit harder about what comes after, when I do. There are some sacrifices that aren't worth the cost."

"That's...a good lesson." Maya took a deep breath, in spite of the pain. "I can't let you do it, though. You know that."

"I know."

Maya hesitated, then blurted out, "There's no point in asking you to come back with me, is there?" She blinked, feeling tears in her eyes. "You don't have to live...like this. We could try to fix what's wrong with the Order."

"Would you come with me? Leave your haken behind, travel out into the Splinter Kingdoms, never look back?"

"No," Maya said, looking down.

Gyre gave a small shrug. "Then it seems likely we'll meet again. Somewhere."

"Somewhere," Maya said. She shook her head. "If you ever want to meet me without a sword in your hand, get word to the palace in Deep-fire. I'll let them know that if someone named Silvereye sends a mes-sage, they should pass it on."

"All right." Gyre started to turn away, hesitated. "Can I hug you, do you think, without squeezing your guts out?"

Maya gave a weak smile. "Beq said hugs are okay, as long as they're gentle."

Gyre stepped forward and wrapped his arms around her shoulders.

Maya clasped hers at the small of his back, pressing her face into his neck.

"I missed you," he said, very softly. "Every day since they took you away."

Maya's throat worked. "I missed you too."

"I hope..." He paused. "Who knows. Be well, Maya Burningblade."

"Be well, Gyre Silvereye." Maya pulled away from him, wiped her tears, and sniffed. Gyre turned away, slowly, and walked up the slope, the constructs following behind him.

Be well, Gyre, Maya thought as he passed out of sight. *I really hope I don't have to kill you.*

Gyre

"You should have killed her, you know. While you had the chance."

Gyre wiped his real eye and straightened up. He felt something tugging on the leg of his trousers, then climbing the side of his body, little claws digging at the leather of his clothes. A tiny spiderlike construct, barely the size of a cat, finished its ascent and settled comfortably on his shoulder.

"Probably," Gyre said.

"Too sentimental, that's your problem," the little thing said. The voice still didn't sound much like Kit's, but it was improving rapidly.

"Speaking of which," Gyre said. "Have you made your decision?"

"You could have asked me at the time," Kit said.

"I think you'd just stopped breathing," Gyre said. "It didn't seem like the best moment." He shook his head and turned to look at the little thing. "I mean it, though. I didn't know if you'd want to... live, like this. I can go back to poor crippled Leviathan, find the Core Analytica, and take it apart. Then you can find your doom at last, if that's what you want."

There was a long silence. Then the construct gave a ripple of its spider legs that might have been a shrug.

"There'll be time for that later, if I feel like it," she said. "I can do it myself, if it comes to that. In the meanwhile"—her voice changed direction, coming from one of the larger constructs beside him as it danced a little spidery jig—"I can see some possibilities. Having a whole swarm of bodies might be useful." Her voice went back to the small construct, shifting on his shoulder. "So what now?"

"Back to Refuge," Gyre said.

"You think they'll want to talk to you?"

"Elariel might," Gyre said. "And I have some ideas I want to see if I can sell her on."

"Your ideas," Kit said, "are always..."

"Yes?"

"Interesting," the tiny construct finished, taking a firmer grip on his shirt. "Let's go."

The story continues in . . .

Book 2 of Burningblade & Silvereye

Coming in 2021!

Acknowledgments

Ashes of the Sun is, depending on how you count, around the twenti-eth novel I've written. Aside from making me feel *ancient*, the thing that surprises me about that fact is that you would think the process would be old hat by now, but it's not. *Ashes* may in fact be my most-revised novel ever, with big chunks thrown away and rewritten; I can only hope the results are worthwhile.

This is not a Star Wars novel, but it definitely originated, back at the beginning, in a series of conversations about Star Wars. My list of people to thank therefore needs to start with Star Wars and everyone who was involved with it (a formidably large group by now) and espe-cially the various authors who wrote novels in that universe, notably Timothy Zahn and Chuck Wendig, as well as David Brin and Mat-thew Woodring Stover for their wonderful *Star Wars on Trial*. Next come thanks to the Red Letter Media crew for the horrifying, insight-ful Harry S. Plinkett reviews of the prequels (maybe lighten up on Rich Evans, guys!) and the participants in a series of conversations at 4th Street Fantasy on the subject, across several years. That includes at least Max Gladstone, Scott Lynch, Arkady Martine, and Seth Dickinson, but also many others who I don't have the time and ability to name. Apologies; my only excuse is that we were in the hotel bar and it was two in the morning.

My editor, Brit Hvide, displayed both great skill and the patience of a saint while I was putting this book together (see the aforementioned chunks thrown away and rewritten) and deserves all the thanks I can give her. Also at Orbit, I'd like to thank Bryn A. McDonald, Ellen Wright, Angela Man, Laura Fitzgerald, Paola Crespo, and Lauren Panepinto. Seth Fishman, my agent, performed his usual miracles in making this book happen. My thanks as well to everyone at the Gernert Company: Jack Gernert, Will Roberts, Rebecca Gardner, and Ellen Goodson. And Rhiannon Held's beta reading, as ever, provided invaluable insight.

My wife, Casey Blair, is always my most important reader, but she went above and beyond on this one, plowing through several iterations in order to have long late-night conversations about plot and character and assure me everything wasn't broken. This would have been a much poorer book without her.

Glossary

agathios (pl. agathia)—A young person in training to be a **centarch**. The **Twilight Order** searches out children with the ability to touch *deiat* and trains them as agathia from a young age. Agathia become full centarchs on being granted their **cognomen**.

alchemy—the process of refining and recombining ghoul **arcana**. Even broken, rotten remnants of the ghouls' organic "machines" can be rendered down into useful by-products, from which an alchemist can create **quickheal** and other medicines, bombs, powerful acids, and a variety of other tools depending on the materials available. The **Twilight Order** forbids alchemy and considers its products *dhak*, so its practice is more common in the **Splinter Kingdoms** than in the **Dawn Republic**. A few products of alchemy, like quickheal, are so useful that the Order considers them legal, **sanctioned arcana**, provided they are made by a few carefully controlled suppliers.

arcana—any tool or implement of **Elder** origin, from rare and powerful weapons like **haken** or **blasters** to **alchemical** creations like **quickheal**. Common people generally have little understanding of the differences between types of arcana.

Auxiliaries—one of the two major branches of the armed forces of the **Dawn Republic**, along with the **Legions**. The Auxiliaries are by far the larger force but, unlike the Legions, carry no **arcana** weapons and armor, relying on ordinary human-made swords, spears, and bows. They are responsible for policing, keeping order, and local defense against bandits and plaguespawn, under the command of the local dux. Sometimes called by the derogatory nickname "Auxies," especially by criminals.

bird—ordinary birds are common, but the term often refers to the large, flightless varieties used as beasts of burden. See **loadbird**, **swiftbird**, and **warbird**.

blaster—an arcana weapon that uses *deiat* in a crude fashion, firing bolts of pure energy that explode on impact. Like any arcana making use of *deiat* and not in the hands of a **centarch**, blasters are powered by energy stored in **sunsplinters** and useless once the energy is expended. The **Legions** use blasters as their standard ranged weapon. Pistol and rifle variants both exist, with the latter having greater range. Since charged sunsplinters can only be acquired from the **Twilight Order** or occasionally scavenged from ruins, functioning blasters are very expensive to acquire and a mark of status.

centarch—one of the elite warriors of the **Twilight Order**, capable of wielding *deiat* through a **haken**, unlike all other **humans**.

Chosen—One of the **Elder** races, along with the **ghouls**. All Chosen could use *deiat*, without the aid of tools like **haken**, and this power made them unchallenged rulers of a continent-spanning empire for centuries, with **humans** serving them. They were wiped out by the **Plague**, but in their final years they founded the **Dawn Republic** and the **Twilight Order**, to help humanity survive in their absence.

cognomen—**Humans** in the former **Chosen** Empire have either only a given name, or a given name and a family or clan name for city dwellers and elites. In addition, some people have a cognomen, a third name that describes some aspect of their history, character, or appearance. Cognomen are granted by general acclamation, not chosen, and trying to pick one's own cognomen is the height of arrogance and opens one to mockery. Cognomen are not always complimentary but can be very hard to shake once applied. They are often two-word compounds: Rottentooth, Boldstep, Halfmask.

For **centarchs**, cognomen have a greater significance. They are granted, not by the centarch's peers, but by the **Kyriliarch** Council when an agathios reaches the status of a full centarch. The cognomen matches the way the centarch manifests *deiat*, and the Council often chooses names held by past centarchs, with the oldest names conveying the most favor and honor.

construct—a semiorganic autonomous servant created by the **ghouls** using *dhaka*. Constructs come in a huge variety of shapes and sizes, but many are roughly humanoid, with specialized construction for their particular role, such as armor, weapons, or extra limbs. They are typically built of artificial muscle and tissue layered over a metal skeleton, and sometimes resemble **plaguespawn**, although the latter are much more chaotic and strange. A device called an analytica provides the construct's ability to understand instructions and make decisions, but only the ghouls understood how these function.

Dawn Republic—A nominally democratic state created by the **Chosen** as their numbers dwindled during the **Plague**. Originally, the Republic encompassed all the land that had been part of the Chosen Empire, but in the four hundred years since the Plague, much of the territory has broken away, forming smaller polities collectively known as the **Splinter Kingdoms**. Even so, the Republic remains the most powerful nation in the known world, with its capital at the old Chosen city of Skyreach.

The Republic has a sometimes uneasy relationship with the **Twilight Order** and its **centarchs**. The Order was charged by the Chosen to defend the Republic and humanity, but not to rule it, and so normally stands apart from the daily running of Republican politics. However, the centarchs collectively wield unmatched power, and in addition the Republic's elite military forces, the **Legions**, rely on Chosen-built weapons and armor that only the Twilight Order can maintain. The upshot is that the wishes and suggestions of the Order carry considerable weight with the Republican government, and centarchs are legally empowered to dispense justice and commandeer any necessary resources in pursuit of their missions.

The Republic is ruled by a Senate, which is theoretically elected, but the franchise is restricted to the wealthy, and senators almost always come from a small group of powerful families. The Senate elects two consuls every year to serve as chief executives. The Senate appoints a dux as military commander and chief magistrate to the various regions of the Republic, typically one per major city. The duxes command the **Auxiliaries**, who handle policing and local defense, with the Legions retained under the consuls' direct control or seconded in small detachments as needed.

Deepfire—A city deep in the Shattered Peak mountains. Deepfire is an exclave, considered **Dawn Republic** territory in spite of being far outside the Republic's borders, connected by a **Gate** under the **Chosen** fortress known as the Spike.

Originally, the mountain that stood where Deepfire is now hosted a major **ghoul** city—perhaps the ghoul capital, though stories are conflicted. The Chosen deployed a weapon of unparalleled destructive power against it. While the nature of the weapon is unknown, it blasted the mountain into a kilometers-wide crater and left a giant fissure in the rock known as the Pit. Immediately afterward, the Chosen's forces began a systematic purge of the ghoul tunnels in the area that had survived the blast.

As the Chosen died out, the **Twilight Order** continued the purges. Humans from the surrounding areas flocked to the crater, since heat from the Chosen weapon—still burning at the bottom of the Pit—kept it warm in the depths of winter, and the Order and **Legion** presence provided protection from **plaguespawn** then devastating the former Chosen Empire. Scavenging in the tunnels eventually became a major industry, and the Order maintained their presence to manage it even after the ghouls had been wiped out.

Modern Deepfire is a divided city. The crater has long since been filled with buildings, and the edge of it marks the formal boundary of the Republic. Beyond that, the mountain is riddled with tunnels, and the people who live in them are called tunnelborn. Tunnelborn are not Republic citizens, and manufactories set up to exploit their cheap labor have become the city's second primary industry. Tension between the tunnelborn and the Republic citizens living aboveground is common, exacerbated by the plentiful opportunities for smuggling and corruption available to Republic officials.

deiat—the power of creation, identified with the fire of the sun. The **Chosen** could draw energy from *deiat* to accomplish a wide range of spectacular feats, from destructive manifestations like balls of flame or bursts of raw force to defensive barriers and more. It could also be used to create unnatural substances, like the indestructible **unmetal**. More advanced uses of *deiat* required specialized tools, now called **arcana**. These devices, when powered by a *deiat* wielder, could accomplish wonders—the **Gates** that wove the Empire together and the skyships and skyfortresses that hovered overhead are notable examples, in addition to more mundane tools like **blasters**, watch charms, water treatment facilities, and so on.

Deiat does have limits. It manipulates physical objects and properties—force, temperature, and so on—and does not interact with biological systems at any level except the crudely destructive. *Deiat* tools also require a continuous flow of power, either from a wielder or a storage device like a **sunsplinter**, and cannot operate without the will of the wielder. In particular, the autonomous **constructs** used by the **ghouls** are impossible to create with *deiat*.

With the Chosen wiped out by the **Plague**, the only wielders of *deiat* remaining are the **centarchs** of the **Twilight Order**, who can use their **haken**—themselves a *deiat*-created tool—to draw *deiat* power, though more weakly than the Chosen could. Why some **humans** have the ability to wield *deiat* and others do not is unknown. Centarchs are typically limited to a particular class of effects—fire, ice, force, and so on—although all can use *deiat* to power arcana such as Gates and **panoply** belts. Only the most primitive of construction techniques are still known, but existing unmetal can be reforged and reshaped, allowing the creation of the armor of the centarchs and the **Legions**.

dhak—Originally, this term referred only to **ghoul arcana** produced using *dhaka*. In the centuries since the **Plague War**, its meaning has expanded and is now synonymous with unsanctioned arcana— arcana not in the very narrow categories approved for safe use by the **Twilight Order**. Possession of *dhak* is illegal in the **Dawn Republic** and grounds for immediate imprisonment or even execution, at the discretion of the arresting official.

dhaka—a form of supernatural power, distinct from the use of *deiat*, originally wielded by the **ghouls**. *Dhaka* allows a wielder to influence biological systems and processes, to accelerate, change, or even give a semblance of life to nonliving things. It can heal wounds and alter living creatures and was used by the ghouls to create a great variety of living and semi-living tools—light sources, weapons, even vehicles. The most noteworthy were **constructs**, automata that could accept orders and act independently, a type of creation impossible even for the **Chosen**.

Any **human** can learn to wield *dhaka*, though the practice can be very dangerous, and much knowledge has been lost. After the **Plague War**, the dying Chosen created the **Twilight Order**, and one of its central commandments was to stamp out the knowledge and practice of *dhaka* forever. This has proven difficult, and the Order pursues *dhakim* down to the present day.

dhakim—a human wielder of *dhaka*. Illegal under penalty of death in the **Dawn Republic**, and even in the **Splinter Kingdoms**, often shunned and likely to be hunted down by **centarchs**. *Dhakim* are widely seen as mad, conducting gruesome experiments and creating horrible diseases. Adding to this perception is the fact that *dhakim* can exert influence over **plaguespawn**, bringing the mindless creatures under their command. Very occasionally, a *dhakim* will establish a reputation as a healer and come to be accepted by their community.

Elder—something of the time before the **Plague War**, approximately four hundred years ago, when the **Chosen** ruled an empire and the **ghouls** lived underground. As most common people are hazy on the distinction between various types of **arcana** and ruins, Chosen and ghoul remnants alike are often referred to generically as Elder.

Forge—The headquarters of the **Twilight Order**, a mountain fortress not far from **Skyreach**. Built with the help of the **Chosen** at the Order's founding, it is a colossal complex, large enough to accommodate the entire Twilight Order even at its height. As the numbers of **centarchs** have shrunk over the centuries, the Forge is now largely empty. It has three **Gates**, the only location to house more than one. The Order's training, storage, and support facilities are located here, as well as the seat of the Council.

Gate—A **Chosen arcana** that allows instantaneous transport from one location to another. A Gate looks like a freestanding unmetal arch big enough to admit a wagon. When activated and powered with *deiat*, it fills with a silvery curtain and connects to a target Gate, allowing free passage between the two simply by stepping through.

Because Gates require a connection to *deiat* to power them and set their destination, only a **centarch** can activate one, and the Gate network is exclusively used by the **Twilight Order**. Many Gate locations are kept deliberately obscure, to prevent enemies of the Order from setting ambushes. In times of extreme danger to the **Dawn Republic**, the Order has used the Gates to transport **Legions**, giving the Republic military unmatched strategic mobility.

ghouls—One of the **Elder** races, along with the **Chosen**. Information about them was suppressed by the Chosen and later the **Twilight Order**, so little is known. They were masters of *dhaka*, produced many **constructs** and biological **arcana**, and lived largely underground. Depictions of ghouls generally show humanoids with bestial features. They rebelled against the Chosen, beginning the **Plague War**, and released the **Plague**, which eventually drove the Chosen to extinction. In retaliation, the Chosen wiped them out. The ghouls are also believed to have created the **plaguespawn** as weapons for use in the war.

glowstone—An inexpensive light source resembling a glassy stone, producing a dim blue light when shaken hard. An **alchemical** creation and generally **sanctioned arcana**.

haken—the most powerful **Chosen arcana**, and the signature weapon of the **centarchs**. Haken resemble bladeless swords, usually adorned with crystals. In the hands of a **human** with the right potential, they allow access to the energy of *deiat*. The wielder can generate a blade of pure energy, shaped according to the manifestation of their talent—fire, wind, force, and so on—and draw power to create a variety of effects or activate other Chosen arcana.

The haken were created by the Chosen in their final days to arm the **Twilight Order** and allow human civilization some access to *deiat*, and the secret of their construction has been long since lost. Fortunately, the centarchs have an instinctive ability to sense haken in general and their own in particular, so when they are lost the Order can generally recover them.

hardshell—A tortoise-like creature used as a beast of burden. Hardshells resemble common tortoises, but on a massive scale, standing nearly two meters tall at the shoulder and three meters at the top of the shell. They are rare and expensive and have to be trained from the egg to be responsive to their handlers' commands. Though slow, they can pull enormous loads and are capable of subsisting on little water and poor forage. They are mostly used in deserts and other badlands where fodder is difficult to find.

human—Humans have always formed a vast majority of the population, both in the former **Chosen** Empire and beyond. After the **Plague War** and the destruction of the **Elder** races, humans are all that remain.

In the lands formerly ruled by the Chosen, the human inhabitants display some differences from baseline humans in the rest of the world. They display a much wider range of hair, eye, and skin tones, are highly resistant to disease, and heal quickly. Women have control over their fertility and must consciously invoke it in order to conceive.

A tiny minority of humans have the ability to wield *deiat* with the assistance of a **haken**, and these are sought out as children by the **Twilight Order** to be trained into **centarchs**. Humans are capable of learning *dhaka*, though the Order works to suppress this as much as it can.

Inheritance, **the**—The founding text of the **Twilight Order**, written by the **Chosen** to provide guidance after their extinction. It gives a brief history of the Chosen, the **Plague War**, and the destruction of the **ghouls**, lays out the ideals and precepts of the Order, and establishes its basic structure and laws.

Kyriliarch—One of the twelve members of the Council that leads the **Twilight Order**.

Legions—One of the two branches of the **Dawn Republic** military, along with the **Auxiliaries**. The Legions are small in number but highly trained and equipped with **arcana** weapons and armor. They use **blaster** rifles and distinctive white **unmetal** armor, giving them power that no conventionally armed force can match.

Though they form the core of the Republic's military and are concentrated against particular threats, the majority of the Legions at any given time are dispersed, sweeping for plaguespawn. The much more numerous Auxiliaries handle local defense, policing, and other duties.

Since only the **Twilight Order** has the ability to recharge **sunsplinters**, reshape unmetal armor, and perform other needed maintenance, the Legions are ultimately dependent on the Order's **centarchs** to sustain themselves. This makes the Republic as a whole reliant on the Order, which has sometimes rankled Republic leadership. Legionaries are often seconded to the Order for duty combating **plaguespawn** and *dhakim* when the centarchs are spread too thin.

loadbird—The most common beast of burden in the former **Chosen** Empire, loadbirds are large flightless birds capable of pulling plows or wheeled vehicles. They look something like emus, standing roughly four feet tall at the shoulder, with a long neck that raises their undersized head much higher. Their legs are overdeveloped and heavily muscled, and their wings are small and vestigial.

Like their cousins **warbirds** and **swiftbirds**, loadbirds are controlled by a combination of reins and whistle commands; the better trained and more amicable a bird is, the more likely it can be directed by whistles alone. Loadbirds can be ridden but are slow and uncomfortable. Bred for strength, they can pull heavy weights alone or in teams.

Loadbirds eat mostly seeds and insects. They dislike **thickheads**, and clashes between the two species are notorious for causing problems.

Order—The **Twilight Order**.

panoply—A type of **Chosen arcana** that creates a defensive barrier, called a panoply field, around the user, absorbing incoming attacks. A panoply needs a constant supply of *deiat* to operate and so is not useful to anyone other than **centarchs**. It will deflect any energy blast or fast-moving object, drawing *deiat* energy from the user in the process.

A centarch using a panoply is impervious to normal weaponry, and the field will even stop blaster bolts or the blade of a haken. However, the energy drain to maintain the field in the face of sustained attack will quickly exhaust the centarch's capacity to draw on *deiat*. Drawing too much power in too short a time will render a centarch unconscious and leave them unable to access *deiat* for several hours. Duels between centarchs are typically fought wearing panoplies, with the loser being the first to be knocked out in this manner.

Physically, the most common form of panoply is a broad belt of thin silver fabric, worn around the midsection, but other varieties exist with the same function.

Plague—a virulent illness that affected the **Chosen** during the **Plague War**. It was released by the **ghouls** in their rebellion against Chosen rule, and in spite of enormous efforts at combating it ultimately proved completely fatal to the Chosen, although it had no effect on humans. It is commonly associated with **plaguespawn**, who appeared around the same time, but the connection is not understood.

plaguespawn—Unnatural creatures created with *dhaka* that have afflicted the former **Chosen** Empire since the **Plague War**. It is commonly believed they were originally created by the **ghouls** as living weapons during the conflict and have run amok ever since.

Plaguespawn have almost infinitely variable forms. They appear as an assembly of organic parts into a vaguely animal-like shape, mostly muscle and bone, from a variety of mismatched sources. They can be as small as mice or as large as elephants, and there are stories of even bigger monsters. In spite of their hodgepodge, ramshackle appearance, they are universally vicious, fast, and deadly.

While they use animal matter in their bodies, plaguespawn are not biological creatures in the normal sense, and are powered by *dhaka*. They do not eat, excrete, or reproduce as true animals do. Instead, their sole drive is to find and kill animals, the larger the better, and humans preferentially above all others. After killing, the plaguespawn disassembles the corpses using *dhaka* and incorporates them into itself, sometimes completely altering its own form in the process. Plaguespawn thus grow larger the more they kill, though there may be an ultimate upper limit on this process.

It's not well understood how new plaguespawn come into existence. Small plaguespawn have been observed to "bud" from larger ones, and areas infested with plaguespawn tend to become more infested over time. On the other hand, areas swept clean and safe for years can suddenly be subject to plaguespawn outbreaks. One theory is that the **Plague** itself is still present in the atmosphere and periodically causes plaguespawn to form spontaneously. The **Twilight Order** maintains that plaguespawn outbreaks are caused by *dhak* and *dhakim*, and hunts them relentlessly.

Dhakim do have a connection to plaguespawn through *dhaka*, and can exert control over them. Absent this control, the monsters are nearly mindless, driven only to hunt and kill. The more powerful the *dhakim*, the more and larger plaguespawn they can control.

The threat of plaguespawn is ubiquitous throughout the former Chosen Empire. In the **Dawn Republic**, a large proportion of the **Legions** at any given time are engaged in plaguespawn sweeps, repeated at multiyear intervals throughout Republic territory. Along the borders, the **Auxiliaries** keep constant watch for incursions. This keeps Republic territory reasonably safe from plaguespawn attack, though the effort involved is enormous and periodic outbreaks still occur. In the **Splinter Kingdoms**, with their lesser resources, such sweeps are impossible and plaguespawn attacks are a fact of life. Towns and villages are walled, houses are fortified, and travelers go well armed. Fortunately, the mindlessness of plaguespawn means they are usually no match for the well prepared.

Plague War—The conflict that brought about the destruction of the **Elder** races and the fall of the **Chosen** Empire. The specific events of the war have largely been lost in the chaos of the times, but an outline is preserved in the histories of the **Twilight Order**. The **ghouls** rebelled against the rule of the Chosen, and when their rebellion was suppressed they unleashed the **Plague**, which eventually wiped out the Chosen completely. The dwindling Chosen, however, were able to exterminate the ghouls in turn, and then founded the **Twilight Order** and the **Dawn Republic** to help their human former subjects survive in the wreckage of their empire.

pony—A small equine sometimes used as a mount or beast of burden. More expensive and less capable than **loadbirds**, **thickheads**, or

hardshells, ponies are relatively rare, and primarily used as status symbols by the wealthy.

quickheal—An **alchemical** creation that functions as an anesthetic, prevents infection, and promotes rapid healing. It can be made either in a liquid form or as waxy, chewable tablets. **Sanctioned arcana** when produced by an **Order**-approved alchemist.

Republic—The **Dawn Republic**.

sanctioned arcana—**arcana** or **alchemical** products approved by the **Twilight Order** for general use, including **quickheal**, **glowstones**, and other staples. All other arcana and alchemical products are considered *dhak* by the Order. Sanctioned arcana is always expensive and in limited supply, which creates constant problems with smugglers selling *dhak*.

skyfortress—The largest class of **skyship** created by the **Chosen** Empire. Only eight of these massive vessels were ever built. During the **Plague War**, they were used to deliver the most devastating of the Chosen's weapons against the **ghouls**. Of the eight, three were lost over the sea in a last-ditch attempt by the Chosen to find land outside their continent-wide empire, in the hopes of escaping the **Plague**. The other five were either grounded and eventually destroyed, or crashed due to mishap or ghoul attack. One, the skyfortress *Grace in Execution*, overhangs the city of Grace and was the original reason for its settlement.

Skyreach—The capital of the **Dawn Republic**, and former capital of the **Chosen** Empire. The heart of Republic wealth and power, and the home of its Senate and ruling class. The huge Chosen buildings that form the heart of Skyreach would be impossible to inhabit without a continuous supply of **sunsplinters** charged with *deiat* to power their elevators, ventilation, water, and so on, and so only here, with the cooperation of the **Twilight Order**, is something like the Chosen's old standard of living maintained. Living in such a tower is a mark of extremely high status, only available to the hugely wealthy and powerful.

skyship—Any of the wide variety of flying vessels used by the **Chosen**. These ranged from small one-man skiffs to the massive **skyfortresses**, generally taking the form of flattened teardrops, with the pointed end being the bow. They were some of the most advanced and complex **arcana** the Chosen created. Many were destroyed in the **Plague War**, and while the **Twilight Order** maintained a few during the first few decades of its existence, they quickly broke down beyond human capacity to repair. No operational skyships are currently known to exist, though there are always rumors among scavengers.

Splinter Kingdoms—portions of the former **Chosen** Empire that have broken away from the **Dawn Republic**. After the **Plague War**, the Republic asserted authority over the entirety of the old Chosen Empire, but maintaining control over such a vast area proved impossible in the face of rebellions and **plaguespawn** attacks. Some regions were abandoned as the **Legions** retreated to a perimeter they could keep clear of plaguespawn, while other cities declared themselves independent under local rulers or ambitious warlords. The Republic crushed some of these rebellions, but strained resources meant that others had to be accepted.

Life in the Splinter Kingdoms is generally more dangerous than in the Republic, without the **arcana**-armed Legions to keep order and suppress plaguespawn. However, this varies greatly from polity to polity. In spite of their name, not all the breakaway states are monarchies—there are free cities, republics, and other political experiments, sometimes changing rapidly as they war with one another. As a general rule, the farther from the Republic they are, the smaller and less stable they become, with larger kingdoms like Grace, Meltrock, and Drail being stabilized by the opportunity to trade with the Republic.

While *dhak* is illegal in the Republic, its status in the Splinter Kingdoms varies. Some attempt to maintain the Republic's ban, while others, like Grace, embrace *dhak* and encourage its creation and sale. Smuggling across the Republic border is a major business. The **Twilight Order** asserts that its centarchs have the right to go anywhere in the old Chosen Empire to hunt *dhak* and ***dhakim***, but as a practical matter some Splinter Kingdoms are openly hostile to Order agents, and they must move secretly there.

sunsplinter—an **arcana** device that serves as a ***deiat*** battery, storing power for future use by other arcana. Most notably used by **blasters** as a power source. Only someone with a connection to *deiat* can refill one, so fully charged sunsplinters are rare and expensive.

sunstone—an **arcana** light source, powered by ***deiat***, which produces bright white light. Controlled by *deiat* and requiring periodic infusions of power to keep operating, so used only by the **Twilight Order** or Republic elites.

swiftbird—A cousin of the **loadbird** and the **warbird**, specialized for riding. Generally resembles a loadbird, but with longer, leaner legs. Contrary to its name, the swiftbird specializes not in speed but in endurance. A warbird might outrun one over the course of a short charge, but a swiftbird can keep up a rapid pace for ten to twelve hours a day with sufficient food and water, allowing riders to cover long distances.

thickhead—A large reptilian creature used as a beast of burden. Thickheads resemble giant lizards, with short tails, tough, scaly skin, and bony protrusions around their skulls. They are tremendously strong and can pull very heavy loads, although their fastest pace is not much more than a walk. They are also very sure-footed and can traverse almost any terrain. Slow and expensive to maintain compared to **loadbirds**, they're used for particularly heavy burdens or as pack animals over bad roads.

Though thickheads look fierce, with their beaks and spiked skulls, they are pure vegetarians and display almost no aggressive behavior. Their smell tends to rile loadbirds, who sometimes snap at them or shy away. When threatened, a thickhead lowers itself to the ground and puts its forepaws over its face, protecting its vulnerable eyes and belly and relying on its tough hide to repel an attacker. Once hunkered down, they are notoriously difficult to get moving again.

Twilight Order—an organization created by the dying **Chosen**, in the last days of the **Plague War**, to give humans the ability to use *deiat* and sustain civilization after their extinction. Key to this purpose are the haken, Chosen **arcana** that allow the few humans capable of drawing on *deiat* to wield its power.

The purposes of the Twilight Order are to defend humanity as a whole, especially from plaguespawn and ghouls; to suppress knowledge of *dhaka* and destroy *dhakim*, as part of that defense; and to make sure the power of *deiat* is wielded for the common good. These themes are laid out in a book called the *Inheritance*, which details the history of the Chosen and the Plague War and explains the goals of the Order.

The core of the Order are the **centarchs**. Every **human** capable of wielding *deiat* that the Order is able to locate is brought to the **Forge** to become an **agathios**, a centarch trainee under an experienced teacher. When they are deemed ready by their master, usually by their early twenties, they receive their **cognomen** and are declared a full centarch. Apart from the **Kyriliarchs**, all centarchs are theoretically peers, and free to choose their own path, though in practice a great deal of deference is paid to seniority and unwritten tradition. Centarchs, wielding *deiat* through their haken, travel throughout the **Dawn Republic** and beyond, fighting plaguespawn and hunting *dhak* and *dhakim*.

The governing body of the Order is the Council of twelve Kyriliarchs. Generally senior centarchs, these members are nominated by the other centarchs, approved by the Council, and serve for life. Only a majority of the Council can issue directions that centarchs are bound by the laws of the Order to accept. The Council sets broad policy for the Order, directs centarchs to particular areas of trouble, and rules on intra-Order disputes and transgressions.

In addition to the centarchs, the Order includes supporting staff of several sorts. The Forge is maintained by hereditary families of servants, who do manual labor in the fortress. An extensive logistics service handles supplies and tracks the vast storehouse of arcana the Order maintains, and a courier service uses the **Gates** to provide rapid delivery of information. Arcanists help maintain equipment and work with centarchs in the field to research arcana. Another group, called scouts, supports the centarchs directly on missions and maintains outposts and intelligence-gathering operations throughout the Republic and the **Splinter Kingdoms**, working undercover where the Order is not welcome.

While the Order is not in charge of the Republic, nor subject to the instructions of the Republic Senate, the two groups maintain an uneasy but close relationship. The *Inheritance* instructs the Order to stay out of mundane politics, to preserve their independence and reduce temptation to corruption. But the Order has traditionally been willing to intervene when the Republic is threatened, and the power of the centarchs is the ultimate guarantor of the Republic's continued status as the most powerful nation in the remains of the Chosen Empire.

unmetal—a material used by the **Chosen** for a wide variety of purposes. Unmetal is lighter than steel but enormously stronger, essentially indestructible except against *deiat*. Even *deiat* takes significant time and effort to damage it. It can have a variety of colors and finishes but is usually identifiable by its iridescent sheen.

With the fall of the Chosen, the means of creating unmetal has been lost, but enormous amounts remain from various Chosen ruins. Modifying and repurposing them is obviously a challenge, however. The **Twilight Order** retains a limited capacity to reforge unmetal, which they use to create equipment for themselves and the **Legions**.

vulpi (pl. vulpi)—a livestock animal raised for meat, with a unique life cycle. They are omnivores and will eat nearly anything, but can thrive on grasses and weeds. Vulpi are born small and helpless, but rapidly grow into boisterous, playful creatures resembling both pigs and weasels. This yearling phase lasts for approximately their first year or two. Toward the end of it, they mate repeatedly, and females store enough sperm to last for the rest of their lives. They then mature into breeders, nearly doubling in size and becoming squatter and ill-tempered. For the following year or more, the females will give birth to litters of pups every eight to ten weeks.

Finally, the mature vulpi enter their final stage of life, during which they are called terminals. They become sessile and increase enormously in size (up to tenfold if provided with plenty of feed), and their legs atrophy and are eventually lost in the vast bulk of their bodies. In this phase they are extremely efficient eaters and produce little waste. On their own, terminals simply die of starvation, but properly tended and eventually slaughtered they produce large amounts of high-quality, pork-like meat. Vulpi is a staple throughout the **Dawn Republic** and the **Splinter Kingdoms**. Culled at the yearling or breeder stage, they can also provide useful leather and other by-products.

warbird—A rarer cousin of **loadbirds** and **swiftbirds**, warbirds are large, flightless birds bred for combat. They resemble loadbirds but retain larger wings, which they flap for stability while kicking. Unlike their more docile cousins, warbirds have long talons on their toes and a sickle-like claw on the back of their foot, and are capable of tearing an unarmored human to shreds.

In battle, warbirds are typically equipped with armor and have blades affixed to their beaks, while carrying an armored rider who fights with a lance or spear. Outside the **Republic** (where the **Legions** with their **arcana** weapons remain the dominant military force) warbird-riding cavalry is often the preeminent military arm.

Warbirds are more difficult to train than their cousins, and more expensive to keep, eating mostly large insects and rodents. They are therefore expensive, and owning one is usually a mark of status.

extras

orbit

meet the author

Photo Credit: Rachel Thompson

DJANGO WEXLER graduated from Carnegie Mellon University in Pittsburgh with degrees in creative writing and computer science, and he worked for the university in artificial intelligence research. Eventually he migrated to Microsoft in Seattle, where he now lives with two cats and a teetering mountain of books. When not writing, he wrangles computers, paints tiny soldiers, and plays games of all sorts.

Find out more about Django Wexler and other Orbit authors by registering for the free monthly newsletter at www.orbitbooks.net.

if you enjoyed
ASHES OF THE SUN

look out for

LEGACY OF ASH
The Legacy Trilogy: Book One

by

Matthew Ward

A shadow has fallen over the Tressian Republic.

Ruling families—once protectors of justice and democracy—now plot against one another with sharp words and sharper knives. Blinded by ambition, they remain heedless of the threat posed by the invading armies of the Hadari Empire.

Yet as Tressia falls, heroes rise.

Viktor Akadra is the Republic's champion. A warrior without equal, he hides a secret that would see him burned as a heretic.

Josiri Trelan is Viktor's sworn enemy. A political prisoner, he dreams of reigniting his mother's failed rebellion.

*And yet Calenne Trelan, Josiri's sister, seeks only to break
free of their tarnished legacy, to escape the expectation and
prejudice that haunt the family name.*

*As war spreads across the Republic, these three must set aside their
differences in order to save their home. Yet decades of bad blood are
not easily set aside. And victory—if it comes at all—will demand a
darker price than any of them could have imagined.*

One

Preparations had taken weeks. Statues had been re-gilded. Familial
portraits unveiled from dusty canvas and set in places of honour.
The stained glass of the western window glittered in the afternoon
sunlight. Come the hour of Ascension it would blaze like fire and
cast an image of divine Lumestra into the hall so that the sun god-
dess too would stand among the guests.

It would not be so elsewhere. In the houses beneath Branghall's
walls the part of Lumestra would be played by a doll, her limbs
carved from firewood and her golden hair woven from last year's
straw. There, her brief reign would not end with the fading of the
sun. Instead, hearth-fires would usher her home on tongues of
flame.

The chasm between rich and poor, ruler and ruled, was never
more evident than at Ascension. Josiri strove to be mindful of that.
For all that had befallen his family, he retained comfort and privi-
lege denied to many.

But a prison remained a prison, even if the bars were gilded and
the guards polite.

Most of the guards.

"That will have to come down." Arzro Makrov extended a finger to the portrait above High Table. "She has no place here, or anywhere else in the Tressian Republic."

Josiri exchanged a glance with Anastacia. The seneschal's black eyes glimmered a warning, reinforced by a slight shake of her head. Josiri ignored both and stepped closer, footsteps hollow on the hall's flagstones. "No place?"

Makrov flinched but held his ground. "Katya Trelan was a traitor."

Impotent anger kindled. Fifteen years on, and the wound remained raw as ever.

"This was my mother's home," said Josiri carefully. "She would have celebrated her fifty-fifth year this Ascension. Her body is ash, but she *will* be present in spirit."

"No."

Makrov drew his corpulent body up to its full, unimpressive height. The setting sun lent his robes the rich warmth of fresh blood. Ironic for a man so pallid. The intricate silver ward-brooch was a poor match for his stolid garb. But without it, he could not have crossed the enchanted manor wall.

Josiri's throat tightened. He locked gazes with Makrov for a long moment, and then let his eyes fall upon the remaining "guests." Would any offer support?

Shaisan Yanda didn't meet his gaze, but that was to be expected. As governor of the Southshires, she was only present to ensure Josiri did nothing rash. Nonetheless, the slight curl to her lip suggested she found Makrov's behaviour tiresome. She'd fought for the Council at Zanya, and on other battlefields besides, earning both her scars and the extra weight that came with advancing years.

As for Valmir Sark, he paid little attention. His interest lay more with ancestral finery . . . and likely in broaching Branghall's wine cellars come Ascension. Josiri had heard enough of Sark to know he was present only to spare his family another scandal. The high-collared uniform might as well have been for show. Sark was too young to have fought against Katya's rebellion. And as for him standing a turn on the Hadari border? The thought was laughable.

That left Anastacia, and her opinion carried no sway.

If only Calenne were there. She'd always had more success in dealing with the Council's emissaries, and more patience. Where in Lumestra's name was she? She'd promised.

Josiri swallowed his irritation. He'd enough enemies without adding his sister to the roster.

"The portrait remains," he said. "This is my house. I'll thank you to remember that."

Makrov's wispy grey eyebrows knotted. "Were it up to me, I'd allow it. Truly I would. But the Council insists. Katya Trelan brought nothing but division and strife. Her shadow should not mar Ascension."

Only the slightest pause between the words imbued challenge. Josiri's self-control, so painstakingly fortified before the meeting, slipped a notch. He shook off Anastacia's restraining hand and took another step.

Yanda's lips tightened to a thin, bloodless streak. Her hand closed meaningfully about the pommel of her sword. Sark gazed on with parted mouth and the first spark of true interest.

"It is my hope," said Josiri, "that my mother's presence will serve as a message of unity."

Makrov stared up at the portrait. "I applaud your intent. But the lawless are not quelled by gestures, but by strong words, and stronger action."

"I've given what leadership I can."

"I know," said Makrov. "I've read reports of your speeches. I'd like to hear one for myself. Tomorrow at noon?"

It was an artful twist of the knife. "If you wish."

"Excellent." He raised his voice. "Governor Yanda. You'll ensure his grace isn't speaking to an empty square? I'm sure Captain Sark will be delighted to assist."

"Of course, my lord," said Yanda. "And the portrait?"

Makrov locked gazes with Katya Trelan's dead stare. "I want it taken down and burned. Her body is ash. Let her spirit join it. I can think of no stronger message of unity."

"I won't do it," Josiri said through gritted teeth.

"Yes, you will." Makrov sighed. "Your grace. *Josiri*. I entertained hopes that you'd lead your people out of the past. But the Council's patience is not infinite. They may decide upon another exodus if there's anything less than full cooperation."

Exodus. The word sounded harmless. The reality was punishment meted out for a rebellion fifteen years in the past; families divided, stolen children shipped north to toil as little more than slaves. Makrov sought to douse a fire with tinder.

"Your mother's memory poisons you. As it poisons your people." Makrov set his hands on Josiri's shoulders. "Let her go. I have."

But he hadn't. That was why Makrov remained the Council's chief emissary to the Southshires, despite his advancing years and expanding waistline. His broken heart had never healed, but Katya Trelan lay fifteen years beyond his vengeance. And so he set his bitterness against her people, and against a son who he believed should have been his.

Makrov offered an avuncular smile. "You'll thank me one day."

Josiri held his tongue, not trusting himself to reply. Makrov strode away, Sark falling into step behind. Yanda hesitated a moment before following.

"Tomorrow at noon, your grace. I look forward to it." Makrov spoke without turning, the words echoing along the rafters. Then he was gone.

Josiri glanced up at his mother's portrait. Completed a year before her death, it captured to perfection the gleam of her eyes and the inscrutable perhaps-mocking, maybe-sympathetic smile. At least, Josiri thought it did. Fifteen years was a long time. He saw little of himself in his mother's likeness, but then he'd always been more akin to his father. The same unruly blond hair and lantern jaw. The same lingering resentment at forces beyond his control.

He perched on the edge of High Table and swallowed his irritation. He couldn't afford anger. Dignity was the cornerstone of leadership, or so his mother had preached.

"When I was a boy," he said, "my father told me that people are scared and stupid more than they are cruel. I thought he'd handed me the key to some great mystery. Now? The longer I spend in Makrov's company, the more I suspect my father told me what he *wished* were true."

Anastacia drew closer. Her outline blurred like vapour, as it always did when her attention wandered. Like her loose tangle of snow-white curls and impish features, the robes of a Trelan seneschal were for show. A concession. Josiri wasn't sure what Anastacia's true form actually *was*. Only black, glossy eyes – long considered the eyes of a witch, or a demon, bereft of iris and sclera – offered any hint.

The Council's proctors had captured her a year or so after the Battle of Zanya. Branghall, already a prison in all but name, had become her new home shortly after. Anastacia spoke often of what she'd done to deserve Tressian ire. The problem was, no two tales matched.

In one, she'd seduced and murdered a prominent councillor. In another, she'd instead seduced and murdered that same councillor's husband. A third story involved ransacking a church. And then there was the tale about a choir of serenes, and indecency that left the holy women's vows of chastity in tatters. After a dozen such stories, ranging from ribald to horrific, Josiri had stopped asking.

But somewhere along the line, they'd become friends. More than friends. If Makrov ever learned how close they were, it wouldn't be the gallows that awaited Josiri, but the pyre.

Pallid wisps of light curled from Anastacia's arched eyebrow. "The archimandrite is foolish in the way only clever men are. As for afraid? If he wasn't, you'd not be his prisoner."

Josiri snorted. "My mother casts a long shadow. But I'm not her."

"No. Your mother lost her war. You'll win yours."

"Flatterer."

The eyebrow twitched a fraction higher. "Isn't that a courtier's function?"

Genuine confusion, or another of Anastacia's little jokes? It was always hard to be sure. "In the rest of the Republic, perhaps. In the Southshires, truth is all we can afford."

"If you're going to start moping, I'd like to be excused."

A smile tugged at the corner of Josiri's mouth. "If you don't show your duke a little more respect, he might have you thrown from the manor."

Anastacia sniffed. "He's welcome to try. But these stones are old, and the Council's proctors made a thorough job of binding me to them. You'll fail before they do."

"You forget, I'm a Trelan. I'm stubborn."

"And where did stubbornness get your mother? Or your uncle, for that matter?"

Josiri's gaze drifted back to his mother's portrait. "What would she do?"

"I doubt she'd put a mere *thing*, no matter how beautiful, before the lives of her people." She shrugged. "But she was a Trelan, and someone once told me – though I can't remember who – that Trelans are stubborn."

"And none more than she," said Josiri. "I don't want to give up the last of her."

Anastacia scratched at the back of her scalp – a mannerism she'd picked up off one of the servants in her frequent forays to the kitchens. Her appetites were voracious – especially where the manor's wine cellar was concerned.

"Might I offer some advice, as one prisoner to another?"

"Of course."

"Burn the painting. Your mother's legacy is not in canvas and oils, but in blood."

The words provoked a fresh spark of irritation. "Calenne doesn't seem to think so."

Anastacia offered no reply. Josiri couldn't blame her for that. This particular field was well-furrowed. And besides, good advice was good advice. Katya Trelan had died to save her family. That was her true legacy.

"I should tell her how things went," he said. "Do you know where she is?"

"Where do you think?" Anastacia's tone grew whimsical to

match her expression. "For myself, I might rearrange the window shutters on the upper floor. Just in case some helpful soul's watching? One who might be agreeable to expressing your annoyance at the archimandrite where you cannot?"

Josiri swallowed a snort of laughter. Regardless of what his mother would have done about the painting, this she *would* approve of. Humiliation repaid in kind.

"That's a grand idea."

Anastacia sniffed again. "Of course it is. Shall we say nightfall?"

That ran things close, but the timing should work. Makrov was due to hold celebration in Eskavord's tiny church at dusk. Afterwards, he'd make the long ride back to the fortress at Cragwatch. It all depended on whether Crovan's people were keeping watch on the shutters.

Still, inaction gained nothing.

Josiri nodded. "Nightfall it is."

Each creak of the stairs elicited a fearful wince, and a palm pressed harder against rough stone. Josiri told himself that the tower hadn't endured generations of enthusiastic winds just to crumble beneath his own meagre weight. He might even have believed it, if not for that almost imperceptible rocking motion. In his great-grandfather's time, the tower had been an observatory. Now the roof was a nest of fallen beams, and the walls stone teeth in a shattered jaw.

At least the skies were clear. The vistas almost held the terror at bay, fear paling before beauty. The town of Eskavord sprawled across the eastern valley, smoke dancing as the Ash Wind – so named for the cinders it gusted from the distant Thrakkian border to the south – brushed the slopes of Drannan Tor. Beyond the outermost farms sprawled the eaves of Davenwood. Beyond that, further east, the high town walls of Kreska nestled in the foothills of the Greyridge Mountains. All of it within a day's idle ride. Close at hand, and yet out of reach.

But it paid not to look too close. You might see the tabarded soldiers patrolling Eskavord's streets, or the boarded-up houses. The foreboding gibbets on Gallows Hill. Where Josiri's Uncle Taymor had danced a final jig – where his mother had burned, her ashes scattered so Lumestra could not easily resurrect her come the light of Third Dawn. It was worse in the month of Reaptithe. Endless supply wagons crept along the sunken roadways like columns of ants, bearing the Southshires' bounty north.

Duke Kevor Trelan had never been more popular with his people than when he called for secession. The Council had been quick to respond. Josiri still recalled the bleak Tzadas-morning the summons had arrived at Branghall, backed by swords enough to make refusal impossible. It was the last memory he had of his father. But the Council had erred. Duke Kevor's execution made rebellion inevitable.

Another gust assailed the tower. His panicked step clipped a fragment of stone. It ricocheted off the sun-bleached remnant of a wooden beam and clattered out over the edge.

"I suppose your demon told you where I was?"

Calenne, as usual, perched on the remnants of the old balcony – little more than a spur of timber jutting at right angles to a battered wall. Her back to a pile of rubble, she had one foot hooked across her knee. The other dangled out over the courtyard, three storeys and forty feet below. A leather-bound book lay open across her lap, pages fluttering.

"Her name is Anastacia."

"That's not her name." The wind plucked a spill of black hair from behind Calenne's ear. She tucked it back into place. "That's what *you* call her."

Calenne had disliked Anastacia from the first, though Josiri had never been clear why, and the passage of time had done little to heal the one-sided divide. Anastacia seldom reciprocated the antipathy, though whether that was because she considered herself above such things, or did so simply to irritate Calenne, Josiri wasn't sure.

"Because that's her wish. I don't call you Enna any longer, do I?"

Blue eyes met his then returned to the book. "What do you want?"

Josiri shook his head. So very much like their mother. No admission of wrong, just a new topic.

"I thought you'd be with me to greet Makrov."

She licked a fingertip and turned the page. "I changed my mind."

"We were discussing the arrangements for *your* wedding. Or do you no longer intend to marry at Ascension?"

"That's *why* I changed my mind."

"What's that supposed to mean?"

A rare moment of hesitation. "It doesn't matter."

"I see." Steeling himself, Josiri edged closer. "What are you reading?"

"This?" Calenne stared down at the book. "A gift from Kasamor. *The Turn of Winter*, by Iugo Maliev. I'm told it's all the rage in Tressia."

"Any good?"

"If you admire a heroine who lets herself be blown from place to place like a leaf on the wind. It's horrendously fascinating. Or fascinatingly horrendous. I haven't decided yet." She closed the book and set it on her knee. "How did the meeting go?"

"I'm to make a speech tomorrow, on the topic of unity."

She scowled. "It went that badly?"

"I didn't have my sister there to charm him," Josiri replied. "And ... he reacted poorly to mother's portrait." No sense saying the rest. Calenne wouldn't understand.

She sighed. "And now you know why I stayed away. If Makrov reacts like that to Katya's image ... I didn't want complications. I can't afford them. And I *do* want this marriage."

Josiri didn't have to ask what she meant. Katya in oils was bad enough. Her likeness in flesh and blood? Even with Calenne at her most demure and charming – a rarity – there was risk. With every passing year, his sister more resembled the mother she refused to acknowledge. Perhaps she'd been right to stay away.

"You think Makrov has the power to have it annulled?"

She shrugged. "Not alone. But Kasamor's mother isn't at all pleased at the match. I'm sure she's allies enough to make trouble."

"Kasamor would truly let her interfere?"

On his brief visits to Branghall, Kasamor had seemed smitten. As indeed had Calenne herself. On the other hand, Josiri had heard enough of Ebigail Kiradin, Kasamor's mother, to suspect she possessed both the reach and influence to thwart even the course of true love, if she so chose.

"On his last visit, he told me that I was the other half of his soul. So no, I don't believe he would. He'd sooner die, I think. And I . . . " Calenne shook her head and stared down at the book. "It doesn't matter."

Josiri frowned. "What? What doesn't matter?"

Calenne offered a small, resigned smile. "I've had bad dreams of late. The Black Knight. Waking up screaming doesn't do wonders for my mood."

The Black Knight. Viktor Akadra. The Phoenix-Slayer. The man who'd murdered their mother. He'd taken root in the dreams of a terrified six-year-old girl, and never let go. Josiri had lost track of how often in that first year he'd cradled Calenne as she'd slipped off to broken sleep.

"Is that why you're back to hiding up here? He'll not harm you, I promise."

"I know he won't." Her shoulders drooped, and her tone softened. "But thanks, all the same."

She set the book aside and joined him inside the tower proper. Josiri drew her into an embrace, reflecting, as he so often did, what a curious mix of close and distant they were. The decade between them drove them apart. He doubted he'd ever understand her. Fierce in aspect, but brittle beneath.

"The world's against us, little sister. We Trelans have to stick together."

565

if you enjoyed
ASHES OF THE SUN
look out for

WE RIDE THE STORM
The Reborn Empire: Book One

by

Devin Madson

War built the Kisian Empire. War will tear it down.

Seventeen years after rebels stormed the streets, factions divide Kisia. Only the firm hand of the god-emperor holds the empire together. But when a shocking betrayal destroys a tense alliance with neighboring Chiltae, all that has been won comes crashing down.

In Kisia, Princess Miko Ts'ai is a prisoner in her own castle. She dreams of claiming her empire, but the path to power could rip it, and her family, asunder.

In Chiltae, assassin Cassandra Marius is plagued by the voices of the dead. Desperate, she accepts a contract that promises to reward her with a cure if she helps an empire fall.

And on the border between nations, Captain Rah e'Torin and his warriors are exiles forced to fight in a foreign war or die.

As an empire dies, three warriors will rise. They will have to ride the storm or drown in its blood.

1. Miko

They tried to kill me four times before I could walk. Seven before I held any memory of the world. Every time thereafter I knew fear, but it was anger that chipped sharp edges into my soul.

I had done nothing but exist. Nothing but own the wrong face and the wrong eyes, the wrong ancestors and the wrong name. Nothing but be Princess Miko Ts'ai. Yet it was enough, and not a day passed in which I did not wonder whether today would be the day they finally succeeded.

Every night I slept with a blade beneath my pillow, and every morning I tucked it into the intricate folds of my sash, its presence a constant upon which I dared build dreams. And finally those dreams felt close enough to touch. We were travelling north with the imperial court. Emperor Kin was about to name his heir.

As was my custom on the road, I rose while the inn was still silent, only the imperial guards awake about their duties. In the palace they tended to colonise doorways, but here, without great gates and walls to protect the emperor, they filled every corner. They were in the main house and in the courtyard, outside the stables and the kitchens and servants' hall—two nodded in silent acknowledgement as I made my way toward the bathhouse, my dagger heavy in the folds of my dressing robe.

Back home in the palace, baths had to be taken in wooden

568

tubs, but many northern inns had begun building Chiltaen-style bathhouses—deep stone pools into which one could sink one's whole body. I looked forward to them every year, and as I stepped into the empty building, a little of my tension left me. A trio of lacquered dressing screens provided the only places someone could hide, so I walked a slow lap through the steam to check them all.

Once sure I was alone, I abandoned my dressing robe and slid into the bath. Despite the steam dampening all it touched, the water was merely tepid, though the clatter of someone shovelling coals beneath the floor promised more warmth to come. I shivered and glanced back at my robe, the bulk of my knife beneath its folds, reassuring.

I closed my eyes only for quick steps to disturb my peace. No assassin would make so much noise, but my hand was still partway to the knife before Lady Sichi Manshin walked in. "Oh, Your Highness, I'm sorry. I didn't realise you were here. Shall I—?"

"No, don't go on my account, Sichi," I said, relaxing back into the water. "The bath is big enough for both of us, though I warn you, it's not as warm as it looks."

She screwed up her nose. "Big enough for the whole court, really."

"Yes, but I hope the whole court won't be joining us."

"Gods no. I do not wish to know what Lord Rasten looks like without his robe."

Sichi untied hers as she spoke, owning none of the embarrassment I would have felt had our positions been reversed. She took her time about it, seemingly in no hurry to get in the water and hide her fine curves, but eventually she slid in beside me with a dramatic shiver. "Oh, you weren't kidding about the temperature."

Letting out a sigh, she settled back against the stones with only her shoulders above the waterline. Damp threads of hair trailed down her long neck like dribbles of ink, the rest caught in a loose bun pinned atop her head with a golden comb. Lady Sichi was four years older than my twin and I, but her lifelong engagement to Tanaka had seen her trapped at court since our birth. If I was the caged dragon he laughingly called me, then she was a caged song-bird, her beauty less in her features than in her habits, in the way she moved and laughed and spoke, in the turn of her head and the set of her hands, in the graceful way she danced through the world.

I envied her almost as much as I pitied her.

Her thoughts seemed to have followed mine, for heaving another sigh, Lady Sichi slid through the water toward me. "Koko." Her breath was warm against my skin as she drew close. "Prince Tanaka never talks to me about anything, but you—"

"My brother—"

Sichi's fingers closed on my shoulder. "I know, hush, listen to me, please. I just...I just need to know what you know before I leave today. Will His Majesty name him as his heir at the ceremony? Is he finally going to give his blessing to our marriage?"

I turned to find her gaze raking my face. Her grip on my shoulder tightened, a desperate intensity in her digging fingers that jolted fear through my heart.

"Well?" she said, drawing closer still. "Please, Koko, tell me if you know. It's...it's important."

"Have you heard something?" My question was hardly above a breath, though I was sure we were alone, the only sound of life the continued scraping of the coal shoveller beneath our feet.

"No, oh no, just the talk. That His Majesty is seeking a treaty with Chiltae, and they want the succession confirmed before they talk terms."

It was more than I had heard, but I nodded rather than let her know it.

"I leave for my yearly visit to my family today," she went on when I didn't answer. "I want—I *need* to know if there's been any hint, anything at all."

"Nothing," I said, that single word encompassing so many years of uncertainty and frustration, so many years of fear, of knowing Tana and I were watched everywhere we went, that the power our mother held at court was all that kept us safe. "Nothing at all."

Sichi sank back, letting the water rise above her shoulders as though it could shield her from her own uncertain position. "Nothing?" Her sigh rippled the surface of the water. "I thought maybe you'd heard something, but that he just wasn't telling me because he..." The words trailed off. She knew that I knew, that it wasn't only this caged life we shared but also the feeling we were both invisible.

I shook my head and forced a smile. "Say all that is proper to your family from us, won't you?" I said, heartache impelling me to change the subject. "It must be hard on your mother having both you and your father always at court."

Her lips parted and for a moment I thought she would ask more questions, but after a long silence, she just nodded and forced her own smile. "Yes," she said. "Mama says she lives for my letters because Father's are always full of military movements and notes to himself about new orders and pay calculations."

Her father was minister of the left, in command of the empire's military, and I'd often wondered if Sichi lived at court as much to ensure the loyalty of the emperor's most powerful minister as because she was to be my brother's wife.

Lady Sichi chattered on as though a stream of inconsequential talk could make me forget her first whispered entreaty. I could have reassured her that we had plans, that we were close, so close, to ensuring Tanaka got the throne, but I could not trust even Sichi. She was the closest I had ever come to a female friend, though if all went to plan, she would never be my sister.

Fearing to be drawn into saying more than was safe, I hurriedly washed and excused myself, climbing out of the water with none of Sichi's assurance. A lifetime of being told I was too tall and too shapeless, that my wrists were too thick and my shoulders too square, had me grab the towel with more speed than grace and wrap it around as much of my body as it would cover. Sichi watched me, something of a sad smile pressed between her lips.

Out in the courtyard the inn showed signs of waking. The clang of pots and pans spilled from the kitchens, and a gaggle of servants hung around the central well, holding a variety of bowls and jugs.

They all stopped to bow as I passed, watched as ever by the imperial guards dotted around the compound. Normally I would not have lowered my caution even in their presence, but the farther I walked from the bathhouse, the more my thoughts slipped back to what Sichi had said. She had not just wanted to know, she had *needed* to know, and the ghost of her desperate grip still clung to my shoulder.

Back in my room, I found that Yin had laid out a travelling robe and was waiting for me with a comb and a stern reproof that I had gone to the bathhouse without her.

"I am quite capable of bathing without assistance," I said, kneeling on the matting before her.

"Yes, Your Highness, but your dignity and honour require attendance." She began to ply her comb to my wet hair and immediately tugged on tangles. "And I could have done a better job washing your hair."

A scuff sounded outside the door and I tensed. Yin did not seem to notice anything amiss and went on combing, but my attention had been caught, and while she imparted gossip gleaned from the inn's servants, I listened for the shuffle of another step or the rustle of cloth.

No further sounds disturbed us until other members of the court began to wake, filling the inn with footsteps. His Majesty never liked to linger in the mornings, so there was only a short time during which everyone had to eat and dress and prepare for another long day on the road.

While I picked at my breakfast, a shout for carriers rang through the courtyard, and I moved to the window in time to see Lady Sichi emerge from the inn's main doors. She had donned a fine robe for the occasion, its silk a shimmering weave that defied being labelled a single colour in the morning light. Within a few moments, she had climbed into the waiting palanquin with easy grace, leaving me prey to ever more niggling doubts. Now I would have to wait until the end of the summer to discover what had troubled her so much.

Before I could do more than consider running down into the yard to ask, her carriers moved off, making space for more palanquins and the emperor's horse, which meant it wouldn't be long until we were called to step into our carriage for another interminable day on the road. Tanaka would grumble. Edo would try to entertain him. And I would get so bored of them both I counted every mile.

Tanaka had not yet left his room, so when the gong sounded, I went to tap on his door. No answer came through the taut paper panes and I leant in closer. "Tana?"

My heart sped at the silence.

"Tana?"

I slid the door. In the centre of the shadowy room, Tanaka and Edo lay sprawled upon their mats, their covers twisted and their hands reaching across the channel toward one another. But they were not alone. A grey-clad figure crouched at my brother's head. A blade hovered. Small. Sharp. Easy to conceal. Air punched from my lungs in a silent cry as I realised I had come too late. I could have been carrying fifty daggers and it would have made no difference.

But the blade did not move. Didn't even tremble. The assassin looked right at me and from the hoarse depths of my first fear my cry rose to an audible scream. Yet still he just sat there, as all along the passage doors slid and footsteps came running. Tanaka woke with a start, and only then did the assassin lunge for the window. I darted forward, but my foot caught on Tanaka's leg as he tried to rise. Shutters clattered. Sunlight streamed in. Voices followed; every servant in the building suddenly seemed to be crammed into the doorway, along with half a dozen imperial guards shoving their way through.

"Your Highnesses, is everything all right?" the first demanded.

Sharp eyes hunted the room. One sneered as he looked me up and down. Another rolled his eyes. None of them had seen the man, or none of them had wanted to. Edo pushed himself into a sitting position with his arms wrapped around his legs, while Tanaka was still blinking blearily.

"Yes, we're fine," I said, drawing myself up and trying for disdain. "I stepped on a sharp reed in the matting is all. Go back about your work. We cannot leave His Majesty waiting."

———————◆———————

"I hate being cooped up in this carriage; another day on the road will kill me more surely than any assassin," Tanaka said, stretching his foot onto the unoccupied seat beside me. "I hope His Majesty pushes through to Koi today. It's all right for him, getting to ride the whole way in the open air."

"Well, when you are emperor you can choose to ride wherever you go," I said. "You can be sure I will."

Tanaka folded his arms. "When? I wish I shared your confidence. This morning proves that His Majesty still wants me dead, and an emperor who wants me dead isn't likely to name me his heir."

It had been almost two years since the last attempt on either of our lives, and this morning's assassin had shaken me more than I dared admit. The way forward had seemed clear, the plan simple—the Chiltaens were even pressing for an announcement. I had been so sure we had found a way to force His Majesty's hand, and yet...

Across from me, the look Edo gifted Tanaka could have melted ice, but when it was returned, they were my cheeks that reddened. Such a look of complete understanding and acceptance, of true affection. Another day on the road might kill me too, if it was really possible to die of a broken heart like the ladies in the poems.

Edo caught me looking and smiled, only half the smile he kept for Tanaka. Edo had the classical Kisian features of the finest sculpture, but it was not his nose or his cheekbones or his long-lashed eyes that made the maids fight over who would bring his washing water; it was the kind way he thanked them for every service as though he were not the eldest son of Kisia's most powerful duke.

I looked out the window rather than risk inspiring his apologetic smile, for however imperceptive Tanaka could be, Edo was not.

"His Majesty will name Grace Bachita his heir at the ceremony," Tanaka went on, scowling at his own sandal. "And make

Sichi marry him instead. Not that Manshin will approve. He and Cousin Bachi have hated each other ever since Emperor Kin gave Manshin command of the army."

Edo hushed him, his expressive grimace the closest he ever came to treasonous words. He knew too well the danger. Like Sichi, he had come to court as a child and was called a guest, a member of the imperial household, to be envied such was the honour. The word *hostage* never passed any smiling courtier's lips.

Outside, four imperial guards rode alongside our carriage as they always did, rotating shifts at every stop. Sweat shone on the face of the closest, yet he maintained the faint smile I had rarely seen him without. "Captain Lassel is out there," I said, the words ending all conversation more surely than Edo's silent warning ever could.

In a moment, Tanaka was at my shoulder, peering out through the latticework. Captain Lassel could not know we were watching him, yet his ever-present little smirk made him appear conscious of it and I hated him all the more. The same smile had adorned his lips when he apologised for having let an assassin make it into my rooms on his watch. Three years had done nothing to lessen my distrust.

Tanaka shifted to the other window and, looking over Edo's shoulder, said, "Kia and Torono are on this side."

The newest and youngest members of the Imperial Guard, only sworn in the season before. "Small comfort," I said.

"I think Kia is loyal to Mama. Not sure about Torono."

Again Edo hushed him, and I went on staring at the proud figure of Captain Lassel upon his horse. He had found me standing over the assassin's body, one arm covered in blood from a wound slashed into my elbow. At fourteen I had been fully grown, yet with all the awkwardness and ill-assurance of a child, it had been impossible to hold back my tears. He had sent for my maid and removed the body and I had thanked him with a sob. The anger had come later.

The carriage began to slow. The captain rose in his stirrups, yet from the window I could see nothing but the advance procession of

His Majesty's court. All horses and carriages and palanquins, flags and banners and silk.

"Why are we slowing?" Tanaka was still peering out the opposite window. "Don't tell me we're stopping for the night—it's only mid-afternoon."

"We can't be," Edo said. "There are no inns within three miles of Shami Fields. He's probably stopping to give thanks to the gods."

Removed as we were from the front of His Majesty's cavalcade, I had not realised where we were until Edo spoke, but even as the words left his lips, the first kanashimi blossoms came into view, their pale petals spreading from the roadside like sprinkled snow. A flower for every soldier who had died fighting for the last Otako emperor. Though more than thirty years had passed since Emperor Tianto Otako had been captured here and executed for treason, it was still a fearful sight, a reminder of what Emperor Kin Ts'ai was capable of—an emperor whose name we carried, but whose blood we did not.

Mama had whispered the truth into my ear as a child, and with new eyes I had seen the locked gates and the guards, the crowd of servants and tutors, and the lack of companions for what they were. Pretty prison bars.

The assassins hadn't been coming for Miko Ts'ai at all. They had been coming for Miko Otako.

"Shit, Miko, look," Tanaka said from the other side of the carriage. "Who is that? There are people in the fields. They're carrying white flags."

"There's one over here too," I said, pressing my cheek against the sun-warmed lattice. "No, two. Three! With prayer boards. And is that...?"

The carriage slowed still more and Captain Lassel manoeuvred his horse up the line and out of view. When the carriage at last drew to a halt, I pushed open the door, stepping out before any of our guards could object. Ignoring their advice that I remain inside, I wound my way through the halted cavalcade, between mounted guards and luggage carts, hovering servants and palanquins bearing ladies too busy fanning themselves and complaining of the oppressive heat to even note my passing.

"Your Highnesses!" someone called out behind me, and I turned to see Tanaka had followed, the gold threads of his robe glinting beneath the high sun. "Your Highnesses, I must beseech you to—"

"Some of those men are carrying the Otako flag," Tanaka said, jogging to draw level with me, all good humour leached from his expression.

"I know."

"Slow," he whispered as we drew near the front, and catching my hand, he squeezed it, gifting an instant of reassurance before he let go. I slowed my pace. Everywhere courtiers and councillors craned their necks to get a better view.

Some of the men blocking the road were dressed in the simple uniform of common soldiers, others the short woollen robes and pants of farmers and village folk. A few wore bright colours and finer weaves, but for the most part it was a sea of brown and blue and dirt. Their white flags fluttered from the ends of long work poles, and many of them carried prayer boards, some small, others large and covered in long lines of painted script.

Upon his dark horse, His Imperial Majesty Emperor Kin Ts'ai sat watching the scene from some twenty paces away, letting a black-robed servant talk to the apparent leader of the blockade. The emperor was conversing with one of his councillors and Father Okomi, the court priest. They might have stopped to rest their horses, so little interest did they show in the proceedings, but behind His Majesty, his personal guards sat tense and watchful in their saddles.

In the middle of the road, Mama's palanquin sat like a jewelled box, her carriers having set it down to wipe their sweaty faces and rest their arms. As we drew close, her hand appeared between the curtains, its gesture a silent order to go no farther.

"But what is—?"

I pressed my foot upon Tanaka's and his mouth snapped shut. Too many watching eyes. Too many listening ears. Perhaps it had been foolish to leave the carriage, and yet to sit there and do nothing, to go unseen when His Majesty was mere days from announcing his heir... It was easy to get rid of people the empire had forgotten.

Only the snap and flutter of banners split the tense silence. A few guards shifted their feet. Servants set down their loads. And upon his horse, General Ryoji of the Imperial Guard made his way toward us, grim and tense.

"Your Highnesses," he said, disapproval in every line of his aging face. "Might I suggest you return to your carriage for safety. We do not yet know what these people want."

"For that very reason I will remain with my mother, General," Tanaka said, earning a reluctant nod. "Who are these people?"

"Soldiers. Farmers. Small landholders. A few very brave Otako loyalists who feel they have nothing to fear expressing such ideas here. Nothing you need worry about, my prince."

My prince. It wasn't a common turn of phrase, but we had long ago learnt to listen for such things, to hear the messages hidden in everyday words. Tanaka nodded his understanding but stayed his ground, tall and lean and confident and drawing every eye.

"General?" A guard ran toward us. "General Ryoji, His Majesty demands you order these delinquent soldiers and their company out of his way immediately."

Ryoji did not stay to utter further warning but turned his horse about, and as he trotted toward the head of the procession, I followed. "Miko," Tanaka hissed. "We should stay here with—"

"Walk with me," I said, returning to grip his hand and pull him along. "Let's be seen like heirs to the Crimson Throne would be seen at such a time."

His weight dragged as Mother called a warning from behind her curtains, but I refused to be afraid and pulled him with me.

Ahead of our cavalcade, General Ryoji had dismounted to stand before the protestors on equal ground. "As the commander of the Imperial Guard, I must request that you remove yourselves from our path and make your grievances known through the proper channels," he said. "As peaceful as your protest is, continued obstruction of the emperor's roads will be seen as an act of treason."

"Proper channels? You mean complain to the southern bastards who have been given all our commands about the southern bastards who have been given all our commands?" shouted a soldier near the front to a chorus of muttered agreement. "Or the southern administrators who have taken all the government positions?" More muttering, louder now as the rest of the blockade raised an angry cheer. "Or the Chiltaen raiders who charge into our towns and villages and burn our fields and our houses and murder our children while the border battalions do nothing?"

No sense of self-preservation could have stopped a man so consumed by anger, and he stepped forward, pointing a gnarled finger at his emperor. Emperor Kin broke off his conversation with Father Okomi and stared at the man as he railed on. "You would let the north be destroyed. You would see us all trampled into the dust because we once stood behind the Otako banner. You would—"

"General," His Majesty said, not raising his voice, and yet no one could mistake his words. "I would continue on my way now. Remove them."

I stared at him sitting there so calmly upon his grand horse, and the anger at his attempt on Tanaka's life flared hot. He would as easily do away with these protestors because they inconvenienced him with their truth.

Slipping free from Tanaka, I advanced into the open space between the travelling court and the angry blockade to stand at General Ryoji's side.

"No blood need be shed," I said, lifting my voice. "His Majesty has come north to renew his oath and hear your grievances, and if they are all indeed as you say, then by the dictates of duty something will be done to fix them. As a representative of both the Otako family through my mother's blood and the Ts'ai through my father's, I thank you for your loyalty and service to Kisia but must ask you to step aside now that your emperor may pass. The gods' representative cannot make wise decisions from the side of a road."

Tense laughter rattled through the watchers. They had lowered their prayer boards and stood shoulder to shoulder, commoners and soldiers together watching me with hungry eyes. Their leader licked his lips, looking to General Ryoji and then to Tanaka as my twin joined me. "You ask us this as a representative of your two families," the man said, speaking now to my brother rather than to me. "You would promise us fairness as a representative of your two families. But do you speak as His Majesty's heir?"

General Ryoji hissed. Someone behind me gasped. The man in the road stood stiff and proud in the wake of his bold question, but his gaze darted about, assessing risks in the manner of an old soldier.

"Your faith in me does me great honour," Tanaka said. "I hope one day to be able to stand before you as your heir, and as your emperor, but that is the gods' decision to make, not mine." He spread his arms. "If you want your voices heard, then raise your prayer boards and beseech them. I would walk with you in your troubles. I would fight your battles. I would love and care for all. If the gods, in their infinite wisdom, deem me worthy, I would be humbled to serve you all to the best of my ability."

His name rose upon a cheer, and I tried not to resent the ease with which he won their love as the crowd pressed forward, reaching out to touch him as though he were already a god. He looked like one, his tall figure garbed in gold as the people crowded in around him, some bowing to touch his feet and to thank him while others lifted their prayer boards to the sky.

We had been careful, had spoken no treason, yet the more the gathered crowd cried their love for their prince the more dangerous the scene became, and I lifted shaking hands. "Your love for my brother is overwhelming," I said to the noise of their prayers and their cheers. "But you must now disperse. Ask them to step aside, Tana, please."

"Isn't this what you wanted?" he whispered. "To let His Majesty see what he ought to do?"

"He has already seen enough. Please, ask them to disperse. Now."

"For you, dear sister."

"Listen now." He too lifted his arms, and where the crowd had ignored me, they descended into awed silence for him. "It is time to step aside now and make way for His Imperial Majesty, representative of the gods and the great shoulders upon which Kisia—"

While Tanaka spoke, I looked around to see the emperor's reaction, but a dark spot in the blue sky caught my eye. An arrow arced toward us, slicing through the air like a diving hawk.

"Watch out!"

Someone screamed. The crowd pushed and shoved in panic and Tanaka and I were trapped in the press of bodies. No guards. No shields. And my hands were empty. There was nothing I could—

Refusing the call of death, I snatched the first thing that came to hand—a prayer board from a screaming protestor—and thrust it up over our heads. The arrowhead splintered the wood. My arms buckled, but still vibrating, the arrow stuck. For a few long seconds, my ragged breath was all the sound left in the sultry afternoon.

"They attacked our prince under a flag of peace!"

The shout came from behind us, and the leader of the blockade lifted his arms as though in surrender. "We didn't! We wouldn't! We only ask that His Majesty name his heir and—"

An arrow pierced his throat, throwing him back into the men behind him, men who lifted their prayer boards and their white flags, begging to be heard, but imperial guards advanced, swords drawn. One slashed the throat of a kneeling man, another cut down someone trying to run. A few of the protesting soldiers had swords and knives, but most were common folk who had come unarmed.

"Stop. Stop!" Tanaka shouted as blood sprayed from the neck of the closest man. "If I do not—"

"Back to your carriage!" General Ryoji gripped Tanaka's arm. "Get out of here, now."

"But they did not—"

"No, but you did."

I followed as he dragged Tanaka away from the chaos and back to the cavalcade to be met with silent stares. Mama's hand had retreated back inside her curtained palanquin, but His Majesty watched us pass. Our eyes met. He said not a word and made no gesture, but for an instant before doubt set in, I was sure he had smiled, a grim little smile of respect. Wishful thinking. No more.

Edo stood waiting at the door of the carriage but slid out of sight as Ryoji marched Tanaka up to it and thrust him inside. He held the door open for me to follow, and I took my seat, trembling from head to foot.

Still holding the door, the general leant in. "Do you have a death wish, boy?"

"I was the one trying to stop anyone getting killed, General, if you didn't notice."

"And painting a great big target on your back while you did it."

"They loved me!"

General Ryoji snarled an animal's anger. "You think it was you they were cheering for? They weren't even seeing you. That was Katashi Otako standing before them once more."

"And I'm proud to look—"

"Your father was a traitor. A monster. He killed thousands of people. You—"

Words seemed to fail him and he slammed the door. A shout to the driver and the carriage lurched into motion. Tanaka scowled, ignoring Edo's concerned questions, while outside, more people willing to die for the Otako name bled their last upon the Shami Fields.

orbit

Follow us:

f **/orbitbooksUS**

🐦 **/orbitbooks**

▶ **/orbitbooks**

Join our mailing list
to receive alerts on our
latest releases and deals.

orbitbooks.net

Enter our monthly
giveaway for the chance
to win some epic prizes.

orbitloot.com